DANIEL B

Daniel Blake worked as a reporter on the *Sun* and the *Daily Telegraph* and then for Control Risks, a company which specialises in kidnap negotiation, clandestine investigations and political risk analysis. He was also one of the youngest-ever contestants on *Mastermind*. Daniel studied at Cambridge and currently lives in Dorset.

DANIEL BLAKE

Soul Murder

HARPER

Harper
An imprint of HarperCollins*Publishers*
77–85 Fulham Palace Road,
Hammersmith, London W6 8JB

www.harpercollins.co.uk

Special overseas edition 2010
1

First published in Great Britain by HarperCollins*Publishers* 2010

ISBN: 978-0-00-728201-2

Set in Meridien by Palimpsest Book Production Limited,
Grangemouth, Stirlingshire

Printed and bound in Great Britain by
Clays Ltd, St Ives plc

*For Michael and Sheila Royce,
whose friendship means more to my family
than they can possibly imagine.*

Acknowledgements

My heartfelt thanks to the usual suspects at HarperCollins and A.P. Watt, especially Julia, Anne, Caradoc, Louise and Rob. I couldn't have done it without them all. Clichéd, but true.

Thank you, as always, to my parents. My mother breathlessly reads every draft in two days flat; my father takes several weeks, punctuated by e-mails detailing ever more esoteric points of discussion. I hope neither ever changes.

Most of all, thank you to my wife Charlotte and our children Florence and Linus, for their endless patience when I shut myself away for weeks on end. They mean the world to me.

Friday, October 1st. 12:15 p.m.

Franco Patrese hadn't been inside a church for ten years.

Ironic, then, that his first time back was straight into the mothership itself; Saint Paul Cathedral, center of spiritual life for close on a million Pittsburgh Catholics.

The bishop himself had insisted. Gregory Kohler had first gotten to know Franco's parents when he, as a young priest, had helped officiate at their wedding. He'd taught Franco and his sisters in the days when priests and nuns could still be found inside the classroom, and over the years had become family friend as well as pastor.

Now he'd offered Franco and his sisters the cathedral. You didn't turn the bishop down, not if you were a good Catholic; and Bianca and Valentina had certainly kept the faith, even if Franco hadn't. Besides, they needed all the seats they could get. Half of Bloomfield – an area of the city so Italian that the parking meters are painted red, green and white – had come to pay their respects to Franco's parents.

Alberto and Ilaria Patrese had been killed five days before. Alberto had gone to pass a truck on the freeway at exactly the moment the truck driver had himself pulled out to overtake an eighteen-wheeler. The collision had flipped the

1

Patreses' car across the central reservation and into the path of three lanes of traffic coming the other way.

They hadn't had a prayer.

The police had come to Franco first, as he was one of them: a homicide detective, working out of the department's North Shore headquarters. When two uniformed officers had approached Franco's desk, he'd known instantly that someone in his family was dead. He recognized the expression on those officers' faces as clearly as if he'd looked in a mirror. He'd had to break similar news many times. It was the worst part of the job, and by some distance. Nothing rips at people's lives like the death of a loved one.

Franco had found the immediate aftermath unexpectedly bittersweet. There'd been tears, of course, and shock giving way to spikes of anger and confusion; but there'd also been rolling gales of laughter at the hundreds of family stories polished and embellished down the years. He'd kept himself occupied with death's legion of petty bureaucracies: police reports, autopsies, certificates, funeral arrangements, contacting relatives long-lost and far-flung. Busy meant less time to think, and less time to think meant more time to be strong, to make sure everyone else was bearing up all right, to deflect even the slightest gaze away from himself.

He was doing it even now, during the funeral service, sat in the front pew with his sisters either side of him and his nephews and niece tucked solemnly between the adults. Determined to be the rock on which the waves of grief could crash themselves out, Franco pulled Valentina close, ruffled the children's hair, and squeezed Bianca's hand when her jaw juddered and bounced against the tears.

The last notes of 'Amazing Grace' faded, and the congregation sat as Kohler climbed the steps to the pulpit. He was in his sixties, with a mane of hair that would have been the envy of a man half his age. The hands he raised as though in benediction of his flock were large and strong, and they did not shake.

Franco tuned out. He heard the grateful laughter when the bishop said something dry and affectionate, but he was miles away, thinking about the things he wished he'd told his parents while he'd still had the chance, and about the things he was glad he hadn't told them. They hadn't known everything about his life, and he had no illusions that they should have done so. He knew they'd loved him, and nothing was more important. But he knew too that loving people meant protecting them.

Somewhere in the distance, Kohler was talking about God, though it was not a God Franco believed in any more. As far as he was concerned, his parents' death had been blind chance, nothing more. Wrong place, wrong time. Why them? Turn it round: why *not* them? You were born, you lived, you died. Mercy and justice and compassion weren't divine traits; they were human ones, and by no means universal. If you didn't believe that, Franco thought, working homicide would soon change your mind. Religion was just a polite word for superstition, and superstition was just a polite word for fear.

Franco hooked a finger inside his collar and pulled at it. He felt suddenly short of breath, and his skin was clammy.

When Bianca looked at him, her face seemed to swim slightly in his vision before settling. Her eyebrows made a Chinese hat of concern and query.

'Is it hot in here?' he whispered.

She shook her head. 'Not for me.'

Franco's ribs quivered with the thumping of his heart. He stood on unsteady legs, stepped over Bianca's feet and walked quickly down the aisle, looking neither left nor right till he was out the huge main door and into the shouty, safe bustle of students from the nearby university ragging each other and putting the world to rights.

3

Monday, October 4th. 8:12 a.m.

The police department offered Patrese two weeks' compassionate leave.

He took two days, and even those didn't really count, given that they were both at the weekend. So he was back at his desk first thing Monday morning, to the unsurprised but good-natured exasperation of his homicide partner, Mark Beradino.

'Sheesh, Franco. You don't want your fortnight, I'll take it.'

Patrese laughed, thankful that Beradino knew better than to kill him with kindness.

Physically, Beradino was pretty nondescript. Five ten, 180 pounds, hair graying but still pretty much all there, and features which were bang-on regular. He was no Brad Pitt, but nor was he a Michael Moore. You could walk past him in the street without noticing; even if you did notice, you'd have forgotten him five steps later. He'd have made a great spy.

But he was a detective; a hell of a detective, in fact.

As far as Pittsburgh Homicide was concerned, he was practically an institution.

He'd been there since the early eighties – most of his clothes looked as though he'd bought them around that time – and he was known on both sides of the law as a good cop. A tough one, sure, one who thought cops should be cops rather than politicians or social workers, but an honest one too. He'd never taken a bribe, never faked evidence, never beaten a suspect up.

Not many cops could say the same.

He and Patrese had been partners for three years – itself a vote of confidence in Patrese's ability – and in that time they'd become friends. Patrese was a regular guest at the condo in Punxsutawney which Beradino shared with his partner Jesslyn Gedge, a warder at the State Correctional Institute in Muncy. Both Beradino and Jesslyn had been among the mourners in Saint Paul's.

'But since you're here,' Beradino continued, 'make yourself useful. We just got a case. Domestic dispute, shots fired, man dead. Zone Five.'

There are six police districts in Pittsburgh, numbered with the complete absence of discernible logic that's the hallmark of the true bureaucrat. Zone Five covered the north-eastern corner of the city; East Liberty, East End and Homewood.

Nine times out of ten, an incident in Zone Five meant an incident in Homewood.

Homewood was Pittsburgh's pits, no question. Homicides, aggravated assaults, weapons and narcotics offenses, prostitution arrests; you name it, there were twice as many in Homewood as in any other neighborhood. It was one of the most dangerous places to live in all of Pennsylvania, and that was saying something.

It was half an hour from police headquarters on the North Shore to Homewood. Patrese and Beradino drove there in an unmarked car; no need for lights or sirens, not when the victim was dead and the uniforms had the scene secured.

You could always tell when you were getting close. First came one splash of gang graffiti, then another, and within a couple of blocks these bright squiggles were everywhere: walls, houses, sidewalks, stop signs.

Our turf. Back off.

Then the pockets of young men on street corners, watching sullenly as the cop cruisers came past; then the rows of abandoned buildings, swallowing and regurgitating an endless stream of vagrants, junkies and whores; then the handful of businesses brave or desperate enough to stay: bars, barber shops, convenience stores, fast-food joints.

Wags from out of town liked to call Patrese's city 'Shitsburgh'. He usually jumped down their throat when they did – he loved this city – but when it came to Homewood, even Patrese was forced to admit that they had a point.

Tragedy was, it hadn't always been like this.

A century and a half ago, Homewood had been *the* place to live. Tycoons like Westinghouse and Frick had kept estates here. Businesses boomed, a trolley system was built, and people couldn't move in fast enough.

And so it stayed till after the Second World War, when the city planners decided to build the Civic Arena downtown. In doing so they had to displace thousands of people, mainly poor black families, who'd been living in the Lower Hill District nearby. Most of them moved to Homewood; and, sure as sunrise, most of Homewood's whites upped sticks and left, fleeing to suburbs further out. The few middle-class blacks who could afford to follow them did.

Then came the riots, here as everywhere else during the civil rights era. With the riots came drugs and gangs with names that sounded almost comic: Tre-8s-Perry and Charles, Sugar Top Mob, Down Low Goonies, Reed Rude Boyz, Climax Street.

Nothing comic about what they did, though. Not then, not now. Drugs and guns, guns and drugs. It was a rare gangbanger who died of old age.

Up ahead, Patrese saw a crowd of people spilling from the sidewalk on to the street. A handful of cops held them back. Across the way, two more police cruisers were pulling up.

The officers held themselves tense and watchful, as well they might. Cops here were the enemy, seen as agents of an alien and oppressive ruling class rather than impartial upholders of law and order.

Patrese and Beradino got out of the car. A few feet away, a young man in a bandana and baggy pants was talking urgently into his cell.

'Yo, tell cuz it's *scorchin'* out here today. And this heat ain't from the sun, you know wha' I'm sayin'?'

He stared at Patrese as he ended the call, daring Patrese to challenge him. The police call it eye fucking, when an officer and a criminal stare each other down. As a cop, you can't afford to back away first. You own the streets, not them.

Patrese and Beradino pushed their way through the crowd, flashed their badges at one of the uniforms, and ducked beneath the yellow-and-black stretched taut between two lampposts.

It was a three-story rowhouse, the kind you see all over Homewood, set slightly up from road level with a veranda out front. Every homicide cop with more than a few months' experience had been inside enough of them to know the layout: kitchen and living room on the ground floor, couple of bedrooms and a bathroom on the floor above, and an attic room with dormer windows under the eaves.

A uniform showed Patrese and Beradino upstairs, briefing them as they climbed.

The deceased was J'Juan Weaver, and he'd been no stranger to the police, the courts, or the prison system. He'd lived in this house with Shaniqua Davenport, his girlfriend, and her (but not his) teenage son Trent.

Shaniqua and Weaver had been running for years, though with more ons and offs than the Staten Island ferry. Before Weaver had been a string of undesirables, who between them

7

had fathered Shaniqua's three sons. Trent was fifteen, the youngest of them. His two elder half-brothers were both already in jail.

You'd have been a brave man to bet against him following suit, Patrese thought.

The uniform showed them into one of the bedrooms.

It was twelve feet square, with a double bed in the far corner. Weaver was lying next to the bed, his body orientated as if he had been sleeping there, with his head up by the end where the pillows were.

The shot that killed him had entered at the back of his head. Patrese could see clips of white bone and gray brain matter amidst the red mess.

Weaver had been a big man; six two and 200 pounds, all of it muscle. There were a lot of sculpted bodies in Homewood, most all of them from pumping iron while inside. Free gym, three hots and a cot; some of them preferred to be inside than out.

'Where are the others?' Beradino asked.

The uniform showed them into the second bedroom.

Shaniqua and Trent, both cuffed, were sitting next to each other on the bed.

Shaniqua was in her late thirties, a good-looking woman with a touch of Angela Bassett about her and eyes which glittered with defiant intelligence.

Trent had a trainer fuzz mustache and a face rounded by puppy fat; too young to have had body and mind irrevocably hardened by life here, though for how long remained to be seen.

They both looked up at Patrese and Beradino.

Beradino introduced himself, and Patrese, then asked: 'What happened?'

'He was goin' for Trent,' Shaniqua said. 'He was gonna kill him.'

That was a confession, right there.

'Why was he going to kill him?'

Silence.

An ambulance pulled up outside, come to remove Weaver's body. Beradino gestured for one of the uniforms to go and tell the paramedics to wait till they were finished up here.

Trent looked as though he was about to say something, then thought better of it.

'We got reports of an argument, then shots were fired,' Patrese said. 'That right?'

'That right.'

'What was the argument about?'

'Oh, you know.'

'No, I don't. What was the argument about?'

'Same kinda shit couples always argue 'bout.'

'Like what?'

'Usual shit. Boring shit.'

'That's not an answer.'

Above their heads, the ceiling creaked.

The detectives might have thought nothing of it, had Trent's eyes not darted heavenwards, involuntary and nervous.

Patrese felt a sudden churning in his gut.

'Who's up there?'

'No one,' Shaniqua said quickly. Too quickly. 'Just us.'

One of the uniforms moved as if to investigate. Patrese raised a hand to stay him, and then slipped out of the room himself.

Up the stairs, quiet as he drew his gun; a Ruger Blackhawk, single action revolver, .357 Magnum caliber, four and five-eighths-inch barrel, black checkered grip.

Surprise was on his side. *Use it.*

He found her, alone, in the attic bedroom.

She was flat on her back; half on the floor, half on a

9

mattress which looked as though it could break new grounds in biological warfare. She was wearing a bra and cut-off denim shorts. The rest of her clothes lay in a pile on top of her right hand, which was hidden from view. Track marks marched like centipedes down the inside of her arms. No wonder Shaniqua and Trent hadn't wanted the cops to find her.

And she was white.

Homewood wasn't a place for white folks.

A few of the more enterprising suburban kids might cruise the avenues in late afternoon and buy a few ounces on a street corner before skedaddling back home and selling it on to their friends at a tidy profit – half the amount for twice the price was the usual – but they stayed in their cars the whole time they were in Homewood, if they had any sense. They didn't walk the streets, and they damn sure didn't go into the crack dens.

So this one must have been desperate. And Patrese knew what all cops knew; desperate people are often the most dangerous.

'Hands where I can see 'em,' he said.

Her body jerked slightly, and instinctively he jumped, his finger tightening on the trigger to within a fraction of the pressure needed for discharge.

Close, he thought, close.

His heart hammered against the inside of his chest.

He was scared. Fear was good; scared cops tended to be live cops.

She opened her eyes and regarded him fuzzily.

Perhaps too fuzzily, he thought.

Was she shamming?

Cops had been killed in these situations before. Places like this, you were on your guard, *always*. It wasn't just the guys with tattoos and biceps who knew how to shoot.

'Lemme see your hands,' he said again.

She stayed perfectly still, looking at him with an incurious blankness.

This wasn't the way people tended to react, not when faced with an armed and armored cop. Sure, there were those who were too scared to move, but they tended to be wide-eyed and gabbling.

Not this one.

Patrese felt a drop of sweat slide lazily down his spine.

Why won't she co-operate?

Two possibilities, he thought.

One, she was so bombed that she didn't know who she was, who he was, where they were or what he was saying.

Two, she wanted him to think all the above, but she was in fact perfectly lucid, and trying to lull him into a false sense of security.

The pile of clothes next to her moved slightly.

She was rummaging around in it.

'Hands. *Now!*' he shouted, taking a quick step towards her.

A flash of black as she pulled something from the pile, bringing her arm up and across her chest.

Patrese fired, twice, very fast.

She was already prostrate, so she didn't fall. The only part of her that moved was her arm, flopping back down by her side as her hand spilled what she'd been holding.

A shirt. Black, and cotton, and nothing but a shirt.

Everyone seemed to be shouting: uniforms barking into their radios, paramedics demanding access, Shaniqua bawling out Trent, Trent yelling back at her.

To Patrese, it was all static, white noise. He felt numb, disconnected.

Should have taken the fortnight's leave, Patrese thought. *Should have taken it.*

Whether he'd followed procedure, or whether he could have done something different, he didn't know. There'd be an inquiry, of course; there always was when a police officer shot someone in the line of duty.

But that was for later. Getting down to the station was their immediate priority, both for questioning Shaniqua and for tipping Patrese the hell out of Homewood.

Beradino took charge, quick and efficient as usual. He told the uniforms to stay in the rowhouse with Trent until back-up arrived to deal with the girl in the attic. Then he and Patrese took Shaniqua down the stairs and out through the front door.

'Don't tell 'em *shit*, Mama,' Trent shouted as they left the bedroom.

She looked back at him with an infinite mix of love and pain.

The crowd outside was even bigger than before, and more volatile to boot. They'd heard Patrese's shots, though they didn't yet know who'd fired or what he'd hit. When they saw Shaniqua being led away, they began to jeer.

'I ain't talkin' to no white man, you hear?' Shaniqua yelled. 'I was born in Trinidad, you know? Black folks don't kiss honky ass in Trinidad, that's for damn sure.' She turned to one of the uniforms on crowd control. 'And I ain't talkin' to no Uncle Tom neither.'

'Then you ain't talkin' to no one, girl,' someone shouted from the crowd, to a smattering of laughter.

Trent was standing at the window, one of the uniforms next to him. For a moment, he looked not like a gangbanger-in-waiting, but like what he was; a frightened and confused teenager.

'I'll be back, my darlin',' Shaniqua shouted. 'I love you for both. Just do good.'

9:38 a.m.

Homewood flashed more depressing vistas past the cruiser's windows as Beradino drove them back to headquarters: telephone pole memorials to homicide victims, abandoned buildings plastered with official destruction notices. The Bureau of Building Inspection spent a third of its annual citywide demolition budget in Homewood alone. It could have spent it all here, several times over.

Patrese, forcing his thoughts back to the present, tried to imagine a child growing up here and wanting to play.

He couldn't.

He turned to face Shaniqua through the grille.

'Is there somewhere Trent can go?'

'JK'll look after him.'

Patrese nodded. JK was John Knight, a pastor who ran an institution in Homewood for young gang members and anyone else who needed him. The institution was called The 50/50, gang slang for someone who was neutral, not a gang member. Knight had also taken a Master of Divinity degree, served as a missionary in South America, and been chaplain of a prison in Arizona. He was a good man, but no pushover; even in his fifties, he carried himself like the linebacker he'd once been, and shaved his black head to a gleaming shine every morning.

That was it for conversation with Shaniqua till they reached headquarters. Patrese didn't bother asking why someone with Shaniqua's looks, personality, and what he guessed was no small amount of brains behind the front she presented to the world, should have wasted her time on the bunch of losers she'd welcomed into her bed, and her life, over the years.

He didn't ask for one reason: he already knew the answer.

There were always fewer men than women in places like Homewood; too many men were in jail or six feet under. So the women had to fight for the remaining men, and fight they did. There was no surer way for a girl to get status than to be on the arm of a big player.

But on the arm sooner or later meant up the duff and, when that happened, the men were out of there. Some were gone so fast they left skid marks. They didn't want to stay around to be pussy-whipped; that was bad for their rep. Far as they were concerned, monogamy was what high-class furniture was made of.

So out and on they went, and in time their sons, growing up without a daddy – or, perhaps even worse, with a step-daddy who cared little and lashed out lots – did the same thing. Beneath the puppy fat, Trent was a good-looking boy. Give him a year or two and he'd be breaking hearts wide open, just as his father had done to Shaniqua.

At headquarters, Beradino logged her arrest with the clerk, found an empty interview room, and turned on the tape recorder.

'Detectives Mark Beradino and Franco Patrese, interviewing Shaniqua Davenport on suspicion of the murder of J'Juan Weaver. Interview commences at' – Beradino checked his watch – 'ten eighteen a.m., Monday, October fourth.'

14

He turned to Shaniqua and gave her the Miranda rights off the top of his head.

Detectives had been discouraged from reading the Miranda script for a couple of years now, ever since Patrese had left the card lying on the table during an interrogation. Several hours into the interview and on the point of confession, the suspect had glanced at the card, suddenly remembered he had the right to an attorney, and shazam! No confession and, in that instance, no case.

'You have the right to remain silent,' Beradino said. 'Anything you say can and will be used against you in a court of law. You have the right to have an attorney present during questioning. If you cannot afford an attorney, one will be appointed for you. Do you understand the rights I have just read to you? With these rights in mind, do you wish to speak to me?'

Shaniqua nodded.

'Suspect has indicated assent by nodding,' Beradino said to the tape recorder.

'You damn right I assent,' she said.

There's usually a time in a homicide interrogation when the suspect cracks, the floodgates open, and they tell the police anything and everything. That time may come several hours into questioning, sometimes even days; rarely does it come right at the start.

But Shaniqua could hardly wait.

'J'Juan dealt horse, that ain't no secret,' she said. 'And sometimes he'd bring his, er, his *clients*' – she arched her eyebrows – 'back to our house, when they were too wasted to get the fuck back to their own homes.'

'You were happy with this?'

'You lemme tell you what happened, we'll get done here a whole lot quicker.'

Beradino was far too much of a pro to take offense. He smiled and gestured with his head: *Go on.*

'No, I weren't happy. I done seen too much of what drugs do, and I don't want no part of it. Not in my house. Every time he brings someone back – black, white, boy, girl, it don't matter – I hit the roof. Every time, he swears it's the last time.

'And every time, like a fool, I believe him.

'But today, when it happens, I've just had enough, I dunno why. We in the bedroom, Trent and I, sittin' on the bed, chattin' 'bout tings: school, grandma – those kinda tings. We talk a lot, my boy and me; we're tight. He tells me tings, I tells him tings. Only man in my life I can trust. Anyhow, J'Juan comes in, says he off out now, and I says, "You take that skanky-ass bitch with you, like five minutes ago, or I'm callin' the police."

'He looks surprised, then he narrows his eyes. Man can look mean as a snake when he wants to, you know?

'"You do that and I'll kill you, bitch," he says.

'Trent says to him, "Don't you talk to my mama like that."

'J'Juan tells Trent to butt the fuck out, it ain't nothin' to do with him.

'"Come on, Trent," I say, gettin' up from off the bed, "let's go."

'"Go where?" says J'Juan. "Go the fuck where? You leavin' me, bitch?"

'"No," I says, "we just goin' for a walk while you cool the fuck off."

'"You leavin' me?" he keeps sayin'. "You goin' to the cops?"

'"You keep on like this," I says, "then, yeah, we're leavin' you. Gonna go live with my auntie in Des Moines. Gotta be better than bein' stuck here."

'I'm nearest the door, J'Juan's standin' by the end of the bed. He's between me and Trent, between Trent and the door.

'He grabs Trent, and says we ain't goin' nowhere.

16

'And right then, I see he's left his gun on the sill.

'So I pick up the gun, and I level it at him.

'He's got his back to me, so he don't see straight away; but Trent sees, and his eyes go like this wide' – she pulled her own eyes open as wide as they'll go – 'and I say to J'Juan, "You leave that boy the fuck alone."

'And he turns to me all slow like, and he says "Put that fuckin' ting down. You don't know what you're doin'."

'And I say, "Trent, come on."

'And J'Juan looks at me, and then at Trent, and then at me again, and he says – I'll never forget this – he says: "You walk out that door, I'll kill this little motherfucker with my bare hands."

'And Trent tries to break free, and J'Juan dives for Trent, and I just shoot him. I said I would, and I did, 'cos he was gonna hurt my boy, right before my eyes, and he does that over my dead body.

'Not my boy. Take me, but not my boy.

'Trent's real daddy's about as useless a piece-a-shit as God ever gave breath to, so no one loves that boy like me. That's why I tell him I love him for both, you know; I love him as his mama and his pops too. Boy needs a daddy, know what I'm sayin'? Boy needs a father like he needs our Father in heaven. But Trent ain't got one. So J'Juan can kiss my ass.

'I shot him, and I ain't ashamed of it.

'Shit, if he walked through that door right now, I'd shoot the motherfucker again.'

Patrese was silent for a moment, and then he laughed; he couldn't help it.

'Now that's what I call a confession,' he said.

Shaniqua looked at him for a moment, and then she laughed too.

'I guess it is. That's the way it happened. But it ain't murder, right? It was self-defense. He was goin' to kill me and my boy.'

'How did you feel when you realized you'd killed him?' Beradino said.

'Feel? Ain't nothing to feel. It was him or me. And if it hadn't been me shot him, it'd have been someone else. He weren't the kinda guy who'd have lived to take out his pension and dandle grandkids on his knee.'

Many people freaked at the sight of a dead body, certainly the first time they saw one. Patrese guessed Shaniqua had seen more than her fair share.

Patrese had charged dozens of suspects over the years, and he'd never apologized to a single one of them. But he wanted very badly to say sorry to Shaniqua; not just for what the law obliged him to do, but also for every shitty thing in her life which had brought her to this place.

Oh, Shaniqua, he thought. What if you'd been born somewhere else, to another family – to any family worth the
name, in fact? If you'd never set foot in Homewood? Never
opened yourself up to men whose idea of fatherhood started
and stopped at conception? Never had your soul leached
from you atom by atom?

'It ain't murder, right?' she repeated.

He was about to tell her things weren't that simple when
Beradino's cellphone rang. He took it from his pocket and
answered.

'Beradino.'

'Mark? Freddie Hellmore here.'

Freddie Hellmore was one of the best-known criminal
defense lawyers, perhaps *the* best-known, in the United
States. A Homewood boy born and bred, he split his cases
between the nobodies – usually poor, black nobodies on
murder charges – and the rich and famous. He was half Don
King, half Clarence Darrow.

Love him or hate him – and most people did both, sometimes at the same time – it was hard not to admire him.
His acquittal rate was excellent, and he was a damn good
lawyer; not the kind of man you wanted across the table
on a homicide case.

'I hear you've got a client of mine in custody,' he said.

'I've probably got several clients of yours in custody.'

'Funny. Let me clarify. Mizz Davenport?'

Beradino wasn't surprised. Someone in Homewood must
have called him.

'Has she appointed you?'

'Has she appointed anyone else?' When Beradino didn't
answer, he continued. 'I'll take that as a no. Put her on.'

'I have to tell you; she's already confessed.'

That piece of news rattled Hellmore, no doubt, but he
recovered fast. He was a pro, after all.

19

'I'm going to have you seven ways to Sunday on improper conduct.'

'We did it by the book, every second of the way. It's all on tape.'

'Put her on, Detective. *Now.*'

Beradino passed Shaniqua the phone. The conversation was brief and one-sided, and even from six feet away it wasn't hard to get the gist; sit tight, shut up, and wait for me to get there.

'He wants to speak to you again,' Shaniqua said, handing the phone back.

Indeed he did; Beradino could hear him even before he put the phone back to his ear.

'You don't ask her another damn thing till I get there, you hear?' Hellmore said. 'Not even if she wants milk in her tea or what her favorite color is. Clear?'

'Crystal.'

Thursday, October 7th. 10:57 p.m.

She'd been in the hospital almost three days now, in the chair beside her sister's bed.

She left only to eat, attend calls of nature, and when the medical staff asked her for ten minutes while they changed the sheets or performed tests. Those occasions apart, she was a constant presence at Samantha's bedside.

Sometimes she talked softly of happy memories from their childhood, conjuring up apple-pie images of lazy summer evenings by mosquito-buzzed lakes and licking cake mix from the inside of the bowl.

Sometimes she fell silent and simply held Samantha's hand, as if the tendrils of tubes and lines snaking to and from Samantha's emaciated body weren't enough to anchor her in this world. And in the small hours, she rested her head against the wall and allowed herself an hour or two hovering above the surface of sleep.

People recognized her, of course, though few seemed sure how they should react when they did, especially in a hospital – *this* hospital – after everything that had happened here. For every person who smiled uncertainly at her, there was another who glared and muttered something about how she should be ashamed of herself.

She acted as though she didn't care either way. She was one hell of an actor.

And now, late in the evening, one of the doctors asked if he could have a word.

'Of course,' she said.

He cleared his throat. 'There's no easy way to say this, so I'll just be straight with you. Your sister is brain dead. Life support is all that's keeping her going.'

'I know.'

'To be honest, with the injuries she received, it's a miracle she's got this far. Multiple gunshot wounds to the head. . . .' He tailed off, spreading his hands.

'So what are you asking me?' she said, even though she knew exactly what was being asked of her.

He swallowed. It was never easy, no matter how often you did it.

'You're next of kin. I need your permission to turn Samantha's life support off.'

It was still a shock to hear it stated so baldly, she thought.

'And if I refuse?'

'Then we get a court order.'

She thought for a moment.

'I understand a certain amount of medical jargon,' she said. The doctor nodded, knowing – as did everybody – what she'd been through in the past. 'Tell me.'

'There's total necrosis of the cerebral neurons,' he replied. 'All Samantha's brain activity – including the involuntary activity necessary to sustain life – has come to an end. We've conducted all the usual physical examinations to find clinical evidence of brain function. The responses have been uniformly negative. No response to pain, no pupillary response, no oculocephalic reflex, no corneal reflex, no caloric reflex.'

22

'You've lost me.'

'Sorry. Eye tests; reaction to light, movement, contact and water being poured in the ears. As I said, all negative. And her EEGs have been isoelectric – sorry, flatline – since she was admitted.'

'And you don't want to waste your time keeping her alive.'

'It's not a question of wanting.'

'It is.'

'It's a question of prioritizing. The damage is irreversible. She's not going to get better. She's not going to improve even an iota from what she is now. The only way, medically, we could justify maintaining life support would be to remove her organs for transplant donation, but . . .' He spread his hands again.

'But she was a junkie, and no one in their right mind would touch her organs with a ten-foot pole. I get it, Doctor. You don't have to soft-soap me.'

'Thank you. Please understand; we don't have the capacity or resources to keep her here indefinitely. Even if we did, she has no reason, no consciousness. She's not living. She's existing.'

She tipped her head slightly and examined him.

'You really believe that?'

'It's fact. It's a medical fact. Medicine's what I believe in.'

When she sighed, it sounded to her like condemnation.

'You square it with your conscience,' she said.

Tuesday, October 12th. 10:08 a.m.

The police look after their own. Always have, always will.

The inquiry into what had happened in Shaniqua's house was conducted by Allen Chance, one of a triumvirate of assistant police chiefs referred to, not entirely without irony, as the three wise monkeys.

The Pittsburgh police department boasted three divisions: administration (the back-room bureaucracy which kept the whole place going), operations (uniformed officers) and investigation, Chance's crew, which along with Homicide included Burglary, CSI, Missing Persons, Narcotics, Robbery, Sex Crimes and Financial Crimes.

Not far north of five foot six, with rimless eyeglasses and the neatest of side partings, Chance looked – and thought – more like an accountant than a cop. Murder clearance rates, targets, statistics: Chance crunched them all with a zeal the Federal Reserve would have envied.

He also knew that the quickest way to send those numbers the wrong way was to hammer the morale of his officers, and the quickest way to do *that* was to leave them dangling when the heat was on.

So his investigation into Patrese's conduct was perfunctory

almost to the point of insult. Independent? Not a chance. Pragmatic? You bet.

Beradino, called as a character witness, testified that Patrese was an excellent detective, that the situation had been fast-moving, and that Patrese had done what any well-trained officer would have.

The suspect had ignored two warnings before making a sudden movement for a hidden object, Beradino pointed out. Patrese's only option had been to shoot.

Chance made appropriate noises about the death being a tragedy. Not the only tragedy of the victim's truncated life, if the toxicological reports were any guide.

On legal advice, Chance did not offer condolences to the deceased's relatives.

Summing up, he declared Patrese's actions and behavior to have been beyond reproach. No charges would be brought, and Detective Patrese would continue with his duties as usual. A press release to that effect would be prepared and released to the media.

Patrese couldn't help feeling he'd dodged a bullet.

PENNSYLVANIA DEPARTMENT OF CORRECTIONS
REPORT OF INVESTIGATION INTO ALLEGED EMPLOYEE MISCONDUCT

INSTITUTION: SCI MUNCY, P.O. BOX 180, MUNCY, PA 17756

DATE OF INVESTIGATION: THURSDAY, OCTOBER 14TH

EMPLOYEE IN QUESTION: JESSLYN H. GEDGE

POSITION: DEPUTY SUPERINTENDENT FOR FACILITIES MANAGEMENT

CASE HISTORY:

Complaints against JESSLYN H. GEDGE were brought on June 23rd by inmate MARA E. SLINGER, number A/38259728-2.[1]

SUMMARY OF ALLEGATIONS:

Inmate Slinger alleges that Deputy Superintendent Gedge:

1. entered into a non-consensual sexual relationship with her;
2. used her position and influence within the institution to maintain this relationship for several months, substantially against inmate Slinger's will;
3. eavesdropped on inmate Slinger's confidential telephone conversations with her attorney;
4. took revenge when inmate Slinger finally terminated their sexual relationship in the following ways:
    4.1. carried out repeated personal searches, strip searches and body-cavity searches on inmate Slinger, sometimes in public owing to the alleged lack of suitable private facilities;
    4.2. scheduled repeated dental examinations for inmate

---

[1] *Subsequent to bringing the complaints, inmate Slinger was released from incarceration on July 12th by order of the Appeal Court.*

Slinger, knowing that inmate Slinger has a phobia of dentists, and that no inmate within the state DOC system has the right to refuse such an examination;

4.3. otherwise harassed inmate Slinger on repeated occasions, applying maximum penalties for minor infractions of prison regulations, including but not limited to: failure to use the shortest route when traveling between two points in the prison complex; stepping out of line in the dining hall; bringing books or papers into the dining hall; giving part of her meals to other prisoners; not taking a full set of cutlery at mealtimes; not eating all the food accepted at mealtimes; and talking to inmates working on the refectory serving line.

4.4. withheld packages addressed to inmate Slinger, or removed certain items before handing such packages over;

4.5. repeatedly confiscated inmate Slinger's prison ID card, in full knowledge that inmates must carry said card at all times except when showering, and that inmates must pay for replacement cards if they lose, destroy or damage said card;

4.6. planted contraband (including money, potential escape tools e.g. nail files, unprescribed pharmaceuticals, illegal narcotics paraphernalia, weapons) in inmate Slinger's cell during searches, and forbade inmate Slinger to be present during such searches on the grounds that her presence would constitute a threat;

4.7. held inmate Slinger down and forcibly shaved her head;

4.8. refused to hand back personal items upon inmate Slinger's release.

SUMMARY OF RESPONSE:

Deputy Superintendent Gedge responded to the allegations as follows:

1. She admitted that she and inmate Slinger had conducted a sexual relationship, but maintained that it was entirely consensual, and that inmate Slinger had in fact initiated sexual contact in the first instance.
2. The answer to this point is implicit in her answer to point 1.
3. On the occasions that she did overhear such conversations, it was while she was monitoring technical faults with the institution's telephone system, and she stopped listening immediately when she realized the conversation was subject to attorney-client privilege.
4. Termination of the sexual relationship was mutual and amicable, and therefore Deputy Superintendent Gedge felt no need for revenge.
   4.1 Deputy Superintendent Gedge carried out all searches in strict accordance with institution policy. On occasion, when all private interview and meeting rooms were being used, searches were carried out in public. Deputy Superintendent Gedge strove to keep these occasions to a minimum.
   4.2 Deputy Superintendent Gedge scheduled all inmate dental examinations in strict accordance with institution policy.
   4.3 Deputy Superintendent Gedge enforced all regulations in strict accordance with institution policy.
   4.4 Deputy Superintendent Gedge checked mail sent to inmate Slinger, removed contraband items, and read letters when she had reason to believe they were being used to plan an escape or other illegal activity. This was all in strict accordance with institution policy;
   4.5 Deputy Superintendent Gedge maintains that inmate Slinger mislaid or deliberately destroyed her ID card on several occasions;
   4.6 Deputy Superintendent Gedge absolutely denies planting contraband items in inmate Slinger's cell;

4.7 Deputy Superintendent Gedge maintains that inmate Slinger shaved her own head to remove traces of illegal drugs in her hair follicles;

4.8 Deputy Superintendent Gedge denies this absolutely.

SUPPORT FOR INMATE SLINGER

Inmate MADISON A-S. SETTERSTROM, prisoner number A/73647829-5, was a former cellmate of inmate Slinger.

She testified that inmate Slinger had repeatedly confided in her that she was unhappy with Deputy Superintendent Gedge's advances towards her, and only acquiesced for fear of negative consequences if she did not.

Inmate Setterstrom said Deputy Superintendent Gedge's behavior after the end of the relationship indicated that inmate Slinger's fears of such consequences had been largely justified.

Several other inmates, speaking on condition of anonymity, also voiced their support for inmate Slinger.

SUPPORT FOR DEPUTY SUPERINTENDENT GEDGE

Lieutenant VALERIE Y. MARGRAVINE testified that the Deputy Superintendent was well respected among her fellow Corrections Officers for her attention to discipline and detail.

Several Corrections Officers stated that Deputy Superintendent Gedge is a devout Christian and a lay minister who presides over services of worship in the institution's chapel on Sundays and other days.

OTHER FACTORS

Inmate Slinger is a high-profile individual whose original conviction attracted substantial media attention, as did the subsequent overturning of that conviction by the Appeal Court. She remains a newsworthy individual.

Any similar media attention in regard to this procedure would be undesirable. The department therefore believes a quick and final resolution to be in the interests of all parties.

Inmate Slinger has signed a confidentiality agreement preventing her from disclosing details of this investigation and hearing to the press, on condition that Deputy Superintendent Gedge receives appropriate punishment.

Deputy Superintendent Gedge has also been the subject of previous complaints from inmates (see cases T637-02, T432-00, T198-96, T791-89).

VERDICT

Pennsylvania Department of Corrections' code of conduct expressly and absolutely forbids all corrections officers from conducting sexual or intimate relationships with inmates.

Irrespective of the validity of the other allegations, Deputy Superintendent Gedge's maintenance of a relationship with inmate Slinger qualifies as gross misconduct and is by itself grounds for immediate dismissal.

Consequently, Deputy Superintendent Gedge is dismissed from her post with immediate effect, and is disqualified from holding any other position within the Pennsylvania Department of Corrections for a period of no less than ten years.

Signed

Anderson M. Thornhill

Anderson M. Thornhill

Governor, SCI Muncy

1:25 p.m.

When Jesslyn pulled in at the truck stop just outside DuBois on I-80, she realized with a start that she could hardly remember a thing about the last hour or so she'd been driving. She'd been operating the car on instinct and muscle memory alone, while her thoughts chased themselves into rolling, tumbling tendrils of confusion.

Her career was over. That much – that alone – she knew. She believed in punishment, and retribution; that was why she'd sought a vocation in corrections. Taking that from her, and in a way which meant she'd never find work in that sector again, was more than she could bear. It was as though Mara Slinger had first led her into evil, then cut her heart out. Here, truly, was the devil.

She wondered whether she should buy a razor here, open the arteries in her wrists, and be done with it all; and even as the thought came to her, she stamped on it with frantic fury, as though trying to beat down a grass fire.

Just the fact that she could entertain such a notion was a deep, shaming sin; 1 Corinthians 3: 16 said: 'Know ye not that ye are the temple of God, and that the Spirit of God dwelleth in you? If any man defile the temple of God, him

31

shall God destroy; for the temple of God is holy, which temple ye are.'

She'd preached that passage repeatedly in the Muncy chapel, knowing that barely a week went past without an inmate trying to take her own life.

Jesslyn stopped her car, a silver Toyota Camry she'd had for a few years, and walked across the parking lot to the restaurant building.

She hadn't eaten all day. She'd been too nervous to eat breakfast this morning, knowing that today her fate would be decided one way or another, and afterwards she'd been given half an hour to pack up all her belongings, hand in her credentials, and get out. No time to say her goodbyes, let alone get some food.

Twenty years' hard work, ripped from her in a flash.

The burger bar smelt like all burger bars do; of cooking oil, sweat and resentment.

Jesslyn walked up to the counter, where a Hispanic-looking woman whose nameplate read 'Esmerelda', and who was too young to be as overweight as she was, regarded the world without enthusiasm.

'Help you?' Esmerelda asked, her tone so polite as to be insolent.

Jesslyn mumbled her order and dropped a ten-dollar bill on the counter.

Fat fingers handed her change and food oozing grease through its wrappers.

Jesslyn went to the far corner of the room, past an EMPLOYEES WANTED sign and a couple of truckers with baseball caps trailing raggedy ponytails.

She was halfway through her burger when the tears came, hot with anger and self-pity. She pressed her hands to her face, not to staunch the flood but in the illogical, childish belief that if she couldn't see the other diners, they couldn't see her.

32

Through the hot rising of mucus in her throat, she repeated silently to herself the words of Lamentations 2: 18. 'Their heart cried out to the Lord, O wall of the daughter of Zion, let tears run down like a river day and night; give thyself no rest, nor let the apple of thine eye cease.'

Friday, October 15th. 7:11 a.m.

Jesslyn left early the next morning, as though she was going to work as usual.

She'd told Mark – Mark Beradino, her partner – nothing. It helped that she liked to keep her work and home lives separate – whatever Mark knew of her job was what she chose to tell him, or not tell him – but still . . . How could she explain it all to him? Where would she even begin?

She had no idea; and, until she did, she figured it was best to keep quiet, and somehow square the silence up between herself and God.

What she *did* know was that the longer she left it, the harder it would be. Every secret she kept from Mark made keeping the next one both easier and necessary.

She hadn't told him about her affair with Mara, so she hadn't been able to tell him about Mara's complaints, so she hadn't been able to tell him about yesterday's tribunal, so she hadn't been able to tell him she'd been dismissed, so she had to go off today to keep the pretence that everything was normal.

And going off today meant she'd have to go off tomorrow, and the next time.

34

She couldn't keep doing that indefinitely; at least, not without somewhere to go and something that would pay her, because corrections didn't pay like Wall Street in the first place, and she didn't have much in the way of savings.

So she needed a job. Not just any job – a job which offered shifts. Prison work wasn't nine to five; like the police, prison officers worked eight-hour shifts, sometimes on the night watch. She couldn't keep up the pretence for long if she took employment as an office clerk.

It didn't have to be a great job. In fact, it almost certainly wouldn't be.

But as long as it paid, and got her out of the house, it would do, at least until something better came along. And she could pass the time by savoring the righteous anger which burned within her. She'd given her life to her vocation, and she'd been cast aside like a piece of flotsam.

That wasn't the way you treated people. There would be retribution; that was not only her right, but her duty too.

She recited to herself the words of Exodus 21: 23. 'And if any mischief follow, then thou shalt give life for life, eye for eye, tooth for tooth, hand for hand, foot for foot, burning for burning, wound for wound, stripe for stripe.'

Burning for burning. Stripe for stripe.

Jesslyn realized she was heading towards Muncy; reflex, perhaps, or providence. Ahead, she saw signs to the DuBois travel plaza, where she'd stopped yesterday.

She pulled off the interstate, parked the Camry, and went back into the burger bar.

Esmerelda wasn't on duty today. At the counter was a guy with acne and eyeglasses who could barely have been out of his teens. His nametag proclaimed him not only to be 'Kevin', but also the manager.

'Help you?' he said, in exactly the same tone Esmerelda

35

had used the day before. Must have been something they taught at burger college.

Jesslyn couldn't remember feeling as demeaned as she did now. Only her faith that God would provide, and that He moved in mysterious ways, forced the index finger of her right hand up and in the direction of the EMPLOYEES WANTED sign.

'I'd like a job, please,' she said.

Monday, October 18th. 6:53 p.m.

'You don't recognize me?' I ask.

Michael Redwine shakes his head. He can't speak, as I've put duct tape across his mouth; and he can't take the tape off or lash out at me, as I've cuffed his hands behind his back. The cuffs are those thin plastic ones, good for one use only.

One use only is all I need.

Besides, the plastic won't last long, not with what I've got in store for him; but by the time he'll be able to break them off, he'll be long past doing anything at all.

His mouth moves furiously around the gag, spilling saliva down his jaw. It takes me a moment to work out what he's saying.

'You're praying?' I ask.

He looks at me with wide eyes and nods.

'That's funny,' I say. 'I didn't think people like you believed in a higher power.'

His brows contract in puzzlement.

I look round his apartment again.

Nothing much wrong with it, truth be told. He lives in The Pennsylvanian, about the most luxurious apartment block in all of downtown. It's built on the site of the old Union rail station, and the arched canopy which covers the main entrance is often cited as the most captivating architectural arrangement in all of Pittsburgh.

The Pennsylvanian has thirteen stories, the apartments getting ever grander the higher you go. Redwine's apartment is on the tenth floor, where the building's loft homes are located: all elegant arched windows, crown moldings, wood paneling and intricately detailed, fifteen-foot ceilings. The windows give on to warehouse roofs and overpasses swooping towards the Strip. Far below me, streetlights glow low sodium.

This, all this luxury, is what you get when you're one of the premier brain surgeons in all Pennsylvania, possibly in the entire United States.

And all this luxury means nothing when you've done what Michael Redwine did, and you're going to be punished like I'm about to punish him.

I open my bag and bring out a red plastic container. It can take a gallon, and pretty much everyone in the world recognizes its shape and what it's designed to hold.

Redwine is screaming mutely behind the duct tape even before I open the lid and let him smell the gasoline.

'Remember what you did?' I ask, beginning to pour the gasoline over his head.

He jerks his body across the floor and tries to stand; anything to get away from the pulsing glugs that mat his hair to his forehead and run into his eyes.

He kicks at me, but I skip easily out of reach, still pouring.

The gasoline is drenching his shirt now, rivuleting down his trousers.

'Remember what you said to me?' I ask.

He throws himself against the wall; to knock himself out and spare himself the agony of what he knows is coming, perhaps, or as a last desperate call for help.

Neither works. He's still conscious, and no one's coming.

'And remember what I said to you?'

When the plastic can's empty, I put it back in my bag.

I take out the juggling torch and the lighter. Then I put the bag by the door, the easier to grab it fast on my way out if I have to make a sharp exit.

I light the torch's wick and look at Redwine. I don't think I've ever seen anyone more terrified in my entire life.

'Isaiah chapter fifty-nine, verse seventeen,' I say. '"For I put on righteousness as a breastplate, and a helmet of salvation upon my head; and I put on the garments of vengeance for clothing, and am clad with zeal as a cloak."'

The torch flares in my hand like the fount of justice. I take a step towards him.

He backs away until he reaches the far corner and can go no further.

He curls himself into a ball and turns his face away from me.

I lower the torch to his shoulder.

10:04 p.m.

From the point of view of a homicide detective, fire scenes are among the most difficult of all to work. What fire doesn't destroy, it damages; and what it damages, the firefighters tend to destroy in their efforts to extinguish the blaze. None of this bodes well for the preservation of evidence. Only bomb sites boast more destruction and disorder.

The fire department had been on the scene within four minutes of first being called, when one of Redwine's neighbors had smelt burning, looked out of the window, and seen large black clouds billowing from Redwine's apartment. The firemen had evacuated the entire apartment block and set to putting the fire out.

It had taken them two and a half hours, but they'd managed it, and had kept it contained to the apartment of origin, more or less. There were scorch marks in the apartment above and those to either side, but nothing worse than that, and no serious structural damage, except to Redwine's apartment itself.

The senior fire officer on site having declared the building safe, Patrese and Beradino pulled on crime-scene overalls, shoe covers and latex gloves, in that order, and entered Redwine's apartment.

They'd been called in the moment the firefighters had discovered both the body – presumed to be Redwine's, though obviously not proved as such yet – and the demarcation line on the carpet next to him.

A demarcation line, in fire terms, marks the boundary between where a surface – in this case, the carpet – has burnt and where it hasn't. More often than not, it indicates the use of a liquid accelerant, which in turn means the fire was started deliberately.

And since very few people choose to start a fire and then hang around inside a burning apartment – suicide by self-immolation is extremely rare – it seemed likely that someone other than Redwine, someone long since gone, had been responsible for both the fire and Redwine's death.

This left two possibilities. Either the arsonist had killed Redwine and then set the fire to cover his tracks; or it had been the fire itself that had killed Redwine.

The crime-scene photographer was already there. Patrese and Beradino watched as he fired off round after round of shots, changing lenses and films with practiced ease.

In close for the serious detail, magnifying things a few millimeters across up to the size of a normal print; mid-range images which concentrated on specific objects; and wide-angle images capturing as much of the room as possible.

He was using both black-and-white and color films. Color is usually better, but gruesome photos are best shown to squeamish juries in monochrome.

Beradino glanced across at Patrese, who read in the furrow of the older man's brow exactly what it meant; concern, that all this would scald Patrese's memories. It was barely three weeks since his parents had perished in a freeway fireball.

'I'm OK,' Patrese said.

They looked round what was left of the room. It was rectangular, though not by much; fourteen feet by seventeen, at a guess.

At either end of the longer side were the windows and a pass-through to the kitchen. The shorter side was bounded by walls, one exterior and one interior.

There were two sofas; a two-seater beneath a window, and a three-seater up against the exterior wall. In the corner between them sat a low, small table, and in the nearest corner to that, where the windows met the interior wall, was a plasma TV.

All of them burnt to the edge of recognition, as was Redwine's body.

His skin was cracked and patched charred black and bright red, splashed with different colors where his clothes had melted on to him. He was hunched like a prizefighter, arms drawn up in front of him and legs bent at the knee.

This in itself proved nothing, they knew. The position was caused by muscles contracting in response to the heat of the fire, and could not indicate by itself whether the victim had been alive or dead when the fire was set.

But the color of the body could do so.

Reddening of the skin, and blistering, tend to take place on a victim who was still breathing rather than one who wasn't.

Beradino crouched down by the body and took a small dictaphone from his pocket. He was gospel strict about making contemporaneous notes. It wasn't just that he couldn't rely on remembering everything when it came to writing things up a couple of hours later back at the station; it was also that making notes forced the investigator to slow down, think, take his time.

After all, the victim wasn't going anywhere.

Beradino looked closely at what had once been Redwine's face.

He didn't think about what Redwine might have looked like in life, as that was no longer relevant. If he thought of anything, it was of over-barbecued meat. The less emotive and more commonplace he could make it seem, the better.

Twenty-five years on the homicide squad hadn't hardened him to things, not really. It had merely made him better at coping with them.

There.

'Around the nostrils,' he said into the dictaphone. 'Beneath the burn marks. Smoke stains, clearly visible.'

The pathologist would doubtless find blackened lungs when he came to do the autopsy, which would confirm it; but for now, Beradino had more than enough to be going on with.

Smoke stains meant inhalation. It was this which had almost certainly killed Redwine – breathing in smoke finishes people off before burning flesh does – but it didn't alter the chronology of what had happened, or the central conclusion.

Michael Redwine had been alive when the fire had been set, and he'd been burned to death.

10:30 p.m.

The doorman was dressed in a suit which, Patrese thought, almost certainly cost more than any of his own suits, and very possibly more than all of them put together.

He tried to ignore this slight on his sartorial standards, and instead read the name on the doorman's lapel badge. Jared Foxworth.

Foxworth handed Patrese two lists.

The first showed which apartments were occupied and by whom, though some of the names were of companies rather than individuals. The Pennsylvanian was a popular locale for corporate lets, allowing companies based outside of Pittsburgh to put up employees or clients here instead of paying for hotels.

The second was a record of every visitor who'd gone up to the apartments today. The Pennsylvanian's rule was simple; you asked at the reception desk, the doorman rang up to the apartment in question, and if you went up, you signed in with him first. If you stayed in reception and waited for a resident to come down before leaving the building, you didn't need to sign in; but Redwine's killer couldn't have done that, as Redwine had been found in his apartment.

44

Anyway, he'd had no visitors at all today, said Foxworth; none, full stop.

There were, he added, no other ways into the building unless you knew enough about The Pennsylvanian's layout to sneak in through the underground parking lot or up the fire escape; but even then you'd have to rely on doors being open that shouldn't have been, and risk being spotted by someone who might ask you what you were doing. Hazardous, to say the least, but not out of the question.

Whichever way Redwine's killer had entered the building, he – of course it could be a 'she' too, Beradino said, but since the majority of murderers were male, they would for simplicity's sake refer to the killer as a 'he', all the while maintaining an open mind – had not had to force the door of the apartment itself. The firefighters had broken down the door when they'd arrived on scene, and they were adamant both door and lock had been intact.

Which in turn suggested two possibilities.

Firstly, that the killer had a key with which he'd let himself in. This might have been a surprise to Redwine, or he might have been expecting it. Perhaps the killer had thought Redwine would be out, and the surprise at finding him in the apartment had been mutual.

Secondly, that Redwine had known the killer, and opened the door to him.

There were two sets of crowds out front. First, the building's residents, who'd been evacuated and were massed under the canopy waiting to be questioned. Second, the rubberneckers who'd heard that there'd been not just a fire but a death too, which was for a dispiriting number of people more than reason enough to drop everything and stand behind police barriers for hours on end.

One of the uniforms was subtly filming the latter group.

Murderers sometimes returned to the scene of their crime; arsonists often did. The detectives would study the footage later, looking for known troublemakers or simply those who looked shifty.

A film crew from KDKA, Pittsburgh's local TV station, were also on site. The event was newsworthy because of The Pennsylvanian's prestige as a place to live, and the fact that the victim had been a surgeon, but the body language of the reporter and cameraman betrayed their instinct that this was not a major story.

Man dies in fire. Tragic, but happens every day. The TV crew would go through the motions and hope for something bigger, more exciting, or quirkier next time.

Beradino and Patrese introduced themselves to the residents and asked if a Magda Nagorska was among them as, according to their records, she lived directly beneath Redwine's apartment.

She was indeed there, and she looked as old as God, possibly older.

If the way they had to shout every question two or three times was anything to go by, Redwine could have been murdered in *her* apartment, perhaps right next to her, without her having heard a damn thing.

'Did you see or hear anyone go into his apartment?' Patrese asked.

'He was a charming man,' she shouted.

'No commotion? An argument? Your apartment didn't shake?'

'It's dreadful, that it happens somewhere like here. *Dreadful.*'

One of the uniforms bit on his hand to stop himself from laughing. It was like giggling in church; the more taboo it was, the more tempting it became.

Patrese didn't think it would do much for the reputation

46

of the Pittsburgh homicide department if he fell to his knees weeping with laughter in front of a potential witness.

They continued in mutual incomprehension for several minutes, before Beradino asked in exasperation: 'Do you have a hearing aid?'

'Lemonade?'

'HEA-RING-AID?'

'Oh yes, but I don't wear it too often. I'm not deaf. Just a little hard of hearing in one ear, you know.'

11:17 p.m.

'How did the killer get in?' Patrese asked, when he and Beradino were in the car.

'That's the sixty-four-thousand-dollar question, isn't it? Well, one of them, anyway.'

That the fire escape and underground parking lot were risky methods of entry didn't mean they were impossible. The parking lot had closed-circuit TV; the fire escape didn't. The cops would trawl through the footage and see what they could find.

Failing either of those, could the killer have been a resident?

It seemed unlikely, to say the least. They'd spoken to all the residents, albeit briefly. None of them looked as though they could harm a fly, and none had an obvious motive to do away with Redwine.

The uniforms would follow up, of course, interviewing every resident properly.

What about one of the doormen? Probably not Foxworth himself – it would be hard to do it on one's own shift, because it would have meant leaving the front desk unattended for too long – but one of the others, who was off shift? A doorman

48

would know all the shortcuts and hidden entrances, and his presence wouldn't be suspicious.

But again, it came back to the same stumbling block: *why*?

Why had Redwine been killed, and why – the second sixty-four-thousand-dollar question – why in that way? Why burned, rather than, say, shot, or stabbed?

To hide something? If not Redwine's identity, then something else?

To destroy something? Forensic evidence, or something less directly connected to the corpse, such as documentation or other items?

As punishment; a cruel and unusual way of murdering someone?

Or were all these delving too deep into something very simple? Had Michael Redwine been burnt to death simply because the killer had felt that was the easiest way of doing it?

Redwine had been a surgeon at Mercy, Pittsburgh's largest and most famous hospital. Mercy was located uptown, a few blocks from The Pennsylvanian.

'We're going to Mercy?' Patrese asked.

'You got any better ideas?'

'Matter of fact, I do.'

Patrese flipped open his cellphone and hit one of the speed dials. A woman answered on the second ring.

'Hey, Cicillo.'

'Hey, sis. Are you on shift?'

'No, at home, all alone; Sandro's taken the kids to his mom's for a few days. Why?'

'Can we come by?'

'Who's we?'

'Me and Mark.'

'Why? What's happened?'

'Tell you when we get there. We're leaving town now. See you in fifteen.'

He ended the call. Beradino looked across at him.

'Who was that?'

'Bianca. My sister.'

'The one who's a doctor at Mercy?'

'The very same.'

Beradino smiled.

There were two ways to find out what Redwine had been like and why someone might have wanted to kill him in such a vile manner. There were formal channels, which involved managers, bureaucrats and warrants; and there were informal channels, which involved the promise of favors owed if you were lucky and good old dead presidents if you weren't.

Either way, there were no prizes for guessing which method tended to be quicker and more effective.

'You're not as dumb as you look,' Beradino said.

'That's the nicest thing you've ever said to me.'

11: 42 p.m.

'What was he like?' Bianca considered the question for a moment. 'He was Harvard med school. That's what he was like.'

'You mean he thought he was God's gift?' Beradino said.

'In my experience, most Harvard med schoolers think God is *their* gift to the world rather than vice versa.'

Patrese laughed. That was his sister in a nutshell, he thought; tell it like it is, no matter the circumstances. Her patients tended to appreciate her straight talking, particularly when it came to diagnosing the severity of whatever they had. Most people with illnesses liked to know what they were dealing with.

She'd been shocked, of course, when they'd told her what had happened to Redwine. You wouldn't wish that on your worst enemy – unless, of course, it was the fact that they *were* your worst enemy which had made you do it in the first place.

But doctors saw an awful lot of life and certainly too much of death, and so they didn't tend to stay shocked for very long. Bianca was no exception.

So now she sat with her brother and Beradino in her living room and tried to think of who might have wanted Redwine dead.

'How well did you know him?' Beradino asked.

'Well enough, but as a professional colleague rather than a friend. You understand the difference? I spent a lot of time in his company, but almost always at work. We rarely socialized. I knew a lot about his life, and he mine, because those details tend to get shared around when you're talking; but if one or other of us had taken a job someplace else, I doubt we'd have stayed in touch.'

'Personal life?'

'Divorced. Couple of teenage boys.'

'Nasty split?'

'Quite the opposite, far as I know. In fact, I remember him telling me once both he and his wife – Marsha, she's called – had been sacked by three successive sets of divorce lawyers because they weren't being greedy enough.'

Beradino and Patrese laughed. Cops appreciated a dig at lawyers as much as anyone else; more than most, in fact.

'Wife and kids still in Pittsburgh?'

'No. They went out west, to Tucson. He used to go and see them several times a year. Hung out with the kids, stayed over at their house.'

'He and Marsha still sleeping together?'

'You'd have to ask her that. But I don't think so. Maybe that was why they split up to start with. He told me once he thought of her more as a sister than anything else.'

'He have anyone else serious?

'Not that I know of.'

'No,' said Beradino thoughtfully. 'I can't imagine they'd have been too happy with him playing happy families with his ex, whatever the real story.'

'But I doubt he ever lacked female company. He was hand-some, he was smart, he was successful.'

'And arrogant.'

'Yes, and arrogant. Most surgeons are. It comes with the

territory. You ask them, they'd call it self-confidence. Patients like a surgeon who's sure of what he's doing. The last thing you need when someone's about to open you up is to find they're suddenly iffy about the job.'

'He was a good surgeon?'

'One of the best. A real pioneer, always looking for new techniques, new ways to make things better. There are people walking round Pittsburgh today who are still here because of Michael Redwine; not just because he saved their lives, but because he did so with methods and equipment which simply didn't exist several years ago, and which he helped bring into being.'

'He ever make mistakes?'

For the first time, Bianca paused.

The house was suddenly quiet, which in Patrese's experience was an event about as frequent as Halley's Comet. If it wasn't Sandro's endless practicing – he was a violinist with the Pittsburgh Symphony – it was the noise generated by three kids blessed with the kind of energy that ought to be illegal.

Vittorio was in ninth grade, Sabrina seventh and Gennaro sixth, and Patrese loved them all to bits. Acting the goofball uncle with them, taking them to Steelers games, playing touch football with them in the backyard till sundown – and telling them that Gramps and Gran were now in heaven, and holding them close when they cried.

'All surgeons make mistakes,' Bianca said eventually.

'You sound very defensive about that.'

'Yes, well . . . Listen, people expect doctors to be perfect, get everything absolutely right every time. But it doesn't always work like that. We're human, our knowledge is imperfect, some symptoms aren't always clear-cut.'

'I don't think Mark intended it to be a value judgment,' Patrese said softly.

Bianca might have been his big sister, but he was still protective of her; that was the Italian male in him.

And he understood her defensiveness, too. Doctors were no different from cops – they looked out for one another. You dissed one, you dissed them all; that was how they saw it.

So they covered each other's backs. Like most professions, medicine was in essence a small world; you never knew when you might need someone to help you out, so you didn't go round making unnecessary enemies. And old habits died hard, even when the person you were protecting was no longer around.

'I'm just looking for why someone might have wanted him dead,' Beradino said.

Bianca nodded. 'I understand. I'm sorry.'

'No need.'

'OK. Every time you lose a patient, you consider it a mistake, even when you know deep down you couldn't have done anything more. That's just the way you feel. And Mike had his fair share of those. I mean, brain surgery, the stats aren't that great. You don't open up someone's skull unless things are pretty bad to start with. But those ones, I'm not counting; they're not mistakes, not really.

'Then there are the ones where, perhaps, if you'd done something different, you might possibly have saved them. But in those cases you don't know till it's too late anyway, and you can drive yourself mad if you dwell on it. If everyone's vision was as good as their hindsight, every optician across the land would be out of work.'

'People sue you for those ones?'

'Sure. If you *could* have done something different, they'll say you *should* have done. So the lawyers get involved, everyone starts slinging writs around, and if you can, you settle before it gets to court, goes public and damages your rep. Comes with the turf, doesn't mean you're suddenly a crappy surgeon.'

She paused again.

'And?' Patrese said, not unkindly.

'And then there are the *real* fuck-ups.'

'Redwine have any of those?'

She nodded. 'One.'

The technical term was 'wrong-site surgery', which barely hinted at how catastrophic such incidents were, and how insultingly, ridiculously amateur they seemed.

Wrong-site surgery was, in essence, when the surgeon operated on a perfectly healthy part of the patient's anatomy, and left the offending area untouched.

The consequences tended to fall into two categories: drastic, and fatal.

Redwine had been scheduled to remove a blood clot from the brain of Abdul Bayoumi, a professor of philosophy at the University of Pittsburgh.

It was a routine enough operation, especially for a surgeon of Redwine's standing; he'd done hundreds in his career.

The clot had been on the left side of Bayoumi's brain.

Redwine had cut into the right-hand side.

Only when he'd got all the way through the skull did he realize his mistake.

He'd immediately closed up the incision, made another one on the correct side, and removed the clot.

In 99 per cent of cases, that would have been it; a near-miss, a bureaucratic snafu, and a story on which the patient could dine out when he'd made a full recovery.

But Bayoumi had suffered complications – Bianca wasn't sure of the exact details – on the side of the brain where Redwine had made the first, erroneous, incision.

The complications had spread, multiplied, and worsened.

Within six hours, he was dead.

'How the hell can that happen?' Beradino asked. 'Don't

you guys,' he caught himself – 'sorry; isn't it standard procedure to have a checklist or something, so this kind of thing gets caught before it occurs?'

'Sure it is,' Bianca said. 'There's a three-step procedure, the Universal Protocol, which is absolutely standard. First, you check the patient's notes and make sure they tally with the surgery schedule. Then you use indelible markers to spot the site where the surgeon's going to cut. Finally, the entire operating team takes a time-out before the start and agrees that this is what they're supposed to be doing.'

'So how can something like this happen?'

'Because a system is only as good as the people using it.'

'And?'

'And in an operating theatre, the surgeon is God. He's captain of the ship; his word goes. So if he says we cut on the left, we cut on the left. And if the notes say otherwise, who's going to tell him, and get yelled at, or worse? Shoot the messenger, you know. Everyone stands around looking at each other, and no one does a thing.'

'Redwine was one of these surgeons?'

'One of them? He was the archetype. He prided himself on not marking sites, as he claimed he could always remember. He didn't think he needed to write things down, like the rest of us mortals.'

'Christ on a bike,' Patrese said.

'Don't blaspheme, Franco,' Beradino said instantly. 'You know I don't like it.' He turned to Bianca. 'How often does this kind of thing happen?'

'Per month, per week, or per day?'

Patrese and Beradino looked at her in astonishment.

'Are you serious?' Patrese said.

'I never joke about my work, Cicillo, you know that.'

Patrese pursed his lips and blew out; Beradino shook his head.

'And this guy's family – Bayoumi – they're suing?'

'I think so.'

'Bayoumi.' Beradino turned the name over, as though inspecting it. 'Arab?'

'Egyptian, I think.'

'What kind of family?'

'Wife, one son.'

'How old?'

'Early twenties, far as I know. Student at Pitt.'

Patrese knew instantly why Beradino was asking. Ask a bunch of Americans chosen at random to play word association with the phrase 'young Arab man', and it was a dollar to a dime that 'hothead' wouldn't be far away.

Call it racism, call it common sense; people did both, and more, and they wouldn't stop till white kids flew airliners into skyscrapers too.

Tuesday, October 19th. 11:24 a.m.

Dr Bayoumi's wife – widow – Sameera lived out in Oakland, the university district. Her apartment was one of three in a large, rambling house with a porch out front and Greek columns propping up the veranda roof.

Mid-morning but with all the curtains still closed, as if to block out hope as well as light, she offered them Egyptian tea: hot, strong and, at least to the palates of two Italian-American detectives, undrinkable without three heaped spoonfuls of sugar.

She was darker-skinned than they'd imagined. Like many Egyptians, and Sudanese, she was of Nubian descent, Arab by culture rather than race.

They spoke in near-whispers, mindful of the enforced twilight and the evident numbness of Sameera's grief.

Beradino, sensing that Sameera would expect the elder and more senior man to take the lead, did the talking.

'As far as you knew, Mrs Bayoumi, was your husband's operation routine?'

'I think so.'

'Dr Redwine didn't seem unduly concerned, when you met him beforehand?'

'No.'

'And afterwards?'

'What do you mean?'

'How did Dr Redwine seem to you, after your husband died?'

'I haven't seen him since then.'

'Not once?'

'No.'

'Have you tried to see him?'

'Of course. But always, he busy. I remember something Abdul always like to say. With great power comes great responsibility. But Dr Redwine not see it like that.'

'Would you say the hospital has been unco-operative?'

'Yes. Very. Not just like that, blocking him from me. I ask for documents, records, and they no interested. Treat me like fly to swat. So I call lawyer.'

She handed them a glossy brochure from the firm in question, a medical malpractice specialist. Patrese glanced at it. Swanky downtown address, shots of a happy but industrious multi-ethnic workforce that wouldn't have looked out of place in a Benetton commercial, and a commitment in bold typeface to 'help you down the path to a better tomorrow'.

'What are your motivations for bringing proceedings, Mrs Bayoumi?'

To many Americans, accustomed to a culture where legal representation can seem not just a right but a duty, the question might have sounded odd. But Beradino figured Sameera had enough first-generation immigrant still in her to make recourse to the law a last rather than a first option.

The consideration she gave the question before answering showed him to be right.

'Abdul and I, we had our own, how you say, parts in the marriage,' she said eventually. 'He go to work, I make the home, look after Mustafa. When Mustafa grow up, we keep the parts the same. Abdul still work, I make home, Mustafa live here still. We all happy that way. Maybe not modern, American, but it work for us.

'And now Abdul gone, where will I find job? I am not educated, not college. Companies, they see my resumé, they say no, no interview, even. So how do I live? That's why I call lawyer.

'I want – all I want – is money Abdul earn between now and he retiring. Not a dollar more. I know it not millions, but it enough. That why lawyer, nothing more.

'I know we can do nothing to make Abdul come back. If you talk of revenge, no, I don't believe in that. And if the hospital say sorry . . .' She made a sound to suggest she thought it unlikely.

'And Mustafa. What does he think?'

'Mustafa his own man now. You must ask him.'

'I understand he's a student at Pitt, is that right?'

'Yes.'

'What's he studying?'

'Chemistry.'

'So that's where we'd find him now? In the chemistry department?'

'Not today. Today, he on outreach. At mosque, in Homewood.'

'We'll go talk to him there,' Beradino said. 'Thank you, Mrs Bayoumi.'

'May I ask favor?'

'Sure.'

'How you say in slang? Go easy on him. For Arab boy, father is most important man in world. To lose that is very hard for him. So for me too. Mustafa is my world now. He my only son. Allah blessed us with him, no more. I lose one man, I no lose another. I do anything for that boy, you understand? *Anything.*'

60

1:09 p.m.

Homewood, Patrese thought; always Homewood. It seemed less a geographical area than a vortex, forever dragging him back in.

On the sidewalk, a handful of youths waved at them, their gestures heavy with sarcasm. Patrese waved back, deadpan, his mind miles away.

After a few seconds, he glanced in the rear-view mirror and saw exactly what he expected; a couple of them flipping the detectives the bird, another pair dropping their pants and mooning.

Patrese laughed. Beradino, swiveling round to follow his gaze, was angry.

'Stop the car, Franco. Let's go bust their asses.'

'Ah, they're just screwin' around.'

'To a marked cop car? You let that go, you let anythin' go. Zero tolerance.'

'You don't like black people?'

'I got nothin' against black people. I'm a good Christian man, Franco. Jesus says that we should accept all men equally. I just don't like *these* black people. If they were white people actin' this way, I wouldn't like 'em any better. Shoot,

61

I'd probably like 'em *worse*.' He pointed forward. 'There, that's the mosque.'

There was a plaque on the building's front wall. *In 1932*, it read, *Pittsburgh became home to the first chartered Muslim mosque in the United States.*

'What a claim to fame,' said Beradino, deadpan. 'Personally, I'd still take the four SuperBowls, you know?'

They stepped inside the main door of the mosque.

It didn't seem like Osama's nerve center, that was for sure. No firebrand preachers hollering death to the Great Satan or burning the Stars and Stripes; no rows of prostrate worshippers facing Mecca. Only the rows of shoes lined up inside on gray plastic shelves gave a hint as to the religion of those within.

It seemed more like a social club than a place of worship. People walked in groups or stood around chatting. Patrese and Beradino, watching this, noticed something pretty much simultaneously; most of the mosque-goers were black rather than ostensibly Arab. They could have been in pretty much any major city.

'Help you?' a man asked.

'We're looking for Mustafa Bayoumi,' Beradino said.

'You'll find him in the outreach center.' The man extended an arm to his left. 'Through the double doors, then first right.'

They followed his directions and, after a couple of further inquiries, found Mustafa alone in an office, entering some data on a computer terminal.

Mustafa was skinny, with cheekbones you could cut your wrists on, hair blacker than Reagan's when he'd been hard at the Grecian 2000, and a neatly trimmed beard. Like his mother, he looked substantially more black than Arab.

Still tapping the keyboard, he looked up. 'Help you?' he said.

They sure were polite round here, Patrese thought. That was two more offers of help than he'd usually get in a year in Homewood.

'We're with the Pittsburgh police department,' said Beradino quietly, 'but we're not going to flash our badges, because we don't want to embarrass you or cause a scene. We just want to ask you a few questions.' He nodded towards a couple of chairs. 'May we?'

He sat down without waiting for Mustafa's assent. Patrese followed suit.

Beradino gestured around the room.

'What is it you guys do here? Outreach – what's that?'

'It's, er, reaching out.'

Beradino laughed, pretending to be offended. 'Hey, educational standards at the PD ain't that bad just yet. I worked that one out for myself.'

Mustafa smiled too. Patrese said nothing, but he admired Beradino's approach; relax them, put them at ease, find common ground.

'Sorry. Outreach is helping people, mainly. We have a day-care facility, programs for entrepreneurs and released inmates, and a health clinic.'

'Pretty impressive.' Beradino sounded as though he meant it. 'Who funds it all?'

'We receive an annual grant from a non-profit organization called the Abrahamic Interfaith Foundation. In addition, Islam obligates all those who can feed their family to give two and a half per cent of their net worth in alms. Many of us give considerably more, both in time and money. Then there are book sales, telephone fundraisers, auctions, banquets; you name it, people have pitched in and helped out.'

'Very good. We could use some of that community spirit round my way. But listen, Mustafa – you don't mind if I call you Mustafa, do you? – we're not here to admire your work, you know that. We'd like to ask you some questions about Dr Michael Redwine.'

Mustafa's face darkened. Patrese supposed that was only natural.

'The man who killed my father, you mean?'

'I'm sure he didn't mean to kill your father.'

'If you shoot someone, detective, and you mean only to wound them, but instead they die, you've still killed them, haven't you?'

Patrese hoped that neither of them saw him wince.

Beradino chose not to answer the question, and parried it with one of his own. 'You know Dr Redwine was killed yesterday evening?'

'I saw it on the news.'

'And?'

'And what?'

'How does that make you feel?'

'Does it matter, how it makes me feel?'

'It does if I'm asking you.'

Mustafa took a deep breath. 'All right. I hope he suffered more than any of us could possibly imagine. That enough for you?'

'Suffered, as in burning in hell?'

'I don't care how. It's not a fraction of what he's caused my mother and me.'

'OK. Let me ask: where were you yesterday evening?'

'At home. I got back about five, and didn't go out again till this morning.'

'Is there anyone who can confirm that?'

'My mother. Of course.'

'Anyone else?'

'No. Just her. I had nothing to do with Redwine's death, so I didn't take the precaution of getting five people to give me an alibi, if that's what you mean.'

64

'I didn't ask whether you had anything to do with his death.'

'Why else are you here?'

'Listen, Mustafa, I'm sorry for your loss –'

'That's what people always say, when they don't know what else to say.'

'– but you being aggressive and giving me static isn't going to help anyone here.'

'Your father still alive, Detective?'

'He is, as it happens.'

'Then don't tell me not to get aggressive. Not till it happens to you.'

Patrese reckoned Mustafa had a point. Best keep that thought to himself.

When it came to unsettling suspects, Patrese knew Beradino was a master. His trick – rather, one of his tricks – was to use their mood against them, as a martial arts practitioner will exploit his opponent's weight and momentum to his own advantage.

If a suspect or a witness was calm, so too would Beradino be, looking to lull them into a sense of ever greater security until they, forgetting he was a cop rather than their best friend, let slip something they regretted.

If, on the other hand, they were upset, as Mustafa Bayoumi was increasingly becoming, Beradino would stoke the fires of their agitation as high as he could until they lost their sense of self-control – and again let slip something they regretted.

Beradino gestured around the room.

'You only help Muslims?' His tone was suddenly snappy, all reasonableness and bonhomie gone as though in a puff of smoke.

'We help our community.'

'You proselytize?'

Patrese knew what Beradino was thinking. Places like

65

Homewood – poor, deadbeat 'hoods where those who didn't seek their oblivion via the liquor store or the crack house were open to almost anything which promised to improve their lot – were fertile grounds for Islamic recruiters.

And everyone knew what *they* were like, because everyone had seen footage of the Nation of Islam: Farrakhan and his bow-tie-wearing, bean-pie-selling disciples who hated whites, Jews, women and gays.

'We welcome those who choose to come to us. Your religion does the same.'

'Our religion was what America was founded on.'

'And what an unqualified success Christianity's been, hasn't it?'

'What does that mean?' Beradino was no longer acting annoyed, Patrese knew; this was the real deal. The two of them had long ago agreed not to discuss religion, because it always ended in arguments; Beradino the devout, Patrese the unbeliever.

'Jesus died for your sins, right?'

'That's right, yes.'

'Then explain this to me. Either that was for everyone's sins right up to the moment he died, in which case we've had two thousand years of some serious bad behavior left unchecked. Or he died for everyone's sins then and for all time; in which case it hasn't helped much, has it?'

Patrese almost laughed. It was a question he'd asked himself, and others, more than once, and no one – not teachers, not priests, probably not even the Pope himself – had been able to answer it properly.

'Not to mention the impeccable behavior of priests up and down the country where young children are involved,' Mustafa continued.

'A few bad apples. Sinners, as we all are. Everyone in your culture's perfect?'

'I look around here, and I see people brought up to believe in the Christian faith. But I also know that, round here, all too often BC means before crack, and AD means after death. That's not good enough. And it's not good enough just to pray and hope everything will turn out all right. We have to go out and do the work.

'And that work starts here. Islam prohibits drugs and alcohol. You stay off those, you can be a productive member of society. You turn to them, and you're just waiting to die. And if the only way out of that is through Islam, then so be it. Because Islam places paramount importance on the education of our children. To be a teacher is a special calling. When I've finished my studies, I'm hoping to teach at the school we're raising funds to build here; preschool to fifth grade.'

'Somewhere to train the next generation of bombers?'

'Not at all. A school where everybody has a strange name, so nobody feels alone. Muslim kids feel like outsiders in public schools. No matter how good those schools are, they can't teach Islamic beliefs and morals. So we will. Kids hate being different; so we'll make them not different. And you know why?'

'I've no doubt you're going to tell me.'

'Because we have to do it ourselves now. Since 9/11, we haven't been able to receive money from other Muslim countries, even from registered Islamic charities.'

'That's damn right. There's a war on.'

Mustafa didn't take the bait. Perhaps he hadn't heard.

'We relied on that money a lot; perhaps too much. That was one of the reasons why, before 9/11, we – the immigrant Muslims – didn't really have that much to do with the black Muslims.

'Then suddenly we couldn't move for surveillance, police raids, airport searches, special registration, and so on. All the time, we had to prove our loyalty to the flag. Still do, every day. I look black anyway, but African-American Muslims sympathize. They know what it's like; not from being Muslim, but from being black.'

He looked at Beradino first, then Patrese; two white men who he felt would never understand, not fully.

'We're all niggers now, basically.'

Thursday, October 21st. 10:26 a.m.

You've seen homicide division rooms umpteen times on the silver screen, and it's one of the few aspects of police work that TV gets right. There really are desks piled high with report forms and coffee cups, and the detectives sitting at those desks really do crick the phones into their necks while pecking two-fingered at their keyboards.

Amidst the barely controlled hubbub of a major homicide investigation, Patrese read the poster above Beradino's head for the umpteenth time that day.

The Fifth Commandment, Book of Exodus, 20, of THE HOLY BIBLE.

Then: *THE OATH OF PRACTICAL HOMICIDE INVESTIGATION.*

Beradino, who'd written the poster and had it typeset himself, had clearly never met a capital letter he didn't like.

Homicide investigation is a profound duty, and constitutes a heavy responsibility. Just as there is no crime worse than taking someone else's life, so there is no task more important than bringing to justice the people who crossed that line. As such, let no person deter you from the truth and your own personal commitment to

69

see that justice is done. Not only for the deceased, but for the surviving family as well.

And remember – 'you're working for God.'

No, Patrese thought angrily; he was working for the city of Pittsburgh. There were times when Beradino's incessant God-squadding really got on his nerves, and this was one of them – not least because he was pissed anyway.

Every cop knows that the first forty-eight hours after a murder are critical. If they haven't got a good lead in that time, the chances of solving the crime are halved as evidence disappears, suspects flee, and stories change.

More than forty-eight hours after Michael Redwine had been torched, Patrese and Beradino had nothing.

Sure, they had an autopsy report, but that just confirmed Beradino's findings – that Redwine, alive when the fire started, had died from smoke inhalation.

And sure, Mustafa Bayoumi's alibi was provided by his mother, and her alone. But it was hard to see what they could do other than take it at face value. Yes, Sameera could have been lying – she'd said she'd do anything for him, after all – but to test that, they'd have to give her the full nine yards, on a hunch that was flimsy at best.

It didn't take much imagination to see how carpeting a recent widow that way would look.

Because Patrese and Beradino had to accept Mustafa's alibi, they had no probable cause to go search the house in Oakland for anything that might connect him to the fire. Even if they *did* get a warrant, and even if he *had* been involved, he was clearly a smart kid. He'd have ditched any clothing and other items that might have linked him to the blaze long before now.

That was how they consoled themselves, at any rate; because nothing and no one else in Redwine's life seemed to point to any other suspects.

70

Every resident of The Pennsylvanian had been interviewed, as had all doormen, cleaners and maintenance workers; anyone with access to the building, in other words. No one had seen anything.

'Either they're on the level, or someone should win a damn Oscar,' Patrese said.

It still didn't answer what had started as the $64,000 question and was surely now into six figures – how had the killer got into The Pennsylvanian?

They retraced Redwine's movements on the last day of his life. He'd been at Mercy in the morning, given a speech at a conference downtown after lunch, and been due to go to the opera – *La Bohème* – that evening. Nothing untoward.

They'd taken twelve officers from the regular police department and used them to turn Redwine's life upside down. No friend, acquaintance or incident was deemed too insignificant or commonplace; everyone was followed up, checked out.

TIE, Beradino told the uniforms, TIE – trace, interview, eliminate as a suspect.

They found zilch. Redwine had been a regular attendee at church, done his part at charity fundraisers, and enjoyed hiking and fishing in his spare time. No embittered ex-girlfriends, no secret gay lovers, no outstanding sexual harassment cases. Even the professional jealousies were no more than the usual found among surgeons, which was to say at once endemic and excruciatingly professional.

All in all, no reason for anybody to have killed Redwine, let alone by such a horrific method as burning alive.

The fire had destroyed any physical evidence worth the name, so Patrese and Beradino could find no joy there either. Instant forensic breakthroughs were strictly the preserve of TV shows titled with snappy acronyms. Pittsburgh PD didn't even have its own DNA lab. It had to use the FBI's, which had a backlog running into the hundreds of thousands.

71

It couldn't use private labs, as their results were inadmissible in court, due to concerns over accountability and maintenance of the chain of custody. Only government facilities were acceptable, though the technical standards at private labs were much higher; not surprisingly, perhaps, given that they were staffed by the best testers, many of whom had left the state sector because they wanted to be paid more, exacerbating staff shortages in public labs and increasing the backlog . . .

Franz Kafka was not dead, clearly. He was alive, well, and living in Pittsburgh.

Nothing of great value seemed to have been taken, ruling out burglary as a motive. Redwine was no serious collector of art, his TV set and computers were still in the apartment (though burnt to cinders, obviously), and everyone who knew him agreed that he never carried more than a hundred bucks or so in cash.

Every known arsonist within Allegheny County was interviewed, bar those already in prison. All of them had alibis for the night in question. Most said they'd pick easier targets than a portered apartment block, and that they certainly wouldn't kill anyone in the process. Arson was a crime against property, not people.

Self-serving bullshit, Patrese thought, but anyway . . .

There was always the possibility that one of the uniforms had stumbled across the crucial bit of information without realizing it. Officers were human, not computers. Long days made them tired, repetitive interviews numbed and bored them. They could miss things and make mistakes, especially towards the end of a shift. But this was the same for every homicide investigation in history. Nothing you could do about it.

There are three nightmare scenarios for cops working homicide cases, and it looked very much as though Beradino and Patrese were facing one of them.

First, that they'd overlooked something so screamingly obvious that, if they ever did find it, they'd almost certainly be carpeted from here to Cincinnati and back again.

Second, that Redwine's murder was a case of mistaken identity, and that in order to find the perpetrator, they'd need to discover first who he thought he'd killed.

Third, that the murder was the type of case that's the absolute hardest to solve; a stranger homicide, where the connection between killer and victim is obvious only to one or both of them.

Killer spotting victim in the street; victim in the wrong place at the wrong time; victim who'd caught the attention of killer; and any or all of these happening for reasons unknown to the police, because they could simply have never imagined or reconstructed them, short of knowing each quotidian incident and occurrence in the lives of every single one of Pittsburgh's citizens, and even the Soviet Union hadn't managed such overwhelming control over its people.

Redwine's ex-wife and sons had flown in from Tucson, their eyes rimmed red with tears and fatigue.

That was the worst part, Patrese felt; having to look these good people in the eye and say yes, we're doing all we can to find the murderer, we're following all lines of inquiry, we're confident we'll bring him to justice; when all the while he knew, and he knew they knew, that what he was really saying was this: we don't have a damn clue.

Not a goddamn clue.

Thursday, October 28th. 3:51 p.m.

Flames leapt high and jagged around the burgers on the grill.

Crammed into a sweltering kitchen, wearing a ridiculous polyester uniform with her hair in a net as though she'd just been caught by a trawler, Jesslyn's anger mashed in tight oblongs.

The interview had been bad enough. Kevin the manager had proved as snotty as he was spotty, sneering at her throughout it all with a contempt he didn't even bother to disguise. Why did she want this job? Why had she left her previous employment? Did she have references? Had she ever worked in the fast-food industry before?

And on, and on, and on, when they both knew this was a minimum-wage job that almost literally a monkey could do, and here was Kevin treating it as though he were personally responsible for choosing the next UN Secretary-General.

She even had to work some Sundays, her religious convictions be damned. Not because Kevin had forced her to – she could have claimed her constitutional right to freedom of religion and threatened him with a lawsuit if he'd even tried – but because she'd done Sunday shifts at Muncy so she could preach in the chapel there. Her suddenly spending every Sunday at home would arouse suspicion in a moron, and Mark was certainly not that.

But even if she *did* find a way to tell him about Mara, she thought, he wouldn't understand, not really. Prison was one of those things you could never explain. If you knew what it was like, you didn't need to be told. If you didn't know, mere words weren't enough.

Prison was a pressure cooker, a place of white heat where life had a suffocating intensity. Friendships, still less love affairs, weren't casual, to be picked up and put down whenever one felt like it; they were life-rafts of survival in a place that tried to crush the soul, raging torrents of defiance and pride in being human.

Within prison walls, the rules changed. What went on inside stayed inside. That was why Jesslyn was so careful to keep her two worlds apart. Mark had some of his colleagues over to dinner or Sunday lunch at their condo from time to time; she never did. Mark brought documents home, discussed work problems with her, gave her tidbits of department gossip; she never did any of that either. If he thought it weird, he'd long since accepted it as just the way she was.

And with Mara, who'd been such a bright shining Technicolor light in the pallors of endless institutional gray . . . well, Jesslyn had been honored, frankly, that Mara, beautiful, radiant, poised, fragrant Mara who somehow kept her poise and fragrance in those conditions, had chosen her when she could have had pretty much anyone.

And then she'd gone. Gone in stages, each of them more painful than the last.

First, Mara had called time on their relationship.

One day, just like that, out of the blue, Mara had said she didn't want to go on with it. Jesslyn had been standing six feet away, yet she'd honestly thought Mara had hit her, such was the physical shock. She'd rushed to the restroom and brought up her breakfast. Food poisoning, she'd said, before going home. They wouldn't see her cry on the prison floor; not then, not ever. Crying was weakness, and weakness was death.

In the weeks that followed, Jesslyn had begged, pleaded, reasoned, shouted and threatened, all to no avail. Sometimes she sought Mara out; sometimes she tried to avoid her. Each time she saw her, it felt as though someone had opened up a wound and started scraping salt into it.

Second, Mara had been released; back into the outworld.

If seeing her had been a torment, Jesslyn quickly realized that not seeing her was a hundred times worse. Even after their split, Mara had been the center of Jesslyn's universe, the point around which she orientated herself and her days.

Now all Jesslyn had was the whisper of Mara's name in corridor gossip, and the few of Mara's keepsakes she'd managed to hold on to, inhaling their scent as though it were the breath of life.

Third, Mara had officially complained about Jesslyn's conduct.

Briefly, surgingly, Jesslyn had hoped Mara had brought the complaints as some warped way of trying to keep Jesslyn in her life. But she could only fool herself for so long and, as the process had ground forwards, Jesslyn had let her feelings curdle towards hatred, if only in hope that it would harden into a carapace around her heart.

She'd always thought of Mara as the innocent victim of an egregious miscarriage of justice. Now, she'd forced herself to damn her as the devil incarnate, vile and evil murderess, fit only for an eternity in hell.

And finally, obviously, when Muncy had given Jesslyn her marching orders.

Jesslyn stared into the flames.

Stripe for stripe, burning for burning.

Was it fair, what had happened to her? Was it fair that murderers, rapists and pedophiles were walking the streets while she was here, frying burgers made of meat she wouldn't give to a dog? Was it fair that she'd given twenty years of her life to trying to make the world a better place, and in return had been given half an hour to pack up and go?

It wasn't just Mara she'd grown to hate, of course. It was everyone who worked the system for their own ends, and then blamed that very system whenever they didn't have the courage to take responsibility themselves. It was lawyers who made people terrified of using common sense; it was media executives who broadcast whatever got them ratings, no matter the harm to those involved; it was judges who gave light sentences; it was doctors who kept alive people any decent society would have executed. It was all these parasites, and more.

Jesslyn sought solace where she always did, in the Book; Ecclesiastes 3: 3–8.

'A time to kill, and a time to heal; a time to break down, and a time to build up; a time to weep, and a time to laugh; a time to mourn, and a time to dance; a time to cast away stones, and a time to gather stones together; a time to embrace, and a time to refrain from embracing; a time to get, and a time to lose; a time to keep, and a time to cast away; a time to rend, and a time to sew; a time to keep silence, and a time to speak; a time to love, and a time to hate; a time of war, and a time of peace.'

Saturday, October 30th. 9:32 p.m.

Patrese's sisters had gone to dinner with Bishop Kohler. Patrese had turned down the invitation. There were probably ways of spending Saturday night which he'd find even less appealing than listening to Kohler mouth platitudes by way of trying to offer spiritual succor, but he couldn't think of any off the top of his head.

Instead, he stood on the balcony of his apartment and looked down over the city.

He lived in a block called The Mountvue on Mount Washington, the hill on the city's south side which rises so giddily that only cable cars can make the ascent. He paid $1,200 a month for the place, at least a third of which was surely for the vista over the city skyline, which would have made postcard sellers kill their grandmas.

Dusk was his favorite time; the moment when the city was held suspended in all its contradictions; halfway between day and night, sanity and madness, picturesque and squalid.

The heart of downtown was called the Golden Triangle, sandwiched between the Allegheny and Monongahela rivers and tapering to the point where the two met and joined the Ohio. On crisp fall evenings like this it did indeed seem golden,

78

the sunlight making the thrusting skyscrapers glow as though in belief that the day to come would hold more than the day just passed.

There was the medieval castle of PPG Place, all battlements and crenellations; there the four interlocking silver octagons of the Oxford Center; there the tallest of them all, the USX Tower, a behemoth of exposed steel columns and curtain walls; there the Grant Building flashing P-I-T-T-S-B-U-R-G-H in Morse code over and again; and there the blue light on top of the Gulf Building which signified that the temperature was falling.

Patrese loved this city. Always had, always would.

He loved the way Pittsburgh held high the best of American values: hard work, unpretentiousness, renewal. Time was, in the heyday of the steel industry, when it had been virtually uninhabitable: palls of smoke so thick that streetlights had burned all day; desk jockeys who'd left their offices for an hour's lunch downtown and returned to find their white shirts stained black; rivers so choked with chemicals that they had burned for days on end.

One writer had called Pittsburgh 'hell with the lid taken off'. He hadn't found much dissent.

But by the early 1980s the steel industry had shut down, and now hillsides above the mill sites had grown lush and green again. Pittsburgh was a riot of hills and valleys, slopes, hollows, streams, gulches too. It spilled out cockeyed across the landscape's folds, taking its cues from the terrain.

It was therefore a city of neighborhoods, little worlds of their own separated by earth or water and rejoined by bridges. Pittsburgh had more bridges than Venice, something of which the tourist board was inordinately proud; that, and the fact that the 'Burgh had been voted America's Most Livable City.

That kind of shit was always double-edged, Patrese thought. The surest way to stop it being Most Livable was to attract all the people who came here *because* it was Most Livable.

There was a sudden explosion of light from below as the sun reached just the right angle to fizz off one of the plate-glass corners on PPG Place. Patrese didn't know whether the architect had designed it so, but he caught his breath every time he saw it happen.

He just wished Pittsburgh looked as good in Homewood as it did from up here.

Sunday, October 31st. 9:24 p.m.

'I'm sorry to disturb you, Father,' I say, 'but I have some sins I'd like to confess.'

Bishop Kohler turns to face me.

I see two competing strands of thought in his expression: the temporal, which says it's late and he wants to be leaving; and the spiritual, which demands he give what succor he can to a sinner.

'Of course, my child,' he says, biting down on his annoyance.

'I won't keep you long. I know you must want to get home.'

Home, in this case, being an eleven-bedroom mansion set in a couple of acres on the border between Shadyside and Squirrel Hill.

Far too large and ostentatious for a man of the cloth, you might think, and you'd be right. I read an interview where he defended his decision to live there. The mansion was given to the church just after the war and has been used by every bishop since; Giovanni Cardinal Montini stayed there once, and later he became Pope Paul VI; it's useful for meetings and putting up visiting dignitaries; and on and on and on.

And yet he knows, as I know, as everyone knows, that what he should do, if he was as humble and holy as he makes out, is go and live in a seminary among those training to be priests, and sell the mansion, using the profits to help with the church's work.

The place would fetch a couple of million on the open market. Imagine what good could be done with that amount of money.

So forgive me if I doubt the sincerity of Bishop Kohler's spiritual commitment.

Still, in the same interview, he said he liked to spend time alone in the Cathedral of Saint Paul, the diocese's mother church out near the university in Oakland; that he preferred on occasion to do the locking-up rounds himself, solo, the better to be alone with God in His house.

Which is why I knew I'd find him here, now, and without witnesses.

Kohler leads me in silence to the confessional. He asks me nothing about myself, I think, the better to maintain the anonymity of the confession. He may know my face, but not my name, nor anything else about me.

He's not to know that, in a few minutes, all this will have ceased to matter for him.

He motions me into one door of the confessional, and himself steps into the other.

The confessional is in classic style; two compartments separated by a latticed grille on which is hung a crucifix. I kneel on the prie-dieu.

I don't know how to begin. I've always thought confession should be between the sinner and their God, with no other human present, so this is difficult for me.

'Has it been long since your last confession?' Kohler whispers.

It's only the two of us in the entire place, but the near-darkness of the confessional – and of the cathedral itself – seems to make whispering appropriate.

'Yes,' I reply.

'Would you like me to remind you of the purpose of confession?'

'Yes.'

'You must confess your sins in order to restore your connection to God's grace and to escape hell, particularly if you have committed a mortal sin.'

'What's a mortal sin?'

'A mortal sin must be about a serious matter, have been committed with full consent, and be known to be wrong.'

'What kind of sins are mortal sins?'

'Murder, for sure. Blasphemy. Adultery.'

He can't see me, but I smile.

'And what happens if these sins aren't confessed?' I ask.

'It's a dogmatic belief of the faith that if a person guilty of mortal sin dies without either receiving the sacrament or experiencing perfect contrition with the intention of confessing to a priest, that person will receive eternal damnation.' He pauses. 'These things are known to all Catholics,' he adds.

'I'm sorry, Father.'

'It must have been a very long time since you last confessed, no?' Another pause. 'In order for the sacrament to be valid, the penitent must do more than simply confess their known mortal sins to a priest. They must be truly sorry for each of the mortal sins committed, have a firm intention never to commit them again, and perform the penance imposed by the priest. As well as confessing the types of mortal sins committed, the penitent must disclose how many times each sin was committed.'

I know that whatever's said in the confessional stays there; this is an absolute, inviolable rule, even if to do otherwise might save lives. Doctors and attorneys can break their pledges of confidentiality in extremis; a priest, never.

So I can tell him, even if everything else goes wrong.

'I have killed,' I say.

Kohler gasps; in horror, surprise, perhaps both. He must think it unlikely, but perhaps the tone of my voice lets him know that I'm not joking.

'How many times?' he asks, more in a croak than a whisper.

'More than once.'

'When did you last kill?'

'Now.'

I'm up off the prie-dieu and out of the door in a flash, pulling the gasoline can from my bag. I throw open the confessional's other door and see Kohler there, his mouth a perfect circle of outrage at this violation of religious etiquette if nothing else.

I splash the gasoline on him. For an old man, he still looks strong, but gentle too. Years of turning the other cheek have left him useless in a situation like this.

In another two seconds, maybe three, he might have reacted to the danger; but those are seconds he doesn't have, seconds I won't give him.

I light the juggling torch and touch it to his face.

His screams echo loud and bounce round the cathedral, and the flames rush from his skin and clothes to the walls of the confessional, leaping orange through crackling wood as I step back and close the door on him, holding it shut for as long as I can stand before the heat drives me back.

It's not long, but it's enough.

'Isaiah chapter fifty-nine, verse seventeen,' I shout, so he can hear me above his screaming and through his agonies. '"For I put on righteousness as a breastplate, and a helmet of salvation upon my head; and I put on the garments of vengeance for clothing, and am clad with zeal as a cloak."'

The screaming stops, and in its place comes a rasped muttering, the words of a dying man, indistinct but their meaning clear if I strain to hear:

'God the Father of mercies, through the death and resurrection of his Son, has reconciled the world to himself and sent the Holy Spirit among us for the forgiveness of sins; through the ministry of the Church may God give you pardon and peace, and I absolve you from your sins in the name of the Father, and of the Son, and of the Holy Spirit, Amen.'

10:12 p.m.

The death of a surgeon in an upscale condo block had merited one mildly disgruntled local TV crew. The death of the bishop brought the national networks out in force. They crammed up against bumblebee-striped crime tape and turned glaring camera lights on anyone who stepped inside the police cordon.

At the edge of that cordon, a uniformed officer met Patrese and Beradino and checked their credentials. When he saw Beradino's name, he touched the checkered band on his hat in respect.

'Have you adapted?' Beradino asked.

Adapt, in this case, was a police mnemonic rather than a Darwinian evolutionary imperative. ADAPT: *arrest* the perpetrator, if possible; *detain* and identify witnesses and suspects; *assess* the crime scene; *protect* the crime scene; and *take* notes.

'All but the first, sir.'

'Who found the body?'

'Passer-by spotted the flames. Kelly Grubb. He's over there.' He indicated a middle-aged man sitting on the trunk of a police cruiser.

Grubb's expression was typical of people who have

stumbled across murder scenes; a mixture, in almost exactly equal parts, of revulsion at the sight and excitement at being part of a police investigation.

'We'll talk to him later. Did he alter the scene in any way?'

'Says he called the fire brigade straight off. Didn't go in, and they sure as hell wouldn't have let him in once they got there.'

'OK.' More degradation of evidence, that was a given once the fire department had done their thing, but there was no point moaning about it. That was their job, to put out blazes, and damn the consequences, forensic or otherwise.

Beradino thought for a moment, looking towards the spot where the fire department had set up an improvised command post. It was right next to where the TV crews had gathered, and a few uniformed policemen were already shooting the breeze there with the firefighters. Beradino turned back to the officer.

'Throw up another cordon, a hundred feet further out than this one,' he said. 'Keep every civilian – TV crews, general public – behind the new one, the outer one. They *start* moanin', threaten to arrest them. They *keep* moanin', make good on that threat.'

'Yes, sir.'

'Good man.'

Patrese understood Beradino's logic. At big crime scenes like this, cops meet up. They haven't seen each other for a while and, since they're used to such situations, they get to chatting, laughing, ribbing each other. They forget there's a corpse nearby. They forget people get offended when they think police officers are being insensitive round the dead. Most of all, they forget there are TV mics around that pick up every word they say.

Patrese and Beradino left the uniform shouting at a colleague to bring more yellow-and-black, and headed towards

86

the cathedral; twin-towered and Gothic, with a statue of St Paul mounted on the center pediment.

There was a poster by the entrance. *St Paul Cathedral*, it read: *a foundation of faith, building a future of hope.*

Patrese shuddered, and stopped. Beradino gripped his forearm.

'Franco, listen. You want me to take care of this one alone? I understand.'

Patrese shook his head. 'No.'

'Come on, Franco. He was a friend of your family's, this is the place you just buried your parents. You got a thousand-yard stare on you. Let me handle this.'

'I told you, Mark, I'm fine.' Patrese managed a weak laugh. 'Vacant stare's probably jet lag.'

'Huh?'

'Extra hour's sleep this morning. When the clocks went back.'

'Yeah.' Beradino looked at Patrese a moment more, and then shrugged. 'OK. You win. Come on.'

The cathedral's main door was open. Before Patrese and Beradino were inside, they could smell the burning – the piquant aroma of woodsmoke and the half-sweet, half-acrid overlay of charred flesh.

Patrese puffed out his cheeks and rolled his head in a circle, counter-clockwise and then clockwise; preparing the body for what the mind was about to suffer.

A few hours ago, he'd been at Heinz Field, watching his beloved Steelers put thirty-four points past the New England Patriots. Now he was at the holding station inside the door, where he and Beradino put on the usual anti-contamination suits, the ones which made the wearer look like a hybrid astronaut cum sewage treatment worker.

Just a normal day in a homicide detective's life, in other words.

The cathedral's nave comprised five aisles beneath pointed

arches and ribbed vaulting. The detectives walked between silent pews and past crime-scene officers and firefighters, men whose concerns – secular, scientific – usually had little place in here.

Focus, Patrese told himself, with a ferocity which made his teeth clench. *Focus*. Don't think about Kohler, and everything he'd been. There'd be time enough for that later. Just work the scene, the way you would any other homicide.

Kohler's body was prostrate on the floor, a yard or so in front of the confessional's ruined timbers; too far simply to have fallen when the confessional collapsed.

He'd tried to escape. Died on his feet, as it were; gone towards death rather than simply waited for death to claim him.

You could mix religion up any way you chose, Patrese thought, believe absolutely in the afterlife and kingdoms beyond this realm; but when it came down to it, simple biological imperatives hardwired into humankind made people fight against the dying of the light. It was nothing to do with soul, or faith, or belief; it was the survival instinct, pure and simple, and it was in you for as long as you breathed.

Kohler looked much as Redwine had; arms raised as though to fight, and clothes – in this case, a bishop's surplice – melted in patches to his skin.

'Who could do this?' Beradino said, and Patrese noted the tremble in his voice. 'To a man of God, in the house of God . . .' He shook his head, as though unable to fathom the limitless depths of mankind's mendacity, and then turned to Patrese.

'I know he was a special man, to you and your family . . .'

'You could say that.'

'. . . and so I promise you, we'll find whoever did this. Just like when a cop's killed, Franco, we'll pull out all the stops. That's my promise to you, right here.'

88

Patrese nodded.

The photographer was snapping dispassionately away, a vulture with a Canon. He glanced up from his viewfinder as Beradino and Patrese came to a halt.

'No chalk fairies, then,' Beradino said.

No one could draw chalk outlines round the body or any other object until the photographers had been and gone. Photographs had to be representations of the crime scene as it was when the incident was reported, or they were inadmissible as evidence. A good lawyer could get a case thrown out of court for less.

'None at all,' the photographer said. 'You train your cops well.'

'Sometimes,' Beradino replied.

Patrese looked around again.

The fire damage was substantially less extensive here than at Redwine's apartment. Not only had the fire department been on the scene within three minutes of Grubb's call, but the confessional had also been set against stone walls to one side of the church. Everything else flammable – pews, pulpits, curtains, altar cloths – was far enough away to have prevented the fire from making the jump.

Patrese swallowed hard, and again Beradino noticed; he knew, too, that Patrese hadn't turned a hair at the sight of Redwine's body, which had been no less horrific than this.

Patrese looked away, more to avoid Beradino's quizzical gaze than anything else.

They set to searching the place.

There were several ways of doing this – spiraling out from or into a central point, dividing the area into zones, shoulder-to-shoulder along pre-designated lines – but Beradino's chosen method was criss-crossing. They'd go up and down the room and then side to side, so that every point was covered twice.

If you missed something the first time, you'd find it the second.

If you missed it the second time, you were in the wrong job.

They used tweezers to pick up objects and bag them, and their elbows to open and close doors. The fewer traces of themselves they left here, the better.

It was lying on the flagstone floor, and Patrese saw it first.

A piece of wood, with what looked like some kind of sculpture attached to it; and broken, that was clear from the ragged edges, smashed rather than cut.

It wasn't hard to recognize what it was. Half the Western world had one.

A crucifix.

More precisely, the bottom half of one.

The top half wasn't far away. The break ran diagonally across Jesus' chest.

'You got these?' Patrese asked the photographer.

'Every which way.'

Patrese squatted down, pulled a transparent plastic evidence bag from his pocket, pushed it inside out and, with the plastic covering his fingers, carefully picked up one half of the crucifix.

It was broken, but not burnt.

Patrese turned it over in his hand.

It felt solid, weighty.

Not the kind of thing which would break if you simply dropped it on the floor.

If you *hurled* it, yes; but not if you just dropped it.

He looked around again.

Nearby, also smashed, were pieces of wood painted in bright gold and red.

Patrese found three, and could fit them together in his

head without needing to check with the photographer again as to whether he could pick them up.

They looked very like the constituent parts of a medieval icon.

'Mark,' Patrese said. 'Look at this.'

'*You* look at *this*, Franco.'

Patrese glanced up; first at Beradino, and then in the direction he was staring.

Beradino was looking at the stained-glass windows high above them; in particular, at the three windows which had been smashed.

11:17 p.m.

Sunday nights in Pittsburgh are more or less traffic-free, so they had a clear run back from Saint Paul to the North Shore.

'I spoke to him just this morning, you know?' Patrese said, gliding the car through lights turning back from green to amber.

'Spoke to who?'

'Kohler.'

'You didn't tell me this.'

'When could I tell you this? We've just been at a murder scene. *His* murder. I'm telling you now. I spoke to him around nine this morning.'

'About what?'

Patrese sighed, and rubbed the bridge of his nose.

'You really wanna know?'

'I don't ask unless I do.'

'OK. This is a little personal, which is why I didn't mention it before. I mean, it's no big deal, it's just . . . I was feeling a bit down, all right? My sisters had gone round to dinner with him the night before. I stayed home, didn't want to go. Probably drunk a bit too much, felt shitty the next morning, was missing my mom and pop, wanted to talk to someone.

92

Bianca was on shift at Mercy, Valentina . . . it was Sunday morning, she'd still have been in bed. So I called Kohler.'

'And how did he seem to you?'

'Totally normal. I didn't really pay attention. I was doing most of the talking. He listened. He could have been cooking breakfast at the same time, for all I know.'

'How long did you talk for?'

'Six, seven minutes, I don't know.'

'You speak to your sisters today?'

'Went to watch the Steelers with Valentina this afternoon.'

'She say how Kohler was last night?'

'Said he was fine. In good humor, in fact.'

Beradino made a moue. 'Little did he know, huh? First Redwine, now . . .'

'There's no guarantee this is even related to Redwine.'

'True. Could be copycat, could be coincidence. Method's the same, location's completely different. Only a few people had access to where Redwine was killed. Here, anyone could have come in off the street, literally. Few buildings more public than a cathedral.'

'Why the smashing of the crucifix? The icon, the windows? None of that with Redwine, was there?'

'Someone who hates religion? Someone who hates Christianity, certainly.'

'Someone like Mustafa Bayoumi?'

Beradino glanced across at Patrese. 'He seemed pretty hostile to it, for sure.'

'So we look at Bayoumi first.'

'Which means we believe the murders *are* connected, until proven otherwise.'

'Yeah.'

'First, we check his alibi. It's just his mom again, no one else, we get suspicious.'

'And we look for any connections between him and

Kohler. Did they know each other personally? Did Kohler do something to piss him off?'

'Or *not* do something to piss him off? Something Bayoumi thought he *should* have done, but didn't? Was the diocese in dispute with the Homewood mosque project? Anything like that.'

'Perhaps it's something less concrete. If it is Bayoumi, maybe he chose Kohler as a symbol – as *the* symbol, the head – of the Catholic church in Pittsburgh?'

Beradino was quiet for a moment.

'Let's not get too carried away with Bayoumi, Franco,' he said. 'Whether it's him or not, we turn Kohler's life upside down, as we did Redwine's. Who had a reason to kill Kohler? Who knew both Kohler and Redwine? We cross-reference every suspect, every witness, every friend, acquaintance, colleague. Some of Kohler's parishioners must have been Redwine's patients, and vice versa.'

'And what else did they share? Were they members of the same country club? Did they play golf together? Were they on the board of the same charity? Were they members of the same professional association?'

'Exactly. And on, and on, and on. Like I said before, Franco, back in Saint Paul, far as I'm concerned, this is like a cop killing. We give it full beans. You don't go round burning bishops. Not on my watch.'

Patrese couldn't help it. It started as a pricking behind his eyes and a flutter in the base of his throat, and then the tears were coming warm and too fast to stop. He wiped angrily at his face, not least so he could keep driving. Tears were weakness.

Beradino was silent, knowing better than to kill Patrese with kindness.

Patrese sniffed hard, twice, and swallowed.

'What kind of man could do those things?' he said. 'What kind of monster?'

Monday, November 1st. 8:22 a.m.

First thing Monday morning, Chance called Beradino and Patrese into a meeting; the three of them in the room, with Mayor Negley on speakerphone like the voice of God.

Howard Negley was a billionaire businessman who'd won the mayoralty a couple of years back. Drawing a token salary of one dollar, he'd proved himself a dynamic presence in City Hall; too dynamic for most of the old stagers there, who'd swiftly found themselves seeking solace in their directorships. Ostentatiously using his business skills and contacts to help regenerate the city, Negley had consciously set himself apart from the endless infighting of career politicos. The public loved him.

'I'm not having surgeons and bishops murdered in Pittsburgh, you understand?' Negley said. 'I *will not* stand by and see it happen. It's bad for the city.'

Bad for your popularity, you mean, thought Patrese.

What Patrese could take from Beradino, as good and honest a cop as you'd find anywhere in the Lower 48, sounded false and shrill from an elected official. Besides, why did Negley always have to talk as though he were addressing a political rally?

95

'Whatever you need to find the killer, you got it,' Negley continued. 'You want more officers, you tell me. You want men from other jurisdictions, I can arrange that.'

It was all Patrese could do not to rotate his tongue in his cheek. To judge from the expression on Beradino's face, and even Chance's, he wasn't alone in his opinion.

Yes, they could have more officers, from inside Allegheny County and outside too, but that wasn't within the mayor's power to offer, let alone make happen.

Typical Negley, Patrese thought. No wonder he'd married a Hollywood actress. The only thing more titanic than the mutual appreciation society would have been the clash of egos.

He put it quickly from his mind, and turned his attention back to the room.

'You should also bring the FBI in on this,' squawked Negley from the box.

Patrese was about to say he'd suggest the same thing – he knew Caleb Boone, the head of the FBI's Pittsburgh office, and thought him a good guy – when he saw Chance look at Beradino, and Beradino shake his head.

'We don't think that's appropriate at this juncture, sir,' Chance said.

Patrese knew Chance was a political animal; few people rose as high in the force as he'd done without being one. But he was also first and foremost a cop. Therefore, as he'd demonstrated at Patrese's disciplinary hearing, he was flatly opposed to anything or anyone which threatened the integrity and independence of the police department.

The FBI was top of that list. It was a turf war, and it was as atavistic and ineradicable as all conflict. There would always be turf; therefore there would always be war.

'Why the hell not?' Negley snapped.

'Because all they'll do is muddy the waters, sir. The more agencies you involve, the more confusion, which helps no one but the killer. Besides, we're perfectly capable of handling this investigation ourselves.'

'The FBI has unparalleled resources. It also tracks extremists – Islamic extremists, other religious fanatics – who might have wanted to do this.'

'Running to the G-Men at the drop of a hat doesn't send out the right message, sir. These are crimes against Pittsburghers. Pittsburghers want to see their own police force solve them.'

'It's obvious you've got a serial killer here, so you must call the FBI in. The Bureau has infinitely more experience than you in dealing with such people.'

Chance actually licked his lips before replying.

'I'm afraid not, sir, on both counts.'

'I'm warning you . . .'

'We don't yet have a serial killer, sir, not necessarily. We have two murders, not necessarily linked. If they *do* prove to be linked, the FBI's own criteria state a minimum of three before a murderer can be considered serial. And even then, we don't *have* to call them in at all. Whether or not to seek the Bureau's help is the decision of the local police department. Right now, we choose not to invite them.'

'Allen, you know me well enough to know I'm not a man you want to annoy.'

'And, sir, *you* know *me* well enough to know I'm not a man who needs to be told how to do my job. I don't tell you how to run the city; don't tell me how best to catch this man.'

Negley was drawing breath to say something else, but Chance beat him to it.

'Now, if you'll excuse us, sir, we have a killer to catch.'

11:30 a.m.

Press conferences were usually humdrum, routine affairs; a few crime correspondents, a couple of detectives, and a department press officer who was underpaid and under-motivated in equal measures.

They'd discuss a bar shooting, a domestic murder, a gang hit. The police would give their side of the story; the reporters would dutifully check names and details; the press officer would make random interjections to remind everyone he existed.

Small-time crimes, small-time meetings. Ninety-nine times over a hundred, they could have convened round a table at Starbucks.

The hacks didn't tend to question the official version of events. If they did, they'd gradually find themselves frozen out of information and access; then their jobs would go to someone else, someone more prepared to toe the line.

Besides, the public appetite for other people's disasters was insatiable. It didn't really matter what the news was, as long as it was bad. Every media man knew the truth of the axiom: 'If it bleeds, it leads.'

But every now and then, those leads slipped from the crime beat to general news.

It could be something shockingly grotesque. There was the floater the cops had pulled from the Monongahela whose skin had slipped off the hands like a pair of gloves; the dog who'd chewed off his owner's face because she'd died and there was no one to feed him; and, most celebrated of all, most gasped at and laughed over, the schizo who'd cut open his stomach and pulled out his guts before cutting them into neat pieces with a pair of tin snips.

Or it could involve someone important. Someone like Bishop Kohler.

The police department found the largest room available, and even so it was bulging at the seams. Reporters brandishing notebooks and voice recorders annexed every chair going; TV cameras ringed the back and sides of the room like a monk's tonsure.

Chance led Beradino and Patrese into the room, holding his hands up as he did so; though whether to acknowledge the assembled multitude or shield his eyes from the popping of flashbulbs, Patrese couldn't tell.

Three chairs had been arranged behind a table. Chance sat in the middle, gesturing that Patrese and Beradino should park their butts either side of him, as though he were Jesus and they the thieves.

Chance's presence was largely symbolic. He was there for one reason only: to show the police were taking this murder so seriously that an assistant police chief would deign to come and break bread with the masses.

This was a double-edged sword, of course. If Patrese and Beradino found the killer, Chance would share the credit. If they failed, they'd fail alone.

Even though he was the junior man, and even though he'd been up half the night consoling his sisters – both of them predictably devastated by Kohler's murder – Patrese did most of the talking.

Beradino despised the media, and made little secret of it. He disliked being second-guessed by reporters he considered uninformed at best and irresponsible at worst, and he hated their tacit demands that the police work to news deadlines rather than at an investigation's natural pace.

Patrese took a more pragmatic approach. He figured that the media were part and parcel of every major homicide investigation, so he might as well accept it. Better to have them inside the tent pissing out than vice versa. The more he could run them, the less he ran the risk of them running him.

Picking questioners with a practiced hand, Patrese performed the traditional detectives' balancing act in such situations: give enough to keep the media happy, not enough to jeopardize the investigation.

He pointed to a man with a mane of hair that would have shamed a lion.

'Ed Sharpe, KDKA. You believe these killings are connected?'

'We're keeping an open mind, but obviously we'd be foolish *not* to be looking for connections. Burning bodies isn't especially common, either as MO or signature.'

MO, *modus operandi*, is the way a killer goes about his business, the things he needs to do to effect the murders as efficiently as possible. Signature is what he needs to do to make the murder worthwhile, be it emotionally, physically or sexually.

The problem for Beradino and Patrese was this. They couldn't be sure whether burning was signature or MO without knowing the killer's internal logic, but finding that logic might be impossible unless they worked out the burning's significance; whether the killer had burnt Redwine and Kohler because it had been the easiest option available to him, or because he'd felt compelled to.

'Andy Rose, *Post-Gazette*. Were the victims alive when they were burned?'

'Not as far as we can establish.' Patrese was proud of his poker face. 'We believe they'd been asphyxiated first, and then set on fire.'

And so, when the crazies started ringing up – as they would, sure as night followed day – and started claiming to have used a silk scarf or gimp ball on the victims, Patrese and Beradino could dismiss them out of hand.

'Jess Schuring, *60 Minutes*. Is it significant that Bishop Kohler was killed in the cathedral? Some kind of religious aspect?'

The poker face stayed on. 'Again, not that we can establish. Probably just the place where the killer knew the bishop would be at a certain time.'

'But some of the stained-glass windows had been smashed.'

Patrese thought fast. The broken windows were visible from the street outside, so there was no point trying to deny it. He'd have to give a plausible explanation instead.

'Preliminary investigations suggest that the heat of the fire shattered them.'

He didn't mention the crucifixes and icons, of course. Nor did he pass on the fact that the fire had also damaged a print of Michelangelo's *Hand of God Giving Life to Adam* – an elderly, bearded God wrapped in a swirling cloak, his right arm outstretched to impart the spark of life into the first man.

Keeping these details quiet was another filter for the lunatics.

'Hugo Carr, *Philadelphia Inquirer*. You think the Human Torch has a previous history of arson?'

'I'm sorry?' It was Beradino, tight-lipped with anger. 'The Human Torch?'

'You know. The *Fantastic Four*?'

'Is this some kind of nickname for the killer?'

'If you like.'

'No, Mr Carr, I don't like. I don't like at all. I don't like giving some cutesy moniker to anyone who does what this man does. I won't be calling him the Human Torch or anything else like that. Nor will anyone else working this case. If they do, they'll be reassigned before they can draw another breath. Is that clear?'

Subdued: 'Yes.'

Beradino gestured towards Patrese: *Go on.*

'We're interviewing known arsonists in the area, of course,' Patrese said. 'We've found indications of accelerant at both scenes, but nothing too sophisticated. Certainly nothing that would rule out, you know, anyone but an experienced firestarter.'

Nothing that would need advanced chemistry, either; but Sameera Bayoumi had told them that Mustafa had spent the previous evening with her, had left for Philadelphia first thing this morning, and wouldn't be back till Thursday.

Patrese looked straight down the lens of the KDKA camera. He knew Pittsburghers would appreciate him addressing them through their own, hometown, channel rather than one of the national networks.

'I'm asking you, the public, to help us on this one. The police can't be everywhere. You can; you *are*. Be our eyes and ears. Please, if you've seen anything, heard anything, noticed anything unusual, ring in and tell us. Don't worry if it seems too small or insignificant or irrelevant. Let us be the judge of that. You never know; your piece of information could be the one that makes the difference.'

That kind of logic – *it could be you* – got people buying lottery tickets, so Patrese figured it was worth a try here. He knew that too much information could, and often did, swamp homicide task forces, but better too much than too little. Given enough time, manpower and luck, you could always find the needle in the haystack.

But if the needle wasn't there to start with, you had no chance.

12:57 p.m.

For a man who'd presumably believed that earthly riches were a bar to the kingdom of God, Patrese thought, Bishop Kohler had sure hedged his bets.

He'd been to Kohler's official residence on several occasions, but it was only now, with the time – and indeed the duty – to search every room from top to bottom, that he appreciated quite how lavish it was.

The house itself was double-fronted, finished in red brick and light gray stone with copper detailing long since oxidized to sea-foam green. Out back, a magnolia tree stood proud in magenta and mauve above perfectly maintained lawns and flowerbeds.

Inside, chandeliers sparkled in shards of silver crystal. Banisters were carved in dark oak and walnut. Intricate reliefs glided across four-square stone fireplaces.

It wasn't just the quality of the house which struck Patrese, but its size too. Nine thousand square feet over three stories. Eleven bedrooms and six bathrooms, plus a library, a morning room, a living room, a dining room, a kitchen and a butler's pantry. Patrese had stayed in smaller hotels than this place.

All for one man, living alone.

It seemed to Patrese a terrible waste – no, more than a waste; hypocrisy and cant of the highest order – for Kohler to have had all this to himself. Sure, part of his job had involved entertaining, and accommodating visitors to the diocese, but still.

Though it was a dull afternoon, the high ceilings and large windows meant that Patrese and Beradino didn't need to turn the lights on just yet. Quiet draped across the house like a blanket; the city may have been all around them, but it had been reduced to a gentle, distant hum, no more.

They were looking for everything and nothing; something, *anything*, which might help them discover who'd killed Kohler.

They started at the bottom of the house and worked upwards.

In the basement was a makeshift gym with a treadmill, an exercise bike, and a rack of free weights. The bike's crank arms were rusty, and a cobweb stretched across the tread-mill's display screen.

The adjacent wine cellar had seen more use. Patrese counted more than five hundred bottles, their racks labeled in Kohler's copperplate: Goosecross Cabernet, Rutherford Merlot.

But there was nothing which could possibly be relevant to the investigation in either room; nor in the living room, the morning room, the dining room, the kitchen or the pantry.

It wasn't just evidence towards the murder they lacked, Patrese thought, but evidence of Kohler's life, full stop. If Kohler had read, it hadn't been for pleasure; the only books on the shelves were religious ones. The TV set looked like it dated from the Cuban missile crisis. There were no videos, no DVDs. A handful of CDs, classical and choral music. No family photographs, of course; Kohler had had no family.

You couldn't give your life to God and live among humans, Patrese thought, not if you wanted to do both properly.

Making a man go so far from his primal urges wasn't natural. It certainly wasn't healthy.

They went into the library.

'We'll find something here,' Beradino said. 'Read your Agatha Christie.'

He was right. They *did* find something there; more precisely, in the top drawer of the antique bureau where Kohler had worked on his papers.

It was a photo of a young man, probably fourteen or fifteen, dressed in the College of the Sacred Heart football uniform. He was squatting on his haunches, his helmet dangling from his right hand, and he was smiling up at the camera.

It was a photo of Patrese.

Not just Patrese, when they searched the bureau further.

Hundreds of children. Patrese reckoned they ranged in age from eleven to sixteen, give or take. Many were in Sacred Heart school uniforms, purple blazers with an elaborate crest on the breast pocket. Some were in football gear; others wore choir surplices. Boys outnumbered girls by about two to one.

All of them were fully dressed. There wasn't even a bare chest in sight, let alone any nudity, and certainly nothing which could be described as in any way sexual.

Beradino was silent, but even so Patrese could sense his relief. He remembered that Beradino, while arguing with Mustafa Bayoumi at the mosque a couple of weeks back, had dismissed abusive priests as bad apples. Beradino *believed*. It would have devastated him to discover that the bishop himself had been a pedophile; that the apples had been rotten not just to the core but to the top too.

'You recognize these kids?' Beradino asked.

'Some of them, yeah. The ones who were there same time as me, sure.'

'The ones you recognize; you guys were his favorites?'

106

'I guess.' Patrese riffled through a few prints till he found a couple of other guys in football uniform. 'Kohler coached the football team. You played football, you were a bit . . .' – Patrese sought the right word – '*special*. Yeah, special. We called him the Pigskin Padre.'

'Pigskin Padre. I like that.' Beradino laughed softly and let a stack of photos fall gently on to the desk, where they fanned out as though dealt by a croupier. 'You have favorite teachers as a kid, so why can't teachers have favorite kids, huh?'

He gestured round the room; not at what was there, but at what wasn't.

'He had no one else, did he?'

2:01 p.m.

They boxed the photos and sent them back by police courier to the North Shore, with orders that every child pictured should be traced and interviewed. The Sacred Heart's administrative office would have contact details for its alumni; they should start there.

At the edge of the police cordon around the bishop's house, a woman with immaculately coiffed dark hair was talking urgently to one of the uniforms. He looked in the detectives' direction. When they'd finished giving the courier his instructions, he hurried over.

'That lady lives next door,' he said. 'She wants to tell you something.'

Patrese sized her up as they approached. Mid-forties, a figure which suggested good genes or a fastidious diet, blouse and skirt tailored just so, and a forehead whose perfection screamed Botox.

Typical Squirrel Hill dame, in other words.

'Yesterday morning . . .' she began.

'Excuse me,' Beradino said. 'You are?'

'I'm what?'

'Your name.'

'My name is Katharine Horowitz. I live there.' She pointed to the nearest house, thirty yards away. It was half the size of the bishop's, which still left it four times as big as Patrese's apartment. 'Yesterday morning, I heard the bishop shouting.'

'Shouting?'

'Yes. Like he was arguing with someone.'

Beradino looked across to Katharine's house, and then back again. 'You heard this all the way from there to here?'

'I was in the garden.'

'On a Sunday morning in November?'

'I had some trimming and clipping to finish off before winter sets in for good. Anyhow, it wasn't that cold yesterday. And so I could see that Father Gregory had a couple of windows open, overlooking his own garden.'

Sunday morning, little traffic noise, no one around. It was entirely plausible she could have heard him at that distance.

'What time was this?'

'About ten.'

'What was he saying?'

'I couldn't catch all of it, but something about how this was all dead and buried, you – the other guy – had no right to bring it up now, show some respect and so on. He was really agitated. I'd never heard him like that before.'

'You said "the other guy". This was a man he was arguing with?'

'Yes.'

'What was *he* saying? What was this man saying?'

'I couldn't hear.'

'You couldn't hear what they were saying, or you couldn't hear the other man's voice at all?'

'I couldn't hear the voice at all.'

'So how do you know he was a man?'

'Because I heard his car draw up about three-quarters of an hour beforehand. I'd just started in the garden then.'

'That might have been the bishop himself, returning from somewhere.'

'No. I heard the bishop greet him, and the man say something back.'

'You catch a look at him?'

'No.'

'The car?'

'No.'

'Pity.'

'Anyone else see this man?' Patrese asked.

'How do you mean, anyone else?'

'Your husband, perhaps?'

The slightest furrow fought its way through the Botox and rippled the perfection of Katharine Horowitz' forehead.

'I live alone, Detective.'

Rich divorcée, Patrese thought instantly; and the look of defensive defiance on her face told him he was spot on.

'When you heard the bishop shouting; this man was still here?'

'I presume so. I hadn't heard the car leave, if that's what you mean.'

'OK. Thank you.' Patrese reached into his jacket's breast pocket and extracted a business card. 'You think of anything else, you have any questions, you just ring the number here.'

'I surely will,' she said. 'Such a tragedy. He was the best of men, Father Kohler.'

Beradino and Patrese walked out of her earshot.

'You phoned Kohler around nine o'clock, you said?' Beradino asked.

'Yeah.'

'So by the time you get off the phone, it's nine ten, give or take. About nine fifteen, according to Katharine Horowitz, Kohler has a visitor. Forty-five minutes later, they're having a pow-wow. You're almost certainly the last person to speak with Kohler before this visitor arrived, you know?'

'I guess. But it still doesn't help, does it? Even if Katharine's timings are a bit out, or mine are, I rang off before anyone arrived.'

'You're sure?'

'I didn't hear a doorbell, or someone else's voice. Kohler didn't break off to answer the door, try to hurry me off of the phone, nothing like that.'

Beradino clicked his tongue against his teeth. 'Too much to hope for, huh?'

Tuesday, November 2nd. 11:54 a.m.

Patrese and Beradino were supposed to see Mayor Negley at ten. They sat in the antechamber to his office, on the fifth floor of the City-County building, for close on two hours, with one or other of Negley's PAs appearing every few minutes to extend the mayor's apologies, reiterate that he'd been caught up in meetings which had gone on much longer than anticipated, and promise he'd be with them as soon as he could.

Standard billionaire behavior. Treat anyone below your own level as supplicants to a medieval king, even when they had a major homicide investigation to run.

Had the meeting just been a progress report, Patrese and Beradino would have gone back to the North Shore long before. If Negley wanted to find out what was going on badly enough, he could make time for them, not vice versa.

But they wanted to see him for another reason entirely.

They'd discovered a connection between him and the two murder victims.

It was almost midday when he finally came bustling in, trailing a comet's tail of advisers and assistants.

He gave both detectives a double-clasped handshake, his

112

left hand clutching their wrists. Every politician Patrese had met did it, presumably in the belief that it made them seem open and sincere. Patrese thought it as phony as a seven-dollar bill.

'Gentlemen, gentlemen. My apologies. This city is a demanding mistress.'

Interesting choice of phrase, Patrese thought.

Negley ushered them inside his office. Patrese was surprised at how small it was, before remembering it was municipal property. In Negley's billionaire incarnation, he probably worked out of something the size of Heinz Field.

Negley took a seat behind his desk and directed the detectives to a nearby sofa. They'd be sitting lower than him. Corporate intimidation 101.

A secretary appeared with tea, coffee and cookies. When she'd gone, Negley clapped his hands together.

'Now. What can I do you for?' He chuckled at his word-play.

Beradino held up a brochure. Glossy, high-end, four-color, its cover emblazoned with the words 'ABRAHAMIC INTER-FAITH FOUNDATION'.

'You're a member of this foundation's board, I believe.'

'Yes, I am. We're all listed in there, aren't we?'

'Bishop Kohler was a director too. We found this in his bureau.'

'Yes, he was. But if this is something to do with the murders . . . The surgeon, Michael Redwine, he was nothing to do with this.'

'He wasn't, no. But Abdul Bayoumi was.'

'I'm sorry, I don't follow. Abdul Bayoumi died a few months ago.'

'Only after Michael Redwine had messed up routine surgery on him.'

Negley's eyes widened.

'I didn't know that. I mean, I knew something tragic had happened in the operating theatre, but not that Redwine had been responsible. I didn't know Abdul well, I'm afraid. I only saw him at foundation meetings.' He indicated the brochure.

'This foundation; what exactly is it that you do?'

Negley switched instantly, perhaps even automatically, into pontificating-politico mode 'Well, Detective, I believe that conflict between the faiths is second only to climate change in the list of issues threatening our society, and therefore resolving that conflict and promoting co-operation is of paramount importance.'

'What exactly is it that you do?' Beradino repeated, deadpan.

Patrese had to bite back laughter, both at Beradino's sardonic tone, and at Negley's complete failure to recognize it as such.

'We facilitate symposiums, joint cultural events, exhibitions, seminars, talks, school programs, those kind of things.'

A lot of jaw-jaw, in other words, thought Patrese; a heap of hot air, and no action.

'Would you describe any of your activities as controversial?'

'Not to right-thinking people, no.'

'You don't, for instance, fund mosques?'

'No. Nor churches, nor synagogues; not alone. Every program we fund, either wholly or in part, must involve at least two of the three Abrahamic religions.'

'Can you think of anything the foundation does which *would* make someone want to kill one of its directors?'

'Nothing at all.'

'Anything about the directors themselves?'

'Quite the opposite. They're all people of the highest integrity. That's why they were invited to join. We picked nine; three each from each of the three faiths.'

'We'd like to give protection to you all. To the seven, er, remaining.'

'I have my own protection, thank you, so you can save a little manpower there.'

'With respect, sir, they're not the police.'

'No, they're not. They're ex-Delta Force. They're a lot more skilled than the police, no offense; and they're certainly better paid.' He smiled. 'I'm sure the other six will appreciate it, however. Is that your strongest lead?'

'At the moment, yes.'

Not just their strongest lead, Patrese thought, but pretty much their only one.

It would take a couple of days to trace and eliminate all the people in the photos found in Kohler's bureau, even with the extra manpower they'd been allocated – a fivefold increase in officers, from twelve to sixty.

In the meantime, those officers had already received several hundred calls, all of which they'd have to follow up. Most would be irrelevant. Some, inevitably, were from wives trying to get rid of their husbands by accusing them of the murders.

Patrese had already recognized one voice as that of a woman who had in the past tried to pin ten separate murders on her husband. He'd given her a phone number.

'This your cellphone?' she'd asked.

'No. It's a divorce lawyer.'

The cops had studied CCTV footage of the road outside the cathedral, traced cars through their number plates, and interviewed their owners. No one had seen a thing.

A homeless man who'd been bedding down opposite the cathedral offered to tell the police what he knew in exchange for twenty bucks. One sniff of his breath had convinced them that the testimony of a man too drunk to remember what day it was would hardly stand up in court, even if by some miracle it *did* lead them to the killer.

They'd checked the list of the cathedral's workers, regular

attendees, friends and supporters against that of Redwine's patients, and interviewed all those who appeared on both. No dice.

They'd discovered that Redwine and Kohler had been members of the same country club in Fox Chapel. They were interviewing the club's management, staff and members; several hundred in all. One former employee, whom the club had dismissed the previous year for embezzlement, had already come briefly under suspicion – he'd written threatening letters to the club after being fired – until the police had discovered that he was already in custody, for mail fraud.

Given the desecration of the crucifixes and icons, they were also checking every Muslim recently convicted of any crime, no matter how small. Allen Chance had impressed on them the importance of subtlety here. They had to pick their way through minefields of political correctness and racial discrimination, and avoid turning a murder investigation into a civil rights issue.

What that meant in terms of Mustafa Bayoumi was anybody's guess.

Wednesday, November 3rd. 9:11 a.m.

The first forty-eight hours after Kohler's murder were already up. Patrese and Beradino both knew that no joy now meant ever-diminishing returns later.

'Forensics have found a strand of hair in Saint Paul,' Beradino said. 'Near Kohler's body, but unburnt. They reckon Asian origin. Probably Pakistan. Heavily treated, so almost certainly female. And cut neatly; not fallen out naturally, not yanked forcefully.'

'A Pakistani woman who'd just been for a haircut?'

'Could be. They're checking hairdressers now. There are no Pakistani women on the cathedral's staff roster, we know that. No Asians at all, actually.'

'Which means nothing. The cathedral's a public place. People come in and out the whole time. That hair could have come from anyone, anytime. You could clean that floor for days, *weeks*, and miss something like that. Or you could sweep it up and then deposit it back there again some time later without knowing. Perhaps it got tangled in the broom fibers and then dropped free again.'

'Exactly. It's the longest of long shots.'

'And the kids in the photos?'

117

'Sacred Heart have identified most of them, and given contact details for everyone they have in their database. Uniforms are working their way through those people as we speak. About two-thirds still live in Pittsburgh, so they're being given priority.'

'And?'

'And nothing, so far. All of them have alibis. Most hadn't seen Kohler in many moons. No discernible motives, that anyone can tell.'

'What are they like now?'

'What are who like?'

'The people. The ones in the photos.'

'How do you mean?'

'Are they, you know, fucked up in some way? Junkies, depressives, suicides?'

'Why do you ask?'

'Looking for a motive for whoever killed Kohler, that's why. Happily married guy with kids ain't gonna wake up one morning and decide to off the bishop, is he?'

'I guess not. Far as I know, they're a pretty standard cross-section. Check the files, if you want. They're in the system.'

Patrese logged on, and soon found that Beradino was right; they *were* a pretty standard cross-section.

More than half were married, about a fifth were divorced, some of them shockingly young. A few gays, a handful with drug problems, or at least problems bad enough to have shown up on their records. There'd be a lot more beneath the surface, Patrese was sure of that; a lot of things that those people wouldn't or couldn't tell the cops. And why should they? Cops were cops, not social workers.

Patrese recognized more names than he'd thought he would. It was like some sort of surreal, virtual school reunion; people whom he'd frozen in his mind at some stage in their teens suddenly reincarnated on the screen in front of him as adults with jobs, and lives, and problems, years and heart-breaks and triumphs and catastrophes away from how he'd remembered them.

'How you've grown!' he recalled friends of his parents saying when he'd been a kid; and *of course* he'd grown, he'd always thought. It would have been a whole heap weirder if he hadn't. So too with these people. *Of course* they'd changed.

Later that afternoon, Patrese went back in front of the media, and tossed them tasty but fundamentally unfilling morsels.

Yes, they were following up multiple leads. Yes, they were aware the first forty-eight hours had elapsed. Yes, they understood the city's shock and outrage.

No, he wouldn't give operational details. No, he wouldn't commit himself to any predictions. No, he didn't want to send a message directly to the killer.

He didn't say what he really thought: that, two murders in – and if Mustafa Bayoumi's alibi held when they finally managed to interview him – what they needed more than anything else was a third.

A third would give them more evidence. A third might persuade Chance to call in the Bureau. A third was what they feared and wanted in equal measures.

Thursday, November 4th. 9:20 a.m.

Of all Pittsburgh's buildings, the Allegheny County Courthouse was Patrese's favorite. It boasted the quintessential architecture of crime and punishment. Massive slabs of Massachusetts granite ran down long sides punctuated with brooding arches and flanked by half-towers, as though the edifice had been lifted wholesale from city gates in ancient Rome.

Richardson, the architect, regarded this building as his greatest work. He'd plundered from across Europe for it: detailing from Salamanca Cathedral for the front tower, still majestically authoritative despite the upstart skyscrapers which now dwarfed it on all sides; Notre-Dame's cornice; the hollow rectangle massing from Rome's Palazzo Farnese; and from Venice the rear campanile and the Bridge of Sighs, through which prisoners had been transported from jail to court and back again.

The courthouse interior was even more thrilling than the façade. The main staircase wouldn't have disgraced the Paris Opera. Levels, landings and staircases seemed to materialize out of nowhere beneath enormous vaulting ceilings.

It was as though Piranesi or Escher had gotten hold of the blueprints and turned it into an arena of spatial paradoxes, a place where the laws of physics were suspended. The Inquisition would have been right at home here, mounting spiked wheels and meat hooks to terrorize the damned far beneath.

In his courtroom on the third floor, Judge Philip Yuricich listened to Beradino making the case for a search warrant against Mustafa Bayoumi – their last, best hope.

Five foot four on a good day, Yuricich held himself slightly stooped and hunched, peering out at the detectives from behind big glasses like an elderly tortoise.

'This man, Mustafa Bayoumi, is our prime suspect,' Beradino said. 'To be honest, he's the only solid connection between the two victims that we have. Both times, his mom has given him an alibi. No one else.'

'You think she's lying?' Yuricich asked.

Beradino shrugged. 'Who can say? We search the place, we might find out more. I know it might be considered a little, er, premature, but . . .'

'You don't have to convince me, Mark. Sure, I'll sign your warrant. These people always look out for each other, you know. They got no respect for the law.'

'These people', Patrese thought, being Muslims; though where Yuricich was concerned, it could just as easily have been blacks, or Jews, or women, or gays, or pretty much anyone who wasn't a WASP like Yuricich himself.

'And when you *do* nail him,' Yuricich continued, 'I'll do my darnedest to make sure I get the trial.'

Friday, November 5th. 7:14 a.m.

They went mob-handed to Sameera Bayoumi's house.

Patrese and Beradino were there, of course, along with ten uniforms. Nine of them were actual police officers; the tenth was Marquez Berlin, whose business card proclaimed him head of the Pittsburgh PD's electronic crime department.

A more honest assessment would have concluded that he *was* the electronic crime department, in its entirety. Blame budget cuts; everyone else did.

Berlin had the pale face and wide eyes of a man who spent a little too much time indoors, and a lot too much time in front of a computer screen. Not that he cared. More than once, he'd spent days online, so absorbed in his work that his body had more or less forgotten its own imperatives to take on food and eject waste.

Now he was draped in one of the department's spare uniforms. He looked an unlikely cop, but that couldn't be helped. All that mattered was that the Bayoumis didn't question his presence there. What Berlin was intending to do may or may not have been unethical, but it was certainly illegal.

Mustafa opened the door. Beradino held the warrant up.

'We have authorization to search these premises. The officers here will conduct this search, while Detective Patrese
and I question you and your mother.'

Sameera appeared at Mustafa's shoulder, eyes wide in fear.
'What's going on?'

'You have no right,' Mustafa snapped. 'Today is our
Sabbath. You are a religious man; you understand the importance of the sacred day. Leave us alone.'

'We have every right. We'll talk in the kitchen.'

Mustafa took the warrant and started reading it, careful
over every line.

'Don't bother,' Beradino said. 'All the details are correct.'

Mustafa ignored him and continued reading till the end.
The details were indeed correct; he couldn't eject the officers on a technicality.

He thrust the warrant angrily back at Beradino. Beradino
grabbed Mustafa's hand and pulled him in close.

'Any more of that, and we'll do this down the station.
Understand?'

Mustafa's eyes flashed defiance, but he was silent.

Beradino let him go, and turned to the uniforms crowded
into the hallway.

'Two of you per room. Search *everything*. Turn the place
upside down. Pay particular attention to Mustafa's bedroom,
you hear? Go.'

They split mother and son up, so they could cross-refer
later and find whether their stories matched. Beradino
interviewed Sameera in the kitchen; Patrese and Mustafa
talked in the living-room. The detectives asked for the smallest
details, time and again; what had been on television that night,
what they'd eaten, what time Mustafa had gone to bed.

Tiny, inconsequential stuff, but lies were much harder to
remember than the truth. If Mustafa or his mother were
lying, and the detectives probed long enough, they'd find it.

Interrogation was like dripping water; sooner or later, it found the opening.

And all the time they were questioning Sameera and Mustafa, it sounded as though the house was alive, around and above them. The dull, reverberating thuds of overturned furniture; floorboards creaking under the weight of heavy footsteps; voices muffled yet urgent as they barked to each other.

Eventually, the uniforms came down with three plastic crates of material.

'You can't take those!' Mustafa yelled.

'We can, and we are,' Beradino said. 'We'll make an inventory and send you a receipt. Thank you for your time.' He said it without inflection; impossible, Patrese thought, to tell whether he was being sarcastic or simply polite.

'This is not the America I thought existed,' Sameera said.

The police went back out to their vehicles. Patrese made sure they were inside their car, with the doors shut and the windows up, before he turned to Berlin.

'You get 'em all in, Marquez?'

'Sure did. A bug in his bedroom, one in the sitting room, and one on the landline. And remote spyware on his PC.'

Sunday, November 7th. 12:15 p.m.

It was the kind of thing that possibly only a trained detective would notice.

Beradino and Jesslyn were in church; their local church in Punxsutawney, the one they'd been attending for years now. The offertory hymn – 'Guide Me, O Thou Great Redeemer' – was being played, and the collection bags were being passed up and down the pews. Each worshipper took the bag, put a folded banknote or two in, and passed it on.

When the bag reached Beradino, he dropped twenty dollars in. Then he handed it on to Jesslyn, who added her own contribution.

Except she didn't.

Beradino gave no sign that he'd noticed, but notice he had.

She'd reached into her handbag all right, and had brought out her hand again with fingers pressed together, as though clasping a banknote.

But in the split second when her hand had gone to the collection bag, Beradino had seen what she'd been holding.

Or, more accurately, what she hadn't been holding.

Her hand had been empty.

Jesslyn always gave money on Sundays; usually ten dollars, sometimes twenty. For her not to have done so was out of character. For her not to have done so, but pretended otherwise, was doubly so.

Beradino thought he should say something; but what? If it came out wrong, she'd either shout at him or give him the silent treatment. He wasn't very good at dealing with either. Best leave it alone. To start a fight or keep the peace; a dilemma pretty much every couple went through pretty much every day.

Perhaps she was worried about him, given the amount of time he spent regaling her with details of the Redwine and Kohler murders, trying to make sense of it all. Home was a safety valve for him, a sanctuary, the one place he could at least try to switch off. If he disturbed that, he'd have no peace anywhere.

The service ended, and they filed out of the church, chatting easily with the other members of the congregation. At the main door, the priest shook their hands.

'That was a wonderful lesson, Jesslyn,' he said. 'Beautifully chosen, beautifully read. Thank you.'

'My pleasure,' she replied.

She was carrying the Bible from which she'd read. A leather bookmark with silk tassels marked her place. While Jesslyn chatted with the priest, Beradino took the Bible gently from her, opened it, and read the lesson again for himself.

He knew it was one of her favorite passages. She'd preached it several times in Muncy, on the occasions when she was pulling the Sunday shifts.

The Book of Isaiah 59: 1–17.

1. Behold, the LORD's hand is not shortened, that it cannot save; neither his ear heavy, that it cannot hear:

2. But your iniquities have separated between you and your God, and your sins have hid his face from you, that he will not hear.

3. For your hands are defiled with blood, and your fingers with iniquity; your lips have spoken lies, your tongue hath muttered perverseness.

4. None calleth for justice, nor any pleadeth for truth: they trust in vanity, and speak lies; they conceive mischief, and bring forth iniquity.

5. They hatch cockatrice's eggs, and weave the spider's web: he that eateth of their eggs dieth, and that which is crushed breaketh out into a viper.

6. Their webs shall not become garments, neither shall they cover themselves with their works: their works are works of iniquity, and the act of violence is in their hands.

7. Their feet run to evil, and they make haste to shed innocent blood: their thoughts are thoughts of iniquity; wasting and destruction are in their paths.

8. The way of peace they know not; and there is no judgment in their goings: they have made them crooked paths: whosoever goeth therein shall not know peace.

9. Therefore is judgment far from us, neither doth justice overtake us: we wait for light, but behold obscurity; for brightness, but we walk in darkness.

10. We grope for the wall like the blind, and we grope as if we had no eyes: we stumble at noon day as in the night; we are in desolate places as dead men.

11. We roar all like bears, and mourn sore like doves: we look for judgment, but there is none; for salvation, but it is far off from us.

12. For our transgressions are multiplied before thee, and our sins testify against us: for our transgressions are with us; and as for our iniquities, we know them;

13. In transgressing and lying against the LORD, and departing

away from our God, speaking oppression and revolt, conceiving and uttering from the heart words of falsehood.

14. *And judgment is turned away backward, and justice standeth afar off: for truth is fallen in the street, and equity cannot enter.*

15. *Yea, truth faileth; and he that departeth from evil maketh himself a prey: and the LORD saw it, and it displeased him that there was no judgment.*

16. *And he saw that there was no man, and wondered that there was no intercessor: therefore his arm brought salvation unto him; and his righteousness, it sustained him.*

17. *For he put on righteousness as a breastplate, and an helmet of salvation upon his head; and he put on the garments of vengeance for clothing, and was clad with zeal as a cloak.*

Monday, November 8th. 8:52 a.m.

From: anon@ucanalwaysbeprivate.tv
To: m.beradino@city.pittsburgh.pa.us;
    f.patrese@city.pittsburgh.pa.us

THIS MESSAGE HAS BEEN SENT VIA A REMAILING
SERVICE

Dear Detective Beradino and Detective Patrese
(Mark and Franco seems too informal, you know? We
don't know each other that well yet, do we?)

I don't like hearing you or anyone else refer to the
victims as innocent. They're nothing of the sort. They
deserved everything they got. Pretty nasty way to go, hey?
I should think so. They merited nothing less.

Nor are you innocent. I heard you have sixty detectives
working on this. *Sixty?* That's one hell of a lot of cops.
Bet you don't assign sixty to a homeless man found shot
in an underpass by the Allegheny, do you? Or to a hooker
sliced and diced out on the Strip?

Those people, the flotsam and jetsam, the detritus,

the losers, they're the usual victims, aren't they? Not for me. They're not my targets.

Oh, I don't think they're angels, far from it. It was their choice to take the first hit of smack, put the extra dime in the slot machine, go with a man they hardly knew and end up with children they can't feed.

But then again, the way they understand choice is hardly the same as the way you and I understand it. Easy to talk about choice when you have good education and a solid job and a nice apartment. Not so easy when you're born poor and get poorer.

But the people I've killed, and the people I will kill, they had a choice, you can count on that. They've had all the advantages in life, but still they've chosen to behave the way they do.

You call me a psychopath, but those I kill are far more deserving of that title than me.

They're guilty, but do you think they feel guilt for what they've done? They're charming, but how deep does that charm go?

Their egos are outsize; they think only of themselves, adoring of their reflection like Narcissus. They like to portray themselves as honest, as men of integrity, but they lie and cheat and deceive. They pretend to feel emotion, sympathy and empathy, but look closer and there's nothing there. And you'll find that whenever anything goes wrong, it's never their fault.

I'm sending this to you two and you two alone, for you to do with it what you will. There are no blind copy addresses you can't see. I could give it to the media. Even though the papers probably wouldn't print it and the networks wouldn't show it, as they're the worst kind of corporate lickspittles, it'd be on the internet within minutes.

But I won't give it to the media, because they're almost

as loathsome as the people they obsess with. They give this case so much coverage for the same reason you put so much effort into trying to solve it – that you think some people are more important than others.

You don't realize that the more important they seem, the more they deserve to die. I don't believe in the hypocritical, moralistic dogma of this so-called civilized society. Look at all the liars, the haters, the killers, the crooks, the paranoid cowards; tremadotes of the earth. You maggots make me sick. I don't need to hear all of society's rationalizations. I've heard them all before. What is, is.

You don't understand me. You are not expected to. You are not capable of it. My experience is beyond you.

Since you clearly have no idea who I am or why I'm doing this, I've made a few suggestions as to how you should go about catching me. I know this is cheeky, but I'll keep taking liberties like this until you find me and take my liberty; if you ever do.

DON'T get too bogged down in details. There's a bigger picture here. Only when you see that picture will you appreciate what you're dealing with.

DON'T believe anything anyone tells you. The only truth is that no one tells the truth.

DON'T trust the officers doing your drudgework. Their aptitude and skills are limited. You're much better than them, though that's not saying much.

DO look inside yourselves. You may find help there.

DO say your prayers at night. You'll need them.

DON'T let your emotions get in the way. They'll only cloud your judgment.

DON'T go with your first judgment, clouded or not. It'll be wrong.

DON'T listen to the drunks, the troublemakers and the village idiots.

DON'T get frustrated. This is going to take a long time for you to solve.

DON'T think too much about it. Just do it.

Sincerely yours, The Human Torch.
(It's a dreadful nickname, isn't it? I wouldn't have chosen it myself. I wouldn't have chosen any nickname, in fact. Nicknames are childish and frivolous. But it seems we're stuck with it.)

'He's not joking about that.'

Marquez Berlin jerked his head in the direction of the first line of the e-mail: *THIS MESSAGE HAS BEEN SENT VIA A REMAILING SERVICE.*

'Not just one remailing service. Two or three, I'd guess.'

The glee in his voice was unmistakable. Like all true computer nerds, Berlin felt inordinately lucky to be paid for doing something which was effectively his hobby. He loved the clarity and logic of computers. By comparison, the real world was messy and absurd.

If there was something to be found in the measureless tracts of cyberspace, you could bet your last dollar that Berlin would find it.

'Which makes the message impossible to trace.'

'Impossible?' Beradino's tone betrayed the remorselessness of his own logic. Computers were created by man; therefore they should have no secrets from man.

'You know how remailers work? If I send you a normal e-mail, I just ping it straight from my account to yours. Even if I don't include my name, finding out where it came from is the easiest thing in the world. E-mails have a heap of information attached; details of the ISP, serial number of the computer which sent it, interface hardware address, so on. ISPs know everything about you. They justify all their checks by saying they're in the name of security. I always think SP should stand for Surveillance Project rather than Service Provider, you know?'

Beradino made a wheel motion with his hand; he wasn't interested in Berlin's opinion of Big Brother. Berlin, for once sensitive to basic human emotions, went on.

'So if I want to keep my identity anonymous, I use a remailer. Rather than send the e-mail to you directly, I send it to a third party, who strips away all those identifying details, replaces them with their own, and sends it on to you.

'But this has its weaknesses, obviously. You know the remailer's details, and he knows the details of the original sender. So if you can lean on him, legally or otherwise, or hack into his system, you can find out where the mail originated.

'So you use multiple remailers.

'The e-mail's sent to the first server. This reorders it and transmits it on to another server, which does the same thing, and so on. Only the first server knows the sender's details, and only the last server – here, ucanalwaysbeprivate – knows the recipient's.'

'Why can't you trace each server back from the one it forwarded to?'

'Theoretically, you can, but these servers encrypt their details. So you're looking at a huge amount of effort to decrypt these. Even if you do manage that, then you have to get every single server to hand over their databases. These servers will almost certainly be based in different countries, which means different jurisdictions, which means different laws . . . you know what I'm saying?'

They did indeed. It wasn't going to happen, at least not this side of the apocalypse.

'And this remailing,' Beradino asked, 'it's easy to do?'

'Pretty much.'

'By normal standards, Marquez, not yours.'

Berlin laughed. 'Yeah, I try to remember everyone's not as talented as me.'

'That's not the adjective I'd use.'

'Hey.' Berlin pretended to be offended. 'You want my help, or not? Yeah, it's easy to do. You have to have a certain amount of basic knowledge, but the thing about the internet is you can teach yourself. Half a brain and a day on Google, assuming you're moderately computer-literate to start with, and you could work this out for yourself, no problem. Much safer than using an internet café, for sure. No worries about eyewitnesses, surveillance cameras, trace evidence, any of that.'

'And you're sure it didn't originate from Mustafa's computer?'

'One hundred per cent. The remote spyware would show us that independently. Hell, the guy doesn't even look at online porn. That's what the web was *invented* for, no?'

'OK.' Beradino patted him on the shoulder. 'Thanks.'

He and Patrese went out into the corridor.

'You think it's genuine?' Patrese said.

'Hard to say. On one hand, there's nothing in this to indicate special knowledge, something only the killer would know, that kinda thing. And whoever wrote it is clearly smart, so they'd know that's what the cops look for, to prove bona fides.'

'And on the other?'

'Is just that. That they're smart. It's well written, it's not the usual rambling illiterate crockashit you get on cases like this. Smart people tend to have better things to do with their time than send crank letters to cops.'

'You wanna ask the FBI their opinion?'

'If I want an opinion, Franco, I'll give you one. The FBI will give us some wishy-washy boo-yah which'll be about as much help as a chocolate teapot. We'll find this guy the same way cops always find bad guys – by being patient and methodical and looking at the facts. No other way. Never has been, never will be.'

Patrese batted his fingers against the printout. 'What about the people he mentions? The ones he says he'll target?'

'What about them? Do you know how many people he could be talking about? Hundreds, maybe thousands. We can't warn them all, even if we want to; we don't know who they are. Releasing this, even *telling* the great and good . . . all that's gonna do is get a lot of innocent folk worried, which'll cause more harm than anything the killer can do.'

'And if he kills again, like he threatens to?'

Beradino sighed. 'You know the answer to that one as well as I do, Franco. He kills again, then we got more evidence to work with.'

Tuesday, November 9th. 5:44 p.m.

All surveillance officers sooner or later discover the same thing: that listening to other people's lives is a lot less interesting than it first seems, certainly once the initial voyeuristic thrill has worn off.

Berlin had installed the listening devices and remote computer spyware in the Bayoumi household four days before. Ever since then, the keystroke logs and phone recordings had fed the monitoring technicians – and the translators too, for when Sameera and Mustafa spoke to each other in Arabic – unrelenting domestic minutiae.

Sameera asking Mustafa if he wanted anything from the grocery store; Mustafa on the phone to the electricity company; a couple of terse conversations with cold callers; Jon Stewart and David Letterman on TV before bedtime. Mustafa forwarding a couple of jokey e-mails to some friends, and checking the news headlines.

Nothing remotely concerning the murders. Nothing even about the way the police had come barging in with their search warrant, which was surprising. Most civilians, confronted with the full might of the law, talked about little else for days afterwards.

It was almost as though Sameera and Mustafa knew the bugs were there.

The listeners were so desperate not to be thought of as slacking on the job that they called Patrese and Beradino the moment they got something out of the ordinary; a phone conversation between Mustafa and an unknown man.

Unknown man: *You coming to the sanctuary this weekend?*
Mustafa: *Not this weekend, sorry. Need to get my stuff together.*
Unknown man: *You sure? Gonna be a lot of disappointment.*
Mustafa: *Can't do nothing about that. Sorry. Next weekend. Ten days from now.*
Unknown man: *Usual time?*
Mustafa: *Yeah.*
Unknown man: *You wanna meet outside?*
Mustafa: *No. Too cold. See you in there.*
Unknown man: *OK. See you when I see you.*

Patrese and Beradino played the tape three times, trying to hear beyond the words: listening for inflections, emphasis, anything which might give them a clue as to who Mustafa's interlocutor was, or what exactly they were discussing.

He sounded young, which was to say, south side of thirty; but then Mustafa was still at college, so it wasn't surprising he'd be talking to people more or less his own age.

'The sanctuary,' Beradino said, rolling the word round his mouth. 'The *sanctuary*. He says that in the first line. Does he mean something religious? Kohler was killed in a church. But not in the sanctuary.'

'What's the difference?' Patrese asked.

'The area round the altar, inside the railings, that's the sanctuary. It's where God dwells. Kohler was killed in the confessional, outside the sanctuary.'

'And how many people know that, Mark? That's a pretty

precise definition. What if "sanctuary" is what Mustafa calls all churches, mosques, synagogues?'

'Could be.' Beradino thought for a moment. 'He said "next weekend", didn't he? So we have ten days till he goes wherever it is he's talking about.'

'We haven't got the manpower to put him under visual surveillance till then.'

'No. But we *can* start watching him from a couple of days before then; say, next Thursday. In the meantime, we keep listening. We listen to every word. Every word. Anything else like this, Marquez, you let us know. Don't worry if it sounds insignificant. Better a false alarm than that we miss something.'

Wednesday, November 10th. 7:46 a.m.

Yuricich comes to the door, unsuspecting.

He has no reason to be otherwise. I don't look in any way threatening, quite the opposite. And this is Squirrel Hill, one of the city's classier neighborhoods; the kind of place where eminent judges live, side-by-side with other pillars of the community, secure in the knowledge that the sun has been placed in the sky expressly to shine on them and them alone.

It's not the kind of place where people get torched to death.

Not until now.

Yuricich opens the door and stands on the porch. If I didn't know better, I'd say he's short because he's bowed down by the weight of the evils he's been tasked with judging; but I know too there's no evil as great as that which lives within his heart.

He looks at me, and at the reason he thinks I'm here, and he smiles; a smile you'd mistake for that of an avuncular grandfather, if you didn't know better.

'I'm sorry,' he says. 'I live alone.'

Alone. In a big house, with trees out front that shield the front door from the road.

Perfect.

'Not to worry,' I say. 'You have a good day, now. Sorry to have bothered you.'

I half turn away from him, and then, as though an afterthought, say: 'I'm sorry, but could I have a glass of water?'

'Surely. Come on in.'

I follow him inside, taking care to close the door behind me, and into the kitchen, where he takes an upturned glass from the draining board and runs the tap a couple of seconds to be sure that it's cold.

'You're out early today,' he says.

'Yes, sir. Not enough hours in the day otherwise.'

His back is to me, and it's the work of a moment to reach into my bag and take out the weapon.

A big old battery in a sock.

Crude, but effective, and so easy.

I swing it in a practiced arc, fast through the air till it bounces hard against the back of his head.

Two cracks; the back of his skull where the makeshift blackjack hits him, and his forehead as he slumps forward on to the edge of the sink.

I worry for a few moments that I've hit him too hard, but he's soon moaning and groaning, and then trying to struggle through what I guess must be a pounding headache as he realizes several things pretty much at once.

First, I've tied his hands behind his back.

Second, I've taped his mouth up so he can't scream.

Third, I'm wearing his own robe, the one he wears in court.

I didn't expect to find it here – I thought he'd keep it in his chambers in the courthouse – but maybe he took it to be cleaned, or maybe he likes to bring it home with him, I don't know, and it doesn't matter.

The robe is black, with the Ten Commandments picked out in gold lettering on the back. Leaving aside the irony of walking around sporting slogans such as 'Thou Shalt Not Steal', 'Thou Shalt Not

140

Commit Adultery' and 'Thou Shalt Not Lie' in a building full of lawyers, judges and politicians, I know Yuricich wears these on his robe – I know this as he tells pretty much anyone who'll listen – because he believes them to be the basis of America's constitution and legal system, and because he sees himself as God's representative in the courts.

'Your God will be judging you soon,' I say. 'Very soon. But before he can judge, there must be a trial, no?'

Terror and puzzlement bounce off each other in his eyes.

'And before there can be a trial, you must take the oath.'

I find a Bible in pretty much the first place I look, which is Yuricich's study. I'm guessing there are probably several more about the place. No matter. This one will do just fine.

I maneuver this Bible into his hands. It's not easy, as they're secured tight behind him and I don't want to undo them, even for a second, but after a couple of false starts we manage it, he gripping the leather cover with trembling fingers.

'Now,' I say, 'repeat after me: "I do solemnly swear that I will support, obey and defend the Constitution of the United States and the Constitution of this Commonwealth and that I will discharge the duties of my office with fidelity."

He mumbles something incoherent from behind the duct tape.

'Say it,' I snap. 'That thing's not coming off, so say it as best you can.'

More gibberish, but it sounds close enough.

'So help me God,' I add.

'Swwwheppmeo'.'

'I charge you, Philip Yuricich, with failing to do exactly what you vowed to do in that oath. You haven't accomplished any of that, have you? You've not supported the Constitution, nor obeyed it, nor defended it. And as for discharging the duties of your office with fidelity – it would make me laugh, if it didn't make me sick.'

Perhaps there's recognition in his eyes now. I've let my voice slip back to normal again, and maybe he remembers it.

141

Maybe not. It doesn't matter either way.

'You, Philip Yuricich, have been responsible for more miscarriages of justice than any other judge in Pennsylvania, possibly the entire United States. You've sentenced twice as many people to death as any other judge in the state, even though you've heard fewer homicide cases than most of your colleagues. You don't like blacks, or women, or Arabs, or gays, or pretty much anyone who's not like you. You apply what you call justice according to nothing more than your own prejudices. You're a disgrace to the office you hold. Do you deny any of this?'

He squeaks dissent from behind his gag, but I don't care.

'You're a defendant's nightmare, a prosecutor in robes. Even actual prosecutors have asked you to tone down your favoritism towards them, haven't they? Thing is, no matter how biased and bigoted you are, in your court, there's still a limit to your power. But not here, not to me, not to my power, not in my court. I'm not just judge. I'm jury too, and I find you guilty.'

He's squirming hard now, desperate and fearful.

'So as judge, I sentence you to death. As executioner, I'm duty-bound to carry out that sentence. And I do so with the words of Isaiah, chapter fifty-nine, verse seventeen. "For I put on righteousness as a breastplate, and a helmet of salvation upon my head; and I put on the garments of vengeance for clothing, and am clad with zeal as a cloak."'

I pull the juggling torch from the bag and touch the lighter to it.

It flares, dangerous and inviting.

And he knows. He knows.

He knows what happened to Redwine and Kohler.

He knows it's happening to him now.

He knows it's a dreadful way to die.

He knows who I am.

He knows.

But he doesn't know what's going to happen to him just before the fire comes.

142

8:44 a.m.

Patrese and Beradino bumped into Freddie Hellmore in the queue for the metal detector at the courthouse entrance. They were due at a pre-trial conference on Shaniqua Davenport's murder charge; first item of business, nine a.m.

Pre-trial conferences – designed to ascertain exactly what charges the defendant would be facing come the trial proper – were usually as dull as ditchwater.

Not that either Patrese or Beradino cared too much. Court appearances were almost guaranteed sources of overtime for homicide detectives. If you'd just finished a midnight–eight a.m. shift, or were scheduled for a four p.m.–midnight one, an appearance during normal court hours meant you had to do double time.

Some of the more enterprising members of the department had been known to pull down six-figure salaries this way. Collars for dollars, they called it.

Hellmore was wearing a tie loud enough to be heard in New Jersey, and the inner lining of his jacket was patterned in army camouflage. Patrese raised his eyebrows.

'I'm going to war on this one,' Hellmore said.

He smiled, but he was serious. Patrese half-expected him to start singing 'Soul Man'.

They passed through the metal arch – no guns in the courthouse, no matter who you were – and started up towards the courtrooms on the third floor.

Patrese had walked through here hundreds of times before, but this was the first time he'd ever ridden shotgun for Hellmore.

It was extraordinary. They'd hardly gone ten paces before they were surrounded by people. Autograph seekers proffered pens. Young men took hurried snapshots on their cellphone cameras. Patrese heard business offers, requests for jobs. A couple spoke breathlessly of an egregious injustice which Hellmore alone could rectify. One guy simply wanted Hellmore to read his poetry.

He, Freddie Hellmore, was the Pied Piper, and he dealt with it all without breaking stride; handing out business cards like a croupier dealing decks in Vegas, rattling off phone numbers for people to jot down, promising a meal here, a cup of coffee here.

He might only have given each person a few seconds of his attention, but when he did, that attention was total. He wasn't searching for someone more important to talk to, nor was he signing autographs without even making eye contact, as was the way with many celebrities.

An outsize character, Patrese thought; but also, in his own way, an authentic one.

Ten minutes later, they made it through the throng to the courtroom.

Amberin Zerhouni, assistant DA in charge of homicide cases, was already there. She was in her early thirties, perhaps a couple of years older than Patrese. Her eyes were the color and shape of almonds, her upper lip formed a perfect Cupid's bow, and a wisp of jet-black hair curled lazily out from under a crimson *hijab*.

By DA standards – hell, by most standards – she was a knockout.

She and Hellmore greeted each other coolly. Lawyers who knew each other well were usually cordial, even friendly, no matter how often they clashed in court. Both sides understood that business was business, and cases were nothing personal.

But this one was different. Hellmore seemed to think he'd got a bum deal here.

Patrese knew the story, at least in outline.

Amberin had wanted to press for murder. Hellmore had called it self-defense.

Hellmore's presence on a case – sometimes even just the *threat* of his presence – had scared many DAs into a plea bargain, downgrading the original charge in exchange for a guilty plea. That way, the prosecution got a guaranteed conviction, the court system had one less trial to deal with, and the defendant got a shorter sentence than they would otherwise have received. Everyone was a winner.

But in Shaniqua's case, Amberin had refused to bargain. Shaniqua had confessed, and no DA in their right mind was going to turn away a confession. Besides, there'd only been one weapon in the room. Weaver hadn't been holding that weapon. He hadn't even been *going* for it. That didn't sound like self-defense to Amberin.

Hellmore had angled for a compromise: involuntary manslaughter.

Again, Amberin had refused.

They both knew why. It was election year, when public officials were obliged to run for office. Being seen as soft on crime was the quickest way to lose the vote. Most DAs would sooner the world knew that they wore their wife's underwear than suspected them of being bleeding heart liberals.

If Amberin wouldn't agree to involuntary manslaughter,

Hellmore had pledged to run BWS – Battered Woman Syndrome, one of the most emotive of all defenses.

Done well, and with a defendant who pushed the right buttons, it gave the jury a hook on which to hang their collective hat. This son of a bitch deserved to die, he was a batterer, he'd had it coming for a long time, we're not going to put anybody in jail for killing this douchebag. That kind of thing.

Most BWS defense lines ran that abuse had psychologically traumatized victims to the point that they were incapable of forming rational thoughts. Therefore, they could not have been responsible for their violent actions.

That Weaver had beaten Shaniqua wasn't in doubt; he'd been indicted before on domestic violence charges. Like many subsections of the American male, few gangbangers were above using their fists to control their women.

No; the question was whether Hellmore could prove that the abuse had been both severe and prolonged. That was never as easy as it sounded. Most victims don't report any more than a fraction of the incidents that occur. Even then, they're as likely as not to withdraw their accusations a day or so later.

So you could never be sure which way a jury would jump with BWS. Twelve men good and true were just as likely to see it as a free 'get out of jail' ticket, or even a license to kill. Getting out of abusive relationships was hard, sure, but there were plenty of ways of doing so without putting a bullet in someone's brain.

That was the logic of the case, on both sides.

Now Hellmore sat with Shaniqua, detailing the myriad of motions he intended to bring: one to dismiss the charges altogether, one to suppress evidence, one to change the trial's venue, one to request a jury rather than a judge sitting alone, and so on.

Shaniqua nodded gravely as she listened, all the while clutching Trent's hand as though her life depended on it.

Perhaps it did, Patrese thought. He gave Shaniqua a little smile.

She regarded him levelly for a moment or two, seemingly more surprised than angry, and then looked away.

Patrese felt like an idiot.

Shaniqua didn't care that he had misgivings about her case, he realized. He'd arrested her and charged her with Weaver's murder. He was five-oh; the enemy.

That was the thing about courtrooms; they were a battle-field. You were on one side or the other. Pretty much the only main players in the middle were judge and jury.

There was no jury today. Just the judge. That's who they were all waiting for.

They were waiting for Yuricich.

11:31 a.m.

They checked Bayoumi's wire-taps first, of course.

The fire brigade had been called to Yuricich's house at exactly 8:30 a.m., when a passer-by had reported smoke billowing from the windows. Though the house was set behind a high hedge, it was on a busy road, well-traveled at that time of morning by commuters and school-run moms.

The fire couldn't have been visible for much more than a few minutes before the report came in; someone would surely have spotted it. Even allowing time for the fire to spread, Yuricich couldn't have been killed much before 7:30, if that.

The wire-taps had Mustafa and his mother holding several brief conversations, in Arabic, at 7:12, 7:37, 8:01 and 8:24. It was at least ten minutes' drive from the Bayoumis' house to Yuricich's, probably more at that time in the morning.

Whichever way you cut it, Mustafa Bayoumi simply couldn't have killed Philip Yuricich; couldn't have got there and back in the time available. And Yuricich wasn't one of the seven remaining board members of the Abrahamic Interfaith Foundation.

Patrese and Beradino would still go and interview Mustafa,

of course. It wasn't just that they might have missed some- thing; it would look suspicious if they didn't. Mustafa had been prime suspect for the first two murders, and he knew it.

If they didn't follow up on a third, he'd wonder how they knew he hadn't done it. From there, it wouldn't be long before he found the bugs and kicked up a stink.

In the meantime, they called in the FBI.

Pretty much had to, in fact. Three murders meant the Human Torch was now officially a serial killer. Even Allen Chance couldn't fight the department's corner, not with a dead judge on his watch to add to a bishop and a surgeon.

Chance mollified Beradino a little by pointing out that the Bureau would be involved purely in an advisory capacity. No Bureau personnel would gather evidence, pursue suspects or attend interrogations without invitation. Those were the rules.

But they both knew things were rarely as simple and clear-cut as that. The more the Bureau became involved, the more control they'd want. They always did.

Beradino knew arguing the toss would be a waste of breath. Chance's support for this as a sole police operation had gone, and it wasn't coming back. And Beradino hadn't survived on the force as long as he had without knowing which battles to fight and which to cede.

The procedure for requesting Bureau assistance is the same across the United States. The police department in question fills in a standard thirteen-page Violent Criminal Apprehension Program (VICAP) analysis and submits it to the Bureau.

The Bureau feeds the data from the VICAP form into its central database to see whether any of it matches known incidents, trends or suspicions. Bureau analysts then pore over everything that comes out and produce a profile of the killer.

VICAP, the Bureau likes to say, doesn't retire, and it doesn't forget.

Since time was tight, however, Patrese sent Caleb Boone, head of the Bureau's Pittsburgh office, a copy of the anonymous e-mail the detectives had received, together with a summary of the murders so far.

'Boone's a good guy,' Patrese said. 'We were at college together. All the time I spent playing football, he was in the library.'

'Probably explains why you're a homicide 'tec and he's a field office head.'

The FBI's Pittsburgh office has federal investigative responsibilities for twenty-seven counties in western Pennsylvania, and all of West Virginia. It's a sizeable beat by any standards. For Boone to be heading it up in his late twenties was some achievement.

Beltway insiders had their eye on Boone. If he didn't screw things up, he could rise very high indeed. Some of them were even muttering about the directorship one day.

Boone e-mailed back pretty much instantly.

Patrese liked that about Boone. He didn't sit on things for hours or days just to make himself look busy, nor did he get underlings to reply on his behalf. If it was urgent, he'd deal with it urgently.

Patrese clicked open the message.

Give you all the help I can on this, buddy. Have cleared my decks and will go over this with a toothcomb. Get back to you within the hour.

Boone was as good as his word. He rang after fifty-six minutes.

'I'm in the lobby,' he said.

12:28 p.m.

Boone had come to them, rather than asking them to come to him. It wasn't so much a question of distance – from the Bureau office to police headquarters was only twenty minutes – as one of priority.

The incident rooms were here on the North Shore, as were the scores of uniforms working the case. Boone had done the right thing, which wasn't to say he'd done the usual thing. The Bureau's reputation for arrogance wasn't entirely unjustified.

Patrese pointed all this out as they went downstairs to meet Boone.

'Darn, Franco,' Beradino said. 'He's jumped in a car, not trekked across the Arctic. We don't have to keel over in gratitude.'

Boone shook Beradino's hand and gave Patrese a light fist pound.

In the incident rooms, they gathered every available uniform – a handful stayed at their desks to man the phones – and introduced Boone, to a smattering of applause; politeness trumping territoriality.

'Thank you,' Boone said. He looked genuinely appreciative.

'Before we start, I'd like to say one thing. I've completed four behavioral science modules at Quantico, so when it comes to serial killers, I know what I'm talking about. I may not be Sigmund Freud, but I know enough. Any of you have a problem with that?'

When no one demurred, he went on.

'Right. I'm going to tell you what I think about these murders, and about the kind of person the murderer might be. It's going to be pretty general stuff. That's inevitable at this stage. If you're expecting me to tell you he's six one with a squint, a Pirates season ticket, a Polish grandmother and a sideline in stamp-collecting, then I suggest you go watch *Psych*. All I hope is that one of you here today remembers one thing I say, and it's that person, and that thing, that leads us to this asshole.'

Boone held up a printout of the e-mail.

'Let's take this e-mail first. First off, I think it's genuine. There's no specific knowledge in there which you could use to eliminate fakes, I know, but everything about it tallies with what I'd expect the killer's personality to be.

'A number of things in this message catch my eye.

'First, look how many questions he asks. Ten in all. Seven of them in the first five paragraphs. Some of these questions are cocky, some sardonic, some disbelieving, some angry, but they're all *questions*. He's inquiring, he's *challenging*. He's got an active mind, he doesn't accept the status quo. He wants to change things.

'He's clearly well educated. Remailing system to remain anonymous. Grammar and spelling, both good. Yeah, you can do spelling with spellcheck, but grammar's harder for a computer to correct, especially without sounding like a computer.

'And his vocab is definitely an educated man's. He makes quite a clever pun on taking liberties. He refers to Narcissus, who's from Greek mythology. And he uses the word "tremadotes". I had to look that one up. It's a type of parasite, apparently. Any of you say you knew that without diving for the dictionary, you're full of BS.'

There was a murmur of appreciative laughter. A bunch of cops were hard to impress, but Boone was playing them just right.

'All these are signs of someone who's not just smart, but wants us to know he's smart. And not just moderately intelligent. Not in his mind. He thinks he's smarter than us, for sure. Look how he says we won't *understand* him.

'So he wants to control us, not vice versa. Look at his list of "dos" and "don'ts". You notice anything? Check the ratio. "Don'ts" outnumber "dos" four to one. He prohibits, he forbids, much more than he enables.' A beat. 'Reminds me of my high school principal.'

More laughter.

'That's the e-mail. Now the murders. Do they tally? Psychologically? I think so. He's organized in what he does. You know, of course, there are two basic types of serial killer; organized, disorganized. Some killers meld the two, but overall most are pretty much in one camp or the other.

'This one is organized, most definitely. He's planned these crimes in advance. He's visualized each one many times before finally going through with it. He's targeting specific people. That means researching their lives, their habits, their routines. He's not just dragging bums into alleyways whenever he gets the heat.

'What's unusual to me is his choice of *site*. Most organized killers operate in three distinct locations. They confront the victims in one place, murder them in a second, dispose of them in a third.

'But here, he only uses one site, each time. Twice it's been their home, once the cathedral. That may be significant, it may not. But the fact he confronts and murders them in the

153

same place *is* interesting. As for disposing – he doesn't. He's not bothered about us finding his victims. Quite the opposite. He *wants* us to find them.

'Three closed locations, and he's got in each time without apparently using force. No broken locks, no shattered door jambs. How does he do it?'

Boone ticked off the possibilities on his fingers as he spoke.

'One, he knows them personally. Two, he feigns distress, pretends he's been in an accident or something. Three, he poses as – perhaps he even *is* – someone with a valid reason to call round: postman, gasman, charity collector, traveling salesman. Four, same idea, but as an authority figure: cop, soldier, teacher, doctor, even a firefighter.

'Which brings me on to fire. Is it MO? Is it signature? Bit of both? He doesn't seem to be using it to obscure the victims' identities, since it's obvious who they are. To destroy evidence, perhaps, but if that's the case, why not torch the whole place? But he doesn't. He just sets the victim on fire. Long as they're dead, he doesn't seem to worry too much if the fire spreads or not.

'Or we could look at the symbolism of fire. Hell springs to mind; hellfire, burn in hell. Perhaps it's something slightly more obscure. Remember all the crowds outside the prison when Ted Bundy went to the chair? *Burn, Bundy, burn*, they chanted.

'If the killer sees himself as executing these people, the victims, perhaps he also sees himself as taking over the role of the state; doing something the state should have done, but didn't, couldn't, wouldn't.

'Remember, too, the importance of the homicidal triad: firestarting, bedwetting, cruelty to animals. Most serial killers exhibit at least one of these characteristics in childhood, and often two or even all three. Perhaps in this case, he had a childhood obsession with pyromania which has lasted into adulthood.

154

'There'll be a reason for the firestarting, that's for sure. What that reason is, we might not know till we find him. Or we might work it out beforehand and find him that way, I don't know. What I *do* know is that the reasoning behind it, whatever it turns out to be, is central to decoding his motivation. Why does he do it?

'In this case – in any case, actually – there are two "whys".

'The first why is what I just mentioned; what drives him?

'In terms of motivation, we divide serial killers into four categories: visionary, mission-oriented, hedonistic, and power/ control.

'We can pretty much rule out the last two. They tend to be associated with sexual arousal, sexual dysfunction and extreme torture, usually with mutilation. There's no sign of any of those here.

'We can also strike visionary. Often as not, visionary killers have schizophrenia or some other mental illness. They get hallucinations, voices in their heads, God talking to them. This makes them unreliable and irrational. But the intelligence and planning our guy's shown – no way he could have done that if he was mentally ill. No way. Not with the kind of psychotic break from reality that real sufferers experience. He might claim insanity when we catch him, but it'll be BS.

'Which leaves us mission.

'Mission killers are organized, stable and intelligent. They don't usually pose or mutilate their victims; the kill itself is the mission.

'He's already stated why they deserve to die; because they're hypocrites, people in power who should know better.

'This gives us another clue. The victims have all been white males. Most people in positions of power are. That means he's almost certainly white himself. Serial killers don't tend to murder across race lines.

'Then there's the second why; why he's chosen to do it *now*.

People don't just wake up one day and decide to go on a spree. It festers in them for years, and only comes out when something triggers it.

'The trigger's something stressful or traumatic, usually one or more of the four "d"s: death, divorce, dismissal, debt. A loved one or close friend dies; a relationship ends, often nastily; you lose your job; financial pressures become crippling. The last two are often related, of course.

'Finally, I want you all to remember something. This is an addiction, simple as that. Nothing alleviates what he's feeling other than the act of killing. The more he kills, the more he wants to kill.

'We can second-guess him up to a point – he's given us some parameters – but they're too wide for us to protect all potential targets, and doesn't he just know it?

'Gentlemen; this son-of-a-bitch is gonna be a hard take-down, and no mistake.'

'Can I have a word?' Beradino asked, when the uniforms had returned to their desks.

'Sure,' Boone said.

'I didn't want to embarrass you in front of anyone there, but this profile . . . no offense, but it seems like the usual baloney cut-and-paste job to me.'

'I'm sorry you feel that way.'

Boone wasn't fazed in the slightest, Patrese saw. He probably got this kind of static off of a lot of police departments.

'Thing is – about all profiles, I guess, not just this one – thing is, they only exist in statistical probability, right?'

'It's a little less haphazard than that.'

'Not much. The moment there's an anomaly, one single anomaly, one deviation from your norm, it all falls down. You say he's a white man, so we're looking for white guys.

But what if he's not? What if he's black, or Asian, or a woman?'

'The profile is a guide. It's not ironclad. It's simply designed to show that some people should be examined with greater care than others. Working the percentages is proven to be the best way of proceeding in cases like this.'

'Not on my cases. Unless that percentage is one hundred, unless it's an absolute dead cert, there's always a chance you're wrong. Then you might as well get chimpanzees to stick pins in pages of the *New York Times* and spell out the killer's name that way.'

'That's not a helpful analogy.'

'Way I see it is this: You want us to take your framework – white, male, educated, organized, all that – and fit the evidence to it. To me, that's putting the cart before the horse. I let the evidence speak for itself, and guide me to the end. You decide what the end will be, and choose what you need to get there.'

'And I bet you we'll end up at the same place.'

'If we do, one of us will have got there by luck, and it won't have been me. So, no offense, but since I'm too old to care what the FBI think of me, I'm going to tell every man in there' – Beradino jerked his head towards the incident room – 'to take your profile and shove it where, er, where the sun don't shine.'

1:39 p.m.

The main morgue for Allegheny County (which includes the county seat, Pittsburgh) is located in the basement of one of the government buildings downtown. It's painted a bilious shade of green which is very nearly, if not very actually, the most unsuitable hue possible for such an institution.

There's the land of the living, up and out in the crisp fall streets; and there's this, the body farm, inside and down, down, like an ancient mythological underworld where the walls sweat death and the odors of chemicals and rotting humans cover and tangle with each other like lovers.

Cliff Lockwood, county medical examiner, moved swiftly, economically and authoritatively round Yuricich's charred corpse.

He placed a rubber body block under Yuricich's back, so that the arms and neck hung down and the chest was pushed up and forwards. That made it easier to cut the chest open.

Though medical examiners are always the ones who study bodies and organs for clues as to cause of death, they often leave the actual dissections to their assistants.

Not Lockwood. He cut better than anyone he'd ever met. Some MEs use ordinary kitchen knives to excise organs, or pruning shears to cut through ribs. These are several times cheaper than specialized medical implements, and do the job almost as well. This isn't fancy microsurgery, where one misplaced nick can be fatal. Fatal's already been taken care of.

Again, not Lockwood. He always used top-of-the-range implements, expense be damned. If it was worth doing, he felt, it was worth doing properly. It may have been nothing more than a matter of pride to him, but pride was everything.

He cut Yuricich open in practiced lines; shoulder to breastbone, each side, and down to the waist.

With a scalpel, he peeled back burnt skin, muscle and soft tissue, and pulled the chest flap up over the face, exposing the ribcage and neck muscles.

He made two cuts on each side of the ribcage, dissected the tissue behind it, and pulled the ribcage from the skeleton.

Quick, decisive cuts above the hyoid bone to remove all the neck organs.

Lockwood reached inside the cadaver and brought them out, murmuring their names dispassionately as he did so: esophagus, larynx . . . and he stopped.

'There's no tongue here,' he said.

Thursday, November 11th. 9:41 a.m.

It may have been Veterans' Day, but it was no holiday for Patrese, Beradino and Boone; not when reading Lockwood's autopsy report over cups of congealing coffee.

The tongue had been removed *ante mortem*, the report stated.

'I don't need an ME to tell me *that*,' Beradino snorted. 'The killer could hardly have reached in and taken the tongue once he'd set the body on fire, could he?'

Patrese grunted agreement, and kept reading.

The most likely method of extraction, Lockwood had written, was with a sharp knife, perhaps a scalpel. The killer would have cut down each side in turn and across the back, as though opening a double-zippered suitcase. The frenum, the flap which anchors the tongue to the floor of the mouth, had been severed, and this was visible even through the fire damage.

'Why?' Patrese said.

As in: why had Yuricich been mutilated, when Redwine and Kohler hadn't?

'Gangs? Gangs cut the tongues from snitches who've blabbed, don't they?'

'He was hardly a gangbanger, though, let alone a stoolie.'

'No, but he presided over several gang-related homicide cases in his time.'

Patrese nodded. He and Beradino had caught some of those killers themselves.

'I know. But were those big news? Little local groups, most of them. Hardly crossed the county line. We're not talking Cali or Medellin. Besides, our gangs, Pittsburgh gangs, are almost totally black. A black dude drives round somewhere like Squirrel Hill, half the locals are dialing 911 before he's reached the first stop sign.'

Beradino laughed. 'OK. You win. Scratch the gang angle.'

Boone got up, walked over to a whiteboard on the wall, and pulled the lid off a marker pen.

What are tongues used for? he wrote.

He penned the answers as they came up.

1. *Eating, or at least tasting.*
2. *Making sounds; talking, shouting, whistling.*
3. *Kissing, licking, foreplay, oral sex.*
4. *Insulting others (sticking out one's tongue).*
5. *Tongue as item of food, e.g. in a meat store.*

'OK,' Boone said. 'How likely is each one?'

'Number five's really out there,' Patrese said. 'Tongue as food. There's nothing in any of the murders to suggest cannibalism, right? Quite the opposite, I'd say. Those bodies are burnt to a crisp.'

'I second that,' Beradino said. 'Scratch five. Scratch one, too; eating, tasting. Yuricich wasn't a chef, restaurant reviewer, food writer, anything like that. He didn't make his living out of food.'

'Could he have been some kind of serious gourmet?' asked Boone.

'Not if he lived in Pittsburgh,' Patrese deadpanned.

They all laughed. Pittsburgh cuisine majors on two things: size, and simplicity. You want *nouvelle cuisine*, drizzled this and sun-dried that? Take the next flight to LA, and leave the supersized portions of mayo and chips to the hardcore steeltowners.

'I reckon we can scratch number four, too,' Boone said. 'Sticking your tongue out at someone, making a raspberry, is hardly the kind of thing you get murdered for.'

'Hardly an insult at all, once you're past puberty,' Patrese said.

'True. So we have two choices. Sex, and speech.'

'Sex first,' Beradino said. 'Yuricich lived alone. Never married, far as we can tell.' He left the implication hanging for a moment, then shot it down. 'I only ever met him professionally, but he always struck me as pretty much asexual. If he'd been gay, actively gay, it'd have got out by now.'

'And if it *had* got out, it would have been an issue,' Patrese said. 'This place ain't the Bible Belt, but nor's it some kind of free-wheeling, anything-goes Frisco. Folks here are pretty conservative, especially those in Yuricich's circles.'

'Maybe he was a secret pussy-hound,' Boone said.

'He didn't look the curb-crawling type.'

'Three-quarters of a working girl's clientele don't look the type,' Beradino said.

Patrese conceded the point with a moue. 'So we go through the runes of his life, as we've done with Redwine and Kohler. Maybe we'll find Yuricich spent all his spare time down the whorehouse. Till then, it's a maybe. That leaves speech.'

'This is where I'm leaning, I have to say,' Boone said. 'What else does a judge do, if not give judgment? When he speaks to pass sentence, his word is law.'

'Even if you don't agree with what he says.'

'And Yuricich could have sparked argument in a phone booth,' said Beradino.

'So we look at his cases,' Boone said. He tapped a manila folder. 'I've got a list of them here.'

Beradino's eyes widened in surprise. 'Courthouse records department told me they couldn't pull that together till after the holiday.'

Boone's smile failed to suppress the satisfaction of his answer. 'The courthouse records department employs two illegal immigrants. I reminded them of that fact.'

Patrese managed not to laugh too loudly. Boone continued, smooth as silk.

'These go back a couple of decades or more. Nothing I can see for Redwine. Yuricich *did* sit on a couple of Mercy medmal cases, but both of them before Redwine arrived there. So rule that out.

'With Kohler, it's a little more interesting. *Brennan-Clark vs Roman Catholic Diocese of Pittsburgh.* You remember that?'

Patrese swallowed the last of his coffee and nodded.

'Kid who'd been abused by a priest, wasn't it?'

'Kid who *said* he'd been abused by a priest,' Beradino corrected.

'Kids don't make that kind of shit up, Mark. Not when it goes as far as a judge.'

'Stuart Brennan-Clark claimed he'd suffered abuse at the hands of a Catholic priest, Moss O'Neill, thirty years beforehand,' Boone said. 'Yuricich ruled there was insufficient evidence to go to trial.'

'How was Kohler involved?' Beradino asked.

'Only by virtue of being bishop at the time the case was brought. He wasn't named in the allegations. I don't think he even knew the plaintiff.'

'Pretty tenuous, then, to think this might be related.'

'Kohler's killer smashed up the church artifacts,' Patrese said.

163

'You get abused by a priest, you might want to take it out like that.'

'Perhaps,' Boone said. 'But not in this case. Not Stuart Brennan-Clark.'

'Why not?'

'He topped himself a few years ago.'

'Because Yuricich threw the case out?'

'Some time after that. He was an alcoholic, had lots of problems. Moved out to Lake Havasu, threw himself under a train. Phoenix field office sent me the details. So nothing there, either.'

'Can I have a look?' Patrese asked.

Boone handed him the case list.

It ran for pages and pages. A record of Yuricich's life, nine to five, Mondays to Fridays, year in, year out.

Patrese split the pile roughly in two and handed one of the halves to Beradino. They began to read.

Less than a minute had elapsed when Beradino said: 'Hey.'

He held up a sheet and pointed. *Commonwealth of Pennsylvania vs al-Rassar, Malik and Ben-Kahla*. I remember those guys. I helped out on the case.'

'They were members of the Homewood mosque, weren't they?' said Patrese.

'Exactly. They were charged under the PATRIOT Act with endangering national security or something. It wasn't long after 9/11. Yuricich found all three guilty.'

'Yuricich? What about the jury?'

'He was sitting alone. Terrorist case. Fifteen years each, they got.'

Beradino, Patrese and Boone looked at each other.

They were all thinking more or less the same thing.

Redwine had botched surgery on Abdul Bayoumi, whose son Mustafa was a member of the same mosque as the three men whom Yuricich had convicted.

If those three had been Islamic extremists – even if they hadn't – what was to stop there being more where they'd come from? Someone who might want to smash crucifixes, shatter stained-glass windows, deface a print of God and Adam. Someone possibly from Pakistan, where the hair in the cathedral had come from. To watch the news, to read the papers, was to be told over and again that Christianity and Islam were at war with each other, and that those at either end of the conflict believed there was no middle ground. You were either for or against.

'Caleb, can you give us the list of all the Muslims you guys are keeping tabs on?' Patrese asked.

Boone paused.

'That's pretty sensitive stuff, Franco,' he said at length.

'Come on, man. We need to check them all out.'

'It's not as easy as that.'

'Hey,' Beradino said. 'You told us you'd help in any way you can.'

'And I will. But there's a lot of sensitive stuff here. Surveillance, operations, deep cover. I can't have you guys just blundering in somewhere and undoing months, *years*, of painstaking work with a few dumb questions.'

'Come on, Caleb,' Patrese said. 'All we want is what's in your files. Names, addresses, radical connections. We find someone we like the look of, something that makes us think, this guy, he could be our man – then we come to you and check we're not pissing on anyone's shoes. OK?'

'I don't know, Franco. Terrorism's our number one priority, you know. Everything has to be cleared through, like, nine levels of managers, and . . .'

'You're head of the field office,' Beradino said. 'Your word goes.'

'Not on something like this. I have to go higher. I have to go to DC.'

'This is a perfectly legitimate request,' Patrese added.

'The guys we're looking at are suspected of terrorism. This is a serial killer.'

'Maybe there's no difference.'

'Huh?'

'Terrorists attack innocent people. They create panic. They attract media attention. They give law enforcement the runaround. Tell me how that's in any way different to what our killer's doing.'

'I have to go higher. I'll ask, and I'll make a good case. That's all I can promise.'

'But –'

'But nothing. It is what it is. Take it or leave it.'

Beradino clicked his tongue in annoyance. 'Every time I deal with the Bureau, you guys are always the same. You swan in and expect everyone else to bend; but the moment *we* ask *you* for something, whoah! You act like we just burned Old Glory.'

'Mark . . .' Patrese began.

'It's OK,' Boone said. 'I understand your frustration. So please understand mine. I'll do what I can. In the meantime, I suggest very strongly we keep this idea under wraps. This could be a PR disaster if we screw it up. Hell, it could be a PR disaster even if we don't screw it up. We all remember how anti-Muslim sentiment spiked after 9/11. I don't want a repeat of that, even on a smaller scale.'

'All right,' said Beradino. It was as near an apology as he'd give. 'Of course,' he continued, 'it might not be about Muslims at all.'

There was a pause; not very slight, and not very comfortable.

They all knew that Yuricich had presided over one case more controversial than all the others put together. It had been so controversial, in fact, that the defendant was bringing what would be – what *would have been*, if Yuricich had lived – a landmark case for bias and misleading the jury.

Landmark because, until now, the Supreme Court had always ruled that judges and prosecutors enjoyed absolute immunity, so they could do their jobs without fear of legal retaliation. However, the Third Circuit Appeal Court had just decided that management failures leading to a wrongful conviction *could* now be prosecuted.

And both Beradino and Patrese had connections to the defendant in question.

Her name was Mara Slinger.

She'd been a Hollywood star; one Oscar already under her belt and, if the pundits were to be believed, more likely to come. She hadn't been proper, hardcore, über-'A'-list – that is, she hadn't been a Julia, or a Nicole – but she'd definitely been on the next rung down, along with the Naomi Wattses and Kate Winslets of this world.

She'd chosen her scripts wisely, mixing popcorn films with serious ones, and she hadn't been scared of taking challenging roles, which was Hollywood-speak for making herself look ugly. Her Oscar had come for a film called *First Lady*, in which she'd played Eleanor Roosevelt, no one's idea of a beauty.

The necessary prosthetics had made Mara unrecognizable, and the way she'd changed her voice meant you wouldn't have known it was her even with your eyes shut. Plenty of actresses would have been too vain to take the role on, but not her, and she'd been good enough to carry it off, her own beauty be damned.

Then Mara had fallen in love with and married a hitherto untameable bachelor, who also happened to be a billionaire businessman and, latterly, mayor of Pittsburgh.

Howard Negley.

Their wedding had been a lavish affair, and their honeymoon had trailed paparazzi. And if Pittsburgh had liked its new mayor, it had gone crazy for his wife.

Even for a city that was newer, cleaner and more confident than before, she'd still been an exotic bird. That she'd chosen to live in the 'Burgh rather than Tinseltown was a vote of confidence in the city which an entire Chamber of Commerce's budget couldn't have bought.

When Mara had said she felt Pittsburghers were the most genuine and hospitable people she'd met anywhere in America – and implied, without quite saying so, that Hollywood was chock-full of fakes, charlatans and weirdos – Pittsburghers had half-considered throwing Howard out and installing Mara as some mayor-cum-queen figure herself.

She'd become pregnant. Supermarket tabloids had rejoiced. The best obstetricians the nation could provide had been summoned to her bedside at Mercy – no Cedars-Sinai or Swiss clinics for Mara – and into a world agog had come Noah, seven and a half pounds of impeccable breeding and genetics.

A month later, Noah had died.

A child's death was perhaps the one thing that could still stop the rapacious press in its tracks. Coverage of the tragedy had been muted and respectful. Even those self-same supermarket tabloids had recognized it was something for which no amount of money, power, looks or talent could compensate.

A year or so later, Mara had become pregnant again. This time round, she'd given birth to a little girl, Esther.

After five weeks, she too had died.

Then had come Isaac, who'd lived for just seventeen days.

The police had opened an investigation, with Beradino as lead detective.

Beradino had arrested Mara on suspicion of killing her babies, all of them; three separate charges of murder.

Mara had denied it, of course.

168

She was a religious woman, a regular fixture at her local synagogue in Fox Chapel. Every movie contract she'd ever signed had barred nude scenes, body doubles or not. She was the last person on earth who'd have killed her children, she'd said.

She'd hired Hellmore to fight her corner, adamant that all three babies had died cot deaths. She'd refused to plead guilty, or claim diminished responsibility, even though she could have got a lighter sentence that way. She hadn't done it, period.

Half the country had agreed with her, and reckoned her the victim of a monstrous witch-hunt. The other half thought her a baby-killer, evil to the core.

The trial had been front-page news throughout the world.

As prosecuting attorney, Amberin Zerhouni had thrown the kitchen sink at Mara, alleging pretty much everything from Mara's resentment of the enforced hiatus in her career to postpartum psychosis via all points in between.

Not all of it had stuck, but then Amberin hadn't needed it all to. Just enough.

The jury had found Mara guilty. Yuricich had given her three life sentences.

Howard, having stood by Mara throughout the trial, had filed for divorce.

Hellmore had worked like fury to have the case reopened. Showman he may have been, but he also knew how to put the hard yards in off camera. Somewhere deep in eastern Europe, he'd found one of Mara's grandmothers who'd lost several children in infancy, and he'd set about proving two things: first, that genetic defects had caused the loss of these children; and second, that these defects had traveled down the maternal line, first to Mara and then to her children.

The Court of Appeal had overturned the original verdict. On a scorching summer morning a few months back, Mara had been freed from Muncy.

Several thousand people, clearly with nothing better to do than trek to a small town in the middle of nowhere and stand around in the blazing sun for hours on end, had been there to witness her release.

Among them had been Beradino, disbelieving and horrified in equal measures. Of every homicide he'd worked, this one – three little children dead before they were six weeks old – had shaken him harder than any other. Much harder.

Far as he was concerned, Mara was guilty as hell. He knew when he'd been lied to, and Mara had made Dick Nixon look like the Pillsbury Doughboy.

So that was Beradino's connection to Mara Slinger.

Patrese's was slightly more tangential, but no less traumatic.

Because the woman Patrese had shot in Homewood, the one he'd thought had been going for a gun when she'd just been reaching for her shirt, the one whose death he'd had to stamp down somewhere deep in his psyche, and even then it didn't, *wouldn't*, stay hidden, it still seeped little bubbles of anguish and guilt and what-ifs; well, that woman hadn't been just another junkie, just another whitey out of place and out of her depth in the ghetto, certainly not as far as Mara Slinger was concerned.

That woman had been Samantha Slinger. Mara's little sister.

Friday, November 12th. 4:00 p.m.

Mara lived in the resolutely middle-class area of Observatory Hill. Her apartment was right on the edge of Riverview Park, which boasted wildlife, trails for hiking, riding and cross-country, and the titular observatory itself, an imposing Greek Revival temple in tan brick and white terracotta topped by domed telescope enclosures.

Except it wasn't her apartment. It belonged to the Pittsburgh police department.

Pittsburgh PD maintains fifty or so safe houses across the city, which they use for people whose lives are deemed in danger; usually witnesses or snitches due to give testimony in upcoming trials.

Mara wasn't one of those, of course, but her safety had been deemed compromised all the same. Since her release in mid-July, she'd received hundreds of death threats: letters, phone calls, e-mails, even parcels full of excrement or dismembered dolls.

So the police had decided to watch over her till the fuss died down and the hordes of crazies moved on to their next target. They'd put her in this apartment on Riverview Avenue;

two officers always inside with her, two more in a cruiser parked outside.

After six weeks, protection had been scaled down to just the two men in the cruiser. Six weeks after that, it had been decreed by whoever decreed these things that there was no longer a clear and present danger to her safety.

The crazies and name-callers had moved on. Only the odd curiosity-seeker was left, and even they didn't tend to hang around too long now there were no crowds in which to pass the time.

The police had left Mara with two things; a panic alarm, which was routed straight through to the nearest cop shop; and a few months to find alternative accommodation.

A couple of weeks after the police had left Mara, Redwine had been killed.

Coincidence? That was what Patrese and Beradino were there to find out.

They were almost at the apartment when Patrese's cell-phone rang.

It was one of the uniforms in the incident room. 'We've found something, sir.'

'Go on.'

'Two small stones in the judge's house.'

'Stones?'

'Yes, sir.'

'What kind of stones?'

'Predominantly pink, with areas of red and white mottling, and a smattering of black spots across the surface.'

'And?'

'There were similar stones at both other murder scenes.'

Patrese sat up straight in his seat. 'Then why the hell weren't they noted?'

'They *were* noted, sir. There's an inventory of items found at each scene. They're in both inventories, but not as stand-alone items. That's why we missed them till now. At the first scene, the Redwine case, they were marked as part of a bowl full of semi-precious stones and pebbles which had been on a table in the living room. And in the cathedral, they were categorized as general debris, presumably brought in on the soles of one of the hundreds of people who'd visited that day.'

Patrese bit back his anger, knowing it was aimed largely at himself.

It didn't matter that the link had been obscure. His job was to find such links.

'There's a geology department at Pitt,' he said. 'Send the stones there. Ask the department to tell us what they are, where they come from, what they might mean.'

'Yes, sir.'

'And good work, whoever spotted the connection.'

'That was me, sir.'

'Then good work to you. Well done. And whatever you do, keep this away from the press. We can use this as a nutjob filter.'

'Of course, sir.'

Patrese ended the call and briefly apprised Beradino of the situation.

Beradino nodded, but his mind was elsewhere; as was Patrese's too, truth be told.

They'd left Boone behind. Technically, they'd done so because Boone's role was purely an advisory one, and having him come along to interview suspects would send out the wrong signals as to the balance of power in this investigation.

They all knew perfectly well that it wasn't the real reason. The real reason was that Patrese and Beradino were probably the two people Mara wanted to see least in the entire world.

Which made them the perfect choices to interview her.

*   *   *

173

There was a picture on Mara's mantelpiece of her on stage at the Kodak Theatre, gym-honed body swathed in Vera Wang and a little gold statuette in her hand. Her smile flashed two rows of preternaturally white teeth, and her eyes crinkled in the warm joy of her peers' adoration.

She sure as hell didn't look like that any more.

She was still pretty, of course, if you looked hard enough. But her skin was almost gray, and her eyes had been pulled downwards by the weight of the bags beneath them. It was prison pallor, recognizable to pretty much everyone who worked in law enforcement, and it took longer than a few months and a dose of civvy street to shift. Both Patrese and Beradino knew plenty of people who'd never looked the same even after a few months inside.

'I wondered when you'd be making an appearance,' she said tightly.

She led them into the sitting room.

It was large enough: high ceilings, tall windows, neutral décor. Bookshelves on the far wall were crammed with paperbacks. On a side table next to the sofa were three black-and-white photographs in silver frames; Noah, Esther and Isaac, all scrunched-up baby faces and white blankets.

If Beradino noticed the photographs, he gave no sign; but then his face couldn't have gotten any tighter than it already was without surgery.

'Please.' Mara gestured towards a couple of armchairs. 'Sit.'

She perched on the edge of the sofa, uncomfortable and nervous. She didn't offer them coffee, tea, or even a glass of water. She wanted them out. You could hardly blame her for that, Patrese thought.

'You know that Judge Yuricich was murdered two days ago?' Beradino said.

Mara nodded towards that morning's copy of the *Post-Gazette*

174

on the coffee table in front of her. The front page carried nothing else.

'Would you mind telling us where you were on Wednesday morning?'

'I was here.'

'Is there anyone who could corroborate that?'

'No, there isn't. I was here alone, Detective.' She paused. 'I usually am.'

'Do you remember what you were doing on the evenings of Monday eighteenth and Sunday thirty-first October?'

'Yes, I do.'

Beradino raised his eyebrows; polite surprise or rancid disbelief, Patrese couldn't tell. He noticed that Beradino was shaking, quivering with tension as he tried to concentrate on the questions he was asking, and on being fair, and playing this one by the book, even down to the smallest detail, when pretty much all he could think about was that this woman had committed the most heinous crime imaginable – not once, not twice, but three times, *three!* – and that, having got her just desserts, she'd then cheated them through a smart lawyer and the bleeding hearts of the appeal court.

'You do? I don't see no diary. You must have a great memory.'

'I was doing the same things those evenings as I do every evening.' Mara paused, an actress' nose for the beat. 'Nothing.'

'Nothing at all?'

'Sitting here. Reading. Watching TV. Going to bed early, hoping I sleep as long as possible. I have no social life. I'm damaged goods, as well you know. No one wants to be seen with me. Not now. Perhaps not ever. I don't go out, 'cos I'm always worried about how people will react. There'll always be people who think I did it.' She raised her eyebrows meaningfully in Beradino's direction. 'All it needs is for someone to say something, even do something, try and attack me, and that's an evening ruined. So I don't put myself out there. Maybe I'm agoraphobic, I don't know. But after all I've been through, I don't even care that much any more either. So no, I don't have an alibi for the eighteenth, or the thirty-first, or last Wednesday, or any other day you care to mention since I left Muncy, because how can I have an alibi when I never see anyone?'

Patrese was about to say something, but Mara was in full spate.

'No, actually, come to think of it, maybe I *do* have an alibi.' She glared at Beradino. 'I know your idea of great detective work is taking a woman who's suffered the biggest tragedy a mother ever could, not once but three times, and deciding the only way to make that worse is to accuse her of doing it deliberately – you don't have children, do you, Detective? No, I didn't think so. No father could ever have done what you did. I wonder whether you even like women?'

She went on before Beradino could answer. 'Anyway, if you do what detectives are *supposed* to do, why don't you go find some of the freaks who used to gather down on the sidewalk outside? The paparazzi, the stalkers, the haters, the bored, the motley crew who'd come to gawp at me, day after day, night after night. Go find them, 'cos I bet some of them were here when those people were murdered, and they'd tell you I couldn't have done it, because I was in here all the time, I hadn't left this apartment, and they'd have known if I had, as there's no way out other than right past them.'

She was breathing hard, and she didn't break eye contact with Beradino once.

'I don't appreciate you speaking to me like that,' Beradino said.

Mara shrugged. 'So arrest me.'

Patrese almost laughed. He was suddenly conscious that

he was being unusually quiet, and realized he was hunching on his seat to make himself appear smaller.

He knew why; because he didn't want to be noticed.

He felt ashamed; the kind of shame he'd known before, perhaps the kind of shame you'd expect when sitting six feet from someone whose sister you'd killed.

'What do you think of Yuricich's murder?' Beradino said.

'What do you mean, what do I think?'

'I mean, how does it make you feel?'

'*Feel*? It doesn't make me feel a thing.'

'You're not glad he's dead?'

'Not in the slightest.'

'Some people might find that surprising.'

'Why?'

'You were bringing legal action against him, is that right?'

'That's right, yes.'

'You felt you had a case against him?'

'Very much so.'

'That must have caused you some upset. Given how, er, how *emotional* this case has been.'

'It did cause me, er, some upset, as you put it, yes. But I wasn't suing because I was upset. I was suing because I felt Yuricich had broken the law. If you think I'm happy he's dead, then no, quite the opposite. Yes, I loathed him, with every fiber of my being. But it's a long way from loathing someone to killing them. Too long to make sense, in fact, at least in this case.'

'Why's that?'

'Isn't it obvious?'

'Not to me.'

'Why does that not surprise me? Whoever killed Yuricich deprived me of my justice. I'll never see him in the dock now. Never see him on the wrong side of the law, for once, beholden to someone else's judgment. Never have the

177

satisfaction of holding him accountable for what he did to me. No; the *last* thing I wanted was for him to be killed. Justice, denied. You think I don't know what *that* feels like?'

'Did you know Michael Redwine or Gregory Kohler?' Patrese asked quickly.

Both Beradino and Mara started slightly, as though they'd forgotten he was there. Mara stared at him for a moment.

'Redwine, no. Kohler, I might have met him with Howard at some point before . . . before it all happened, but I don't remember. If I did, he clearly didn't make a big impression on me. If you're asking me whether I killed them . . .'

'That wasn't what I was asking.'

'Come on, Detective. You two aren't here to wish me happy Shabbat. You ask me whether I knew them, you ask me whether I killed them, one leads to the other. No, no, no. I didn't kill either of them. I have no reason to want either of them dead. None at all. None at all.'

She glanced out of the window. It was late afternoon, and the sky was blackening.

'Now, if you'll excuse me; it's nearly dark, and Shabbat starts at sundown.'

Saturday, November 13th. 10:16 a.m.

Pittsburgh receives more rain than Seattle, a point it likes to ram home on occasion. Today was such an occasion. Outside the windows of Hellmore's office, the rain came down in sheets, blankets, curtain-rods – hell, practically an entire bedroom suite.

Patrese and Beradino looked round the room. Wall space was clearly at a premium, with hundreds of pictures of the man himself in grin-and-grips with the great and good: Shaq and Magic, Denzel and Will, Jesse and Al. Dotted in the few remaining spaces were framed copies of multi-million-dollar checks Hellmore had won for his clients. Patrese recognized a couple of names from police brutality cases.

Hellmore came in at a quick trot. 'Sorry I'm late; and I have to go out again now.'

His tie was another marvel in Technicolor.

'Who's your supplier?' Patrese asked. 'Stevie Wonder?'

Hellmore laughed, which Patrese took to be a good sign. 'The day I take fashion lessons from the cops is the day I know it's all gone to shit.'

Patrese remembered the statement aimed at potential clients on the home page of Hellmore's website. *The police and prosecutors do* not *have your best interests in mind after a murder charge is made. Their job is to quickly convict you based on the evidence obtained and move on to the next case.*

It was safe to say Hellmore was not a natural fan of the police force; but equally safe to say he took each member of that force as he found them. Patrese made the effort to get on with him; Beradino less so, especially since the Mara Slinger case.

'Listen, detectives; can we do this later? Unless you want to come with me?'

'Where are you going?'

'See my dad.'

Beradino and Patrese looked at each other.

'Sure,' Patrese said.

'You won't be so sure when we get there, especially if he's refused his pills. Still, on your own heads be it. We'll talk in the car.'

'The car' was another integral part of the Hellmore legend; a Rolls-Royce in beige ('racing gold', he insisted) with a number plate that read 'SUE YOU'.

'Don't both y'all sit in the back,' Hellmore said as he clicked the remote. 'People will think it's *Driving Miss Daisy*.'

Beradino pulled rank and took the back seat. Patrese rode shotgun.

Hellmore pulled out into downtown traffic, light on a weekend.

'My right of way, asshole,' he hissed at a car passing close across his bows. 'Where were we? Oh, yeah. Dad lives in a nursing home; sorry, a senior citizens' home. As if giving it some bullshit euphemism is going to make people forget the residents check out only one way – feet first.'

'Good home?'

'Mount Lebanon.' Mount Lebanon, south-west of the city center, was about the most characterful of Pittsburgh's more affluent suburbs, with its hilly bricked streets and hotchpotch of houses; older mock-Tudors, bungalows, four-squares. 'Best that money can buy. Not that he appreciates it. He's an ornery bugger, specially since he had a stroke. Anyway, we'll be there soon enough. What can I do for you in the meantime? You wanna know who had a reason to do Yuricich?'

'If you would,' Beradino said from the rear, deadpan.

'Shit. Take your pick. Half of Homewood, for a start. Yuricich was a racist fuck, man. Didn't like black defendants. Sure as hell didn't like black lawyers. But you guys already figured out that a bunch of black dudes in Squirrel Hill gonna stand out like titties on a pork pie, so it ain't any of the brothers.'

'You were bringing a suit against him for bias and misleading the jury in the Mara Slinger case, is that right?'

'Damn right. Not just him. Lockwood, too. You know, the asshole ME.'

'Clifford Lockwood is a respected professional,' Beradino said levelly.

'Not from where I'm looking. You remember his bullshit statement about the odds against it *not* being murder? That was what sunk Mara. But it was bullshit. The math was flawed. One of the math professors at Pitt proved it, right after the trial. But it was too late by then. And Lockwood knew it was bullshit all along. Fucking knew it.'

Everyone who'd followed Mara's trial – which was to say, pretty much everyone in the country – remembered that moment.

As well as being medical examiner for Allegheny County, Lockwood was director of pediatric forensic pathology at the Children's Hospital of Pittsburgh, responsible for investigating suspicious child deaths throughout western Pennsylvania. He wasn't just any old expert; he was authority, he was the oracle.

This was what he'd said on the witness stand.

'There's no evidence that cot deaths – sudden, unexpected,

181

seemingly inexplicable deaths – run in families. There is, however, plenty of evidence that child abuse does.

'We work on a simple principle which has yet to be proved wrong. One cot death is a tragedy. Two is suspicious. And three is murder.

'Look at the evidence. All three children seemed entirely healthy before suffering sudden, fatal collapses. The autopsies showed no evidence of illness. I should know; I carried them out.

'In a family like this one – a high-income, professional, health-conscious, non-smoking family – the odds of an infant dying by chance alone is around one in 8,500.

'The odds of two infants dying by chance alone are therefore this figure multiplied by itself, which works out as one in almost 1.75 million.

'And the odds of three infants dying by chance alone' – and here Lockwood had paused, as though daring the jury to try and work out in their heads how ridiculously large the next, crucial figure would be – 'are more than one in 600 billion.

'In other words, one in a hundred times the current population of the world.

'If you played the lottery every week, and those were your odds of winning, you know how long you'd have to play before you could be sure of hitting the jackpot? More than a billion years.'

'So Lockwood,' Hellmore said, 'we're looking to do for perjury. I'd do him for being a smarmy fuck too, if I could. You remember what else that motherfucker did? The bouncy chair Mara had put her babies in was admitted as an exhibit. And that . . . Jesus, I still can't believe it. Lockwood looked round the room, looking for the laugh, and said loudly, "I didn't realize we were that short of chairs." And then, *and then*, he came over at lunchtime and said: "I always try to be sympathetic towards the mothers. This is terrible for me, it must be awful for you." I told him to fuck off.'

He eased the Roller across the Fort Pitt Bridge.

'We can still get Lockwood, of course. But Yuricich . . . it would have been legal history, man.' His eyes glittered; the words 'legal history' were music to the ears of a crusader like Hellmore. 'Expert witnesses have long been fair game, but not judges and prosecutors. We'd nailed Yuricich, we'd have opened the floodgates. All those fucked by the system would have got a crack at it too.'

'Why not Amberin?' Patrese asked.

'Amberin did her job. I got no problem with that. Nor does Mara. Amberin was there to prosecute. That's what she did. Yuricich *wasn't* there to prosecute, but he might as well have been. I've seen some bent judges in my time, and he was right up there. Too in love with himself, too. You know he used to leave the courthouse during lunch breaks in the trial, go round the souvenir stalls outside and buy up figurines and T-shirts of himself?'

'And if you'd won? If Yuricich had lived, and you'd taken him to court, and won? What would that have meant?'

'For him? A ruined career, I hope.'

'You *hope*?'

'Damn straight. Honest mistakes honestly made are one thing. What Yuricich did to Mara – and lots of others, let's face it – was something else entirely. And you know how much compensation Mara gets for that? None. Zilch. Not a dime. People get millions when they scald their dumb asses with hot coffee from Micky D's, but not when they spend years inside for something they didn't do. Not in this state, at any rate. All Mara got was a shrug of the shoulders and an "oops". She deserves more.'

Patrese half-turned and glanced at Beradino.

Beradino was as expressionless as the Sphinx.

11:08 a.m.

The Golden Twilight Senior Citizens' Home at Mount Lebanon was clean, well-appointed, and lacking any semblance of warmth.

Notice boards were spattered with offers for this, that and the other, almost all of it costed. The only poster without a dollar sign anywhere to be seen was one asking the residents to become donors for the UPMC Willed Body Program. *Benefit science after you've gone*, and so on.

That apart, it seemed to Patrese to be the kind of place where they knew the price of everything and the value of nothing.

The home's manager, Walter de Vries, met them at the entrance. A ring of graying hair skirted the flanks of his bald scalp. Beneath it, his face was round and bland.

'Good to see you again, Freddie,' he said, shaking Hellmore's hand vigorously.

'You too, Walter. How's Dad?'

'Not too bad, this week. A bit up and down. No more than usual.'

'Still accusing you of everything bad?'

'A little. But don't worry. We get that the whole time,

184

and not just from him. Goes with the territory. It don't mean nothing. You get to that age, folks start losing their faculties. It's sad. We just try to look after them best we can, let them hold on to as much dignity as possible. It's all we can do. All anyone can do.'

He gestured through into a sunroom. 'He's in there. Have to dash, but good to see you again. Anything you want, you be sure to let me know.'

De Vries hurried off. They went through into the sunroom.

Old Man Hellmore was sitting in a wheelchair. He was slightly hunched and looked indefinably shrunken, but there was no missing the dancing sparks in his eyes as he glared at Beradino and Patrese.

'The fuck are these guys?' he snapped.

'Morning to you too, Dad,' Hellmore Jnr said equably. 'How you been?'

'I said, who the fuck are these guys?'

Patrese was going to point out that he'd actually said 'the fuck are these guys?' rather than '*who* the fuck are these guys?', but figured there was a time and place for grammatical pedantry, and this was neither.

'Dad, meet Franco Patrese, Mark Beradino.'

'You cops? No, don't answer. Course you are. Clear as the noses on your faces. You carry yourselves like cops. Don't ever do undercover, guys, you want my advice. OK, Mr De-tec-tives, maybe y'all can clear up a mystery for me. My son here come see me every week, but he never come on his own. He always gotta bring someone else with him. You figure that shit out?'

'Dad,' Hellmore said, in a tone half-warning and half-exasperated.

''Cos if you can't, you guys ain't much by the way of detectives.'

'Dad, let's not do this now. Not in front –'

'Not in front of the guys *you* brought?' Old Man Hellmore never took his eyes off Patrese. 'How you doing, hotshot? You worked it out yet?'

Patrese looked at Hellmore, who shrugged apology.

'Families is families,' Patrese said eventually. 'This is not my beef.'

'Then you a chickenshit,' said the old man. 'You know damn well why he never come on his own. There someone else here, he reckon I can't make a scene.'

'I'm a busy man,' said Hellmore. 'It saves time to conduct meetings in the car on my way here. That's all it is. I'm not ashamed of you, Dad.'

'Then why you shove me in this shithole?'

'This shithole costs eighty grand a year! I could put you in the Hilton for less.'

'It's a *shithole*. You put gold plate onna turd, it still a turd. S'all 'bout the money with you, ain't it? You know where your money goes? I sure as hell don't. It don't go nowhere I can see. Not to employin' anyone who looks like they actually enjoy their fuckin' job, for a start.'

'Dad, this is rated one of the best nursing homes in Pennsylvania.'

Patrese and Beradino exchanged glances. They both had the impression that this argument had been played out many, many times before.

'Then whoever rates it is a fuckin' moron. Come and stay for a day or two and see what the place is really like. They *abusin'* me, Freddie.'

'They're not abusing you, Dad. I come every week, and I've never seen them be anything but professional.'

'They *know* you come every week, dumb ass. They put on a big fuckin' song and dance for you, and the moment you out the door, it's back to the same old shit. They shout at me, they cuss, they ridicule me – when they not ignorin' me, that is. I tell 'em I can't think for the pain, they tell me it's arthritis. I know what arthritis is, dammit. I've had arthritis twenty years, and this ain't it. Assisted livin'? Assisted dyin', more like. They even bitch at me when I try and have a cigarette, like it's some damn crime or somethin'. I have to wheel this damn contraption outside just to light up. No smokin' in the building. It's like the fuckin' Nazis. Come on, Freddie. Take me outta here and lemme come stay with you.'

'You're too old for that, Dad. You're too old to be left on your own, and I'm never there, I'm always at work.'

'Then work less.'

'I can't work less. I made the commitment, Dad. I don't want to sit on the couch scratching my ass and watch things fall apart bit by bit. I try to fulfill that commitment, every day.'

'Yeah; commitment to the law, not to anyone who loves you. You wanna use the law, start by suin' everyone in this damn place, from that fool de Vries downwards. You too busy givin' your time to folks you don't know. You don't give your time to me, or to your women, your kids. Shit, Freddie, between your law and the fact you can't keep your pecker in your pants, s'no wonder you never kept a relationship.'

'Choices I made, Dad. Anyway, those folks I gave my time to deserved justice.'

'Not many of them.'

'All of them.'

'Some of them, at best. Like that Mara broad. Damn disgrace, what happened to her. Best thing you ever did, getting her off of all that. I don't mind you givin' time to her. You brought more broads like her here, I'd be a happier man.'

'You brought Mara here?' Beradino asked in surprise.

'Damn right he did,' said the old man before his son could reply. 'You couldn't move for slippin' over the droolin' tongues of the old buzzards in here. She sure brightened the place up. Talked some sense, too. You know what she said?'

Hellmore rolled his eyes. 'Dad, you bring this up every time I come here.'

''Cos it's *true*. She said even though your parents get like children, they still your parents, they always been your parents, they always gonna be your parents, and forgettin' this is dishonorin' them, takin' their dignity away. Yeah, your relationship with 'em is different from when you was a kid, but it's still a relationship God has made for you.' He smiled. 'She a fine lady. What she up to now?'

Sunday, November 14th. 3:33 p.m.

Beradino, home alone, paced the living room in endless loops.

Seeing Mara again had shaken him. *Physically* shaken him, as though he'd got the jitters or something. Beradino believed in evil, as a malevolent force in itself rather than simply the absence of good; and he believed evil was in every molecule of Mara, body and soul. It oozed from her in sludgy trails.

How not everyone could see that, he had no idea.

It was the Sabbath, the day God had set aside for rest and reflection. Jesslyn was on shift, out of reach, but Beradino very badly wanted to talk with her.

He hadn't really slept the last couple of nights, his mind churning in livid eddies; Mara, Mara, Mara. He should have mentioned it earlier, but Jesslyn had seemed preoccupied, as she often did these days, so he'd kept quiet.

He couldn't keep quiet any longer.

He needed to let it out, work it through. Talking to himself wouldn't do it. He needed someone who understood, and that was Jesslyn. Only Jesslyn could make sense of Mara. She'd seen her at close quarters, year after year. She knew her better than anyone. Jesslyn had no illusions about what they were dealing with.

It was through Mara that Beradino and Jesslyn had met, in fact; an irony which never failed to make Beradino wince, that the best thing in his life could have come from the worst.

He'd taken a special interest in Mara's incarceration, wanting to be sure she was getting no special privileges; that every day, and in every way, she'd be reminded of what abominations she'd perpetrated.

In the course of this, he'd met Jesslyn, who ran the roost at Muncy and took, if possible, an even dimmer view of what Mara had done than Beradino did.

They'd started exchanging first e-mails, then phone calls, always about Mara, their common purpose. But soon the conversations had begun to last longer and roam wider, taking in their respective lives, politics, hopes, fears and, most of all, faiths.

Beradino's Christian beliefs were the bedrock of his life, but sometimes he felt them as something more passive than active; deep strata, always there but rarely called upon.

In contrast, Jesslyn held her Old Testament high, like an army's standard. Born and brought up a Southern Baptist, her father a preacher in Yazoo City in Mississippi, she wanted eyes for eyes, teeth for teeth, fire and brimstone, and woe betide those who didn't repent or acknowledge their misdeeds.

There was another reason why Jesslyn felt what Mara had done so deeply. Because she, Jesslyn, had never been able to have children.

For someone who believed so deeply in God, and that children were God's blessings, this had been a terrible blow. Jesslyn had accepted her own barrenness as God's will, imposed for she knew not what purpose; but what she had never been able to accept, not while the world turned, was someone so blessed as Mara turning that fortune back on itself by doing what she'd done to those poor innocents.

Jesslyn had wanted nothing more than for Mara to go to

the chair; all appeals over, all petty human maneuverings and legal technicalities exhausted, and an evil woman finally alone in front of whatever God she professed to follow.

She'd wanted to be there. She'd have hit the switch herself, if they'd have let her.

But they'd never put Mara to death; she knew that too well.

Talking about all this, and much else besides, Jesslyn and Beradino had become friends; a friendship which had soon, perhaps inevitably, blossomed into more. They'd kept their separate apartments for a while, but Pittsburgh and Muncy were four hours apart, too far for regular visits when they both worked odd hours; so, when they'd been sure this was going to last, they'd selected Punxsutawney as more or less halfway between the two places, and moved in there together.

They'd both been round the block, as it were; one failed marriage each, followed by a succession of go-nowhere relationships gone nowhere.

Was this a big, passionate love?

Perhaps not, but then they'd found each other at a time when they both expected less out of life than they'd done in their younger days.

Working homicide and corrections, you saw a lot of the worst that human nature had to offer. It knocked much of the idealism out of you, but it also made you realize you were on the side of the angels, no matter what your limitations were. And it made you see how much worse things could be, and how much worse off than you people could be, so you settled for the hand you'd been dealt.

Beradino dialed Jesslyn's cell again, more in hope than expectation.

He was put straight through to voicemail, again. That wasn't surprising. She turned her phone off when she was on shift, and she certainly didn't carry it with her on her rounds. Inmates would have killed for it.

191

But Beradino wanted to talk to her *now*. He couldn't wait till she came home.

Well, he probably could, but he wanted to be doing something. Sitting round the house was going to drive him insane.

Better to get in the car and go to Muncy. He could meet her when she came off shift, surprise her, take her somewhere nice for dinner.

The traffic was light, and he made good time on the interstate. But near the DuBois exit, he felt a slight quivering behind his cheekbones, and knew instantly what it was; the strain caused by stifling yawn after yawn, testament to his broken sleep.

Best not to keep driving like that. Beradino had seen enough RTAs to know the slogan was true: tiredness really did kill.

Cup of coffee, stretch legs, deep breaths, and he'd be good to go again.

He turned off at DuBois and pulled into the service stop.

There was a burger bar here; he'd get a coffee.

It would probably taste like dirt, but so long as it had caffeine, he didn't really care. Besides, it couldn't be any worse than the department coffee. Nothing could be worse than that; nothing this side of a slurry pit, at any rate.

The burger bar was almost empty. He walked straight up to the counter.

There was only one server there. She had her back to him, arranging paper-wrapped burgers in their various racks. Hair up beneath a ridiculous cap. The things they made these people wear, he thought. As if the salary wasn't demeaning enough.

'Excuse me,' he said.

She turned round, corporate smile plastered bright on her face.

Monday, November 15th. 9:49 a.m.

Frenzy in the incident room: a Chinese parliament of men barking down phones, passing on leads, checking arrangements for press conferences, or shouting purely to relieve the frustration that still, *still,* they had no concrete suspects, let alone an arrest.

Sound and fury, and nothing.

The only person in any way calm was Beradino, and even that was surface only.

He was far, far away, endlessly replaying in his head everything that had happened yesterday when he'd come across Jesslyn in the burger bar off of I-80.

His surprise. Her surprise. Her embarrassment. His bewilderment. The manager's anger when she couldn't bring herself to serve the next guy in line. Beradino's anger at the manager being a jerk, and at Jesslyn dressed up like a fool, flipping burgers, what the heck . . .?

She'd quit on the spot, of course. He'd have torn the place apart if she hadn't, and the Lord knew Beradino wasn't a violent man.

In the car on the way home, she'd told him what had happened.

Mara had made complaints about her. Muncy, fearing bad publicity, had caved in.

Then we sue the prison, Beradino had said.

No, no, Jesslyn had replied. Mara had a case, loath as Jesslyn was to admit it. Jesslyn had been over-zealous; she had harassed Mara. The Lord knew Mara deserved it, but the Lord didn't make prison laws, more was the pity. Any court was going to side with Mara, particularly after what she'd been through.

Why hadn't she told him any of this before?

Pride, she'd said; pride, shame, guilt. Regular human failings. She'd wanted to tell him, but every day that had gone past – that she'd let go past – had made it harder and harder. She should have told him, she knew; and he'd never realize how sorry she was that she hadn't. But she was telling him now, even if only because she had no choice.

Beradino had forgiven her; that was the Christian thing to do. You love someone, you forgive them their sins. Then he'd told her to be strong. They, perhaps alone, knew what Mara had done; they weren't blinded by her beauty, or in love with her like most everyone else seemed to be.

To give Jesslyn strength, he'd made them recite Psalm 23 together.

The LORD is my Shepherd; I shall not want. He maketh me to lie down in green pastures; he leadeth me beside the still waters. He restoreth my soul: he leadeth me in the paths of righteousness for his name's sake. Yea, though I walk through the valley of the shadow of death, I will fear no evil: for thou art with me; thy rod and thy staff they comfort me. Thou preparest a table before me in the presence of mine enemies: thou anointest my head with oil; my cup runneth over. Surely goodness and mercy shall follow me all the days of my life: and I will dwell in the house of the LORD for ever.

Now, here in the incident room, Beradino had told the other cops he was thinking, searching for some bright spark of an idea which would help them find the killer. They left him alone after that, but they wouldn't do so indefinitely.

9:55 a.m.

Patrese's phone rang. He pressed his hand close over his free ear just so he could hear himself speak.

'Patrese.'

'Detective Patrese, it's Lionel Wheelwright here.' Great name, Patrese thought. 'I'm professor of geology at Pitt.'

'Hi. Thanks for calling.'

'No problem. The stones you sent are pink granite.'

'OK. What does that mean?'

'It means they're pink granite.'

Patrese laughed. 'No; I mean, is there anything special about pink granite?'

'Nothing at all. It's very common worldwide.'

'Do you know where they might have come from? What part of the world?'

'Not without further analysis. I can't even tell you at the moment whether they've been found naturally.'

'Naturally?'

'As opposed to already being cut and treated. Pink granite's used for a whole bunch of purposes. Construction, lot of construction. Like most granites, it makes good dimension stones. You'll find it in staircases, floors, walls, kitchen countertops, that kind of thing. Sculptures and monuments, too, more and more. It's more resistant to acid rain than marble.'

'Could you find out where the stones came from? With more tests?'

'Sure, but we'd have to bill you. Those tests can be expensive.'

'No problem. Mark the invoice for me and send it here. Thanks.'

'Thank *you*. Glad to be of help.'

Patrese put the phone down, and immediately it rang again.

Thinking the connection with Wheelwright hadn't been closed properly, he picked up and said: 'Professor?'

There was a soft chuckle the other end; a female chuckle, slightly breathy.

'Not exactly. Probably not ever.'

'Who's this?' he asked, though he knew exactly who it was.

'Detective Patrese, this is Mara Slinger.'

10:10 a.m.

'She did *what*?' Beradino spluttered.

'She asked me round to dinner.'

'And you're going to go?'

'Why not?'

'*Why not?* Since when did you become a moron?' Beradino wiped the back of his hand across his forehead. 'Because she's a *suspect*, Franco.'

'Last time I looked, talking to suspects was our job.'

'Talking to them, as in interviewing them, sure. Locking them up and telling them of their right to remain silent, ditto. Having an intimate *tête-à-tête* with them, no.'

'It's not an intimate *tête-à-tête*.'

'What is it, then?'

'It's dinner.'

'Just the two of you?'

'I guess.'

'Then it's a *tête-à-tête*. Look, Franco, she's famous, pretty, you're flattered . . .'

'Don't patronize me, Mark.'

'. . . but she's trouble. Trust me on this. She manipulates everyone round her.'

'Come on, Mark. You're not exactly unbiased, are you?'

'No, I'm not. But I'm also right. I don't know what her game is, but there *is* a game, you can bet on that, and she's playing you like a Stradivarius. I know what she's really like. She knows I know. Maybe she wants to get you on her side, drive a wedge between us.'

'It's just dinner. Nothing else.'

'You're determined to go?'

'Yes. I might get some information out of her. Catch her off guard.'

'I doubt it.' Beradino sighed. 'But if you're determined, then OK. But you be sure it's just dinner. You get involved with her . . .'

'I'm not going to get involved with her.'

'. . . you so much as peck her on the cheek, I'll request a new partner. I'm a Christian man, Franco. I have morals, I have faith. She has neither.'

'She's a devout Jew. She asked us to leave before Shabbat the other day.'

'She believes in one thing: herself. Nothing else. Be careful, Franco. Here's something to think about: Why on earth does she want to see *you*? You killed her sister. Someone killed my sister, I wouldn't be inviting them round, that's for sure.'

'Well, that's part of it, I think.'

'What?'

'She said she wanted to talk about that. And so do I. I want to talk about it.'

Tuesday, November 16th. 7:24 p.m.

Something was happening out there, Patrese thought as he drove rain-slicked streets.

It had started with a single internet tribute site, its tone one of smug, knowing semi-irony. Then it had spread exponentially, the number of Google hits jumping by the hour, replete with semi-illiterate bulletin boards scrawled in moronic sub-English.

Next, the first T-shirts had appeared, luridly sloganned with love hearts and leaping flames, and there'd been a couple of jokey mentions on radio shows, little quips about striking a blow for the little guy, and suddenly it was official.

The Human Torch had become a cult figure.

Patrese took a deep breath and tried to tamp down the churning in his stomach. He was often nervous before going on a date, especially a first one, even if that wasn't the kind of thing you admitted when bantering with the guys.

But this was hardly a normal first date. It wasn't a date at all, come to think of it.

For a start, there was the issue of Mara's sister, which he'd spent so long suppressing and was now rushing to the surface fast enough to give him the bends.

200

Then there was the very fact of who Mara was. It wasn't every day you got asked to dinner by an Oscar winner who'd been first convicted and then acquitted of triple murder. Maybe Jack Nicholson would have taken it in his stride. Not Franco Patrese.

He parked outside Mara's apartment building, and got out of his car. It was a third-generation Pontiac Trans Am GTA, '87 model; deep burgundy paint, gold flat-mesh diamond-spoke wheels, 5.7 V8, north of 150,000 miles on the clock, electronic gauge cluster. It spent as much time in the garage as out of it and cost him a small fortune, but he loved it, and had vowed to drive it literally into the ground.

He rang the bell, and Mara buzzed him up.

She was waiting for him in the doorway to her apartment. A touch of make-up, not too much; just enough to put color in her face. Simple skirt, simple blouse. Hardly the supervixen of Beradino's nightmares.

A formal handshake, awkward on both sides. He'd brought her a bottle of wine, Chilean red, determinedly neutral; nothing vintage, no cheapo paint-stripper either.

'Here,' she said. 'Let me take your coat.'

'Something smells good,' he said, as she hung his coat on a hook by the door.

'Seafood gumbo. You like?'

'Very much.'

'November in Pittsburgh, it's the nearest we're going to get to New Orleans.'

Mara had a bottle of white already open, chilled from the fridge. She poured two glasses, and clinked hers to his.

'Thanks for coming over, Detective Patrese. I really appreciate this.'

'You can call me Franco, you know.'

'Franco,' she said, as though trying it on for size. 'Nice name.'

She paused. Patrese felt suddenly vertiginous, the way he

201

always did when about to break up with someone he liked, knowing they'd have to talk it out, and that he'd hate every second of it but find a curious sense of relief when it was all over.

No small talk. No pleasantries. Straight in. Let's get on with it.

'I don't blame you,' she said.

He studied her carefully.

'Really?'

'Really. Oh, I *did*, of course. I thought you were just a trigger-happy cop full of adrenalin and testosterone, and that you got your kicks shooting anyone you considered scum. And of course, what I'd been through before with your, er, with your *partner*' – it seemed as though she couldn't bring herself to say Beradino's name – 'made me hate the cops even more.'

'I can see that.'

'Then I thought about it a bit. I remembered things I'd seen in Muncy, the way fights blow up' – she snapped her fingers – 'bang! out of nothing. Well, not quite nothing, obviously; there's an atmosphere, some tension on the block, but there's always that, there's always something bubbling, you just live with it, but once in a while it explodes, no warning. Not like the movies, where there's a bit of pushing and shoving beforehand. One minute, everything's normal; the next instant it's full-on, girls kicking and punching and scratching until the guards come and pull them apart.

'And I wondered if it had been like that for you.'

Patrese rotated his wine glass in his fingers, not daring to speak.

'I tried to imagine what it must be like, on a raid like that, pumped up so hard you think you're going to burst, and it's like those prison fights, there's only two kinds of people, aren't there? Those who want to hurt you, those who want to keep you safe. So you're there and you come across Sam,

202

strung out of her head – *again* – and you think she might be a danger, 'cos everyone in that house is a danger, right?

'*I* know she wasn't. You know she wasn't, *now*. But not then. And I thought, can I really blame you for that? Thing is, I saw in those fights that these are split-second decisions. I had a sheltered life, I guess, till then. But most all those girls live their lives like that, minute to minute, never thinking ahead. You do something that takes half a moment, but the consequences live with you for a whole lot longer.

'And then I started wondering what it must be like for you, having that in your head, every day. A split second, and then consequences, running on and on. You seem like a decent man, so I'm presuming it must have affected you.'

Patrese nodded, clenching his teeth against the lump in his throat.

'And if that's so, I want you to know two things. First, like I said, I don't blame you. I did, but I don't any more. I *can't* any more. And second – and this is even harder for me to say – if it hadn't been you, it'd have been someone else.'

'Huh?'

'Sam was lost to us long before you shot her.'

'That don't make it better.'

'It's not supposed to. But it's true, it is what it is. I'm not going to go into her life story – you probably know a lot of it already, it all came out after her death – but basically she had it all. We had a great childhood, loving parents, all that. She had talent, looks. Much more than me. No, no, that's not false modesty on my part; she really did. She was amazing. And she couldn't cope with it, with any of it.

'I've never taken drugs in my life, not one; not even aspirin. They tried to give me anti-depressants and all sorts after my babies died, and I wouldn't take them. But Sam, she'd do anything going. Drugs I hadn't even heard of, all mixed together. She was in the ghetto when you found her.

203

Nice middle-class Jewish girl. She shouldn't have been there in a million years. You know how desperate she must have been, to end up in a place like that.

'And that's what she was – desperate. She didn't care any more, Franco. She hadn't cared for a long time, to be honest. She was never going to get better. So whether it had been you, or an OD, or a random bullet in crossfire, or a drunk driver in the wrong place at the wrong time . . . she wasn't going to grow old and read Dr Seuss to her grandkids, put it that way. And that kills me to say, because I'd give anything for it to be different, but it's true, and it's only right you should know that.'

He was silent for a long time after she'd finished speaking, trying to find the words which would take him through the door she'd opened. And when the words did finally begin to come, he felt as though he was having to pick them from out of a minefield, one by one. They came to him reluctantly, haltingly.

Patrese told Mara he felt his life was divided into two parts, before and after; and the moment in the middle was Samantha herself.

She was the first person he'd killed. He could never go back from that.

There *was* a line, but once you stepped over it, the line disappeared. You took a life, and instantly you were apart from the huge majority of the human race who'd never done – who could never do – such a thing.

You weren't like normal people any more. You were different. You were tainted.

Most of all, you were empty.

He'd never felt such a – such an *absence*, as after killing Samantha.

Beradino had rationalized it for him, of course. Patrese had done what he had to do, no more and no less. It was just one of those things. A lot of guys had been through similar experiences. You just had to pick yourself up and get on with it.

So that's what Patrese did. It was that or go under. But it didn't mean he forgot about it.

Cops like to joke about things, even – especially – things which are beyond the pale. They do so with sick humor, gallows humor, the kind of remarks that shock normal folks. They mean nothing by it; it's just their way of dealing with the unthinkable. Firefighters and ambulance crews do the same thing.

Patrese could joke with the best of them; but never about Samantha.

He knew the Slingers were Jewish, and he often thought of what the Talmud says; that whoever destroys a soul, it is considered as if he destroyed an entire world.

'Then think of the very next line,' Mara said instantly. 'Whoever saves a life, it's considered as if he saved an entire world. You catch the person doing these things, these burnings, and you'll save lives, you'll make amends. It won't bring Sam back, but it'll mean someone else doesn't lose a loved one.'

He excused himself and went to the john, more to compose himself than through any pressing call of nature. When he returned, Mara was ladling out the gumbo. He took a mouthful, making appreciative – and genuine – noises.

'You're surprised?' she asked, a faint smile wafting round her mouth.

'Should I be?'

'Maybe not. I just thought you might think I think myself too grand to cook.'

'That's a lot of thinks there.'

She laughed. 'Sam always told me I think too much. I get a lot of time to do it, nowadays. Not to mention Muncy. A whole lot of time to think in there.'

'You come to any conclusions?'

'Lots. Sometimes I reckon none. You don't want to hear about that, though.'

'Why not?'

'Well, men never do. You go to a man with a problem, he wants to solve it. Go to a woman, and she listens.'

'You want me to listen?'

'It's a long story.'

'I got all night.'

She arched her eyebrows at him, amused. *All night?*

'OK.' She handed him the bottle of white. 'You're going to need a full glass. Maybe more than one. Where do you want me to start?'

'Begin at the beginning.'

'Why not? Why not indeed? But where's the beginning?'

She paused a moment, collecting herself; as though she were about to go on stage.

'The beginning's on Broadway,' she said suddenly. 'That's where it is.'

On Broadway I played Medea: daughter of King Aeetes; niece of the sorceress Circe; granddaughter of the sun god Helios; and wife of Jason, leader of the Argonauts, finder of the Golden Fleece.

Medea, whose husband left her for the king of Corinth's daughter.

Medea, who in revenge murdered the children she'd borne Jason.

> *In vain, my children, have I brought you up,*
> *Borne all the cares and pangs of motherhood,*
> *And the sharp pains of childbirth undergone.*

Of all the roles I've ever played, both stage and screen, it was in every way the most; the most harrowing, the most difficult, the most corrosive, the most exhausting, the most exhilarating, the most horrific, the most fantastic.

Screeching and vengeful, convinced she's given up everything for a man who then betrays her, Medea has violence in that part of the human soul which should be buried forever. She stalks the stage, ranting and raving through the heartbreak and horror of a private hell she's destined never to escape. She's compassionate and intelligent; hateful and insane.

> *You will nevermore your mother see,*
> *Nor live as ye have done beneath her eye.*

Euripides wrote Medea almost 2,500 years ago. In all that time, filicide has stood as society's most aberrant act. For a woman to kill her child is the ultimate taboo.

I didn't break that taboo. Whatever they say, I didn't break that taboo. I was never Medea, no matter how hard they tried to prove that I was. I played Medea before I became a mother. I could never, ever have played her afterwards.

Far worse to have been a mother and lost your babies than never to have been a mother at all. As a mother, I didn't live life for myself, and now my babies are gone, I don't want to again. I feel aimless and empty; a proper, total, terrifying emptiness, where the absence of anything, *everything*, becomes so oppressive that it generates a force all its own, something atavistic and primal, stripping away thousands of years of evolution and progress and civilization in searing recognition of the fact that we're all animals, we're all part of the natural order, and there's something so terribly, terribly wrong when that order gets ripped apart.

Beradino comes round a couple of days after Isaac, our third, has died. He seems a nice man, offering his condolences and saying how dreadful the whole thing is. Then he asks if I understand why the police need to make an investigation. Of course, I say. Not only do I understand, but I welcome it; maybe it'll give me the answers I crave, and tell me why my babies keep dying. Is it something genetic? Or did the doctors miss something? I've got nothing to hide, I tell Beradino. I know the police will be on my side; that's their job, isn't it, to protect and serve?

'I just can't believe this could happen three times,' I tell Beradino.

'Neither do I,' he replies.

I should have known, then; but I was still blind to the way everything looked. He comes back the next day. He says they've found post-mortem abnormalities in Isaac's autopsy which tally with similar abnormalities in Noah and Esther. He's discovered the cause of the children's deaths.

'Well?' I ask. 'What did they die of?'

He looks momentarily pained, but I still don't realize why; I think it must be some ghastly disease whose details he wants to spare me. I don't yet realize that what pains him is *me*, or rather what he thinks I am.

'Mara Slinger,' he says, 'I'm arresting you on suspicion of the murders of Noah, Esther and Isaac Negley.'

The strange thing is, even down at the station house, I'm still quite calm. I know I didn't kill the children, therefore there's no way I can be convicted of their murder, therefore this is all a huge mistake, or some crossed wires, or the police department covering itself. I'm bewildered rather than frightened; I've got nothing to hide, so if I co-operate, this whole thing will sort itself out. Nothing to hide means nothing to fear.

I've always believed in authority, and its fairness. Sure, mistakes are made, but in the greater scheme of things, good always wins out. I've no history of abuse or mental illness, nothing the police can use to make me look suspicious. I've never been in trouble with the law in my life, not even drunken high jinks at college. I was always a goody two-shoes. Sometimes, when I got invited to parties I thought would be too wild, I said I couldn't go 'cos my mom had said no, even if I'd not actually asked her.

Beradino brings in three cardboard boxes: one marked

Noah, one Esther, and one Isaac. Inside is every trace of our babies' existence: clothes, toys, books, changing mats, cards of congratulations and condolences, certificates of birth and death, imprints of their feet, locks of their hair. It's everything that ever signified they were alive. Before, they were memories; now they're evidence.

Hellmore comes to see me.

'The way I see it,' he says, 'we've got one chance of beating this.'

'What's that?'

'I want you to plead insanity.'

Truth is, I've wondered many times since all this began whether I'm going mad. I know there've been cases where people do the most terrible things and somehow completely and genuinely forget every last thing about them, like they're in some trance or fugue state. Of course I don't think I'm one of those, but then if I was I guess I wouldn't know.

'Women make lousy criminals, by and large,' Hellmore continues. 'In the US, there's only two types of crime women commit as often as men: shoplifting, and infanticide. We still view children as the mother's property, and destroying your own property is the act of a crazy person. So if we plead insanity and the jury accept that, you'll be sent to a mental health institution, not a jail. In such an institution, your progress will be monitored, and at some point in the future a judge can declare you sane and have you released. And in a mental health institution, you'll get help.'

'I don't need help.'

'You'll need help if you go to prison, that's for sure.'

'I'm not going to prison, I'm not going to a mental ward. I didn't do it.'

'The jury might not agree.'

'They will if we tell them the truth.'

'Trials aren't a search for truth.' He holds up his hand

against my gasp of disbelief. 'I know, I know, they should be, but they're not. Trust me. A trial's a game with complex rules, and whoever plays those rules better wins. It's like football; you have an offense, a defense, and an umpire. Or think of it as a stage play, an act. It's all about presentation and prejudice. It's a crapshoot. My job's to get you off, end of. Anything I can do to that end, I will.'

'But if I plead insanity,' I say, 'won't that be an admission of guilt?'

'An admission of guilt is pleading guilty. This is not guilty, by reason of insanity.'

'But I'd still be saying I did it.'

'Yes, that you did it, but you weren't responsible for your actions.'

'But I didn't do it.'

'Like I said; whether you did it or not is irrelevant.'

'I'm not admitting something I didn't do.'

'Then you're greatly reducing your chances of being acquitted.'

But I stand firm. I plead not guilty.

Howard starts to distance himself from me. He does it slowly and gradually, so gradually that he may not even know he's doing it himself. When I question him, he denies it. But I know. Maybe he's beginning to wonder whether I actually did it after all; maybe he's just preparing himself in case I'm found guilty. He doesn't ask me straight out whether I killed them, but he doesn't have to. Even if I'm acquitted, he's always going to wonder, deep down, I'm sure of it.

The trial approaches. I find comfort in the scriptures. I receive hundreds of letters pointing me to various verses which they think will give me strength. I know there are many people out there praying for me. I have faith; all this is being sent to test me. I don't know why. Maybe I'm not supposed to know.

Every night, before I go to bed, I read the same passage. *Even though I walk through the valley of the shadow of death, I will fear no evil: for thou art with me; thy rod and thy staff they comfort me.*

Finally, the trial arrives. I know what the cameramen want; tears, vulnerability, blood. They crowd in on us as we walk into the courthouse, shutters whirring and snapping, reporters yelling moronic questions as the cops elbow a path for Hellmore and me. The cameramen want Hollywood, like I've given often before. I'm not giving it to them today, I won't.

I've learned to numb myself over and over against everything happening to me. I weep, but only behind closed doors. I'm an actress. I can cry fake tears on demand, so I can staunch real tears too. I'll cry for you if you've paid ten bucks to sit in a cinema for two hours; I won't when all you have to do is switch on your TV. Court TV is showing every second of open proceedings. Later, they'll boast that ratings had been even higher than for OJ's trial, like I should be flattered or something.

I take the oath, swearing on the Old Testament, the Hebrew Bible; the truth, the whole truth and nothing but the truth.

The prosecutor, Amberin Zerhouni, sets off down looping, swooping lines of questions, designed to catch me out, turning truths into half-truths and doubts into lies, throwing up a myriad of little aspersions, none of them especially convincing in themselves, but weave them all together and they began to look quite persuasive.

She suggests that having children was damaging my Hollywood career; that I resented the drudgery of looking after newborns; that I didn't get a nanny because having someone else around would have made it difficult if not impossible for me to have killed my children; that I didn't try CPR on any of my children even though I knew how; that I suffered from post-natal depression but refused to accept it or seek treatment;

212

that perhaps that depression mutated into postpartum psychosis, something far scarier, a mental break, a descent into distorted reality made even more dangerous by the fact the sufferer's often unaware that she's unwell.

Did I ever hear God speak to me? Did God ever order me to do things I wouldn't normally do? Did God ever order me to harm my babies? Did I ever think the world's a bad place and I've done wrong by bringing children into it? Did I think I was saving their souls by killing them? Did I think God took my children up?

A Muslim questioning a Jew in front of a Christian judge. One nation, under God.

Innuendo and slur from nothing, time and again. It's like a nightmare, where little bits come back in their own time, and never when you want them to. I get small details wrong and contradict myself, and I know these are actually signs of innocence; only the guilty get everything absolutely right, because they've practiced their deception again and again. But tell that to the jury.

Then there's Lockwood.

He starts talking about autopsies and dissection in the cold impersonal language of medical investigation, and I just take myself away to happy times, little baby things, my darlings asleep in their cots or on my chest, the wonderful trust and warmth they had for me; an unconditional love that I bounced back to them a hundred times over. They weren't court exhibits or physical shells; they were real, living, breathing people.

And I keep thinking: Lockwood, a man, is talking about mothers and babies like he knows the first thing about us. This is an arena for women. Men don't know, can't know, won't know a fraction of it.

'I'm not afraid to put myself in danger for my beliefs,' Lockwood says. 'Child abuse is an issue I feel strongly about, even if the public finds it uncomfortable, and they tend to shoot the messenger. People like me who write about it, speak about it, point it out – we're unpopular messengers. But it's a price I'm prepared to pay, over and again if need be. As Jesus said: "There is no prophet without honor except in his own country."'

The prosecutor asks Lockwood if he'll demonstrate how I killed my children. A doll is brought in, and Lockwood takes the jury step by step through what he thinks I did. I can't watch; not him, or them, or anyone. It's obscene, revolting – *wrong*, most of all, but when he's finished some jurors are in tears, and one is glaring hatefully at me. The jurors want the drama; they want me to be guilty. They've seen book deals, movie deals; they want to be one of those who find Mara Slinger guilty, to be there at this car-crash moment in American culture.

I played Medea, once upon a time, in a different lifetime. I also played Elizabeth Proctor, falsely accused of witchcraft in *The Crucible*. Nothing has changed in three centuries. It's a witch-hunt, and I'm the witch.

Hellmore does his best, and his best is considerable. He describes the case as the most unfair one he's ever come across, one which flies against all known standards of decency and conscience. I've already lost what I prized most in life, my children – and now they want to punish me some more for it? Worse, they want to charge me with something for which they've got no evidence?

And why've they got no evidence? Because no crime's been committed, that's why. In most murder cases, no one disputes that murder occurred; the question's whether the accused did it, or someone else. But here, the facts aren't simply that I didn't commit murder, but that no one did. No one knows why Noah, Esther and Isaac died. There has to be a reason; three children don't die for no reason. But that reason isn't murder.

Cot death is a mystery, he says. It's baffled the greatest medical minds for two thousand years. And, not to cast aspersions on the prosecution witnesses, but to be a great doctor, you have to have humility as well as humanity. But the doctors called by the prosecution are arrogant enough to think they know everything; ask them any question you like, and the one answer you'll never hear is 'I don't know.'

Medicine clearly doesn't know everything; if it did, no one would have to do any more medical research. But billions of dollars are being spent on research every day. In the meantime, we go with what we have. Perhaps if my babies had died a few years from now, their deaths would be easily explained, and I wouldn't even be questioned, let alone be put on trial. What's unexplained today may be perfectly well understood tomorrow.

Hellmore brings in experts who propose alternative theories: a vasovagal shutdown of the nervous system, where the baby vomits and the vagal nerve, stopping the child breathing to prevent inhalation of the vomit, slows the heartbeat down to fatal levels; breakdowns of the immunity system; or autosomal inheritance, where a condition is passed from generation to generation, sometimes manifesting itself when the genes are dominant, sometimes lying dormant when the genes are recessive. But that's all they are – theories.

And so to the closing statements. The prosecutor goes first, and she starts by asking the jury to be silent for three minutes so they can experience the amount of time each child endured me smothering them before dying.

Even the showman Hellmore has no comeback to this. He's reasonable, he's calm. With so much divided opinion about this case, he says, whatever you believe could be wrong, and that sounds very much like reasonable doubt to him.

Yuricich could make an indication as to how he's thinking.

He doesn't. He's mindful of the need to be fair, he says; unspoken is the implication of another celebrity trial, with everyone remembering the travesty of justice that was OJ. He reminds the jury not to be swayed by high emotions, but instead to use clinical assessment of the facts, even though none of them are clinically trained. He urges them not to flinch from returning a guilty verdict if they think that's the right one, even though they may reach that conclusion with heavy hearts. He sends them out, and says they may not return for days.

They're back in six hours; and I know instantly, just from their faces, that they've found me guilty.

Up till now, I've always thought the verdict would, in a funny way, make no difference, as no punishment could be worse than the all-consuming anguish of losing my babies. I've even wondered sometimes whether death would be a release, and that's something no Jew takes lightly; Judaism teaches that suicide is one of the most serious sins of all.

But now I know it *does* make a difference.

'Have you reached a verdict?' Yuricich asks the foreman.

'We have.'

'And is that verdict the unanimous decision of you all?'

'It is.'

'On the first charge, the murder of Noah Negley, how do you find the defendant: guilty or not guilty?'

'Guilty.'

'On the second charge, the murder of Esther Negley, how do you find the defendant: guilty or not guilty?'

'Guilty.'

'On the third charge, the murder of Isaac Negley, how do you find the defendant: guilty or not guilty?'

'Guilty.'

'God has given me over to the impious; into the clutches of the wicked he has cast me,' says Job. 'I was in peace, but

216

he dislodged me; he seized me by the neck and cast me to pieces. He has set me up for a target; his arrows strike me from all directions. He pierces my sides without mercy; he pours out my gall upon the ground. He pierces me with thrust upon thrust; he attacks me like a warrior. I have fastened sackcloth over my skin, and have laid my brow in the dust. My face is inflamed with weeping and there is darkness over my eyes, although my hands are free from violence, and my prayer is sincere.'

The woman waiting for me at the prison entrance was wearing a Kevlar armored vest to protect her from shanks, spikes and knives. I expected her to be some big, butch dyke, all shaved head and tattoos, but she was nothing of the sort. She was pretty, small and petite, no bigger than me. She looked nice, friendly, reasonable; the kind of person who'd be firm but fair, someone who'd manage to remain conscientious in a place like this. I looked at the name on her badge. JESSLYN GEDGE.

She searched me, removing any items which she deemed contraband and placing them in a large envelope which she said would be returned to me on my release. Was there something in her voice which suggested she didn't expect that day to come for a very long time, or was I imagining it? Into the envelope went my watch, my wedding ring, pictures of my children, letters, and the Star of David from around my neck.

'Can I keep that?' I asked as she removed the Star. 'It's for my faith.'

She fingered the chain. 'What's this made of?'

'Gold.'

'Solid gold?'

'That's right.'

She put the Star of David in the envelope. 'Chain lengths and medals must not exceed the dollar amount and sizes listed in Department policy DC-ADM 815.'

'It's for my faith,' I repeated, knowing that I sounded pathetic.

I was taken to the RHU, the Restricted Housing Unit. The RHU has four wings, named Alpha through Delta. Alpha is for violent inmates, Bravo has those with mental problems and self-harmers, and Delta houses offenders under the age of 21.

I was in Charlie – the one where they put lifers. When you get someone in Charlie, you know they did it. You'd think that would make them more violent – that, and the fact they've got nothing to lose, no need to behave well and try to impress the parole board – but the opposite's true. If you're in Charlie, that's your home for life, so you might as well accept it. Rocking the boat just makes things harder.

The first few weeks seemed to go on for ever. Everything was new, scary, tiring; it was all grotesquely alien, everything planned and circumscribed. Hands through the door opening to be cuffed before we could leave our cells; no going anywhere without keys turning in locks ahead of and behind us; plastic cutlery, plastic mugs, plastic food.

Other inmates tried to make their cells like home: photographs, pictures, personal items. I refused. I wouldn't let myself settle in, because I knew I'd be out one day, and when that day arrived, I wanted to be able to pack up and go in thirty seconds flat. I learnt fast that the only way to deal with things was to harden myself against them, grow a carapace and wrap it round myself.

The choice was simple: shut down, or go under. No anger, no tears. I tried to pretend it was all happening to someone else, as though the real me was in storage somewhere and a fake me was putting in the time there. I felt like a pencil drawing that'd been half-erased, my lines all faint and blurry. It was as though there was a spirit of despair in the prison, an actual spirit, a ghost, moving from inmate to inmate. When it landed

218

on you, when it was your turn, you had to endure it till it moved on again. I was one of the lucky ones; it never stayed around me too long. Others had it much worse; it's no wonder there are so many zombies in there, stuffed full of the bug juice of antidepressants and mood regulators whose names sounded through the pharmacy like roll call: Phenergan, Vistaril, Elavil, Sinequan, Mellaril, Thorazine, Stelazine, Triavil, Desyrel.

Some women just looked blankly into space; some were monkey mouths, talking, talking, talking; some, the smack-heads, would smash up their cells, so out of it they didn't care, they didn't feel pain, even when they were dragged away with their arms behind their backs and their thumbs bent back double. Smack's a better bet than dope in there; smack clears the system in three days, dope stays in for a month. What's more likely to beat the urine test?

I'm not really sure what I thought my fellow inmates would be like, but I know now what they're not. They're not big-time gangsters, nor serial killers, nor mafia kingpins, nor kidnappers, nor embezzlers. Most of them were there because they were accessories to crimes committed by men, or for things like prostitution, pickpocketing, shoplifting, robbery, drugs. Small-time stuff, mainly. Criminals, or victims? I wasn't scared of them, at least most of them. If anything, I felt sorry for them.

Everyone talks about gangs in prisons, but there weren't many in Muncy. Maybe it was because we were all women; forming gangs is tough when everyone wants to be in charge. There was less violence than I thought there'd be, too, again maybe because we were women; we'd talk to each other so much that incidents usually got defused before they could boil over. What violence there was in Muncy was just as often women turning on themselves as it was on others; there was a lot of self-harming.

And a lot of suicides, too. I saved one woman, someone

just brought into Charlie, who tried to hang herself with shoelaces. She nearly made it, too; her eyes were bulging, her tongue lolling between blue lips. She'd tied the laces so tight round her neck that I couldn't get my fingers underneath them to pry them off, and of course we weren't allowed anything sharp. I called the guards, and they came just in time, panicking; they'd land in a whole lot of trouble every time someone topped themselves. I saw the woman a day or two later, when she got back from the sanatorium. I heard she was about thirty seconds away from the beginnings of irreversible brain damage, and she came over to me. I thought she was going to say thanks.

'You stupid fucking BITCH!' she yelled. 'What the fuck did you do that for? Now I'm on suicide watch, and I can't take a fucking step without being watched. Thanks for fucking NOTHING. Next time you poke your nose into my business, I'll fucking KILL you, you understand? KILL you!'

She didn't kill me, of course. In fact, the next time I saw her, she apologized, and said she was just shocked that I tried to help her, because it'd been a long time since anyone had done something decent for her. She was called Madison Setterstrom, and she was a cop-killer, an unrepentant one at that; she must have been about the only person in there who'd admit she was guilty. Pretty much everyone else claimed to be innocent, so much so that it was almost a standing joke; people'd ask 'What are you in for?' but never 'What did you do?' because everyone knew the two were different.

Not Madison. She was proud of what she did, and she couldn't stand the Pepsi Generation, the newer, younger prisoners who lacked respect for the old-school ways. We became buddies. She was my only true friend in there, not least because she was the only one who couldn't give a fig about my celebrity or my story. Everyone else was either impressed by the fact I was a Hollywood actress, or couldn't wait to tell me what an evil cow I was. Madison was neither. She just took me as I was.

I never cracked, never answered back; do that, and they'd know that they'd got to you. I'd just take myself to another place, and say to myself over and again that they were not going to break me. Oh, they tried. And every day you had to fight the battle again, because if you broke once, you'd break forever.

One day, Hellmore arrived to see me. He'd got good news and bad news, he said; which did I want first? I said the bad news; get it out of the way. The bad news was that Howard wanted a divorce, and here were the papers. I felt sick. I'd long stopped wondering whether this was coming, knowing it was simply a question of when – Howard hadn't been to see me once in all the time I'd been here – but it didn't make it any easier when I finally saw it in black and white.

I took a few deep breaths, and asked for the good news. The good news, he said, was that he'd seen a doctor friend of his the night before, and they'd discussed this rare, newly discovered gene disorder known as Long QT Syndrome, which damages the pumping chambers of the heart, some-times fatally. The thing about Long QT is that it can miss a generation or two before striking again, and he'd remem-bered something I'd said to him when preparing our defense; that my grandmother had lost several of her children very young.

He wanted to go see my grandmother and have her tested for this Long QT thing, and perhaps other genetic disorders too. I told him it was a nice idea, but my grandmother was living in Poland, and didn't speak any English. She lived for a while between the wars in Cleveland, which has a big Polish population – which was why she never had to learn much English, and she'd have forgotten even that meager amount so many decades on – but she and her family went back to Poland in 1938, and never managed to get out again; first because of the Nazis, then because of the Soviets.

So he traveled to Poland. Only Hellmore would go that far. He went to Poland, got an interpreter from the American embassy in Warsaw, and tracked my grandmother down to the village where she was living. A remote village in the middle of nowhere, and he turned up, probably the first black man any of them had ever seen. She told him she had twelve children and lost five of them before they were eight weeks old. Three of those five were born while she was living in Cleveland. He asked her whether they ever found a cause of death for the children, and she replied simply: 'This is something Jehovah takes care of. We leave it to Jehovah.'

So he explained what'd happened to me, and how he believed in my innocence and wanted to get me out, and said that if they could test her and find that she had this thing, or indeed anything else, then that might help me. They took her to Warsaw – she might have been ninety-five, but she was tough as old boots, well able to handle such a journey – and they tested her. And guess what? He was right. She *did* have this Long QT thing.

Suddenly, the whole case was blown wide open. Hellmore returned to America, and came to visit me pretty much every week, each time with another breakthrough. He said he'd found that Lockwood suspected this might be the case, or that it was at the very least a possibility, and hadn't disclosed it to the defense as he was obliged to do. Not just that; Lockwood also withheld research he'd been conducting at the time of the trial, which showed plenty of evidence that attempts to resuscitate children could and did cause rib fractures.

The retinal hemorrhages which he said couldn't have been caused post-mortem – and which he therefore held up as an example of my guilt – turned out not only not to be hemorrhages; they weren't even retinal. They were actually on the choroid, a layer of tissue next to the retina. Lockwood also got the measurements of siderophages in the lungs wrong. Though they were high, they weren't nearly as high as he'd said they were, and were within the limits which could be caused by inhaling blood during resuscitation attempts.

All this, Hellmore said, gave us more than enough grounds for an appeal. He had to take it to the state appeals court first, but if that failed, we'd go federal. But we didn't need to. The state court heard it, and the science was on our side this time. The judge said he could find no convincing evidence that my children's deaths had been caused by injury, but he could find a lot of evidence that pointed to a genetic disorder.

He also slammed the way the original trial was conducted. He accused Lockwood of over-simplifying and withholding relevant data, and of covering up his mistakes; at least one of the autopsies, he said, was a textbook example of how *not* to do one. The state judge said Yuricich was biased and unprofessional; he also criticized the prosecutor for not being on top of her witnesses, though he recognized that, not being a medical professional herself, she had to take their findings at face value, and was therefore not as culpable as they were.

I was going to be released. I could hardly believe it. Madison embraced me. She's originally from Norway, and in Norwegian, she said, the word for a miscarriage of justice is *justismord* – 'justice murder'. Miscarriage is an altogether more forgiving word; it suggests an accident, an act of God. The Norwegians have kept the term 'murder', because they know that's exactly what a wrongful conviction is; something dreadfully, horribly destructive. Something deadly.

The day I walked free, what struck me most of all was the sunlight; so bright and searing, so white, as though it came from the heart of a thousand atom bombs. I stood outside the gates, next to Hellmore, thousands of people corralled behind hastily erected crash barriers. Half of them were for me, chanting 'Who do we love? Mara!' The other half kept up an endless rhythm: 'Guilty! Guilty! Guilty!'

Hellmore took the microphone, and the crowd slowly quietened down.

'The justice system is like Amtrak,' he said. 'It can be old and creaky, but it gets there in the end. Today is a victory for all those who believe in justice. I'm sorry it took so long, but better late than never.'

He handed me the microphone. My voice came out faint, quavery. I've never been as good at speaking my own words as I am other people's.

'With all respect to my fantastic lawyer,' I said, 'today is not a victory. Not for me, not for anyone. There are no winners here. We have all lost. If I feel anything, it's relief, no more than that. Relief that the courts, and hopefully the people of America and elsewhere too, finally believe in my innocence. That's the only comfort I take. In every other respect, my nightmare goes on. It will never end. I will never get my babies back. I will never know the joys, heartaches and totality of being a mother. I ask you all for nothing except one thing; that I may be allowed some privacy to grieve for my little ones in peace, and try to make sense of what's happened to me.'

Patrese was silent for a long time after Mara finished; so long, in fact, that eventually she prodded him and said, with a weak smile; 'Say something.'

His face showed his shock. He felt flayed, raw, like an anatomical drawing.

The smile he offered in return was no less faint than hers had been. 'Like what? You've just pulled your soul inside out. Tell me one thing I could say which won't sound totally inadequate.'

She reached across the table, careful not to knock over a wine glass or trail her sleeve in the gumbo, and entwined the fingers of her right hand in his.

'I'm sorry, Franco.'

'You're not the one who should be sorry.'

'Well, I am. I didn't mean to lay it on you like that, straight out of the blue. It's just . . . I haven't spoken about it all for such a long time, and so it just came gushing out. Thanks for listening. It means a lot. More than you can imagine.'

She made no move to take her hand away. Nor did he.

Patrese remembered what Beradino had said to him about getting involved with Mara, and wondered what Beradino would say if he could see them now. You could probably have heard the explosion in Baltimore.

Patrese figured Beradino had got Mara all wrong.

'I should go,' he said.

Mara nodded slowly. 'I guess you should.'

'Early start tomorrow.'

'You don't have to justify it, you know.'

'I know I don't. But still.'

'Why?'

'Because . . . I've really enjoyed myself.' He laughed. 'Strange, given what we've talked about, but . . . I'd like to do it again sometime. With a few more jokes.'

'Me too.'

He took his hand from hers and stood up. She followed him into the hallway.

'Thanks again,' he said, shrugging on his coat. 'And the gumbo was awesome.'

'Take care of yourself, Franco.'

He kissed her on both cheeks; and the moment after that was too long, too close.

'Do you really have to go?' she whispered.

He nodded. 'No.'

Wednesday, November 17th. 4:56 a.m.

It wasn't far off dawn before Patrese left, dazed and confused.

It had been years, Mara had said, since she'd been with a man; since before prison, before the trial, before her arrest, even before Isaac had been born. *Years*. Literally.

Which explained, Patrese guessed, why she'd been so tentative to start with, and why she'd then seemed suddenly unleashed; primal, wild, ravenous.

He could flatter himself and think it was his unique skill and charisma which had set her aflame, but he knew women well enough to know otherwise. If it hadn't been him, it would have been someone else.

What Mara had needed hadn't necessarily been him, Franco Patrese, but simply someone who'd pay her attention, give her a chance, make her feel . . . well, he'd been going to say 'like a woman', but perhaps the more prosaic truth was that she'd simply needed to feel *alive* again.

Or was he just protecting himself from whatever consequences there might be?

Out on the sidewalk now, he smiled through a yawn. After all, there were few men alive who didn't, at a basic level, relish the feeling of leaving a new lover's apartment at five in the morning. If Mara had been vulnerable, perhaps he'd needed it too, in his own way. And it wasn't like he'd gotten her drunk and taken advantage of her, was it?

He dug in his pocket for the Trans Am keys.

Suddenly, he was pitching forward and down.

It caught him by surprise, and he was tired, so he was almost on the ground before he realized he hadn't tripped.

He'd been *pushed*. Propelled hard from behind; attacked.

Patrese had played enough football to know how to fall properly, and done enough police training to know how to fight, all repeated so often it had become instinct.

He took the impact on hands and forearms, keeping them loose to absorb the shock; you broke bones when you tensed. The moment he touched concrete, he was rolling; fast on to his left side, as moving targets were harder to hit, and then immediately on to his back with his hands up to block a weapon or lash out. You couldn't fight unless you could see your opponent.

His attacker was a man, that was for sure, but that – and the fact he had body odor that wouldn't have been out of place on a goat – were just about the only things Patrese could tell with certainty. The man had a baseball cap pulled low on his forehead, and a heavy coat buttoned up to his neck.

Patrese kicked out, upwards and hard. He heard a sharp crack as his foot connected with the man's left hand; and with a yelp the man was gone. By the time Patrese got to his feet, the man was halfway down the street, sprinting towards the main road.

Lunatic? Wannabe mugger who'd reckoned late that Patrese wasn't a soft target? Patrese didn't know, and to be honest didn't much care either. It was the city, it was the small hours, when only the freaks were out. Shit happens.

He picked himself up and patted his pockets. Keys, wallet,

cellphone; all present and correct. No broken bones. Probably a couple of bruises.

He unlocked the Trans Am, got in, and turned the key in the ignition.

Nothing.

He sighed. This was happening more and more. The garage had fixed it a couple of times, but still the starter motor kept cutting out. What did he expect? The car wasn't exactly in the first flush of youth.

He got out of the car and pulled the steering wheel as far round to its left side lock as it would go. Slowly, manually, Patrese turned the Trans Am round in the road, his right shoulder pressed against the windscreen pillar, until he was facing back down the length of the street.

With a clear run, he got the car moving at something above walking pace, leapt in, and turned the key again. The engine fired like it had never missed a beat in its life.

8:23 a.m.

Patrese arrived at headquarters a few hours later. Beradino was already there.

They regarded each other levelly, Patrese as deadpan as he could manage. He'd practiced a couple of times in the bathroom mirror before leaving home, hoping the slight traces of red in his eyes wouldn't betray his lack of sleep.

'Enjoy yourself?' Beradino asked at length.

Serious? Wry? Joking? A bit of all three? Patrese couldn't tell.

Patrese shrugged. 'Interesting.'

'You find out anything?'

'Nope. Nothing useful to the case, any rate, if that's what you mean.'

'You gonna see her again?'

'It was *dinner*, Mark.'

Answering the question by not answering it; a technique used, wittingly or not, by any number of crime suspects over the years. Even before the words were out, Patrese was cursing himself, sure that Beradino would follow up; but either Beradino didn't notice, or didn't care, because he changed the subject immediately.

'OK. We got some good news. Well, a little bit anyway. We managed to connect Kohler and Yuricich.'

'How?'

'Well, they knew each other socially, for a start.'

'That's hardly surprising. A bishop and a judge. High society, and all that.'

'True. But that's not what I'm talking about. You remember the hullabaloo last year about removing the Ten Commandments monument from the courthouse?'

Patrese nodded. The Supreme Court had decreed that the monument, located in the concourse of the Allegheny County Courthouse, represented government endorsement of Christianity, violating the constitutional separation of church and state.

Four separate groups had descended on the monument: workmen, to remove it; protestors, to try and prevent them from doing so; police officers, to remove the protestors; and, inevitably, TV crews, to record the whole thing.

'Well,' Beradino continued, 'they were both protesting about it. Kohler and Yuricich, both trying to keep the monument where it was. Look.'

He ran digital downloads of segments taken from network news broadcasts.

Here was Yuricich railing to CBS. 'It's a sad day when the moral foundation of our law and the acknowledgment of God has to be hidden from public view to appease a federal judge. Forbidding the acknowledgment of God violates the First Amendment's guarantee of free exercise of religion. We will fight this; you can be sure of that.'

NBC had Kohler in altogether more reflective mode. 'Is it such a bad thing to think about not killing, not stealing, not lying, not committing adultery? Is it so bad to talk about honoring one's parents? Or to think about a power greater than oneself – about God or some higher deity? Or to set aside just one day a week as a spiritual day, separate from the material strivings of the other six days?'

On ABC, Yuricich was tub-thumping again. 'I wouldn't just keep this monument here. I'd put one in every court-house in the land, and in every school too. They'd be better than metal detectors and security guards. They'd be a divine flak jacket to curb violence and save society.'

His hair disheveled and his eyes staring, Yuricich looked like some sort of Old Testament prophet – a little deranged, certainly.

'What about Redwine?' said Patrese.

'No sign of him. Berlin's run every tape three times, all the way through.'

'Redwine was a Methodist, right?'

'Right. But sort of Methodist-lite. He wasn't a regular church-goer.'

'Which makes him odd man out of the three.'

'Not if you count Mustafa Bayoumi.'

'You think we were on the right lines to start with?'

'Mustafa's got a reason to kill Redwine. Islamic extremists have got a reason to kill Kohler and Yuricich. And those extremists . . .'

'. . . are all on the Bureau's database.'

'You ring him. He's your buddy.'

'You mean, *you* pissed him off last week.'

'I'm sure he's heard worse.'

Patrese dialed Boone's number – cellphone, of course, so he wouldn't be shuffled through endless layers of Bureau secretaries. Boone answered on the third ring.

'I was just about to phone you,' he said.

'Really?'

'Yeah. About the guys we've got under surveillance?'

'That's just what I was calling about.'

'Er . . . We can't share the list with you, I'm afraid.'

'*What?*'

'I tried, Franco, I really did. I took it as high as I could. I fought your corner.'

'Why did they say no?'

'Usual BS. Operational security, Chinese walls, compromise possibilities.'

'*Jesus.*' Patrese jerked his head in frustration. Beradino rolled his eyes.

'I'm really sorry, Franco,' Boone was saying. 'If it was up to me . . .'

'I know. And I appreciate that. Listen, Caleb, tell me one thing.'

'I can't promise, but try me.'

'Is Mustafa Bayoumi on your list?'

'Hold on.'

Down the line came the sound of a door closing; Boone ensuring he wasn't being overheard. The walls of Bureau offices had larger ears than most, Patrese thought.

'OK,' Boone continued. 'No. Mustafa Bayoumi's not on our list.'

'A Muslim chemistry student, and he's not on your radar?'

'He *was*, for a coupla years. But he did nothing wrong all that time, so we took him off. We haven't got infinite resources, Franco. You know how many people we have under surveillance?'

'How many?'

'Across the entire jurisdiction of this office – western Pennsylvania, West Virginia – about seven hundred.'

'*Seven hundred?*' That was covering just a state and a half of the fifty in the union, plus DC. Even allowing for geographical and demographic variations, a conservative extrapolation of that number across the country meant the Bureau must have about thirty thousand Muslims under active surveillance. It really was a war, Patrese thought.

'That's right.'

'What kind of people?'

'All this is strictly background, yeah?'

'Course.'

'What kind of people?' Boone made the question rhetorical. 'Take your pick. Radical mosque preachers. Disaffected youths, some with criminal records, possibly ripe for conversion as they try to find some meaning in their shitty lives. People in sensitive positions; you know, nuclear scientists, defense contractors, those sort of people. And names passed on by NSA for inappropriate web use; logging on to jihadist websites, Googling bomb-making instructions, that kind of stuff.'

'That can't be legal.' Patrese knew it sounded naïve, but he hoped he hadn't yet surrendered himself totally to the cynics. Wire-tapping prime murder suspects was one thing; handing over web weirdos was a little too Thought Police for Patrese's liking.

'What can't be legal?'

'NSA. Google history.'

'You want legal, Franco, or you want to get blown up?'

Thursday, November 18th. 3:07 p.m.

The Cathedral of Learning at Pitt is less a skyscraper than a Gothic totem.

An academic ark of classrooms, laboratories, lecture rooms, libraries, conference rooms and offices, it rises forty floors above the Oakland campus; high, proud and stepped. Its hub is not at the top, perhaps strangely for such a magnificent edifice, but right on the ground floor; the Commons Room, a miniature cathedral with ceilings of soaring vaults, walls which echo with the hum of languid footsteps and studious chatter, and an outcircling of smaller rooms decorated according to national stereotype; tenth-century Armenian, folk-style Norwegian, Byzantine-era Romanian.

It was in the Commons Room that Patrese met Wheelwright.

Wheelwright was small and dapper, dressed in a green sports jacket, brown slacks and dusty brogues. His only concession to mild professorial eccentricity was a red and black bow tie.

He had two sheets of paper with him. The first was his invoice, which Patrese folded and pocketed without opening. However much Wheelwright had charged, it wasn't Patrese's problem. The second was Wheelwright's findings as to the origin of the pink granite pebbles.

'Before I tell you what we've found,' Wheelwright said, 'I want to tell you briefly *how* we found it, so you can make up your mind as to whether we've been accurate enough for you.'

'OK.'

It was often this way with experts, Patrese knew. They wouldn't give you straight answers to straight questions; they had to take you through the whole process first, and woe betide anyone who tried to hurry them up. Perhaps it was a legacy of too many exam questions demanding not just the right answer but also that you 'show your reasoning'.

'First, we found they were from the Arabian-Nubian Shield.'

'Which is?'

'An exposure of Precambrian crystalline rocks, mostly Neoproterozoic in age.'

'How big is it?'

'It covers most of Israel, Jordan, Egypt, Saudi Arabia, Sudan, Eritrea, Ethiopia, Yemen and Somalia. Thing is, the shield's actually two sub-shields, separated by the Red Sea. The Arabian's the east side, the Levant and Arabian peninsula. The Nubian's the west, North Africa. So we had to work out which of the two sub-shields the pebbles come from. This involved checking microscopic variations in their gravity, magnetic, structural and isotopic characteristics.' Wheelwright indicated the paper. 'They're from the Arabian shield, the eastern side. The figures are there.'

'You can't be more specific?'

'Sure we can. And we have. Each shield is divided into microplates or terranes; you know, like individual sectors, areas, but several thousand square miles each. By elimination and subatomic analysis, we've narrowed the place of origin down to the Midyan terrane.'

'Which is where?'

'It borders the Red Sea on its east and north shores, and covers the north-western strip of Saudi Arabia and the north-eastern corner of Egypt, the Sinai Peninsula.'

'You say Saudi Arabia. Does it include Mecca?'

Wheelwright shook his head. 'Too far south.'

'Medina?' Medina is the second holiest city in Islam.

Wheelwright shook his head again. 'Too far east. The most popular place for visitors in the terrane is Sharm el-Sheikh. You know it?'

'No.'

'On the Egyptian side, right on the Red Sea. Big tourist destination. You dive?'

'No.'

'Amazing diving. *Amazing*. Some of the best in the world; hundreds of coral reefs, more than a thousand species of fish. My wife and I go every year. They hold Middle East peace conferences there too, you know.'

'Fat lot of good *they've* done.'

But Patrese was already thinking something completely different.

He was thinking that Mustafa Bayoumi was originally from Egypt.

4:01 p.m.

Patrese found Mustafa in the chemistry department, just coming out of a lecture.

Mustafa's face was briefly, almost comically, thunderous when he saw Patrese; but his classmates' curious glances clearly persuaded Mustafa that discretion was the better part of valor.

Rather than risk an embarrassing scene, Mustafa swallowed his anger and walked over to Patrese.

'You looking for me, Detective?'

'Sure am. You got some time to talk?'

Mustafa looked around suspiciously, as though expecting Beradino to materialize like some malevolent swampland bunyip.

'I'm alone,' Patrese said. Beradino had stayed back at North Shore to keep an eye on any progress in the investigation. 'Just a chat. Nothing formal. I'd appreciate it.'

Mustafa looked at his watch. 'I've got an assignment starting in half an hour.'

'That's cool. It won't take that long. Buy you a coffee?'

'Sure. There's a café down the corridor there.'

'I know. I was a student here myself.'

'Chemistry?'

'No. But I had the hots for a chick who did.'

A brief, crooked smile appeared on Mustafa's face, and vanished just as abruptly when he remembered that Patrese was the police, the enemy.

The café was almost deserted. Even so, Patrese instinctively chose a corner table. Corner tables gave good sightlines; they were also harder to eavesdrop.

'So,' Mustafa said, when Patrese had returned from the counter with the coffees, 'what have you come to talk about?'

Patrese didn't really know, to be honest. He hadn't formulated any plan beyond the vague notion that being conciliatory towards Mustafa might reap more dividends than constantly harassing him.

Mustafa clearly responded better towards Patrese than he did towards Beradino. Perhaps Patrese could make use of that. If not, he'd hardly have lost much.

'I came to tell you I'm sorry,' Patrese said, winging it.

'Sorry?'

'If you think we've been too harsh on you. I know we've got a murderer to catch, but . . . Look, my mom and dad were killed in a car crash a couple of months back. Straight out of the blue, like it must have been for you when your father died. And it's awful, I know it is. I know the shock, the disbelief, the numbness, the anger. It's different for everyone, of course, but I do have some idea of what you must be feeling. And maybe we should have taken more account of that.'

Mustafa nodded, but said nothing.

Patrese had a sudden idea; a longshot, but no worse for that, perhaps.

'I know you were close to your dad,' he continued. 'My parents, for me, were always somewhere I could find solace, love, comfort, all without conditions. They were a, er . . .'

he feigned stumbling for the right word, all the while watching Mustafa carefully, '. . . a *sanctuary*, I guess.'

No reaction to the word 'sanctuary'. None at all.

And Patrese couldn't try again without risking suspicion. The only way they knew Mustafa was intending to go to the sanctuary this weekend, wherever and whatever it may be, was through an illegal wire-tap.

Mustafa was silent for a few moments, and then said: 'You know *The Godfather*?'

'I'm Italian-American, Mustafa. It's pretty much part of my DNA.'

Mustafa smiled. Perhaps Patrese was getting somewhere.

'You remember the first line?'

'Of course. "I believe in America."'

'My father believed in America. Told me a thousand times how lucky we were to be living in the land of opportunity. Every week, he used to read me the Declaration of Independence and the Gettysburg Address. You know the way people who give up smoking are suddenly the most zealous anti-smokers around? That was my father, about America. He believed America was a place where your name, your color, your creed posed no barriers to your success.'

'And you didn't agree with him?'

'The war on terror is the war on Islam. There are no two ways about it.'

'That's not what I asked.'

'Yes, it is. How can this be a place of tolerance when Muslim brothers are being killed in Iraq and Afghanistan, while here we are stopped, searched, harassed, taken from our homes without evidence, and even shot, all for no reason other than our beliefs?'

Mustafa was still looking at Patrese, but now it was almost as though he were looking *through* him, to a place Patrese could never see. He seemed almost to have been tripped by something; his own Queen of Diamonds.

'You always quote 9/11 to us,' Mustafa said, his voice rising slightly, 'as though that alone is justification for persecuting us until the end of time. Well, I ask you this: how many people died in 9/11? And how many have died in Iraq and Afghanistan? We have suffered many 9/11s. *Many* 9/11s.

'Enough is enough. You will find an immutable truth not of your religion or ours, but of human nature; that you can only push people so far before they explode. There can be no debate or discussion when you kill Muslims. You attack us, we attack you. You bomb us, we bomb you. You strike at our people, we strike at your people.'

Patrese opened his mouth to interrupt, but Mustafa was in full flow.

'The Koran allows us to fight in armed struggle against those who wage war against us. We must fight and kill the infidels wherever we find them. We must capture them. We must lie in wait for them in every place. Fight against them till there is no more oppression and all worship is devoted to Allah alone. Fight for the future of America. Allah created the whole universe; it's all worthy of praise. America doesn't belong to anyone but Allah. He's put us on this earth to live wherever we want, and to implement *sharia* everywhere. The only laws will be *sharia* laws, the only courts *sharia* courts.'

Sharia was Islamic law. Yuricich had been a judge. Another connection.

'Only by such a system can the degeneracy of this country be reversed. Every day, and in every way, you see a society without moral standards, without faith, without direction. Drastic measures must be taken, and we must all take them. No one is too small to make a difference. Whoever sees something evil should change it with his hand. If he cannot,

241

then with his tongue; and if he cannot do even that, then in his heart. That is the weakest degree of faith.

'These measures must be taken as follows. Since Islam, submission to the will of God, is the only religion ever given to the human race, all those who follow other creeds must be punished. All those whose characters are flawed because they drink alcohol or consume drugs must be punished. All those who indulge in deviant sexual relations and bring up children out of the sight of Allah, out of his holy institution of marriage, must be punished. All those who injure others, and exploit others, and kill others, must be punished.

'The Koran says those who disbelieve will have garments of fire cut out for them. It says they will have from hellfire a bed and coverings; thus do we reward the unjust. It says there will be some to whose ankles the fire will reach, some to whose knees the fire will reach, some to whose waists the fire will reach, and some to whose collarbones the fire will reach. And it says the unbelievers will not be able to ward off the fire from their faces, nor from their backs, and they will not be helped. The fire will come to them suddenly and confound them. They will not be able to avert it; nor will they be given respite.'

11:52 p.m.

It was a sad day – night, rather – Patrese thought, when he couldn't sleep for thinking about religion. But that was the truth.

He lay on his back, watching the headlights of passing cars wash across the ceiling. He was alone, albeit reluctantly so. Mara had come round earlier, laughingly wanting him to cook for her this time; and he'd gritted his teeth and told her it was a bad idea.

You can't be that bad a cook, she'd said.

No, he'd replied; not the cooking. *It* was a bad idea; it, this, them. The judge who'd sentenced her had been murdered. Patrese's own partner had originally arrested her. To get involved with her would be unprofessional. It wasn't that he didn't like her, far from it, but . . .

She'd started crying. He'd have preferred it if she'd slapped him.

He wanted nothing more than to lose himself in the heady, early days of someone else, plump and lush with the joys of mutual discovery. He wanted *her*, and for many of the reasons he knew he shouldn't; because anything they had would have to be clandestine, because she was damaged, perhaps even because it would be some sort of atonement for what he'd done in that fetid Homewood attic.

She'd left, sniffing back tears. She really liked him, she'd said; and it sucked, to find someone you really liked and not to be able to have them, even for a little while.

To stop himself from feeling guilty, even though he knew he shouldn't – once a Catholic, he thought ruefully, always a Catholic – Patrese was worrying about what Mustafa had said, and about the way in which he'd said it. He'd seemed almost *possessed*, Patrese thought.

A surveillance team had been due to start watching Mustafa from eight o'clock the following morning – taking into account the Islamic Sabbath on Friday, the start of the weekend in which he was due to visit the mysterious sanctuary. Patrese had been so alarmed by Mustafa's ranting, however, that he'd brought their start time forward twelve hours. So far, they'd called in nothing unusual.

As far as Patrese was concerned, religion did three things – divided people, controlled people, and deluded people. It didn't matter whether it was the kind of bile he'd heard Mustafa spewing in the café earlier, or Yuricich and Kohler hanging on to their courthouse monument of the Ten Commandments. It ended up pretty much at the same place.

If God had made man in his own image, Patrese thought, why had he made man so flawed – so disrespectful, thieving, covetous, murderous, lying and adulterous, in contravention of the commandments? Even if you believed in original sin and the fall, why had God let that happen?

Most of all, how could you apply something as proscriptive and inflexible as the commandments to the endlessly complex business of life? That was just bumper-sticker ethics, pure and simple. Surely you should do the right thing because you had empathy and understanding of what was at stake, not because dogma and an outdated set of tribal taboos legislated thousands of years ago compelled you?

Patrese didn't like people who took religion lock, stock and barrel, with no attempt at separating out its various parts; and he especially didn't like them when they had influence over ordinary people's lives, as Kohler and Yuricich had done.

And yet, and yet . . .

If what Yuricich had told the networks was right, the commandments underpinned pretty much the entire legal system; a system which, as a police officer, Patrese was sworn to uphold.

Patrese may have fallen away from religion, certainly in terms of being a believer, but it – the institutions, the rituals, people's need for faith, pretty much everything – still had a hold on him. It intrigued him, scared him, dragged him back when he least wanted it to – such as now, in the small hours.

Logical reasoning beat blind faith, he told himself.

So he worked out three reasons as to why the commandments were wrong.

Firstly, they were confusing. Should you honor a father who abused his children or battered his wife? Should you not kill even if killing saved lives? Should you have killed Hitler, for example, had you ever had the chance? What was an image of God, exactly? How could you not covet – you couldn't stop yourself *thinking* bad things, only acting on them? And so on, and on, and on. The commandments were fuzzy; and to unfuzz them, you had to use your own brain, your own moral compass.

Secondly, they were inadequate. Could they tell us the right thing to do about any of humanity's million and one problems? About climate change, racism, national debt, capital punishment, gay rights, overpopulation, abortion, social breakdown, unemployment, war, terrorism, obesity? Not as far as Patrese could see. You might as well consult the menu of the pizza joint round the corner, for all the enlightenment the commandments gave.

Finally, they were absolutist. Ridiculously, absurdly absolutist, to the point of being immoral. They admitted no exceptions, period. If a man's children were starving and the only way to feed them was to steal food, he must not steal, even if his children die. Imagine running on a road and being told to keep to the road, whatever happens. The road goes off the edge of a cliff. Do you go over with it?

That was that, Patrese figured. Yuricich had clearly been talking shit.

But still, as he finally drifted away, tiny fingers of doubt nipped and pulled at him. What if he was wrong?

Friday, November 19th. 10:37 a.m.

The surveillance team outside the Bayoumis' house – more precisely, a new two-man shift, taking over at dawn – reported into headquarters every hour. They knew that Mustafa was still inside the house, because they hadn't seen him leave, but they couldn't tell what he was doing inside.

Marquez Berlin, on the other hand, *could* tell what Mustafa was doing, because Berlin could see exactly what Mustafa was looking at on his computer.

It was a video clip, ten minutes long, an amateur recording. A crowd of men, Middle Eastern by the look of them. It was taken during the winter, as the men were all wearing thick coats. They were chatting, laughing, singing. A few of the younger men were digging a hole in the ground. One of them paused to exchange pleasantries with the cameraman. He didn't seem to have a care in the world.

After a few minutes, there was a sudden surge of excitement among the crowd. A quick, whirling shot of sky and ground as the cameraman turned to find the source, and then a shape wrapped head to toe in a white sheet was carried into shot and placed in the hole.

The shape was clearly human, with legs and arms trussed.

247

Berlin choked back the gag reflex in his throat, and dialed Patrese.

'You better come here, Franco. Like, *now*.'

Patrese was there inside a minute, with Beradino following close behind. They crowded round Berlin, peering at the screen in fascinated horror.

It was impossible to tell whether the trussed shape was male or female. The hole came up to its waist, leaving the torso and head visible.

A loud voice shouted out instructions. The shape was very still.

It only moved when the first stone knocked it sideways.

'Jesus *Christ*,' Patrese said.

Beradino was too shocked to notice the blasphemy, let alone admonish Patrese.

On screen, the shape righted itself again; and again it was hit.

There were stones falling wide or short, but plenty were making contact too; glancing blows which barely seemed to register, heavier impacts which each time knocked the shape a little further left or right, back or forth.

Each time the shape was hit, it took a little longer to right itself again.

Patrese wondered why the shape didn't struggle more. He guessed it was already resigned to its fate.

'It's his Sabbath,' Patrese said, meaning Mustafa. 'Who the fuck watches this shit on their holy day?'

The sun was behind the camera, and the shadows of the stoners writhed, stretched across the ground, grotesque in the exaggeration of their gesturing.

Stones gathered round the shape like cairns.

The white sheet was turning red very, very fast.

Patrese, Beradino, Berlin; they could barely watch.

Even towards the end, when the shape was lying prone,

half-in and half-out of the hole, no one in the crowd seemed shocked or subdued. None of them seemed to worry that something similar might happen to them, or to appreciate the gravity and finality of such a punishment.

In fact, it looked like it hardly seemed a punishment to them at all, let alone an act of community retribution for whatever crime the poor unfortunate had committed. It was just entertainment, a bunch of guys come to enjoy a good stoning and catch up with some old friends in the process. This was the modern version of family picnics at the old Wild West hangings, or the crowds who used to gather to watch the slaughter of gladiators in early Rome.

'Can you imagine this happening in the West?' Patrese said, as much to himself as the others.

'Savages,' Beradino spat. 'Darn *savages*.'

'Remember, we don't know Mustafa's watching this,' Berlin said.

'This is real time, isn't it? He's watching it right now.'

'We don't know, *legally*. We can't do a damn thing about it.'

'You can't imagine it, can you?' Patrese continued, gesturing at the screen. 'Any of this. It just wouldn't happen here. It's not our mindset.'

Beradino turned slowly towards him.

'If that's the case,' Beradino said, 'and if we're right about this being an Islamic thing, then why shouldn't the burnings be following some equally inaccessible logic?'

'Inaccessible only if you know nothing of Islam.'

'Exactly. My point, *exactly*. So we need to know something of Islam.'

Patrese found a spare terminal and started searching the Koran online.

It didn't take him long to see that the Koran, like the Bible, was open to any number of interpretations, depending on how deranged, literal, fanatical or autistic you were. Believing every

249

word was inflexible doctrine had driven men to fly planes into the Twin Towers. Patrese found it hard to understand people whose world was so Manichean; but understand them he might have to, if they were to solve this case.

Reading the entire Koran from start to finish would have been too time-consuming, and probably too confusing. If it took scholars a lifetime to understand the Koran fully, as Patrese knew it did, he was hardly going to nail it in a couple of hours flat.

The more he read, however, the more he realized how little he knew. He was learning Islam on the hoof, and it was nowhere near enough for what he needed.

What he needed was an expert, and he knew just where to find one.

Saturday, November 20th. 2:48 p.m.

East Carson Street, the main artery of the South Side Flats, is a long drag dotted with bars, restaurants and clubs. Depending on the time of day it is, successively, not yet open, lively, edgy, and downright dangerous.

Patrese took Amberin there some time between not yet open and lively.

He'd booked a table at Fat Heads, an unashamedly jock-style bar which is an East Carson institution. Patrese had been going for years with his college buddies. He'd even made it into the Wall of Foam for surviving the beer tour, which had involved working his way through the place's impressive array of craft and specialty beers.

There was much about those visits Patrese couldn't remember, for obvious reasons, but he could still match drinking sessions to the beer in question, their names curiously evocative: Long Trail Harvest, Boulder Obovoid Stout, Southern Tier Pumking, Stone Arrogant Bastard Pale Ale, Rogue Dead Guy Ale, and so on. Small wonder that some people called Pittsburgh a drinking town with a football problem.

He'd worried slightly that Amberin was too sophisticated for this place. Had he met her at college, she'd have been the kind of girl whom football jocks like him jeered at for being too cool and self-possessed, all the time finding her cool and poise intimidating – but that was also part of the reason for taking her there. He wanted to put her slightly off guard. If he'd gone to see her during working hours, the meeting would have been too formal, the two of them circumscribed by their roles. Here, however, they could drop the labels of DA and detective, at least partly.

Moreover, he worried she'd react badly when he told her what he was thinking. He'd made plenty of scenes in Fat Heads in his time, but they'd all been of the drunken antics variety, and none had involved an irate assistant DA.

He worried for two reasons.

First, she might get defensive. Patrese didn't know Amberin well, but it was obvious she was proud of being a Muslim, if only from the *hijab* she always wore. She could easily regard his theory as a taint on all Islam, even – especially – if he was right. After all, it had taken only nineteen hijackers to spark a war seemingly without end.

Secondly, it would mean involving Amberin directly with the case, which would bring its own difficulties come prosecution. But he needed a practicing, thoughtful, intelligent Muslim, and she was the most obvious choice. *Not* to have used her would surely have been the greater dereliction of duty. He'd have gone to bin Laden himself if need be.

Amberin looked around her as they sat down. 'This is great.'

'Really?'

'Sure. That's pretty cool, for a start.' She indicated a collage of people wearing Fat Head T-shirts in all kinds of weird and wonderful places: a US Marine under the crossed swords monument in Baghdad; a trade delegation outside the Taj Mahal; people in front of the Eiffel Tower, in Tiananmen Square, even at Everest Base Camp.

'Have you ever been here before?'

'No.'

'Would you have ever come if I hadn't invited you?'

'Of course not. Which is why it's great. I might even invest in one of those.' She indicated a display case of T-shirts saying *Beer Rescue Squad* on the front and *Saving Society From Bad Beer* around the neckline at the back.

'You're joking?'

'Try me.'

They ordered. Fat Heads did all the usual things – burgers, chicken, subs, salads, soups, and so on – but for the full experience, you had to go for one of their trademark head-wiches; a sandwich, only bigger. Amberin plumped for a Bay of Pigs – *like an invasion of your stomach*, the menu said, *a Cuban sandwich gone nuclear!* – full of roasted pork, ham, Swiss cheese, pickles and honey mustard dressing.

'Pork?' Patrese asked.

'Sure.'

'But isn't pork . . .'

'Tasty? Yes.' She laughed. 'I wear the *hijab*, but I eat pork.'

Patrese laughed, surprised. 'You're the Pick'n'Mix Muslim.'

'Most of us who live in America are, to some degree or other. We have to be.'

Unencumbered by any religious picking or mixing, Patrese went for the Artery Clogger; two fried eggs topped with slices of ham, crispy bacon, melted American cheese, lettuce, tomato, onion and mayo.

Amberin read the Clogger's description from her menu. *'If Elvis was alive, he'd love this!'* She looked at Patrese. 'I can't help thinking that Elvis isn't alive precisely because he *did* love things like this.'

'Ain't that the truth.'

She was, he thought, proving more fun in two minutes out of work than in all the time he'd known her in it.

'So,' she said, 'you wanted to pick my brains.'

'Yes. And I don't have to tell you that all this is confidential.'

'No. You don't.'

Patrese told her what they'd found at the murder sites, and the possible connections with Islamic extremism. He mentioned his suspicions about Bayoumi, but didn't tell her about the wire-taps, the remote computer spyware, or that Beradino was back at headquarters waiting for Mustafa to make a move towards his mysterious sanctuary. She listened to it all without speaking, and waited till he'd finished before replying.

'It's possible,' she said.

'That's all? *Possible*?'

'Yes, that's all. It's *possible* that whoever's doing this could be a Muslim, sure. But if you're talking about the stones coming from that part of the Middle East, why not a Christian, or a Jew? Christians and Jews live there, too.'

'In much fewer numbers than Muslims.'

'There are fewer Muslims in Pittsburgh than Christians, aren't there? You're looking for a minority, it works both ways. If the hair's from Pakistan, why not a Hindu or a Buddhist? Or he could be something else entirely, like, I don't know, like one of those guys who thought the world was going to end in the tail of a comet; you remember them? Mass suicide cult.'

'Hale-Bopp.'

'That's the one. The joke's on all of us if it turns out they were right, isn't it?'

Patrese laughed. 'Just assume for the moment . . .'

'You know what they say about *assume*.'

'That it makes an *ass* out of *u* and *me*. I know. Detective training 101. But anyway. Just *assume* for the moment that the killer *is* a Muslim. Then what? Why burn them?'

'Burning has pretty much the same kind of symbolism in

Islam as in Christianity, particularly, you know, punishment in the afterlife.'

'Muslims believe in hell?'

'Sure. And that the more evil you are, the more you'll suffer. Some people just get smoldering embers under their feet, but they end up with their brains boiled anyway. Others are burnt till their skin's roasted through, then they get a new skin, and it all starts again. Or they're dragged into Hell on their faces.'

'Which kind of people suffer the most?'

'The Koran says that hypocrites will be in the lowest depths of the fire, and that they'll find no helper there for them.'

Patrese started. The anonymous e-mail had referred to the victims as hypocrites.

'But you can't just pluck these things out of context, Franco,' Amberin continued. 'Listen, you want to know about the Koran?'

'Yes.'

'Then you have to begin at the beginning. The Koran's made up of *ayat*, verses. Some of these *ayat* are clear and unambiguous; these passages are called *mukhamat*. Other passages, *mutashabihat*, are ambiguous or metaphorical. The first ones, *mukhamat*, form the Koran's foundation. They deal with fundamental beliefs, pious rituals, explicit laws, that kind of law. *Mutashabihat*, in contrast, describe aspects of faith whose nature can't be truly known, is up for debate, and has both outer meanings, *dhahir*, and inner meanings, *baatin*. Scholars have argued about these for more than a thousand years. They'll still be arguing a thousand years from now.

'Now, I can tell you what I believe, along with the vast majority of Muslims. I believe the Koran does *not* say that God belongs to one people. In fact, Islam's the only major faith not to be named after a prophet or a group of people, but a concept, submission to the will of God. The Koran doesn't say that God is wrathful and unloving. It doesn't say that *jihad*

255

is a holy war against the non-believers. *Jihad* actually means the struggle for good against evil, and is therefore something everyone should practice, regardless of their faith. The Koran doesn't discourage interfaith dialogue and co-operation. The Koran doesn't hate women. I can tell you all that, and I believe it all to be true. But there are also people with their own take on it, and that take is very different to mine.'

'Different enough to be doing something like this?'

'There were people who flew planes into skyscrapers, Franco.'

Patrese nodded, conceding the point. 'And have you come across any?'

'Any what?'

'People whose take on it is very different to yours.'

'Here?'

'Yes.'

She shook her head. 'Not that I can think of.'

'Sure?'

'Sure.'

'Anyone who comes to mind, no matter how ridiculous it seems.'

'Franco, I told you, I can't think of anyone.'

'Amberin, this is a murder investigation, and . . .'

'Don't lecture me. I know full well what it is. I do a lot of sensitive work with people, a lot of stuff done in confidence, and I'm not going to betray that. But I've been around as many homicide cases as you, and I know what to look for. If there's something or someone I think might be involved, you'll be the first to know.'

'But . . .'

'But nothing. That's the best you're going to get.'

The headwiches arrived, each of them the size of Rhode Island. Tacitly agreeing a truce, they tucked in.

'Look at the couple over there,' she said. '*Without* turning . . .'

Patrese had already turned his head, of course.

'I can't believe you could be so indiscreet,' she laughed.

'I can't believe you could see them without turning your head.'

'Women have got better peripheral vision than men, that's why.'

'Anyway, what about them?'

'*Massive* argument. Massive.'

'You heard them?'

'Not here. Before they arrived.'

Patrese looked at them again, more subtly this time.

'They look entirely normal to me,' he said.

'Franco, how the hell are you a detective?' She drew the sting from the words with a light laugh. 'Do you just switch your brain off when you clock off? Can't you tell they've had a fight? It's so obvious.'

She went round the room after that. That couple are bored with each other. Those two guys there are bitching about their wives. That big table, a birthday party, she's with him but wants to be with the other guy, and so on.

'You haven't noticed any of that?' she said.

'It's a woman thing, clearly.'

'Clearly.'

'Tell you what I have noticed.'

'What?'

'I've noticed every entrance and exit, and how to get there as quickly as possible. There are two blown light bulbs over in that corner that need replacing. That guy over there has read the same page of the *Post-Gazette* three times.'

'Bet you noticed the waitress.'

Patrese shook his head. 'Not especially.'

Amberin laughed again. 'I hope you're a better detective than you are a liar.'

11:43 p.m.

It was almost midnight when the surveillance team finally called in.

Mustafa Bayoumi was on the move.

If Mustafa suspected he was being watched, he gave no sign. He sauntered out of the house as though he didn't have a care in the world, climbed in his Saturn, and set off without a backward glance, even the one in his rear-view mirror required by the traffic code.

The watchers kept an open line to a speakerphone on the North Shore as they tailed Mustafa through quiet residential streets and on to Fifth Avenue, heading south-west.

'That's back towards town,' Patrese said.

Mustafa stayed on Fifth all the way past the Mellon Arena, and into downtown.

'*Making a right on Grant,*' said the speakerphone.

'Perhaps he's coming to see us,' Beradino murmured. 'He's going the right way.'

Patrese shook his head. 'I don't think so.'

'Why not?'

'I dunno. I just don't.'

'*Making a right on Liberty.*'

Liberty Avenue led away from the bridges to the North Shore and up towards the Strip District. The Strip is a rectangle of about twenty blocks by five, hard up against the cityside bank of the Allegheny. In its time, it had been first the industrial and then the economic center of Pittsburgh. Now, it was party central: funky loft apartments, farmers' markets and boutique shops by day, edgy bars and night-clubs by night.

Not exactly the natural stomping ground for a good Muslim boy, Patrese thought.

'Making a left on 17th.'

Definitely the Strip. Mustafa had ignored the previous turning, which led to a bridge over the river and up to East Allegheny.

'Left again on Penn. Suspect is slowing. Looking for a parking spot.'

Beradino leaned into the speakerphone. 'Driver, stay with the car, please. Shotgun, get out and maintain visual on foot, you understand?'

'Yes, sir.' A slight chuckle, and then: *'Sir, you ain't gonna believe this.'*

'Believe what?'

'There's a queue stretching halfway down the block, people waiting to get in a bigass new trendy nightclub, and it's called. . . .'

Patrese, suddenly realizing, finished the sentence. 'The Sanctuary.'

The Sanctuary was an old Slovak church, now deconsecrated and converted. Thick brick walls meant little sound leaked on to the street outside, but the lights and lasers thrusting upwards through the octagonal cupola rose high into the night sky.

Patrese went in alone. Dressed in jeans and a paisley shirt, he could just about pass for one of the hip young professionals who comprised the club's clientele. Beradino, no matter what clothes he wore, could not. At best, he'd look like someone's dad; at worst, like a cop. Either way, he'd stick out like a pork pie in a synagogue.

The dancefloor was packed, several hundred people caught frozen-strobed in an infinity of strange contortions. Patrese was momentarily tempted to join them and abandon himself to primal, sweaty pleasure; try and dance away all the shit he dealt with every day. That's what everyone else here was doing, he thought; stressful, busy jobs five days a week, two nights to enjoy themselves.

A day on homicide shift would show them what real stress was.

He climbed an elaborate half-spiral staircase up to the mezzanine level, past the DJ boothed in the old pulpit. A smiling waitress dressed as a Catholic schoolgirl stood aside to let him pass. Smiling back at her, Patrese was glad Beradino hadn't come in. Waitresses as Catholic girls; he'd have tried to close the whole place down for that.

An area of the mezzanine was roped off; private party. Patrese checked that Mustafa wasn't among the guests, and then leant on a rail and looked down at the revelers below; those on the dancefloor, those by the plexiglass bar.

There.

Mustafa was standing alone, in a corner, nodding his head in time with the music. His eyes darted round the room. Patrese presumed he was looking for whoever he'd arranged to meet here, the voice on the wire-tap.

After a few moments, a blond man in a turquoise shirt approached Mustafa.

Turquoise Shirt leant in close and shouted something in Mustafa's ear; pretty much the only way to be heard above the music.

Mustafa nodded and shouted back; a single word, repeated

for emphasis. Second time round, even at this distance, Patrese managed to lip read perfectly.

Thirty.

Turquoise Shirt nodded. Mustafa slipped past him and headed towards the stairs which led downstairs. Turquoise Shirt followed.

Downstairs were the toilets; Patrese had seen the sign on the way in.

Women went to the toilets in pairs as a matter of course, but men almost never – especially two men who, from their body language, looked to have only just met.

In fact, Patrese could think of only two possible reasons.

If it was the first, why not just go to a gay club?

And if it was the second, who better to deal with than a chemistry ace?

During the hour or so in which Patrese watched him, Mustafa disappeared to the toilets seven times. He was dealing something, that much was obvious to a moron, and a dollar to a dime said MDMA. Not only was Turquoise Shirt now dancing as if he'd personally experienced the Second Coming, but Patrese remembered reading about a case in New Jersey where a chemistry major had made about half a million bucks from manufacturing and distributing MDMA. It was one way of funding college, Patrese supposed.

And so much for Mustafa hating Western decadence, too; unless, of course, he'd justify it with some spurious garbage about helping destroy the system from within.

The easiest thing would have been to bust Mustafa's ass there and then; catch him red-handed, send the pills off to be analyzed, and sling him in the cells. But that could invite explanation as to how Patrese had happened to go, by himself, to the one club in all Pittsburgh Mustafa was visiting, which would in turn risk blowing the wire-taps. Better to be subtle, and perhaps keep the knowledge of what was happening here as a joker to be played at a later date. Softly softly catchee monkey, and all that.

Sometime around half past one, the lights dimmed, the fog machines started belching out enough smoke to hide Mount Rushmore, and the opening bars of Madonna's "Like a Prayer" reverberated around the club.

This was clearly some kind of ritual here, if the crowd's manic cheering and rush to the dancefloor was anything to go by. Patrese smirked. The song's video – burning crosses, stigmata, Madonna writhing around the black Jesus – had always made him laugh. He figured Madonna's love-hate attitude to religion was pretty much his own.

Through the smoke, he saw Mustafa pull out his cellphone, read a message – he must have had it set to 'vibrate', Patrese thought, he'd never have heard a beep above the music – and set off from his corner once more.

This time, however, he wasn't going down to the toilets.

He was heading for the door. Patrese followed.

The night air was sudden and cold after the warmth of the club. Mustafa pressed his cellphone to his ear with one hand and pulled his coat tight round him with the other. Patrese, twenty yards behind, couldn't hear what he was saying, but from Mustafa's tone and cadence, he was asking for directions; asking where his interlocutor was.

Apparently satisfied with the answer, Mustafa ended the call, shoved his cellphone back in his pocket, turned the corner and headed right, down towards the railroad lines and stockyards by the river. The streets here were much less well lit than the main drag of 16th. It was the kind of place you'd go if you didn't want to be seen; the kind of place you could also get mugged, or worse, if you didn't have your wits about you.

Patrese walked on the balls of his feet, hands loose by his side; ready for anything.

Up ahead, Mustafa stopped.

A figure materialized from the dark; a black man, Patrese saw, dressed in baggy pants and an orange puffa. The kind of guy who'd never have got past the rope at The Sanctuary, in other words.

He handed Mustafa an envelope. Mustafa took a step backwards, into the pool of watery light from the nearest streetlamp, and opened the envelope, the better to count the money inside. The black man stepped forwards with him, also into the light, and Patrese saw his face, clear as day.

It was Trent Davenport.

Transaction done, Mustafa and Trent went their separate ways; Mustafa back towards The Sanctuary, Trent down towards the 16th Street Bridge. Patrese followed Trent.

The moment Patrese was sure Mustafa was out of earshot, he called out: 'Trent!'

Trent spun round; surprised, scared.

'Don't run,' Patrese said. 'I know what you got. I saw you take it. Running's just gonna make it worse. Run, and I *will* bust your ass.'

Trent looked wildly round; not for escape, Patrese saw, but for something else.

Patrese worked it out fast, even as he closed the gap across to Trent.

Homewood was twenty minutes' drive away. It was too late for the buses, and no taxi driver in their right mind would go into Homewood after dark.

So Trent must have got here by car. But he was too young to drive. Someone must have brought him here, and that someone must have been taking him home again.

And that someone would have stayed the hell away while Trent was buying the drugs, in case he got caught. Get caught, and you were on your own. That's how the gangs work;

263

they get teenagers to collect and deliver the drugs. Teenagers are less likely to be stopped, so the thinking goes; and, if they do it well, it's part of their initiation. From there, they'll gradually graduate to bigger, better things in the gang.

'Let me see 'em,' Patrese said.

'I dunno what you talkin' 'bout, man.'

'Let me see 'em, Trent, or I'll slam you against that wall, and it *will* hurt.'

'Man, they see you, they're gonna kill me.'

Patrese held out his hand, impassive. Trent looked round again. Sullenly, he pulled a small plastic bag from his pocket and held it out.

'They ain't for me, man. They ain't personal use.'

Patrese took the bag and opened it. A hundred pills, at a guess. Ain't personal use, damn straight.

Trent was gabbling. 'You confiscate that, man, I really am dead, I ain't shittin' you. That a thousand bucks' worth, right there, and it ain't my dead presidents.'

Ten dollars a pill; reasonable wholesale price.

Patrese thought fast. He had three options here.

One, he could confiscate the pills. But if Trent went back to Homewood with no money and no pills, the gangbangers would think he'd run off with their cash himself. They'd kill him, no questions asked. At the very least, they'd hurt him bad.

Two, he could arrest Trent. But if he did that, he'd be condemning Trent to the endless labyrinths of the justice system. Once you were in, you never got out, not really; not as a young black man in the inner city. Your name was known, you were marked. The cops had their eye on you. That, too, was a death sentence. It was slow, it was insidious, but it was a death sentence just the same.

Three, he could give Trent a thousand bucks, keep the pills himself, and let Trent return to whoever had sent him with some bullshit story about how Mustafa had never showed, and here's their money back. But that would leave Patrese a grand out of pocket, and have as close as made no odds to zero impact on Pittsburgh's drug supply.

'You recognize me?' Patrese asked while he thought.

'Sure, man. You the cop who arrested my mama. What you here for? You get a bonus for doin' the whole family?'

Patrese knew what he had to do.

He picked a single pill out, and handed the bag back to Trent.

'Hey man, they *count*.'

'They're not going to miss one. And Trent?'

'Yo?'

'You got a brain in your head. Think about why I'm doing this.'

Sunday, November 21st. 12:39 p.m.

Jesslyn broached the subject as Beradino was driving them back from church. She couldn't think of a way to ease into it gradually, so she cut straight to the chase.

'I'm going to see Mara tomorrow,' she said.

Beradino glanced sideways at her, eyebrows arched. 'You're doing *what*?'

'I'm going to see Mara.'

'I heard what you said. I want to know *why*.'

''Cos she rang and asked me.'

'What, and you just *agreed*? After everything she's done to you?' Beradino took his hands from the wheel and clapped them to his temples in frustration. 'Shoot, Jesslyn. I've listened to *weeks* of you telling me about how Mara deserves to die, and suddenly off you go like a puppy dog. What's going on?'

'I'm going 'cos it suits me.'

'How's that?'

'There's something in it for me. Something I need.'

'Like what?'

'Money.'

Beradino looked across at her again; suspicious, this time. Wary.

'What's that?'

'I've got something of hers. Something she'll pay for.'

'Go on.'

'Her Star of David.'

'What?'

'Solid gold. Wears it round her neck.'

'How have you got it?'

'By accident. She handed it in when she arrived at Muncy. It must have got mixed up with my stuff somehow. I didn't even notice till she rang to ask me.' First lie.

Beradino narrowed his eyes. 'How does she have your number?'

'It was on the tribunal documents, under my personal info section.' Second lie.

'What on earth was it doing there?'

'Someone messed up. Should have taken it out. Didn't. It happens.'

Beradino nodded. He'd seen enough incident statements with the witness' contact details accidentally included to know that this kind of mistake did indeed happen.

'And this Star of David,' he said. 'You're going to make her pay to get it back?'

'She *offered* to pay.' Third lie.

'You shouldn't let her. It belongs to Mara, Jesslyn. You want to give it back, give it back. But it's not yours to sell. Especially not a religious icon like that.'

'She *offered*. Darn it, Mark, it's not like she can't afford it. She's still got millions stashed away, I bet. And I need the money.'

'We got enough money.'

'No, we haven't. Not long term. Look. Mara cost me my job. Now she wants to pay me. Maybe it's guilt money. No matter. She's paying, I'm taking. End of story.'

Beradino thought for a moment.

267

'You want to hurt her?' he asked.

'I want her to suffer for what she did.'

'What she did to her babies, or what she did to you?'

'Both. Her babies more, of course.' That, at least, was true.

'The law's the law, Jesslyn. You know that well as I do.'

'God's law, Mark. God's law. Not man's law.'

'Jesslyn, you go see her, you don't touch a hair on her head, you understand me?'

'Nothing I could do would be a fraction of what she deserves.'

'Not a hair on her head. She's a free woman now. I don't like it any more than you do, but she was tried and acquitted in a court of law, and we have to respect that.'

'She should never have been –'

'– but she is. Take her money if you want, but nothing else. Promise me.'

'I'm just going to –'

'Promise me.'

Finally, grudgingly, like a sulky teenager: 'I promise.'

4:44 p.m.

Patrese wondered how many lies he told each day. He always lied for a good reason, he thought, but lie he did; and if most of them weren't outright lies, then they were certainly sins of omission.

For example, he'd told Beradino that Mustafa had gone to The Sanctuary to deal drugs, and that he, Patrese, had gotten hold of one of Mustafa's pills to send off for testing. What Patrese *hadn't* told Beradino was that he'd got the pill off of Trent.

And Patrese had told Mara he'd spent yesterday seeking advice about Islam and the Koran, as that was an avenue the police investigation into the serial murders was considering. What he *hadn't* told her, for obvious reasons, was that he'd sought the advice off of Amberin.

It was late afternoon, Sunday. Mara had asked him to come round. She wanted to show him something, and no, that wasn't a euphemism, a come-on, or a pretext. She knew what was and wasn't on offer, and though she didn't like it, she respected it.

He kissed her awkwardly on the cheek. She poured him

some coffee, and set it down next to a cardboard box which brimmed with sheets of paper.

'There are two more just like this. Three boxes in all, each of them chock full.'

Letters, Patrese saw. Hundreds of letters, perhaps thousands.

'What are they?'

'Take a look. I want you to *understand.*'

'Understand?'

'Franco, even if you don't want me . . .'

'It's not that.'

'OK; even if you feel you can't be *with* me, at least appreciate this. You're pretty much the first person who's listened to me since I got out. That means something to me. These letters are why that means something.'

Patrese tipped the letters on to the bed and flicked through them.

This was one of the things about police work, he knew. You do it long enough, you come across so many wackos, kooks, headcases, nutjobs, screwballs, crackpots and psychos that you begin to wonder whether there's anyone sane left in the country.

The letters Mara had received came from at least forty states (few people put their addresses, but the envelopes had postmarks), and the vitriol expressed in them was staggeringly virulent, if rarely articulate.

Some people had quoted passages from Revelation. Some had attached drawings of what they'd do to her if they ever caught her. Some had written long screes of verse outlining the myriad of ways in which she'd sinned. One letter consisted simply of the word 'BITCH' written over and over again, on for twenty-six pages. Another denounced her for being a 'Zionist whore' and part of the 'Jewish media conspiracy'.

Patrese jabbed an angry finger at it. 'Conspiracy, *bullshit,*' he said.

'You don't believe in conspiracy theories?'

'Not one. Not JFK, not 9/11, not Area 51, the Apollo moon landings, Oklahoma City, Paul is Dead, the New World Order, the Bilderberg Group, the Illuminati, or anything else you can think of. You know why? In all my time on the force – on this planet, come to think of it – I've yet to meet one person in a position of any authority who could find his own asshole with a mirror.'

Mara laughed. 'Ain't that the truth.'

'Why do you keep all these?'

'Why? To remind me.'

'Remind you of what?'

'That no matter how bad my life is, there are plenty of people out there with so little going for them that they get their kicks by spewing hate to total strangers.'

Patrese nodded, and turned his attention back to the letters.

An entire section came from Mara's personal stalker; no celebrity was complete without one, he guessed. An unprepossessing Hawaiian man called Alika Manuwai (he was considerate enough to attach his name and address to each letter, and often several photos too), he was quite a scribe; especially keen on long, rambling, repetitive letters detailing the torrid extent of his love for her, the joy he could bring her (especially as opposed to certain no-good, flaky billionaire mayors), and the inevitability of his and Mara's eventual union.

'What's this?' Patrese asked. 'He's written in some kind of, like, child language. "Peepo tink I mento", "I wen cry", "God goin do plenny good kine stuff fo yo". What the hell does that mean?'

'It's Hawaiian Creole. Pidgin language. And Honolulu PD checked him out. Say he's weird, but harmless.'

'Harmless? Brainless, more like. If he ever does something, he's practically given you his Social Security number. We could find him in three minutes flat.'

'He's no threat to you for my affections, put it that way.'

'I should hope not.'

'Any case, there's a restraining order against him. He's not allowed within five hundred yards of me.'

'I thought you said he was harmless?'

'*I* think he's harmless. Hellmore doesn't. And it was Hellmore who filed for the restraining order. He says you can never be too careful.'

A couple more letters quoted various passages from the Koran, either on their own or alongside the Bible and Talmud, as though to prove Mara was damned whichever God happened to hold sway in the afterlife. Another letter suggested Mara move to Saudi Arabia or Afghanistan, where women were treated as she deserved to be. This, Patrese assumed, was not supposed to be a compliment.

Wondering whether there was any link, no matter how tenuous, between this kind of bile and the killings, he held up the letters in question. 'Can I keep these?'

'If you like.'

'Come to think of it, why haven't you given these to us before?'

'You? You mean the police?'

'Yup.'

'My faith in the police isn't exactly at an all-time high. Present company excepted, of course. Here. Look at these.' She fished out two letters from the pile. 'These are *really* weird.'

Patrese read them. They were typed and unsigned, but clearly both written by the same person. The first one ran as follows:

```
Dear psycho baby-killing bitch,

Fucking bitch you should suck on a shotgun
and do everyone a favor. They should of
```

given a broomstick encrusted with broken glass to the other shitbag's in prison with you and let them use it on you. I would love to beat the ever living tar out of you rip your blackened still-beating heart right out of your chest.

However, the LORD JESUS says I shouldn't, because the LORD JESUS says for us to control our sinful impulse's.

May the LORD JESUS rule over GOD's people forever Amen.

The LORD JESUS says that in the end many false teacher's like Darwin and Mohammad will rise. I will not be swayed because I have met GOD. You say you heard GOD talking to you you're a fucking bitch liar. Only the true believer's can hear the LORD our GOD.

You and your lie's aren't fooling anyone. You're fake through and through that's why you're an actress scum faker not a truthful bone in your body. I saw you on TV with your Oscar acting like it was a big surprise and how humble you felt and I wanted to scratch your eyes out vile woman evil woman so smug and insincere.

You say you didn't kill those poor little babe's you're a filthy filthy liar.

If we claim to be without sin we deceive ourselves and the truth is not in us. If we confess our sin's HE is faithful and just and will forgive us our sin's and purify us from all unrighteousness. If we claim we have not sinned we make HIM out to be a liar and HIS word has no place in our live's.

The word of the LORD our GOD 1 John 1: 8-10.

Those angel's didn't ask to be born you gave them tombstone's before they could talk. Your son's will never play ball learn to drive or give their mother grandchildren. Your daughter will never attend a prom or walk down the aisle in white on her wedding day.

Million's of women would give anything to have children and would love and cherish them every minute of the day but they can't. You were given that most precious of gift's and spat it back. The LORD must have a reason for letting you do this. The LORD is great HE is kind and HE is forgiving.

Well this is not all there is. You are going to be held accountable for your action's. I hope they are worth an eternity in what I hear is a pretty uncomfortable place. All the blood money you and your shyster lawyer make won't help you down there. Fucking kike's scratching each other's back's. You get some big book deal too? Your greed is greater than your shame but your evil will never prevail.

For the word of God is living and active. Sharper than any double-edged sword it penetrates even to dividing soul and spirit joint's and marrow it judges the thoughts and attitude's of the heart.

The word of the LORD our GOD Hebrew's 4:12.

Watch your thought's for they become word's.

Watch your word's for they become action's.

Watch your action's for they become habit's.

Watch your habit's for they become character.

Watch your character for it becomes your destiny.

Your destiny will be decided by the LORD. Vengeance is mine saith the LORD. Even the most righteous are but filthy rags before HIM.

GOD has granted me great faith and understanding and as long as the earth endures I will fear no evil for GOD is with me. The Truth will shine like 1000 sun's. May the LORD JESUS rule over GOD's people forever Amen.

[unsigned]

And the second one:

Dearest darling Mara my precious and sweet one

I'm sorry I should never have sent you that other letter, if I could take it back I would.

I didn't mean all the thing's said
there, I wrote it coz I was angry at
you coz I thought I'd never see you
again after you left without even saying
goodbye.

Like all of us I am an imperfect
sinner but I know the LORD JESUS will
have mercy if we truly repent our sin's.

I want to be with you do you think that
could ever happen? Just the two of us
like the song goes, we could go live on a
beach in Mexico or somewhere where no one
would bother us or care or any of that.

But I know you probably don't want
that because you misunderstand the way
I've behaved towards you. I've tried to
explain but word's aren't my strong
point as you can probably tell from
these letter's!

Well it's not too late, we can always
clear the slate and start again can't we?

Can't we say we can say it please?

Most of all I know you didn't do what
they said you did with your baby's and
that. Your a good person and there's no
way you could have done that I know that
now. All those men in the courtroom, what
do they know of the way women think?

The LORD our GOD moves in mysterious
way's and only HE knows why he's sent
this on to you but you can rest assured
the reason will be perfect.

'The LORD shall judge the people; judge
me, O LORD, according to my righteousness,

and according to mine integrity that is in me.'

Remember too the word's of Job: 'Naked I came out of my mother's womb and naked I shall return: the LORD has given and the LORD has taken away; blessed be the name of the LORD.

I've seen you at your window a few time's and you always look so beautiful but sad too, if I could somehow wipe away all the tear's and hurt believe me I would do just that no matter what it cost me.

I stood among all those freak's and idiot's outside your apartment and they all think they know you, but they don't, they're fooling themselves, they read the Enquirer and think they know you and it's wrong, no one knows you like I do and certainly no one love's you like I do.

No offense but you're better off without Howard if he never kept the faith and ran off with the little whore next door the moment you were in Muncy.

GOD has granted me great faith and understanding and as long as the earth endures I will fear no evil for GOD is with me. The Truth will shine like 1000 sun's. May the LORD JESUS rule over GOD's people forever Amen.

[unsigned]

'Weird indeed,' Patrese said.

Monday, November 22nd. 7:20 p.m.

This will shock them, that's for sure.

It'll shock them because they're too hidebound in their thinking. Since they've already found three dead white men, they assume the next victim will also be a white man. They assume it because that's what the profiler's told them, or that's what they've read in those endlessly tedious screeds of psychology literature; that the chosen, like me, never kill across lines of race and gender. They simply can't appreciate that I'm different; different in every way from what's gone before.

The fear is all too real with this one. She – yes, she – knows beyond doubt what she's done. Redwine may not have been sure, Kohler probably didn't have time to think, and it would have taken Yuricich days to go through all the people he'd wronged. But this time, I've no need to disguise myself. So she knows. She knows who I am, and so she knows what she's done. She knows her scriptures, she tells me; she finds solace in her faith. She'll need it now, I tell her.

I look round the apartment, savoring the moment.

I remember almost nothing about the first time I killed. There was too much going on in my head; the logistics, the endless checklists to make sure I hadn't overlooked anything, but most of all, the *battering in my psyche. Life's so ingrained in our culture. Everything's geared to preserving and prolonging it, from all the doctors and pharmaceuticals money can buy down to the language itself: live life to the full, get a life, life imprisonment, life partner. We're conditioned to make lives, and save them; not take them.*

So to cross that line is an irreversible shock. When you first kill, in fact, you kill two people; not just the victim, but yourself too. Your old self is gone, and in its place is a new persona. I'm no longer part of humanity, not really, and nor do I care. I have no faith in mankind any more. I am the one who will be redeemed, not them, because I am performing the work of a higher power. Those who can't understand that have only themselves to blame. Most of the world worship at the feet of an all-powerful, no matter what name they use for their deity. And if you believe in a god, then you believe in an afterlife, where the good go to one place and the evil to another.

I know where this one, this victim, is going.

'Isaiah chapter fifty-nine, verse seventeen,' I say. '"For I put on righteousness as a breastplate, and a helmet of salvation upon my head; and I put on the garments of vengeance for clothing, and am clad with zeal as a cloak."'

7:58 p.m.

Patrese went home via Mara's apartment, which wasn't much of a via. In fact, it was almost exactly the opposite direction.

He didn't know why he wanted to see her, which was to say he knew exactly why, and it wasn't something he was particularly proud of.

The polite, acceptable answer was that he felt protective of her, especially since he'd seen the bilious letters she'd received, and that he wanted to check she was OK.

That was all true, but it wasn't all of the truth. He was drawn to her. He wanted to see her, get his fix while still denying himself the whole of it, the real rush. Temptation; resistance; control. Something to lift him from the frustrations of his day, which had been the usual rigmarole of dead-end leads and tail-chasing.

Patrese turned into Mara's street, and suddenly Tom Petty was singing alone on the car stereo, the chorus to 'Free Fallin', vaporizing in Patrese's throat.

Down the other end of the street, by the entrance to the park – right outside Mara's apartment block, in other words – three fire engines had slewed across the road.

Beneath flashing blues and reds, the firefighters swarmed

like ants; unrolling hoses and raising cherry-pickers, their movements shot through with the unflustered urgency of men who did this every day.

Patrese gunned the TransAm hard, as fast and as close to the fire engines as he dared. He was out and running almost before he'd come to a halt.

One of the firefighters moved to block his path.

'Hey! Fire scene, buddy. Stay out.'

Patrese ripped his badge from his belt and held it high. 'I'm a cop.'

'I don't care who you are, man. That place looks like Saddam torched it.'

Panic rising in Patrese's gut, gushing to fill the gap between what was in front of his eyes and what was coming up fast from the back of his mind. He looked around wildly, hoping to see Mara sitting on the back of a fire truck with a blanket round her; shocked and scared, no doubt, but at least still alive.

There was no sign of her.

'Is there anyone left in there?' he blurted.

The firefighter puffed his cheeks out. 'We found one.'

'Is she alive?'

'Not a chance, bud.' The firefighter paused. 'You said "she". But we haven't called it in to the cops yet. You know her?'

8:05 p.m.

Patrese took himself into the park, away from all the commotion.

Round the back of the observatory itself, he slumped on to a whitewashed stone bench, glacier cold through the seat of his trousers, and inhaled the winter air so deeply and violently that he began to feel light-headed.

Focus, he told himself, *focus*.

Easy to say; a damn sight harder to do, when a woman he'd made love to a week ago was now burnt to a cinder.

Patrese had seen what had happened to the others. They'd ended up as charred lumps of meat scarcely recognizable as the people they'd once been, the people who had, pretty much until the moment they'd been killed, walked and talked and laughed and loved, paraded their strengths and hidden their weaknesses.

They'd been like the rest of us, in other words. And now they were anything but.

Patrese hadn't known Redwine. He'd met Yuricich a couple of times. Kohler had been a family friend. None of them had evoked in him a fraction of what Mara had.

Mara was dead; the thought ran through Patrese's head

like a loop. Mara was dead. Mara was dead, Mara was dead. She'd lost her babies, she'd lost her freedom, and now she'd lost her life; pain upon pain upon pain. Why would one person deserve all this? They wouldn't, that was why. It was just chance; and therefore there was no God.

Patrese felt detached. It wasn't the lazy cliché of it being like it were happening to someone else, but rather that he seemed to be seeing and feeling it all through a thin layer of gauze. He knew it was shock, and he knew too that he must use it while it lasted. Mara's murder would hit him for real soon enough, and when that happened, he wanted to be alone. No one knew about him and her, and that was how it had to stay, even – especially – now she was dead. Anything else would pose more questions than answers, and the balance between the two was lopsided as it was.

To clear his head, Patrese shook it hard, as though he were a dog leaving water.

After a few moments, when he was satisfied he'd got his workings right and hadn't missed anything, he called Beradino.

'Mark, it's me.'

'What's up?'

'We got another one.'

'Who?'

'Mara Slinger.'

Beradino's silence was loud through the static.

'Mark?' Patrese continued. 'You hear me? Mara Slinger. Dead. Fire. *Capisce*?'

'Yeah. Sorry. Mara Slinger. Dagnabbit. You sure? How do you know?'

'I heard the fire called in on the scanner.' That Patrese should have been listening to the 911 frequency in his own car was perfectly plausible; lots of emergency service personnel did. 'Hauled ass to Obs Hill.'

'You there now?'

'Yup.'

'You been inside the apartment yet?'

'Nope. Firefighters still trying to get the thing under control. Be a while yet.'

'Wait there for me. Get the uniforms to throw up cordons, and wait there for me.'

'Will do.'

After ending the call, Beradino stared at the wall for a long, long moment, hoping to find an answer in the blankness of white paint.

There had to be an innocent explanation, he thought. Jesslyn had promised him she meant no harm. *Promised* him. And where he came from, that still meant something.

But Beradino knew too that Jesslyn was full of hate, and also that she'd kept her dismissal from Muncy secret for several weeks. In fact, he'd only discovered it by chance. Left to her own devices, she'd still be working in the burger bar now.

Since she'd hidden that from him, she'd almost certainly hidden many other things too. Working homicide for close on three decades had shown Beradino that, deep down, no one really knows anybody else. If he'd had a dollar for every time someone had told him that the killer was the quietest, nicest guy on the block, he'd be living out his retirement on Grand Cayman.

He picked up the phone again and dialed Jesslyn.

She answered on the third ring, crying great, racking sobs.

And he knew.

Beradino felt his head slump forward, as though his neck muscles were no longer up to the job of keeping it upright.

'What have you done?' he wailed. 'What on earth have you done?'

She tried to say something, but it came out as gibberish. Beradino took a deep breath, trying to compose himself.

'I'll be home later,' he said. 'I've got to go to her apartment now. Anybody there suspects anything, I'll think of something to head 'em off. When I get home, we'll talk. We'll figure this out. We'll figure out a way, I promise.'

9:12 p.m.

One man, looking at his dead lover, giving not a hint of the turmoil within.

Like Beradino, Patrese was professional enough to do exactly what he'd been trained to; walk the grid, record his impressions, look for anomalies. He noted that the body was in the middle of the living room, in the same hunched position – half fetus, half boxer – as the others had been. That was fire for you, he thought bitterly.

The fire itself had ravaged the living room, but the men with hoses, ladders and a frankly insane amount of bravery had got to it before it could spread much further. That had spared the kitchen, bathroom and bedroom the worst of it, and kept the apartment more or less intact.

Kept a lot of Patrese's DNA about the place too, no doubt.

Patrese had spent years cursing the slowness of the over-worked forensics system, where getting a DNA sample analyzed could take months. Now that very inefficiency was his best hope. By the time they got round to running the tests, perhaps the whole thing would be done and dusted.

His thoughts were interrupted by a commotion outside the apartment door.

'I know exactly who you are, sir,' one of the uniforms was saying, 'and you still can't come in.'

'The fire department have declared it safe. Let me in.'

Patrese knew the voice, but he couldn't immediately place it.

'Yes, sir, but this is still a crime scene, and . . .'

'Let me see her!'

Patrese recognized it now. The voice was that of Howard Negley; billionaire, mayor and, most pertinently in this instance, ex-husband.

Neither Patrese nor Beradino were quick enough to intercept Howard before he came into the room and saw the carnage.

He took one look, groaned deep in his throat, and rushed through to the bathroom.

Whatever Howard had eaten for dinner, it was all coming straight back up again. Patrese and Beradino listened in silence as he vomited, dry-retched, moaned again, and finally flushed the john.

'That's not on,' Patrese said.

Beradino nodded; he knew exactly what Patrese meant.

'You gonna tell him,' Patrese continued, 'or shall I?'

'I'll do it.'

Beradino sounded a little reluctant, Patrese thought; but it was hard to lay down the law to someone like Howard Negley, even when you were in the right.

The moment Howard emerged from the bathroom, Beradino went over to him.

'You've contaminated this crime scene from here to kingdom come,' Beradino said. 'Your footprints there, your performance in the bathroom.' The latter rankled especially, Patrese knew; bathrooms could offer rich pickings for trace evidence. 'I've a good mind to arrest you for obstruction of justice.'

'That's my wife there!' Howard shouted.

Wife, Beradino and Patrese noted pretty much instantaneously; not ex-wife.

Prison divorce rates were astronomical, certainly for any sentence of more than a year; they ran at something like 80 per cent when the husband was incarcerated, and close on 100 per cent when the wife was.

But divorce proceedings could last longer than a David Lean film. Even assuming that both parties co-operated, that there was a signed agreement covering all financial issues, that the court wasn't backed up, and that the stars were perfectly aligned, you were looking at six to nine months.

Without those conditions in place, the whole thing could take literally years, especially when rich people were involved. Poor folks never take long to divorce; half of fuck all is fuck all. Rich people, as F. Scott Fitzgerald had noted, are different.

Beradino and Patrese drove Howard home, and they talked on the way. It wasn't so much that they suspected him – though of course they both had reason to try and deflect attention from their own differing clandestine involvements with Mara – as that any information from a victim's ex-husband was welcome.

'How did you hear about this?' Beradino asked.

'Allen Chance called me. I was at dinner in town. I came straight here.'

He was dressed billionaire casual: pink polo shirt beneath a golf jumper the color of cut grass, and mustard slacks with creases sharp enough to disembowel the unwary.

'You were with your lady? Miss Ellenstein?'

'I was. My driver took her home after dropping me off.'

'You think she was upset you wanted to come see this scene?'

'She can be upset all she likes.'

288

'OK. Now, you mind telling me how close you were to finalizing the divorce?'

Patrese was momentarily surprised at Beradino's bluntness, and then figured that Beradino was trying to get as much information out of Howard as possible while Howard was still shocked, before he composed himself properly and reverted to his usual Master-of-the-Universe shtick.

Besides, Howard knew he'd messed up by blundering into the crime scene. Since Beradino would be perfectly entitled to follow through on his threat to arrest him, even now, Howard probably reckoned a bit of co-operation wasn't a bad idea at all.

'A couple of weeks, a month maybe.'

'So pretty much deal done?'

'Pretty much.'

'How much was the settlement?'

'It was complex.'

'That's not what I asked.'

'You been divorced, Detective?'

'Matter of fact, I have.'

'Then you'll know Pennsylvania's an equitable division state.'

'I didn't have too much to divide, equitably or not.'

'I'm sorry to hear that.' Howard didn't sound sorry in the slightest. 'But you'll remember, I'm sure, that each spouse owns the income they earn during the marriage, plus the right to manage any property in their sole name. But whose name's on what isn't the only deciding factor. Instead, the judge divides marital property *fairly*.'

'And fair don't necessarily mean equal. I remember *that* bit.'

'You got it. So Mara's holding out for what she feels is fair.' Neither detective corrected Howard's errant choice of tense; it was all too common in such situations. 'But she

289

and I have got rather different ideas about what "fair" is. And it's not helped by the fact she has no idea – *no idea* – about money. She's got this agent in LA who's been ripping her off for years, but does she do anything about it? No sir.'

'You got this agent's name?'

'Guilaroff. Victor Guilaroff.'

Patrese raised his eyebrows. Victor Guilaroff had been a contemporary of his at Sacred Heart. In fact, Victor's photo had been among the hundreds they'd found in Kohler's house. Small world.

'So, back to my original question,' Beradino said. 'How much are we talking?'

'Neighborhood of twenty million.'

Patrese whistled. 'That's a pretty respectable neighborhood.'

'Ain't it just?' said Beradino. Then, to Howard: 'And now she's dead, you hold on to everything?'

'That's right.'

'You realize twenty million dollars is reason enough for murder, least where I come from?'

'And *you* realize, Detective, what proportion of my wealth twenty million represents? No? I don't wish to sound boastful, but I'll tell you; less than half of one per cent. Half of one per cent of *your* salary is a few hundred bucks. Would *you* kill for that?'

'I know plenty of people who've killed for much less.'

But they took Howard's point. Year after year he rode high in the Forbes list, even though his philanthropy was as legendary as his earnings. He gave away more than a hundred million dollars a year – including his mayoral salary, in lieu of which he accepted a symbolic dollar – and liked to compare himself to Pittsburgh's greatest son, Andrew Carnegie. Offing his wife over relative peanuts just didn't seem likely.

'And anyway,' Howard said, as though it had only just

occurred to him, 'I couldn't have killed her. I was at dinner in town. People saw me.'

'But you're a man of influence. You could easily have arranged for someone to have killed Mara, someone professional.'

Howard only just avoided treating the question with the disdain they all knew it deserved. 'I *could* have done, Detective. But I didn't.'

'Had you seen Mara since her release from jail?'

'No.'

'When *did* you last see her?'

'The day she was convicted.'

'You didn't go see her in prison?'

'No.'

'Not once?'

'No. She'd killed my kids. Would *you* go see someone who'd killed *your* kids?'

'But you came here tonight?'

'She's dead. I wouldn't have wished that on her, even her. I wanted . . . Listen, this is hard to express. It's very confusing.'

'Care to be more specific?'

'I'm not sure I can.'

'Not sure you can, or not sure you will?'

'Not sure I can. Imagine what it's like, won't you? You go through the biggest nightmare a man can have, you think it's all over, you're just about to get yourself back on track . . . and then everything you know gets turned on its head. So I tried not to think about it too much. It was easier that way.'

'But?'

'But she was still the mother of my children. I loved her once, I really did. I . . .'

He tailed off.

Smart enough to make billions, Patrese thought, but not smart enough to unravel the mysteries of the human heart.

And if that sounded like criticism, it wasn't meant to be. It wasn't as though Patrese had worked too much of it out himself.

They passed the rest of the journey in silence. There was something bugging Patrese, something not quite right, though he was damned if he could work out what it was. He couldn't quite quell the stab of irrational jealousy he felt at hearing Howard talk about Mara, but he knew that wasn't what was gnawing at him.

Howard lived in Fox Chapel, six miles north-east of Pittsburgh. It would have been more surprising if he didn't. Fox Chapel is the Beverly Hills of Pittsburgh, though without the palm trees. Pretty much anyone who's anyone in Pittsburgh society lives here: the Heinzes; the Kaufman super-market dynasty; and, most importantly as far as Patrese was concerned, Rocky Bleier, former Steelers fullback and four-time Superbowler. Fox Chapel is 95 per cent white and 5 per cent Asian. The only black people seen here are either domestic staff, lost, or casing joints.

They glided past ornate gates and manicured lawns: Fox Chapel Golf Club, Fox Chapel Field Club, Fox Chapel Racquets Club. Patrese remembered Groucho Marx's view on such places, and couldn't help thinking he had a point.

The only establishments more in evidence than country clubs were churches. Patrese counted a Methodist, an Episcopal, a Presbyterian and a Lutheran, all within a couple of blocks. One way or another, he was unlikely ever to end up living here.

They pulled into Howard's drive, and stopped outside the house. Beradino got out of the car and opened the rear door for Howard.

'Because you can't do it from the inside,' Beradino explained. Howard might not have had to open a car door himself for many years now, but Beradino was damned if he was going to be thought of as a chauffeur.

'Thanks very much,' Howard said.

He was halfway to his front door when Beradino called out.

'Actually, we'd like to talk to Miss Ellenstein too.'

10:09 p.m.

Even by Fox Chapel standards, the house was something else. The floor was black-and-white checkered marble, and twin mahogany staircases curved up and round to meet each other at a gallery fifty feet above.

Ruby appeared at the top of the stairs. She was five four and 100 pounds, of which at least ten were plastic; and her hair, skin and teeth all came in shades rarely, if ever, found in nature. She and her former husband had lived in the house next door to this, and her swapping horses, as it were, had caused quite a stir in the press at the time.

'Down in a sec,' she trilled.

Howard ushered them into a living room roughly the size of Heinz Field. A maid came in with coffee – no alcohol for the detectives, not while on duty – and when both master and servant had left, in walked Ruby.

This was just a chat, they emphasized. Neither she nor Howard were under any kind of suspicion. This was routine police procedure, to interview ex-partners.

She said she understood.

Beradino asked her normal, unthreatening questions to start with. Did she work? She was on a few charity boards.

What were her hobbies? She liked going to the gym. What had she had for dinner tonight? Alfalfa sprouts and prune juice.

Patrese somehow stopped himself from laughing out loud at this last one.

'It must be hard,' Beradino said.

'What do you mean?'

'Your situation. All the publicity, all the controversy.'

Ruby opened her mouth to say something, stopped, and then suddenly jumped up, ran over to the bookshelf, grabbed a paperback, ran back and thrust it at Beradino.

'That's what it's like,' she snapped. 'It's all in there.'

Patrese looked across at the cover. *Rebecca*, by Daphne du Maurier.

He remembered the story. A young woman marries an older, wealthier man, and finds that his first wife – the eponymous Rebecca – still casts a pall over his life from beyond the grave.

'I'm sorry,' Ruby said. 'I know I should be all calm and collected about it, but you wouldn't be if you were me, and you wouldn't expect me to be, not if you know the first thing about women. She hangs over *everything*. Everybody knows the story, everybody has an opinion on what happened – on what *they think* happened – and more often than not *I'm* the interloper, *I'm* the harlot, scarlet woman, trollop, slut, whore. *I* didn't kill *my* children! She did, and suddenly *she's* Sandra bloody Dee. How did that happen? She killed her children – the worst thing any mother can ever do, bar none – and she *did*, no matter what that clever-ass lawyer and those idiot judges say.'

Beradino nodded.

Harden yourself, Patrese thought. *Think without passion.*

He reckoned Ruby could only have been this desperate to unburden herself if she hadn't told Howard what she really thought, for whatever reason. Anyone who felt herself heard would never have gone off like this. And Ruby never used Mara's name. It was always she, she, she. Never Mara.

'Are you glad she's dead?' Beradino said.

'Yeah. Yeah, I am. I hope she's burning in hell right now. That may not be the sensible thing to say to you guys, but it's the truth. I'm *thrilled* she's dead. I'd be even more thrilled if it felt like she was dead.'

'How do you mean?'

'She's here, in this house, everywhere; every room's got something of her in it. Her being dead won't change that in the slightest.'

'This was where she lived with Howard?' Patrese asked.

'Yup. It's insane, that he hasn't moved. He says he won't run away from where it all happened. Like he has to face it down or something. Such a *male* thing to do. I keep on at him, Can't we move, can't we move? Somewhere we can start anew, just the two of us. I don't want to stay here. It has bad memories for me, too, you know.'

'How come?'

'I used to live next door. That's how we got together. I wasn't getting on with my husband, and every day I'd see Howard with all the stuffing knocked out of him, that bitch in jail, his babies dead. All that money and power, they didn't matter. That's when I fell for him. It wasn't because of his money, no matter what people say. I fell for him when all his money meant nothing.'

Tell it to yourself often enough, Patrese thought, and you'll start to believe it.

10:56 p.m.

'What did you think?' Beradino said, when they were back in the car.

'She's a piece of work, ain't she?'

'You know it.'

'Whichever way you look at it, he's her meal ticket. She got him when he was low. Now she lives in fear he'll be off the moment he stops needing her support, or the moment she loses her looks.'

'And he hasn't moved out of the house where his kids died. That had been me, I'd have moved like a shot. Wouldn't you?'

'Sure.'

'So where's his motive to kill Mara? Nowhere. But for Ruby, different story.'

'Mara out the way, she can try and get Howard to marry her – then she's set for life whatever happens. She's an operator. She's one of those people who feels they owe it to themselves to be beautiful, skinny, successful, healthy; to be more than – I don't know, to be more than what we all are.'

'Which is?'

'A collection of random cells. Ruby reckons she can beat

that. She reckons with enough aerobics, prune juice, alfalfa and surgery, she'll live to a hundred and twenty, and by that time science might have worked out how to get her to live forever.'

'Jeez Louise.' Beradino shook his head at people's unending stupidity. 'You eat nothing but alfalfa and prunes, even if you don't live to a hundred and twenty, you'll feel that old.'

They laughed.

'But if it is her, how does it fit in with the other murders?' Patrese said.

Beradino puffed his cheeks. 'That, I don't know.'

They were silent for a moment, then Patrese said: 'Can I ask you something?'

'Sure.'

'You asked Ruby whether she's happy that Mara's dead.'

'Yeah.'

'But what about you? Are *you* happy Mara's dead?'

Beradino looked angry for a moment, reflex at having his professional integrity questioned, and then his face softened.

He nodded. 'That's a fair question. And good on you, for asking it. Yes, I'm happy, because she killed those babies, and I'd have strapped her into the chair myself for that. But that doesn't mean I don't want to find the killer. I do.'

'What if it was just her murder we were investigating?'

'Even then. Sure, I care about the other victims – some more than others, but that's life, even when it's death, if you know what I mean – but I care just as much about the challenge. The murder, this murder, any murder, is . . . I don't know, an affront to my intellectual vanity. Here's the crime, here's the criminal, and he's saying: Come on, gimme what you got, let's see if you're up to cracking this baby.

'All those bleeding-heart detectives on TV, they don't exist, not in real life. You know that, Franco. You know that too well. You know which TV detective I like the best? Poirot.

298

'Cos Poirot doesn't give a hoot. Behind his mustache and his hair lotion and his little-gray-cells, he doesn't. Give. A *hoot*. It's a game to him, that's all. That's the best you can hope for from a really good cop, that he cares about the game. Nothing else. You hate blacks, Jews, gays, women, Arabs, it don't matter. City don't employ you to hold hands and be Gandhi. It employs you to catch killers. End of.

'One of the best detectives I knew was a racist, all the way through. He'd catch twelve, fifteen murderers a year; the victims, always black. Victims' families loved him. But if a black family moved in next door, he'd run the father through the computer to find out if he had charges. It's who he was. Not nice? Darn straight. But tell it to the Marines.'

'I consider my question answered.'

Beradino laughed. 'I'm sorry. Didn't mean to rant. But you asked.'

Tuesday, November 23rd. 1:28 a.m.

It was past one in the morning when Beradino finally got home.

He hoped Patrese had noticed nothing abnormal about his behavior earlier. That business with Howard contaminating the scene had almost caught him out – he'd usually have been on to something like that in a flash – but he figured he'd covered up his hesitation well enough. Surely he could be excused for acting a little oddly round this particular murder scene, given his history with Mara and her babies?

And now he had to sort things out with Jesslyn.

Half of him was dreading the confrontation; the other half wanted to get it over with. Even without it, he'd probably get little or no sleep tonight. He always found it hard to rest in the immediate aftermath of being called to a homicide. If you saw the carnage which resulted from one human killing another, and you then slept like the dead yourself, there was something not quite right with you.

He stopped the car in the parking lot outside the block where he and Jesslyn shared a condo. Looking up at their windows, he saw that all the lights were off. There wasn't even the faint curtain-diffused glow of a bedside lamp.

That was strange. Sure, it was late, but after everything that had happened tonight, Jesslyn was surely still awake.

Unless . . .

No, Beradino told himself firmly. *No.* She was a fierce Christian, and believed suicide was the ultimate sin. There was no way she'd take her own life, no matter how extreme the circumstances. Absolutely no way.

So why were the lights off?

Maybe she wasn't at home.

Come to think of it, he hadn't seen Jesslyn's silver Camry in the parking lot; but then again he hadn't *not* seen it, either. He hadn't looked specifically for it. It could easily have been there, and he just hadn't noticed.

Still; if she wasn't at home, where would she have gone?

He had no idea.

Or what if she *was* at home, but wanted him to think that she wasn't?

Possible; but why?

The answer came pretty much simultaneously with the question. Why? Because Beradino was the only one who knew Jesslyn had killed Mara.

Which made him a target.

Darkened house. Target. Ambush.

He pulled his gun from its holster.

Jesslyn had been incoherent on the phone to him earlier. Panicked, confused, angry, scared . . . she was all these, and any of them could make her lash out. He was bigger, and stronger. The element of surprise was all she had. He had to be on guard.

On the landing outside the condo's front door, Beradino scooted silently across the carpet, low to the ground in case Jesslyn was watching through the fish-eye spy hole.

Still crouching, he pushed against the door with a splayed hand.

Shut.

Slowly, he pulled his house keys from his pocket, fingers spaced between each key to keep them from jangling against each other.

He found the one for this door, inserted it very slowly in the lock, and turned till he felt the resistance from the tumblers stop.

Absurd, he thought, to be behaving like this outside his own front door.

Beradino tensed, took a deep breath, and flung himself against the door as hard as he could, his momentum taking him forward and down into the room, rolling instantly away from the door with gun held out in front of him, sighting down the barrel, looking for movement in the dark reaches of the room beyond the pale puddle of light from the hall.

Nothing. No one.

He clambered to his feet and switched the light on.

The room was empty.

He went through the condo fast, checking each room as he'd done a thousand times before on police raids. Empty, empty, empty. No Jesslyn hanging from the shower rail, coming at him with a carving knife, or crouched shivering tears in the corner.

No Jesslyn at all.

He opened her closets. Half her clothes were gone, as were her toiletries and a couple of suitcases. No sign of her handbag, purse, keys or phone.

He dialed her cell, and was put straight through to voice-mail.

'It's me,' he said, hardly waiting for the tone. 'You're not here, you've gone. Ring me. Come back. Whatever you think you're doing . . . you can't do it this way, Jesslyn. You just can't. I said we'll sort it out, and we will. But you have to trust me.'

He ended the call, and wiped his hand across his face.

It was going to be a long night.

4:17 a.m.

Long before the first pinking of dawn, Beradino gave up on any prospect of slumber, and drove back to North Shore. He was in good company there, as police headquarters never really sleep. Even on the graveyard shift, when the place is almost empty and most of the people who *are* there move with the deliberate slowness of deep-sea divers, there's no escaping the purposeful, remorseless, electronic hum of the platoons of machinery which reduce faces to pixels and individual lives to number strings, but without which the world no longer runs.

It was to this endless network that Beradino now turned.

He requested details of Jesslyn's bank balance, and notifications whenever her car was spotted or she used any kind of bank card. To ensure that these alerts went to him and him alone, Beradino assigned them to a case number from the previous year: a homicide in Beltzhoover which remained unsolved but was no longer under active investigation. That way, anything which came in about Jesslyn wouldn't form part of the current inquiry.

The bank information came back inside fifteen minutes. Jesslyn had withdrawn her daily limit of $500 twice in the previous twelve hours: first at an ATM in Allegheny Center, 21:32 last night; and then at an ATM in Punxsutawney, 00:02 this morning.

By now, several hours later, she could be anywhere.

Beradino knew he could still come forward and report what had happened. They'd put out a statewide, even a nationwide, manhunt for Jesslyn, and a dime to a dollar they'd have her in custody by the weekend.

That was the sensible thing to do; he knew that. But he knew too that once her name was out, once it was known she was one hundred miles and running, she'd never get a fair hearing; not from the cops, not from the public, not from the jurors. Manhunt meant guilty, end of.

Keep this hidden now, and there was no going back. This was his last, best chance. If he didn't take that chance, and he was found out, he'd never be able to explain his way out of it. So every moment he waited both reinforced and compounded the lie.

It wasn't a contest. Not really. Not when it was someone you loved. Beradino didn't want to be alone again. He knew there was nothing greater than love, because he knew too how vast and cold was the darkness beyond love.

Beradino walked into the incident room and surveyed the handful of uniforms who'd been manning the phones during the night shift.

'Right,' he said. 'What have you got for me?'

8:49 a.m.

If Lockwood had found that performing an autopsy on a woman whom his testimony had once helped convict was in any way strange, unsettling, or simply poetic justice, he made no hint of it in his report. Nor did that report tell Patrese and Beradino anything they hadn't seen in the three previous cases. Mara had been burnt alive. Like Redwine and Kohler, but unlike Yuricich, her tongue was intact at the time of death.

Nor did the detectives claim much joy elsewhere. Beradino said he'd already asked Jesslyn whether there could be a connection between Mara's murder and anything that had happened during Mara's incarceration in Muncy, and been assured there couldn't; Mara had been a model prisoner. No beefs, no conflicts, no revenge.

Mustafa Bayoumi had been home all the previous evening, as he was most nights of the week. Increasingly, it seemed his Saturday-night excursions were the start and end of his social life.

'But we keep the Islamic angle in mind,' Beradino told the morning progress meeting. 'Mara was Jewish, remember. Maybe that makes her just as obvious a target as Kohler and

306

Yuricich; you know, men who were defenders of the Christian faith.'

'And maybe we should have thought of that earlier,' Patrese said.

'How so?'

'Well, it's not exactly news that Jews and Muslims don't get on, is it?'

'Then maybe *you* should have suggested that before, Franco, rather than being a smart-alec Monday-morning quarterback.'

Beradino regretted the words, and the tone in which he'd spoken them, the moment they were out of his mouth. The uniforms were staring at him in surprise, as was Patrese. Beradino never lost his rag; never. That was one of his hallmarks.

'Sorry,' he said. 'I didn't mean it to come out that way. Sorry, Franco.' Patrese raised a hand; *Fuhgedaboudit*. 'This whole case is getting to me, I guess. Yes, you should have thought about it earlier, but that goes for all of us.'

'Even if we had jumped to it, what could we have done?' Patrese said, helping Beradino save face. 'Protect every Jew in Pittsburgh? Even every prominent Jew? Of course not. We don't have the manpower. Mara didn't do anything to piss the Muslims off especially, far as we know, apart from being Jewish. And it's hardly as though the killer's gonna go after Seinfeld and Woody Allen next, is it?'

That got a laugh.

'OK,' Beradino said. 'What if we're right about the Islamic connection, in the other three murders, but not this one? What if this is a copycat?'

'It can't be. Forensics found two pieces of pink granite, same as before. Copycats don't know about the stones.'

'They don't know *officially*; it ain't been in the press. But think of all those who actually know about the stones.'

307

Beradino ticked the groups off on his fingers. 'Everyone in this room, plus half the rest of the building. Guys at the Bureau. Geology guys at Pitt. Say even one of them has a few beers, has a big mouth, tells his buddies about it – and you know it happens, no matter it ain't supposed to. Those buddies tell other buddies. Sooner or later, it comes to some wacko who wants to get rid of Mara. He thinks if he makes it look like part of this series, it won't point the finger at him. He gets some accelerant and a couple of stones – Wheelwright said pink granite's very common . . .'

A few of the uniforms were looking skeptical. Beradino couldn't blame them. He was fishing. He knew it, and they knew it, though of course they didn't know why.

'The stones come from the Middle East,' Patrese said. 'Not the nearest shop.'

'So we get Wheelwright to test these ones, just like the others. In the meantime, we keep an open mind, yeah?'

Anything to keep the hounds from Jesslyn.

There was a knock at the door.

'Come.'

Summer McBride, one of the forensic analysts, appeared.

Blonde and almost always smiling, she was well-named, though sometimes the summer in question seemed to be hurricane season. She could be fearsomely feisty, especially to those who dared suggest that computer technology was making human fingerprint analysts increasingly redundant.

'Got quite a lot,' she said. 'Too much fire damage in the living room, but in the rest of the apartment, no problem. At least four sets; one of them Mara's.'

'How do you know?' Beradino said.

'How do I know what?'

'How do you know one of them was Mara's? Her hands were burnt to a crisp.'

'I cross-reffed to the prints taken when she was arrested for killing her children.'

Beradino nodded approval; smart work.

Summer continued. 'The other three sets remain unknown. I've put them in IAFIS to see if there are any matches.'

IAFIS was the FBI's Integrated Automated Fingerprint Identification System, which Boone had made available to them for the duration of this investigation. The largest biometric database in the world, it was the civil libertarians' *bête noire*.

Beradino didn't know whether Jesslyn's prints would be on IAFIS. She didn't have a criminal record, that was for sure, but he wasn't certain whether or not she'd have been required to give them in her capacity as a state employee. He seemed to recall a big brouhaha over the issue, and a lot of jumping around about constitutional rights and all that; but he couldn't remember which way the decision had fallen.

'And get this,' Summer added. 'The other sets, the ones that weren't Mara's? All three were in the kitchen and bathroom – but only one of them was in the bedroom.'

She looked round the room, smiling as they all worked out the implication.

'Mara had a lover?' Beradino's tone suggested a cure for cancer was more likely.

'She had at least three visitors.' Forensic analysts rarely offer suppositions. They regard their remit as simply finding the dots. It's up to the detectives to join them up.

'One of whom looks to have been a lover.'

'And one of whom looks to have been a killer,' Patrese added.

Beradino looked at him. 'Unless lover and killer are the same person.'

11:06 a.m.

The crowd outside Mara's apartment was growing with every hour that had passed since the announcement of her murder. By mid-morning, there looked to be around a thousand people out front. Some were making shrines to her, candles glowing softly like votive offerings in front of makeshift photographic triptychs. Others held placards marked 'baby-killer'. In death, as in life, Mara divided opinion.

One of the uniforms was up on the roof of the block, filming the crowd down below. The police had done this for every murder. Killers sometimes returned to the scene of their crime; arsonists often did.

The footage was relayed back via video link to monitors in headquarters, where Patrese and Beradino watched in real time.

In every crowd there's the drunk, the clown, the trouble-maker, the junkie and the fool. They were all represented here, and in multiples.

There was a sound link too, though the officer doing the filming didn't say a word. This was the professional – and therefore the unusual – thing to do. Films like this had to be handed over to the defense if proceedings ever made it to trial, and it didn't look good if the cameraman decided to grade the women out of ten, crack unfunny jokes, or break wind. All three had happened in cases Patrese had worked on.

Berlin was running a face-recognition program on the footage. He'd hijacked a copy of the newest software a few months ago, and had to be dragged away from using it at every opportunity. He'd once spent three-quarters of a Pirates match filming the crowd at PNC Park, and pronounced himself thrilled when the computer managed to identify more than fifty convicted criminals in the crowd.

Surprised? he'd asked. Only that there weren't more, Patrese had replied.

Not that computer face recognition was perfect. It was pretty good at full frontal faces and anything up to 20 degrees off, but beyond that, further towards profile, it was hit and miss. The good old human brain and eye combination was much better.

Which was how Patrese came to recognize, standing right in the middle of the crowd and wailing loud enough to have been part of Bob Marley's backing band, a man with eyeglasses and a fat face.

Alika Manuwai. Mara's lovelorn Hawaiian stalker. The one who'd attached photos of himself to his letters. The one whom Honolulu PD had described as harmless.

Patrese thought fast. Manuwai lived in Hawaii. Mara had been killed around twelve hours ago. Factor in a couple of hours before her death was officially announced, the scarcity of late-night flights, the time spent waiting for connections...

If Manuwai could have got from Hawaii to Pittsburgh in that time, he deserved his own superhero movie franchise.

Which meant he must have been in Pittsburgh before Mara was killed.

11:35 a.m.

Three uniforms lifted Manuwai from the crowd without trouble. He seemed almost pleased to see them, though not as pleased as some of the rubberneckers nearby. Manuwai's caterwauling had been getting on their nerves. Italian mommas at funerals cried and carried on less than he'd been doing.

Real or feigned, Manuwai's distress by itself meant nothing. He could easily have killed Mara before being overcome by grief. Cops saw it all the time; people who murdered their loved ones in red rage, and only afterwards realized the enormity of what they'd done.

OK, Manuwai and Mara had hardly been loved ones in the conventional sense; but if his letters were anything to go by, there was no doubting the veracity of his feelings for Mara – or the tenuousness of his grip on reality.

The uniforms frisked Manuwai, of course. If they found drugs, they'd tell Patrese and Beradino, who could use it as a bargaining chip for information later on. Not that the uniforms had any reason to suspect drugs, though; so, if it came down to it, they'd claim they'd frisked Manuwai for officer safety, in case he'd been carrying a concealed weapon. Anything else would have violated his constitutional rights.

312

Then they slung him in the back of a cruiser, brought him into North Shore, printed him, put him in a cell, and called up the incident room squawk box.

'We got your man. Cooling his heels in 149.'

'Thanks,' Patrese said into the speakerphone.

'Watch out for his BO, man. Dude's got a half-life like plutonium.'

Patrese laughed. 'I want my suspects docile, sweet-smelling and non-contagious, but the world's an imperfect place. One of the three will do just fine. Which one don't really matter.'

The cells were in the basement, strung out either side of a corridor. Patrese and Beradino took the elevator down.

'Gotta take a leak,' Beradino said as they passed the restrooms. 'See you in there.'

Patrese opened the door to cell 149. The uniforms had been right about Manuwai's BO, that was for sure. Place smelled like a damn farmyard.

Manuwai was sitting on the cot. He looked up at Patrese, and his eyes widened.

'I know you,' he blurted, and then tried to choke back the words, as though he'd said something he shouldn't have.

Patrese was about to assure Manuwai he *didn't* know him when he caught sight of Manuwai's left hand; or, more precisely, what was on it.

A plaster cast.

1:13 p.m.

Manuwai started gabbling; the same Creole pidgin in which he'd written his letters to Mara, now spattered out in rapid, machine-gun syllables.

'Oh man, I sorry. I sorry for hittin' ya, I wasn't sleepin' in so long, and you know I love her, fo sure, she an angel on dis earth and now she in heaven and I go kill myself to be with her again, she sent from Holy God above to suffer and save us all, ya know? Ya a good man, Detective, ya a lucky man fo goin' with her, of course it don' mean nothin', you nothin' fo her, she jus' waitin' fo me, but . . .'

Patrese was hardly listening. He was thinking fast, knowing he had to get it right first up. Beradino would be here inside a minute, and in that time Patrese had to do two things: first, persuade Manuwai – simple, deluded, possibly mildly retarded Alika Manuwai – to keep quiet about Patrese's sleeping with Mara; second, not to let Manuwai know how important this was to Patrese.

'Alika, shut up.'

'I jus' tellin' ya . . .'

'No. Listen to me, 'cos I want to help you.'

'Ya do?'

314

'Yes. *I* do. But my colleague won't. You're in big trouble, you know. I could have you up for assault and for breaking your restraining order like *this*.' Patrese snapped his fingers. 'Combine the two, you're looking at fifteen to twenty, easy. But I don't care too much about that. What I *do* care about is finding out who killed Mara. You help us with that, I'll forget the assault, and see what I can do about the restraining order. But you *don't* help us, I'll bring it all down on you. You understand?'

Manuwai nodded meekly. Patrese continued.

'So if my partner, Detective Beradino, asks you what happened to your hand, you tell him you fell over. He's a real stickler for justice, you know? He finds out the truth, he might decide to press charges himself. Then you're screwed.'

Manuwai nodded again.

'Good man,' Patrese said.

Beradino appeared at the door. 'We ready?'

1:20 p.m.

They took the smallest and barest interview room available. This was standard practice. Most detectives like the following: a room with as little space and as few distractions as possible; chairs with no arms to prevent the suspect from getting too comfortable; two detectives there, one talking, one listening; and no table, which mean they can get close to the suspect, invade his personal space, unsettle him.

'I'll start off,' Beradino said *sotto voce* as Manuwai sat down.

Patrese nodded. Beradino had made his name as a closer, a detective who could close cases by getting the suspect to confess. Some detectives excelled at canvassing, some at forensics, some at finding those who didn't want to be found. Beradino's forte had always been interviewing.

So he'd do the talking; Patrese would listen, take notes, and watch for things Beradino missed. Even someone as good as Beradino found it hard to ask questions *and* get every last detail of a suspect's reactions at the same time.

What Beradino wanted above all from Manuwai was, of course, a confession to Mara's murder, if only to buy him enough time to find Jesslyn.

316

What Beradino asked, to put Manuwai at his ease, was: 'You like Pittsburgh?'

'Neat,' Manuwai said. 'Neat, da city.'

'Really? You think it's a dive, you can say, I won't be offended. Franco here, he loves the place, loves it so much he should get paid by the tourist board; but me, I can take it or leave it. What you been up to here?'

'I try fo tink.'

'You have to *think* to remember what you did a few hours ago? Come on, man. Your memory's not allowed to be that bad till you get to my age.'

Manuwai laughed. 'I wen walk round town.'

'Where did you go?'

'All round.'

'Like where?'

'Er – da Strip. I wen go da Strip.'

'What did you do there?'

'I wen chill, man.'

Beradino gestured at Manuwai's cast. 'How did you do that?'

Manuwai looked at Patrese. Patrese did his best to remain expressionless.

'You don't need Detective Patrese to tell you how you got a plaster cast, I'm sure,' Beradino said. 'How did you do it?'

Manuwai looked back at Beradino. 'I wen fell over.'

'How did you do that?'

'Tripped. Too much fo drink, you know?'

'Here? In Pittsburgh?'

'No. Honolulu.'

'What were you doing at the Strip?'

'I wen chill, man.'

'Where did you go? You remember the names? Bars? Clubs?'

Manuwai thought for a moment, then shook his head. 'Jus' places.'

Beradino leant forward and touched Manuwai's knee. As

any suspicious wife knows, it's much harder to lie to someone who's touching you.

'Dis importen', ay?' Beradino said.

Patrese almost shook his head in admiration. Beradino was mimicking Manuwai's speech pattern without seeming to be disrespectful. It was a tricky balancing act; Patrese knew he couldn't have pulled it off.

'I know, cuz.'

'And we know you weren't at the Strip. *You* know you weren't at the Strip. You came to Pittsburgh to see Mara, and you were outside her house. You can help us here, Alika.' Beradino lowered his tone, making Manuwai lean closer to hear him; bonding them by proximity, if not yet by intimacy. 'Tell us what happened. Tell us what you did.'

Beradino didn't use the word 'murder' or anything like it. Those are very final terms, and suggest to even the densest suspect that there's no way out.

Patrese winced. Accusing Manuwai of killing Mara would make him defensive.

'Honest fo God, I neva done one ting.'

Beradino kept his head bowed as he listened, as though he were priest to a penitent. He was too much of a pro to show an iota of what he was thinking, though both Beradino and Patrese knew Manuwai was lying. The moment a suspect says 'honest to God' or anything like that – 'honestly', 'frankly', 'sincerely', 'believe me', 'I'm not kidding', 'would I lie to you?' – it's a sure sign he's as shifty as Dick Nixon.

'You know the story of Pinocchio, Alika?'

Manuwai smiled, the child in him surfacing. 'Fo sure.'

'You know how his nose grows when he's lying? Turns out it ain't fiction. When people lie, the stress makes blood flow to their extremities. Your nose grows. So does your Johnson. Want us to pull down your pants and see if you're messing with us?'

Manuwai giggled. 'No, man.'

'You think this a game?' Beradino barked suddenly.

Manuwai's head jerked up, his eyes wide with shock. Patrese's, too. Even if this was for effect, it was very unlike Beradino. That was twice in a few hours he'd lost it.

'You think this is *funny*? Tell you what; you wanna have fun, I'll go and call the Operator. You ever heard of him? No? He's a big guy round here. You know why he's called the Operator?' Manuwai shook his head, tears springing from wide eyes. ''Cos he likes phones, that's why. It's good to talk, he says. You wanna know what he'll do to you? First he'll slam a phone book on your head, time and again. Hurts like heck, but doesn't bruise the scalp. You know what that means? *Do you?* It means no one'll believe you when you tell 'em what happened. Then the Operator – he's only just getting into his stride now – next thing he does, he gets one of those old-style cranked telephones, you know? They generate electricity when they're wound up. He runs some naked wires out the back of the phone. He puts some on your face, some on your balls. Then he tells you he's gonna make a long-distance call. A hundred bucks says you'll be squealing you killed her before he dials the number. And you know what? Sometimes he dials anyway, just for the heck of it. I'll go get him now.'

Beradino pushed his chair back and started for the door.

Through his gulping tears, Manuwai shouted: 'I neva kill her, but I see who did.'

Beradino turned round slowly, and retook his seat at half-pace; trying not so much to intimidate Manuwai as to give himself time to think.

'You were in her apartment?' he asked at length.

'No. Neva.'

'You ever try to get in, see her?'

'Neva. Neva, neva. Dat her place. She entitled to her privacy.'

Beradino nodded. Restraining order or not, Manuwai was way too immature to have approached Mara directly. His passion for Mara was almost certainly genuine enough, but based on such an artificial construct – movie star, tragic mother, brave victim, stoic sufferer, vindicated heroine – that at the deepest level he wasn't even interested in who Mara had really been. The popular narrative of her life wasn't just enough for him; it was the line which he'd never cross for fear that, like the wizard in Oz, the reality wasn't half as good.

'Where were you, then?'

'On da avenue. Riverview Avenue.'

'Outside her apartment block?'

'Not quite. Up da street a bit, on da other side.'

Keep talking round the issue. If he gets too near to implicating Jesslyn, there might be time to steer him away.

'You didn't want to make yourself too obvious?'

'Dat right.'

'Because of the restraining order?'

'Dat right.'

'You were on foot, or in a car?'

'Both. I hire car and sit in it. Sometime I go to park.'

'Park? Park the car?'

'No. Park, at the end of da street. With da absurdity.'

'Absurdity?'

'You know. Big white thing. To watch stars.'

'Observatory.'

'Dat's what I say.'

Beradino smiled thinly. 'What were you doing in the park?'

'Walkin' round. Stretch da legs. Fresh air, ya know?'

It would also have done Manuwai no harm to move around like that, Patrese thought. If he'd sat too long in the car at any one stretch, one of the neighbors would eventually have seen him and called the police.

'How long had you been outside the apartment?'

'I came over last week. Monday.'

'Eight days ago?'

'Dat right.'

'You come over often?'

'Time and money. When I have both, I come.'

Patrese opened his mouth as though to say something. Beradino reckoned Patrese was wondering why he was going round the houses this way.

He had to ask Manuwai directly. To delay any further would look suspicious.

'So,' Beradino said, 'last night. You saw the man who killed her?'

It was a leading question, of course, with the implicit assumption that Mara's killer was male. That was the best Beradino could do. And if Manuwai said Mara's killer was a woman, Beradino would be sunk.

It felt to Beradino as though empires could have risen and fallen in the time before Manuwai answered, though he knew too that it was probably less than a second.

Manuwai shook his head. 'Did na see him.'

Beradino blinked quickly; relief.

Manuwai, worried this might not constitute sufficient 'help', looked imploringly at Patrese. Patrese nodded in as encouraging a way as he could.

'You told us a few minutes back that you *did* see him,' Beradino said.

'I see his car.'

Lord have mercy, Beradino thought.

'What kind of car?'

Manuwai smiled, eager to please. 'Toyota Camry. Silver.'

Beradino kept his face pluperfectly blank. 'You're sure?'

'Sure. I like cars. Wanna Corvette one day. Wanna Z06, yellow.'

'You didn't catch the plate?'

'No. I sorry.'

'How come you saw the car, but not the driver?'

'I wen go take leak, 'cos I drink too much coffee. Whole thermos, ya know. Keep me warm, keep me wake. Make me go pipi. I come back, silver Camry's there, right outside apartment. I wait a bit. Den I hungry, so I go get eat. I come back, car gone. Den I see da fire, so I dial 911.'

'You were the one who called it in?'

'Sure. She dying in dere. But dey get dere too late. An' she dead. It not right.'

Beradino gestured with his head to Patrese: *outside*. They stepped into the corridor.

'He seems on the level,' Beradino said.

'I think so.'

'You know the Camry's the most popular car in America?'

'Is it?'

'Read it the other day. Sell half a million a year. And silver's one of the most common colors for any car. Some boo-ya about good resale values.'

'So looking for a specific silver Camry's gonna be like trying to find a particular yellow cab in New York City?'

'You got it.'

'Well, it is what it is. What do we do with him?'

'We could bust him for breaking the restraining order, but . . .'

'But what's the point?'

'Exactly. She's dead. He's not going to harm her now, is he?'

The quicker Beradino got Manuwai away from Pittsburgh, of course, the less likely he was to pipe up and remember anything that might point to Jesslyn's involvement. And Patrese had to fulfill his half of the bargain he'd struck with Manuwai.

Letting Manuwai off suited them both, even if each knew only the half of it.

Patrese pulled out his cell and rang Summer McBride's extension.

'Hey,' she said. 'You want his print results?' They'd sent Manuwai's prints up to her for comparison against those she'd found in Mara's apartment.

'No, I just rang to hear your voice.'

'Flattery will get you everywhere.'

'That's what people keep telling me. Yes, print results, please.'

'No match. Unless he wore gloves the whole time, he wasn't in there.'

'Thanks.'

'No problem. By the way, the tests came back on that pill.'

'Yeah?'

'MDMA.'

'You're sure?'

'I popped it myself, and felt love for everyone. Even you.'

Patrese laughed. 'Very scientific. Thanks, Sums.'

Patrese ended the call and went back into the interview room.

'Dere gonna be funeral fo her?' Manuwai said. 'I like fo go.'

'Go back to Honolulu, Alika,' Patrese said, not unkindly. 'Find someone real.'

(TRANSLATED FROM THE ORIGINAL ARABIC)

SAMEERA BAYOUMI (SB): Mustafa, have you seen the news? Another burning! Have the police been in contact with you?

MUSTAFA BAYOUMI (MB): No, I haven't seen the news. Who is it?

SB: That actress. The one who killed her babies.

MB: Mara Slinger?

SB: That's her, yes.

MB: No, nothing from the police. Maybe they've finally realized it's not me.

SB: Well, for killing those lambs, she deserves it. You remember your Koran? No soul shall bear the burden of another.* Murder must be answered by murder. 'Retaliation is prescribed for you in the matter of the slain.' What kind of country are we living in, Mustafa, that people do these things?

*Translator's footnote: According to the Koran, humans don't carry the sins of Adam and Eve, the original sin which prompted the Fall of Man, but only their own good and evil deeds. Therefore, the purest state a human can achieve is that of a newborn baby, who's sinless and whose heart lives in a state of complete submission to Allah.

The prophet Muhammad said that every child is born in a state of natural inclination to worship Allah alone. Before its earthly incarnation, every human soul converses with Allah. 'And whenever your Lord brings forth their offspring from the loins of the children of Adam, He calls upon them to bear witness about themselves. "Am I not your Lord?" – to which they answer "Yes, indeed, we bear witness."' Babies are born with this original pledge to Allah in their subconscious, and parents must nurture that spirituality into remembrance.

MB: Don't start that again, Mother. I have to go now, or I won't make it in time.

SB: Where are you going?

MB: The hardware store. I've got to get some stuff to put the shelves up.

SB: Oh yes, I remember. Will I see you for dinner?

MB: Of course. As always.

Wednesday, November 24th , 9:37 a.m.

'This is WDVE, 102.5 on your FM dial.'

WDVE was the city's most popular radio station, heavy on classic rock, comedy sketches and sports news; aimed squarely and unashamedly at men under the age of thirty-five, in other words.

'You listen to this stuff?' Beradino asked in mock horror.

'Sure do, Grandpa. Some of us think music didn't end in 1812, you know.'

Patrese was driving them through the snow to the airport, from where they'd go separate directions. Patrese was heading west to LA, where he'd interview Victor Guilaroff, Mara's agent; the man whom Howard Negley had accused of stealing from her. Beradino was traveling south, to Mississippi. Among Mara's boxes of hate mail (which she'd kept in her bedroom, and which had therefore escaped the fire) were some from the Magnolia State which were so virulent and unrestrained that Beradino wanted to check them out himself.

That Jesslyn was originally from Mississippi, and that in the past she'd fled home more than once when upset, was of course purely a coincidence.

Both men also felt they'd benefit from a change of scene,

no matter how short. They'd be away for at least a couple of days, as tomorrow was Thanksgiving. The world and his wife were traveling across America. Patrese and Beradino had both had to pull rank to get themselves on the flights today, but there was no way they'd make it back to Pittsburgh till Friday at the earliest.

They'd left a clear chain of command in the incident room, Boone had promised to lend any help he could, and of course they'd be in constant contact both with North Shore and each other.

Patrese left the TransAm in the long-term parking lot. In the terminal, they checked into their respective flights, had a coffee, went airside, shook hands, and made for their respective gates.

11:44 a.m.

Crammed on to the last spare seat in his departure lounge, hard up between a wall and a man who spilled over into Beradino's space in cascades of drooping cream flesh, Beradino tried to stop his mind from racing.

He reminded himself what he knew for sure.

He knew that Mara's murder was the first to have occurred since he'd discovered that Jesslyn had lost her job at Muncy; and that now Jesslyn was nowhere to be found.

He knew that all four murders had taken place since Jesslyn's dismissal.

He knew that Jesslyn hadn't been on shift at the burger bar when any of the first three victims had been killed, as he'd obtained a copy of her records from Kevin, the spotty, insolent manager. He'd told Kevin he needed them for a tribunal, before slipping him a hundred bucks for his trouble and another hundred for his silence.

He knew that seismic events, such as being fired, are often the trigger for people to start acting out violent and traumatic emotions which they've previously kept hidden.

He knew that Jesslyn's views on crime and punishment were strong, inflexible and shot through with her religious beliefs.

That was what he knew for sure.

Here was what he *didn't* know.

He didn't know why Jesslyn had selected any of the victims bar Mara, apart from the point she'd made in her e-mail about them being hypocrites. Far as he knew, she'd never even met Redwine. She *had* met Kohler a couple of times, most recently at the funeral of Patrese's parents, and each time she'd been thrilled just to be in the presence of a real-life bishop. And Yuricich had been as convinced of Mara's guilt as Jesslyn herself was. It wasn't his fault that Mara had been freed on appeal.

He didn't know why Jesslyn had cut Yuricich's tongue out.

He didn't know what Jesslyn meant with the pink granite pebbles, or where she'd got them from.

He didn't know why Jesslyn, the most God-fearing person he'd ever met, had destroyed the crucifix and icons in Saint Paul Cathedral.

The answers, he reckoned, must lie not just in Jesslyn's obsession with Mara, but somewhere deeper, somewhere in her Baptist preacher upbringing. Find Jesslyn, and he'd find out *why*.

Finding her, however, was the problem.

4:51 p.m. (Pacific Time)

Patrese was drenched in sweat by the time he reached Guilaroff's office at the Beverley Hills end of Wilshire Boulevard. His flight out of Pittsburgh had been delayed by snow on the runway, but Los Angeles was enjoying an unseasonable heatwave. Even late in the afternoon, the temperature was still in the mid-eighties, a thick, smothering heat beating up at Patrese from asphalt and windshields.

Patrese gave his name to the receptionist before slumping on to a sofa shaped like Mae West's lips. The air-conditioning vent was right above his head, and he shifted position slightly to get as much cold air as possible. It felt like a shower.

'Hey! Franco Patrese!'

Guilaroff came striding into the lobby, arms open wide as though he were a game show host expecting applause. The little Patrese recalled about Guilaroff from school – Patrese had been a couple of grades ahead – was of Guilaroff as a short, chubby, nondescript kind of boy. Now, fifteen or so years on, Guilaroff had turned into . . . well, a short, chubby, nondescript kind of man.

Patrese got up and put out his hand.

'Good to see you again, Victor.'

'Great to see *you*, man.' Guilaroff ignored the handshake, and went straight for the hug. Patrese patted his shoulder with a certain bemusement. He and Guilaroff hadn't been friends at school, and they'd probably never have seen each other again had it not been for the coincidence of their respective involvements in Mara's life, and yet here Guilaroff was, greeting him like the prodigal son.

'Terrible business about Mara,' Guilaroff continued, untangling himself. '*Terrible* business. Help you any way I can. But listen, it's nearly five o'clock, it's Thanksgiving tomorrow, and the office ain't a place to be on a day like this. Why don't we do this thing over a brewski? I know a great little bar round the corner. What you say, bubbaloo?'

Patrese thought fast. Some people are more forthcoming with the police when they're uncomfortable and disorientated; others are more prone to let things slip when they're relaxed. He reckoned that Guilaroff, used to endless meetings of bluff and brinkmanship, would fall into the second category. Besides, Patrese needed a beer badly enough to qualify for a remake of *Ice Cold in Alex*.

'Sure,' Patrese said.

5:28 p.m. (Pacific Time)

Hollywood agents take movie stars and bigwig producers to the Polo Lounge or The Four Seasons, but they sure as hell don't take out-of-town cops there. They take them to the Coronet in West Hollywood, where the lights are low and the booth walls high.

Guilaroff clinked his bottle of Coors against Patrese's.

'So. Mara. Like I said, help you any way I can.'

'What did you do for her?'

'I was her agent. I represented her.'

'Which involved what?'

'Sending her scripts, pitching her to studios, negotiating her contracts, making sure she was happy with her career path, holding her hand . . .'

'Metaphorically, or literally?'

'Strictly metaphorically. Rule one: never fuck the client.'

Like Mara would have given you the time of day, Patrese thought.

'And she paid you – what? A retainer? A salary? A commission?'

'Fifteen per cent.'

Patrese whistled. 'Nice rate.'

'I'm worth every dime, I assure you.'

Patrese wasn't sure, but he thought he remembered Guilaroff as having been on the end of some nasty bullying at Sacred Heart one time; nasty enough to have gotten the police involved, let alone the school board. That kind of thing could work one of two ways. Either you let it destroy you, or you nursed the hatred, moved town, reinvented yourself and worked towards success with a furious ambition.

'How did you get to work for her?'

'Excuse me?'

'Hey, I don't mean it as an insult. I'm just curious. How do agent and star meet?'

'Oh. OK. The agency I work for, she was with us already. The guy handling her retired; got burned out, went to Montana, Idaho, some place like that. I'd met her a couple of times, and she liked me.'

'This was all before her court case, obviously.'

'Sure.'

'So you must have been young back then.'

'Twenty-four years old, when I first started working with her.'

'Vote of confidence in your ability.'

'I guess she saw I was talented. And she liked that I was from Pittsburgh, you know? Steeltowners stick together, and all that. So there we are.'

'Your fifteen per cent. How does that work? When she got paid, who got the money first? Her? You? Both of you?'

'Me. The agency. Everything came to me first; that's standard.'

'Then you deducted your percentage and transferred the remainder to her?'

'You got it.'

'There can't have been that much coming in when she was in jail, right?'

'Not true. A lot of back-end stuff – you know, payments tied to a movie's gross – kept coming in from things she'd done earlier in her career. Complex stuff. Hollywood accounting procedures make rocket science look like the two times table.'

'Would you say she was financially savvy?'

Guilaroff cocked his head slightly, trying to work out where this was going.

'How do you mean?'

'I mean, you said this stuff is complex. Was she on your ass the whole time, questioning this and that about her finances, or did she just accept what you sent her?'

'She trusted me, so she knew what I sent her was correct.'

Interesting, Patrese thought. That wasn't what he'd asked. He swigged his Coors.

'Her husband reckons you were ripping her off.'

Guilaroff's eyes flashed wide. 'Her husband's talking shit.'

'You don't sound surprised to hear this.'

'I'm not. He rang me personally one time to tell me just that.'

'How did you react?'

'I told him we had better lawyers than him, and if he wanted to find that out for sure, all he had to do was repeat it.'

'And did he?'

'No.'

'What would you say if I wanted to take a look at your accounts?'

Guilaroff laughed. 'I'd say you're out of your jurisdiction here, you haven't got a warrant, and you probably don't know your way round a balance sheet anyway.'

Asshole, Patrese thought. He kept his expression and tone neutral, though. Just two old school buddies having a beer.

'And I'd say you're right on all three. But say I could find a way round all those, what then? You'd be happy for me to look at your accounts?'

'My accounts in general, no. We deal with big stars, and they don't like people knowing how much they have. But Mara, now she's dead? Sure.'

It was the smart answer, Patrese knew. It made Guilaroff look co-operative, but they both knew it would take weeks for a warrant to work its way from Pennsylvania to California, and months while Guilaroff and his lawyers used every stalling trick in their no doubt extensive playbook.

Still. Playbook meant game, and game meant tactics.

'Great. I'll get on it the moment I'm home.'

'When you heading back?'

'Friday. No flights tomorrow.'

'You're gonna miss Thanksgiving?'

Patrese shrugged. 'Demands of the job. My family understand. Yours?'

'Mine what?'

'Your folks. They still live in Pittsburgh? You come back home a lot?'

'My folks still live there, yeah. Same old house as they ever did. But I haven't been back in, like, forever. Eight, nine years, I reckon. My folks come see me here from time to time – not this year, this year they're with my sister in Michigan – but I don't go back there. Home is here, my man.'

'You don't like Pittsburgh?'

Guilaroff was silent for a second. 'Honestly?'

'Honestly.'

'I *hate* it. Why do you think I came out here? I got sunshine, money, chicks.'

'Why do you hate Pittsburgh?'

'I hate the weather. I hate the people. I hated school.'

'Sacred Heart?'

Guilaroff finished his Coors and gestured to the bartender for two more.

'I wasn't like you, Franco. I remember you from school,

man. First-choice running back for, what, two years in a row? Three?'

'Three.'

'I remember you on the grid. Whole school used to come watch, you know? Every time school was on offense, we didn't look for the quarterback. We looked for you.'

Patrese remembered it too; the handoffs from the quarterback, the heart-pounding rush into the tunnel of bodies in midfield, ducking, weaving, muscles working faster than thought itself as he'd jink towards the glimmering chinks through the darkness, run to daylight, run to daylight, as though the noise from the crowd was physically prising open the gaps in front of him, and then out into the open prairie and the long run for home, defenders floundering in his slipstream as the crowd rose and stamped and his teammates thrust their arms skywards, Go, Franco, go, go, go.

Nothing else in his life had ever come close.

'I was just a nobody,' Guilaroff continued. 'Bet you don't even remember me from school? Before this whole thing came up?'

'Sure I remember you.'

'Really?'

'I recognized your name when I heard it. I recognized your face in the photo.'

'Photo?' Guilaroff looked puzzled. 'What photo?'

'The photo we found in Kohler's desk.'

'No one told me about this.' Guilaroff sat forward, his face flushed. 'What the hell? What kind of photo?'

'You got something to hide?'

'No. No, not at all. But . . . It sounds weird. What would *you* say, if you found your photo in the desk of a man you hadn't seen for fifteen years?'

'I did.'

'You did what?'

'Find my photo in his desk. And yours, and hundreds of others, kids from Sacred Heart. Normal photos, yearbook photos. Someone should have been in touch with you earlier; I'm sorry. I thought we checked out everyone involved, to see if they knew anything about his murder. You know he was murdered, right?'

'Yeah. I read about it.'

'How did it make you feel?'

Guilaroff dug the heels of his hands into his eyes and rubbed hard.

'I hated that school, Franco. I was unhappy, and I got no support from anybody who should have given it to me, Kohler included. For a man of God, he sure didn't behave in an especially Christian way. So I didn't feel anything when I heard. OK?'

'I get you.'

'If you ask me, school's bullshit, deep down. Take someone like me. Total nobody at school. Look at me now. I do well for myself, I reckon. I do more than well. What you are at school don't determine shit.'

Patrese wondered what Guilaroff was implying, if anything? That it worked in reverse too? That it was a fall from grace for someone like Patrese, one of the school demi-gods, to be now eking out a public-sector salary as a steeltown cop?

Guilaroff gestured round him. 'You should come here too, Franco. To LA. Plenty of opportunities for a guy like you. Hollywood homicide. Beverly Hills cop. I know some guys on the force here, I could help you out. You interested?'

Patrese shook his head.

'Your demons don't vanish just 'cos you run from them, Victor,' he said.

338

Thursday, November 25th. 2:29 p.m. (Central Time)

Beradino's life was neatly parceled into a triptych: good, nondescript and bad.

Good was the view from his window; open roads and rows of crops marching out of Yazoo City like ants to the horizon, and the start of the Mississippi delta.

Nondescript was his room. Bog-standard chain motel: neat, clean, less than no soul.

Bad was pretty much everything else.

He'd trawled Yazoo City, hoping against hope that he'd see Jesslyn walking down the street, or eating in one of the restaurants she'd taken him to on their trips here, or praying in church, or . . . or anything, really.

He'd rung Jesslyn's sister LeAnn, who lived outside the city with her husband and what seemed like a million kids. The conversation had told Beradino everything he needed to know, and nothing he'd hoped for.

'Hey, LeAnn,' he'd said. 'It's Mark, your brother-in-law.'

'Hey, Mark! Happy Thanksgiving, honey.'

'And to you.'

'Bet it's cold up there in Punxsutawney, hey?'

'Matter of fact, I'm in Mississippi.'

'You are? You nearby? Come on over. We got food for plenty.'

Which had meant Jesslyn almost certainly wasn't there. If she had been, and if she'd been lying low, LeAnn wouldn't have invited him over.

'I'm too far away, I'm afraid. I'm in McComb. Working some interstate case.'

'On Thanksgiving? Hope they're giving you double time. It's not right. Not on Thanksgiving. How's my sister? She home alone? I rang her earlier, but no answer. She never calls, she never writes . . . you tell her not to forget her family, you hear? Spending all that time with those whackjobs inside must be messin' with her head.'

LeAnn was many things, but an actress, never. No way had Jesslyn got in touch with her since Monday, let alone confided in her.

Beradino had been sorely tempted to leap in the car and go over there anyway, with due regard for how long a notional journey from McComb would have taken. In normal circumstances, he could think of few things he'd rather do than be surrounded with love and laughter while stuffing his face – and in LeAnn's house, your face stayed stuffed, most of all on Thanksgiving, when you could hardly see over your plate once you'd taken your share of turkey, cranberry sauce, stuffing, gravy, winter squash, sweet potatoes, hominy, green bean casserole, cornbread, pumpkin pie and pecan pie – but there was no way he could go there and pretend everything was OK.

The hotel was doing a special dinner, too, but that was hardly the same. Besides, he'd be eating on his own, and Thanksgiving was all about family. Other diners would either pity him or invite him over, and he didn't want either.

He remembered reading somewhere that the name *Yazoo* came from the Native American for 'river of death.' It seemed bitterly appropriate.

340

Friday, November 26th. 3:49 p.m.

Patrese and Beradino met back at Pittsburgh International Airport, by the statue of Franco Harris, the Steelers' greatest ever running back and the man after whom Patrese had been named.

Franco Harris Patrese, that was his full name, and damn proud of it he was too.

Harris – the original Harris – had in his prime looked like Othello, with fierce dark eyes and an aquiline nose. He'd had a black father and an Italian mother (they'd met in Europe at the end of the war), and as a result had been wildly popular with Pittsburgh's Italian population, who'd dubbed themselves 'Franco's Italian Army' and worn army helmets with his number, 32 – the one Patrese had worn through high school and college – painted on them.

Patrese's father had been just about the biggest fan in all the Italian Army; such a fan, in fact, that the day Patrese had been born, Alberto had been not at his wife's bedside but a thousand miles away in New Orleans, watching the Steelers win their first SuperBowl and Harris be named MVP.

Waiting by the statue, Patrese thought about Harris, and football, and Pop. He thought about how Pop hadn't been

341

there when he'd been born, and hadn't been there when Patrese had needed him most; and he'd thought about how the first had never bothered Patrese and the second always would.

They drove back into town. The road snaked through rolling hills and countryside, past outlying towns and hints of creeping urbanization, but with no sign of Pittsburgh itself. You can see Manhattan pretty much all the way in from JFK; but here, a few miles from Pittsburgh, you could be anywhere.

Then they dived down into the Fort Pitt Tunnel, drove through half a mile of claustrophobic darkness, no sense of the outside world, and wham! Pittsburgh in all its glory; city, skyscrapers and bridges suddenly exploding into view as if they'd materialized from nowhere.

There's no city in America, perhaps the world, which has an entrance so thrilling. Each time Patrese came through it, it was like a rebirth.

That was what they needed right now, he suddenly realized. A rebirth, a reboot; an entirely new approach to the Human Torch. They had to accept that everything they'd assumed might be wrong.

They had to start again.

5:10 p.m.

'Of all the victims, which one was most likely to have been killed?' Patrese asked.

'What do you mean?'

'I mean, who had most enemies?'

Beradino thought for a moment. 'Mara, I guess.'

'Yeah. Mara, by miles. Half the country hated her, it seems sometimes.'

'So?'

'You remember when Boone first did his profile? Remember what you accused him of? You said he was making the evidence fit the theory.'

'Yes, I remember.'

'That's what *we've* been doing. We've been chasing Bayoumi, and Muslims, and wacko letter-writers down South, and this, that and the other, and we've got *nowhere*. We've got to go back, do it the other way round. Evidence first, then theory. And which victim has the most potential evidence? Mara.'

'So what do you propose to do?'

'Turn her life upside down.'

'We've done that already.'

'Not all of it.'

'What have we missed out, then?'

'Muncy.' Beradino opened his mouth, but Patrese cut him off. 'I know what you're going to say, but hear me out. I just thought of it, driving through the tunnel, coming up here into the city. I wondered whether that was what Mara felt when she was released. You're used to walls, darkness, no view of the outside world, and then in an instant everything's in your face, there's a million ways you can go. System over-load. So I thought of Mara and Muncy, and that made me think in turn: where better to look for clues to a murder than in prison? And I know you already asked Jesslyn. But she's a guard. I bet she doesn't know a fraction of what goes on in there.'

'She knows *everything*. She rules the roost there. And she said Mara was a model prisoner; never got into trouble, sat in her cell, read her scriptures, had no beef with anyone. Too much of a chicken to take on anyone who could fight back, you ask me.'

'Well, double-checking can't do any harm.'

'You're wasting your time, Franco.'

'It's my time to waste. Let's find out what the brass *don't* want us to know.'

'How? You want to infiltrate? You want to go undercover as an inmate? It's an all-female prison, Franco. What the heck you think this is? *Some Like It Hot*?'

'Not infiltrate.'

'Then what?'

'Use someone already there.'

'A prisoner?'

'Of course.'

'Yeah, that'll work. 'Cos prisoners really love cops, don't they?'

'They do if we find an incentive.'

Monday, November 29th. 9:23 a.m.

The incentive Patrese had in mind needed both Amberin and Hellmore to OK it, so he had to wait till Monday to pitch it to them.

They met in Amberin's office in the courthouse. Beradino had told Patrese several times this was a non-starter, but Patrese was determined, and Beradino knew he couldn't keep pouring cold water on the plan without Patrese eventually getting suspicious of his motives. So Beradino went along too, and hoped that either Amberin or Hellmore would nix it.

Coffee poured and biscuits offered, Patrese outlined his idea.

Background first. Mara had told Patrese that she'd made one particular friend in Muncy; an inmate called Madison Setterstrom. So if there *was* a connection between these murders and something that had happened to Mara in prison, Setterstrom was the most likely person to know something about it.

Thing was, Setterstrom wouldn't tell the cops directly. Not in a month of Sundays. Beradino had pointed out that cops weren't flavor of the month in prisons, and in Setterstrom's case they could magnify that tenfold. She was doing life for killing a cop during a convenience store robbery, and had said at the trial that her only regret was that she hadn't taken out more of the fuckers. Her exact words.

The admission had scuppered her 'not guilty' plea, but that was another matter.

So the cops had to get Setterstrom to talk without letting her know she was talking, as it were. The best way – perhaps the only way – was to get her to share a cell with someone who'd prize the information out of her, over a period of weeks or months if that was what it took, and then report it all back to them.

Of course, that someone would need an incentive.

That was why Patrese was here. He wanted Shaniqua to be their informant.

Shaniqua was a damn sight more intelligent than people gave her credit for, he said. She'd be good at winkling out information without making it obvious. She could talk, exchange confidences, do all the things women did so well. The plan would never have worked in a male prison; put two men in a cell together, and two years down the line they'd still be discussing beer, football and sex.

In return, as the carrot, the incentive, Patrese wanted Amberin to downgrade Shaniqua's charge from murder to voluntary manslaughter.

Voluntary manslaughter was the most Patrese knew he'd get. There wasn't a prosecutor in Pennsylvania – in the entire country, in fact – who'd agree to involuntary manslaughter, the next step down, in any case where a firearm had been used.

If Amberin agreed to voluntary manslaughter, and Shaniqua accepted that, they'd be in business. It might all come to nothing, but at least Patrese would have tried, gone out there and done something rather than just chase his tail round headquarters.

What Patrese didn't say was that downgrading the charge would also help Shaniqua, and that was the least he felt she deserved.

Amberin listened to the plan, all the way through, without saying a word.

'Absolutely not,' she said when Patrese had finished.

Hellmore jumped in. 'Why not?'

'We went through all the options first time round. What's changed between then and now? Nothing. So the charge stays the same.'

'You've got no sympathy with Shaniqua?'

'Personally, or professionally?'

'Both.'

She blew her cheeks out. 'Personally, yes, a little. Sounds like Weaver was a terrible man. But no one forced Shaniqua to be with him. No one held a gun to her head and said, "You must be with this man."'

'Well, he did. Weaver did.'

'So *she* says. That's a matter for the jury. My job's to uphold the law, not be some spokeswoman for the sisterhood. So professionally, no, no sympathy. Sorry. I can't afford to.'

'Can I try and persuade you?' Patrese said.

She laughed. 'Sure. I'd like to see you try.'

'Me too,' Hellmore said. 'She's a hardass, Franco, in case you ain't noticed.'

'OK,' Patrese said. 'Let's start at the beginning. Self-defense is a complete defense against any charge of murder, isn't it?'

'Yes.'

'Now, I know this case isn't self-defense pure and simple.'

'No.'

'But isn't it also true that if a person acts in the honest but unreasonable belief that self-defense justifies the killing, then this is a deliberate homicide committed without criminal malice – in other words, manslaughter?'

347

'Yes.'

'And that the word "malice" is used in the definition of murder where the act is both an intentional killing, and without legal excuse or mitigation?'

'Franco, you been raiding Grisham's backlist again?' Hellmore said.

'Yes,' Amberin said, in answer to the original question.

'Well, that was Shaniqua's situation. She thought she had to kill Weaver to prevent him hurting her or Trent. She was wrong, but she still held that belief honestly.'

'Or she'd just had enough and thought this was an easy way out?'

'It wasn't like that.'

'Oh, you were *there* when it happened? It was the kind of argument Shaniqua said they'd had a million times before, if I remember rightly. She hadn't felt the need to blow Weaver's brains out on any of those occasions, had she?'

Probably not the need, Patrese thought, but almost certainly the urge.

'Come on, Amberin,' said Hellmore. 'You know well as I do that women are much more likely to kill a male partner than they are to kill anyone else, especially when that partner's abusive. You know too that recidivism rates for such crimes are extraordinarily low.'

'I'm not prosecuting Shaniqua on what she might do in future, Freddie. I'm prosecuting her on what she did in the past, on what she's done already.'

'I know that. But look at it from her point of view.'

'That's your job, not mine.'

'Damn it, Amberin,' Patrese snapped.

She rounded on him, eyes wide with fury. 'Don't you *dare* talk to me like that.'

'Then *listen*. What happened in that bedroom just before Shaniqua shot Weaver, you can't treat that like, I don't know,

348

like an altercation in a bar between two guys who can't handle their beer. It wasn't a fair fight. She's smaller, she's weaker, she's scared for her son. She *can't* walk away.'

'She could call the police.'

'In Homewood? On a domestic violence charge? Would you? Ghostbusters would come quicker, let's face it.'

Amberin was silent. Patrese and Hellmore exchanged glances; first blood to their cause? Patrese hurried on, anxious not to lose momentum.

'So what's Shaniqua supposed to do? Wait till he hits her again? Or *stabs* her? Or *shoots* her? She does any of those, and all she's agreeing to is murder by installment. Her murder, and probably her son's too, if he's a witness. So we come back to the start. Was Shaniqua's fear of Weaver correct? On this occasion, probably not. But was it *reasonable*? Yes. And that's what matters. That's what matters in law, isn't it?'

She was silent. Wavering, Patrese felt; he *hoped*.

He'd done the heartstrings. Hellmore weighed in with the pragmatics.

'Come on, Amberin. We both want to maximize our opportunities here. You can't be sure a murder charge'll be sound, can you? But a manslaughter charge will stick, I bet you that. And I'll take voluntary manslaughter like a shot, you know that. You've got a good conviction rate. You want to jeopardize that?'

Another pause, and then Amberin smiled. 'Franco, you should be a lawyer.'

'I'm presuming that's a compliment.'

She laughed. 'I guess it's normally the most heinous of insults – sort of like "You should be a realtor" or "You should be a politician" – but in this instance, yes, it *is* meant as a compliment. All right. I'll do it. I hope it works out for you.'

Beradino's face wouldn't have shamed a veteran of Texas Hold 'Em.

Tuesday, November 30th. 4:15 p.m.

Patrese went to Muncy alone. It was both his choice – he figured his chances of persuading Shaniqua were better on his own, as he reckoned he'd had something of a rapport with her – and Beradino's too. Beradino had said he'd had a few run-ins over Jesslyn's pay scale with Anderson Thornhill, the prison governor, and would therefore prefer it if Patrese didn't mention his name. Best to keep Beradino and Jesslyn out of this altogether, they'd agreed.

The journey to Muncy was almost all interstate, and Patrese had his brain as well as his car in cruise control as the signs rolled past the windows: I-79 North, I-80 East, I-180 West, Route 405 South. All four compass points. He found that oddly pleasing.

The final road into Muncy, lined with maple trees, was unexpectedly, disarmingly tranquil. The limestone administrative block, all faded charm and white cupola, could have been the heart of a small rural college; not an Ivy League hothouse, perhaps, but somewhere in the second or third divisions, where the pace of life was gentler and the students probably much more content.

Patrese pulled into the parking lot, where he could see

things that shattered the illusion; things like fences, razor wire, security cameras, even searchlights.

His status as a police officer didn't exempt him from the usual searches, which in an odd way reassured him. Visitors were searched not just to stop them deliberately bringing in contraband, but also to be sure they'd got nothing on their person which could be used as a weapon if they were taken hostage.

So Patrese surrendered his Ruger Blackhawk, his keys, the change in his pocket, his cellphone and what seemed like half the accoutrements without which he, along with 99 per cent of his fellow Americans, couldn't get from dawn to dusk and back again.

Thornhill was a thin man with eyeglasses and a studious air which appeared much more suited to the college campus of Patrese's alternative Muncy than the realities of a state correctional institute. He wasn't especially happy about Patrese's request, though this seemed to be more of a resentment at police interference than any great concerns that Patrese would in any way harm the running of the prison.

Patrese understood Thornhill's attitude, and didn't hold it against him. Most police officers would be similarly ambivalent if a prison governor marched into *their* office and started trying to shift *their* personnel around.

Thornhill made some noises about the difficulty of housing a remand prisoner like Shaniqua with a convicted killer such as Setterstrom, but found a solution to this in the very next sentence. Prisoners were always being moved; sometimes for their own safety, sometimes through sheer weight of numbers. The authorities could think up several plausible excuses for unlikely pairings.

Curiously, perhaps, Thornhill didn't want to know *why* Patrese wanted Shaniqua moved. Perhaps he'd guessed. Perhaps he simply preferred not to get involved, and figured

351

that Patrese must have decent reasons if he was asking in the first place. If Shaniqua agreed to it, he said, that was fine with him. Patrese wondered whether Thornhill was this hands-off in all aspects of his governorship. Maybe all those women cooped up together frightened him.

Patrese met Shaniqua in the visitors' room. It took him a moment to recognize her. It wasn't her features that had changed, but her expression; a wariness to the set of her jaw, a deadness in her eyes. Three and a half decades in the ghetto hadn't knocked the sparkle out of her, but a couple of months in jail had.

'My favorite detective,' she said.

'What's my competition?'

She laughed. 'Not great. Now, why you here? You ain't come four hours from the 'Burgh for the good of your health.'

'I've come with an offer from the prosecutor.'

Shaniqua hissed with her tongue against the back of her teeth. 'The fuck that bitch offerin' me? Rat poison?'

'Plea bargain.'

'Plea bargain?'

'She's prepared to downgrade your charge. If you plead guilty to voluntary manslaughter, she'll drop the murder charge.'

'The fuck does that mean?'

'It means that instead of facing life behind bars, you'd be looking at four and a half to seven. You behave yourself, you'll be out earlier.'

'And in return?'

He smiled. 'How do you know there's an "in return"?'

'Don't shit me, Detective. Ain't no such thing as a free lunch. Everybody here knows that. Shit, half of them are in here for tryin' to prove there *is* a free goddamn lunch, one way and the other.'

'OK. In return, we want you to get information from

352

another inmate, and we want to put you in the same cell as her.'

Shaniqua regarded Patrese levelly for a few moments.

'I know what you're thinkin',' she said.

'What am I thinking?'

'You're thinkin' I was gonna say to you straight off, fuck that, I ain't doin' that, I ain't no fuckin' snitch.'

Patrese shook his head. 'No. I wasn't thinking that.'

'For real?'

'That's what I'd have expected most people to do. But I don't think you're most people. Which is why I want you to do this.'

'Well, I figure you ain't a bad guy – shit, by the standards of the police' – she pronounced it almost as two words, *poh-lease* – 'you're practically Captain America. So I figure you must have a good reason for aksin' me.'

'I do.'

Patrese explained about Mara, and Madison Setterstrom, and what they were looking for – which was to say, they didn't really *know* what they were looking for, so all they wanted Shaniqua to do was get in there, get to know Madison, don't push too hard, but try and become friends with her and get her to open up slowly, gradually, naturally, unsuspectingly. Put that way, it sounded easy. It might be anything but.

'Deal?' Patrese asked.

Shaniqua shook her head. 'Uh-uh.'

His shoulders slumped. 'Can I ask why not?'

'Sure you can aks. I might even tell you.' She laughed. 'I ain't takin' no plea bargain from no one, for one very simple fuckin' reason. *I didn't do it*. Not murder, not manslaughter, none of that. It was self-defense, end of. That's what happened, that's what I'm pleadin'.' She held her hand up. 'I don't give a fuck it might be the sensible thing to do, to take that skanky old plea bargain. I'm doin' what's right. It's nothin' but a game to them, and I ain't playin'.'

'Please, Shaniqua. Mara didn't do what she was accused of either, I'm sure of it.'

'Don't try that emotional blackmail shit on me. You're better than that.'

'OK. But I wouldn't ask you if it wasn't important.'

'Oh, I'll share a cell with that Madison ho', no problem.'

Patrese felt his forehead knot in confusion. 'You will?'

'Sure. But I ain't pleadin' guilty to no manslaughter. And 'cos I ain't takin' the bargain, I want somethin' else.'

'I'll have to get that authorized,' Patrese said. 'Don't worry. There are procedures for this kind of thing, it won't be a prob—'

'You think I mean *cash*?' Her eyebrows arched like an angry cat. 'You think I'd aks you for dead *presidents*? Shit, Franco. Who the *fuck* you take me for?'

Patrese couldn't remember the last time he'd felt so small. People talk about wanting the ground to swallow them up or being able to rewind time. It was moments like this that Patrese realized these weren't simply figures of speech. He'd rather have run butt naked round Heinz Field than underestimated Shaniqua like that.

He looked at the floor. He couldn't bear to meet her gaze. 'I'm sorry.'

Shaniqua exhaled. 'Accepted. Forget about it.'

'Thank you. So what do you want in return?'

'I want you to keep an eye out for Trent.'

It was on the tip of Patrese's tongue to say 'Is that all?' but he caught himself just in time. He could get away with being crassly insensitive once, but not twice; not with someone as sharp and proud as Shaniqua.

He debated whether to tell her about Trent, Bayoumi and the MDMA.

On one hand, it would show him, Patrese, in a good light, that he'd already tried to show Trent the right path. On the other, it would anger and alarm Shaniqua, and she'd be able to do nothing about either.

For now, at least, he decided not to mention it.

'Of course I will,' he said. 'But why me? Hell, Shaniqua, I'm not even from Homewood. I'm not even black.'

'Exactly.' She wagged her index finger at him. '*Exactly*. Homewood's the damn problem. When you last see a U-Haul movin' someone *into* Homewood? You know the world outside, Franco. You ain't in that Homewood state of mind. You know there's more than the choice between sellin' drugs and workin' at Taco Bell, and you know that choice is only a damn choice if you're not the one havin' to make it.

'I want Trent to respect the law. I want someone to show

him the police don't have to be the enemy all the time. You're a good man, you can show him that. You know why? 'Cos you believe. Maybe you don't even know that yourself, but you *believe*. I know you seen some bad things, I can tell that just by the way you hold yourself, but you wake up each mornin' believin' today'll be better than yesterday and worse than tomorrow. You do, don'tcha? And you can't put a price on that.

'Don't get me wrong. JK's a good man too – you know JK, the pastor who's lookin' after Trent? – he's a helluva good man. But he's got a whole heap of boys to look after. Will Trent be special to him? No. He can't be. Shit, Franco, I don't want you to adopt the little man or shit like that. Just keep an eye on him now and then till I get out. And that ain't gonna be in four to seven on no goddamn plea bargain. That's gonna be when the jury acquit my ass first off.

'Lemme tell you somethin', Franco. The other night in here, I made myself a promise. I promised myself I ain't never gonna love another man again. Every man I ever loved, they're all dead, or they're in jail, so they might as well be dead, 'cos these prisons kill your ass quicker than rat poison. And why are they inside? Because of bullshit, man, over kids' stuff. "You call me this, I call you that." It's all bullshit.

'But Trent's different. He's my *son*, man. I don't have no choice about lovin' him. You have kids? No? Then you don't understand. You don't, not properly. The moment you become a daddy, you'll understand. You'll understand you can't *not* love your kids. Every day, if I don't get up and say a prayer, I can't make it. And I say that prayer for him, for Trent, no one else.

'And I tell him, he better not be a gangbanger. Not now, not ever. I'm gonna hurt him if he is. They better not give him nothin', he better not do nothin' for them. I told him,

"I know some of your friends are dealers. You can talk with them, but don't let me catch you hangin' on the corner where they sell. I done struggled too hard to try to take care of you. I'm not gonna let you throw your life away." That's what I told him. But I know how hard it is. Boys don't become gangbangers 'cos they're bored after school and need somethin' to do. Shit no. Gangs ain't no fuckin' *playgroup*. You seen them toolin' up for a rumble, ain'tcha? They goin' to *war*, man. They goin' to fuckin' *war*, and it's bullshit, like every war ever is. Some of those kids wanna die, Franco; they wanna be remembered as a goddamn fallen soldier, they wanna be put out of their misery, but they sure as hell don't wanna do it themselves, 'cos that's the coward's way out, ain't it? So they go to war hopin' they catch a bullet. They're scared, but they ain't *allowed* to be scared. So what do they do? They dress it up into bullshit about retaliation and honor. But bullshit is bullshit. I always been knowin' that. I refused to be a "straight G", you know, a girl who gets to be a bigshot gang member by doing the things the boys do. Always refused. You know what my biggest fantasy was? You wanna know? You'll laugh your ass off. I'll tell you. I wanted my life to be just like *Ozzie and Harriet*.'

Patrese didn't laugh. He knew all too well what she meant. Gangs are like pedophiles. They draw you in subtly, grooming you, a little here, a little there, carry a message, paint a graffiti tag, run some drugs, take a gun, one step further each time, one more brick in the wall of your resistance knocked away, so it's hard to tell even where the point of no turning back is, let alone whether you've passed it.

By the time you get to the initiation ceremony, the formal acceptance of your status, you're pretty much in anyway. And once you're in, you're in forever, both as far as the law's concerned – penalties and jail time are bumped up almost automatically whenever a crime is considered gang-related – and also in the eyes of your fellow members. Gangs are like lobster pots; there are several ways in, but only one way out, and you don't tend to be around to see that route.

Patrese remembered a case where a couple of Homewood gangbangers had found religion and decided to leave the gang. No way. They'd been executed. They'd had no intention of ratting on their former comrades, but that had made no difference. Patrese had arrested the man who'd shot them, and asked him why he'd done it. 'There's no getting out of this motherfucker,' he'd replied. 'Not Jesus, not nothin' gets you out.'

Cure is therefore pretty much impossible. Once you're in, you're in. The outlook for prevention – catching them before they make it through the door – is slightly better, and slightly better is pretty much all you ever get in Homewood. If Patrese had thought that busting Trent's ass would make a difference, he'd have done it, but he knew that arrest, caution, even jail had never stopped a single person from joining a gang. All they did was make sure the police were on your case too.

There was a wailing from across the other side of the visiting room; a wailing so visceral that every head snapped round towards the source.

Another inmate was with her children – two little girls, hair in bunches, the elder one no more than five – and they were clearly at the end of their visiting time. The debris of their visit – plastic bricks, coloring books, jigsaws, fairy tales – was scattered across the floor, and the little girls were clinging to their mother as if they'd never see her again. She was down on her haunches, the better to clasp them to her, and her entire body was shaking, as though racked not by ordinary sobs but by tremors of the earth itself.

Everyone else in the room stopped their conversations; not just because they could hardly hear themselves think over her wailing, let alone hear someone else talk, but also because it seemed somehow discourteous to the intensity of her agony to do anything other than hold themselves in suspended animation.

Three guards pulled mother from daughters, not without kindness, and ushered the children out of the room. Patrese looked at the guards as they went past. Their faces were blank, absolutely wiped of expression. It was the only way they could deal with it; the only way anyone could deal with it, if you saw it as often as they did.

The woman staggered out of the room in the other direction; back towards her cell, towards another week before the whole thing would be repeated.

'Happens every day,' Shaniqua said. 'You can't touch them afterwards, not for hours sometimes, else they just break down. Just don't say anythin' when they go quiet. We all have it here, man. Everyone just clampin' down on all that shit inside them. If we all overflowed at once, this place'd need a 911 to Noah and his ark.'

Patrese's time with Shaniqua was up soon afterwards. He reclaimed his belongings from security at the entrance, and walked back to his car – a squad car, not the TransAm, so there was at least a vague possibility he might make it back to Pittsburgh without breaking down.

He had a vague, uneasy feeling which took him several minutes to crystallize, and it slightly surprised him when he managed to articulate it. The responsibility Shaniqua had given him, he felt, was the equal of the task he had in solving these murders.

He started the car, turned the headlights on against the darkness, pulled out of the gate, and headed up Route 405. It was a couple of miles to the interstate, no more.

He wasn't halfway there when a massive bang sent the car slewing across the road.

6:04 p.m.

Police driver training had its uses.

Patrese didn't panic. He battered down the lurch of surprise in his stomach, steered into the skid, felt the front wheels regain their grip, and eased the car straight again.

His first thought was that he'd had a blowout, but he scotched that a moment later. The car was still riding smoothly, with none of a flat tire's juddering and listing.

In any case, the bang hadn't sounded like a blowout. It had been more of a metallic report, as though something had struck the car.

A deer? He didn't know if there were any around this area, but animals could be a hazard pretty much anywhere outside built-up areas.

He slowed and pulled towards the side of the road, intending to stop, get out and examine the damage to his car and whatever had hit it. If it was an animal, and it was in pain, he had his sidearm; he'd do the humane thing and put it out of its misery.

He was just coasting to a stop when the car was hit again.

This time, Patrese saw him.

Well, not *him*, exactly. He saw a nondescript sedan with

its headlights off, which was why he hadn't seen it first time round. In the darkness, with all that was happening, he couldn't get any more than a glimpse of the driver, not even enough to tell if it was a man or a woman.

Patrese hit the gas and fishtailed away from him.

He came again, clipping Patrese's offside rear and sending him into a half-spin.

It was bizarre, but Patrese felt as though only half of him was concentrating on driving. The other half was trying to work out who the hell his assailant was.

Was it Patrese in particular he was after? Then he must have been lying in wait for him, either in the Muncy parking lot or in a turning off Route 405 outside.

If that was the case, it begged the question of who knew Patrese was there. Beradino, Amberin and Hellmore were the first three who sprang to mind, followed by a good proportion of the police department and DA's office respectively. Patrese had hardly advertised his trip, but it wasn't a state secret either; anyone in police HQ or the DA's department could have found out about it.

Then, of course, there were the prison staff. They all knew he was here. If they were worried about him finding something, how better to nip it in the bud than try and kill him, or at least give him a warning serious enough to make him think twice?

So the answer to Patrese's question – who knew he was there? – was, give or take, around two hundred people.

The other possibility was that the attack wasn't aimed at him personally at all, and was just dumb chance; some junkie or dipso bombed out of his head and having his own kind of fun.

Patrese corrected the spin. The sedan came again, and this time Patrese was ready for him. He yanked the steering wheel hard over, and caught the sedan flush on the fender. The sedan veered across the road and on to the verge, sending clouds of gravel and dust billowing into the arc of Patrese's lights.

This was fun, Patrese thought; no, more, it was *exhilarating*. He was enjoying it. He felt *alive*. He shouted something; half challenge, half exhortation.

Once more the sedan aimed for him. Patrese hit the brakes, watched as the sedan sailed across his bows, and then he stood on the gas and took the assailant broadside on. The sedan spun across its own axis, off the road and out of sight.

Patrese pulled to a stop, took his Ruger Blackhawk out of the glove compartment, turned the engine off, pocketed the key and got out of the car, low to the ground in case the mystery attacker had other means of finishing what he started.

He crouched by his open door, checking that every bit of him which should be working was. There'd be a few bruises in the morning, possibly some whiplash too, but right now there was far too much adrenalin chasing itself round his body for him to feel any of it.

He counted a minute. No sign. If the attacker had been coming for him, he'd surely have been here by now.

Patrese went across the road in a half-crouch, so as not to give his silhouette against the night sky.

The sedan had come to a halt in a field about thirty yards from the road. Patrese approached it cautiously, trying to keep himself to the driver's blind side.

When he was a couple of yards away, he took a deep breath and launched himself at the car, grabbing the door and yanking it open in one movement.

The sedan was empty.

Patrese looked around, but couldn't see anyone.

For a moment, Patrese thought the attacker might have hit him with the oldest sucker punch in the book – drawing him out so he could make off with his car – but then remembered he'd been smart enough to take the keys out, which automatically set the immobilizer.

That minute Patrese had spent waiting by his car had allowed the attacker to escape.

Ah well, Patrese thought. He had the man's car, and presumably a whole heap of forensic evidence inside.

He called Muncy police and got them to send a trailer for the sedan. They said they didn't have the facilities to test forensics, so he told them to take it all the way back to Pittsburgh. They'd run tests there, and sign off on all the jurisdictional hoo-ha later.

Then Patrese got back into his car, which was a substantially more interesting shape than it had been ten minutes previously, checked that everything which should work did work – as indeed he'd done with his own limbs – and set off for Pittsburgh.

He was shaking half the way back home, and it wasn't with anger.

Wednesday, December 1st. 8:18 a.m.

The sedan which had run Patrese off the road outside Muncy was in the pound the next morning. Patrese rang Beradino, and they agreed to meet down there.

A quick check once the mud had been scraped off the number plate had given them the owner's name and details. He was a Thomas Monroe of Muncy, and he'd reported the car, an ageing Chevy Nova, as having been stolen a couple of hours *before* the attack had taken place.

Muncy PD had checked him out, and said he was genuine. He worked nights as a security guard, and had been on shift when Patrese had been re-enacting the Indy 500.

That the car was from Muncy suggested local involvement. This, if true, would mean that the culprit was either simply some joker who'd picked Patrese at random, or one of the prison staff. If it was the latter, they'd have to have moved very fast, given that the car had been reported stolen two hours before the attack, and that Patrese hadn't been at the jail much longer than that.

When Beradino arrived, he cast a weary eye over the damage.

'What does yours look like?' he asked.

'Pretty much the same.'

Beradino opened the Nova's door and hauled himself inside. 'Right. Let's see if we can find anything which might tell us who this punk was.'

Clutching the steering-wheel for balance with one hand, he leant across and opened the glove compartment.

'Er, detective?' said one of the tech boys.

'What?'

'We haven't dusted it yet.'

Beradino sat upright again and glared at him. 'Why the hell didn't you say so?'

He pulled himself out and gestured towards the car. 'All yours.'

9:29 a.m.

Patrese rang Amberin and Hellmore to tell them that Shaniqua had agreed to his plan.

'Didn't think it was gonna happen for you, I have to be honest,' Hellmore said.

'Why not?'

''Cos Amberin ain't in the takin'-shit business. But you didn't let her play you. I'm impressed, man. I know there's some static between cops and defense lawyers, so sometimes you need to cut through the bullshit and give props where they due. For what it's worth, I'm impressed.'

'Thank you,' Patrese said; and meant it.

'Hope Shaniqua finds out whatever it is you want her to. Oh – that reminds me. About Mara. She never changed her will.'

'Huh?'

'I was clearing up some loose ends yesterday on her estate. Turns out the will she wrote when she and Howard first got married, she never changed it.'

'Which means what?'

'Under state law, if you're getting divorced, an existing will's valid right up to the moment the judge signs the final decree.

If your will leaves everything to your spouse, as Mara's did, and if you die before the divorce is over, as Mara did, then the spouse gets everything.'

'Everything?'

'Everything. It don't matter if proceedings been going on for years, it don't matter if one or both of you's living with someone else, it don't matter if the whole thing's gonna be signed off in twenty minutes' time. You're in or you're out. No such thing as legal separation, not in Pennsylvania.'

'How much is everything, in this case?'

'Close on ten mill.'

'Ten mill? Jesus. Why didn't she change her will?'

'You tell me. I kept on at her to do it – even got one of my associates to draw one up for her – but she always said yeah, yeah, I'll do it, and then just left it till next I bugged her about it.'

'Did she want to get Howard back?'

'"Get him back" as in "win him back", or "get him back" as in "punish him"?'

'I meant "win him back", but I guess either.'

'She never said so, but I reckon. She didn't want the divorce to start with, she stalled it as much as she could. But what did she expect?'

What indeed, Patrese thought; what indeed?

Howard hadn't just saved himself twenty million dollars with Mara's untimely death; he'd actually made another ten million, whether he knew it or not.

Patrese wondered if he and Beradino had been too hasty in taking Howard at his word the other night, when he'd told them that even millions of dollars were a drop in the ocean for him. In Patrese's admittedly limited experience of dealing with very rich people, he'd worked out two things. First, as far as most rich people were concerned, too much was never enough. Second, most fortunes looked a lot less secure on closer inspection than they did at first glance. Extravagant net worth assessments were always impressive, but as often as not they were at best exaggerated and at worst downright fiction.

Either way, it was easily sufficient reason to go and see Howard again.

Patrese rang Howard's office. Howard wasn't there. His secretary said he was in a meeting at the Renaissance; downtown's newest and swankiest hotel, a brownstone building of rather severe beauty hard up on the south bank of the Allegheny, from where it looked across the river right into the diamond of PNC Park baseball stadium.

Patrese and Beradino headed for the Renaissance.

The hotel doormen gave them the once-over, expressions suggesting the detectives were clearly a couple of rungs down the social ladder from the Renaissance's usual clientele. Patrese resisted the urge to flash his badge. They had every right to be here.

'I need to take a leak,' Patrese said once they were inside. 'Too much coffee.'

'OK. You find the john, I'll wait for you here.'

They approached reception, intending to ask where they could find the restrooms. A young woman was a few paces ahead of them.

'I'm here to see Mr Negley,' they heard her say.

They stopped dead.

'Is he expecting you?' the receptionist asked.

'Oh yes.'

'Can I have your name?'

'Ava.'

Patrese and Beradino looked at each other. Howard's secretary had told them he was in a meeting. Some kind of meeting.

The receptionist dialed a number. 'Mr Negley?' she said brightly. 'I have an Ava for you. Yes, yes. Thank you.' She replaced the receiver and turned back to Ava. 'Room 915. Ninth floor.'

'Thank you.' Ava headed towards the elevator bank on the far side of the lobby.

The receptionist looked at Patrese and Beradino. 'Can I help you?' she said.

'No,' Beradino replied. 'Thank you. We know where we're going now.'

Ava pressed the button for the elevator. One set of metal doors slid open, and she stepped inside. The detectives quickened their stride to make it in with her.

She gave a brief smile, the way you do at people who've just snuck in between closing doors. 'Which floor would you like?' she asked.

Patrese glanced at the control panel. The number '9' was illuminated.

'Looks like we're already going there,' Patrese said.

'Are you staying here?' Beradino asked, playing the jovial conversationalist.

She hesitated for a moment. 'Yes. Yes, I am.'

'They got some of those fancy credit card keys here? I bet they have. I love those things. Mind if I have a quick look at yours?'

She stared at him without speaking.

The floor indicator pinged, the doors opened, and they all stepped out on to the landing. Ava glanced at the signs on the wall and headed in the direction of room 915. Patrese and Beradino followed.

All the way to the door of 915, in fact.

10:47 a.m.

Howard's reaction to their appearance followed an entirely predictable sequence. Open-mouthed shock gave way to self-righteous anger, which in turn elided into a cold-eyed assessment of the situation, the second transition given a helping hand by Patrese's suggestion that, if Howard didn't want to co-operate, they could just ring Ruby and let her know where they all were and what a fun time they were having.

There was a bottle of champagne open, and Howard had poured two glasses. He offered them to Beradino and Patrese with a smile, as though he'd been expecting them all along. They shook their heads, but Patrese smiled back. The mayor had style.

Howard came clean pretty much immediately. As they all knew, Ava was from an escort agency; and, again as they all knew, escorting is legal. An agency can dispatch individuals to provide social or conversational services. What it can *not* do is arrange a contract for sexual services, or even hint that such an option might be available. If the escort and the john agree to have sex once they're in each other's company, that's neither the agency's fault nor its problem, at least technically.

The whole thing is shot through with hypocrisy, of course. Everyone knows what's really on offer and how best to skirt the legal line in providing it. No one in their right mind pays thousands of dollars for a little small talk and no action. Hell, if all you want is conversation and intellectual stimulation, you can hire Henry Kissinger.

Terms and conditions vary from agency to agency, but it's not uncommon for the girls and the agency to split the fees fifty-fifty, with the girls keeping anything they earn on top, like tips or extras for rough stuff. So the state makes agencies gain licenses and pay taxes, both of which swell government coffers, and direct the police to crack down on streetwalkers instead.

'Come on,' Howard said. 'This happens the whole time. People like me, with high-powered, high-pressure, high-stress jobs, we need an escape, a release. How do you think we get these jobs, hey? By having sex drives the size of Texas, that's how.' It sounded like something from Dr Ruth, but he didn't seem embarrassed in the slightest. 'You elect men with big balls and high testosterone, and then expect us to behave like eunuchs?' He shook his head. 'Uh-uh. No, sir. It's high sex drives that get you into positions of power to start with.'

'And they can get you out of them too,' Beradino said.

Howard turned on him. 'What are you, Detective? The moral majority?'

'I'm not making a judgment. I'm simply pointing out the truth. If this came out, how long do you think you'd last as mayor?'

'And you think that would be a good thing? You don't think I'm a good mayor? You think it's just coincidence that the city budget's gone from a billion-dollar deficit to a billion-dollar surplus on my watch? Or that more police are on the streets and crime's down? Or that all the "America's Most Livable City" stuff just *happened*?'

371

He didn't once ask them to consider whether he'd suffered enough already. Many people in Howard's situation would have fallen back on the trauma of the Mara case and tried to lay on the emotional blackmail that way. For all his money, power, ambition, drive and intellect, what had happened to his wife and children had clearly cut Howard to the core, and he was as much a fuck-up as anybody else who'd undergone that kind of ordeal would have been. But he didn't use it as an excuse, and Patrese admired him for it.

They had the fate of one of America's richest men in their hands, at least potentially. It felt almost headily surreal. For the first time, Patrese appreciated a fraction of what it must be like to have the power of life and death over someone; to be a surgeon, a soldier, a serial killer.

'Did you know your wife hadn't changed her will?' Patrese said.

Howard didn't look fazed in the slightest. 'Mara's affairs were her own business,' he replied. 'She never listened to me about money, about lawyers. Nothing.'

'Her entire estate goes to you. Ten million dollars.'

He shrugged. 'I'll give it to charity.'

'All of it?'

'Every last cent.'

'As part of your annual philanthropic efforts?'

'*On top of* my annual philanthropic efforts.'

Patrese was suddenly conscious he still needed to take a leak.

'Excuse me,' he said to Howard. 'Could I use your bathroom?'

'Sure,' Howard said, and pointed to a door across the room. 'Just in there.'

'Thanks.'

Patrese walked in, turned on the light, shut the door – and had a sudden, almost muscular, flash of realization.

While driving Howard back to Fox Chapel from the scene of Mara's murder, Patrese had thought then that something was wrong, that he'd missed something.

He now knew what that was.

Patrese shook, zipped, flushed, washed and stepped back into the hotel room.

The atmosphere was so awkward it was almost comic. The other three were standing around like strangers at a cocktail party who'd exhausted their reserves of small talk. Howard was gazing lustfully at Ava; an encounter with the law was too trivial to derail his libido, clearly. Ava looked slightly concerned; probably wondering if she was still going to get paid. And Beradino had the air of a chaperone from a bygone age, knowing that the other two wanted him to leave and that they'd be getting it on pretty much before the door had closed behind him.

'Well,' Patrese said, 'that's good, isn't it? Everything sorted out.' He went over to the table and picked up one of the champagne glasses. 'This calls for a celebration, no? Anyone want to join me?'

They all looked at him as though he was mad.

'No?' Patrese shrugged. 'OK. No problem. Mark, can I have a word? Outside?'

Patrese and Beradino went out into the corridor. Patrese was still holding the champagne flute, and hoped Howard hadn't noticed the way in which he was gripping it: very lightly, and as near the rim as possible. Not a very natural way to hold it.

'I'm going to ring Summer and get her to meet us at head-quarters,' he said.

'Huh?'

'I want her to check some fingerprints.'

11:31 a.m.

'Yup,' Summer said.

'You're sure?' Patrese asked.

'Positive.'

She'd dusted the champagne glass, which had Howard's fingerprints all over it from when he'd initially offered it to Patrese. That was why Patrese had picked it up by the rim, so as not to damage any of those fingerprints.

Once Summer had found a good print, she'd checked it against those at Mara's apartment. There had been four separate sets there; one belonging to Mara, the other three as yet unidentified. Beradino knew one of those three belonged to Jesslyn; Patrese knew another belonged to him.

Howard's prints were a dead match for the final set.

'The set that was found in Mara's bedroom?' Beradino asked.

'No. Not that one.' No, Patrese thought; he knew who *that* set belonged to. 'His prints were in the kitchen and bathroom.'

'Still,' Beradino said. 'The night Mara was murdered, Howard told us he hadn't seen her since the day she was convicted, right? When he saw her body he went to the bathroom to throw up, which explains his prints being there. But he *didn't* go in the kitchen, did he? Which means he must have visited before, to have left prints there. When Mara was alive.' He turned to Patrese. 'How did you know?'

'From when he threw up. Like you said, he took one look at her body and rushed to the john. But he didn't ask *where* the john was. He knew already, even though he said he'd never been to her apartment before. When I asked him tonight if I could use the bathroom, he showed me which door I needed – in a room with only two doors, the bathroom door and the main door, and we knew which one the main door was because we'd come in through it.'

Beradino clapped Patrese on the shoulder. 'Well done, young man.'

Patrese felt absurdly proud.

11:45 a.m.

The whole fingerprint thing had taken so little time – ten minutes each way between the Renaissance and headquarters, and twenty minutes of Summer working her latent print magic – that they were back in Howard's hotel room within the hour.

'You think he'll still be there?' Beradino asked on their way up in the elevator.

'Heck, yeah,' Patrese replied. 'If I'd paid the going rate for Ava, *I'd* be getting my money's worth, even if an entire SWAT team was kicking down the door.'

Ava was in a robe which revealed less of her undoubted charms than most men would have liked. Howard was in a shirt and underpants, looking rather less like a Master of the Universe than usual.

'Get your clothes on and get out,' Beradino said to Ava.

She grabbed her dress from off of the floor and hurried into the bathroom. Beradino and Patrese waited in silence till she came out. She picked up her handbag, glanced around the room to see whether she'd left anything, walked up to them, spat in both their faces, and left the room.

'Classy,' Patrese said.

'Very,' Beradino replied.

Beradino explained to Howard what they'd found. He said they must be mistaken. His legs and arms were crossed, his hands hidden. Underdressed, or something to hide? Or both?

They probed a little more, and still he parried. But his eye contact, his Clintonesque *you're the most important person in the room* shtick, was gone. He kept looking towards the door, as though he couldn't wait to get out.

There are three elements to a liar's voice: pitch, speed and volume. The pitch gets higher as stress contracts the vocal cords; the speed slows as the liar tries to formulate the lie; and the volume decreases as the liar thinks things through, being careful not to catch himself out.

Howard's voice was high, slow and quiet. In addition, he touched his nose, rubbed his eyes, pulled his ears and scratched his neck; none of them sinister in themselves, but a pretty powerful indication en masse that right now he was telling more porkies than Pinocchio.

'This is how it is,' Beradino said. 'We'll keep on here, or we can go down the station. We'll grill you for three hours, then we'll bring in some new guys. Just when you think you might have convinced us, you'll have to start over again with another pair who won't want to believe a word you say. And they'll be fresh and alert. They're used to this kind of stuff. There's two types of people in this world, you know? ESSO guys and non-ESSO guys; ESSO, in this case, being Every Saturday and Sunday Off. Homicide 'tecs are non-ESSO guys. They're in good shape, because they have to be. You, on the other hand, will be tired, trying to remember what lie you told and who you told it to. They'll ask you the same old questions again and again. You know how demoralizing that is? I'll tell you; most suspects, if they haven't spilled already, confess within an hour of the first shift change. That's how demoralizing it is.

379

'There you go,' Beradino concluded, ever reasonable. 'Your choice.'

'I didn't kill her,' Howard said.

'I'm not saying you did. You hear me say you did? Franco, you hear me say he did?' Patrese shook his head. 'No, Franco heard nothing neither. I'm just saying your prints were all over Mara's apartment. You disputing that?'

'I didn't kill her.'

'But you were there?'

'Yes,' Howard said, so softly that they had to strain to hear him.

It all came out after that.

Howard had gone to see Mara just the once; not long before she'd been killed, but after the police protection had been lifted. He hadn't told Ruby, of course. She'd have gone *apeshit*; she wouldn't have understood, not in the slightest.

To tell the truth, he wasn't sure he understood either. Why had he gone? He didn't really know. No reason. Lots of reasons. To see how Mara was doing, after everything she'd gone through. To apologize for having doubted her, and explain why he'd done so. The evidence against her had seemed so incontrovertible, he'd been so distraught, he'd wanted someone to blame and she'd seemed the obvious person.

How had Mara reacted to his visit?

God, that was the worst part. She'd been so goddamn gracious and understanding, it had made him feel ten times worse. She'd said she didn't blame him, it wasn't his fault. No, he'd said, it *was* his fault. He shouldn't have abandoned her, he should have stuck by her. Maybe they should try again; not for children, of course, but as a couple, try and put it all behind them and start over.

His suggestion, or hers? His, definitely. His.

They'd cried, and hugged, and . . .

The cold knot which suddenly clenched tight in Patrese's stomach told him where this was going.

. . . somewhere, somehow, the hug had turned into a kiss, and the kiss into – well, they could guess, couldn't they? Both of them shaking with tears even before it was over. And afterwards? Go away and think about it, she'd said, and she'd do the same. They had a lot to sort out.

Patrese clenched his jaw so hard he thought his teeth would break.

Liar, he wanted to say. *Liar. She never mentioned you; not once. You might have been in the apartment, but you never made love to her.*

2:12 p.m.

They'd checked Howard's alibis for all four murders not long after Mara had been killed, but for form's sake they checked them again. Watertight, the lot. At the time of the murders, Howard had been, respectively, at a cocktail party, giving a television interview, at a breakfast award ceremony, and out having dinner. His attendance was corroborated by at least twenty people for each occasion. His 'meetings' with the likes of Ava aside, Howard lived a life that was almost unrelentingly public. Good for a mayor; bad for a serial killer.

'You read that thing in the paper the other day?' Beradino said. 'About how politicians and millionaires exhibit typical characteristics of psychopaths?'

'No, but I can imagine. Charm, narcissism, egotism, manipulation, low boredom threshold, promiscuity . . . the list goes on.'

'You want it to be him? You want Howard to be our man?'

'It would solve our problems.' *They weren't looking for Mara's lover any more.*

'It sure would.' *Sure would take the heat off Jesslyn.*

Patrese wondered whether – hoped that – Howard was lying about having made love with Mara. He remembered what Mara had said about Howard's lack of reaction to their children's deaths. Pathological deceit and absence of empathy are also high on psychopathic checklists. It's not that psychopaths don't know how to show emotions, Patrese knew; it's that they don't even know how to *feel* them.

Thursday, December 2nd. 2:56 p.m.

Patrese had asked to be informed if Trent was ever brought into Central Booking. He got his first notification a little over twenty-four hours later, when two patrolmen arrested Trent for tagging – spraying graffiti markers.

Patrese went down to the basement and checked Trent's cell number against the list. He was right at the end, last cell along. Patrese walked all the way down the corridor, unlocked the cell door, and walked in.

For a moment, he thought he'd got the wrong room. There was only one place to sit, a concrete bench, and that was empty.

Then he saw the dangling legs away to the right, just above his eyeline; kicking hard, spotless and laceless Timberlands beneath baggy jeans.

Oh no. Oh Jesus no.

Patrese moved quicker than thought; one arm round Trent's waist to take the weight, the other reaching upwards for whatever Trent had used as a noose. Dammit, Patrese thought, the uniforms were supposed to take laces and belts from suspects. It was pretty much the first thing you did after doing the fingerprints.

There was no noose. No belt, no cord; nothing. Just a hand which batted angrily at Patrese's, and a voice shouting 'Get off me! Get off me, man!'

Trent wasn't hanging himself. He was trying to escape through the ceiling panel.

Patrese wrestled Trent down and on to the concrete bench. Trent lashed out a couple of times, but Patrese was too quick and smart for him. He swayed easily away from the blows and pinned Trent's wrists to the bench. Trent tried to kick Patrese's back.

'You do that one more time,' Patrese snapped, 'you're gonna be in more trouble than you can possibly imagine.'

'Fuck you, man. Let go of me.'

'You stop thrashing about like a dying fish, I'll let go.'

Trent gradually subsided his wriggling. Patrese pushed himself away and stood up. Trent sat upright, adjusting his clothes with sullen defiance.

Patrese saw a pair of gloves sticking out the back of Trent's jeans. Cloth gardening gloves, to be precise. A lot of young men wore them to protect their hands during a fistfight; either that, or Homewood had more budding Theodore Paynes than River Farm ever did.

'This your first offense?' Patrese asked.

'First one I been *caught* for.' Sullen bravado.

'OK, so you probably won't be charged this time. Next time, different story. If I'd busted you outside The Sanctuary the other night, you'd already be on remand, you know? This is not the way you want to go.'

'How the *fuck* you know which way I wanna go?'

'I'm telling you. This is not the way.'

'And *I'm* tellin' *you* . . .'

Patrese grabbed Trent's collar and pulled his face close. 'You're telling me *nothing*, you understand? You're in a police station. My turf. While you're here, you'll listen to me. Is that clear?'

'Listen, man . . .'

'Is that fucking clear?'

Trent looked briefly like the frightened, confused young man Patrese had seen the day they'd taken Shaniqua away.

'Yeah,' he said. 'Yeah. Sorry.'

Patrese let Trent go. Trent picked at his shirt again.

'Sorry,' Trent said again.

'Why do you do it?' Patrese asked.

'Man, it weren't nothin'. We was just . . .'

'No. Not why *did* you do it, the tagging. Why *do* you do it?'

'What you mean?'

'Why the gang? Why do you want to be in the gang?'

Trent smiled. 'Man, *everyone* wanna be in da gang.'

'Why?'

Patrese knew the answers, of course; but he wanted Trent to say them out loud. Maybe that way he'd think about them; question them.

'Respect,' Trent said. 'Dead presidents, hoes. Be the big man. It's excitin', yeah?'

'Hanging out on street corners is exciting?'

'No, man. Goin' for a rumble is excitin'.'

'You spend a lot more time hanging out on street corners than going for a rumble, I can tell you.'

'Man, what you know about it anyway?'

'I work homicide, Trent. Homicide means gangs, often as not. I know more than you think. I know more than you do.'

'Man, I get this shit off of J-Dog da whole time.' J-Dog, Patrese presumed, being John Knight. 'This make-yourself-a-better-citizen shit.'

'You keep on like this, Trent, you'll end up in jail, or you'll die, or both. You can't do a thing with your life if you're dead or serving twenty-five. Think of your mom.'

'My mom's in jail. *Remember?* She ain't here with me.'

And that was it in a nutshell, Patrese thought, whether Trent knew it or not. Trent wanted the gang because he wanted a family. All his real family were either locked up, dead, or otherwise long gone from his life. The gang was a substitute for all that, even though it would eventually eat itself; because how could a gang compensate for all the brothers dead or inside, when so many of its members would end up going the same way?

You joined a gang to belong, and it turned out to be undependable. You joined it for excitement, and it turned out to be boring. You joined it for protection, and it turned out to make you more vulnerable.

Shaniqua was right, of course. Homewood was the problem; the place, the mindset. It was all very well Patrese telling Trent not to get involved, but Trent would only listen when he had alternatives, and alternatives meant getting him out of there.

When the arresting officer had cautioned Trent and told him he didn't want to see him back here, not *ever*, not unless he'd just graduated from police academy, Patrese said he'd drive Trent back to Homewood.

'This your car?' Trent said as they approached the TransAm.

'Yup.'

Trent pursed his lips and nodded. They got in. Patrese turned the key. The starter motor turned wheezily over, considered its options for a few moments, then decided that today was a good day to actually do some work and start the V8.

'It always sound that bad?' Trent asked.

'Always. Half the time, it don't even start.'

'You should get another car.'

'No way. Not till the rust is all that's holding this thing together.'

388

They passed Heinz Field. Patrese nodded towards it. 'You ever been?'

Trent snorted. 'No, man.'

'You don't like football?'

'I *love* football, man. But when a brother like me gonna get to Heinz Field?'

'You play?'

'Sure.'

'What position?'

'Safety. Free safety, mainly.'

'You like playing there?'

'Yeah, man. Love it. Stand back, watch the play unfold, see it all before me. I got all the options. Cover the receiver, smack the halfback, blitz now and then. *Love it.*'

By Trent's standards, Patrese figured, that was a veritable soliloquy.

'Yo, man, can I aks you somethin'?' Trent said.

'Sure.'

'J-Dog said you won the Heisman at Pitt. That true?'

'That *is* true. I did.'

'Man. *Man.* The Heisman, that's some serious shit. But you a bit short for bein' a quarterback, ain'tcha?'

'Why do you think I was a quarterback?'

'Why? Only quarterbacks and runnin' backs ever win the Heisman, right?'

'Not always – you might get a wide receiver now and then – but pretty much, yeah. Why can't I have been a running back?'

Trent laughed, as though this was the most ridiculous thing he'd ever heard. ''Cos you *white*, man. White folks don't play runnin' back.'

He had a point. Not a single NFL team, and precious few college outfits, had a white running back on their starter roster. No one really discussed it, because it – the Great

Disappearing White Running Back – was all bound up with America's great unmentionables, race and culture.

Scientists will tell you it's racial; that blacks have denser bones, less body fat, narrower hips, thicker thighs, longer legs and lighter calves than whites. Then in the next breath they'll tell you whites are more intelligent, so no one can accuse them of bias; give with one hand, take with the other.

But it was just as much a question of social pigeonholing. The fewer whites who played at running back, the fewer whites who were encouraged to. It worked the other way too, of course. There hadn't been a black NFL quarterback, not a regular starting one at any rate, until the late seventies. Not because they hadn't been good enough, but because they hadn't been white enough.

'I did,' Patrese said. 'I played running back.'

'They give you static about it?'

'Did who give me static?'

'Anyone.'

'Sure they did. Coaches, mainly. Told me to bulk up and play tight end, else I'd never get a place on the starting roster.'

'They told you that 'cos you were white?'

'That's right.'

'Just 'cos you were white?'

'Just 'cos I was white.'

'Nothin' to do with some other guy being better than you?'

'Just 'cos I was white.'

'Shit, man.' Trent smiled. 'Then you got a small idea what it's like to be a nigga.'

Saturday, December 4th. 11:03 a.m.

Mustafa Bayoumi was working with a fury which was controlled, ice-cold and, above all, righteous.

The chemistry department at Pitt was deserted, which was how he liked it when doing things that weren't strictly legal. He had an entire laboratory to himself, and he laid out his ingredients across the workbench with the precision of a television chef.

First, hydrogen peroxide and acetone. When he mixed them together, they'd make acetone peroxide, a by-product of MDMA. It was his MDMA making that had first given Mustafa the idea for what he was doing now.

He continued arranging his precious items. Chapatti flour. Cardboard tubes. Flashlight bulbs. A nine-volt battery. Electric wires. Metal pipes cut to various lengths. Ball bearings, washers, nuts, screws, tacks, nails. And a camouflage hunting vest bulging with pockets: six bellows on the chest, a hand-warmer on each side, two on the inside, and a couple on the back.

The camouflage pattern was immaterial to Mustafa's purpose – he'd be wearing the vest under a large overcoat, so it wouldn't be on show – but the vest's shape was important. Explosives belts tend to 'print'; their sharp edges catch the fabric of the clothing outside them, thus revealing their shape. Vests fit both body and clothes better, and are therefore easier to conceal.

Once Mustafa had all the items where he wanted them, he stepped back from the bench and took several deep breaths to keep his thoughts clear.

He had no doubts that he was doing the right thing. The Human Torch had shown him that; this way, the public way, was the only way.

Look how the serial killer had everyone in his thrall. The cops, the media, people in the street, the whole city itself: they seemed to talk about little else. They didn't know exactly who the Human Torch was, but they sure as anything knew *of* him, and took notice of what he did. The apparently random, one-off killings took lives, gained vast amounts of attention, and set a city on edge.

Mustafa wanted to do just the same thing. He wanted people to take notice of him too, give him some of their mind. And not the kind of attention the cops had been paying him, either, thinking he must be involved in all those murders. What gave them the right to keep on and on at him, when they had absolutely no evidence?

It was just as he'd told the detectives right at the start, when they'd first come to see him in the mosque; all Muslims were niggers now. If it wasn't these murders they were on his tail about, sooner or later it'd be something else. If it wasn't him on the receiving end, sooner or later it'd be someone else, hassled, harassed, never given a moment's peace, all because they were Muslims, wore beards, didn't believe in what the Americans did, didn't want their way of life.

The Americans wouldn't want his way of death, that was for sure.

If Mustafa's father had still been alive, he'd have said Mustafa was insane to be doing this. Abdul had believed there was always a route to compromise, if only both sides were prepared to seek it. But Abdul was no longer here to turn the other cheek. Mustafa believed in an eye for an eye. He'd had it with bowing down to the infidel. The infidel would bow to him.

Americans would doubtless wonder how a son could do this to his mother, especially so soon after she'd lost her husband. But Americans were weak. All the wastrel, self-indulgent fools who'd bought Mustafa's pills in order to find brief respite from the soulless, godless vacuums of their lives had shown him that. They were weak, but they believed their lives to be of paramount importance.

Mustafa knew his life, like that of everyone in the world, belonged only to Allah. It was Allah for whom he was fighting, and Allah for whom he would die. His mother would understand. And she'd be all right financially, for a while at least. Selling MDMA had made him upwards of forty thousand dollars, which he'd stashed in a bank account for her.

Mustafa cast all this from his mind. It was time to make the bomb, for which he needed every ounce of concentration he could muster. Making the bomb wasn't difficult, but it needed precision, patience, and time.

He'd chosen acetone peroxide as the base for several reasons. He had worked with it before, it was the easiest of several possible explosives to get hold of and prepare, and it was undetectable to sniffer dogs. But it was also dangerously unstable; so much so that Palestinian bomb-makers, many of whom ended up missing hands or with skin streaked in burns from where they'd misjudged preparations, called it something else entirely.

They called it Mother of Satan.

Sunday, December 5th, 10:10 a.m.

Patrese had two season tickets to the Steelers. One he always used himself, but who he took with him varied. He'd gone with Pop quite often before this year, and also with Beradino. Sometimes he'd take one of his sisters, or perhaps a college buddy.

What with one thing and another, however, he hadn't yet asked anyone to today's match, even though it was the Turnpike Rivalry: the Steelers against the Cleveland Browns, the most visceral of all Steelers match-ups. Hardcore Steelers fans would accept losing to every other team on the roster – even their two other great rivals, the Cincinnati Bengals and the Baltimore Ravens – as long as they beat the Browns. It was always hammer and tongs, a special day whether your team won or lost, whether the game itself had been close or a walkover.

With this in mind, Patrese knew *exactly* who he'd take to Heinz Field.

10:38 a.m.

There was a grim constancy about Homewood. Summer or winter, spring or fall, you saw the same faces in the same places doing the same things.

On each corner ran a conveyor belt of drug deals. It wasn't as obvious as it sounded, of course; even in Homewood, people don't sell drugs in plain view. But if you know what you're looking for, the players aren't hard to spot.

There are always five of them, not including the boss, who if he has any sense (and since he's the boss, he usually does, else he doesn't stay boss for long) keeps himself well away from the scene.

There's the lookout, who keeps his eyes peeled for the law and whose cellphone has the quickest speed dial in the West. There's the steerer, the punters' first point of contact, the maître d' of the street corner, rattling off menus and prices. How much? How much for how much? Next comes the moneyman, who takes the punters' cash.

Now we're at the sharp end, because here comes the golden, cardinal, number one, forget-your-own-name-before-you-forget-this rule of drug deals; keep the money and drugs separate.

Once the moneyman has your cash, and not till then, the slinger gives you the drugs. The slinger's the only one of the gang who physically handles the drugs in this transaction, and is therefore the most liable to be arrested, which was why gangs often used juveniles as slingers, because the courts treat them more leniently.

And finally comes the gunman – hidden, of course, on a rooftop or behind a hedge – watching, waiting, trigger finger at the ready in case the whole thing goes to shit and he has to shoot his way out of it.

Patrese counted this scene, with minor variations, on six consecutive street corners.

This life, this so-called life, was what Shaniqua feared for Trent.

Not just for him either, Patrese thought. He saw a young mother, couldn't have been out of her teens, two little boys already, and she was cooing sweet nothings into her cell-phone while her kids tugged uncomprehendingly at her leg, seeking the attention she was giving to the guy on the other end of the line.

That was the next generation of steerers and slingers, right there, those two cute little boys. You didn't need to be Nostradamus to predict their future.

Patrese arrived at The 50/50 and got out of the car. There was no point locking the TransAm's doors; if someone wanted to break in, they'd do so anyway. Locking the doors only meant they'd have to cause damage.

Patrese found Knight in his office, changing out of his priest's robes; he'd just finished his Sunday service.

'I've come to ask Trent if he wants to go to Heinz Field with me,' Patrese said.

'I'm sure he would. Heck, if he doesn't, I will.' Knight laughed. 'No, it would be good for him. He was talking about you the other day, you know.'

'Who? Trent?'

'When you brought him back from the cop shop. Talking all about the crazy white dude who won the Heisman for being a running back.'

Patrese felt ridiculously, stupidly proud.

'But listen,' Knight continued, 'you can't just go in there and ask him if he wants to come, not in front of his buddies. They'll think he's a snitch, or you're a fag, or both. He'd never live it down.'

'So what should I do?'

'Say you want to talk to him some more about that tagging incident.' He paused. 'Can I be frank here?'

'Sure.'

'Franco, I don't know you from a bar of soap, but you seem a good man. What you're doing for Trent, not too many people do those things these days. But be careful. Kids like Trent, they don't trust adults, period. They especially don't trust men. Too many men come and go in their lives. They're there with them, then they're inside, or six feet under. No one hugs these kids. They think everyone's out to get them; they'll hustle you just to stop you hustling them first. So once you start this, you can't stop. You can't start on trying to help Trent and then walk away because you're too busy or he's being a jerk. You got to be in it all the way. If you're not, if you haven't got that commitment, then go now. I won't think any the worse of you, Lord no. The only thing I won't let you do is raise his hopes and then shatter them again. That's worse than having no hope in the first place.'

Patrese nodded. He knew Knight was right, and he appreciated him saying it.

He found Trent in one of the communal rooms, sitting on the floor with three other youths about his age. They were poring over a copy of *Guns 'n' Ammo*.

Trent looked up and smiled for half a second before remembering that his buddies were watching.

'Yo,' he said, voice dead neutral.

'Yo,' Patrese replied, feeling about as uncool as a dad dancing at a wedding. 'Can I have a word? About the tagging?'

'You wanna word *now*?'

Patrese nodded. 'Now.'

'OK.' Trent got up and walked towards Patrese. The other three watched warily.

Patrese gestured for Trent to follow him from the room. When they were out of the others' earshot, Patrese stopped.

'Hey, man, I got a caution for that,' Trent said before Patrese could speak, 'and you told me that was it. So what's this about?'

'I'm trying out a new interviewing technique.'

'Yeah? The fuck am I, some sorta guinea pig?'

'I thought we could discuss it further at Heinz Field this afternoon.'

Trent was about to snap something back when he realized what Patrese had said.

'Heinz Field?' Trent asked.

Patrese nodded.

'The Browns are playin' there, that right?'

Patrese nodded again.

'Yo; lemme check my diary.' Trent paused half a second. 'I checked. I'm free.'

11:15 a.m.

Everyone has a last morning of their life, thought Mustafa; but only the privileged ones know for sure exactly when that last morning is, and can therefore make all the arrangements they need for entry into paradise.

The last tufts of his beard lay clumped in the basin. He ran his hand round his jaw, wincing slightly at the tenderness of skin now clean-shaven for the first time in years. The face which returned his gaze from the mirror looked younger and more innocent than he knew it was.

No one would give him a second glance; not till it was too late, at any rate.

Mustafa washed the remnants of his beard down the plughole, sluicing with water and fingers till the basin was clean again. Then he took a vial of flower water and dabbed it on his face and hands. As with the removal of his beard, this was a vital part of correctly preparing his body for what awaited him.

He returned to his bedroom and dressed carefully; underpants, socks, pants, shoes, two T-shirts, and the camouflage vest. Each of the vest's numerous pockets contained one or more of the metal pipes he'd cut to length, and every pipe was filled with an assortment of ball bearings, washers, nuts, screws, tacks and nails. The vest was heavy on Mustafa's shoulders, and he had to adjust it several times before he found a comfortable position which didn't dig into his skin too much.

He was proud that he'd done all this himself, without a single piece of help. Some attacks needed a whole team of people; one to select the operative, one to select the target, a couple of engineers, one to plan logistics, one to get the operative to the target, and so on. Not this time. Mustafa was a pure solo artist. A legend.

He'd set his video camera on a tripod in one corner of his bedroom. He went over to it, switched it on, pressed the 'record' button and returned to his chair, already placed so as to be dead center in the picture.

When he spoke, his voice was clear and strong, and he didn't stutter.

'To Allah belongs the power and the majesty. I beg Allah to accept this action from me, knowing I make it in all sincerity, and to admit me to the highest station in paradise, for verily he grants martyrdom to whomever he wills.

'To my mother, I beg you not to cry for me, but instead rejoice in happiness and love what I have done, for Allah loves those who fight for his sake. Mother, keep your heart sealed to this religion. Hold tight to the rope of Allah, and don't let go. Pray your five daily prayers so you may be saved from hell.

'I am forsaking everything for what I believe. My religion is Islam, obedience to the one true God, Allah, following the footsteps of the final prophet and messenger Muhammad. But for this I am pursued, left unable to go about my daily business by a godless government which perpetuates atrocities against my people all over the world. My creed and color deny me the freedom your constitution promises. I salute the

400

man known as the Human Torch who is killing the prominent people of this city. Between us, we will make you listen.

'To the people of America, I say this. Your support of your government's actions makes you directly responsible, just as I am directly responsible for protecting and avenging my Muslim brothers and sisters. As the areas in which you can move freely shrink to nothing, I will make you see what it feels like to be one of the hunted. I will make you fearful of sitting in a café, of visiting the mall, of riding the bus. We are at war, and I am a soldier. *Allahu Akbar.*'

12:35 p.m.

Patrese found it amusing, and touching, to see Trent out of his natural environment.

Trent walked round Heinz Field with his eyes wide and his mouth hanging open, as though he were prime witness to an alien invasion rather than one of thousands making a weekly pilgrimage. He gawped at everything; at the scalpers selling tickets outside the stadium, at the tailgate parties in the parking lots, at the sea of black and gold in the stands. Here, Trent wasn't a gangbanger in waiting, or a teenager trying to cover up confusion with a mask of toughness, or even a young man whose mother was going on trial. Here, he was just a kid at a ball game, knocked sideways by the sound and the spectacle.

Patrese had been to watch the Steelers probably more than a hundred times in his life, but seeing the wonder and excitement in Trent's eyes made him feel somehow that he too was seeing it through fresh eyes. For the first time, Patrese felt he understood why men love being fathers; he understood the source of the vicarious, deep-rooted thrill at the everyday and familiar being made new and enthralling again.

Here came the Dawg Pound, the Browns' most hardcore

402

fans, decked head-to-foot in orange and brown, singing loudly and posing for TV cameras. Here were stalls selling serried ranks of Terrible Towels, yellow hand towels which had become a staple item for any serious Steeler fan.

Everywhere was laughter and anticipation, a rivalry which came from being similar; both industrial towns in the north-east, both with waterfront stadiums, both with rabidly partisan fans. The rivalry was about battles played hard, won hard and celebrated hard. It was about not just the desire but the atavistic *need* for a rivalry like this. When it had at one stage looked as though the Browns franchise might be relocated away from Cleveland, Steelers fans had joined the protests in huge numbers, standing alongside their oldest and bitterest rivals. Both clubs needed the juice of such an ancient contest, understanding that they were diminished without the other.

Patrese didn't insult Trent by making explicit the unspoken message of all this; that if you need rivalry in your life – and most people, certainly most young men, do – then make it this rather than what you're heading for. People die in gang shootouts. They don't die in stadiums on the banks of the Allegheny or Lake Erie.

Everyone was here to celebrate, honor and renew that rivalry.

Everyone except one.

12:47 p.m.

In purely scientific terms, a bus would probably have been Mustafa's best target, especially at this time of year when all the windows would be closed to keep out the cold. A sealed environment would intensify the force of the blast and maximize its killing potential; the shock wave tearing lungs and crushing other internal organs, a hail of shrapnel piercing flesh and breaking bones, and an exploding fuel tank causing burns and respiratory damage.

But in terms of the wider psychological effect which Mustafa was seeking, a bus was a non-starter. He knew he had to hit the people of Pittsburgh where it hurt, which meant targeting something they loved.

People didn't love the bus. They rode it to work and back, a purely functional way of getting from A to B. Catching the bus was no more exciting than breathing.

People liked their public buildings – their theatres, their galleries – and their parks, for sure, but attacking these places would sting the city rather than tear its guts out.

No, there was only one thing all Pittsburghers loved.

The Steelers.

2:38 p.m.

Berlin didn't often come into work over the weekend, but he was running a big diagnostic check on the department's crime database, and it needed checking every twenty-four hours. If he left it unsupervised all weekend, and something went wrong, it would take him half the following week to fix; but this way, he'd lose a day's work at most.

The system was running slowly, and it took him a few moments to work out why. Someone had switched the download destination of the Bayoumi wire-taps to the hard drive on which Berlin was running diagnostics. The department didn't have people listening to the taps round the clock any more; it was just too much manpower. Now, they were simply saving the files and checking them every day.

Sound files take up a lot of memory, and saving them to the wrong drive was a simple mistake, easily corrected. Berlin clicked on the mouse to move the wire-tap files, but his finger was too fast. The mouse registered a double-click and opened the first file before he could cancel the command.

Mustafa Bayoumi's voice came through the computer speakers.

To Allah belongs the power and the majesty. I beg Allah to accept this action from me, knowing I make it in all sincerity, and to admit me to the highest station in paradise, for verily he grants martyrdom to whomever he wills.

Berlin listened all the way through, hardly daring to breathe. It was a joke, surely? Or perhaps some kind of weird rehearsal? A film, a play?

He listened again. It sure didn't sound like a joke.

He rang the incident room, skeleton-staffed on a Sunday.

No, said the bored uniform manning the phone, neither Beradino nor Patrese were there. Their cell numbers? Sure. Hold on a sec. A shuffling of paper, the sound of coffee being slurped, then the uniform was back on the line, reading out the numbers. Berlin scribbled them down with a shaking hand.

He dialed Beradino's first.

'Beradino.'

'Marquez Berlin here. You gotta listen to this. It's from the Bayoumi wire-tap.'

Berlin played the sound file for the third time.

'Jeez Louise,' Beradino said, when it had finished. 'This was recorded when?'

Berlin looked at the timecode on the file. 'A bit over three hours ago.'

'That's all there is? Nothing else?'

'I'll check.'

There was only one file recorded more recently. Berlin clicked on it. Two voices, this time: Mustafa and Sameera, speaking in Arabic.

Down the line, Beradino sucked his teeth in frustration. 'Doggone it. Translators aren't in today, are they?'

'Doubt it.'

'OK, Marquez, listen to me. I'm home in Punxsutawney.

406

I'm leaving now, but it's a couple of hours from me to you, and we might not have that time. Ring Patrese and play that file to him. Then I want you take a couple of uniforms and haul ass to the Bayoumis' house. You remember where that is?'

'Sure.'

'Tell Patrese to meet you there. Find out from Sameera where her son's gone.'

3:15 p.m.

Patrese wasn't answering his phone – it just rang and rang before going to voicemail – so Berlin went to Sameera's house without him, taking the first uniforms he could find.

Sameera answered the door with a strange cowering defiance.

'What you want?' she said quickly. 'Why you not leave Mustafa alone?'

'Where is he?'

'He not here.'

'Where? Where's he gone?'

'I don't know. He not tell me.'

'We're going to have to search the place.'

'You need warrant.'

'We have reason to believe your son intends to perform a suicide bombing.'

Sameera's eyes opened wide, like a cat's. '*What?*'

'You heard. Now let us in.'

She stood aside a split second before they barreled through the door.

If her reaction had been genuine, and there was no reason to suppose otherwise, Sameera clearly hadn't heard Mustafa's suicide message, which meant he'd probably recorded it in his bedroom. Berlin led the uniforms up there.

The video camera was in the corner. One of the uniforms turned it on and began to scroll through the recordings, while Berlin looked round the room. There were a handful of prints on the walls, scenes of deserts and mosques. The books on Mustafa's shelves were either scientific or religious. His jackets, shirts and pants hung in the closet; underwear was folded in drawers. It was all very neat and tidy; unnervingly, unnaturally so. Hell, Berlin thought, even the trash can was empty.

Almost empty.

There was one thing in there: a label, trailing a plastic tag. Berlin bent down and picked it out.

Congratulations on buying genuine official Steelers merchandise, the label said, next to the three-starred Steelmark logo.

The shop sticker was on the back. *LGE STLRS JCKT, BLK/GLD. $149.95.*

Berlin walked out of the bedroom. Sameera was standing in the corridor outside.

'Mrs Bayoumi, was your son wearing a Steelers jacket?'

She nodded.

'Was it new?'

'Yes. He buy it the other day. I don't even know he like football.'

Berlin went back into Mustafa's bedroom and looked in the closet. There were two overcoats in there, both more than up to the job of keeping the wearer warm even in a Pittsburgh winter.

'Why would you buy a brand new Steelers coat,' Berlin mused, 'when you've got two perfectly good overcoats here, and you don't even like football?'

'To blend in,' one of the uniforms said.

'Like, at a football match,' added the other.

409

3:34 p.m.

It was turning into one hell of a match.

The Browns had gone out of the blocks at a fearful pace; ten points up after the first quarter, fourteen clear at half-time, back to ten going into the last quarter. The Steelers had hardly got a look in. Passes had gone to ground, tackles been missed, punt returns fumbled. Patrese hadn't seen them play this badly in a long time.

And the crowd had kept singing and shouting, louder and louder.

It was that which had really grabbed Trent in his vitals, Patrese saw; that the Steelers fans hadn't gotten down on their team because they were losing, but instead had ramped up the support, up a gear, and another, and another. Each time the Browns had scored, where you might have expected a deflated hush, the stadium had erupted in defiant noise: Come on, Steelers, *come on*, back and at 'em, we shall overcome, we love you whatever, cut us and we bleed black and gold.

It was part of Steelers folklore that the team never thrived more than when it was dissed, knocked, kicked to the curb. The surest way to make them lose was to tell them how good they were and get them complacent. It was that old steeltown thing; they were always underdogs, and they loved it. The Steelers liked being in a corner, they said, because in a corner no one can come at you from behind.

And now, slowly, with the clock running down, back they came.

Third and goal, a flurry of movement behind the scrimmage, and suddenly there was Ben Roethlisberger, Big Ben, the first Steelers quarterback to be spoken about seriously as a successor to the legendary Terry Bradshaw, scrambling over from a couple of yards out for the touchdown.

Trent was on his feet, his arms rising to punch the air – and the upswing accidentally knocked Patrese's cellphone out of his coat pocket and on to the ground.

'Shit. Sorry, man.'

'No worries.' Patrese bent down, picked the phone up and checked it for damage. It looked OK.

Missed calls: 11, the screen said.

Patrese raised his eyebrows in surprise. The noise of the crowd must have masked the ringing, and the thickness of his coat deadened the vibrations. He scrolled through the menu to see who'd called.

Beradino, North Shore, a couple of numbers he didn't recognize, and voicemail.

He phoned Beradino first of all rather than wade through endless messages. Beradino picked up almost before Patrese had heard it ring.

'Franco! Where the heck have you been?'

'I'm at Heinz Field. Sorry, didn't hear . . .'

'Heinz Field? Holy moly, that's where Bayoumi is.'

'What?'

Another breaking wave of crowd noise. Patrese jabbed his finger into his free ear so he could hear Beradino properly.

'Mustafa Bayoumi. He's there, at Heinz Field. He's going to blow himself up.'

411

Patrese was too much of a pro to waste time asking Beradino if he was joking.

He thought fast. Heinz Field held sixty-five thousand people sat close together, side by side and front to back. An explosive vest could kill perhaps fifty people first off, injure a whole heap more, but that wasn't the half of it. The blast would set off the mother of all stampedes to get out of the stadium as fast as possible, and that would kill the same amount of people again, maybe even more.

'I'm on it.'

'Get your butt over to the stadium control room. There's a bunch of uniforms on the way. Stadium security have been told to look out for anyone acting suspicious, but not why, or what he's doing.'

'How come?'

'Fewer people who know, fewer people who can panic. But they need you to ID him, Franco. You're the only one there who knows what he looks like.'

'Where are you?'

'On the interstate, hauling ass. *Go.*'

Patrese ended the call and turned to Trent. 'Stay here. I'll be back.'

Trent was so engrossed in the game, he barely noticed.

Patrese hurried from the stands and into the bowels of the stadium. A steward in a vest fluorescent enough to be seen from space directed him to the control room.

Four times along the way, unsmiling men in suits blocked doorways and asked with menacing politeness whether they could help. Four times Patrese showed them his police badge, and four times they swung open the portals for him.

In the control room now, screens banked high on every wall; the crowd, parceled into endlessly shifting sections. Whoever you were, wherever you were sitting, you were being watched.

'We've already checked the ticket sales roster,' said one

412

of the stadium staff. 'There's no record of a Mustafa Bayoumi. So either he booked in a false name, or he bought a ticket from a scalper outside.'

Patrese nodded. The match was in its fourth quarter, so the scalpers would have long gone. No point looking for them, let alone questioning them.

'What do you want him for, anyway?' said someone else.

Patrese didn't answer. He ran his eyes from screen to screen, skimming the sea of faces. Bayoumi's skin tone alone wouldn't be enough to mark him out, especially on a day when people were wrapped up tight beneath hats and scarves. Bayoumi looked more black than Arab, and plenty of Steelers fans were black, as were half the squad.

No; what Patrese was looking for was something which *jarred*.

Sporting crowds are homogenous entities. They move more or less as one. Heads swivel in synchronicity to follow the action, bodies tense in communal excitement or frustration. It was the anomaly which Patrese was seeking; the one who looked like everyone else, but wasn't behaving like it.

There.

A man with eyes lifted high and unfocussed in a thousand-yard stare. A genuine fan would never have worn an expression like that, especially during a game like this.

'Zoom in there,' Patrese said.

Buttons tapped and trackballs span. A face filled the screen. It looked like Mustafa, but the man had no beard.

'Can you go in closer?'

Another zoom.

Through the cluster of pixels, Patrese could see what looked like mild tan lines, a lighter area of skin round the jaw and mouth.

The kind of mark a freshly shaved beard would leave, in fact.

413

'That's him,' Patrese said. 'Where's he sitting? Where's that camera?'

'Lower Level West. Block 135.'

'No one is to approach that man but me, do you understand?'

Patrese left the control room at a jog. By the time he was back in the wide concrete walkways under the stands he was running fast, almost knocking over a pregnant woman with a sign over her bump saying 'Baby's First Game'.

He wondered why Mustafa hadn't detonated the bomb already. Perhaps he was plucking up the courage to do it. Perhaps he was waiting for the match to reach its climax, for maximum effect.

Patrese didn't know, and he didn't much care either. All that mattered was that he got to Mustafa before Mustafa decided to detonate. That was their only option. Anything else – a Tannoy announcement, a SWAT team, an attempt to clear the stadium – would simply alert Mustafa to the fact they were on to him, and that would be it. Mustafa would never let them take him alive.

Patrese saw the entrance to Block 135, and headed towards it.

No. Going that way would put him straight in Mustafa's sightline. Better to enter the stand at the next block along and come at Mustafa from the side and behind.

Patrese went in at 136. A short flight of stairs took him into the main body of the stand, where he turned back on himself and climbed to the highest row of seats in the block, hard up against the overhang of the level above.

From here, he could get to Mustafa as quickly and stealthily as possible.

Two minutes to go, three points between the teams. The Steelers on offense, second-and-10, thirty-two yards out.

Patrese looked through the crowd, trying to sort through

the visual clutter – towels, arms, movement – and get a fix on Mustafa.

Roethlisberger took the snap from the center, backpedaled into the pocket, and surveyed his options.

There. Mustafa, his mouth working furiously. Talking to himself. Praying.

Roethlisberger waited, and waited, and waited, arm cocked, checking events downfield; looking at the patterns his wide receivers were running, looking for the angle, the space, all the time keeping half an eye on the frothing, churning maelstrom of the big guys in the middle of the park, the Browns' linebackers grappling with the Steelers' offensive linemen, thousands of pounds of muscle and aggression colliding like crazed rhinos.

Patrese on the move now, hurrying down the clear aisle behind the final row of seats. He held his left hand ahead of him to barge past anyone who got in his way. In his right, he gripped the Ruger Blackhawk tight inside his coat.

One of the Browns' linebackers broke clear. A Steelers' hand clutched in futile desperation at the linebacker's ankle and banged the turf in fury when he missed; and *still* Roethlisberger waited.

Patrese ran down the stairs towards Mustafa's row.

The linebacker was still a stride away from Roethlisberger when the quarterback, with a sniper's deathless cool, finally saw the opening downfield he'd been waiting for. He shimmied half a pace to his right, just enough to give himself the space to clear the linebacker, and in the same moment he launched the ball, the power coming not just from the sling of his arm but all the way through his twisting trunk.

Every pair of eyes in the stadium followed it, apart from two.

Patrese was at the end of Mustafa's row now; ten yards away, maybe less.

Roethlisberger's throw wasn't a perfect spiral, but it didn't matter. It went just where he'd been aiming; the exact spot where wide receiver Hines Ward was arriving in the middle of three defenders.

Patrese pulled his gun out, and even with the drama on the pitch, the people nearest him saw what was happening and began backing away, shouting, staring, shrieking.

Ward leapt, reached, caught, tumbled to the ground, and bounced straight up again, the ball held above his head and his mouth gaping in triumph. Touchdown. *Bedlam.*

Mustafa turned towards the commotion at the end of his row and saw Patrese, Ruger Blackhawk held in two hands front and center, bead drawn on Mustafa.

It seemed to both of them, locked deep in their concentration, that all the noise and tumult faded away.

Mustafa moved his hand towards his pocket.

Detonator, thought Patrese. *Detonator.*

'Hands out!' he yelled, loud as he could, louder than he'd ever yelled before, just to be heard above the torrent of noise in the stadium. 'Show me your fucking hands!'

Patrese would have to go for the head. A body shot could still allow Mustafa to press the detonator, or even set it off straight. Some detonators were sensitive to heat, shock or friction, and a speeding bullet tended to boast all three.

No; it would be a headshot, or nothing.

'Hands where I can see 'em,' he shouted at Mustafa, *again,* that was the third time, and in that moment Patrese realized why he hadn't taken the shot yet; because *hands where I can see 'em* was exactly what he'd said to Samantha Slinger before he'd shot her.

He'd been wrong then.

But he wasn't wrong now, was he?

Take the shot, godammit, he told himself; *take the fucking shot.*

The Muslims call it *bassamat al-farah,* the smile of joy; the

416

luminous, transcendental ecstasy brought on by the impending martyrdom of a true believer. When Mustafa gave Patrese this smile, he looked so happy that, just for a moment, Patrese didn't see Mustafa's hand dart towards his pocket.

Just for a moment; no more.

Patrese squeezed the trigger, faster than thought, and Mustafa's head exploded.

Not all of him. Just his head, split like a watermelon and gone in puffs of blood.

Monday, December 6th. 8:30 a.m.

Boone was a one-man Big Brother, on your screen no matter how often you switched channels. Sharing a sofa with Diane Sawyer on *Good Morning America*; behind a desk with Matt Lauer on *The Today Show*; video-linked to Harry Smith on *The Early Show*, not to mention *Fox & Friends*, *BBC World News Today*, and probably even MTV and the Cartoon Network, given half a chance.

Boone's line, as agreed with Chance, was that the shooting of Mustafa Bayoumi had been a Bureau operation carried out after receiving specific intelligence about the Heinz Field attack. This was the only way to sidestep any tricky questions about how Mustafa's intentions had been known ahead of time. The Bureau's powers of surveillance under the PATRIOT Act were vastly greater than the police's.

Boone declined to be drawn on the exact nature of the intelligence received, the name of the agent who'd shot Mustafa, or any other operational specifics.

The networks tried to link the attempted bombing with the Human Torch murders, of course. They wanted Boone to join the dots for them: Mustafa had killed Redwine in revenge for Redwine's botched operation on his father before

418

murdering the others and trying to go out in a blaze of glory. That's how they wanted it.

Sorry, Boone said, but that simply wasn't plausible. Yes, there were similarities. The triggers that could turn a serial killer's fantasies into reality applied to terrorists too. Mustafa had always flirted with radicalism, but he'd only made an irrevocable leap to it following his father's death. Increasingly disillusioned with mainstream America, bereft of the man who'd been his rudder and anchor no matter how often they'd argued, and angry at the way Abdul had died, Mustafa had struck out in the most destructive way possible.

Thing was, Mustafa's anger had been diffuse, unfocused. He'd ranted and raved about the evils of American society, but (Redwine apart) hadn't singled out any individuals for opprobrium. On the other hand, whoever was doing the burnings – and no, Boone wouldn't use the nickname he knew the media was fond of – was very focused indeed.

Mustafa had alibis for each of the killings. None of the forensic evidence found at any of the scenes matched him. Far as they could tell, he'd shown no special interest in the case; no newspaper cuttings scrapbooked at home, no discussions with friends or colleagues. Many serial killers loved talking about their cases, returned to the scenes of their crimes, and even tried to insert themselves into the investigation by hanging out at police bars and discussing the case with off-duty officers.

Whichever way you cut it, Mustafa was not their man, not for the burnings.

The killer could still be a Muslim extremist, of course, but it hadn't been Mustafa. He'd been a failed terrorist, and he'd never been a serial killer. He'd wanted to kill hundreds. As it was, he'd killed no one at all. Not even himself.

6:32 p.m.

Pittsburghers reacted to what had happened at Heinz Field with indignation, affront, and fury. Crowds gathered at each of Pittsburgh's seven mosques. Protestors railed against Bayoumi's actions and demanded arrests, deportations, executions, the lot. Muslims gathered in counter-protest, furious that they should all be tarred with one brush, and pointing out that they had American passports and paid American taxes. A rally downtown turned into a riot. Muslims were attacked on the streets for no apparent reason other than their religion. That the victims were of Arab origin rather than black, and therefore more obviously and visibly Muslim, seemed to bear this out.

Inevitably, there were those in the Muslim community who wanted to – and did – strike back. A bunch of hotheads went on the rampage in Homewood, and it needed almost half the city's riot squad to stop the carnage turning into civil war. Central Booking hadn't seen anything like it in years.

Meanwhile, Patrese spent three hours in debrief with Chance and Boone, recounting every last detail he could remember about the shooting. They told him he'd done a

420

hell of a job, but they couldn't recognize it publicly, given the official line that this had been a Bureau operation. Patrese couldn't have cared less. He didn't particularly want to play the hero, especially if putting his name out there would encourage another disaffected Muslim to seek revenge on him personally.

He thought of something Mustafa had said in his video message: *I am pursued, left unable to go about my daily business by a godless government which perpetuates atrocities against my people all over the world. My creed and color deny me the freedom your constitution promises . . .*

Had Patrese been too zealous in his pursuit of Mustafa? Was that what had tipped Mustafa over the edge: that Patrese had been round after every murder, probing, questioning, worrying away at him like a terrier?

There was no way of knowing for sure, he guessed. But even if he *had* been the difference, what else could he have done? He'd been doing his job; yes, with zeal and thoroughness, but those were what usually got cases solved. Except this one.

Patrese was leaving North Shore when his cellphone rang. He looked at the caller display and his eyes widened in surprise: Amberin.

'I'm ringing to see if you're OK,' she said, the moment he answered.

'Yeah, I'm fine. Er . . . thanks.' He couldn't keep the curiosity out of his voice. He hadn't expected her to phone; hadn't even wondered whether she would, in fact.

'That was a heck of a brave thing you did, Franco. I'm sure lots of people have told you that already, but I . . . Hold on a second.'

Patrese heard a shout in the background.

'Amberin?' he said.

'I'm here.' Her voice was strained and twisted.

'What's wrong?'

'I'm being followed.'

'Where are you?'

'Just left the courthouse. Crossing Smithfield at 4th. Franco, there's three of them, three guys, and they're . . . they're shouting things, racist things . . .'

'Stay on Smithfield.' Smithfield was a large street, well lit and busy. 'Find a shop or something, a department store.'

'Franco. *Hurry.*'

The naked fear in her voice on that last word had Patrese sprinting to the nearest cruiser. No matter that Amberin was a kick-ass assistant DA who'd faced down psychopaths across a courtroom. On her own, at night, with three men behind her, she was a woman, no more and no less, and as vulnerable as all women were to the stupider and cruder end of the male species.

Patrese turned on his blues and twos and sliced through the North Shore traffic.

He trusted there were enough people around Smithfield for the men following Amberin to think twice. They were probably just punks, too much beer inside them and picking on someone they thought was an easy target. Every cop had met hundreds like them; assholes who looked tough and talked loud, but took off like scalded cats at the first sniff of a real fight. That's what he *hoped* they were, at any rate.

It took him six minutes to get to Smithfield. As he pulled up, he rang Amberin's cellphone. No answer. No sign of her, either.

What he *could* see was a crowd of people gathered on the pavement.

For a moment, Patrese thought it must be the men who'd been following Amberin, but there were too many of them for that, and in any case the crowd was largely static.

Someone was making a phone call; another person was crouched down. Their body language reeked concern, and they were massed around something.

Someone.

Patrese leapt from the car and shouldered his way through, shouting: 'Police officer, I'm a police officer, let me through.'

Amberin was curled on the floor in a fetal position. Her face and *hijab* were covered in blood. Her eyes were open, and she was both conscious and lucid, telling those around her that she was OK, and that all she needed was not to be rushed.

'Franco,' she said, when she saw him.

The others stepped back a bit to allow Patrese through. He crouched down at her side.

'I came as fast as I could.' It sounded desperately inadequate.

'They jumped me. Called me an Arab bitch, told me to go back to my cave.'

Patrese looked up and round at the crowd. 'Anyone see what happened?'

Two or three people said they had. Amberin's attackers had hightailed, but they'd still have enough eyewitness statements to get descriptions of them.

An ambulance and a patrol car arrived. The cops started taking witness statements; the paramedics put Amberin on a stretcher and lifted her gently into the back of the ambulance. Patrese followed them to Mercy, where he ignored Amberin's protests that he should go home. He waited while the doctors patched her up, checked her for concussion and broken bones – negative on both counts – and sent her on her way.

He said he'd drive her back to her apartment.

'Thanks, but you don't have to. You've already done more than enough.'

'You want to wait half an hour for a taxi? Or you want a lift courtesy of the city?'

'You must have better things to do than go out of your way to drop me home.'

Patrese thought for a second, and then shook his head. 'No, I don't, actually.'

Amberin laughed. 'OK. Then yes, I'd like a lift, thanks.'

She winced as she settled in her seat and fastened the belt.

'Where to?' Patrese said.

'South Side. Above the Flats.'

It wasn't too far from Patrese's own stomping-ground of Mount Washington, at least as the crow flew, though the roads tended to take rather more circuitous routes through, across, up, down and round Pittsburgh's extravagant topography.

Patrese pulled out of the hospital parking lot.

'I don't mean to state the obvious,' he said, 'but . . .'

'What?'

He gestured at her bloodstained *hijab*. 'Don't you think it might be wise not to wear that for a while?'

'I've got plenty more at home.'

'Not that particular one. The *hijab*, period.'

She chuckled. 'I know what you meant.'

'Well?'

'You're probably right, but I don't care. I'm going to keep wearing it.'

'Why?'

'Because I *want* to. I wear it to show my attachment to my culture. My pride in my religion. My identity, something a little bit separate from this McDonald's world.'

'It's not, er, a bit . . .'

'Oppressive? No. You want to see oppression? Every American woman is forced to look the same way – not

424

through law or force, but through something just as potent, the relentless bombardment of images saying this is how you must look, this is the ideal, always be skinny, wear short skirts, look hot, let guys know you're up for it.'

'It's not the same.'

'It *is* the same. You're a man, you don't understand; it doesn't hit you where it hurts. But it does for girls, and *that's* oppression. The *hijab* is feminist expression, because it forces people to judge me by my character rather than my looks. It protects my dignity. If that's not liberation, then what is?'

'Men don't have to wear them though, do they?'

'No. No, they don't. But Muslim men have to do things that Muslim women don't, and vice versa. And before you tell me women are second-class citizens under Islam; no, they're not, and if you think they are, you don't know what the hell you're talking about. You know when Muslim women were given the right to keep their surnames when married, the right to receive and bestow inheritances, manage their own financial affairs, get divorced? The seventh century. Parts of the West didn't grant those kind of rights till the sixties. The *nineteen* sixties.'

Amberin in full flow, brimming with passion and energy even after having seven bells knocked out of her by pond life; Patrese shook his head in admiration, and more.

'But the Koran –' he said.

'You want to see sexism? In the Bible, Eve comes from Adam's rib, and she lures him into eating the apple. In the Koran, she's created equal, and she doesn't tempt Adam. Satan tempts them both.'

'What about Afghanistan? What about Saudi Arabia?'

'What about them?'

'Women covered head to foot. Banned from driving. Can't go anywhere unless there's a man with them. You support that?'

425

'Not at all.'

'But that's Islam.'

'No. That's *culture*, that's oppressive governments, and I hate it far more than you ever could. But it's nothing to do with religion. Look at it the other way. What are the three biggest Muslim-majority countries in the world? I'll tell you: Indonesia, Pakistan and Bangladesh. And they've all had female leaders. How many women presidents has America had?'

Patrese held up his hands. There was no answer.

'That's far more serious than what I choose to wear on my head. See, Franco, you look at the *hijab* and think of it as gender discrimination. You see cultural restraints on individual behavior and call it oppression, because you're American and that's the way you see the world. No, don't dispute it, I'm not saying that's right or wrong; it is what it is. But for lots of cultures, mine included, communal standards *aren't* seen as inhibiting individual freedoms. Quite the opposite, in fact; they're seen as part of belonging to a group whose cultures and values are important to those individuals.'

'But your head?'

'What about my head?'

'Your head's where your face is, your individuality. You subsume those?'

'I cover my head, Franco, not my brain. Does your brain stop working when you put a hat on?' She laughed. 'Don't answer that. Listen, I may be a Muslim, but I'm an American too, just as much. This country lets me practice my religion, wear what I choose and be respected for my choices. To me, that's real empowerment. I'm sorry Mustafa Bayoumi felt otherwise, and I'm especially sorry he chose to show it the way he did. But he's not me. He's not the vast majority of Muslims, either.' She pointed towards a side street ahead. 'Make a left there.'

It was an eclectic neighborhood, where new condo blocks touched shoulders with teetering rickety rowhouses one room wide and four stories high.

'There.' Amberin indicated a block on the right. 'The Angel's Arms.'

The Angel's Arms was a deconsecrated church turned condo block, a stern and handsome redbrick building in the Romanesque revival style with a tall square entrance tower which rose glowering from the slopes.

'A *church*?' Patrese said. 'Interesting choice.'

'I like to think so.'

They pulled up in the parking lot.

'You hungry?' she asked.

'I guess.'

'Then I'll cook you some supper.'

'You don't have to do that.'

'And you didn't have to give me a lift.'

8:08 p.m.

There were towering columns in Amberin's kitchen; the vast main windows of the living room were arch-topped beneath a domed ceiling with ornamental plasterwork; and a seven-foot stained-glass rosette looked to be a fully restored original.

It was quite a place.

Amberin cooked chicken and rice. Here, on her own turf and free from the endless demands of being a woman in a man's world, she seemed much softer. She was no longer wearing her *hijab*. Her white shirt was rolled up to the elbows and slightly creased across the shoulders, and thin strands escaped from the clip which held her hair up. When she smiled, it was with a soft crinkling of skin rather than a sharklike flash of teeth.

Not that it made her easier to read. If anything, it made her even harder to read than before.

In other circumstances, Patrese might have assumed that any woman who invited him round to her apartment at night was keen on taking things further. But with Amberin, he couldn't help feeling that it may just have been a mixture of professional interest and a caring personality, and that she'd have done the same for anyone.

He couldn't get a lock on her intentions, not at all; and it was almost with a start that he realized he liked her.

Yes, he'd been drawn to Mara too. Funny that he should have had designs on two women who'd faced each other across a courtroom in the most bitter and charged of circumstances; or perhaps not so funny, whether peculiar or amusing. And yes, dating Amberin would come with its own difficulties. But he liked her.

Not just because he couldn't work her out; not just because she was dusky beautiful and altogether too exotic for a hardscrabble Pennsylvania steeltown; not just because she was bright and feisty and principled; and not just because she straddled two cultures, and even she didn't know where the boundaries between the two were.

It was all of these, of course, but more too.

She *felt* right. She *smelt* right.

And when Patrese realized this, he realized something else too; that all humans are animals, and like animals, they sense things at a gut level. So either he felt and smelt right to Amberin or he didn't, and either way there was nothing he could do about it.

By happenstance, *First Lady* – the film about Eleanor Roosevelt for which Mara had won her Oscar – was showing on cable. Patrese and Amberin sat with their plates on the sofa, close but not touching, and watched it together.

'You forget it's her, don't you?' Amberin said, during the first commercial break.

You did indeed, Patrese thought.

The most famous scene in the movie was about halfway through. Eleanor and FDR have both just begun affairs; Eleanor with her bodyguard Earl Miller, Franklin with his private secretary Missy LeHand. In the marital bedroom that night, both husband and wife not only recognize the arrangements, but also accept and even encourage them, knowing that the extent to which they want each other to be happy is matched only by their mutual inability to provide such happiness.

It was one of those scenes during which you hold your breath, and only realize you've been doing so once the scene is over.

But there was nothing spectacular about it; no flashy shots, fancy camera angles or extravagant monologues. It was underwritten and underplayed. Neither Eleanor nor Franklin ever alluded to the situation directly. Instead, they did it all with euphemism, pauses, and minuscule adjustments of their bodies and faces. It was magic.

When Amberin turned towards Patrese, her eyes were wet.

'It's such a tragedy,' she said. 'For someone that talented, to do what she did . . .'

'*If* she did.'

'If she did, if she didn't; it's a tragedy whatever the truth of it is.'

He nodded, unable to think of anything to say; and he was suddenly aware that they were both holding themselves very, very still, waiting for the other to move first.

It was Amberin who broke the spell, but not in the way Patrese had hoped.

'I've got an early start tomorrow,' she said.

Tuesday, December 7th. 9:48 p.m.

'Can I help you?' he says.

'Yes. I think you probably can.'

His eyebrows furrow. 'Are you a resident here? Are you one of ours? I'm afraid I don't recognize you, and I pride myself on knowing everyone here, you understand.'

'I'm just visiting.'

'Then I'm afraid you'll have to come back another time. Visiting hours are over for today. You can visit the residents between ten a.m. and six p.m.'

'It's not the residents I've come to see.'

'No?'

'It's you.'

He's puzzled, I can see, but not alarmed; not yet.

There's a watercooler in the corner of his office. I gesture towards it.

'Could I have a glass of water, please?' I ask.

'Of course.' He goes over to the watercooler, pulls a cup from the dispenser, and holds it against the faucet under the tank.

One smack on the back of the skull with the battery in the sock, and down he goes.

I don't worry about witnesses; we're alone in the office, and the rest of the complex is an old people's home. The few people who can see well enough to give the police a description of me probably can't remember what they had for lunch that day. They're hardly going to be the most reliable of witnesses, are they?

I cuff his hands behind his back and slap him to consciousness. He peers at me with woozy eyes.

'Scream, shout, do anything other than talk, and I'll hurt you,' I say.

'I don't understand.'

'I think you do.'

'Are you confused? Would you like help?'

'I know what you do to the residents here.'

'What are you talking about? We provide them with care that's second to none.'

'You take their dignity from them.'

'This is absurd. Let me get you some help.'

'You take their dignity in life, and you take their dignity in death.'

'We . . .'

'SHUT UP! Do you know what your staff do? Let me tell you. They don't give the residents the medicine they need. They deny them food. They restrain them forcibly and leave them like that for hours. They wrap towels round their heads to stop them breathing. They let them wallow in their own waste. You think that's dignity?'

'That's not true.'

'Residents have complained, haven't they?'

'There are always complaints, in any senior citizens' home.'

'That's not an answer.'

'OK. A few people have complained, yes; but they're not in good health. They're senile, distressed, prone to fantasy. Every single allegation we get, I check it out. Every one is baseless. I'd know if there was something like that going on.'

He's gabbling now, he's nervous.

I pull the torch from my bag.

'Oh no,' he says. 'Oh no, no, not that. No. Please. Please. I beg you.'

'Isaiah chapter fifty-nine, verse seventeen,' I say. '"For I put on righteousness as a breastplate, and a helmet of salvation upon my head; and I put on the garments of vengeance for clothing, and am clad with zeal as a cloak."'

He screams. It's no use. They're all deaf as posts here. No one will hear him.

10:32 p.m.

The fire brigade had evacuated the Golden Twilight nursing home while they tried to stop the blaze spreading from de Vries' apartment to the rest of the building. By the time Beradino and Patrese arrived, the residents were huddled in small groups on the driveway. Most sat in wheelchairs, all of them wrapped in as many blankets as they could find against the savage, clear coldness of a December night.

'Hey! Hotshot!'

Patrese recognized the voice at once. It was Old Man Hellmore. He went over.

'Fuck the fire, man.' The flames, reflected, danced in Old Man Hellmore's eyes. 'A few more minutes, you gonna have folks here dyin' of hypothermia. Y'all gonna keep us outside, least let us move a bit nearer so we can get the warmth from the fire, you know what I'm sayin'?'

'I'll have a word with the fire brigade.'

Patrese was halfway towards the firefighters when he heard Old Man Hellmore shout out again. 'Full marks for compassion, hotshot. No marks for doing your job.'

Patrese turned round. 'Huh?'

'Don't you want to know who killed de Vries?'

'I was out here having a cigarette. Had to give the smokin' Nazis the slip, as there's some damn fool curfew, everyone in their room by nine thirty, like we're damn schoolkids or something. Can't smoke in the room, else it sets off the alarm and all hell breaks loose. I fought at Midway, for Chrissakes. I'd known I was fightin' for a country a man can't even have a smoke in, I'd have gone over to the Japs.

'Anyhows. Out I come, just there, ten feet from where we are now, and I spark up. Hell of a headrush, smokin' when it's this cold, you know? I'm enjoyin' my smoke when, from right over there' – he indicated the door to de Vries' apartment, about twenty yards away and swarming with firefighters – 'I see this little old lady come out.'

Patrese and Beradino looked at each other.

'I think she must be one of ours, one of the residents here, but I don't recognize her. Sure, it's dark, and she's a way away, but we got the streetlamps on, and my eyes aren't too bad, least not for distance vision. Can't read a damn thing close up, mind. I wonder who she is, but I'm not, like, suspicious or nothin'. She comes out of the apartment, gets in her car and drives away.'

'Did she look agitated? Did she drive away fast?'

Old Man Hellmore shook his head. 'Cool as you like. So I didn't pay it no mind. I thought maybe she'd come to see de Vries about livin' here – I could tell her a few home truths, if she asked me – maybe she was a friend or somethin', I don't know.'

'Could she have been a former resident?' Beradino asked.

Old Man Hellmore laughed. 'This a one-way street, man. When your residency goes from current to former, it's 'cos

435

you're six feet under. Where was I? Oh, yeah. She drive away. Few minutes later, I see the first flames, just as I'm finishin' my cigarette. I wheel the chair inside like I'm Mario damn Andretti and hit the alarm.'

'Did you see what kind of car she was driving?'

'Sure I did. Toyota Camry. Silver.'

Wednesday, December 8th. 9:12 a.m.

It wasn't just the car that Old Man Hellmore had clocked. He'd also remembered the first two letters of the license plate, DG, and that the plate itself had blue letters on a white background, with a blue band across the top and a yellow one along the bottom. That's the design of the Pennsylvania state plate. Cars registered in Pennsylvania are given license numbers with three letters, a period, and four numbers.

The license number of Jesslyn's silver Camry was, Beradino knew, DGY•7462.

For reasons obvious to him, if to no one else, Beradino took personal charge of the vehicle hunt. He confirmed with the Pennsylvania Department of Motor Vehicles that the plate design in question had come into force near the end of 1999 – before that, it had been yellow lettering on a solid blue background – and that numbers were issued sequentially, beginning with DAA•0000 and ending with DXX•9999, before moving on to the 'F'-series (no 'E', for reasons best known to the bureaucrats). A 'DG' beginning, which could cover anything from DGA to DGX, indicated a 2001 issue.

There were more than eight thousand silver Camrys which matched the description.

'Let's start with the cars registered in Pittsburgh and Allegheny County,' Beradino told the uniforms. 'If you get no joy there, then move wider.'

Jesslyn's Camry was registered to their home address in Punxsutawney, a couple of hours' drive from Pittsburgh. It would give Beradino maybe forty-eight hours' breathing space, which was the best he could reasonably hope for. He'd already tried to delete Jesslyn's details from the DMV database, but the department's remorseless computer had advised him that he didn't have the requisite authorization. Sooner or later, therefore, the uniforms would find Jesslyn on the list.

'Any of those cars that have been reported stolen, of course you check them immediately,' said Patrese. 'Nothing to stop our killer having stolen the car first.'

'What about looking at the owner's age?' asked one of the uniforms. 'If it's, like, an old lady we're looking for.'

Patrese shook his head. 'It's not an old lady. No old lady I've ever met could carry out killings like this. It's someone *disguised* as an old lady. That's how she gains entry into the victims' houses. Who turns an old lady away? No one, that's who. No one feels threatened by them. Hell, no one even *notices* them.'

Every cop knows it's better not to be noticed than not to be recognized. No one recognizes a man running down the street with a stocking over his head, but they sure as hell notice him. Old ladies, on the other hand, are about as invisible as you can get.

'Maybe it's not even a woman,' Beradino said. 'Could be a fellow in drag.'

Patrese shook his head again. 'No. It has to be a woman.'

'Why?'

'Because her disguise is good enough to get her into victims' houses, and then keep those victims off guard for as long as it takes to subdue them. Putting on some dowdy clothes, plunking on a white wig and giving herself a stoop wouldn't fool Stevie Wonder, let alone a five o'clock shadow and hairy arms. In fact, you ask me, this isn't even just basic make-up. This is professional stuff.'

'Professional stuff?'

'Proper kit. Theatre kit.'

11:41 a.m.

Patrese went to the O'Reilly Theatre downtown, where a quick phone call had secured him a slot with Maxine Park, one of their make-up artists.

Maxine Park was built like a shipping hazard and sported an orange bandana above purple eye shadow, which made Patrese fear for her cosmetic skills – did she ever look in a mirror? – but he needn't have worried. She knew her stuff, and then some.

'You can get old-age kits online or in stores,' she said. 'Anything from kits for kids' parties, which are fun but no more, to proper theatrical ones, as good as anything we use here. I'll give you the names of the main manufacturers, if you like.'

'Please, yes. But this is something the person in question would need to apply regularly, probably by herself. Would that be possible?'

'Sure. Difficult, in parts, but easily possible, if you've got time and patience.'

'How long would it take?'

'To apply? Coupla hours on, twenty minutes off.'

'Would she need to be skilled?'

'Not really. You can get videos showing you the process, either on their own or as part of the kits. A little practice goes a long way in this business.'

'And good make-up would fool people?' Patrese knew the answer, but he wanted to be doubly sure; the killer had tricked quite a few people along the way.

'That depends.'

'On what?'

'On how suspicious they are. Most people, they see an old lady, and they think, that's an old lady. If they've got no reason to be suspicious, then they won't be, not even when you're quite close to them. People see what they want to see. You could make it good enough to pass any normal encounter, no question.'

'You're sure?'

'I can prove it, if you like.'

'How?'

'I can age you so people who see you every day won't recognize you.'

First Maxine cleaned his face with something called Sea Breeze, to remove surface oils which might stop the latex stipple she was going to use later from sticking.

Using a make-up sponge for even coverage, she put on Patrese's face, neck and ears a base layer slightly lighter than his natural skin tone. Old-age complexions tend to be on the pale side, she explained. Next, she used high-light and shadow on his forehead, nose, cheeks and around the eyes to make his skin look saggy. White make-up took care of his eyebrows, with transparent powder taking the shine off.

Then came the main part; stretch and stipple. Stretching each section of his face, neck and hands in turn, she stip-pled on a modified latex solution; two layers each time. Still holding the skin, she ran a hairdryer over the section in question, powdered it, and finally let go.

The effect was amazing. Suddenly Patrese's entire skin was wrinkled; properly wrinkled, old person wrinkled.

Then it was just touching up; deepen some lines with greasepaint, add liver spots and freckles to break up the smooth areas, put a pad inside each cheek to sag and pouch them, and fix the wig on top.

'This wig feels really natural,' Patrese said. 'Is it real hair?'

'Sure is. Asian.'

'I'm sorry?'

'Ninety-nine per cent of wigs come from Asia.'

'Why's that?'

'Economic, mainly. There are many more people there than in America or Europe. Certainly many more who need to sell their hair for money.'

He thought for a moment. 'Anywhere particular in Asia?'

Maxine tipped her head slightly, as though unbalanced – or impressed – by the specificity of the question. 'The best ones come from India and Pakistan. Their hair's less stiff and forms slight waves, which looks good on wigs.'

The hair in Saint Paul Cathedral had come from Pakistan, Patrese remembered.

Wig in place, Patrese looked at himself in the mirror. He'd expected to see some likeness, but he literally couldn't recognize the man who stared back at him. He felt so dislocated that he had to say something out loud to reassure himself it was still him, but all that did was freak him out that an old man was speaking in his voice.

Maxine said she'd get a list of old-age kit manufacturers and fax them over.

'Go on,' she said. 'Go back to the police station, and see how long it takes till someone recognizes you.'

She lent Patrese an old man's jacket from her props store

442

to make the disguise even more convincing. Still in make-up, he left the O'Reilly, got into his car, and drove north across the Allegheny. He used his swipe card to get through the security gate at headquarters and went up to the homicide department, where he walked through the middle of the room, in Maxine's make-up, an old man's jacket and his best effort at a doddery geriatric gait.

He'd been working day in, day out with these people – all police officers, all trained to be observant – for more than two months.

Not a single one recognized him. Not a single one.

3:03 p.m.

Maxine Park faxed over the list of companies which manufactured old-age make-up kits within the hour. Patrese gave it to a couple of uniforms who weren't checking the Camrys, and told them to get the companies' mailing lists and order books. Pay special attention to any kits sent to Pennsylvania addresses in, say, the six months before the first murder, he said, and make sure to cross-reference with the license plate lists. If a name and address appeared on both, that was a red flag, right there.

Patrese and Beradino took themselves to an empty room and tossed ideas around.

There were now five victims. Two of them were directly connected to the Mara Slinger case: Mara herself, of course, and Yuricich. A third, Walter de Vries, was also linked, albeit very tangentially; he ran the nursing home where the father of Mara's lawyer was living. For the other two, Kohler and Redwine, nothing.

If these killings *were* something to do with Mara's case, there were at least two women they could look at: Ruby Ellenstein, the mayor's girlfriend, and Amberin, who'd originally prosecuted Mara. If either of them owned a Camry, or had sent off for a professional make-up kit, they'd be in the frame. But neither seemed likely, which probably meant these murders were nothing to do with Mara's case at all.

Make the theory fit the facts, Patrese remembered, *not the other way round.*

Given they had precious little by way of theory, that was hardly a problem.

By the end of the day, they didn't have much more by way of facts either. Neither list, the license plates or the make-up kits, had yet thrown up any likely suspects, let alone a name which appeared on both. Though they still had a long way to go checking through these lists, and they both knew this was how many crimes got solved – through repetitive, clerical drudgery – that didn't stop the lack of speed and results from being immensely frustrating.

For Patrese, at least.

For Beradino, of course, it was his only hope.

Thursday, December 9th. 5:45 p.m.

'Mark? It's Summer.'

This was the call Beradino had been dreading. He knew it straight away, just from the tone of her voice. She had news for him, and he wasn't going to like it.

'Hey.' He tried to keep his voice as neutral as possible.

'Can I come and talk with you?'

'Sure. Now?'

'Please. And if you've got somewhere quiet, that would be best.'

'Secret stuff, huh?'

'You got it.'

In the couple of minutes before Summer made it up from the basement, Beradino tried to work out how best to play this.

Summer must have found Jesslyn's fingerprints in Mara's apartment. They'd have to interview Jesslyn. She wasn't around. They'd ask Beradino when he'd last seen her, and either he'd lie, and they'd bust that one open soon enough, or he'd tell the truth, and bring seven tons of Shinola down on his head. Either way, his career would be finished. He probably wouldn't even qualify for the police pension.

By the time Summer arrived, Beradino was no nearer the answer.

They found an empty interview room. Summer looked terrified; torn.

'I don't know how to say this,' she began, 'but we've got a match from Mara's apartment, and I don't know who to talk to. I don't want to be the one who tells tales out of school, but I can't hide what we found, I double-checked it, *treble*-checked it, because I couldn't believe it at first . . . and well, you should know, I guess, you're in charge of this investigation, and it impacts directly on you.'

Beradino felt for Summer. It wasn't her fault that things had come to this, and nor was it fair on her, that she should have to be the one to break it to him.

This was it, he guessed.

A strange sense of calm came over him. He was out of options. All he could do now was tell the truth. Everything else was history.

'You found her fingerprints?'

Summer looked puzzled. 'Mara's? Of course. It was her apartment. No, the match I'm talking about is the semen.'

Beradino's head felt as though it were plunging down a helter-skelter. Semen? Mara's lover? This wasn't about Jesslyn at all.

'You found her lover?'

'Yes.'

'Well, who is it?'

Summer looked as though she was going to cry. 'It's Franco.'

Beradino was far too smart and streetwise to confront Patrese immediately. This was information, and information was power – especially when it proved that his deputy had not only jeopardized the integrity of an investigation, but had also lied to Beradino about it when directly questioned.

That Beradino's own record on lying and jeopardizing the investigation wasn't exactly spotless was neither here nor there. He knew about Patrese; Patrese didn't know about him. It was the Eleventh Commandment: thou shalt not get caught. When this was all over, Beradino would find a way to square it with God and with his own beliefs, but he didn't have time for that right now.

All police officers have to give fingerprints and DNA samples, so their traces can be eliminated from consideration by crime-scene analysts. Patrese's fingerprints had also been found in Mara's apartment, but that was easily explicable. Even Beradino knew Patrese had been there three times; when the two of them had first gone to interview her, when Patrese had gone to dinner there, and when they'd attended the murder scene. He'd been wearing gloves only on the last occasion.

But there was absolutely no reason for traces of Patrese's semen to have been in the apartment – apart from the obvious, of course.

Summer would be expecting him to do something about Patrese. She hadn't given Beradino the information for the good of his health. If she saw Beradino covering this up, who knew what she might do? She might accept it; she might cry blue murder.

So inaction was not an option; but nor did Beradino have to rush thoughtlessly into things. He had a few hours, a couple of days maybe, to work out his next move.

He went back into the incident room. Patrese was on the phone, grinning across his face and hopping from foot to foot.

'OK. OK,' he was saying. 'I'll be there as soon as I can.'

He ended the call and turned to Beradino, eyes shining. 'That was Shaniqua,' he said.

And there went Beradino's safety margin, vanished in a fingersnap.

'What did she say?'

'Her exact words?' With affection, Patrese imitated Shaniqua's voice. '"I gots somethin' for you, detective man." That's what she said.'

Beradino sat down, thinking furiously.

Two let-offs in direct succession was too much to hope for. He'd dodged a bullet with what Summer had found; lightning didn't strike twice. Why else would she have called, except to tell Patrese about Jesslyn? Prisons were rife with gossip, even more so than offices. At least in offices, people had something else to do other than gossip. Not so in prison. An hour's exercise, ten hours' sleep, thirteen hours' gossip.

Beradino had already tried to put the frighteners on Patrese by running him off the road outside Muncy, but that hadn't worked. So maybe now was the time to bring up Patrese's involvement with Mara? He could throw Patrese off the case for misleading him. Someone else would have to go interview Shaniqua, sure, but Beradino himself could do that, and make up something back at headquarters about what she'd told him. By the time anyone found out the truth, this case would be long over.

Mulling all this over, Beradino was only half-listening to what Patrese was saying.

Patrese was on the phone to Thornhill, the governor at Muncy, trying to fix a visiting time. It was already late afternoon; there was no way Patrese would make it from Pittsburgh to Muncy before the inmates were confined to their cells for the night. Beradino could only hear Patrese's side of the conversation, but even so it was clear that Patrese's attempts to bend the rules weren't going smoothly.

'No, I understand that, but . . . I'm asking for one exception . . . It's hardly a precedent, is it? I mean, how often do you get this kind of request? . . . No, of *course* I don't want a wasted journey . . . This is urgent police business . . . By the time I get a warrant, it'll be tomorrow anyway, so I might as well wait till then, mightn't I? . . . No, thank *you*. Fuck you very much.'

Patrese slammed the phone down.

'Fucking petty jobsworth *asshole*.' He pointed at the clock. 'I've been here ten hours today. I'm outta here. I'll go see Shaniqua first thing tomorrow, so I'll be back here in the afternoon. On my cell except when I'm in jail.'

A few uniforms laughed, waving sketchy goodbyes to Patrese.

Beradino didn't even notice. He'd just realized something.

Something absolutely critical.

6:37 p.m.

I see him come home; find a parking space, get out of his ridiculous car, head for his apartment block. His movements are shot through with anger's jagged jerkiness. He must have had a bad day at work.

Behind and below me, Pittsburgh spreads low and wide. Like him, I love this city, I really do; just not some of the people who live here.

It's only been two days since de Vries, so they won't be expecting another one so soon. That's the trick, I know; mix it up a bit. I left ten days, give or take, between each of the first four. Let them get used to a regular rhythm, then pull the rug from under their feet. A couple of weeks from the fourth to the fifth; leave it longer, get them worrying. And now this one, hard on its heels. Slow, slow, quick quick, slow. Keep them on their toes and off balance.

Patrese's now twenty yards from the Mountvue's front door. His hands are stuffed in his pockets and he's walking fast, with his head down against the cold. I break cover and begin to shuffle along the sidewalk towards him, slow and pained, making myself as decrepit and unthreatening as possible. It's not enough just to dress as an old lady. I have to act the persona all the way through.

6:39 p.m.

Hunched against the cold, Patrese only looked up when he got to the Mountvue. When he did, there was someone right in his face, materialized from nowhere. He jumped back, startled and breathing hard.

'Jesus Christ! You almost gave me a heart attack.'

'I told you before, Franco. Don't blaspheme.'

Beradino's here. Where did he come from? What's he doing? What does he want? He looks grave. They're talking. I have to abort this run. I've missed my chance, at least for today; can't go through with it this time. I'll have to reschedule.

Turning round or stopping would look suspicious, so I keep shuffling, right past them, without missing a beat. Just another little old lady heading back to her lonely bedsit. They don't even notice.

They're on their way inside the apartment block, their faces both furrowed: Patrese's in puzzlement, Beradino's in concern, or at least that's how it looks to me. What's happened? What's going on? If it's something drastic, it'll be in the news.

I take deep breaths. Calm, steady. No drama. There'll be other opportunities.

6:41 p.m.

Patrese took off his jacket and holster and hung them in the hall. In the living room, he removed his tie and watch, placing them on the table. He offered Beradino a hook for his coat, a beer and an armchair. Beradino took none of them.

'I hauled ass here for a reason, Franco. There's no way of soft-soaping this, so I'll just get straight to it. Forensics have matched the semen found in Mara's apartment.'

'Yeah, we know that already. To Howard.'

'No. To you.'

'Don't be ridiculous. That's impossible.' Patrese's voice sounded shrill, even to his own ears. 'Impossible.'

'None of Howard's semen was found there. Either he was lying about making love to her, or he used a rubber. Your semen *was* there. Just dinner, you told me.'

'Just dinner. That's all it was.'

'And?'

'And what?'

'And what else?'

'There must be a mistake, Mark. Forensics make mistakes. Look at what that guy Lockwood said during Mara's trial,

454

about the odds of her killing her children being billions to one. That turned out to be bullshit, didn't it?'

'There's no mistake here. It's a DNA test. It matched yours exactly. *Exactly.*'

'I still . . .'

'Don't insult my intelligence, Franco. You're not some two-bit punk who reckons people will eventually believe you if you just keep lying. You're better than that. If you're not, I certainly am. So let's do this the easy way, eh?'

Patrese was silent.

'You want to think about it?' Beradino continued. 'OK. No hurry. I got all night. But while you think, there's something else you should be aware of.'

'What's that?'

'You remember Katharine Horowitz?'

'Who?'

'Kohler's neighbor.'

'Oh, yeah.'

'She told us someone came round the morning Kohler was killed. Someone Kohler had a huge row with.'

'I remember.'

'I know who that person was.'

'You do? Who?'

'You.'

'It was you arguing on the phone with Thornhill just now which gave me the clue. I was thinking how disjointed conversations sound when you can only hear half of them, and I remembered something Katharine said; that when Kohler was arguing that morning, she could only hear his voice, no one else's. We'd presumed the other person was cowed, or trying to be placating, or whatever; keeping their voice low.

'But what if they weren't there at all? What if they were on the other end of the phone? That would explain why she'd only heard one voice, wouldn't it?

'The records show Kohler wasn't using the phone at the time Katharine said, around ten o'clock that morning. The nearest call, either before or after that time, was the one you yourself had made an hour earlier. *Exactly* an hour earlier.

'Then something else you did just now gave me the second half of it. You pointed at the clock in the incident room and said you'd been in the office too long and were going home. The clocks had gone back an hour the morning Kohler was killed, hadn't they? And when they go back, or go forward, folks often forget to change the time, especially that first

456

Sunday. What if Katharine was one of them? What if the timings she'd given us were still summer time, not daylight saving?

'She said she heard a car draw up at around nine fifteen, Kohler greet the visitor, and then the argument at ten. But what if that person – *you* – had arrived at *eight* fifteen, left sometime before nine, and *then* rung Kohler and had the argument? That would match the time on the phone records, wouldn't it? And the phone records would always have the right time; they're automated.

'There was still one thing that bothered me. If Katharine heard the visitor's car arrive, why didn't she hear it leave? But if the visitor was you – in fact, *especially* if it was you – that's perfectly plausible. You'd have gone there in the TransAm, which makes up its own mind about whether or not it's going to start each time. The drive from the bishop's house slopes down to the road below. If the TransAm didn't start when you left Kohler, you'd have had to roll it down the slope and get enough speed in the wheels to turn the engine over. By the time the ignition caught, you'd have been pretty much at the road, out of Katharine's earshot.'

The fight had gone out of Patrese's face. Beradino knew he had him.

'So, Franco; what's this all about?'

Patrese was silent for a long time, but it was the silence of someone standing on the edge of a precipice, trying to find the courage to jump, to work out the right words, rather than that of a determined stonewaller. Beradino let it play out.

'I couldn't do it face-to-face,' Patrese said. 'I still felt like a little boy. On the phone, he was just a voice. On the phone, I could tell him.'

'Tell him what?'

'Tell him I was going to bring him to justice.'

457

I wanted to be a priest when I was growing up.

I wanted to be a priest because Kohler was our local priest in Bloomfield, and he was a cool guy. He wasn't some fat, balding weirdo like lots of priests. He was quite young, and sporty, and didn't patronize us. He told us silly jokes and played ball with us.

Bloomfield's about as Italian as Rome, and Kohler was Irish, but no one ever held that against him. My father used to joke with Kohler that he was like Tom Hagen in *The Godfather*; you know, the Robert Duvall character, the Irishman who becomes Don Corleone's right-hand man.

Kohler did everything. He baptized the young, conducted Mass and first communions, performed wedding ceremonies, taught religious studies at school, took us on outings. Everything. I can't remember a time when he wasn't around. We'd have trusted him with our lives. All our parents did.

I became an altar boy – hard to imagine now, I know. It may even have been at Kohler's suggestion, I can't remember. I *do* know, now if not then, that he was very good at working out who was vulnerable, who'd be amenable to his advances. He was a Jedi master at that shit; seeing who had a vacuum in their lives that needed filling. I was one of the ones he homed in on.

Pop was rarely there; not properly, not the way you need your Pop to be. Oh, he was *there*, of course, he wasn't one of those deadbeats always trying to dodge child support. Quite the opposite, in fact; he worked his nuts off to provide for us. But restauranting ain't an easy job, and if your peak work hours are other people's social time, your own spare time – your own family time – is what suffers.

Pop treated everyone like his best friend. It was great, of course, and it said a lot for him, a lot that was good, but it got so you felt if everyone was special, then no one was special. Pop paid all his customers so much attention, it felt like there was none left over for us. Sure, Pop was jovial, demonstrative and flamboyant, but all my life, I can't recall a single conversation we had that you could call intimate. Not one, on either side, when he poured his heart out to me, or vice versa.

Kohler identified this very fast. He'd been round our house often enough to see it. And he was very, very good at doing what he did.

I don't mean that grudgingly. I mean that, years on and knowing what I know now, I can see how skilful he was. He *groomed* us. All of us. He was a family friend in the truest sense of the word, a friend to the whole family and everyone in it. Different things to each of us, of course; but he left me in no doubt that I was the one he thought was very special.

He groomed me most of all; and he did it with sophistication, professionalism even. He didn't just force himself on me one day. No; that would have been too vulgar.

Not one step until we'd taken the step before. Inviting me to stay behind after choir practice to watch a bit of football on TV. Sharing with me the dregs of his whisky nips. Asking me to sit on the arm of his chair and rub his sore shoulder. Each one very innocent on its own, little parts of the kaleidoscope of growing up.

Then a porno mag, which he claimed he'd confiscated from one of the other boys. A short lecture about the evils of temptation and the devil. 'Are you aroused? Are you aroused? Let me see. Let me feel if you are.

'You *are*.'

Of course I was. I was just about starting puberty. I got aroused by a gust of wind.

'No, Cicillo' – he used my family nickname – 'this won't do. You're too special a boy to get your kicks from looking at this filth. I'll show you the right way. I'll help you. I'll *protect* you. You're lucky to have this opportunity. You might find it uncomfortable at first, but don't worry. You'll get used to it. It's like your first beer, your first cigarette. They're rites of passage, and if they seem horrible at the time, it's only because you're not used to it.'

The first few times were just kisses and cuddles. Then clothes started to come off; first shirts, then pants, finally underwear. He'd fondle me, and ask me to fondle him. Fingers, hands, mouths.

Finally, one day, he said: 'This might hurt a bit.'

And it did.

You hear that pause, Mark? That's not silence. That's the sound of a child's spirit being broken.

When something like that happens, that act – you see, I still can't say it out loud, what he did – there's no way back.

I was like a broken vase. I put myself back together again, I glued the cracks up, and from the outside I looked the same as I ever did. But I was never the same again, not properly. I was never whole again.

Even then, I knew the exact details of what Kohler was doing weren't the important things. What was important wasn't what he was doing, but that he was doing it at all.

Each time, afterwards, he'd ask me; did you enjoy that? I always said yes. Sometimes I even meant it. That was the worst part; no, not the worst part, but certainly the most confusing part. I got erections. I came. I was with a man when I did these things, so I must be gay. And gay was the one thing you could never be at school.

Where the other guys were bragging about getting with girls – almost total bullshit, of course, though at the time we all took it as gospel, little forays into an unknown world – I was with Kohler. I was submissive, I was dominated, it was my job to give him pleasure rather than the other way round.

But I also enjoyed it sometimes. I'd let him do it to me. So it must have been my fault, in some ways. Must have been. Because otherwise I could have stopped it, no? I played football. I could look after myself, I could protect myself from harm.

And yet I chose not to.

I don't know how long the abuse went on for, I honestly don't; exact timings must be one of the things I blocked out. More than a year, less than two, if I had to guess. Not every day, of course, not even every week. When and how often weren't the issue. The issue was that every time, there'd be a next time, until I got big enough to say no, that was enough, there'd be no next time.

And when I *was* big enough, that's what I went to tell him. He must have sensed something; shit, he was that good at seeing who was ripe for it, he sure as hell should have been good at seeing who wasn't going to take it any more. Before I could say a word, he told me it was over – 'it', like it had been some big love affair. I'd lost my looks, he said. I no longer gave him pleasure.

I should have been relieved, and I was; but I was also hurt, as he knew I'd be. He'd had the power from the start, and he made sure he still had it at the finish. Not a single

461

thing in my dealings with him had been on my terms, and he made sure it ended that way.

I fucking *hated* him for that.

I thought stopping it would be the end of my problems. It wasn't. In some ways, in fact, it was just the start.

I started to get nightmares, and even bizarrely violent daydreams, when moments I'd had with Kohler came back to me at the most random times. I became numb and number. I'd go through the motions, but I'd sleepwalk through each day. I'd look at everyone around me reacting in all the ways you're supposed to, all the hundreds of emotions human beings can experience, and I couldn't feel a damn thing. I couldn't concentrate, I couldn't sleep, I jumped at the slightest sound.

Football was my salvation, and my torture. My torture because, even more than in normal life, there was no bigger sin in the locker room than being gay. If someone called someone else a fag, and meant it, that was an act of aggression not far short of Pearl Harbor. Being gay was being someone the others couldn't trust, the weak link in the team ethos. Watching your buddy's back was good. Checking his butt was bad.

I worried all the time in the showers that I'd get a boner. All those naked guys, and me thinking I was gay. It was bound to happen sooner or later, wasn't it? Unless you did what I did, which was hang around in the locker room, chatting with the other guys so as not to make it too obvious, until everyone else had finished their shower and I could go in alone. Meant I always got a cold shower, 'cos everyone else had used up all the hot, but that was a price worth paying.

And my salvation, because I loved it. I was a running back, short and stocky, sharp and elusive, low to the ground;

a scat back. The big fullbacks tend to run north—south, straight lines, up and down the field. The smaller ones, the halfbacks, run east—west, looking for the gaps. I ran every which way. I'd have given a compass motion sickness.

When I ran, I'd imagine Kohler's face beneath my feet. Stamp, stamp, stamp. When I was hit and got hurt, I'd imagine his face at the point of impact; whichever linebacker had taken me out had also smashed his face in. I ran ahead of this tsunami that was on my heels, because I feared it would swamp me the moment I stopped. Keep running. Never stop, never face it, never let it catch me.

At Pitt, I made the Panthers, the varsity football team, in my freshman year. Out there, on the grid, I was free. I didn't have to worry about Kohler or my studies or even the laws of physics, it sometimes seemed, as I'd dodge half the defense to score searing touchdowns.

I loved everything about it; not just the matches, but the razzmatazz, the feeling that I was one of the big men on campus. At home games, students would carry standards and form a tunnel for us to run through on to the field while the Pitt Band played 'March to Victory'.

In my senior year, we won the Sugar Bowl and I won the Heisman, the trophy for the best college player. There was some serious pedigree in that little trophy. OJ had won it, as had Tony Dorsett, Earl Campbell and Marcus Allen. If I could be half the player those guys were . . .

I was placed in the NFL draft. Every night for a month, I prayed the Steelers would get me. But I guess I was no longer sold on God after what Kohler had done, and God knew this; because the Steelers missed me, and in the second round I was picked up by the Minnesota Vikings, the team the Steelers had beaten to win the SuperBowl the day I was born, January 12th, 1975. You had to laugh.

Summer in Minneapolis, pre-season, the press on my ass,

463

as they always were with the Heisman winner. Routine training session, nothing special. A running drill, two linebackers closing in, and I'd already seen the gap between them and was shifting to get through it.

But the grass was wet where the sprinkler system had been left on too long. My cleats caught in a patch of mud. I went one way. My knee went the other. It sounded like a shot. I collapsed like a cheap deckchair.

The surgeon who operated on me said it was the worst knee injury he'd ever seen. In time, I'd be able to walk again, even run – in a straight line. But jink, twist, dodge and swerve – no way.

I was never going to be a pro footballer.

I'd carried so much of myself in that ambition, not least in trying to flush Kohler's poison out of my system. Football had been keeping me sane. Without it, I'd have to find some way of letting out all the poison.

I went to see a therapist, after much agonizing; after all, seeking psychotherapy wasn't the manliest thing to do, was it? And I'd had more than my fair share of worrying about not being a man, hadn't I? Ironic, that seeking help for not being a man made the problem worse.

I asked for a woman therapist, of course. I tried to seduce her; but I was clumsy about it, and my ineptitude saved me. She brushed me off, not unkindly, and gradually unpicked the mess that was my head.

She was the very first person I'd told. It wasn't just for me that I kept it secret. It was for my family too. They loved Kohler, they'd had him round to the house a hundred times, he was their friend. They'd entrusted all their children to him at one stage or another. To tell them what had happened would be to tell them that they'd failed as parents. You're supposed to protect your children. They hadn't protected

464

me; but how were they to have known? How were they to have known what Kohler was really like? If they had known, they wouldn't have let me anywhere near him.

Would they?

I'd tried to find out whether Kohler had ever done anything to my sisters Bianca and Valentina, but they always seemed uncomplicatedly pleased to see him whenever he turned up, so I guessed he hadn't. It had only been me who made excuses never to be alone in the same room as him; football practice, exam revision, upset tummy, whatever.

The therapist told me I was feeling guilt, which came from believing I'd done something wrong. I'd done nothing wrong; that was where this started and stopped. I wasn't responsible for the abuse. It had been Kohler's decision, all the way along. And even if I *had* initiated some of it – I hadn't, but even if I had – it would still have been Kohler's responsibility to say no. He was the adult, I was the child; he had the understanding and the experience that I hadn't.

I also felt shame, which was like guilt but at the same time quite different. Shame was a painful feeling of inferiority, of unworthiness, of being ridiculed or held in low opinion by somebody. Shame carried the fear of being judged and disapproved of. I was ashamed because I'd enjoyed some of my trysts with Kohler, but that was no reason, she said. Boys could be physically aroused even in traumatic or painful situations. It didn't mean that they wanted the experience or understood fully what it meant at the time.

There was, she said, one more thing which set my case apart from other similar ones; the question of Kohler's vocation. Kohler, like all priests, was seen as having a quasi-magical function, in bringing Christ's presence to the faithful. A priest was the closest thing to God on earth.

If you were close to the priest, therefore, you were close to God. Conversely, if you were betrayed by the priest, you were betrayed by God. What Kohler had done to me wasn't simply physical abuse. He'd also ripped from me the spiritual security that other children found with a consistent, unsullied belief in God.

It was soul murder.

On one hand, the Church preached enlightenment on issues such as poverty, immigration and peace. In other areas it was still in the Dark Ages, and nowhere more so than in its attitudes to priests and their sexuality. Repressing natural impulses just encourages rather than discourages sexual abuse. If being gay was wrong, official thinking seemed to go, the best way to make up for it was to be a priest, and reclaim the lost moral ground.

Knowing all this was a help, but it wasn't enough. I knew Kohler had to be punished. I couldn't have been the only one he'd abused. Perhaps I could have saved a lot more kids if I'd only spoken up earlier; all that's needed for evil to flourish, after all, is for good men to do nothing.

I could bring the case myself, and maybe others would join me once I'd set the ball rolling. There *would* be others, I was sure of that. Men like Kohler don't just offend once; they do it again and again. And when we found those photos in his desk, I knew. He wouldn't have touched all the kids in the pictures, sure, but some of them, definitely.

Remember that guy Guilaroff, Mara's agent, who I went to see in LA? His picture was in there. Kohler did it to him too, sure as eggs are eggs. Everything Guilaroff said about Kohler, and about Sacred Heart. He hated the school, hated Kohler. He was one of the unlucky ones, like me. I'd bet a year's salary on that.

So yes, I could bring the case myself. It wasn't the kind of thing I wanted my fellow cops knowing, but if that was the way it had to be, that was that. It would be my word against his, and Kohler would deny it, of course. His lawyers would send private dicks to sift through my trash and try to discredit me. I could deal with that.

I could deal with everything except my parents knowing. I loved them too much for that. I had to sort it out without them. And that meant not sorting it out, everything else be damned.

I made two promises to myself. First, I'd do nothing about it while my parents were still alive. Second, I'd do *something* about it once they were no longer here. I wouldn't just sit on my ass and say, oh, let bygones be bygones, let Kohler live out the rest of his life in peace, because it all happened a long time ago.

Not for me it didn't. The memories don't go away, and they never will. Nor does the legacy they've left. It's with me for ever, shot through my core like writing in a rock-stick. I can't forget about it or get over it. The best I can do is keep it in a box, but it doesn't just stay there, docile. Every day, it wants out; and every day, I struggle to keep it down.

7:02 p.m.

They sat in silence for long minutes after Patrese had finished.

There'd been enough hints, Beradino thought, if only he'd known how to look. There was Patrese's overarching dislike of religion, of course, even though Beradino still thought the reaction excessive. How could you hate an entire religion, all religion, because one man had done you harm? Beradino's own faith was stronger than that.

Beradino thought back to the night they'd found Kohler's body.

He remembered the thousand-yard stare on Patrese's face outside Saint Paul, when they'd been about to go in and examine the scene. Beradino had asked if Patrese had wanted him, Beradino, to do this alone, and had said he understood. No, Patrese had replied. That *no* hadn't been to Beradino's offer of going in alone, Beradino now saw; it had been to Beradino's belief that he understood.

Beradino had also said Kohler was a special man, and Patrese had shot back a deadpan *You could say that*. At the time, Beradino had thought Patrese's mild sarcasm was in response to Beradino's understatement of Kohler's qualities. Now it turned out Patrese had meant something diametrically opposite.

468

Most obviously, Patrese had broken down that night while driving back to North Shore. *What kind of man could do those things?* he'd said through his tears. *What kind of monster?* Beradino had thought he'd been talking about the killer. He hadn't. He'd been talking about Kohler.

'Why didn't you tell me earlier?' Beradino said at last.

'About Kohler, or about Mara?'

'Either. Both.'

'Personal involvement with two of the victims, conflict of interest – you'd have thrown me off the case, wouldn't you?'

Beradino nodded. Here was his opportunity, served up as though on a silver platter. 'And I still would. I am. Take a leave of absence, Franco.'

Patrese shook his head. 'I've got to see Shaniqua tomorrow.'

'Don't worry about that.'

'What do you mean, don't worry? She's got something for me. This could be it. This could be our breakthrough.'

'I'll go see her.'

'She won't talk to you, Mark, you know that, not with the whole Jesslyn angle. She trusts me, and me alone. She asked me to look out for Trent, you know.'

'Franco, you're off the case. That's final. I'll cover for you, spin an explanation.'

'At least let me go see Shaniqua, find out what she has to say . . .'

'No.'

'. . . and after that, if you still want, *then* I'll take the leave of absence.'

'I said no.'

'Why? This could be the breakthrough, and you don't want to know? Why the hell not? Tell me why.'

'It's not up for discussion, Franco.'

'Why don't you want to hear what she's got to say? Are you worried about it? You think it's going to involve Jesslyn

469

or something?' Beradino's face must have betrayed the truth of this, for he saw Patrese's eyes widen. 'You *are*. My God, Mark. You know what Shaniqua's going to say, don't you? You never wanted me to go in the first place. You tried to steer me away from tapping Shaniqua, and . . . *steer me away*, that's it, it was you who ran me off the road that night outside Muncy, wasn't it? Of *course* it was. So stupid, not to see it till now. You knew where I was going, you had a reason to want me out of the picture. You stole that sedan rather than use your own car, so it couldn't be traced, and the next morning, when the sedan was in the police pound, you crawled all over it before Forensics had got to it, so when your fingerprints were found inside, there was a perfectly rational explanation.'

'You're talking nonsense, Franco.'

'Tell me where I'm wrong, then.'

'Nonsense. All of it.'

'Yeah? Then let me go see Shaniqua, and we'll see, once and for all.'

'No.'

'You can't stop me.'

'Yes, I can.'

'What are you going to do? Arrest me?'

'That's *exactly* what I'm going to do.'

Beradino had his gun out almost before Patrese realized. Patrese's own Ruger Blackhawk was in his holster, hanging in the hallway. Beradino was standing, while Patrese was sitting in the depths of his sofa. It was no contest, in every way.

Patrese laughed; half disbelief at the absurdity of the situation, half nervousness that this was actually for real. 'On what charge?'

'Well, we could start with five counts of murder, couldn't we?'

7:24 p.m.

It was ludicrous, of course, but it was also strangely logical, at least once Beradino had outlined his reasoning.

Patrese had a cast-iron reason to want Kohler dead, that was beyond doubt. He'd also been Mara's lover, and who knew what had transpired between them? Men killed their lovers the whole time. Perhaps Patrese had found out Mara was still sleeping with Howard, and killed her in a jealous rage.

As for the other three victims; well, that was what questioning was for, wasn't it? You questioned someone when you didn't know all the answers.

Then there was the circumstantial evidence.

Serial killers typically need a trigger, something stressful or traumatic, to push them from fantasizing about murder to actually carrying it out. That trigger is usually one or more of the four 'd's: death, divorce, dismissal and debt. Patrese's parents had been killed a few weeks before Redwine's murder – and in a fireball too, the same way these five victims had met their end. Add to the mix Patrese's shooting of Samantha Slinger, and you didn't have to be Perry Mason to argue for a disturbance in the balance of his mind.

A vast proportion of serial killers – even by the most conservative estimate, more than nine in ten – have suffered abuse while growing up. Not all victims of abuse become killers, of course, but almost all killers have suffered abuse. Again, Patrese fitted the bill.

And Patrese hated religion because of what Kohler had done to him. Kohler's killer had smashed crucifixes, icons and religious prints. The connection was clear.

'What about the old lady?' Patrese said. 'How do you explain the killer was me, when we've already decided it must be a woman using the old lady disguise?'

'*We* didn't decide that at all. *You* told us it must be that way; and why wouldn't you, to throw us off the scent? And then you came into the incident room with the make-up on, after you'd been to the O'Reilly, and not a single person recognized you. If the make-up's that good, it doesn't matter if you're man or woman.'

Beradino motioned Patrese to get up from the sofa, very slowly, hands in the air. From a low, soft sofa, it was harder than it sounded. Patrese needed three attempts before he had enough momentum.

'Turn round,' Beradino said. 'I'm going to cuff you.'

Proper handcuffs, too, not the flexible plastic ties that were ten a penny. Beradino had come prepared. Patrese tensed his hands as the cuffs went on.

'Let's go,' Beradino said.

8:15 p.m.

Beradino put Patrese in the cells at North Shore. He needed Patrese out of the way, somewhere secure, and he figured this was as good a place as any. Yes, it would set tongues wagging all over headquarters, but that didn't worry Beradino; quite the opposite. He didn't publicly mention the possibility of murder charges just yet, but he *did* drop the news about Patrese's histories with Kohler and Mara round the night staff in the incident room, knowing their sympathy for Patrese would be limited.

Cops don't tend to be judgmental about their peers' personal failings – most of them have more than enough of those themselves – but they *do* take a dim view of anyone who withholds information vital to an investigation. These guys had been busting their chops for weeks, months, to try and find the killer. Patrese had held back at least two critical pieces of information. He wouldn't really be flavor of the month.

Beradino left strict instructions with the duty officers about how they were to treat Patrese. No one was to talk to him, bring him food or liquid, or even check through the door grille to see if he was OK. Whatever Patrese said, whatever

473

wild accusations he might make, they were to ignore him. Patrese was in a world of trouble, Beradino said, and that went too for anyone who helped him, even in the smallest way.

What Beradino wanted was for Patrese to spend a night in complete isolation, and see how amenable that made him to walking away from the case. Beradino had even put Patrese in the end cell, right down the far end of the corridor, to keep him as out on a limb as possible. He, Beradino, would be back in the morning; fed, watered and rested, unlike Patrese. Then maybe they could come to some kind of arrangement.

The one concession Beradino had made was to take Patrese's cuffs off. There was no reason to keep a suspect cuffed when alone in a cell, providing laces, belts and neckties had been removed beforehand. That was department policy. Besides, keeping the cuffs on would just give Patrese something to complain about, which might in turn tempt one of the duty officers to remove them, and get chatting, and then . . .

10:10 p.m.

Patrese lay on the cot and stared up at the ceiling, his mind whirling. It was cold down here, and the regulation-issue blanket was too thin and scratchy to be much use. If he was to get any sleep, he'd need a coat, a woolly hat, maybe even some gloves.

Gloves made Patrese think of Trent, who'd been in a cell just like this, gardening gloves peeking from his hip pocket . . .

Not in a cell just like this, Patrese realized. In this very cell.

With the dodgy ceiling panel.

Maintenance should have repaired the ceiling panel by now – Patrese had put in a request the day after he'd caught Trent trying to escape – but they'd still clearly not gotten round to it. Patrese had lost count of the number of times he'd cursed bureaucratic inefficiency, but he'd never been so glad to find it as he was now.

Standing on the concrete bench, he could reach high enough to dislodge the panel. From there, it was simply a question of having enough strength to haul himself up through the gap. It had been almost a decade since Patrese had done pull-ups to failure at training camp, but he still had enough muscle memory and raw strength to make it. He was up and through on his second attempt.

He starfished himself, to spread his weight as widely as possible, and looked round. The panels were all part of a false ceiling, with the real ceiling a couple of feet higher. Electric wires and three or four pipes snaked through the crawlspace; the buildings' arteries and veins, hidden from casual view.

There was a small window at the far end of the crawl-space. If Patrese flattened himself and leopard-crawled across the top of the panels, he could make it to the window. He had no idea where it led to, but it had to be worth a shot, especially when he totted up his other options: a big, fat zero.

He went slowly, carefully. Time was not the issue. Beradino's interdiction against the duty officers checking on Patrese would work in his favor, as it should be many hours – with luck, not till Beradino himself arrived the following morning – before they discovered he'd gone.

No; the issue was stealth. The last thing Patrese wanted to do was alert someone by making too much noise or – worse – crashing through the panels into another cell below. So he took his time, testing his weight each time before moving forward.

Patrese didn't know how long it took him, as he didn't have a watch, but he was drenched in sweat by the time he reached the window.

The window was hinged at the top. He eased it open, looked through – and saw the underside of a car, parked a few feet away.

Of course. The cells were in the basement, so a window above their ceilings would be pretty much at ground level. This was the building's main parking area.

Patrese waited a few minutes. No one walked past. It was night; the parking lot was pretty deserted.

He decided to risk it.

Moving fast now, he wriggled through the opening and on to the tarmac, staying low till he got his bearings.

Heinz Field was dead ahead. Beyond that, the river.

He thought about hot-wiring a car, but that risked drawing attention, and attention was the last thing he wanted. Better to go on foot. It was two or three miles back to his apartment. Not too long, if he ran it. Besides, running would keep him warm.

With no laces and no belt, he didn't so much canter as shuffle, but he didn't care. Every step took him further from North Shore and nearer the Mountvue.

Friday, December 10th. 2:13 a.m.

He didn't have his keys, of course, but that was no problem. The Mountvue wasn't anywhere near upmarket enough to have a doorman, but it *did* have a caretaker, Chad, who lived in a small basement apartment and had sets of every resident's keys.

Patrese buzzed Chad, feigned giggling drunkenness – 'a night out with the boys,' he slurred, 'you know how it is' – and got his spare key. 'Thanks, man. Appreciate it. Give it back in the morning. Sorry to wake you. Peace.'

The clock in his apartment said it was past two in the morning, though Patrese felt wide awake. He changed into jeans and sweatshirt, put his watch back on, grabbed a holdall, and began slinging stuff in it. He didn't know how long he might need to be on the road for, and he wanted to be as self-sufficient as possible, so he packed toiletries, warm clothes and whatever non-perishable food he could find in the place. Then he strapped on his holster, and put his wallet, keys and cellphone into the pockets of his jeans. A quick check to make sure he'd left nothing vital, and then he was out of there; lights off, door locked, and who knew when he'd be back?

He checked both ways, up and down the street, before crossing the short distance to the TransAm. It never hurt to be careful.

No one was around. The coast was clear.

The TransAm started first time. Patrese smiled. Surely that was a good omen?

He nosed through deserted city streets, always wary of passing patrol cars – a couple came past, sirens wailing, but they were hurrying some place far from him – and, almost before realizing it, he found himself on the interstate.

Next stop; Muncy.

8:00 a.m.

Thornhill had said Patrese could come see Shaniqua any time from eight o'clock onwards. Patrese was there right on the dot.

The security rigmarole seemed to take twice as long as he remembered, though Patrese knew that was just his impatience talking. As before, he surrendered every personal item; wallet, phone, coins, keys and – of course – firearm.

After what felt like several eons, he was ushered through to the visiting room. A few minutes later, Shaniqua appeared.

'OK,' she said – no preamble or pleasantries; maybe she was as excited as he was, in her own way – 'here's the skinny. I been talkin' a lot to that Madison bitch. She ain't all that bad, actually, once you get her to open up. I think she walk around puttin' on this big ol' don't-fuck-with-me act, but that ain't her at all, not really.

'Anyways. Accordin' to her, Mara had this ting with one of the guards. This *ting*, you know what I'm sayin'? Like a love ting. Love affair. Happens the whole time in here. And not just any ol' guard, either. This guard, she be, gotta get the title right, she be deputy superintendent for facilities management, you know these people, ain't nothin' they love more than some big ol' job titles.'

480

Patrese knew where this was going, but he kept quiet; not, he felt, that he could have gotten a word in edgeways, even if he'd wanted to. Once Shaniqua started off, you had to let her run her course.

'She's the boss player on the block. She's in charge of – let me get this right again – unit management, facility security, and all corrections officers. Like I said, she's the boss player, her word goes. She says jump, you say how fuckin' high, you know what I'm sayin'? Anyways, she gets a big ol' fuckin' bee in her bonnet about Mara. They get it on. And then, after a few months, Mara pulls the plug. This woman, this guard, she goes *batshit*. She wants revenge. No fury like a woman scorned, you know? Especially when it's another woman doin' the scornin'. Mara steps out of line, even this much' – Shaniqua held her thumb and forefinger a millimeter apart – 'and her ass gets banged up in solitary.

'All this time, Mara's bein' cool and shit. She turns the other cheek, every time, like she's fuckin' Gandhi or somethin'. But everybody sees it, man; everybody sees what the fuck's goin' on, and peeps here don't like that shit, not when it's so fuckin' blatant, you know what I'm sayin'? Every motherfucker in here got a fuckin' sixth sense for injustice. So Madison says to Mara, either you complain, or I'm sure as fuck goin' to, 'cos this shit ain't right. So Mara complains – this is before she's released, you know – and it goes all the way up to the governor, and there's some other peeps called to give evidence, peeps like Madison, this takes, you know, some time, by which time Mara's released, so she ain't even here no more, and cut a long story short, couple months back, this guard's given the sack. Fuck you, bitch, *fuck you*, you Audi 500 O-U-T outta here, and you can kiss my black ass on the way through.'

'Shaniqua?'

'Yo.'

'What was this guard's name?'

'I ain't told you that? Sorry. Gedge. Jesslyn Gedge.'

No wonder Beradino hadn't wanted him to come here, Patrese thought.

'That good enough for you?' Shaniqua said.

'Oh, yes. You can say that again. You're a marvel, Shaniqua.'

'Shit, Detective. Sheeeit. Ain't no one told me that before. If I weren't black, you could see me blush. Now, *quid pro quo*, like the doctor says to Clarice. My boy. Trent. You been lookin' out for him like I aksed?'

Patrese told Shaniqua about his encounter with Trent in the cop shop, what they'd talked about there, and how they'd gone to Heinz Field to watch the Steelers take down the Browns.

'Yeah, man,' she said. 'He a hell of a footballer. When he play in the NFL, we can go watch his ass. Hospitality suites, champagne and oysters, you know it.'

'I'd like that.'

'But you gotta keep on him, Franco. I know you a busy man, but once in a blue fuckin' moon ain't enough. You gotta build up a rapport with him, you know?'

'I know that.'

'Else he gonna go to shit. He *will*, man; he will. He'll go to shit, 'cos I know what he capable of, man, I know he can get sucked in, I know he can be a dumbass, and then I'll be doin' all this shit for fuckin' nothin', you know? For *nothin'*.'

Patrese was about to reply, but something in Shaniqua's words jarred. He played them back in his head, trying to find what had caught his attention.

Two phrases, he realized. *I know what he capable of*, and *I'll be doin' all this shit for fuckin' nothin'*.

It seemed outrageous, what Patrese was thinking; and it also made perfect sense.

'Shaniqua,' he said.

'Yo.'

'Trent killed Weaver, didn't he?'

She said nothing.

Patrese was flattered, in a way. They'd obviously got to a stage where she wouldn't lie to him, not directly, even if she wouldn't answer him straight either.

He saw how it must have happened that day in Homewood. It had been Trent who'd been standing by the windowsill, next to the gun, and Shaniqua who'd been by the bed. Weaver had therefore gone for Shaniqua, not Trent. And it had been Trent who'd shot Weaver, not Shaniqua.

It made more sense that way, psychologically; that Weaver should have attacked his woman, his first target for abuse over the years; and also that Trent, unencumbered by blood ties to Weaver and ever more cognizant of his own ascent to manhood, should have picked up the gun and said, That's it, enough is enough.

Then they'd swapped places, in every way. Shaniqua had taken the rap for what her son had done. If she'd been the one to kill Weaver, she had a decent chance of pleading BWS and walking free, claiming that years of abuse had driven her to it. But if the killer had been Trent, he'd have no such defense.

Yes, he'd come to his mother's aid; but why only then, why not on all the occasions before? Patrese knew exactly how the jury would see him; just another Homewood punk, a fuck-up in waiting. Likely as not, he'd have been found guilty, and that would have been it. His last, best, first, only hope gone.

Patrese was right; he knew he was. Nothing else could explain why Shaniqua had said *I know what he capable of.* Every other mother Patrese knew thought her son the Archangel Gabriel, even when confronted with direct evidence to the contrary. And it certainly explained why Shaniqua had been so happy to confess right off the bat. Any lawyer would have told her to shut the hell up, which in turn would have risked the truth coming out. This way, however, she could transfer all the heat from Trent on to her own shoulders right from the start, and back her chances with a sympathetic jury.

Patrese couldn't have begun to tell her how much he admired what she was doing.

'Trent killed Weaver, didn't he?' he said again.

'Franco, you got my confession. That's what happened, man. Just like I said.'

He was about to ask her again, and then he had a thought.

If she told him the truth now, what would he do? Would he go back to Amberin and say, Look, here's what happened; let's lock Trent up too, keep Shaniqua in for obstruction of justice, and just fuck up as many lives as we can in one go? Or would he think this is what Shaniqua has chosen to do, because this is what being a parent is all about, protecting your own child, no matter what the cost to you?

Put that way, it was hardly a question.

'Just like you said,' he replied.

She smiled. 'We understand each other, Franco, you know?'

He knew indeed.

8:34 a.m.

Thornhill confirmed that Jesslyn Gedge had been dismissed for improper conduct. The Pennsylvania Department of Corrections maintained the highest standards of integrity and probity, and any officer who fell short of these . . . yadda, yadda, yadda.

'Mr Thornhill,' Patrese said, 'I'm a police officer, not a press conference.'

Thornhill gave a thin smile. 'Of course.'

'Do you have a copy of the proceedings I could see?'

'Of course.'

Thornhill went across to his filing cabinet, opened the top drawer, flicked through the folders, brought one out, and handed it to Patrese. It was a full account of Jesslyn's dismissal; complaint forms, tribunal minutes, citation, judgment, legal counsel, the lot.

Jesslyn had written a longhand submission in her own defense. Patrese recognized the handwriting at once; it was the same as that on the two letters Mara had shown him in her apartment, one of them hateful, the other pleading for reconciliation, both of them liberally peppered with Bible quotes and admonitions about the Lord Jesus.

Patrese looked at the proceedings' relevant dates.

Mara had brought her complaint on June 23rd, and had been released on July 12th.

Jesslyn had been fired on October 14th. Redwine had been killed four days later.

Divorce, debt, death – or dismissal. From a job she'd regarded as a vocation.

You do the math, Patrese thought.

8:51 a.m.

Patrese had been in the cell more than twelve hours, Beradino calculated. He'd be tired, cold and hungry by now. Perfect timing to put the pressure on.

Beradino's first thought when he walked in was that he'd got the wrong cell. His second was that one of the duty officers must have moved Patrese, or even let him go, in direct contravention of Beradino's orders. Someone was going to catch hell for this.

Then he saw the hole where the ceiling panel had been.

8:53 a.m.

'Thornhill.'

'Mr Thornhill, Mark Beradino here. Is Franco Patrese with you?'

'You've just missed him, I'm afraid.'

'What do you mean, just missed him?'

'He was here with me a few minutes ago.'

'What did he want?'

'He wanted to know about Jesslyn Gedge.'

'What did you tell him?'

'I told him the truth.'

'Mr Thornhill, Franco Patrese is no longer part of the police force. In fact, he's a murder suspect. He escaped from custody last night. That makes him a fugitive from the law. Can you lock your prison down? Make sure he can't get out, if he's still on the premises?'

'Only if I activate the breakout alarm.'

'Then do that, please.'

'You have no jurisdiction . . .'

'I don't care. Do it, or I'll have you charged with obstruction of justice. *Now.*'

8:55 a.m.

'Wallet. Cellphone. Keys, two sets. Coins, assorted. One sidearm, Ruger Blackhawk .357. Sign here, please.'

Patrese held the inventory sheet flat with his left hand, scribbled his name with his right, and pushed it back to the prison officer. 'Thanks.'

'No problem. You have a good day now.' She gestured towards the double set of security doors. 'You remember how they work?'

'Sure. The outer set won't open till the inner set's shut.'

'You got it.'

The inner doors opened as Patrese approached. He stepped through them and into the small area between the two sets of doors. Patrese wondered what they called this area. An airlock? A pod? No man's land?

The inner doors closed behind him.

The alarm was so sudden and loud that for a moment Patrese felt as though it was actually ringing inside his head. In the confined space, it seemed to come at him from every direction at once, wailing sirens and flashing lights hammering him, trepanning, like he was the unwitting subject of some giant experiment.

Through the bedlam, he realized something: the outer doors should have opened by now. That they hadn't meant the alarm must have overridden their mechanism, which in turn meant it couldn't be a fire alarm, as a fire alarm wouldn't trap people inside.

If it wasn't a fire alarm, it must be an escape alarm. Instant shutdown.

He looked at his watch. It was just before nine; easily time enough for Beradino to have discovered he was no longer at North Shore. Beradino would know instantly where Patrese had gone. He'd have rung Thornhill, told him that Patrese had escaped custody, got him to shut the place down . . .

Patrese looked back at the officer who'd signed him in and out. She shrugged, raising her hands in helplessness. *Nothing I can do, pal.*

Then he saw her pick up the phone, cupping one hand over her free ear and the other round the mouthpiece so she could hear and be heard over the sirens.

Her mouth moved in silent demands. *What? Can't hear. Speak up.*

She listened for a few seconds, and then looked at Patrese; puzzled, suspicious.

They were on to him. Which meant he only had one option left.

He pulled out his Ruger Blackhawk and shot the hell out of the outer doors' lock.

8:56 a.m.

Patrese crossed the parking lot to his TransAm like an Olympic sprinter. No one else could get out of the building till the alarm was turned off, of course, but he couldn't bank on his head start being more than a few seconds; a minute or two, at most.

He flung open the car's door and dived in.

Please start, he thought. *Of all the times, please start.*

It didn't, of course. Twice consecutively was too much to ask.

In the main building, the alarm suddenly stopped. They'd be out on him in a flash.

Patrese jumped from the car, wedged his right shoulder against the windscreen pillar, and began to push.

Nothing. The car wouldn't move.

He pushed harder. *Come on. Come on.*

Still nothing.

The handbrake, he thought. *Didn't take the handbrake off. Doofus.*

He leant inside, snapped the handbrake down, and pushed again. This time, the TransAm began to roll forwards.

A shout from the main gate. Patrese didn't even look. He was running now, the car gathering speed ahead of him.

The crack of a bullet, the whistle of the air round his head as it passed by.

Lucky once. He might not be lucky twice.

He stopped pushing, jumped in and twisted the key in the ignition, one seamless movement honed to perfection through years of practice with this damn machine. The engine fired and he was gone, fishtailing out of the parking lot with two snaking lines of black rubber behind him and the steering wheel bucking in his hands.

9:00 a.m.

Patrese made straight for the interstate.

It was a risky strategy – freeways are much easier for the police to check than a myriad of minor roads – but Patrese wanted to get as far from Muncy as possible, as fast as possible. The local cops would throw up roadblocks at various distances from the prison, and he wanted to be outside them all by the time they did so. Besides, he didn't know the back roads round Muncy, and taking to them would just invite the police to run him to ground and corner him like a fox before hounds.

Patrese had already turned his cellphone off when he'd first entered Muncy, but now he took the battery out too. Phones still send signals to the nearest masts every few minutes when they're off, but not when they've literally no power to work with.

If the phone links up with just one tower, that tower can judge the distance to the phone, but not the direction; that is, it could be anywhere along the edge of an imaginary circle. If a second tower gets the signal too, it can also plot an imaginary circle, thus narrowing the location to the sector where the circles intersect. A third tower will make the intersecting sector much smaller, pinpointing the location to within a few hundred meters. A few hundred meters wasn't much on the open road.

Then he turned on his police scanner. He didn't know the frequencies the cops round here used, so he set the scanner to search; lock on to a channel, listen for five seconds, hunt for the next one. A fire in Pennsdale. A water main burst at Seagers. RTA on route 15 southbound out of Sulvan Dell, EMS en route.

And the Muncy Police, together with the Lycoming County Sheriff's Department, rushing to the State Correctional Institute, all units to be on the lookout for a burgundy TransAm, gold wheels, suspect armed and dangerous, use deadly force if required.

Well, Patrese thought, he'd shot his way out of prison and was listed as an escaped fugitive. What else did he expect?

The first thing he had to do was ditch the car. Silver Camrys may have been ten a penny, but burgundy TransAms certainly weren't. Driving this thing around, he might as well put a neon sign on the roof announcing his identity.

There was a service stop up ahead, at mile 194. Patrese pulled in, heading for the busiest part of the parking lot. The TransAm would be less visible in the midst of a block of other cars than way out on its own at the edge.

He glided to a halt and turned off the engine.

The service stop restaurant was filled with the breakfast-time crowd, all deep into their newspapers while chowing down their grits and waffles. If Patrese stayed low between the cars, the vehicles themselves would block him from the diners' sight.

He was looking for a car which was cheap and old. The newer the car, and the more expensive it was, the better security it would have; and Patrese needed to be in, out and gone without screwing around with deadlocks or immobilizers.

494

Three spaces down from him was a two-tone Pontiac Sunbird hatchback that must have been a couple of decades old, and had definitely seen better days in that time.

Perfect.

Patrese got out of the TransAm, clipping the police scanner to his belt as he did so. He popped the trunk, took out the holdall and a small canvas bag toolkit which he always kept there, shut the trunk again, and then moved casually along to the Sunbird.

He opened the canvas bag and picked out a thin strip of spring steel a couple of feet long, an inch or so wide, and with two staggered notches at the bottom. A Slim Jim, a lockout tool, beloved of locksmiths and cops worldwide.

Making sure the Sunbird was shielding him from anyone who happened to be looking out of the restaurant window, Patrese eased the Slim Jim between the passenger door's rubber seal and window glass, and slid it down into the door itself. There was a rod in there which connected the locks, and if he could only find it . . .

There.

The Slim Jim's notch caught, Patrese pulled gently, and the locks popped.

He opened the passenger door, put the holdall in the footwell, and slid across to the driver's seat. From his toolkit, he took a screwdriver, a pair of wire strippers and some insulated gloves. He'd had to hotwire the TransAm often enough, when it was jerking him around. Now, he'd do the same to the Sunbird.

Using the screwdriver, he prized off the plastic panels around the ignition tumbler, revealing a panel trailing six wires; blue, red, purple, green, black and orange. What such wires' respective colors signify varies not only between manufacturers but even between a single manufacturer's models; there's no universal code.

495

But chances of the schematics matching are higher if you stick with the same manufacturer, which was why Patrese had chosen a Pontiac. In his TransAm, the 'on' wires were purple and green, the starter wires black and blue.

Patrese put on the gloves, took the wire clippers, pulled the four wires in question from the Sunbird's ignition, stripped an inch or so off the end of each, and touched them all together.

The engine fired almost before the wires had sparked. If Patrese had believed in God, he'd have blessed every Pontiac engineer ever born.

11:00 a.m.

Patrese headed towards Pittsburgh, into the eye of the storm.

There was method in his madness, of course. They'd be expecting him to run *from* them in his beloved TransAm, at least to start with, so he'd blindside them by running *to* them in a Sunbird. Besides, he knew how to hide himself in Pittsburgh better than he did anywhere else, and he also wanted – *needed* – to prove what Beradino had done. Quite how he was going to do that, he didn't yet know. He'd have to find some way of getting to Boone, or to Chance, and convincing them of the truth.

If he couldn't get it all resolved today, and had to spend the night – maybe several nights, given that tomorrow was the weekend – where would he go? The cops would already have been to see his family and friends, so there'd be no safe haven there. Hotels, motels and hostels were too easy for the police to check. He could always hunker down in an abandoned building with the homeless and the winos, but half those guys would shop their own grandmas for a 40-ounce bottle.

All of which meant he *had* to get it resolved today, one way or another.

The closer Patrese got to Pittsburgh, the better he could pick up city police chatter on the scanner, and what he heard alarmed him. Pittsburgh police use twelve channels, and Patrese was prime topic of conversation on both Channel 8, frequency 453.950, which the detectives use, and Channel 12, 458.3625, reserved for tactical operations.

Again and again came his physical description. A voice from the Allegheny County Sheriff's Department, saying they'd disseminated the APB and were standing by for further instructions. Another voice said he'd spoken to both the suspect's sisters, and told them to dial 911 the moment Patrese tried to get in touch with them. There were men at Patrese's apartment, turning the place upside down. Someone said every local TV and radio station was carrying news of the manhunt.

Patrese flipped on the radio. They weren't lying. He was lead item on that, too, top of the hour: *Law enforcement have launched a state-wide manhunt for Detective Franco Patrese, who escaped from custody last night and is suspected of carrying out the Human Torch killings which he himself was investigating.*

Beradino had gone nuclear, Patrese thought. He knew he had to get Patrese before Patrese got him, and so he'd thrown the kitchen sink at it. Accusing Patrese of the murders was the only way Beradino could mobilize such a massive manhunt. If you were going to lie, Patrese thought, lie big.

Beradino must also have known Patrese would be using the scanner if he was in Pittsburgh, but there was no way round that. You can't co-ordinate a manhunt on cellphones or secret frequencies; you have to keep everyone in the loop, otherwise one hand doesn't know what the other's doing. If a suspect is listening in, too bad. Even the most resourceful fugitive can't run forever.

498

11:07 a.m.

'Clinton County Sheriff's Department, you've requested police assistance, how may I help you?'

'My car's been stolen.'

'What's the make, color and license plate number, please?'

'Pontiac Sunbird. Light blue, dark blue. Two-tone. Nevada plate, 740JEF.'

'And your name, sir?'

'My name is Ryan Green.'

'Thank you, Mr Green. Where was the vehicle stolen from?'

'Rest stop on I-80. Mile 194.'

'And that's where you are now?'

'Yes, of course. I can't exactly go anywhere, can I?'

'A patrol car will be with you within the hour.'

'An *hour*? You can't get someone here quicker than that?'

'There's a state-wide manhunt for an escaped fugitive. All our units are assisting with that. I'm sorry, sir.'

12:37 p.m.

In the suburbs now, stop lights making his progress jerky, Patrese felt more exposed. Drivers don't look at other drivers too much on the interstate; they do in urban traffic, picking their noses as they wait for the lights to go green. Sooner or later someone would recognize him, and they'd call in a description, send in the hounds.

Patrese flicked through the scanner's channels again, if only to know that the usual quotidian run of law and disorder went on without him.

Pittsburgh's six police districts are covered by three radio channels. Patrese first turned to Channel 1, frequency 453.100, which covers zones One and Two: downtown, North Shore and the Strip, among others. The cops were waiting for him here, that was for sure, in case he chose either to come back to headquarters or tried to take his case to someone in authority downtown; Howard, for instance, or Amberin.

Channel 2, 453.250, covers zones Three and Six: Mount Washington, where he lived, and the South Side. They were *definitely* waiting for him here. Half the force was probably at his apartment already, he thought; the other half would be at Fat Heads.

Which left Channel 3, 453.400, zones Four and Five: Oakland, Squirrel Hill, Bloomfield, Homewood. Oakland was where Patrese had been to varsity, Bloomfield was where he'd grown up. Obvious places for him to head to, sooner or later.

Not Homewood, though.

Patrese smiled to himself. They'd *never* think of looking for him in Homewood.

1:04 p.m.

Patrese's all over the news. A robot blonde stands outside police headquarters and breathlessly tells her microphone, the camera and the nation in that order that this is the largest state manhunt in recent history, and that the Pennsylvania Governor is considering calling in the National Guard if need be.

Robot Blonde says Patrese was arrested last night on suspicion of carrying out the Human Torch murders, but he escaped from custody sometime in the night. He was then involved in a shootout earlier this morning at the State Correctional Institute in Muncy, where Hollywood actress Mara Slinger, one of the Human Torch's victims, was imprisoned for killing her three babies, a sentence later overturned on appeal.

Robot Blonde clearly doesn't have a clue why Patrese might have gone to Muncy, and she spends several minutes offering theories which get increasingly outlandish and ludicrous. But the cops – Beradino at least – must know that Patrese didn't do it. Which means Beradino must know why Patrese went to Muncy; because that's where the answer to the Human Torch is.

Which means Patrese has information Beradino would kill for. Hence the manhunt.

Patrese's alone, probably friendless.

Everyone's looking for him, including me.

Everyone's looking for me, too, including him.

The answer's obvious. We should collaborate.

Two fugitives, helping each other. But he doesn't know why I want him. He doesn't know what a lucky escape he had last night. He doesn't know I won't miss twice.

I'll help him, give him a safe haven, and then I'll kill him.

Two fugitives, helping each other. One fugitive, killing the other.

1:16 p.m.

Clinton County Sheriff's Department had said a patrol car would be with Ryan Green within the hour. In the event, it was more than two.

A heavyset officer with a goatee beard too small for his face clambered out of the driver's seat. 'Mr Green? Sorry we took so long, sir. One heck of a busy day today. I'm Officer Schmidt.'

Schmidt took a notebook from the breast pocket of his jacket. 'Now, your vehicle – a Pontiac Sunbird, is that right? – was stolen at around what time?'

'I was eating breakfast in there from nine till around ten. Came out, car had gone.'

'You didn't see anything suspicious?'

'Apart from a big gap where my car should have been?'

'Sir, you giving me static is not going to help matters, is that clear? I meant, you didn't see anything suspicious from the restaurant? No one acting weird?'

Green shook his head. 'No.'

Schmidt walked over to the restaurant window, wanting to see exactly what kind of view a diner would have of the parking lot. He looked back at the serried ranks of parked cars, and that's when he saw it.

A burgundy TransAm. With gold wheels.

The one every law enforcement officer in Pennsylvania was looking for.

1:22 p.m.

Knight was just about to begin a Bible study group when Patrese walked in.

'Hey, Franco,' Knight said; as if nothing had happened, which meant Knight can't have known. If there was one place in Pittsburgh where folks wouldn't have heard the news, Patrese thought, it was Homewood. 'You come to see Trent?'

There were a dozen or so teenagers in the room, Patrese saw, Trent among them.

'I was just, er, passing, and . . .'

'Then stay. Join the study group. Stay and pray with us.'

'That's kind, but it's not really my thing.'

'Come on, man,' Trent said. 'Just for a little while.'

Patrese stayed.

Sitting in a spare chair, the only white guy there, he felt the tension and anxiety begin to seep out of him for the first time since the previous afternoon.

Knight began to talk about the way in which Jesus had always represented the poor and excluded, the easily despised, the demonized, those whose burdens were more than they could bear; and Knight did it all without once sounding superior or judgmental. He had a calm about him that was soothing. Patrese could tell from the faces of those in the study group that he wasn't the only one who thought so.

They weren't bored, fidgety or disrespectful. They listened, they asked questions, they nodded when they got an answer that made sense. Patrese knew these kids weren't saints; few kids are. But nor could he sit here and reconcile what he was seeing with what he knew of their record sheets down at Central Booking.

Police work is marked by the underlying philosophy that might is right. Every year the cops declare war on the gangs, saying they're going to take Homewood back block by block, street by street, house by house. They call in help from an alphabet soup of agencies: SWAT, FBI, DEA, ATF. They lay confiscated weapons out like dead fish at press conferences, and push slack-eyed gangbangers into the back of cruisers in front of TV cameras.

And yet it seemed to Patrese, not to blow his own trumpet, that an afternoon at Heinz Field had probably done Trent more good than the endless cycle of arrest, trial, prison, release and arrest had ever accomplished for any of his brothers.

Patrese thought of what he'd seen in Homewood, and realized suddenly that the more pertinent question was what he *hadn't* seen. He *hadn't* seen sports halls or swimming pools, playgrounds or basketball courts, baseball diamonds or football pitches, supermarkets or department stores. He'd seen vacant lots and boarded-up homes. That was pretty much it; and that was where the problem was, surely?

All the arrests the cops made; what did they accomplish? They took some bad boys off the streets and put them inside for a while, sure. Then out came those bad boys again, not changed in the slightest. Jail didn't make you better; Patrese had only had to talk with Mara to know that. Jail took people out of society's way, that was all.

If you've got a floorboard that needs fixing, there are three things you can do. You can leave it as it is, till one day it trips someone up and hurts them; you can put a rug over it and not think about it any more; or you can get your toolkit out and mend it.

Those, Patrese figured, were society's options with kids like these. We could leave them as they were, which was more or less abandoning them. We could put a rug over them and lock them up, out of sight and mind. Or we could do what Knight was doing here and now, and try to fix them into becoming productive members of society.

Patrese wasn't suddenly going to run off and sing songs with Joan Baez, but perhaps every cop needed, sometime in his life, to question what he was doing and why he was doing it. Patrese didn't know what the answers were – hell, he didn't even know what some of the *questions* were – but he realized now that the two cases which had informed his life these past few months, and the way in which they'd gradually become intertwined, were two halves of a whole.

Jesslyn was the Old Testament avenger, punishing people for who knows what, an eye for an eye until the whole world was blind. Shaniqua was the New Testament; a woman who loved her son so much she'd sacrifice herself for him.

And how could you understand the Bible when its two constituent parts were at such odds with each other?

Patrese dragged himself back from his thoughts to what Knight was saying. Knight had moved on from Jesus, it seemed, and was now talking about other ways in which the Bible sets out guides for the ways in which people should live their lives.

'How many commandments are there in the Old Testament?' he asked.

'Eleven.' Trent, smirking.

Knight raised his eyebrows, playing along. 'That so, Trent? I only remember ten, but maybe I'm mistaken. What's the eleventh?'

'Thou shalt not get caught,' Trent said.

Everyone laughed, Knight included; then he was straight back to serious. The commandments are there for many reasons, he said. They're there to help us enjoy happiness, peace, long life, contentment, accomplishment, and all the other blessings for which our hearts long. They're there to show us the difference between right and wrong. They're there to protect us from danger and tragedy.

The commandments cover the whole duty of man. They're the law of God, and the law of God is perfect, so the commandments cover every conceivable sin. The commandments are so serious, in fact, that in Biblical times the punishment for breaking them had been death.

That got everyone's attention; Patrese's included.

And the other thing about the commandments people forget, Knight said, is how restrictive they are. Of the ten, eight are prohibitions. Only two are positive exhortations to do things rather than injunctions against doing them.

Something tugged at Patrese here, something he couldn't quite place, but which he was sure was important.

They're forbidding, the commandments, Knight continued; and they're permanent, too, which was why they'd been carved in stone; on two tablets, which Moses had brought down from Mount Sinai.

There was a strange rushing in Patrese's ears, as though all the fizzing synapses in his brain had sparked their own electrical storm.

Wheelwright had said the Sinai peninsula in Egypt was part of the Midyan terrane, where the pink granite had come from.

Two tablets, with the commandments on, brought down. From Sinai.

Two stones at each murder site; two pebbles, of pink granite. From Sinai.

Now Patrese saw what had tugged at him a moment earlier. In the commandments, there are only two 'do's, but eight 'don't's.

Just as there had been in the e-mail which the killer – which *Jesslyn* – had sent them, about the 'do's and 'don't's of a homicide investigation.

Jesslyn, with her Old Testament fire and brimstone. Jesslyn, railing against sinners.

That was why she was killing the victims. That was *why*. That was the pattern. That was it. They, her victims, had transgressed the commandments. That was what it said in the Bible, and so she took it as absolute truth.

As the word of God, in fact.

Thou shalt have no other Gods before me.

Thou shalt not make unto thee any graven image, or any likeness of any thing that is in heaven above, or that is in the earth beneath, or that is in the water under the earth. Thou shalt not bow down thyself to them, nor serve them: for I the Lord Thy God am a jealous God, visiting the iniquity of the fathers upon the children unto the third and fourth generation of them that hate me. And shewing mercy unto thousands that love me, and keep my commandments.

Thou shalt not take the name of the Lord thy God in vain, for the Lord will not hold him guiltless that taketh his name in vain.

Remember the Sabbath day, to keep it holy. Six days shalt thou labor, and do all thy work: but the seventh day is the Sabbath of the Lord thy God: in it thou shalt not do any work, thou, nor thy son, nor thy daughter, thy manservant, nor thy maidservant, nor thy cattle, nor thy stranger that is within thy gates. For in six days the Lord made heaven and earth, the sea, and all that in them is, and rested the seventh day: wherefore the Lord blessed the Sabbath day, and hallowed it.

Honor thy father and thy mother: that thy days may be long upon the land which the Lord thy God giveth thee.

Thou shalt not kill.

Thou shalt not commit adultery.

Thou shalt not steal.

Thou shalt not bear false witness against thy neighbor.

Thou shalt not covet thy neighbor's house, thou shalt not covet thy neighbor's wife, nor his manservant, nor his maidservant, nor his ox, nor his ass, nor any thing that is thy neighbor's.

1:40 p.m.

Patrese began at the beginning, in every way.

If Jesslyn was murdering according to the commandments, she was surely doing so in strict numerical order; a pathology so precise in its insanity wouldn't brook random matchings of victims with transgressions.

So. First murder, and first commandment; Michael Redwine, and *Thou shalt have no other Gods before me.*

Bianca had said Redwine was a typical Harvard med school graduate, thinking God was his gift to the world rather than vice versa. Redwine was a surgeon, therefore he played God, whether he liked it or not; when you were under his knife, he had absolute power of life and death over you. At such moments, surgeons don't just think they're God; they *are* God.

Had Jesslyn killed Redwine simply because he was a surgeon, or was it something he personally had done? Something to do with Mara, in particular? But they'd checked that already. Redwine had never operated on Mara, and wasn't involved in any of the awful business with her children.

Come back to that one.

Second murder, second commandment. Gregory Kohler,

and *Thou shalt not make unto thee any graven image, or any likeness of any thing that is in heaven above, or that is in the earth beneath, or that is in the water under the earth. Thou shalt not bow down thyself to them, nor serve them: for I the Lord Thy God am a jealous God, visiting the iniquity of the fathers upon the children unto the third and fourth generation of them that hate me. And shewing mercy unto thousands that love me, and keep my commandments.*

Crucifixes, icons, stained-glass windows smashed, the Michelangelo reproduction defaced. All images of God, in one form or another; but the Bible holds that all men, even geniuses like Michelangelo, are mortal, and therefore by definition incapable of capturing the essence of a deity who has no shape or form.

It seemed a very literal interpretation of the commandment, Patrese thought; but then again, so was killing someone for transgressing it. Jesslyn's pathology might be extreme, but it was at least consistent.

Third murder, third commandment. Philip Yuricich, and *Thou shalt not take the name of the Lord thy God in vain, for the Lord will not hold him guiltless that taketh his name in vain.*

Yuricich's tongue had been cut out – for taking the Lord's name in vain.

Like all public officials in Pennsylvania, Patrese included, Yuricich had taken an oath: *I do solemnly swear that I will support, obey and defend the Constitution of the United States and the Constitution of this Commonwealth and that I will discharge the duties of my office with fidelity.* At the end, the oath taker can, if they wish, add *So help me God.*

Patrese hadn't done so on his turn, for obvious reasons. Yuricich would definitely have done so, for equally obvious reasons. But his handling of Mara's case, among others, had given the lie to that pledge.

Fourth murder, fourth commandment. Mara Slinger, and

Remember the Sabbath day, to keep it holy. Six days shalt thou labor, and do all thy work: but the seventh day is the Sabbath of the Lord thy God: in it thou shalt not do any work, thou, nor thy son, nor thy daughter, thy manservant, nor thy maidservant, nor thy cattle, nor thy stranger that is within thy gates. For in six days the Lord made heaven and earth, the sea, and all that in them is, and rested the seventh day: wherefore the Lord blessed the Sabbath day, and hallowed it.

Patrese stopped, not knowing what to make of this. Of all the many things Mara had been accused of, surely failure to observe the Sabbath wasn't one of them? Mara had been Jewish, so her Sabbath was Saturday – technically, Friday sunset through Saturday sunset – rather than Sunday; but did that make a difference?

While filming any of her movies, had she been on set during those times? Almost certainly. She'd done theatre too, so Patrese figured any Friday-night performance would technically have been a breach of her Sabbath. But was that really it? If you started killing people for breaching the Sabbath, you could pretty much pick any stranger at random, sure in the knowledge they'd transgressed at some stage. Even Jesslyn herself must have worked Sunday shifts at Muncy.

Was Patrese missing something? He wasn't sure. Another one to come back to.

Fifth murder, fifth commandment. Walter de Vries, and *Honor thy father and thy mother: that thy days may be long upon the land which the Lord thy God giveth thee.*

This one was obvious. Even Patrese remembered enough from Bible school to know the fifth commandment enjoins respect not merely on one's actual parents but on all elders, those in the twilight of their lives who've seen much of what the world has to offer and call it experience. Walter de Vries had been charged with looking after these people. If the

515

complaints of Old Man Hellmore and others were anything to go by, he'd failed them miserably.

Patrese slapped his face lightly to keep himself alert.

There'd been five murders already. If he was right about the pattern, there'd be five more to go, in strict sequence. Knowing what Jesslyn's criteria were might help him anticipate her choice of victim. He looked at the list again.

Sixth commandment, the most basic and reductive one of all. *Thou shalt not kill.*

Patrese felt something warm and hateful clutch at his entrails.

He himself had killed, hadn't he? He'd killed Samantha Slinger.

She hadn't died instantly. He remembered that like it was yesterday; the hope, tight and burning within him, that she'd somehow make it, lying there with her life soaking the floor beneath her as the paramedics swarmed and injected and shouted, what kind of drugs has she taken, what kind, tell us *now*.

She'd been on life support. He'd wanted to go and see her. No way, Chance had said; absolutely no way. Him visiting wouldn't look good, in legal terms, if this ever went to court. Patrese hadn't cared what it looked like, in legal terms or any other. He'd wanted to go see her, even though she was in a coma and wouldn't know he was there. He'd have been going for himself rather than for her. But he'd still wanted to.

Her family had been there. They certainly wouldn't have wanted him anywhere near them.

And eventually, after a few days, they'd turned Samantha's life support off.

Bianca had told him once that whether to end a life was a decision pretty much every doctor had to take at some stage during their career. In an ideal world, they'd keep everyone alive for as long as they could. But this isn't an ideal world, and comatose patients take up time, resources and bedspace they never even know about.

So, sooner or later, a doctor will say to the relatives, Listen, there's nothing more we can do. Your loved one might yet live for years in that bed, but they'll never regain consciousness. They're in deep coma without detectable awareness. They are, to all intents and purposes, existing rather than living. They're brain dead.

If the skill of the doctors is all that's keeping someone alive, withdrawing that skill is what will kill them, or let them die, depending on your view of the semantics. As a doctor, you have to judge that margin, walk that line. You have to play God.

You have to play God.

Bianca would know. He needed to talk to her.

The police had already been on to her, in case he phoned. Maybe they even had someone sitting with her right now, especially if she was at home. He couldn't remember what shifts she was working this week. If she was at work, he could go through the hospital switchboard, but that would be lunacy; they'd put him in a queue, trace him and swoop.

Which meant he had to ring her cellphone. But he couldn't remember the number.

It was programmed in his own cellphone, of course, but he'd never had cause to memorize it. So he'd have to use his own cell, and risk the cops triangulating his position. There are more phone masts in cities than there are in the countryside, and the accuracy of triangulation is therefore much greater; not a few hundred meters, as it is out in the sticks, but a few tens, if that.

If he did this, he'd have to be on his way out of here straight afterwards.

517

He needed to know. There was nothing else for it.

He put the battery back into his cellphone, turned it on, and hit Bianca's speed dial.

'Jesus, Franco,' she said the moment she answered. 'What have you done?'

'Nothing, and you know that. It's a big frame-up.'

'Are you OK? Where are you?'

'I'm fine. Where are you?'

'At the hospital.'

'There any cops with you?'

'No. But they want me to call them when you make contact.'

'Listen. In life-support cases, when the machine's turned off; do hospital records state which doctor authorized it?'

'What's *that* got to do with anything?'

'It might have everything to do with it. Please. Just trust me.'

'Of course I trust you. And yes, they do state it.'

'And that doctor – does it have to be the surgeon who originally operated?'

'No. Not at all. Any doctor senior enough can do it, once they know the facts of the case and feel qualified to make a diagnosis.'

The police had checked all the operations Redwine had performed, Patrese knew, but not every decision he'd made as a doctor.

'If I give you the patient's name, can you check for me?'

'Is this important?'

'Critical.'

'OK. Because there are computer checks, and they'll want to know why . . .'

'Samantha Slinger,' he said, simply.

Bianca caught her breath. '*Jesus*, Cicillo.'

'It's for the burning case. Trust me.'

He heard the tapping of her fingers on the keyboard; then another intake of breath, much sharper and more urgent than before.

And he knew.

Bianca read it in a low monotone.

'Cessation of Samantha Slinger's life-support mechanisms was authorized by Dr Michael Redwine.'

Patrese pressed hard on the bridge of his nose. Redwine had played God, even though there was little else he could have done, and he'd paid the ultimate price.

'Thanks. I'll see you. I love you.'

Patrese ended the call, thinking furiously.

Was there no end to Jesslyn's obsession with Mara? Clearly not.

He was about to turn his cell off again when he saw he had a text message. He didn't recognize the sender's number. He clicked it open.

Looks like they're looking for us both. I didn't do it. I know you didn't too. I know who did. Let me help you. Meet? J.

1:52 p.m.

Patrese worked out his options.

He didn't buy Jesslyn's claims of innocence for a moment, but that wasn't the point. What did she know? What did he know?

There was no reason for her to assume he'd worked out either her disguise or the pattern of the killings yet, which meant she didn't know he knew he was next in line. Therefore the promise of help was a trap; lure him, and then kill him.

He could turn this to his advantage. He'd meet her, apparently willingly, but arrest her before she could do anything. That way, he'd have proof not only of his innocence but also of Beradino's complicity, which was why he'd come back to Pittsburgh in the first place.

Yes, it was a trap, but he'd be trapping her, not vice versa.

He didn't want to go anywhere private or enclosed, just in case she got a jump on him. She'd killed five people already; he had to afford her the respect of caution. What he wanted, therefore, was somewhere public, but not too busy. It was freezing outside, so he could wear coat, scarf and baseball cap without attracting attention, and that would keep his identity from any but the nosiest passer-by.

He thought for a moment, wondering what would be a good location.

The idea came to him in a flash. He looked at his watch. It was almost two.

Sure, he typed back. Meet you at Warhol Museum at 3.

1:56 p.m.

'Attention all units. Attention all units. Please be advised suspect's cellphone has been triangulated to Homewood district, corner Frankstown and Collier, error margin twenty-five yards. All Zone Five units to proceed to location immediately. Repeat, suspect believed to be driving two-tone blue Pontiac Sunbird, Nevada plate, number seven, four, zero, period, Juliet, Echo, Foxtrot. Suspect is believed armed and dangerous. Approach with caution. Use deadly force if necessary.'

1:57 p.m.

He hasn't given me long; a couple of hours, at most. It'll only take me fifteen minutes to walk to the Warhol, but what about the make-up? That's a couple of hours in itself.

Which makes me wonder: does he know about the disguise? Has he worked it out? If so, best not to risk it this time. Not if he's expecting an old lady.

I'll go as myself. That'll surprise him. And surprise, just a little bit, is all I need.

2:23 p.m.

Beradino stood in the middle of the incident room and sucked his teeth.

Zone Five had just radioed in. They'd missed Patrese. They'd found out where he'd been – at The 50/50 – but no one there knew where he'd gone, or if they did, they weren't saying. Zone Five were now asking whether Beradino wanted them to arrest everyone in The 50/50 and bring them in for questioning? They'd harbored a fugitive, after all.

Beradino thought for a moment.

'No,' he said. 'Even if one of those guys *does* know something, by the time we get it out of them, this whole thing will have moved on several stages. Besides, Knight does some good things for those kids. I don't want to start a riot in Homewood.'

Where are you, Franco? Beradino thought. *Where are you heading?*

'Sir!'

Beradino looked round. One of the uniforms was brandishing a printout.

'What you got?'

'The old-age make-up kits.'

Beradino had almost forgotten about them, what with everything else going on; and, in terms of keeping Jesslyn hidden, any news on this front was bad news.

'We've got slightly bigger fish to fry than that, haven't we?'

'Three kits sent to Magda Nagorska at The Pennsylvanian, 1110 Liberty Avenue,' the uniform said excitedly. 'That's where Redwine was killed, wasn't it?'

Magda Nagorska. The Pennsylvanian.

Beradino must have looked like a guppy fish, his mouth dropped so far open.

Magda Nagorska was the deaf old woman who'd lived beneath Redwine.

2:45 p.m.

Arguably the three most striking of Pittsburgh's several hundred bridges are the co-ordinated trio of suspension spans painted in Aztec gold which cross the Allegheny at Sixth, Seventh and Ninth Streets. They commemorate three famous Pittsburghers – Roberto Clemente, Andy Warhol and Rachel Carson respectively – and Patrese had always been struck by the symbolism of that choice. It said much for the city, he thought, not just that a baseball player, an artist and an environmental pioneer should be immortalized side-by-side, but also that such eclecticism was seen as normal.

He'd left the Sunbird in an out-of-the-way parking lot after hearing on the scanner that they knew he'd switched cars, and he'd walked the last bit into town. It was a cold day, and a man wrapped to the nines attracted no attention, just as he'd predicted.

Standing on the riverbank, he waited a couple of minutes, just to check there was no reception committee at either end of the bridge. If the police sealed it off when he was halfway across, his only option would be over the side and into the Allegheny, which was hardly going to be tropical at this time of year.

Satisfied that the coast was clear, Patrese crossed the bridge.

The Warhol Museum, a few hundred yards up from the north end of the eponymous bridge, is a cream-toned, terra-cotta-clad warehouse: exactly the kind of industrial site the artist had used for his studios. Inside, it still feels like what it once was, with stone walls and airy, cavernous rooms.

Patrese paid the entrance fee, took a small map of the museum from the desk, and began to walk round, looking for all the world as though he were just another art lover.

He checked his watch. Ten to three.

2:51 p.m.

A SWAT team went into The Pennsylvanian; they were taking no chances.

They split into four groups. One guarded the building's perimeter at street level, one took the rooftops, one went up the fire escape, and the fourth went with Beradino through the lobby and up the stairs. Once he'd realized there was no way he could call them off, he'd insisted on coming with them, in an ever-receding attempt to keep Jesslyn's identity to himself, or at least be there for her when her luck finally ran out.

No knock on the door, no polite requests to have a word; a battering-ram to the lock and in they piled, eyes flicking left and right over the sights of their rifles, fast through the rooms, barking *clear, clear, clear.*

The place was empty.

Beradino stepped inside the living room and looked around.

How the heck had Jesslyn afforded this place? How the heck had she stood in front of him the last time he was here, Redwine still too hot to touch, and presented a face, a body, a voice, an entire persona that wasn't her own?

How the heck had he failed to recognize her, his own partner?

Then again, he'd also failed to recognize Patrese when *he'd* had the make-up on, and he spent more time with the two of them than with anyone else in the world. Just went to show, he thought; you never know anybody else, not really.

You never really know yourself half the time, come to think of it.

If Beradino knew where Jesslyn was, he could still lead them away from her.

There were books in the shelves, some washing-up on the sideboard. She couldn't have left in a tearing hurry, as the place was pretty tidy, but equally it didn't look like she'd packed for a major journey.

Her cellphone was still here, for a start, sitting on the kitchen table. Beradino picked it up, his fingers brushing the keys.

The screensaver disappeared, and he found himself looking at the messages menu.

One message in the inbox. From Patrese.

Sure. Meet you at Warhol Museum at 3.

The SWAT leader was peering over Beradino's shoulder. Another second, and Beradino could have deleted it. Too late now.

'Let's go, sir,' said the SWAT leader. 'Let's go take them both down.'

2:58 p.m.

It wasn't the Campbell's soup cans or the Marilyn Diptych which snagged Patrese's attention. Instead, it was Warhol's Death and Disaster Series: *Orange Disaster #5*, orange-tinted photos of an electric chair isolated in a room with a sign blaring SILENCE; *Green Car Crash*, in a similar vein; a CAT scan of someone's skull.

These were Warhol's versions of old *memento mori* paintings, Patrese realized. Warhol understood death; he understood that we're little souls carrying round corpses, nothing more. And when you get to be that corpse, Patrese knew, it's not pretty. The body bloats, it purges, it bleeds. The only people to have it right in two thousand years, Patrese reckoned, were the Vikings. When it was his turn, he wanted to be like them; he wanted to be cast off in a burning boat and left to the flames.

He dragged his thoughts back to the present, and checked his watch for what felt like the hundredth time. A couple of minutes shy of three o'clock.

Distant footsteps, echoing round the concrete spaces. The soft hum of machinery.

'Franco.'

530

He spun round. No one there. Just soup cans and Brillo boxes.

'Over here. Through the pillows.'

Off the main exhibit space was a smaller side room, around which helium-filled foil pillows were being gently buffeted by a fan high on one wall. On the far side of the room, swimming in and out of view behind the pillows, was Jesslyn. She too was wrapped in coat, hat and scarf, clearly as paranoid as he was about being recognized.

Patrese closed his fingers round the Ruger Blackhawk in his coat pocket.

He remembered reading somewhere that these helium pillows represent a basic personality test. If you take the straightest route through them, bashing them out of the way, it shows you're no-nonsense but unimaginative. If you dodge and weave, working the angles and anticipating the gaps, determined that none of the balloons should so much as touch you, it means you see things from different angles and don't mind going off at a tangent.

All bullshit, of course; but he zigzagged anyway, jink, jink, breathe and stop.

'We've got a lot to talk about,' Patrese said as he reached her.

'We sure do,' she said, unwinding the scarf from round her face,

and knowing that Patrese's shock when he sees me will buy me time

and the recognition was a physical blow, so much so that for a moment Patrese thought she must have actually reached out and punched him, right in the solar plexus.

It wasn't Jesslyn.

It was Mara.

3:00 p.m.

Thoughts tumbled through Patrese's head like acrobats; logical deductions made lightning fast, time slowing as his brain raced.

Two women had been in Mara's apartment that day. One of them had killed the other and then left, never to be seen again. Beradino and, latterly, Patrese had both assumed Mara had been killed and Jesslyn had escaped.

Now Patrese saw the truth; it was the other way round. And because the body had been burnt, and because there'd been three previous victims, no one had questioned whether it was Mara's or not. Why should they have done?

For the switch to work, of course, Mara and Jesslyn must have been roughly the same size. Patrese remembered what Mara had told him about her arrival at Muncy, when she'd first met the woman who was to be her nemesis.

I expected her to be some big, butch dyke, all shaved head and tattoos, but she's nothing of the sort. She's small and petite, no bigger than me, and she's quite pretty.

Small and petite, Patrese thought, *no bigger than me.*

Maxine Park had said people see what they want to see.

532

If you've no reason to be suspicious, you can easily be fooled. The cops had seen what looked like Mara and what they'd had no reason to believe *wasn't* Mara. A lot of negatives in that sentence, but all adding up to one undeniable truth; they'd been fooled.

Patrese didn't even bother to consider motive. Mara had every reason to kill the victims; so much so, in fact, that faking her own death was perhaps the only way she could have continued to evade suspicion.

He wondered where and when the idea had first come to her. Perhaps it had been less a blinding flash than a slow accumulation of realizations, starting with what she'd seen every day during her trial: the Ten Commandments, sacred text in all three Abrahamic religions and backbone of the justice system, printed on Yuricich's robes.

Then, when that system had failed her, she'd had countless hours in jail to brood, plot, refine, and watch as the pieces fell slowly into place; the final, crucial, achingly satisfying one being the fact that she could turn her tormentor Jesslyn into her patsy.

Jesslyn must have gone to Mara's apartment with malice on her mind; otherwise why would Beradino have assumed she, Jesslyn, was the killer, and gone to such lengths to protect her? She'd probably never realized, until it was too late, that she'd been walking into a trap.

Mara had been unrecognizable as Eleanor Roosevelt in *First Lady*. On set, she must have sat in the make-up chair day after day, hours each time, watching, listening, asking questions, seeing how she was gradually transformed into someone else.

It was a hell of a plan, and a hell of an execution, in both senses of the word; Patrese had to give her that.

All this flashed through his head, sensed and understood if not properly articulated, in a couple of seconds, and during that time he was too stunned to do anything other than stand and stare.

Which was exactly what Mara had counted on.

Patrese wasn't even beginning to draw his gun when Mara pulled from behind her back the makeshift blackjack which had served her so well; battery in a sock, the staple prison weapon. Up fast and round she whirled it, hard against Patrese's temple before he could block it, and down he went as though someone had cut his strings.

3:04 p.m.

For a moment, when Patrese came round, he had no idea where he was, and he felt no pain. Then the recognition of the gallery – Mara had closed the door of the small side room, sealing them off with the silver helium pillows still bouncing happily around – together with the agonies pulsing in his head, and the realization there was a gag in his mouth, all hit him at pretty much the same time.

The room swayed, and he put his hand down to stop himself falling; except his hands were fastened behind his back, and he was already sitting down, his butt on the floor and his back against a wall, so he toppled sideways with a lack of elegance that would in other circumstances have been embarrassing.

Very clever. He'd have thought about applauding if his hands had been free.

She'd secured them with plastic cuffs; he could feel the texture against his skin. A few years before, plastic cuffs had been pretty much the preserve of the police, but now you could get them anywhere; uniform and equipment retailers sold them in stores and online. Hell, you could make half-decent ones yourself just by going into a hardware store and buying some electrical cable ties. It wasn't exactly arduous to get a gun in America; why would it be hard to get some plastic cuffs?

But they had their limitations too. They could be broken by people who were very strong, or very strung out on drugs, and they could be cut or melted.

Patrese wasn't either of the first two, and if the other murders were anything to go on, by the time the cuffs had melted, he wouldn't be around to take advantage of it. So if he was going to get free, he'd have to somehow cut them himself.

But how?

She'd leant him near a small corner, where the wall jagged away at right angles to accommodate a window alcove. If Patrese leant slightly to his right, he could place his wrists against this right angle; and if he rubbed hard enough and fast enough, he might be able to wear away the plastic on the cuffs enough to split them.

It would hurt like hell, because whatever damage he was doing to the cuffs he'd be doing to his skin too, but it was that or die like a human barbecue, and put that way, it wasn't much of a choice.

Keeping his body between his wrists and her, so she couldn't see, Patrese began to rub in small, quick motions. Even if she saw it, he hoped she'd think he was simply shaking with fear; not an unreasonable assumption, given the circumstances.

She came across the room with the gasoline can. The top was off; he could hear the gasoline sloshing inside, and smell the rich fumes as they wafted into the room.

Splashing it on him now, running into his eyes and nose as he gasped through the gag for air, panicking for a brief moment that he might asphyxiate here and now even before she lit the flames.

Patrese kept rubbing his wrists against the plaster. His skin was wet with what he presumed was blood, and each abrasion sent jagged shards of pain darting through his body, but he didn't care. Pain was good. Pain meant his plan might be working, he might be rubbing the plastic away.

Pain meant he was alive.

She had the torch in her hand, and was flicking the lighter open.

Patrese had a sudden, hysterical urge to know whether she'd ever really cared for him at all; but he guessed here was his answer, right here.

He looked away. Pleading would do no good. Nothing would stop him from dying apart from his own ability to free himself.

He wasn't going out like the others, he told himself. He was younger, and stronger, and he was a cop, and she wasn't going to beat him, not as long as there was breath in his body.

He's shaking, his body giving little jerks against the wall. He's scared. Good.

He knows what happens next, he's seen it five times before already. He knows how the bodies look, how they smell. He knows what a horrible, horrible way it is to die.

He deserves it, and he knows that too, deep down.

I remember what we shared, what we did together. It means nothing. It never did.

I turn to him and speak.

'Isaiah, chapter fifty-nine, verse seventeen. "For I put on righteousness as a breastplate, and a helmet of salvation upon my head; and I put on the garments of vengeance for clothing, and am clad with zeal as a cloak."'

There was more give in the cuffs now, Patrese was sure of it. His wrists were agony, from being scraped against the wall and the cuffs themselves, but he gritted his teeth against the inside of the gag and kept going, drive on, drive on against the pain.

Then a snap, so sudden it made him jump, and his hands were free.

He comes up fast from the floor, his arms swinging round to the front, all wet and slick with blood and the cuffs falling away from them, and somehow he's managed to break free.

I spark the flame on the lighter and thrust it in his direction. He sways away fast and scared, a fencer dodging a parry. He's not wild-eyed; he's calculating, and that makes him more dangerous. I could rush him and touch the flame to him, but he's bigger and stronger than me, and he could close with me; grab me and hold me to him so we both burn.

He pushes his matted hair back from his forehead, rips the gag from his mouth, and snarls. I pick up the gasoline can again, to use it as a shield if need be.

And then the world explodes.

They come flying through the door; men in body armor and hockey helmets, sighting down the barrels of rifles which are as much a part of them as their own limbs, hollering and whooping to disorientate me and keep their own adrenalin high.

Then they stop dead, as I've got the lighter in one hand and the gasoline can in the other, and Patrese's drenched in gasoline from head to foot.

'Drop 'em,' they shout. 'Drop 'em, and step away.'

'You won't fire,' I say. 'None of you will fire.'

'Hands EMPTY!' they shout.

'None of you will fire,' I say, as though I haven't heard, 'because bullets create sparks, and sparks start fires. So even if you hit me, he'll go up in flames.'

And while they process this, I flick the lighter shut, take the rest of the gasoline, and empty it. Over my own head.

'No!' Patrese shouted.

It's something they train you for at police academy, because any officer might face it one day; the moment in a situation where the perpetrator realizes it's not going to end the way they intended. That's when things really get dangerous.

That's the point Mara was at now.

She'd missed killing Patrese, let alone whoever she had in mind for the last four. So this was going to end only one of two ways: their way, or her way.

And she was right; they couldn't shoot, not without risking that fatal spark.

She took four quick steps backwards, right to the other side of the room, just in case they tried to rush her; and she flicked the lighter open again.

'I have walked the same path as God,' she said. 'By taking lives and making others afraid, I have done God's work.'

'Not this way, Mara,' Patrese said.

'Yes,' she said. 'This way.'

It would be dark outside soon, Patrese thought; and with sunset came Shabbat.

Mara sat down, sparked the flame on the lighter, and touched it to her face.

It was Mara's stillness which haunted Patrese. Flames billowing beneath rolling clouds of black oily smoke, transforming and destroying her: the high, salty odor of burning flesh, her skin blackening and charring, skin and clothes melting into one; and all the time she burned, she never moved a muscle nor uttered a sound.

The SWAT team fell on her, beating and smothering the flames with their own bodies. She, and they, were taken to Mercy. The SWAT guys got away lightly, all things considered. They'd suffered several epidermal burns and a couple of dermal ones, but none had gone full thickness, down to muscle or bone.

Not so Mara.

She was horrifically burnt; third-degree over more than half her body, in fact. She'd survive, but would need multiple grafts; how many, the doctors couldn't say. What they *did* know was that the fire had damaged her larynx so badly she'd never talk again, and smoke inhalation meant she'd have respiratory difficulties for the rest of her life.

4:30 p.m.

Patrese went through Mara's apartment in The Pennsylvanian and pieced together what she'd done.

After killing Jesslyn, Mara had taken Jesslyn's car, keys and phone, driven to the Punxsutawney apartment Jesslyn shared with Beradino – Beradino, of course, being at the murder scene – and taken enough items to make it look like she'd gone on the run. And after *that*, she'd disappeared to The Pennsylvanian – she was officially dead, and very recognizable to boot – and only ventured out in full old lady make-up.

But swapping places with Jesslyn was only the half of it. In fact, Mara had created an entire new identity for herself. A new identity meant a social security number, a bank account, credit cards, passport: everything she'd need to start a new life, in other words. An identity started with a single piece of paper, without which nothing else was possible; a birth certificate.

But Mara couldn't have got just any old birth certificate, especially one of someone else still alive. The risks of the duplication being discovered were too great. Nor could she have got one of someone too old still to be alive, as the social security computers would have picked it up.

What she'd needed was the certificate of someone who was no longer alive. Identity fraudsters frequently trawl graveyards or cemeteries, looking at headstones to find someone who fits their bill.

The Allegheny County Clerk of Courts, located in the main courthouse on Grant Street, had issued a passport at the end of July to one Magda Nagorska, confirmed by her birth certificate to have been born in Cleveland, Ohio, on May 14th, 1932. What the ersatz Magda Nagorska had understandably failed to add was that the real version had died little more than a fortnight later, on May 31st of the same year, and was buried in St Stanislaus' Church in Cleveland's Warszawa district.

Patrese remembered from Mara's trial that her Polish grandmother had lived in Cleveland between the wars. Magda Nagorska, in fact, had been Mara's aunt; one of her grandmother's children who'd died in infancy of what Hellmore had later identified as Long QT syndrome, a connection which had been the starting-point for getting Mara's conviction overturned.

Mara's choice of The Pennsylvanian might have seemed counter-intuitive – surely the more people around, the more chance of her being rumbled – but Patrese knew the number of people is far less important than their attitude. Large apartment blocks are full of transients, people staying a few months here, a few months there. They often work or party long hours, and have neither the time nor inclination to get to know their neighbors. In smaller communities, on the other hand, everyone notices a stranger, and everyone knows everyone's business.

Mara had kept detailed files on all her victims, past and future.

Howard was to have been next in line, for violating the seventh commandment, *Thou shalt not commit adultery.*

Number eight, *Thou shalt not steal*, was Mara's agent Guilaroff, who had indeed been stealing from her. She'd made meticulous lists of the amounts. It wasn't that she hadn't known; she'd simply chosen to bide her time and exact her own revenge.

Number nine, *Thou shalt not bear false witness*, was Lockwood, the man whose testimony had done so much to help convict her in the first place. He'd sworn on the Bible to tell the truth, the whole truth, and nothing but the truth. He hadn't done so.

The last one, *Thou shalt not covet*, was Ruby, and covet she certainly had. She'd been Howard's neighbor before becoming his lover, Patrese remembered. Ruby, like everyone else, had coveted what she'd seen, especially what she'd seen every day.

5:55 p.m.

Beradino wasn't on Mara's list, but she'd destroyed his life just the same.

Once he realized Jesslyn was dead, he crumpled. It all came out in a huge rush, the kind of confession police officers dream of; a torrent of names, places, reasons, tumbling over each other in the penitent's desperation for absolution, and stopping only when he was completely spent.

He was dismissed with immediate effect and charged on four counts: unlawful imprisonment; aiding and abetting; hindering an investigation; and obstruction of justice. Yes, Patrese thought, Beradino had done what he'd done for love, and love makes people do the strangest things.

But his actions – or, more precisely, his inaction – had caused deaths. Whichever way you cut it, Beradino was looking at a stretch inside, and cops tend to be not much higher than child molesters in prison pecking orders.

Beradino asked to speak to Patrese. Patrese thought about it for a while, and then went to see him in his cell.

Beradino apologized for everything.

It's a bit late, Patrese replied. You wanted me dead.

No, Beradino said, not dead; just out of the picture.

547

Well, Patrese countered, those two tend to amount to the same thing when you've got half the state's police running around.

'I've been a good cop,' Beradino finished. 'You might not think so right now, but I have. I've always fought for what I thought was right. And now I ask: Why? There are still bad people out there; always have been, always will be. I've tried to keep it in perspective, to remember that just because death and violence are the norms of my life, they're not that of most people's. Most people want nothing more than to be happy. They might disagree about what makes them happy, but they want to get there. That's all I was looking for. Happiness. Is that too much to ask? Me, you, all of us, Franco, we're that little Dutch boy with his finger in the dyke. You can never conquer evil, but maybe you can keep it at bay, keep the darkness at one remove. If that's all you can do, that has to be enough.'

Yes, Patrese thought. Not only did it have to be enough, but it *was* enough. The darkness only won if you let it.

Patrese thought of Kohler, and the vile things Kohler had done to him, and he realized that already he was seeing that at one remove. He'd never have killed Kohler himself, but he wasn't in the least bit sorry that Kohler was dead.

Kohler had known what kind of man he was. He hadn't needed a trial or a jail sentence to show him. His own torments, let alone anything his God might choose to inflict on him, were punishment enough.

Saturday, December 11th. 9:43 a.m.

Amberin stopped by Patrese's apartment after breakfast.

'I can't stay,' she said. 'My mom's in the car outside. I just wanted to check that you're OK.'

'Probably not yet, but I'll get there.'

She kissed him once, very softly, on the mouth, and then drew away.

'I'm sorry,' she said.

'Don't be.' He tried to smile. 'Don't be sorry at all.'

'Well, I am.'

'Why?'

She touched his cheek and buried her head in his shoulder; then she looked him straight in the eye, because she knew she had to tell him straight and not flunk it by mumbling into his shirt.

'My mother's taking me to an Islamic dating convention.'

'An Islamic dating convention? That as bad as it sounds?'

She laughed. 'Worse. The tenth circle of hell. Dante would add one specially for it if he was still around. Five thousand people at the convention center down by the Allegheny, you know? Po-faced miked-up facilitators marching round saying' – she put on a mock-solemn voice – '"It is important to the family system of Islam for our sons and daughters to match

549

well." Matrimonial registration forms, everything your future mother-in-law could want to know, and they want to know *everything*: hobbies, sports, visa status, height, weight, religious participation, family information. Fathers wanting to get daughters married off before they go to college so they won't be single during Spring Break. My mom will scope out every man there, and she'll tell me about each one: "Yes, his looks matter. His personality matters. But if he's not aware and fearful and loving of Allah, he's not going to be right. If he doesn't follow Allah's laws, he won't be able to treat you right."'

It was Patrese's turn to laugh. 'OK. But why does this make you sorry?'

'Why do you think?'

Patrese flushed. 'Well, I wasn't sure whether you . . .'

'Of course I do. That night you took me home, I wanted you to stay more than anything. But my parents are traditional. They wouldn't understand what I see in you, and that's nothing to do with who you are or aren't, it's simply the color of your skin and the God you worship, or in your case don't worship. They want me to find a nice Muslim boy, settle down, have kids. They don't want me dating white men, people who aren't from our race or culture.'

'But you're . . . you're you, Amberin. You have a mind of your own. Hell, more than anyone else I know, pretty much. You really care what they think?'

'Yes. Of course I do.'

'No, I didn't mean it like that. I meant . . .'

'I know what you meant. And I see why you think it. But I could never do it to them. No matter how much I like you – and I do, believe me, I do – I couldn't even introduce you to them. They could never know you even exist. I had to tell my mom I was picking something up from a girlfriend.' Amberin wiped at the corner of her eye with the end of her little finger. 'And that's why I'm sorry.'

Sunday, December 12th. 3:12 p.m.

It was two days before they let Patrese see Mara. She was so heavily bandaged that only the doctor's notes at the end of the bed, and the permanent presence of a policeman by her bedside, could confirm her identity.

He had to ask her some questions, he said.

Since she couldn't speak, and her hands were too badly damaged to write, the hospital had rigged up a laptop for her to communicate. The pinky finger on her right hand had escaped the worst of the fire, more by luck than judgment. It was the only digit she could put any pressure on whatsoever, so she'd peck away at the keyboard with that. Painfully slow, but better than nothing.

'I'll ask, you type,' he said. 'Is that OK?'

Yes, *I tap.*

I wonder if he'll understand; properly understand, that is.

I was tried, convicted and sentenced under a legal system based not on God but on the blindness, stiffneckness, foolishness and self-righteousness of the idiots who think they have the power, righteousness and wisdom to make laws. Only God can govern us through His most perfect and holy laws – the Ten Commandments.

My God is not a God of benevolence, but one of justice. He moves in mysterious ways; what seems incomprehensible today may, with His guidance, be crystal clear tomorrow. So I asked Him: why?

You were not meant to be a mother, He replied. You are a warrior princess, hardened by the ordeal you have suffered. I have tested many, and discarded them all; they were weak and unwilling, so I cast them by the wayside. What I've put you through has shown the true nature of those who stood before you and deprived you of everything you held dear. They clothe themselves in the garments of the righteous, but when the scales fall from your eyes, you will see them in their true colors, and you will know what you must do.

The Book of Hebrews says there is no forgiveness without the shedding of blood.

They'll punish me here on earth for what I've done, because they're pygmies and understand nothing. But God won't punish me. Everything I've done has been for Him. Every life I've taken, be it the ones too good for this world and the ones who deserved punishment alike, has been for Him, because He told me to do so.

I've done His work, and he knows that.

I turn my attention back to Patrese.

'We'll take this slowly,' he says.

I nod.

'OK. Let's start at the beginning. Let's start with the first murder, when you killed Michael Redwine.'

I type with excruciating, exquisite slowness, a letter at a time.

Michael Redwine was not my first murder.

See ... Evil

J . S . Raynor

Published by Dolman Scott Ltd 2015

ISBN: 978-1-909204-74-4

Dolman Scott Ltd
www.dolmanscott.co.uk

DEDICATION

I would like to dedicate this book to my family. My wife, Aleth, son James and daughter Kimberley all suffer the effects of having to live with someone whose mind is always in the midst of new story ideas or engrossed in typing manuscripts in the office.

In addition, I would like to mention how the Royal National Institute of Blind people's Talking Book library has inspired me. After many years of being unable to read physical books, I felt liberated when, in 2011, I bought my first talking book device and started reading their books. In the first four years after this, I had read one hundred and seventy books. The superb stories created by such magnificent authors as Lee Child, Stephen King, Tom Clancy, Nelson Demille, Jack Finney, Dan Brown, Tess Gerritson, Dene Koontz, Harlan Coben, Robert Ludlum, James Herbert and E. L. James have all intrigued and Inspired me into using what I hope is an ability to create all the stories I have written so far. My wish is that I can continue to write stories for many years to come.

After sponsoring the production of a talking book version of Dan Brown's "Inferno" in 2013, I would like to sponsor many others should sales of my work permit me to do so.

CONTENTS

PROLOGUE

Captain Alex McCloud looked up when he heard the all-too familiar sound of sniper-fire. It seemed uncomfortably close to the base camp at Kandahar. "Jack! Quick! Come with me!" The two men ran towards the camp entrance and soon saw the crumpled bodies of two Afghan soldiers who had been guarding the camp's main entrance gates. A third soldier was calling out for assistance and trying to revive the two unfortunate men who were, obviously, beyond any earthly assistance.

Alex and Jack were soon by the man's side. The young captain was familiar with all three Afghans who had been willing to assist American and British forces in an attempt to rid the country of the Taliban insurgents. To make it worse, all three men were related.

"Did you see the attackers?"

"Yes, Sir." He looked devastated at the loss of his cousins. "There were four Taliban." He turned and pointed. Alex looked and saw a vehicle racing away from the camp. Four figures were in the battered vehicle as they made their escape.

Alex wasted no time and ran with Jack towards a light-armoured vehicle. "Watkins! Adamson! Come with us, quickly!"

Within seconds,the four were in their vehicle and racing in pursuit of the killers.

Alex had been assigned to take charge of flushing out groups of Taliban fighters entrenched near to the villages where they could intimidate and keep pressure on frightened residents. Now he had a job to do. "Just get this right!", he said to himself.

While Jack drove the vehicle, his foot pressed hard on the accelerator, alex was on his radio, instructing a helicopter pilot to take off and assist in this dangerous task.

After a few minutes driving at speed, on poorly-maintained roads, through village streets, the car entered open countryside with just the occasional small group of dwellings. The car with the Taliban fighters came to a halt near to a mainly open area. They jumped out of their vehicle and ran away in the direction of a simple building. It was one of several similar buildings in this area.

Jack pulled up, without getting too close to the other vehicle, in case it had been booby-trapped. All four ran after the escaping insurgents.

the first three Taliban fighters were easy to dispatch as they, seemingly, made easy targets. When another fighter retreated into the small, ordinary-looking building, Alex's unit followed, unaware that this was a deadly trap.

As the man ran inside, he quickly hid behind a stack of boxes, waiting for the British soldiers to enter. When he was satisfied that several soldiers were inside the building, he shouted "Praise be to Allah!" and detonated a huge bomb, ensuring not only his own death, but that of several of the infidel fighters.

In the explosion that followed, Alex's Sergeant and best friend, Jack Prentice, was literally torn to pieces, while Corporal Doug Adamson was decapitated and a third soldier, Private Bill Watkins lost both legs.

Alex felt the full force of the blast, his clothes immediately catching fire, while he received a great deal of shrapnel wounds to his face and one side of his body.

Luckily for him, the force of the explosion hurled him away from the structure and out of further danger from the now, fiercely-burning building. a second huge explosion ripped through the air, making it impossible to retrieve what was left of the bodies of his three unfortunate comrades.

Alex was uncertain what happened next, but, somehow, he stumbled away from the blazing inferno that had trapped them and, after collapsing, was quickly dragged away by his fellow soldiers who had disembarked from the helicopter and had come to his aid. While enemy snipers were firing at Alex, he was quickly rolled on the ground to extinguish the flames from his burning clothes. Alex was not only dazed, but also completely blinded from the frags which had, painfully, torn into his face, making it impossible for him to help himself. Blood streamed down his shattered face, giving the young soldier a ghoulish appearance, somewhat reminiscent of a horror movie.

As the men in his troop realised Alex's difficulties, they literally picked him up and carried him to the helicopter which, thankfully, had returned for them. It was pretty undignified, yet life-saving, as they bundled their inert Captain inside. They all scrambled in quickly after him, allowing the heavy machine to lift off, while still being targeted by small-arms fire.

Alex remained unconscious for about three hours, coming round in the military hospital at Camp Bastion.

He would always remember that day vividly. The antiseptic smell, the air of quiet efficiency, but most of all, the strange feeling of isolation. Not just the fact that he was lying in a hospital bed, but, for all he knew, the on-going battles could be a million miles away, or even ended, though he knew this was impossible.

He turned slightly in his bed in a vain attempt to get a little more comfortable and winced from the sharp pain.

Out of the darkness, a familiar voice gave him a start. "Hello, Alex. You're back with us, then?"

Alex recognised the deep, now calming tones of Derek, his commanding officer.

He wasted no time and asked the all-important question, "What happened to my men?"

There was an uncomfortable, meaningful pause before the reply came. "A secondary explosion prevented us from getting the others out. Prentice, Adamson and Watkins didn't make it, I'm sorry to say."

Alex had dreaded the bad news, but had feared the worst. "Oh, shit! What a mess! I should have guessed that it was a trap."

Major Derek Connolly could not agree with the young officer. "Don't blame yourself, Alex. If we did not react in case everything was a trap, we would get nowhere. The important thing, now, Alex is to get you better and out of that bed."

Dreading the answers that may be given, he asked the next-important question. "What happened to me? Why can't I see anything?"

Again, another short, yet meaningful pause. "You received about twenty per cent burns, mainly to the left side of your body. The frags caused extensive scarring, particularly to your face and upper body."

"What about my eyes?"

"I'm sorry, Alex. The front portion of both eyes was damaged and the probability is that loss of sight to both eyes could be permanent."

Alex felt as though he had been hit by an express train, metaphorically speaking. Burnt skin and frag wounds could heal, but the news that he would never see again, hit Alex badly. He took a deep, involuntary breath in before asking, "Are you certain about my eyes?" He feared that he knew what the answer would be, even before Derek replied.

His commanding officer sounded apologetic. "The front portion of both eyes was damaged so severely that corneal implants could not even be considered. I am terribly sorry, Alex, but that is the situation as explained to me by the medics."

Right then, Alex wished that he had died in the battle, along with his men. He could not understand why his own life had been spared, while his future had been so finally and brutally destroyed. "There's no future in the army for a blind soldier", he thought, somewhat bitterly. He could not imagine life without sight, unable to see the magic in a woman's smile or the wonderment in a child's innocent face. Even to see the creases and fine lines in his own face as he aged, would be denied to him. His silence said everything.

Alex's feelings of hostility and despair were not aimed at Major Connolly. He knew that it was his superior's job to be honest, sometimes to the point of brutality, with the men in his command. One of the disadvantages of climbing up the ranks was the inevitable task of breaking bad news when a death or serious injury occurred.

"Listen, Alex. Tomorrow you will be flown back to the U.K. where you will receive the very best medical treatment. If there is any way that your sight can be restored, then it will be done. I'm just telling you the situation as it is at this moment. Okay?"

"Sorry, I didn't mean…"

"It's alright, Alex. I do understand your frustration. We now have to put our trust in the specialists back home."

The flight back to England was a very sobering experience. Alex was one of three who were on stretchers along with one female and five male soldiers whose injuries were less severe, allowing them to sit in normal seats.

It was heart-wrenching to realise that, as well as the injured, there were two soldiers in coffins. Soldiers whose lives had been cut far too short. "What a fucking mess!" he thought. For the men in his own unit who had died in the huge explosion, their bodies would remain in that God-forsaken country, the dignity of being buried on British soil being denied to them. All that was left was the memories of these three brave individuals.

Within a couple of hours after landing, Alex and the other seriously injured soldiers were flown, by helicopter, to Queen Elisabeth Hospital at Edgbaston in Birmingham.

This famous hospital was only opened the previous year and had a world-renowned reputation for the care and rehabilitation of military personnel injured in conflict zones.

The care Alex received was superb. He was fortunate to have burns which were not quite deep enough to need skin grafts. There were many blisters from his shoulders down to his abdomen, causing him extreme discomfort, but, with a great deal of patience and expertise by the medical staff, they would, eventually, be replaced with new skin.

Debbie and Susan handled him with the same care as they would for a premature baby. They gently bathed him, applied liberal quantities of lotions and dressings, where appropriate. The bed in which he lay had an electric ripple-effect mattress, designed to prevent contact sores normally associated with lying in one position for protracted periods of time.

The injuries to his face were, however, a major cause for concern. The metal fragments had torn deep into the flesh and it took surgeons four hours to remove any remaining pieces of metal and repair the facial tissue as much as possible.

CHAPTER ONE :

20ᵗʰ. APRIL, 2011

*"*Shit!" The bandages were unbearably tight around Alex's head and he wished somebody, anybody, would loosen them enough to ease the throbbing pain in his damaged skull. There was little of his head not tightly bandaged apart from his nose and mouth. He tried, with fingers that did not feel like his own, to fumble with the bandage, but, try as he might, he was still unable to find a loose end. "Shit! Shit!" He was not, under normal circumstances, the kind of guy who casually uttered even this mildest of profanities, but, now, in his present situation, it actually felt quite excusable.

The effort exhausted him and he gave up, sinking back onto the bed, defeated and deflated. Naively, he hoped that nobody had observed him pulling at his bandages, but a nurse had and rushed over to his bedside. "Alex! Please leave your bandages alone. They are tight for a reason."

Alex grunted. He knew Debbie, the nurse, was correct, but this did not lessen his feelings of frustration. He lay exhausted from his futile efforts.

Sensing his frustration and sadness, Debbie softened a little. "Is there anything I can get you, Alex?"

There was not a hint of humour in his voice as he replied, "How about a new body?"

She gave a wan smile. "Listen, Alex. You do have a good body, believe me." She was not just saying this to please him. Debbie had seen him naked many times and wished she had a guy with such a muscular frame in her own life. With Alex, "everything", and she really meant "everything", was in the right proportion.

Debbie was single and, at twenty-eight, after a few forgettable relationships, wondered if there would ever be someone special in her own life. Her past sexual partners had, to put it simply, not come up to expectations. Why a man should think that a two or three minute fumble should be enough to satisfy a woman, she could never comprehend. Why is it that men find it impossible to understand what a woman really needs? Her blushes, at these most intimate thoughts, went unseen. "You're healing well and, with a little patience, you will make a full recovery."

If anyone knew what his body was like, it was Debbie and her colleague, Susan, who worked alongside her. Ever since Alex had been flown from Afghanistan and brought into the Intensive Care Unit, three weeks earlier, these two women had bathed, cleaned and assisted him to use the bedpan and probably knew every inch of his body in far greater detail than anyone else, even including himself. They had fed him intra-venusly when he was incapable of looking after himself as a result of the heavy cocktail of drugs necessary for pain relief.

He struggled to speak clearly, his voice not following his thoughts, coughed a little and then tried again. "I could do with a drink, please, Debbie. My mouth is so dry."

"Of course." Debbie pressed the controls to raise the head of the bed, making it easier for her difficult patient to drink. She placed the cup into Alex's hand and, using a straw, he gulped down a few, welcoming mouthfuls of fruit juice. "Thanks, Debbie. That's much better. I'm sorry for being such a pain in the butt." He laid back, irritated that even the slightest effort, such as sitting up, exhausted him. He had never felt so incapable and useless as he did now. He felt that his abilities had been reduced to that of a baby and not a very intelligent one, at that.

"Don't worry, you are getting better and I am not joking when I tell you that we have had much worse patients than you." She hesitated, uncertain if she should tell Alex of one of her more memorable experiences which had left her in tears, but, then, after only a moment's hesitation, continued, with some bitterness in her voice. "About ten months ago, a Colonel Peter Bower was admitted into this unit. He had lost his leg, after being caught in a Taliban suicide bombing. He received the same amount of attention as everybody else in Intensive Care, but this had never been quite enough for him. One day, I had been late with his medication, as a consequence of one of the more critically ill patients dying. I was upset as the unfortunate young soldier had been a war hero and, to my mind, the string of obscenities and insults from the Colonel was completely unjustified and unnecessary." Brushing away a tear at these painful memories, she added, "I could never imagine you emulating the officious Colonel."

After hearing her story, Alex realized how truly dedicated all the nursing staff were and, in that moment, he was determined not to make their jobs any more difficult. "I am so sorry, Debbie."

"Don't worry about it. It's all part of the job and I really do love my work." The diligent nurse adjusted Alex's bed again, using the remote control, made certain he was as comfortable as possible and, quietly, returned to her nurses' station.

He could smell her perfume as she had leaned over him and the sweet, distinctive scent had lingered even after she had moved away. "Nothing wrong with my sense of smell", he thought. This was not the only sense which had survived, but had, like most young men, always been lurking, just beneath the surface. "Wonder if she is good-looking?" He imagined that she had slim, attractive features. Bright, seductive eyes, small, angular nose and full, soft, delightfully-tempting lips.

Alex did know that she had long, silky hair as it had touched his arm when she had leaned over him a few days earlier. He felt certain that, had Debbie strictly followed hospital regulations, she should have had it tied back, but there had been occasions, perhaps on her late shift where she had, temporarily, let her hair down.

"Wonder what colour her hair is?" He could ask her, but, for some inexplicable reason, felt a little reticent. In his mind, her hair would be black, long and silky, contrasting against her soft, milk-white skin. He imagined her naked, displaying her small, firm breasts, slim waist and slender hips. He knew that he may be disappointed if the reality did not meet up to his erotically vivid imagination, but, well, it helped to pass the time. "Bet she's great in bed", he thought, remembering stories in his youth of the many sexual antics indulged in by members of the nursing profession when off or even on duty, but, of course, that did not mean that these rumours were true. Still, imagination worked wonders when the body was incapable of much, if any action.

Apart from this interest in the females looking after him, Alex's feelings were a mixture of anger, boredom and regret that he was unable to see or do anything useful for himself, just as if he was an infant, once again.

Before all this, he was a picture of physical fitness. His six foot two inch, fourteen stone muscular frame enjoyed the admiration of both men and women alike, when he was a twenty-four year old captain in the British Paratroop regiment.

He not only had strength of body, but was extremely confident, self-disciplined and perfect material for the strict requirements of the British army.

At twenty, he had undergone the rigorous training at Sandhurst Military Academy, leaving as a commissioned officer. He had wanted active service and, when he was posted to Afghanistan in two thousand and nine as a second lieutenant, he knew that this was exactly what he wanted. Alex certainly did not relish the idea of a regular occupation, which meant a mindlessly, boring, nine to five desk job, five days a week for the next forty-odd years. For many, this would have been perfectly acceptable and infinitely preferable to having no job at all. For Alex, it would be like living in a permanent state of limbo, with no challenges and no excitement.

He had wanted action, adventure and, of course, a certain degree of danger. His parents, however, were not so convinced and, fearing for his safety, tried to persuade him to take a less leading role in military activities.

Even at the age of six, the energetic youngster had declared that, when he was grown-up, he was definitely going to be a soldier. All through school, as well as achieving good results in academic subjects, he had excelled at swimming, rugby, football, gymnastics and long distance running. He not only had great strength of body, but was also determined enough to excel in anything which would assist his military future.

It was not as if there had even been anyone in the close family with a military background. His father, James, was a barrister and his grandfather, Richard, an accountant, both, in Alex's opinion, quite sedentary, extremely boring occupations.

The one exception to this was his Mother's brother, Uncle Robert. After ten years in the Royal Air Force, he was now a senior pilot with Singapore Airlines. He was the only one who could understand the hunger for military action, so apparent in the youngster. When he had the opportunity to talk to Alex in private, he would tell of his own military experiences, particularly his missions in defence of the Falkland Islands and, generally, encouraged the attentive Alex, even creating a degree of tension with his sister and brother-in-law, when they realized how his words were influencing their son. Yet nothing would dissuade the determined youngster from his goal.

Both Louise, his mother, and James, knew that their son had ambitions to have a combat role and were disappointed, though not surprised when he left the U.K. for a six month tour of duty. During this time, he had shown great courage and strength of character and a worthy example of a commissioned officer.

Alex had been involved in many risky maneuvers, coming close to death on numerous occasions. In one of these he managed to rescue a teenage girl and her family after they were threatened and attacked by the Taliban. This was all because the girl was determined to be well educated, something which the Taliban seemed to fear and do their best to prevent. The girl had been injured, but, thanks to the intervention of Alex and his combat group, not seriously. Alex could not understand the mentality of Taliban thinking. Do they really fear domination by women? Is this why females seem to be so dominated by men and repressed within the Islamic faith? He had heard of young, unmarried women who had been brutally, stoned to death after being discovered in an intimate relationship, while the man, apparently would , escape without fear of any punishment. Why should women accept anything less than full equality?

It was a great relief for his proud parents when he safely completed his six month tour of duty and returned to the U.K., as a newly-promoted Captain Alex McCloud.

He had everything going for him. A career he loved and Helen, his fiancé, who had been an important part of his life for the past three years.

The problems started when he returned to Kandahar Province in Afghanistan in December, two thousand and ten. The troubles were escalating and the Taliban were proving to be ever more resourceful in their efforts both to evade and attack foreign troops.

CHAPTER TWO :
22nd. APRIL, 2011

When Helen, Alex's fiancé, visited him just three days after his return to the U.K., he felt apprehensive about her possible reaction. There was a slight hesitation when she entered the ward and then, without saying a word, she walked up to his bed and planted a tender kiss on Alex's lips. It had been five long months since they had last kissed, but the taste of her lipstick and the smell of her perfume reminded him of much happier times. Also, on that day, five months ago shortly before he went out to Afghanistan, they had done much more than just kiss, but, how long would it be before he could make love, again? How long before he could be a real man?

She gripped his hand tightly. Although Helen considered herself lucky that Alex had survived the conflict, it was heart-breaking to see him in his present condition. "How are you feeling, darling?"

"Better now that you're here, sweetheart." It seems like ages since we were together." He relaxed a little, yet, within a few seconds, a virtual black cloud appeared at the back of his mind and, somehow, something seemed different and troubling.

All his life, Alex had been self-confident and assured, but now, nothing seemed certain any more. Did he have anything to look forward to? Would Helen still want to marry him, now that he was blind? He wished he could see into the future, if only to know what to expect.

"Are you in a lot of pain?"

"The medication helps. The pain-killers make me feel so drowsy that I do sleep quite a lot. Then, there are the head-aches, far worse than I've ever experienced. At least I'm alive, unlike poor Jack."

Helen knew of Alex's long friendship with Jack and would have liked to give him a big hug, but she dare not, in case it caused him even more pain. "Oh, Darling, I'm so sorry."

Helen sat on the chair at the side of the bed and, tenderly, held his hand. It was as if it was made of delicate china and may break if she held it any tighter. "When are the bandages going to come off?"

"I don't know. The staff change the bandages regularly to clean and check how the flesh wounds are healing, but I really don't know how long it will take."

Helen sympathised. "Oh, it must be awful. I suppose it will take a while for your eyes to heal before you can see again?"

Alex was stunned by this question. "Did my parents not tell you about my eyes?"

Her blushes went unseen. "Well, yes. They said both your eyes were damaged, but I thought that surgery would be possible to recover some sight." She was already regretting the fact that she had asked what now seemed like a really stupid question.

The hopelessness in Alex's voice was evident as he replied, "You have no idea how much I wish that was true, but the ophthalmic surgeon told me that there was too much damage to both eyes to ever have the possibility of seeing again."

An awkward silence fell on the young couple, broken only by Alex's parents and younger sisters, Lucy and Amelia, entering the single ward. His mother sensed the tension between her son and potential daughter-in-law, but knew better than to make the situation worse by enquiring about the noticeable chilly atmosphere.

Messages from relatives and friends, some quite humourous, were passed on to Alex by his parents and the conversation soon took on a lighter tone.

Lucy found the sight of her brother in such a bad way, deeply upsetting and shed many tears while squeezing his hand tightly. Thirteen-year old Amelia was equally upset, but, somehow, was managing to stem the flow of tears, having shed so many when she first heard the news about her big brother's suffering extensive injuries.

Later, when all visitors had left, Alex thought again about Helen's question. He had a sickening feeling that everything that had happened over the past three years between him and Helen was soon to fall apart. She had not said anything more about his lack of sight, but the disappointment in her voice said it all. Why should anything spoil his chances of a happy marriage? His depression deepened, noticed by the vigilant medical staff.

Alex realised that, over the next few weeks, Helen's visits became less frequent. He had feared that this may happen, but hoped that her feelings were too strong to be affected by his hopeless medical condition.

On top of this, he suffered from many chilling nightmares, where he re-lived the experience which had so effectively changed his entire life. Re-living the agonizing death of his friends and comrades terrified him beyond belief, each nightmare scribing deeper and deeper into his already tormented soul.

On several occasions, the nursing staff had to waken him as he screamed and threshed around in his bed, with the potential to damage his slowly-healing wounds.

When Helen did visit, he could sense an emotional barrier between them. She did try to say all the right things to lift his spirits, but there was now an emotional chasm where once their hearts had been deeply entwined. It now, almost, seemed a relief when visiting time came to an end, as he found it difficult to hide the hurt he was feeling inside.

He surprised himself when he admitted his concern about Helen to Jane, the psychiatric counsellor, a middle-aged woman with a soft, caring voice, who listened attentively to the young man's worries.

"It's not uncommon for relationships to suffer after such a trauma. You may find that she resumes the relationship when you are more mobile. Would you want that?"

Alex had to think about his own feelings for Helen. "I think so, but I do feel that I am now a huge disappointment to her."

"Don't be so hard on yourself, Alex. Many blind people can still lead a full, active life."

Even the word "BLIND" made Alex aware of a deep-rooted fear. Why was this five-letter word so short yet so powerful with his emotions? Why should it happen to him?

"I know, but I never wanted to depend on somebody else. I'm the one who should be looking after my partner."

Jane could understand his feelings of inadequacy. In her job, she had come across similar situations many times and saying the right words to injured servicemen was never easy. "Give yourself time and I feel certain that your situation will improve."

He knew she was probably right and tried, with great difficulty, not to worry about his own situation and difficulties.

To Add to Alex's anxiety, the painful headaches persisted. For this reason, the specialists responsible for his care decided to carry out a brain scan.

The anticipation of this worried the young soldier even more, as the thought of having not only lost his sight, but also having impaired mental abilities would be just too much for him to accept.

Peter Jacques, the Neuro-surgeon who analysed Alex's brain scan, tried to be re-assuring. "In most respects, your brain scan appears to be absolutely normal, Captain McCloud."

The "in most respects" part of the surgeon's statement caused immediate concern to Alex. "Just what does that mean?"

"Let me explain. As far as we can establish, there are no adverse reactions. This means that there is no impairment to your mental abilities."

"Good." Alex felt a little easier, but still knew that there must be something more to explain. "So how is my brain different?"

The surgeon sounded reassuring. "There are signs of increased activity in the right hemisphere, which usually means a heightened cognitive reasoning. This could have been caused by the impact on your skull when you were injured in Afghanistan."

Still puzzled, Alex asked, "Is that a good thing?"

"Oh, yes. Individuals with higher activity than normal in this area tend to be more aware, more perceptive and, in some cases, have an unusual gift or talent, such as increased memory retention or the ability to mentally calculate complex mathematical calculations."

This took the young man by surprise. "You mean that I may now be a genius?"

The specialist, who was quite a big guy, laughed with surprising volume. It was almost a "Brian Blessed" laugh. "Genius is a bit of an emotive term, but certainly mental capabilities higher than the average and, don't forget, the down side is the problem of continuing headaches."

"Those bloody headaches!" Alex would happily exchange any improvement in his mental abilities for the absence of mind-numbing pain.

The surgeon smiled, apologetically, though this went unseen. "I can prescribe medication, but, as you probably know, their effectiveness diminishes and can lead to higher, undesirable doses. I would be grateful if you could keep me informed of any unusual side-effects you may notice. I'll put my card on your bedside cabinet.

Alex thanked him for the information, but doubted if he was ever likely to phone the surgeon with any amazing revelations.

For now, his future did not seem to lie much beyond this bed and in this hospital.

Gradually, over the course of the next few weeks, he was allowed out of bed more often as his body slowly began to heal from the burns. It did come as a relief to be able to stand up after such a long time when he was unable to leave his bed. His legs felt weak and he was shocked to find that he had lost over two stones in weight.

With regular physiotherapy, exercise and a good supply of food, he would be able to regain his body mass, again, yet this would do nothing to bring back his sight. It came as a fantastic relief when the dressings were finally removed from around his head. The scarring from the shrapnel wounds was annoying and the nurses had to keep reminding Alex to leave them alone without picking at them.

Before the bandages had been removed, Alex wondered if there would be any vision left at all. A faint light, perhaps? Moving shadows as people crossed his line of vision? Anything at all would give him some sign of hope, but the inky blackness which surrounded him told him that his dreams were just that. Pointless, stupid, hopeless dreams!

It was the worst feeling he had ever experienced to be immersed in a pitch black, inky sea of nothing. How deep was this seemingly bottomless, empty pit? Would it ever come to an end?

As he thought about his hopeless, current situation, Alex suddenly remembered an earlier part of his life which, in some ways, was reminiscent. When he was about fifteen, he had a phase when he was crazy about pot-holing. He knew that it could be dangerous, but enjoyed the excitement of finding, as yet, undiscovered underground caverns.

It was on one of these expeditions that he nearly lost his life. His group was making its way back to the surface and, without warning, a sudden rock fall blocked his path. What made it worse was the fact that he was isolated from his friends, the rock fall separating them. His torch had been damaged by the fall, leaving him on his own and in complete darkness. He had many anxious thoughts during his imprisonment and wondered if this was how his life was going to end.

It took several hours of delicate rock removal before the emergency services could release him from this cramped, unlit space. It was an experience he hoped never to repeat and, yet, his current situation had so many similarities.

After this brief exposure to unseen natural light in his present world, small, individual protective dressings were placed over each eye, these being concealed by dark glasses.

In the middle of Alex's feelings of desperation and hopelessness, he thought of his best friend, who had lost his life in the explosion. For Jack Prentice, the blackness would be everything and permanent. For him, he would not feel the soft touch of the nurse's skin or any other woman's, come to that. No earthly exercise would strengthen his muscles. Poor Jack. There was now a huge gap in his life with the death of this best friend.

Alex had first met him at Secondary school. A tall and, at that time, quite skinny boy with a cheeky, infectious grin. He had always had the nickname of "Jack Sprat", from his build, but it never bothered him. The two eleven year olds made friends immediately. Intellectually similar, the two had remained in the same teaching group throughout all their school years. They had joined the cadets together and it was obvious that both were destined to lead a military career.

Both had achieved ten, high-grade GCSE passes and were able to continue studying for their "A" levels. The divergence came during this time.

Jack had fallen for Suzanne, a good-looking, nicely proportioned girl from their form.

Their somewhat stormy relationship had cost Jack any decent grades in his exams, spoiling his chances of going to Sandhurst, much to the disappointment of his parents. Jack had admitted to Alex that, when he should have been studying Maths and English for exams, he was, instead, enjoying studying the birthmarks on Suzanne's nicely-rounded backside.

Meanwhile, Alex had resisted the attention of several girls to concentrate on his studies. He did, however, remember how envious he was of Jack who lost his virginity at least two years before himself. "What is it like to come inside a woman?" he asked enviously.

"Fantastic! Mind-blowing! There's just no comparison, especially when you both come at the same time. To feel her body give that final shiver of excitement and then just collapsing into each other's arms. Amazing!"

Alex could see the longing, lusting look in Jack's eyes, desperate for the next time when he and Suzanne could make love, again, adding to Alex's own frustration at never having come anywhere close to screwing around. Jack did realize how envious Alex was and tried not to say anything more to frustrate his friend.

It did make Alex wonder if holding back his sexual desires was worth it. There were several girls in his year who he felt attracted towards and had a feeling, no, a certainty that they probably would have gone to bed with him if he had had the courage to approach them. He had put his studies above everything else and had been rewarded for his efforts, but was it worth it?

The two friends still kept in touch even though their paths were leading in slightly different directions. Jack had many girl-friends after Suzanne, none lasting more than a few months. He then joined the army at nineteen, while Alex was at Sandhurst.

Alex had found the fitness and leadership tests harder than he could ever have imagined, but, thankfully, he was accepted by the world-famous military academy. After twelve months of even more rigourous training at Sandhurst, it was gratifying to be able to enlist in the same battalion as Jack and the two companions continued their friendship as though nothing had happened.

Of course, there now was a difference. Jack had more military experience, but his rank as sergeant was less than Alex's position as second lieutenant and, in the British army, keeping within one's rank level was important.

Alex had ignored this so-called protocol and had treated Jack as his equal.

On that fateful day, it was Jack who led the charge into that cursed building, only to be blown apart by the Taliban's bomb. Alex felt so deeply affected by the loss of his good friend and the memories of thirteen years growing up together was precious to him.

Alex was also saddened by his departure from Intensive Care as he had grown fond of the two nurses who had looked after him, particularly Debbie. He liked her sense of humour and had a good feeling whenever she was near. It was the contrast between Debbie and Helen which played on Alex's mind. Debbie accepted him as a man and treated him normally, while Helen... Well, Helen must have had her own reasons, but, when she had visited him only a few days earlier, she had broken off their engagement.

"I'm so sorry, Alex, but I don't think I can handle what has happened to you. I do feel terrible."

"Well, fuck you, Helen Dennison! So you bloody-well should!" thought Alex, but he said nothing

"Tears filled her eyes as she continued, I think it better we leave things alone for now and see how we feel after a while. But, I'm not certain I could manage to be a good military wife."

Alex's anger was bubbling under the surface, yet he restrained himself. She must have realized the possibilities of him suffering injury or death as his ambitions for a military career had always been known to her. "If that is what you want, Helen." He remained cool, distant and impassive.

Again, she repeated, "I'm so sorry."

He remembered how they had met. His parents had organized a big celebration for his twenty-first birthday, which, fortunately, coincided with his military leave. Helen Dennison had been the Occasions manager at the Hilton hotel selected for his celebration. There had been a mix-up in the catering arrangements for the seventy-five guests expected at Alex's party. Helen had managed to resolve the problem with quiet efficiency, but still felt it necessary to apologise to him in person.

As the two met, the chemistry between them was instant. Within days, they had their first romantic date and, within six months, they were engaged. Alex's career made it difficult to arrange the wedding, especially since both parents wanted to organize huge celebrations and, ironically, they were to be married two months after his current tour of duty. Now, that had all disappeared with Alex's hospitalization and Helen's change of heart.

That was the last he had seen of her after three beautiful, enjoyable years together. Three years of laughter, love and passion. Many times, he had imagined having at least three, possibly four children with Helen. A life full of happiness and companionship. He felt deflated and cheated and was more scared of the future than at any time in his life.

How he hated the Taliban for what they had done. The death of three of his comrades, the loss of his eyesight resulting in the ending of his military career and, to cap it all, the woman he loved had now finished their relationship.

A memorial service had been held for Jack and his comrades, together with other soldiers whose lives had been cut far too short through the actions in Afghanistan, but, sadly, Alex's condition prevented him from attending. He did, however, 'watch' the news on television, where the memorial service was covered in detail, with a very moving, descriptive commentary.

He felt a mixture of anger and sadness at such unnecessary loss of life and Alex realized that, even though his eyes were useless, his tear ducts were still functioning.

Since Alex was now more mobile, he was able to use the bathroom, giving him back some of his dignity. He had been given so many bed-baths and had suffered psychologically by having to use bed-pans, that he actually felt liberated when he could use the toilet in private. Debbie had shown him where everything was located in the bathroom and he soon mastered the controls on all the appliances. Alex had always preferred to shave using the traditional wet razor, feeling that they gave a much closer shave than their electric equivalent. He had thought that it would be impossible to shave without being able to see his image in a mirror, but, in fact, it was an unnecessary luxury.

In reality, one just had to feel round the face, instinctively knowing which areas to avoid.

One morning, Alex was feeling particularly depressed by his hopeless situation and, while shaving, he suddenly realized that he could end all his problems. The solution lay in the small, plastic-handled Gillette razor which he was now holding. All he had to do was to slice into either his neck or wrist. He stood motionless for what seemed an eternity, thinking of his situation. "Would anybody really care if he was dead? He still longed for a military career, but without sight, how could this ever be possible? "The wrist is probably easier. All I have to do is find the main artery, slice into it and the heart would do the rest pumping the life-blood out of my body." He felt for the pulse, knowing that one quick slice of the razor would be enough. "What happens, though, if Debbie finds me before I am dead? She would do everything to try and stem the blood flow and, after that, I would not be allowed to use a razor again.

In addition, I would be put on a suicide watch and everybody would think I was a coward." Then another thought hit him. "How would it affect my parents and younger sisters? Could I really put them through so much heartache?"

Alex mulled over all these thoughts and, after what seemed hours rather than minutes, pulled himself together when he heard Debbie's voice through the door. "Are you alright, Alex? Do you need any assistance?" The vigilant nurse had noticed how quiet Alex was and decided to check.

"Fine, thanks, Debbie. Almost finished shaving."

"Good. I have your medication here, when you are ready." Alex would have been surprised to learn that the nursing staff was already keeping a close eye on their patient. The depth of his depression had been noticed and all staff had been advised to be alert to the possibility of suicide.

Alex finished shaving, washed his face, patted it dry and applied after-shave. In those few seconds, he had decided that it would be incredibly stupid to end his life and was determined to face the future, whatever it may bring.

CHAPTER THREE :
15th. JULY, 2011

The move from the I.C.U. was not to another ward in the same hospital. Instead, Alex was driven over ninety miles to Moorfields Eye Hospital in London. He felt useless at having to be guided to enter and exit the car, almost hitting his head on the car roof, yet he could not complain about any of his treatment or the attention given to him.

The nurses were sad when it came to the time for Alex to leave the ward which had been his home for the past four months. Debbie, in particular, surprised Alex by giving him what could only be described as a passionate hug and a tender, meaningful kiss on the lips. He had always liked her but was surprised by the emotion expressed by her. He had to admit that he enjoyed and responded to it warmly, re-living the experience many times during his long drive.

At Moorfields, he was escorted to the consulting room of a Professor Goldman. "Please take a seat, Captain McCloud." His voice was confident, warm, yet professional. It seemed odd that, after many years of assessing individuals by their looks and actions, this luxury was no longer afforded to him. Everything had to be ascertained by voice alone. As to Professor Goldman's age, a voice was not the easiest way to assess. Alex guessed that he was, probably, in his late forties, plus or minus ten years. The young soldier's hand was placed on the arm of the offered chair. Clumsily, he took a seat.

"As you are no doubt aware, your eyes suffered a great deal from the explosion. Both corneas were damaged beyond repair or possible transplant." He paused, but, without any response from the young soldier, continued. "Normally, in such circumstances, both eyes would be completely removed and inactive prosthetic replacements inserted."

"Why do you say, 'normally'? Why am I different?" Alex was puzzled. His eyes were useless, so why not take the bloody things away?

The Professor spoke in a relaxed manner, un-phased by Alex's almost hostile reaction. "This standard procedure can still be carried out, but I wanted to put an alternative suggestion to you."

"Is there any alternative?" Alex could not imagine why they were dragging out this painful, psychological torment.

"When the medical team dealing with your injuries contacted me, they described the trauma in detail. There had been considerable scarring of tissue, particularly around the eyes, with a possible loss of aqueous Humor, which is ninety-nine percent water, indicating probable permanent loss of sight. As a result, I asked them to keep the remaining receptive areas of your eyes protected with a special dressing which would assist in preserving what remains of the retina. You were probably not even aware of this but, by taking these precautions, we now have an alternative to permanent blindness."

Was this the reason why he had seen nothing when the bandages were removed? Had there really been another layer he was not aware of? Alex's curiosity was now getting the better of him. "Tell me more."

"Well, if the eyes are removed completely, then there can never be any chance of seeing anything again as the optic nerve would be severed."

"Stating the bloody obvious", thought Alex.

"In your case, the retinas and the optic nerve connections are still intact, while the front portion of the eyes is severely damaged."

Alex's attention and hopes were raised by the professor's words. "Does it mean that I may be able to see again?"

"I don't want to raise false hopes, but, at Moorfields, in conjunction with the University College of London's Institute of Ophthalmology, we have been carrying out a great deal of research into synthetic lenses and pupils. We are at the point of looking for somebody to test the very promising results of our research."

Alex was stunned by the professor's words. "You want me to be a guinea pig?"

The professor chose his words carefully, fully aware that Alex already felt hostile and defeated by his current loss of sight. "We are at a very advanced stage of research and feel ready to test it in a live situation. Ideally, we need a physically fit person who is self-disciplined. Would you be interested?"

Alex now understood why he had been the obvious candidate for the research and he realised that many who lose their sight would not be suitable. "I'm interested, but I need to know more before I agree."

"That's fair. What do you want to know?"

It was obvious what Alex's first question would be. "Will it enable me to see normally, again?"

"There is a fair chance, but it may never approach the full vision potential of normal sight. The human eye is a truly fantastic piece of engineering and any man-made replacement is bound to be inferior."

Alex's hopes lost some of their initial expectations. He had heard of light-sensitive chips being used where normal sight was impossible. While successful, the resolution was extremely limited and could not provide much visual use. The ability to distinguish between light and dark, with vague, shadowy images did not appeal to this impressionable young man. In Alex's mind, a low-resolution camera built into spectacles and with a connected battery pack would not give him much useful vision and would probably make him look decidedly odd.

Curiously, the professor seemed to realise what Alex was thinking. "You have probably heard about chip implants, but, let me assure you, Alex, what we have achieved here is infinitely superior to those early implants."

"In what way?"

"What we have achieved is almost a complete replacement for the eye. The only parts we retain are the retina and the connecting optic nerve." It was obvious from the professor's voice that he was proud of the achievements of his team. "Powerful micro-electronics are embedded into the prosthetic eye, giving it capabilities never thought possible."

Alex thought of a potential flaw. "Electronics need power. How do you achieve this?" He did not wish to have unsightly wires coming out of his head, leading to an external battery pack. "I don't want to look like Frankenstein's monster", thought Alex.

"You're quite correct. Micro-photo-voltaic cells are used to generate the tiny amount of power needed." Before Alex could ask the next obvious question, he continued, "Capacitors are used to store the power for up to twenty-four hours, so as long as the wearer has some stimulus from natural daylight or even artificial light every twenty-four hours, that is sufficient to power the devices without the need for any external electric source."

Alex's curiosity was now aroused. "I'm impressed. Tell me more about the resolution and, is it monochrome or colour vision?"

"Over the past few months, we have managed to increase the resolution from eight hundred by six hundred to nineteen hundred and twenty by twelve hundred. The colour palette is sixteen and a half million. Do you think that is enough?" The professor had deliberately emphasised the word "colour" to leave Alex in no doubt about the capabilities of his prized invention.

"Those specifications sound like those of a computer monitor or television."

"That's true. The basic technology is identical. In truth, the human eye can only distinguish about ten million colours, so the spec is more than enough."

Alex now had hope in his voice. "It does sound remarkable and 'yes', I am extremely interested."

The professor slid open a drawer and, carefully, lifted out a small package. "This is an earlier prototype, but it will give you some idea of the size. He handed the device over to Alex, who turned the tiny object around in his hand, feeling it's shape and size. It was about twenty-five millimetres in diameter, yet not a perfect sphere. The front portion was of smaller diameter than that where the retina resides at the back of the eye.

"How does the weight compare to that of a natural eye?"

"A typical weight of a human eye is about twenty-eight grams, while the one in your hand weighs thirty-two grams when filled with the necessary fluid. The extra weight is marginal, but quite manageable. The muscles surrounding the eye can handle up to about thirty-six grams."

Satisfied that these remarkable implants could give him sight once again, Alex agreed to stay at Moorfields for the next few weeks to undergo testing, fitting and training.

Professor Goldman took him to one of the many laboratories within the hospital and asked Alex to lie on a bed. He needed to inspect the remains of Alex's eyes and carefully removed the dressing from one of his eyes. "Excellent! The tissue in the orbit appears to be in good condition and there is no sign of retinal detachment."

"If my eyes are still working, wouldn't I be able to see something, now? Even just light?" To Alex's logical mind, this was an inconsistency.

"Sorry, Alex. I should have explained. The dressing is in two parts and, in here, I dare not remove the lower. This can only be done in absolute sterile conditions and when you are anaesthetised." This did sound logical to Alex, yet there was still a big question in his mind.

"What I can't understand is why the micro-electronics are necessary. Surely, if the retina is still working, all it needs is a small lens to focus the image on the retina?"

Professor Goldman had anticipated this question. He knew Alex was intelligent enough to work out this simpler solution. "There is a good reason, but I am not the person to explain it to you." He looked at his watch. "The person who can tell you more will be arriving in about forty-five minutes. Until then, I would ask you to be patient and, hopefully, everything will be explained."

Alex was curious about the identity of this mysterious individual. The Professor carefully replaced the dressings around Alex's eyes and then escorted him to a comfortable room where he would be staying for the next few weeks.

He introduced Amy, a nurse at Moorfields. "She will show you where everything is in your room. We want your stay to be as comfortable as possible. I'll see you later."

"Hello, Alex. Do you mind if I take your hand to show you where everything is?"

"No, not at all." She took hold of his right hand and, with great care and understanding of his situation, showed him the location of his bed, chairs, locker and wardrobe.

Her hand was cool and gentle as she placed his on each item in the room. "Where's my case?"

"Don't worry. It's in the bottom of the wardrobe. I can help you unpack, if you wish."

"It's okay, Amy. I'll manage. What about the toilet? I hope it's not far."

"You have your own private bathroom and toilet. Come, I'll show you."

Again she took his hand and led him into a well-fitted bathroom. There was a bath, shower, toilet and washbasin, all positioned to make location easy.

"It's like a four star hotel. From what you have told me, I even have my own television in the bedroom." Again, Amy showed him the controls on the uncluttered remote, making certain that he knew how to use it.

"Is everything okay now, Alex?" She had a very pleasant, soft voice with a slight, almost imperceptible Irish accent. "Is there anything else I can do for you?"

There was, but he knew it would not be included in her job description. He smiled at her. "No, thanks. You've been very helpful."

"If you do need assistance, just pick up the phone and ask for me. If I am off duty, ask for Helen."

The mention of this second name brought back painful memories of his ex-fiancé. Amy noticed the sudden change in his expression at the mention of her colleague's name. Are you alright, Alex?"

Snapping out of his thoughts, he regained his composure. "Yes, difficult memories returning. Sorry, I ..."

"Don't worry, it's understandable. Right, I'll leave you in peace. Just remember, if you have a shower, don't wet the dressings around your eyes."

As soon as he was on his own, Alex checked the time on his talking watch. He had requested some way of knowing the time and date several weeks earlier and had been provided with a fairly bulky wrist-watch which had a strong, rather sombre-sounding male voice. Sometimes, he found the voice extremely irritating, but, at least, he knew what time of day it was. "Four-thirty. Probably another thirty minutes before my visitor. Enough time to freshen up." As he carefully washed his hands and face and changed into more formal clothes, hopefully suitable for the visitor, many troubled thoughts ran through his mind.

When he had been in hospital in Afghanistan, he had clearly been told that the chances of having any useful vision were minimal. This had been reinforced by the medical staff at the hospital in Birmingham and, yet, he was now given the opportunity of having his sight restored. Why? Something had obviously changed, but what?

A knock on his door disturbed his thoughts. He opened it. "Are you ready to meet your visitors, Alex?" It was Professor Goldman.

"Visitors? As in plural?"

"Yes, there are two people I would like you to meet. I'll escort you to the Board room where we can talk in comfort."

Alex took the offered arm of the Professor and followed him along the winding corridors. He still felt uncomfortable and embarrassed holding onto a man, while he was perfectly happy to be escorted by a woman. Somehow, it offended his masculinity.

CHAPTER FOUR :
15ᵗʰ. JULY, 2011

As they entered the board room, Alex heard chairs being scraped on the floor as the strangers stood up. Who could they be? Alex was curious to find out.

Professor Goldman spoke. "Could you introduce yourselves, please?"

"Certainly." The first man walked up to Alex, took his hand and shook it firmly. "Brigadier General Paul Marshall. Pleased to meet you, Captain McCloud." His typically-military voice indicated someone not just of high rank, but something even more exclusive and important. There was no way in which Alex could accurately determine the appearance of this senior official, but he imagined a stout, erect figure with gingery-coloured hair and even possibly a tidy moustache. He was probably one of a long line of military leaders in his family and had no doubt that there would be many portraits of all these on the walls of his ancient manor.

In spite of all this, there was something about him that Alex did not like. Was it something in his voice or mannerisms? Alex could not work out what it was, but, for whatever reason, he felt wary of this distinguished army officer. His experience of many, but not all senior army officers had never instilled him with much confidence. In fact, he considered many to be pompous, arrogant pricks. "Guys do not get to his rank by being nice", thought Alex.

The man relaxed his grip, allowing the other person to move closer to Alex. This voice surprised him even more than the Brigadier General's.

"Major Jennifer Sherlock. Very pleased to meet you, Captain."

Her handshake, while not as strong as the Brigadier General's was warm, firm and conveyed a great sense of discipline, confirmed by her senior rank. The most surprising fact was that she was not English. Her voice sounded American and, yet, not quite.

With a sudden inspiration, he asked, "Do I detect a slight Canadian accent in your voice, Major?"

She laughed. "Well noticed. My family came from Canada, but we moved to New York when I was twelve. So my accent is a mix of both countries. Probably the worst."

Professor Goldman, eager to get the meeting under way, interrupted these pleasantries. "Shall we all take a seat?"

Alex's hand was placed on the arm of a comfortable chair. All four took their seats. It was the Brigadier General who started the conversation. "I'm sorry for the lack of information given to you, Captain McCloud. Hopefully, we can clear up any confusion or mis-understandings."

"Good! I would like to know why the use of micro-electronics is necessary, but, even more, I would like to know why I was told that I probably would never see, again."

"That is understandable. I must admit that, when you arrived in the field hospital, the specialist there felt there was too much damage to your eyes to retrieve any useful vision."

"So what changed?" Alex was not going to be over-awed by this senior-ranking official.

"One of the specialists at the military hospital in the U.K. found that while there had indeed been major damage to both eyes, he felt that parts of the retina may still be functioning and receptive enough to provide some useful vision, providing the remainder of the eyes could be prosthetically replicated."

The Professor spoke. "This specialist contacted me at Moorfields to explain your prognosis and enquired about our recent research. The problem is that not all the retina's receptive area survived. Focusing light through a conventional prosthetic lens would provide some useful sight, but the field of vision would be severely limited, perhaps even distorted." He paused to let this information be absorbed by the attentive Alex. "The technology we have been developing here can overcome this problem by electronically manipulating and enhancing the image before it is received by the retina"

Alex understood what was being said, but still had a problem. "But, why all the secrecy?"

The Professor continued. "The fact is that our research is just that. If this micro-implant is used, you would be the first person on the planet to receive it."

"And that is where we came in," the Brigadier General interrupted. "As head of Military Intelligence at MI6, your situation is of considerable interest to us."

"But, why?" The frustration in Alex's voice remained.

"Perhaps I can help. Have you heard of Augmented Reality?" It was the softer voice of Major Sherlock.

"Yes." Alex was hesitant. "I've heard of it being used in video games."

"It has much wider use than just on games. The military already use it in some situations and it can prove very useful. I work in a small, elite unit in the U.S. Defence Department, where the benefits of Augmented Reality are studied and utilised to our advantage. But, we are still at an early stage."

Alex was beginning to understand. "So you want to create Augmented Reality within my eyes?"

"In a nutshell, yes."

Alex could sense the excitement in her voice. These people wanted to use Alex as a human guinea pig. But, there was still something that had not been said. He felt that he was missing something. He raised his head and, hopefully directing his question at Professor Goldman, asked, "There's a catch, isn't there? What are you not telling me?"

The Professor remained quiet, but the Brigadier General gave a little cough and answered Alex's question. "You are quite correct, Captain McCloud. To the outside world, you must still appear to be blind. Nobody, apart from a select group of people, must know that you can see. This military advantage must not be known to the individuals your missions will involve."

Everything had now dropped into place, but Alex's anger was rising. The events of the past few months raced silently through his tormented mind. "I don't know whether any of you know, or even care about this, but my fiancé dumped me because she could not handle the probability of looking after me, as a blind person, for the rest of my life." There was silence in the room. Had he been unfair to expect something, anything from these three disperate individuals? "I'm sorry, it just upsets me to think about how my life has been turned upside down and you want to meddle with my eyes to suit your military needs."

Professor Goldman broke the silence. "You don't have to make a decision just now. Take as long as you want."

Alex ignored this and asked, "If I do agree, what do you want of me? You would want something for such an investment?"

Major Sherlock picked her words carefully. "Criminals and terrorist groups, both here and in the States, are becoming ever more resourceful and we feel this technology could bring many benefits. We would like you to undertake specific special missions jointly between British and American forces. For this, you would receive jointly from the two Governments, payment of two hundred and thirty thousand U.S. dollars each year. That's about.."

"One hundred and fifty thousand pounds," interrupted Alex, as he swiftly calculated, using the approximate exchange rate of one point five dollars to the pound. This was a considerable amount and far more than he had been paid by the British Government during his military career and even more than David Cameron, the present Conservative Prime Minister. It was a very attractive inducement.

If he turned down the offer, he would receive injury compensation and a meagre pension. It could be a very uncertain future without the means to earn a decent living. He could go back to living with his parents, but this would be a burden on them and what would happen as they became old and infirm? He did not want to imagine such a bleak, empty future.

His thoughts were interrupted by the Brigadier General. "On top of your salary, we would provide a place for you to live, rent-free, here, in London."

With the current property prices in the capital escalating at an unprecedented rate, this was an even greater inducement, but it was not this which changed Alex's mind. He knew that the thought of being on secret missions with their inherent danger, intrigued him. "Okay. I will agree to be your guinea pig. Just don't get it wrong. My future depends upon it."

The three men and one woman stood up and handshakes were, again, exchanged. Alex was surprised to hear Major Sherlock say to the professor, "I'll cancel my return flight to Washington and book into a local hotel."

"My secretary will assist you in finding somewhere to stay. There are many hotels within a short distance from Moorfields. The Crown Plaza at Shoreditch is only about ten minutes walk from here."

Alex could not resist the temptation to ask, "What is your involvement in the next stage of my treatment, Major?"

"The electronics developed here at Moorfields needs some software enhancement to include the facility to add A.R. and that is my specialty. I will be here as long as is necessary. I'm afraid that you are going to see a lot more of me."

This thought excited Alex and, if she looked as good as she sounded, the day when he would be able to see again could not come too soon.

The Brigadier General added, even though Alex had not asked the question of him, "My involvement here is finished, for now and I'll leave you in far more capable hands. I will be more involved when the missions commence. I wish you every success, Captain McCloud." With this, the senior military man left the room. Alex had the impression that he probably enjoyed being the centre of attention, but, for him, he felt relieved when the senior officer had left the room.

"Would you like to take my arm, Captain?" Surprisingly, it was not the professor who offered this, but the much preferable, Major Sherlock.

"Yes, thanks." Alex wondered if she understood his discomfort in being guided by a man. He did realise while they were walking along the corridor, that she was quite tall. Perhaps five feet nine or ten? He found it difficult to guess her age, but, with her rank, the probability was that she was older than him. Perhaps in her late twenties or early thirties?

After leaving Alex at his bedroom, she went with the professor to the office, where she could organise her accommodation.

Alex remembered how, less than two weeks earlier, he had contemplated suicide and was thankful that he had not had the courage to take his life.

His spirits now lifted, Alex did feel more optimistic about his future and decided he needed to re-build his military physique. He was not in bad condition, but had not carried out any strenuous exercise for a long time. He changed into tracksuit pants, sweatshirt and trainers.

Fifty press-ups, a break and another fifty was a good start. He wished he had the pull-up bar to strengthen his arm muscles and checked the door frame to see if it was able to take his weight. He had to admit to himself that the door frame construction was not designed for a twelve or thirteen stone man to suspend himself from and had to make do with stretching exercises. Still, it was a start.

He was sweating when Amy knocked on his door. "I've brought your dinner, Alex."

She wheeled the trolley in the room and served Alex's meal, placing his plate and cutlery on the adjustable table, positioning it so that Alex could sit in a comfortable chair.

His exercises had given him an appetite and he managed to persuade the young nurse to give him an extra portion of beef and fries.

After eating his fill, he pushed the table to one side and was about to relax, when he heard a knock at the door. He thought it would be the nurse, coming to clear away the dishes. "Come in, Amy."

He was surprised when Major Sherlock entered the room. "I hope you don't mind me disturbing you. I'm at a bit of a loose end in my hotel and thought it may be a good opportunity to find out a bit more about you."

Alex was pleased. "No problem. Pull up a chair, Major."

She laughed. "Let's get rid of these military titles. Please call me Jen."

"Okay, that's fine by me. What do you want to know?"

Jen was very probing and particularly interested in his childhood, asking many questions about his family, education and military training.

He answered all her questions as accurately and honestly as he could and then decided to balance the conversation a little, by asking, "Which part of Canada do you come from?"

Her gentle laugh was quite pleasant and endearing. "You won't have heard of it. Innisfil is a tiny town on the west shore of Lake Simcoe in Ontario. When I lived there the population was less than thirty thousand and nothing much ever happened."

"Was this the reason your family move to New York?"

"In part, yes. There was little opportunity to do much in such a tiny, rural place. My parents wanted me to have better chances than they had."

"Any regrets?"

It did not take much thought for her reply. "None at all. Don't get me wrong – Innisfil is a beautiful place, but, if I had stayed there, I would probably now be a logger's wife with half a dozen kids running around the house and an addiction to anti-depressants."

They both laughed. Alex sensed that Jen put career above family life, from her remark. "Is there a Mr. Sherlock?"

Again, she laughed. Her character was relaxed and quite amiable, bolstering Alex's thoughts about her. "Only my dad! I travel around too much to settle down and I love my job."

Alex had guessed that this would be her answer. "I can tell that you are very enthusiastic about your work." Alex was feeling a bit restless and as he moved to become more comfortable, he accidently pressed the button on his talking watch. As the stentorian male voice announced that it was nine forty three, Alex apologised. "Sorry, I didn't mean to press it. It's a bit too sensitive. You know, I can't stand the voice."

She seemed surprised. "Why? It sounds quite manly."

"That's the problem. It gives me a shock, especially when I press it accidentally, which happens quite a lot. I would have preferred a more soothing, softer voice."

Jen showed interest. "Let me have a look at your watch, Alex." He slipped it off his wrist and handed it to her.

It was quite bulky, with an analogue display and four buttons, two on each side of the face. Thoughtfully, Jen said, "We need to provide some interface between the chips in your eyes and the Internet. We could include this within a wristwatch and engineer a more acceptable voice at the same time."

"Really?" Alex was impressed. He was constantly amazed by the miniaturization of complex electronic circuitry.

"We could easily manufacture a much smarter watch, combining all the functions needed." Jen stood up. "Anyway, it's time I was leaving you in peace and going back to my hotel

Alex had enjoyed the evening, even the probing questions and deep discussions about his background. Still, he felt certain that they would be seeing a lot more of each other and was quite happy with this situation.

CHAPTER FIVE :
JULY, 2011

O ver the next two weeks, Alex's patience was severely tested, as numerous measurements were taken and software tweaked to optimise the quality and reliability of the tiny chips. He was desperate to reach the point where he could see something, anything. To him, the past few months of blackness had seemed an eternity, even to the point where he had difficulty remembering what it was like to have normal vision. Just to see the rich greens of grass or bright, blue skies seemed far too difficult to recollect. His frustration, together with his continuing headaches had been making him feel quite irritable and ill-tempered, but, somehow, he managed to repress his inner anger.

True to her word, Jen retained a keen interest and, when she was not working, spent many hours with Alex.

Even with all the attention, he still had a strange, empty feeling. A feeling that would not leave him, no matter how hard he tried to shut it out. One evening, he was in his room, eating his dinner. The radio was on in the background. He had come to hate the silence and used the radio for company. Almost like a child's soother.

The five o'clock news was, however, depressing with riots being sparked off in London, following the fatal shooting of twenty-nine year old gangster, Mark Duggan by a Police marksman in tottenham, the previous day. Anger was spreading at what seemed, to many, to have been an assassination, since Duggan was, apparently, unarmed, although a gun was found only twenty feet away, suggesting that Duggan had discarded it on seeing the Police.

Thankfully, the music was more up-lifting in Simon Mayo's "Drive Time". On Radio Two. Since it was Friday, listeners could request the artist and soundtrack they would like him to play.

One listener was talking excitedly about his girl friend. The two of them would be travelling to Barcelona for a romantic holiday, the following day and he wanted to hear music which reminded him of her, particularly the colour of her eyes.

It was his choice of music which caught Alex's attention. "Brown-eyed girl" by Van Morrison was requested. This track, released long before Alex was even born, superbly sung by the talented Morrison, had words which seemed to be so relevant to Alex. The song was still frequently played on the radio and, now, Alex listened to every word and phrase in great detail.

The guy who requested it probably had never really listened closely to all the lyrics as they were painfully reminiscent of Alex's own situation and not one of lovers about to go on holiday together.

Helen's eyes were, indeed, a beautiful, deep shade of brown, but the song was remembering the times together before they had separated.

"Our hearts were thumping, you, my brown-eyed girl" was remembering the good times, but, as with Alex, they were now, only distant memories.

Even the words, "slipping and sliding all along the waterfall, with you" had a significance to Helen and Alex's relationship as they had this same experience, two years earlier while walking along a narrow, slippery path near to a powerful waterfall in the Cumbrian hills on a hot, August day.

"So hard to find my way, now that I'm on my own, my brown-eyed girl." Alex was missing Helen more than he had expected and, like Van Morrison, similarly, finding it so hard.

He wondered if Morrison had suffered a similar, painful break-up of a wonderful relationship, inspiring the emotional words in this truly memorable song. He sat motionless for several minutes, turning the skillfully-crafted words around in his mind. Illogically, he now both loved and hated this emotional song. He was on the edge of tears, held back only by a stubborn belief that this was not something a real man should do.

Eventually snapping out of his morose mood, he finished his meal, but was still troubled by these pervasive thoughts.

There came a time when no further work could be done at Moorfields, as the final chip had to be manufactured in a special facility, which was more normally used for assembling the complex electronics used in satellites. Even so, the production would be given top priority and constructed in a very short time frame.

Noticing that Alex was becoming ever more restless, Jen asked, "Would you like me to go with you for a walk outside the hospital?"

"Would I? That would be great! I'm tired of being restricted to my room and the laboratory."

Jen smiled, understanding his frustration. "Right, I'll call at your room in fifteen minutes and we will see how far you can walk. I've checked with Professor Goldman and he says that it's fine."

"Good. I don't know what to wear. Is it cold, outside?" After being restricted to keeping indoors for so long and no visual feedback from the outside world, he felt uncertain.

"It's actually quite bright, sunny and fairly warm. A perfect day for a walk."

As they emerged from the hospital entrance, Alex breathed in the fresh air and held on to Jen's arm as they walked down the steps onto City Road. This was the old entrance, as Jen preferred to use this rather than the newer Cayton Street entrance around the corner.

She guided him expertly, letting him know as they approached any steps up or down.

He found her pace quite comfortable. Not too fast or slow and felt quite confident in her care. He was wearing dark glasses, but, even so, some people, occasionally, still managed to bump into him.

He accepted their apologies, without complaint, when they noticed his situation, but, in truth, he really did not mind. Alex felt so exhilarated by the new feeling of the sun on his face, the noise of the city and the strange array of smells in the air. He was like a baby, learning new sensory feelings and felt relieved that the bomb in Afghanistan had not damaged any of his other senses.

They did not walk very far from the hospital, since both hardly knew their way around this bustling city and did not wish to get caught up in the current riots which had now spread to other parts of the U.K. Jen did, however know the route to her hotel in Shoreditch and used this knowledge to their advantage as they walked around the streets of London.

Jen was fairly talkative as they strolled along their route and, as Alex had already noticed, conversation with this young, vibrant woman was quite easy. As a comparative new-comer to London, she was fascinated by the Royal family, particularly Princes William and Harry.

"What I can't understand is why the Royals need so many Palaces. Apart from Buckingham Palace, there's also Kensington, St. James and Hampton Court Palaces." After a moment's thought, she added, "And then there's Windsor Castle as well! Just how many Palaces does the Royal Family need?"

"You have a good point, but, after so many years of Royalty, it's inevitable that they accumulate many historical buildings."

"Yes, but who pays for the upkeep and maintenance of all these buildings?"

"Partly through tax payments, but the Queen does pay for a large part of the cost of upkeep. Tourism also brings in a terrific income to offset all the expense, so it's not quite as bad as you may think." After a moment's thought, he added, "At least we don't have to maintain Nonsuch Palace!"

Jen almost did a double take. "Nonsuch Palace? It sounds like a Disney creation."

Alex laughed, half-expecting such a reaction from someone who lived across the Atlantic. "Henry the eighth decided to build the best Palace in the world to celebrate the birth of his first son and named it 'Nonsuch' because there would be nothing as good to compare it with."

There was a hint of curiosity and, perhaps, a slightly mocking tone in her voice as she asked, "So what happened to ..." Jen paused, finding it difficult to repeat such a strange, untypically British name. "Nonsuch Palace?"

Their discussion was temporarily interrupted at this point, as they crossed over the busy road, Jen guiding him, particularly at the up and down kerbs.

"Poor Henry never saw its completion. He died a few years before it was finished. Apparently, it did live up to its name and was built in Henry's hunting grounds, in Surrey. It passed down the Royal lineage and by the sixteen eighties, it was in the hands of Charles the second, who, foolishly, gave it to one of his mistresses."

"So, it's no longer a Royal Palace?"

"Worse than that. His mistress had enormous gambling debts and had the building torn down, selling all the materials to pay off her debts. From that point on, Nonsuch Palace ceased to exist and became 'No such Palace'!"

Jen laughed. "I really don't know whether I should believe this story, or not. It has a strange, yet ridiculously plausible sound to it."

"Would I lie to you?" Alex smiled, knowing how strange this story must have sounded. He had thought the same when Helen had told him of this long-demolished Royal building, but the internet had confirmed the facts.

"Check it on Google and you'll see the facts." Alex found conversation with Jen easy and knew that he really enjoyed her company.

After walking for nearly two hours, they returned to the hospital and back to Alex's now very familiar room. As he sat on the bed, he said, "It's crazy, Jen. I feel exhausted and, yet, what we have done today is nothing compared to normal daily Army routines."

"Don't worry. You have been inactive for quite a while. It will take time to get back into shape."

Alex smile was one of gratitude. "I know. Thanks so much, Jen. I'd be lost without you. Literally!"

"No problem. I enjoy your company."

He stood up and, hoping his effort would not seem too clumsy, took hold of Jen and leaned in for a kiss. This had been a mis-calculation on his part. She pulled away and stood back from him, surprised at his bold approach. "Sorry, Alex. I'm not sure that's a good idea."

The young man dropped his hands, feeling foolish and admonished. Naively, he asked, "Why? You just said that you like me?"

There was almost a note of exasperation in her voice. "I do, but I want to keep our relationship professional. The last thing I want is to return home and try to maintain a long-distance relationship. Sorry, but it's just not going to work, Alex."

He could see the sense of her argument, but still had hoped for a better response. Over the past few weeks, when they had spent many hours together, he had felt great comfort in Jen's company, but, more than that, he had longed to make love to her. When struggling to fall asleep at night, he had, on many occasions, imagined Jen pulling the covers back and climbing, naked, in beside him, her wandering hands discovering every intimate part of his body. Her fragrance and the touch of her skin, although only in his imagination, had aroused him and he wished these fantastic, sensual dreams would, somehow, come true. "Perhaps there is someone in her life, back in the States", he thought.

For Jen, the budged attempt had not been a complete surprise. Again, over the past few weeks, she had noticed a change in Alex. She felt that he was now getting over Helen and probably felt that she was fair game for a new romantic involvement. Jen did really like him, but felt it was too soon for such a relationship. For her, it was nearly three years since she had been intimately close to anybody and was still hurting from the experience. The thoughts of her ex-lover filled her mind and brought great sadness to her.

Their thoughts and discussion were interrupted by the arrival of Professor Goldman. He was excited and, if he did sense the awkward situation, he showed no sign. "Alex! We've just received the prosthetic eyes from the lab. We are lucky the package managed to reach here, considering all the riots in London and around the country."

"Great!" His enthusiasm at the news was slightly tempered by the continuing violence and Jen's, not unreasonable, rejection. "When can they be fitted?"

The Professor looked at his watch. "We have some final test to ensure that everything is okay, but I see no reason why we can't fit them tomorrow morning."

It would be a relief to end his world of blackness and Alex knew that, if it was not for the dedication of this brilliant Professor, this chance would not even be possible. The ophthalmic surgeon left the young couple to return to his work.

Recovering himself, Alex said, "I'm so sorry, Jen. Of course, you are right."

"It's alright, Alex. I can understand your situation and, I guess, you're still missing Helen."

The mention of his ex-fiancé's name made Alex realise that Jen's words rang true. The pain of separation was immense and it would be very difficult for any other woman to ever replace her and, yet, he knew Jen was someone very special. He felt incredibly stupid for making such an amateurish pass and blamed it on his sexually-starved hormones.

Jen suggested that Alex get a good night's sleep, ready for the work of the following day. She held his hand and kissed him gently on the cheek, which Alex, gratefully, accepted as consolation.

He still found difficulty sleeping, thinking about his fudged attempt at intimacy with Jen. Was she really a "Helen substitute" or was she someone he wanted to have a long-term relationship with?

CHAPTER SIX :

In a quiet road in London, not too far from Moorfields Eye hospital, Tony Bradbury was at the wheel of his smart, six-month old Mercedes "C" class. He was quite early for his meeting and drove at a leisurely pace. Twenty-eight year old Tony was a confident, successful criminal who had made most of his money from dealing in drugs. He would never deal with end-users, preferring to act, instead, as a "middle man", or, as he preferred to think of himself, as a "Wholesaler".

Over the past few years, he had enjoyed spending the fruits of his crimes on numerous luxuries, giving him the confidence of one who has "made it". A smart, west-end apartment, expensive personal jewellery and a bank balance in excess of two million all helped to make Tony feel extremely confident and untouchable.

Sitting behind him, in the rear passenger seat was heavily-built Jake Mitchell, Mark's business partner of five years and his 'muscle'. Both men were looking for possible traps, never trusting anybody they were involved with to do exactly as expected. Tony and Jake were armed and ready to kill anybody who may decide to cause them a problem.

Tony parked the car at the quiet entrance to an ancient-looking warehouse, as agreed with their contact.

"I don't like this area", said Jake. "There's something about this that gives me an uneasy feeling."

"Relax, Jake. Just keep your eyes alert and we'll be alright."

Within a few minutes and precisely on time, a man of medium build, probably in his early thirties and carrying a briefcase, approached the car.

Tony unlocked the doors and

Opened the front passenger door just enough to indicate where the man should go.

Pulling the door fully open, he took the front passenger seat and placed the briefcase on his lap. After closing the door, the man said, "Impressive car, Tony."

"It should be for the price I had to pay." Tony did not like small-talk and asked, " Do you have all the money?"

"Of course. Do you have the goods?"

Tony almost felt offended, but ignored the question and lifted a briefcase on to his knees. "You show me the cash and I'll show you the drugs."

The man seemed quite casual as he turned his briefcase to allow inspection of the contents. He flipped the catch and lifted the lid. A high-pressure "whoosh" of eight litres of sevoflurane gas was instantly released, giving just enough time for the man to fit a small, protective breathing mask, before the effects could be felt by him.

For Tony and Jake, there was no such escape, both men losing consciousness within three seconds. Jake had started to draw his gun, but was unable to complete his defence.

The rear door opened and another man, similarly fitted with protective mask, slipped into the vacant seat. He shut the door and held out his hand, expectantly. The man in the front seat took two long icepicks out of the brief case and handed one to the other. Within seconds, both Tony and Jake had the icepicks rammed into the backs of their necks and up into their brains, ensuring that their deaths would be swift and with minimum loss of blood. Some had spilled out of the small wound and run onto the expensive, tailored shirt and suit worn by Tony.

One man opened the window just long enough to dissipate the gas and make it possible for their masks to be removed. The dark-tinted windows on the Mercedes had assisted these two killers in this carefully-executed plan. They were meticulous as they wiped their prints off anything they had touched.

Danny Jackson and Paddy Conroy stepped out of the car, each carrying a briefcase. One had not much more than a small amount of cash and the mechanism for releasing the gas, while the other contained three kilos of high-quality cocaine.

Once they had walked far enough away from the Mercedes to avoid suspicion, Paddy took a phone from his pocket and dialed a number. His message was brief and concise. "Business transaction completed successfully."

Danny smiled and said, "Gianni should be very pleased with today's work."

Paddy agreed. "Shame about the car. I wouldn't mind one like that, myself."

The two men continued their walk until they reached their own car a few blocks away. Satisfied at the success of their mission, they drove away from the area.

CHAPTER SEVEN :
9th. AUGUST, 2011

Alex lay, anaesthetized on the operating table, a clamp holding his head steady, allowing the gowned surgeon to begin this very delicate operation. The tiny dressings which had been protecting the retinas were removed and the prosthetic shells, complete with their miniature electronics, were gently inserted into the vacant orbits. The clamps holding the facial tissue were slowly released, allowing the muscles to grip the shells and fill the anterior chambers with aqueous humor.

When he was satisfied that Alex's replacement eyes were correctly aligned, Professor Goldman motioned to Jen to inspect the final appearance. He lifted the eye-lids gently to show Major Sherlock.

"They appear fantastic and so real-looking. I just hope that Alex is going to be able to see, again."

"We will know as soon as he comes round from the anesthetic."

A very groggy Alex began to come back to consciousness about forty minutes later. While under anesthetic, he had experienced a strange, almost realistic dream of two men being silently killed, which, considering his military background was not surprising, yet, for some inexplicable reason, he felt that this was closer to home than Afghanistan. The pain in his head seemed too much to bear, yet this eased as he returned to full consciousness.

As his mind cleared, he realised that a mask had been placed over his eyes and moved his hand to take this away. Professor Goldman noticed. "Are you ready, Alex?"

"Yes, of course. I've longed for this moment."

The surgeon gently lifted the mask off and helped the younger man to sit upright. "Tell me what you can see."

Alex prayed that this was going to work and looked in the direction of the Professor's voice.

There was definitely something different. The inky blackness had disappeared and, was, now, replaced with a pale, insipid-looking mist surrounding him, but, then, he noticed that the mist was gradually becoming more and more patchy with haphazardly-positioned blotches of other colours slowly invading his visual field. "Yes! I can see some light!" Concentrating his efforts, he stared intensely at the older man. "How do I focus the image?"

"Exactly the same as you have always done. Just look at the object you wish to see and the muscles will adjust the focal length to achieve the sharpest image. The electronics in your new eyes are self-calibrating themselves for optimum acuity. It may take a little while getting used to."

As Alex stared at the Professor, the image slowly changed from a blurred, fuzzy outline to a more distinct shape in his brain. He could see a figure dressed in a light-green, surgical gown. Gradually, the details became sharper and the man was smiling at him. "I can see you!"

Professor Goldman took off his surgical cap. "What colour is my hair, Alex?"

With noticeable enthusiasm in his voice, he answered, "Mainly black, but I can see some greyish areas!"

"Isn't that just typical of my luck! Give a guy sight and the first things he notices are my grey hairs! Don't look too closely or you will also see the wrinkles on my forehead."

They laughed and then Alex realised that there was another person in the room. He turned his head to see a woman standing close to the wall on his left. She was quite tall, had short, blonde hair, clear, blue eyes and pale golden skin. "Jen? Is it you?"

She laughed. "Right first time, soldier. I deliberately stayed out of your main field of vision to see if you noticed me. The implants appear to be working."

The smile she gave him made Alex realise that the reality was even better than his vivid imagination. She truly was beautiful. Her amazingly-bright, blue eyes seemed to sparkle in the stark, fluorescent light of the operating room. Alex's thoughts began to meander through new tracks. "Wow! What a beauty! Sorry, Van but no more brown-eyed girl. Elton John's 'blue eyes' suddenly seemed more appropriate."

"How many fingers am I holding up?" asked Jen.

Without any hesitation, he answered, "Four!"

"Correct. Now, how many?"

Alex saw Jen swiftly move her hands, concealing them behind her body. "I don't have x-ray vision, so I've no idea. You are holding your hands behind your back!"

"Great!" They all laughed, happy that this scientific gamble now appeared to be a success.

The professor, eager to be assured that everything was working, said, "Now, Alex, look at the chart on this panel and read the letters for me, please." The Professor switched the rear illumination on the reading test page.

With increasing confidence, Alex read down the screen, only finding difficulty with the very bottom line.

"Don't worry, Alex. Look at the bottom line again and concentrate. Really focus on working out what the letters are."

To Alex's amazement, the letters became larger, making it possible to read every single character, without any difficulty. "Fantastic! I can zoom in, just like a camcorder! How do I zoom out?"

Again, the Professor chuckled. "Look away from the smallest letters and the zoom will decrease. You had better zoom out before you look at my hair, again, or you will see even more grey hairs!"

Alex was like a small child with a new toy. Fascinated, he looked at everything in the room, zooming in and out, at will. He even sneakily zoomed in on Jen's face, hoping that she did not realise that she was being studied at close quarters. "Why is it that women from North America and Canada seem to have such perfect teeth?" Alex thought. Her lips were full and delightful. She was wearing pale pink lipstick which seemed to have a sparkle. He did wonder if this had been applied especially for his benefit, but, whatever the reason, she looked superb and absolutely stunning.

Bringing him back from his thoughts, the Professor added, "Just like a camcorder, if you zoom in too much, the image will be pixilated, but I'm sure you can live with that."

"Yes, I certainly can. This is truly amazing! Thank you both, so much." The smile on Alex's face said it all.

The Professor asked, "Are you okay for me to make some further tests of your eyesight?"

With his new-found vision, Alex's mood had lightened considerably. "Yes, of course. I'm ready for anything."

Professor Goldman smiled and, now, Alex could see his expression clearly. More clearly than he had ever imagined possible. "Come into the other room and we will carry out a field of vision test. Alex remained motionless, now used to being escorted from room to room. Realising what he had done, he cursed himself for being so stupid and meekly followed the other two into an adjacent room.

"Take a seat, here, Alex." He took the offered seat. The older man placed heavy spectacles on Alex and placed a disc in the frame to cover his right eye. "Now, rest your chin on this support and look directly at the spot in the centre."

Alex was facing into a large black hemisphere and concentrated on the white spot at its centre.

He was handed a small unit with a prominent push button. "When I start this equipment, you will see another white spot close to the midpoint. It will move away from the main spot and I want you to press the button when it disappears out of your field of vision. Okay?"

"I understand, Professor and ready when you are."

The older man started the unit and the second white spot began to move away from the centre. Alex waited until it had disappeared from his field of vision and quickly pressed the button. The spot swiftly returned to the centre and, this time, moved in a different, random direction. About ten minutes later, a complete field of vision had been mapped and stored for Alex's left eye.

After the disc was removed from the spectacle frame and inserted to cover his left eye, the whole process was repeated.

The ophthalmic surgeon turned the lights up in the room and spread the computer printouts on the desktop in front of him.

"So, how's my field of vision?" Alex nervously enquired.

After a painfully long pause, Professor Goldman looked up at Alex. His face held a broad smile. "Fantastic! Your field of vision is even better than we had expected or hoped for. The accepted normal field of vision is about ninety-five degrees out, sixty degrees up, seventy-five degrees down and sixty degrees in. This is typical for a man in his early twenties, but, in your case, we have managed to extend this by another five degrees in all directions." The Professor looked with incredulity at the printed results.

"Quite remarkable!" he exclaimed and then added, "Even your blind spot is minimal. It is the brain which fills in the gaps created by the blind spot where the optic nerve is attached, but, somehow, the electronics have also compensated and assisted in the process."

Alex's face lit up at the news. "Congratulations, Professor. You've created prosthetic eyes with superior capabilities to normal human eyes. Thank you so much."

Jen had been listening and joined in with the praise. "It is a truly great achievement. When the A.R. is activated, the vision will be even more super-human."

"There's another test I would like to carry out before we make a start on the enhancements." The Professor operated a dimmer control which adjusted the level of lighting in the room. After turning it quite low, he said, "Tell me how much detail you can see now that the light level is low."

Alex looked around the room. "I can tell that the light level is lower, yet... It's strange! I can see everything in perfect detail."

"Excellent! Now, see if you can read this." The Professor lifted a sheet of paper off the desk. He had, previously hand-written a message on the paper and now held it facing Alex.

The young man laughed. "My birthday is in three days time. Friday, twelfth of August."

The Professor was lost for words. He turned the paper to face Jen. "Can you read this?"

Jen stared at the paper and shook her head. "No, I can't make out a thing." The Professor turned up the light until she could read the message.

"That's incredible! You already have the best vision in the world, even at low-light levels.

Alex was elated. "This is a terrific early birthday present."

Jen decided that now was the time for the next phase. She handed a small box to Alex.

Inside, he found two smart, brushed-stainless steel wristwatches. They had the appearance of high-priced Swiss-made precision watches. "Now they're cool-looking watches! Thanks, Jen."

"You're welcome. The two watches are identical. I felt it prudent to have a backup in case one gets damaged or lost. Oh, and they're waterproof down to fifteen feet."

He placed one on his wrist, admiring his new, stylish timepiece. It had a neat digital display and, to Alex's surprise, there were no buttons as he had expected.

When he commented on this, Jen replied, "it's touch sensitive. Just touch the display at the right side."

When Alex did this, it came as a pleasant surprise to hear Jen's voice emerge from the tiny speaker. "The time is eleven thirty-five a.m."

Alex laughed. "That is such an improvement on my present talking watch. Your voice is so clear, yet calming."

"Thanks for the compliment, Alex. Now press the lower edge of the display."

When he did as instructed, the voice on the watch said, "Today is Tuesday, the ninth of August, two thousand and eleven."

Jen gave him further instruction on how to set the alarm by touching the top of the display. "Now, here comes the tricky bit, Alex. Look at me and then touch the left and right side of the display at the same time. I think this is going to be a bit embarrassing, for me, at least."

Alex wondered what she meant, but tried it. To his amazement, text appeared at the top of his field of vision. It read, "Jennifer Kimberley Sherlock, Rank Major, Nationality American/Canadian. Marital status single. Date of Birth May 11, 1984. Occupation Advanced technology researcher U.S. State Defence Department."

Alex was stunned. "Incredible! How on earth does it work?"

Jen proudly explained. "The image from your eyes is fed, via the watch to a powerful image recognition computer and, providing it can find a match in the database, the text is relayed back to your eyes. As soon as you look away, the text will clear

Intrigued, Alex turned his head to look at the Professor. The earlier text was replaced with new information, reading, "Daniel Michael Goldman, title Professor, nationality British, date of birth January 4 1961. Marital status Widowed. Position head of Advanced Ophthalmic research at Moorfields Eye hospital, London, England."

"Wow! This is mind-blowing!"

Jen, proud of her contribution, added, "Sorry the date format is not European. The data is U.S. based, so month comes before day, but I'm certain you could live with that."

"Please don't apologise. What you have developed is truly fantastic."

"It could lead to information overload if this was permanently on, so, to stop it, just touch the left side of the display, again."

He did this and, instantly, the text disappeared.

There's more", said Jen. "Touch the left and top of the display, together."

Again Alex did as instructed and was shocked at what happened next. Instead of seeing what was in the room, a new image appeared in his eyes, but he was uncertain about what was being displayed. "What is it showing?"

"This is the tricky one. Many spy satellites are constantly monitoring the earth and, what you can see is a real-time image looking down on this part of London. You should be able to make out the outlines of Moorfields and the surrounding roads. Try concentrating on one part of the image, say, the road next to Moorfields."

As he did so, the image zoomed in, until it was possible to see fine detail such as people and cars moving along the busy road. "This is unbelievable! But, it's presumably only this good on a fine day?"

Jen shook her head. "That was a major consideration when designing the software. If the weather is cloudy or during the night, infra-red cameras take over, allowing you to see human activity at any time, day or night, even through heavy cloud cover."

Alex was now beginning to understand the military significance of the project. This is why it all had to be kept a secret. "Dare I ask how much all this technology is costing the American and British tax-payers?"

Jen hedged the question. "You really don't want to know. Let's just say that it was over a million dollars."

This did not surprise Alex. "So, I'm the man with the million dollar eyes?"

Jen laughed. "I suppose that, allowing for inflation since 'the six million dollar man', that's probably about right just for the eyes!"

The young man felt like a character out of X-Men; someone with super-human powers and just hoped that this "gift" would benefit the world. He had a thought. "If I am supposed to be blind, it is going to be difficult for me, now that I've got superhuman eyes."

Jen handed a small case to Alex. "Try these on."

Alex looked at the pair of spectacles she held out for him. "Won't it reduce the capabilities of my eyes if I have to wear dark glasses?"

"Not with these. To anybody else, they look like any ordinary pair of sun glasses, but the lens is specially made to allow you full freedom of vision." She looked very confident. "Try them on."

Alex seemed doubtful, but took hold of them and put them on. "That's amazing! I can see as clearly as though I was not wearing them. And, they look quite fashionable."

"Good! I'm glad you like them. We fashioned them on the 'Ray-Ban' sun glasses brand."

Professor Goldman looked at the newly-confident young man and felt very satisfied with the results of his extensive research.

He had been working on this project for over three years and had wondered, on many occasions, if anybody would ever benefit. Alex's injuries had made him the ideal recipient and, at last, he felt vindicated.

On many occasions, Daniel Goldman had been severely criticized by his colleagues who felt that he was wasting his time and, more importantly, precious research budgets. Still, he had persisted, even more since the death of Pamela, his wife of twenty-seven years, to breast cancer in two thousand and eight. Always a dedicated worker, he now spent even more long hours, working late into the night on his "Special" project.

When he fully realized the military significance of his work, he had contacted the Ministry of Defence. At first, they showed little interest, but when the deeply-committed Professor mentioned the possibility of adding Augmented Reality to the prosthetic eyes, their interest soon became apparent.

He realized the extent of their interest when he was invited to a meeting at MI6 at Vauxhall Cross, where he had to sign a secrecy agreement. That was where he met the larger than life, Brigadier General Paul Marshall for the first time. He was invited to explain, in great detail, how the high tech prosthetic eye worked and how soon a fully-working version would be available.

He gave himself a tight deadline of six months and, with new impetus, managed to keep to his schedule.

During this period, Major Sherlock flew in from the States to join in the progress meetings and, very soon, she was a significant contributor to the design of the miniature circuitry and software contained within the eye.

"Do you need me for any further tests, Professor?"

Alex's question brought Daniel back to the present. "No, not for now. What do you have in mind?"

The young man hesitated a little. "I want to see how I look in the mirror in my room. Does that sound vain?"

"No, not at all. It's very understandable and quite natural. Can you find your way to your room?"

"I think so. You will hear me, if I get lost."

Alex was about to leave the laboratory when he had a sudden thought. "What happens if I have a shower or get caught in a heavy downpour? Are the eyes waterproof?"

Professor Goldman laughed. "I suppose it's a logical question, but the answer is that the electronics in the prosthetic eye are in a sealed unit encased within a resin shell, making them completely impervious to any moisture. Even if you dip your head under water, there will be no problem."

Satisfied with this answer, Alex smiled. "Whew! That's a relief!"

It seemed so strange to walk along the maze of corridors back to his room without assistance, but he managed it without too much difficulty, as he could now, clearly, remember the route. As soon as he was in his room, he stripped naked and stared at himself in the full-length mirror on the inside of his wardrobe.

Alex smiled and the man in the mirror smiled back at him. Was this really what he looked like? Four months of seeing nothing had eroded, even changed, what he thought was his appearance. Of course, his features were slimmer through loss of body weight while inactive in a hospital bed.

The areas down one side of his body which had received most of the burns were still pinkish and quite noticeable, but he felt that in a few more months time, they would have blended in. Thankfully, his manhood had escaped mutilation during the bomb blast and should still have the capacity to satisfy a woman's needs. "Hope that's not going to be too long a time," he thought.

The hair on his head was growing back where it had been shaved before his many operations to remove the frags. There were still numerous scars on his head and body, and his face looked a bit uneven in skin tone following the scarring, but, of course, what Alex was really interested in were his eyes. Would they appear realistic or obvious imitation replacements? He hoped that they would look more realistic than those of a ventriloquist's dummy.

Nervously, Alex edged closer to the mirror and looked at his "bionic" eyes. He had to admit that the Professor had done a brilliant job in re-creating them. How many times had his mother commented on how sharp and bright blue they were? Just like his father's and now, science had re-created perfect copies. He found it incredible that the eyes he was looking at and through had been made by man.

He was fortunate that his eye-lids had escaped damage during the bomb blast, as this would have presented many problems in retaining the prosthetic eyes securely in place.

Feeling very satisfied with the results, Alex dressed again. His room had one window. It was quite small, but, now, bright sunshine streamed into his room, highlighting a rectangular strip on his bed and the wall beyond. He moved closer to the window and peered through with some curiosity. It over-looked City Road and with the strong, afternoon sun, London seemed so bright and colourful.

When he had walked around the area with Jen, his imagination had filled everything in drab, varying shades of grey, but, now, red, blue, green and a multitude of other colours met his incredulous gaze. He found it difficult to tear his eyes away from this new spectacle and enjoyed watching the rich, vibrant colours of the cars, people and buildings. "Who ever said that London was a drab, dull place?"

Just then, he noticed a plane, high in the sky. At first, it seemed tiny, but then his eyes zoomed in on the craft, giving Alex an idea. He touched the left and right areas on his watch and, within seconds, text appeared at the top of his vision. It read, "Aircraft : Boing 737. Flight BA211 from London Heathrow. Destination Stockholm, Sweden. ETA 17:50"

This clever feature intrigued him. He could have spent many hours just identifying objects in his field of vision. "What a fantastically clever device! How come I managed to be the lucky guy with vision second to none", Alex mused. Reluctantly, he cancelled the text with another touch on his watch and, with some difficulty, returned to the present. Feeling very satisfied with his new eyes, he dressed once again.

His first thought was to phone his parents and tell them of his good news, but was brought back to reality by the words of the Brigadier General echoing through his mind. "Only a select few must know of the new-found vision."

If Alex's parents knew about his superior eyesight, it would not take long before aunts, uncles and cousins became aware and, after that, who knows? A casual remark to a journalist and the press would soon have his story on the front page. Publicists would be pestering him constantly to tell his story and, then, the whole world would know. This scenario must be avoided, at all costs and he knew that his secret could not even be shared with his own close relatives.

Alex knew that he would like to visit his family and sought out Professor Goldman to ask his advice.

He did confirm Alex's fears. "Your family and friends must not know the extent of your vision, as it may endanger future military missions. But, I do think it a good idea to visit your family, especially as it is your birthday on Friday. Another day and we should be finished with all the tests, so why don't you phone your parents and make some arrangements?"

Alex desperately wanted to see his family, but could envisage several problems. "But, how do I travel to Bury St. Edmunds as a blind person, when I can see? I can't just walk up to my parent's house and knock at the door!"

Jen was listening with interest to this discussion. "Perhaps, I can help, Alex."

"How?" Alex could not see any obvious solution.

Jen said, "There is one other combination of keys on your watch which I had not told you about, yet. Try touching the top and bottom contacts together."

Alex did as suggested and, suddenly, he was again immersed in a sea of inky blackness. The super-human vision he had known for just a few hours had disappeared in an instant. "God! How do I get it back?"

"The same touch contacts again will resume full vision."

Alex touched his watch and smiled as his eyesight was, again, fully restored. "That was so scary. To go back to nothing after what I have seen today, was truly depressing."

"But, at least, it would be convincing." Jen could see that Alex still seemed doubtful. "Listen, Alex. I could drive you there, if you wish." After a moment's thought, she added, "You could introduce me as someone who works at Moorfields."

Alex looked surprised. "Would you do that for me, Jen?"

"Of course, if it will help you out of a problem. And my work here is just about finished, anyway."

Professor Goldman seemed happy with this compromise and added, "I can provide you with a white stick and other aids to reinforce the impression."

Alex considered the idea. "Okay, I'll phone my parents, this evening."

His mother was thrilled to hear from him, but rebuked him for not keeping in touch. "You always seem to be away on your birthday, but we will make this one very special. It's a bit short notice, but we will manage."

He knew she would pull out all the stops and interrupted her before she could get far into her planning. "Mum, I don't want a big party. Just you, Dad, Lucy, Amelia and Grandmother. I don't want all my relatives gawping at me while I'm struggling with the food on my plate."

She did understand his apprehension and agreed to keep the celebrations just within close family members.

"Would you like us to pick you up, on Friday?"

He had wondered if she would ask this and replied, "No, thanks. It's not necessary. One of the staff here will give me a lift."

She sounded surprised. "Really? Okay, see you on Friday."

He was thankful she had not asked further questions about his escort. He knew that, as soon as his mother met Jen, she would begin, mentally, preparing for a wedding. She had been upset when Helen had finished with her son and, not surprisingly, thought it a cruel, selfish decision and, at the slightest excuse, would make derogatory remarks about her very nearly daughter-in-law.

CHAPTER EIGHT :
12th. AUGUST, 2011

O n Friday, Alex had wanted to pay for the hire car, but Jen had insisted that her "expenses" included the cost of any transport during her time in London. "Think of it as a birthday present from me and the American taxpayers", she said, with a firmness which denied further argument.

Considering that, back in the U.S., she would have been driving on the other side of the road, she was, obviously, a confident, skilled driver. They wound their way out of the capital. The Audi sped along the M11 towards Cambridge, where they turned onto the A14following Alex's directions. His parents lived midway between Bury St. Edmunds and the village of Woolpit in Suffolk. It seemed really strange to Alex, as they drew nearer to his family home. It was a mixture of fearful anticipation, of excitement and anxiety. When they were within half a mile, Alex touched the contacts on his watch, once again, thrusting him back into a chilling blackness.

He had described the house location to Jen and, when he felt the car swing off the road and into the curved drive, he knew the time had come. Alex remained in his seat until Jen came round the car and offered him assistance. He heard the front door of the house open on his left and knew that his mother must have seen them arrive. Of one thing he could be certain, his mother and sisters would be studying Jen, thinking that she may be a potential marriage partner for Alex. Jen handed him his overnight case from the back of the car and directed him towards the entrance door.

It was his mother, Louise, who spoke first. Jen helped Alex to step into the wide hallway, where his mother took hold of him and gave a hug as though she had not seen him for years. "Alex! You are looking so well. Introduce me to your friend."

Freeing himself from the hug, Alex said, "This is Jen. Jen, meet my mother, Louise." As they exchanged greetings, Alex asked, "Are Lucy and Amelia here?"

Lucy's voice seemed to tremble a little as she said, "I'm already here, Alex. Come on, give me a big hug as well."

As they held each other, Alex felt terrible. He knew his eighteen year-old sister was emotional because of his faked 'blindness'. How he wished that he could switch on his eyes and see his family properly.

As Lucy loosened her hold on Alex, thirteen-year old Amelia moved in. Although she was at least nine inches shorter than Alex, he could tell that she had grown a little since they had last seen each other. Her voice was also a little shaky as she asked, "How are you feeling, Alex?"

"I'm fine, Sis, and happy to be home again." The obvious emotion in Amelia's voice touched him. Although he had always teased Lucy, the age difference between him and Amelia made him very protective of his little sister. In truth, he would have done anything to care for and protect either of his sisters and he felt extremely proud of both of them.

Alex's father, James, was not at the house. It was only four fifteen and another two hours before he was likely to arrive home from the office.

"Shall we go into the lounge? Would you both like a drink?" Louise was fussing as she always had when faced with a new situation. Two now faced her. Her son returning home unable to see his family and Jen, a young, attractive woman who obviously cared enough for Alex to bring him to their house. So many questions she wanted to ask, whilst accepting that it would be impolite to do so.

Jen guided Alex into the large lounge, although he probably could find his way around the house without difficulty. His problem was the fact that he would not know just where his mother and sisters would be. Jen was now used to this situation and led Alex over to the chair offered by his mother.

The voice of Alex's eighty-two year old Grandmother, Elizabeth, did sound a little tremulous as she asked "How are you feeling, Alex?"

"I'm fine, thank you. How about yourself? Do you still have a problem with your balance?" Ever since her mid-seventies, Elizabeth had problems with her inner ear, causing her, on occasions, to lose balance.

"Oh, I can't complain. My balance is worse in the morning, particularly when I have just woken up." She gave a little sigh of resignation. "But I'll survive."

He felt certain that she would be around for many years to come. Louise's mother was a very strong-minded woman and the only survivor of her generation in the family. Her husband, Robert, had died of lung cancer in two thousand and seven, while his father's parents had both been killed in a car accident in nineteen ninety four. Stupidly, this had been caused by a drunken driver smashing head-on to their car at seventy miles an hour. Alex had been eight years old at the time, but he still remembered them with sadness. Amelia had not even been born at the time of the accident and Lucy was too young to remember them as she was only one-year old. Alex had always felt cheated that only one of this older generation was still alive.

Earlier that day, Louise had collected her mother from the warden-controlled flat, where she was determined to look after herself. She always insisted that she did not want anybody to make a fuss of her, just because of her age. Thankfully, she did still have a very sharp mind.

"Tea, coffee or fruit juice?"

Jen chose black coffee, while Alex asked, "Do you have any Tropicana orange juice?" He particularly enjoyed this drink "with bits" as the manufacturer had so proudly promoted in their adverts on television, as if it was clever to miss juicing all the flesh of the orange. Still, it was a favourite of Alex's and his mother knew it.

"You know we will always have your favourite drink in the fridge", said Alex's mother, with a knowing, yet unseen, smile.

A few minutes later, as he sipped the refreshing drink, it reminded him of Wham's hit song "Club Tropicana" released in the eighties. Whenever he had this drink, he remembered the video of George Michael, Andrew Ridgely and the two bikini-clad backing singers. Although this was before he was born, he had seen and enjoyed watching this video numerous times, as a young teenager. He remembered ogling the scantily-clad gorgeous girls.

The interrogation was about to start. "How long are you staying for, Alex?"

"Only until Sunday. Jen's giving me a lift back." Alex knew what her next question would be and he was not disappointed.

"Would you like to stay here, Jen? We do have a spare room." This was true. It was a large, five-bedroomed detached house, worthy of Alex's father's occupation as a barrister, but Louise's hopes were about to be dashed.

"No, thanks, Louise, but it's good of you to offer. I'm visiting some friends in the area." This last statement was not quite true. During their drive from London, Alex and Jen had agreed that it would be less embarrassing if she stayed in a hotel. The two had stopped in Bury St. Edmunds and found that the Angel hotel had a single room available for a couple of nights.

Louise seemed disappointed, perhaps feeling that possible future wedding plans would have to be shelved, yet again. All she wanted was a secure and happy life for her son and Jen seemed perfect material for a potential match. Louise could never forgive Helen for 'dumping' her son, just because of his loss of sight.

The small talk continued for a while, until Jen decided she would leave Alex with his family. "I'll pick you up about eleven on Sunday morning, Alex."

He went out with her to the car. He spoke quietly to prevent being overheard. "God, it's difficult! I really wish I could switch my eyes on, again. I miss seeing them."

"Just relax and enjoy being with your family. You'll be fine."

"I'll try. Hope you enjoy your stay at the Angel hotel. It's very historic. Apparently, Charles Dickens has stayed there, but I think he checked out some time ago." Jen laughed and gave him a hug and climbed into the Audi. He waited until her car had driven onto the road before he turned back towards the house.

Lucy came out and took his arm. "I'll help you, Alex. Do you want to go to your room, yet?"

"Yes, please, sis. I could do with freshening up." He knew the layout of the house perfectly, but realised that he may accidently catch one of the many expensive ornaments his mother had accumulated over the years and positioned around the house.

Once in his room, he took off his shoes and relaxed on the bed. As he lay, there, he touched the contact areas on his watch. It came as a great relief to see once again. He looked around his room and realized that nothing had changed since he was last at home.

The large dressing table still had the long-abandoned games station, on which he used to spend hours playing, mostly, military games.

"You spend far too much time playing dangerously-sadistic games. An absolute waste of time!" his father would say, but, even then, it was a precursor to him joining the army, which both his parents had feared.

The stack of DVD's lined several shelves. Alex wandered over and picked out a few. He had most of the James Bond collection, even dating back to the days of Sean Connery and, more recently, Daniel Craig as the famous secret agent. Even as a small boy, he had enjoyed playing with Action Man soldiers and anything else with a military connection.

Pride of place on the cluttered top was a model of a British Chieftain tank, which he had painstakingly constructed from an Airfix kit, when he was about twelve years old. Alex had spent many hours assembling the model and even more, accurately painting it in fine detail.

He still felt proud of this miniature symbol of his dreams. And ambitions

Alex stood there for several minutes, his eyes scanning the mementos of his childhood.

At last, he snapped out of his memories and wandered into the en-suite bathroom. He quickly freshened up, tidied his hair and then switched off his eyes, ready for his family.

As he opened the bedroom door, Lucy soon re-appeared, ready to escort him downstairs. He felt guilty, remembering how horrible he had been to Lucy when he was in his mid-teens. He had teased and made fun of her, but, now, she cared enough about him to be ready to help, when necessary.

Lucy had always been terrified of spiders and he remembered how he collected as many as he could find only to leave them tactically positioned around her room to scare the wits out of his younger sister. He particularly enjoyed placing the larger ones close to the pillows on her bed for maximum effect. Lucy's screams when she found these eight-legged monsters could be heard right through the house. It would always take a while for her to calm down and, quite justifiably, she would accuse Alex of planting these monsters just to frighten her. He now felt really bad for his role in these typically-teenage brother pranks.

They sat together in the lounge, Louise occasionally excusing herself to go into the kitchen, where she checked the slowly-cooking dinner, which smelled fantastic to Alex. Even though the food had been good at Moorfields, it could never compete with his mother's home cooking.

His Grandmother had fallen asleep and was, gently, snoring.

Alex was trying his best to avoid saying much about himself, preferring, instead, to quiz Lucy on her "A" level examinations which she had recently finished, but, as yet, did not know the results.

"I feel fairly confident, but just hope that I have done well enough to be accepted at Cambridge." In some ways, Lucy was, like her brother, determined to aim for a particular career. However, in her case, her parents were in favour of her studying medicine. Alex knew that she was a hard worker and felt certain that she would succeed.

As for Amelia, she was enjoying the six-week break from school. She was, like her older sister, studious and hard-working, but enjoyed any break from the regimented school timetable.

Around six thirty, the sound of the key in the front door could be heard and he knew his father had arrived home. He walked straight into the lounge and up to where Alex was seated. "Good to see you, son." He knew that the hand on his shoulder would be as much as he could expect. He could never remember being hugged by his father, but, at least, he had not avoided the word "see" in his greeting. So many people, when faced with a blind person would jump through verbal hoops to avoid this simple, yet obvious, word.

"Hi, Dad. How's work?"

The older man gave a little chuckle. "Relieved that the case I've been working on recently has been delayed as the defendant tried to commit suicide, otherwise I would have been in Manchester Crown courts, today. I'm just pleased to see you on your birthday."

Alex knew that he was, indeed, fortunate to see his father. As a barrister, he could be away for days at a time, working on cases around the country. His mother had become used to James' long absences and kept herself busy for most of the time.

This evening, all six of them enjoyed celebrating this twenty-fifth birthday and Alex really appreciated the meal, so superbly prepared by Louise. Alex's grandmother had a few too many glasses of wine and, once again, became quite drowsy after the meal.

Of course, there were presents for Alex. A warm, branded jumper, expensive after-shave lotion and a box of chocolate liqueurs were the type of presents he could always appreciate. Lucy and Amelia had joined together to buy him an I-tunes voucher.

There was a tricky moment when James asked, "What of the future, Alex? Are you going to be looking for work?" Alex had been dreading this question, but, before he had chance to answer, his father continued. "I've many good contacts and probably could get you an office job of sorts."

Alex could have screamed. Even after all that had happened, his father was still trying to control his life, pushing him towards a boring, business-orientated occupation. "I've already been contacted by the Army occupational resources division and they are keen to employ me as a military advisor. They will even help me to find some accommodation in London."

How he wished he could have seen the look of surprise on his father's face, as he responded, "Really? Well, that's great!" The lack of enthusiasm in his father's voice was very noticeable, but Alex did not care at all and hoped that Brigadier General Paul Marshall could really change his life for the better.

Later in the evening, Louise took her, now, somewhat relaxed mother back to her flat, after the old lady had given Alex a longer than expected, comforting hug.

CHAPTER NINE :

The following day was spent quietly with Louise, Lucy and Amelia bringing Alex up to date with family news, while his father, predictably, was working on case notes in his study.

It was a happy, gentle, relaxing day, several hours being spent in the large garden, enjoying the warm, August sunshine, while being in deep conversation with his mother and sisters.

It was Amelia who noticed his watch, asking, "That's a cool-looking talking watch, Alex. Can I hear what it sounds like, please?"

He really had no choice and gently touched the display. Jen's voice sounded very clear in the quietness of the garden, where the only other sound to be heard was that of birds singing. "The time is two-forty-five p.m." He touched the other contact area. "Today is Saturday, August the thirteenth, year two thousand and eleven."

It was his mother who commented. "The voice on your watch sounds just like your friend, Jen."

"Damn!" thought Alex. He had never thought about possible consequences of having Jen as the voice on his watch. He had no option but to lie. "Jen is an expert in micro-electronics and worked with the R.N.I.B. in designing this new watch and offered to use her voice in preference to the usual male voice."

"Really?" Louise was particularly surprised by this information and wondered, again, if there was something Alex was not telling them about his friendship with this young woman. "It must be nice to hear her voice, when she's not there."

Lucy and Amelia were not as interested as Louise in their brother's relationships, both agreeing that his watch was really cool and trendy.

Somehow, he managed to get through the rest of that day without any further problems, even occasionally, switching his sight on to catch a sneaky look at his family.

It seemed so strange to be sleeping in his old bed, once again and, by Sunday morning, he had been brought up to date on all the news.

Although Alex had enjoyed being with his family, it had been a stressful time and he felt relieved when Jen arrived at the house on Sunday morning. He gave Lucy, Amelia and his mother a big hug and popped his head around the door of the study, where his father was, as always, working on case notes.

"When will we see you again, son?"

"I honestly don't know, but, during the next few weeks I will be training with a guide dog. I'll keep in touch by phone."

He sighed with relief as he settled in the passenger seat of Jen's car. As soon as they were out of the drive, he switched his eyes on again. "I'd like to go back to London a different route, Jen, if you don't mind a little diversion."

"Not at all. We've plenty of time and it's a lovely day. Where would you like to go?"

"If we turn left at the next junction and keep on that road for four or five miles, we should arrive in a place called Woolpit."

"That's a strange-sounding place. Sounds a little creepy."

Alex laughed. "Creepy is a good description. I've been fascinated by the place since I was a boy. Apparently, its name is nothing to do with wool. I understand that it used to be called Wolfpit, which derives from the pits that villagers used to dig to trap the roaming wolves."

"Really?" Jen sounded as though she did not quite believe him. "How long ago was this?"

"Oh, well over a thousand years ago. But, that is only part of the story. During the reign of King Stephen, in the early eleven hundreds, a boy and his sister suddenly appeared in the village."

"What's so strange about that?" Jen was clearly puzzled, yet, at the same time, intrigued by this curious tale.

"Their skin was bright green, their clothes unusual and they spoke in a strange language."

"You must be kidding?" Jen wondered if Alex was telling her a tall story.

Alex's expression was serious. "It is well documented, so I feel certain that it was true. The children had appeared out of a cave near one of the many ditches and the story goes that they lived in an underground colony in a place called Saint Martin, but had lost their way and, on coming out of the cave, were stunned by the brilliant sunshine. A group of reapers found them unconscious and carried them to the village."

Jen found the strange tale incredible and asked, "What became of them?"

"Both children were baptized, but, unfortunately, the boy died after a short while because he would not change his life-style and only ate green beans, yet his sister adapted, learned English and ate many other foods. Apparently, her skin colour became more normal as she grew into a young, somewhat loose, woman. She called herself Agnes Barre, married a nobleman and had children."

"That is one hell of a weird story. So why do you want to go there, now?"

"I suppose it's just my curiosity. Woolpit is only a small village and I wonder what it looks like from the sky!"

Jen now understood. Alex had time to think about the possibilities of seeing the world in a different light using his new-found super-vision. Within a few minutes, they were in the centre of the village and managed to find somewhere to park their car, next to an ancient pub. It was a beautiful, sunny August day and the couple took a seat in the paved garden area at the rear of the fourteenth century Swan Inn.

A waitress took their order and, within a few minutes, Jen was sipping a soft drink while Alex enjoyed a glass of real ale.

Alex looked thoughtful. "It's strange to think that, after nearly nine hundred years, there could be many descendants of the green girl in the area."

Jen thought for a few seconds and, smiling, said, "I think the waitress may have looked a little green, but perhaps that was with envy at seeing me with you."

Both laughed and agreed that it was a fascinating story.

Casually, Alex touched the contacts on his watch and, immediately, his field of view had been replaced with a satellite image of the whole area.

He could see the roof and garden of the Swan Inn and the impressive St. Mary's church, nearby, with the narrow, winding roads surrounding them.

He concentrated on the garden of the Swan Inn and, as the image zoomed in, he could even make out the tiny figures of himself and Jen. Alex was tempted to wave his arm, but did not want to look like an absolute idiot. Although he had never been to New York, he understood that, in Times Square, anybody could appear on a huge advertising screen, if they positioned themselves in the right place, within the square. He now understood the reason why so many people did the craziest things just to appear on the screen, for all to see.

He moved his gaze around the village, but still could not explain, even to himself, what he was hoping to see. Buildings, houses, woodlands and roads, but, as far as he was aware, nothing out of the ordinary.

Then he spotted it. At first, it just looked like a mark on one of the roofs in the village, but as he concentrated on this area, the different color of this one roof became more apparent. He remembered what Jen had said about his vision through the spy satellites. Infra-red detectors could identify areas of different temperatures, usually to locate human activity. What he was seeing now was one building where the roof temperature was, apparently, significantly higher than that of the surrounding buildings.

Jen had noticed Alex's change of concentration and asked, "What is it, Alex?"

"I.. I don't know." He dropped his voice to avoid being overheard. "I think there is a building on fire."

"Are you sure?"

"I suppose there could be an innocent explanation, but I can't think of one. All I know is that this one roof has a difference of some sort. It can only be that it is much hotter than other surrounding roofs."

Jen took command of the situation. "Drink up and we'll check it out."

The two drained their glasses and left the Swan Inn. They walked arm in arm, through the village towards the building in Alex's vision. As they approached it, Alex switched from overhead vision to look at the buildings from a normal perspective.

As he did so, a young, dark-haired man was just entering one of the houses in this quite elderly block of terraced houses. It was at the end of this group of buildings where Alex had noticed the heat source and, from this viewpoint, everything seemed quite normal. Alex had expected to find flames licking at the windows, but heavy blinds prevented any chance of seeing inside the building. It was not just one house that was affected. The same pattern of a strong heat source and blinds at all windows applied to the last four houses in the block.

"Perhaps the heat source hasn't reached full combustion point, yet", said Jen, thoughtfully.

A sudden inspiration hit Alex. "Don't make it too obvious that we are looking at the houses, Jen. I think it could be a Cannabis farm. The temperature has to be much higher than normal to cultivate the plants."

"You could be right – it makes sense. What we do not want is to get caught up in an investigation, so I'll phone my contact here in the U.K. and get him to alert the local authorities." She pulled out her mobile, keyed in the number an spoke quietly, passing on the address of the properties. Satisfied that they could do nothing more, she said, "Police will be here, shortly. I think it's time we left Woolpit." Alex agreed and they walked back to their car.

Inside the house, a young, nervous-looking man watched the couple on a CCTV monitor. He knew they had been looking at the houses with some interest and pressed a few keys on his mobile. He wasted no time on introductions. "Moving out, immediately. Parties interested in properties."

The person on the other end of the line understood perfectly the meaning of the brief, coded message and gave a simple acknowledgement.

The young Italian man swiftly put the phone in his pocket. He was sweating profusely, partly through the intrusion by these strangers, but also because of the demands of hundreds of plants requiring a great deal of heat and moisture. Plaster was bulging on the walls and ceilings and many, rough holes had been made through the entire structure. The cost of setting up this Skunk Cannabis farm had been over thirty thousand pounds, but, since the output could generate forty times this, every year, it was a very effective investment. The owner of the houses had no idea of what his properties were being used for, but was satisfied that, at least, he was being paid a regular rent. This would, now, come to a swift end.

There was no way that any of the equipment could be removed in the time available, but the man moved quickly around the plants within these four adjacent houses, cutting off the heads of some of the female flowers and dropping them into a leather pouch. He threw this, together with some of the monitoring equipment into a large holdall and hurried through to the back of the houses.

Taking one last look at this once-profitable place, he realized what a mess the building now looked with sodden plaster on walls and ceilings, with access between the houses made through rough openings in the party walls.

Walking swiftly, he escaped along the narrow passages, trying to avoid being observed and made his way to a small area of waste land.

Still nervously looking around, he climbed into an ancient van and drove away, knowing that this cannabis farm would no longer be profitable for his organization.

Alex and Jen said nothing as they drove back through Cambridge towards London, aware that, in just a few more hours, they would have to go their separate ways. Both had enjoyed their time together over the last few weeks and, although Jen did not want a relationship, they had become good friends. Or, was it more than that? Alex mused, that, perhaps, he was getting more like his mother, just wanting him to settle down and have a family. Louise would have loved to become a grandmother, but Alex pulled himself together. He had a job to do and the time was approaching when he had to repay the British and American Governments for the gift of sight.

The couple, both subdued by their imminent separation, said little as they walked to his room at Moorfields. Once there, Alex switched his sight on again. He looked at Jen and felt certain that there was a hint of tears in her eyes.

"I'm going to miss you, Jen."

"I know. I feel the same about you." She paused, searching desperately, for the right words, hoping this separation would not be too painful for either of them. "I've no choice. I have to go back to the States, now that my work here is done."

Alex smiled with a look of resigned understanding. "I know. I do understand. If you ever feel like a holiday, I could show you around the sights of Britain."

"I might just do that. I would really love to visit all the tourist places except, perhaps, that creepy place, Woolpit, one day. Take care and keep in touch, Alex."

He laughed at her reference to the strange, historical village. The two hugged and, then, Jen was gone. Once again, Alex was on his own, with an uncomfortable, empty feeling in his heart.

For the rest of the day, he lazed in his room and his only visitor was the nurse who brought his evening meal. Professor Goldman was absent, as he was taking his first weekend off in a long time, now that his research work was complete. Even he would miss the endless days of concentrated effort and would feel strange and empty, now that he had achieved his goal of creating artificial sight for a blinded soldier.

Alex noticed a small folder on his bedside cabinet and, now that he had the vision to read again, he scanned through the information. It contained a brief history of Moorfields Eye Hospital. Apparently, it was the first specialist Eye Hospital in the world and was opened as The "London Dispensary for diseases of the eye" and ear in eighteen hundred and five by John Cunningham Saunders. Initially, it had been set up as a charitable institution, opened to assist soldiers returning from the Napoleonic Wars in Egypt. Many had contracted trachoma, a blinding, tropical form of Conjunctivitis.

The hospital had moved to its present site on City road in eighteen ninety-nine. It retained its charity status until nationalization in nineteen forty-eight, but had to be rebuilt after receiving a direct bomb hit during the Second World War

It was quite amazing how the hospital had changed from its historic background into a high-tech centre of excellence, known throughout the world.

After this brief period of education, Alex felt restless and, for that evening, he just lay on his bed, listening to Radio 2. "Listening" was not really the right word as the music and the presenter's voice just drifted through his brain without registering anything.

What had puzzled him was why he had chosen to go to Woolpit. It was as if something had drawn him there. Perhaps the gift of "special sight" had something extra? Did he have a sixth sense and, if so, why?

He did watch the BBC news that night and heard the newsreader talk about the discovery of a cannabis farm in a quaint Suffolk village. Nobody had been arrested as the houses had been found to be deserted. It had not been a major news item, but Alex smiled to himself, knowing that he and his new-found special sight had been responsible for its discovery and loss of income for the illegal growers.

CHAPTER TEN :

15th. AUGUST, 2011

By nine the next morning, Alex had packed his bags, ready to leave the hospital after a total of four weeks in this famous institution. When his visitor arrived at ten thirty, Alex said his farewells to the diligent staff and gave particular thanks to Professor Goldman, who had made such a fantastic difference to his life.

The un-named man introduced himself as Alex's driver and escorted him out of the hospital to the car park. Alex had been told to remain 'blind' for this journey to the Ministry of Defence offices. Within forty minutes, he was walking along the quiet corridors of a large, anonymous building. Eventually, they reached the room where Alex felt certain that he was to meet the Brigadier General.

He was not mistaken. The greeting was executed with the same regimented stiffness and precision as at their earlier meeting. Once the escort had left the room, Alex switched on his eyes and looked around the richly-furnished office. A seat was offered to the young man and he was introduced to the other three individuals around the table.

Adrian King, Paul Adams and Kristin Asher were polite and fairly quiet in comparison with their more senior colleague.

"Every person in this room is familiar with your situation. That is that you lost your sight in battle and have had prosthetic replacements which have capabilities far superior to that of the human eye." Alex remembered how he was told that only a few, select individuals would know his secret. Presumably, these were the few apart from Jen, the Professor and some senior officials within the American Defence department. "I would be grateful if you could demonstrate the capabilities to my colleagues."

"How? What can I do to convince everybody in this room?" As he was talking, Alex looked closely at everyone around the table.

"Don't worry. We are all familiar with the current relatively-low resolution of implants within the eye. If you can describe us, this will give an indication of the quality and extent of your vision."

Alex said nothing as he considered. "Okay." He looked first at the Brigadier General and was surprised how close his impression was to reality. "You are quite tall. Probably six feet three, have slightly-greying ginger hair; a neat moustache and ..."

Alex zoomed in to check the colour of his eyes. "And green eyes. Your tie is Maroon with grey patterns." This description was even more detailed and accurate than the group had expected.

What Alex did not mention to these individuals was the watch worn by the Brigadier General. His superior vision had identified a Cartier and one of the most expensive fashion watches available. "He must be on a damn good salary to afford one of those", Alex thought, somewhat surprised.

He continued, "Adrian – You have short, black hair, silver-framed spectacles, a dark, blue suit, white shirt and a grey tie. Paul, you also have black hair, a bit longer than Adrian's. Your suit is mid-grey, white shirt and a light-blue tie."

He paused to look at the only female in the room, knowing that he had to be particularly careful in his description of her. "Kristin. You have shoulder-length blonde hair, bright blue eyes and you are wearing a pale-green blouse and light-grey skirt. You also have a fine, gold chain around your neck. A tear-drop pendant hangs from this chain."

All four, particularly Kristin, were smiling and noticeably impressed. Alex could also have guessed their ages, but the possibility of getting them wrong stopped him from giving this extra information. Marshall was probably in his mid-forties, while the other three appeared to be in their early to mid-thirties.

"Excellent! Your descriptions are precise and accurate. Now, as you know, we have a place where you can live in London. After this meeting, you will be driven there and tomorrow you will begin training with a support dog."

"I thought it was going to be a guide dog?"

"To the public, it will appear as a guide dog, but, in reality, it is a Police dog with some extra training. In this way, the dog will act not just as your eyes, but more for your personal protection."

Alex was impressed. "I hope I can get on with the dog or else it may attack me, instead."

The military man smiled. "I'm certain that it will be a successful partnership." Alex noticed that the Brigadier

General had a habit of playing with the end of his moustache. Alex was still puzzled by his feelings about this man as there was nothing to suggest a threat, but, still, the uneasy feeling would not escape him.

The older man turned to his colleagues and continued, "Now, I would like you to describe your job functions to Alex. You first, Adrian."

The young man cleared his throat. "I am coordinator for Terrorist and serious crime Investigations Intelligence Unit. My role is to direct you to specific objectives and locations where you will assist in observing known suspects. Whatever you do, you do not speak to any local Police officers about your observations. You will contact only me for directives and feedback. I report back to the Brigadier General."

"Quite impressive", thought Alex. "He seems fairly young for such a responsible position". "Okay, understood", Alex replied.

There was something about Adrian's voice which sounded vaguely familiar. After a moment's thought, he realized that Adrian sounded similar to the London-born presenter and actor, Stephen Fry. Alex had seen this well known personality on television many times and his articulate voice had been heard by the millions of fans who watched Qi on BBC television. Alex wondered if Adrian had a similar sense of humour to the ebullient Fry, or did the similarity end with the voice?

It was, now, Paul's turn. "My role is in micro-electronic aids for operatives. I suppose you could think of me as 'Q' in the James Bond films, but not as glamorous a role. In addition, I am responsible for maintaining the electronics in your communications watch."

Alex had to admit that he did not look like a 'Q'. "Not really a geeky guy", he thought. "Sounds interesting."

He did wonder just what role Kristin would play

She cleared her throat. "My role is as coordinator between British and American Intelligence. You probably won't hear much from me as Adrian will provide me with the feedback for the States. Without American assistance, this project would never have got off the ground. Understandably, they have insisted on full and complete information on your progress and assignments."

"That's fair, considering that they are paying towards the cost. Okay." Alex had a sudden thought. "Adrian, what happens if I do get stopped by the police? Is there anything I can say or show to make certain they don't interfere with my assignment?"

"After our meeting, Paul will take you to an office in this building, where your official I.D. will be created. It should only be shown to the emergency services as a last resort."

"Okay, that's understood. Also, how do I contact any of you, if I need to?"

Paul answered. "You will be given a mobile phone, shortly. Although it looks like any other smart phone, it has dedicated and encrypted channels for communication with all of us."

Their discussion ended, Paul took Alex to an operations room. There was an air of quiet efficiency in the large, organized room. Several people sat at desks, all typing and concentrating on their individual screens.

Paul approached a middle-aged, balding man at one of these workstations. "Anthony. Do you have Captain McCloud's i.d. ready?"

The man smiled and slid a drawer open. He retrieved a small, neat wallet and handed it to the senior officer. "It was completed just a few minutes ago."

Paul opened the wallet and studied the i.d. "Thanks. That's fine. How about the mobile?"

Before Paul had finished his question, Anthony had produced what looked like a smart i-phone from the same drawer.

"Excellent. I'll show you how to contact us, Alex." Paul indicated the keystrokes to call the different disciplines at the headquarters and then handed the phone and i.d. to Alex. The two of them left the office, Paul directing him back to where Adrian was patiently waiting.

"All done?"

"Yes. Captain McCloud, now, has his new I.D. and mobile phone." Alex guessed that Adrian was the senior of these two men. "Okay, Paul, I'll take over, now."

He escorted Alex back to a waiting car. He shook his hand and said, "This man will take you to your new accommodation and, tomorrow, you will be picked up and taken for training with your support dog."

"How long before my first assignment?"

Adrian considered his question. "That depends on how you get on with your dog. Hopefully, within a few weeks."

Alex thanked him and slid into the passenger seat of the black Ford Focus. The driver said nothing as he engaged the gears and accelerated into the traffic. He obviously knew London well as he made many turns down the less busy roads, avoiding the traffic snarl-ups so familiar in the capital city. Eventually, he pulled up in front of a group of Georgian terraced houses. "You have an apartment on the ground floor at number twenty-one. I will show you around."

The young man climbed out and opened the door for Alex who had already switched his sight off. He took the arm of the driver, who was also carrying Alex's suitcase. There were five steps up from the pavement level to the front door which was shared by all the apartments. The man showed Alex a small keypad at the side of the door.

"The combination number for entry is nine four six two"

Alex had a look at the keypad. He could feel a slightly raised marker on one of the keys. "Is it the same as a telephone keypad with one at the top-left?"

"Absolutely right. See if you can find the correct sequence."

Alex pressed the keypad and, after hitting an enter button, the lock on the door was released. He pushed it open and stepped into the large hallway, followed by his driver, who closed the main door.

"Your entrance is the first door on the left, hopefully making it easier for you to find."

Alex soon found the doorway to his apartment. He felt for a keyhole, but there was none. "How do I get in?"

The driver explained. "There is a small, flat plate just under the handle. When you place your i.d. against it, it should open."

Alex was already impressed by the security and took his i.d. out of his pocket and used it, as instructed. The electronic lock clicked smartly and he could push the door open. He stood back, allowing the driver to enter first.

"We are now in a hallway, with three doors off. The one in front of you is to the living room, one further along to a bathroom and the one at the end is the bedroom."

He pushed the door open and the two men walked into a large, living room. "It's a living and dining room and there is just one more door to the kitchen. Would you like me to show you the rooms in more detail?"

Alex was desperate to switch his eyes on, but did not know if the driver was aware of his bionic eyes, so said, "It's okay. I'll manage. Thanks for your help... I don't even know your name."

"Terry." He said this quietly and with an obvious reluctance, as though he preferred to remain anonymous.

"Okay, Terry. What time will you pick me up, tomorrow?"

"Nine o'clock. Please be ready." The driver seemed to be very precise and had a noticeable lack of humour in his voice. He placed Alex's suitcase against the wall.

As soon as Terry had left, Alex touched the contacts on his watch and was then able to see his new apartment in full detail. It was a good-sized room, about nine metres by five. A comfortable room with clean, un-cluttered lines already furnished with a sofa, two chairs, a dining table and storage cupboards. He was impressed to see that a forty-two inch slim Samsung television was mounted on one wall.

He wandered through to the kitchen, to find it equally modern and comfortable. The kitchen units seemed to be very recent and there was everything he could possibly need, including washing machine, tumble dryer, kettle and even a Tassimo coffee-maker.

Alex wondered who had lived here before him and how long ago. Eager to see the bedroom, he went back into the hall and down the bright corridor to the end door.

This was equally impressive with a double bed, complete with good-quality bedding. He walked up to the large, built-in wardrobe and pulled the door open, half-expecting to find a complete rail of clothes, but, not surprisingly, there was nothing except some spare hangers. Still, it was immaculately clean, leaving him no cause for complaint.

The last room to inspect was the bathroom. It was not big, but had everything he could need, except a bath, but this was something he could easily live without.

A marble shelf with a large, illuminated mirror over it ran along the whole of one wall. A smooth, built-in washbasin was in this shelf, while a toilet was on the opposite wall at the far end.

In the remaining corner, behind the door was a shower, but this was different from anything he had ever seen before.

It was a corner shower cubicle, with sliding doors and a touch-control panel on the inside. An instruction manual soon revealed that the shower could be controlled either from within the cubicle or from a small, hand-held remote control unit. Alex did not wish to read the comprehensive instructions at this time, but, by glancing through, he discovered that it had a monsoon shower, hand-held shower, high-pressure side body jets and a built-in radio.

The final sophistication was the facility to use the shower as a steam-room, even having a built-in seat to relax upon. This really impressed Alex and he determined to make good use of all the features.

Now that all areas of the apartment had been checked, Alex returned to the kitchen, opened the fridge and looked to see if there was anything to eat. To his surprise, there was milk, margarine, some fresh fruit and vegetables and even frozen pizza and several ready-to-cook meals in the freezer.

"Somebody has taken a lot of trouble to make me feel comfortable", he thought.

In a cupboard near to the fridge, he found a set of four cups, saucers, mugs, plates and dishes, containers of sugar, tea and coffee.

A few minutes later, Alex was relaxing in one of the comfortable chairs, drinking a mug of hot chocolate, feeling quite pleased that he now had a decent place to live and a pretty good income from the British and American Governments.

For the rest of the day, he did very little, unpacking his few possessions and watching television. He knew the hard work would start the following day.

A sudden thought crossed Alex's mind. He pressed the numbers on his recently-issued i-phone and was soon connected to the automated bank information line. It had been several months since he had last used this facility, but he managed to remember his password sequence and pin number. His balance was thirty-nine thousand, two hundred and sixty-three pounds and fifteen pence. It was quite a bit more than he had expected, but knew that his salary would have been paid in while he was in Afghanistan and the Queen Elizabeth hospital.

It was when he checked the individual credits that he realized he had been paid over seven thousand pounds in the last few weeks. This meant that he was already on the payroll in his new employment with the Defence department. With over seven thousand pounds going into his account every month, he was certainly not going to be short of funds.

Even with all his comfort, Alex had difficulty sleeping that night. Everything seemed so strange and unreal, increasing his anxiety level. Why did everything seem so alien? Would he have to live the rest of his life lonely and alone? Was there really any future for him? To his annoyance, his headaches still persisted and the usual pain killers made absolutely no impression.

When he did, eventually fall asleep, he found himself in a weird, troubling dream. His dead friend, Jack, kept reminding him of their thirteen-year friendship. In the dream, both boys were aged about fourteen and, fuelled by their teenage hormones were seeking female friendship. Karen Simpson had become quite close to Alex, but, to his annoyance, Jack managed to entice her away. She was the one girl Alex had ever fancied while at school, and for a few months he distanced himself from Jack for this selfish action. It was not as though there were no other girls around, but Alex felt that Jack had deliberately stolen her from him to cause annoyance and it had worked.

This was the one time their friendship was seriously tested, but, after Karen started seeing another boy, Alex and Jack became good friends yet again. Alex awoke from his sleep, the dream still fresh in his mind. He had actually forgotten this time eleven years earlier and realized that he and Jack had not always been the best of friends, but, as far as he could remember, this was the only real rift between them. Eventually, he fell back into a more relaxed sleep, this time without troubling dreams.

He was already awake when his alarm sounded at six-thirty, the following morning. After a shave, he enjoyed the super-sophisticated shower and, by eight-thirty was ready for what promised to be an unusual day.

As expected, Terry appeared exactly at nine. Alex allowed himself to be guided to the car after making certain that the apartment was secure.

CHAPTER ELEVEN :
16ᵗʰ. AUGUST, 2011

Terry said very little during the forty-minute journey and seemed unresponsive to Alex's pleasantries. He did wonder if this was really Terry's character or perhaps, in his line of work, was he supposed to be deferential and remote? The journey was only punctuated by the sound of the windscreen wipers, struggling against a particularly heavy downpour. Even with this annoyance and the heavy traffic, Terry never said a word or even uttered a curse.

Again, it was a relief when they arrived at the training centre. Terry escorted Alex to the reception area and said that he would return at for-thirty.

The receptionist led Alex to an office where he was introduced to Kate, A pleasant sounding woman, who Alex guessed, from her voice, was in her late thirties. He was gradually becoming used to assessing individuals by their style of greeting and the subtle nuances apparent in their voices. What did surprise him was the feel of her hand. For a woman, it was quite large, with thick, rough fingers. A vision of a farmer's wife came into his mind.

"Please take a seat, Captain McCloud." He did as instructed, not knowing just what to expect of this very new situation. "I felt it may be helpful to explain just how we are hoping to help you, following your loss of sight."

"Right," thought Alex. "She doesn't know the true situation." "That would be helpful", he replied.

"The centre has been provided with a dog which has, previously, been trained in a military environment. Our job has been to enhance this training to provide the necessary abilities to work as a guide dog."

"What type of dog is it?"

"Ah, Elsa is a beautiful German Shepherd. It's been a delight to work with her over the past few weeks. She's been very well trained already and is a highly intelligent dog." Alex could tell from the tone of her voice that she had enjoyed training his future guide dog and held some attraction for Elsa.

"Over the next few days, we need to assist you to learn how to control and react to Elsa's movements."

"How long will it take for this training?"

"It is too early to know until we can assess how well the two of you work together. Would you like to meet her?"

"Yes, sure." Alex felt a little nervous at this prospect, but, in a way, he wanted to get it over with.

"Good! I'll show you the way." She took his arm and led him out of the main building and into the kennels. The smell was unmistakable. Not dirty, more the characteristic odour of several dogs living in close proximity. Alex could hear the scrabbling sound of claws on concrete as Kate approached, each dog hoping to be the one she was seeking.

"Elsa! Come here!" Alex could hear the panting of one dog as it rushed towards the familiar figure of Kate. She unfastened the door and quickly slipped a lead over the head of the energetic animal. "Down, Elsa!" Her voice was firm and commanding. Turning to Alex, she said, "Elsa is a really lovely dog. She's been a pleasure to train. Give me your hand, Captain McCloud."

"Please call me Alex. I'm a civilian, now", he lied. As he, nervously, held out his hand, Kate placed it on the head of what seemed to be a very big animal. Immediately, the dog turned her head upwards and started licking the palm of his hand, as though she had known him for ever. Alex stroked Elsa's head gently, the dog enjoying the attention. Hot breath could be felt as Elsa again lifted her head, still obviously receptive to every stroke.

"Take hold of her lead in your left hand and I will guide you to the open training area." He did as instructed and, trusting his two guides, one on each side, he walked gingerly out of the kennels, Elsa pulling eagerly.

Kate led them to a point in the area, where she said, "Okay, take the lead off Elsa and instruct her to sit. You must say it firmly and stress the 'S' sound of the word."

He did as instructed and held the lead loosely in his hand. "Sit, Elsa!"

Kate spoke quietly. "You need to say it with more conviction, Alex. She has got to really understand that you are now her master. Be very firm, yet do not shout."

He tried again, extending the 'S' sound. Although he could not tell, Kate said, "She is sitting. Now praise her – Say, 'Good girl, Elsa' and stroke her head."

Again, he followed her instructions. He was surprised that, even after only a few minutes, he felt a strangely-reassuring attachment to this animal.

"Okay, Alex. Now I want you to tell her to 'stay'. Again, be firm and repeat the command several times."

"Okay. Stay, Elsa. Stay!"

Kate watched with satisfaction. "Now, keep repeating the command while moving further away from her. Try to be casual and don't move too quickly." Kate had already moved a few feet away. "Follow my voice and, remember, keep repeating the command, but also praise her at the same time."

Alex followed her instructions precisely and felt that, already, he had the start of a trusting relationship with this dog.

"Good girl, Elsa! Stay!"

"This should be the easy part. When you are ready, just say 'come'. Then give her lots of praise." Alex could detect a smile in Kate's voice.

"Come, Elsa!" The dog instantly bounded towards him, almost knocking him over. It was obvious to anybody that Elsa and Alex were going to get on fine. Elsa's tail was wagging vigourously and she was licking his hands as though she had known him for years.

"Excellent! Now we should put her on the lead again and we will return to my office." Elsa walked at Alex's left side as they returned to the small office. Kate showed Alex the position of the chair. "When you are seated, instruct her to lie down."

By now, Elsa was getting used to Alex's vocal commands and, immediately, lay down near his feet. She was a fairly big dog and occupied quite a large part of the floor.

After this, Kate went through all the procedures they would be covering over the next few days. For the rest of the day, he received further instruction on how to handle his new "eyes". The hardest part was shortly after four o'clock, when Elsa had to return to the kennels. It was obvious to Alex that the dog was sad at this end to several hours of working with her new master. Alex stroked her head soothingly as he sensed the change in Elsa's demeanor.

When Terry arrived prompt at four thirty, Alex was equally saddened by their separation and said little throughout the journey.

Back at his flat, Alex's feelings of emptiness and loneliness deepened. In an effort to pull himself out of this morose mood, he picked one of the ready made meals from the freezer and followed the instructions to heat it up in the microwave. "Got to build up my strength and stamina, but I just hope that it will all be worth the effort."

Again, the silence annoyed him intensely. He turned on the radio, hoping for company and found Simon Mayo's evening programme on Radio Two. It did help to ease him out of his dark mood. He relaxed, listening to the business news with Rebecca Pike, followed shortly by the listeners' humourous confessions. The microwave pinged, bringing him back to reality.

His dinner was a tasty, chicken and rice meal, which he followed with fresh fruit. At least his stomach was satisfied, even though his soul was not.

At about seven, he picked up his mobile and phoned home. He was pleased when his sister, Lucy answered. "Hi, Sis! Did you get your results?"

She sounded excited. "Yes. I've got three A's. I can go to Cambridge!"

"Fantastic! I'm so pleased for you, Lucy. I'm certain you'll make a fine doctor."

"There is a lot of work before I get that far, but I'm so happy just to get my grades."

Alex knew that his sister had worked hard and was thrilled by her success. " I have some news for you. I have a new girl-friend, Sis."

For a few seconds there was a stunned silence. "Really? Who is she?"

He could hear the surprise in her voice and had difficulty in stopping himself from laughing. "Yes. Her name is Elsa and she is not some Scandinavian beauty, but an eighteen month old German shepherd dog!"

"Oh, Alex!" She began giggling and told her mother what her brother had said. "Hold on, I'll put Mum on to speak to you."

For the next fifteen minutes Alex had to tell Louise the events of that day in every minute detail. His mother had never been keen on dogs, preferring, instead, pets of the feline variety. Still, she was fascinated by Alex's description of his day.

"You must keep me informed on your training, Alex. I think you are so brave to get on with your life, after all that has happened." She sounded so proud, making Alex feel incredibly guilty about concealing the truth from his family.

Over the next few days, he and Elsa worked closely together, both being instructed by the ever-capable Kate, who appeared quite impressed by the rapid progress for dog and master alike. It was up to the guide dog trainer to decide just when Elsa should be allowed to stay full time at Alex's place and, confident in their abilities, she told Terry, as he dropped Alex off, that day, that she would drive him and Elsa to his apartment, later in the afternoon.

When they arrived at his place, it came as a surprise to Alex that Kate knew her way around the apartment. She explained that she had been called to assess the premises to determine if they were suitable for a guide dog, even before Alex had moved in. In addition, she had organized the construction of a drained concrete "run", where the dog could urinate and defecate. Alex was thankful that all he had to do was hose the area down daily to flush away all the waste material.

Kate had brought other items with her. A feeding bowl, water bowl, a large bag of dog food, grooming brush, Elsa's harness with handle and a dog bed were all provided, presumably paid for by the British Government. It was certainly well organized, but would he be worth the expense and effort?

"Okay, Alex. I think I'm done here. Is there anything you need to know before I leave you?"

"Not that I can think of, just now."

"Well, if there is anything, just give me a call. When you need more dog food, we can get it for you and, if there are any problems with Elsa's health, the Vet I recommended will assist you."

"Great! Thanks for all your hard work, Kate." Elsa was at his side as he walked to the main door to his apartment. Alex had wondered if Elsa would want to return to the centre with Kate, but was relieved that she stayed close by his side, seemingly accepting Alex as her new master.

As soon as Kate had left the building, Alex again "switched" on his eyes. "Now, Elsa, I want you to keep this little secret between us. Okay?" He looked at his new partner and was impressed by Elsa's appearance. The dog's coat was predominantly black with contrasting shades of brown, some almost golden in colour and her long face was mainly brown. As he stared at her, she, similarly, looked up into his face, her black eyes seeming to acknowledge his secret. There was an obvious intelligence in this new partner. To his surprise, as the dog was sitting, it lifted its right paw, as if expecting Alex to take hold of the outstretched paw. As he grasped it, he knew that there was a deep understanding between them. The two looked at each other for, what seemed like hours, yet, in fact, was probably only about fifteen seconds. It was as though the dog was reading her master's mind, absorbing all the facts with a new-found knowledge.

Kate had made it quite clear to Alex that keeping regular feeding times was important and he intended following her instructions precisely. At six, he poured the dog food into her bowl, added water and placed it on the kitchen floor. As soon as he let go of the bowl, Elsa greedily attacked the food. Alex was amazed how quickly the dog finished her meal, lapping up the food and water and then licking around the bowl to devour every last scrap.

He followed this by taking her out to the run on the lead and was pleased that the dog was happy to relieve itself onto the drained area.

That evening seemed very strange to Alex. He was relaxed, watching television, while Elsa lay on the floor, near to his feet. Somehow, it felt like they had been together for a long time, not just a matter of days.

Alex had read the background to German shepherd dogs, purely out of his own interest.

As its name implies, the dog was initially bred to help sheperds in the German valleys. They were strong animals with an intelligence which only needed visual signals to follow the shepherd's commands. The breed gained an unfortunate reputation during the Second World War, when the Nazis used this powerful breed to attack and keep control of prisoners in concentration camps. They were given an alternative name of "Alsatian", in the nineteen seventies to distance the connection to their Nazi training, but, several years later, the name of "German Shepherd" became more accepted, again. They, together with Labrador Retrievers, were favoured by the Guide Dogs Association as they had the perfect temperament and intelligence to guide and care for their blind owners.

CHAPTER TWELVE :
SEPTEMBER, 2011

The next big hurdle for Alex was to venture outside his apartment with Elsa, in harness, guiding him through the streets of London. Fortunately, Kate would be accompanying them until she was satisfied that Elsa was proficient enough to leave them on their own. The main problem was that Alex knew little of London streets and, even more important, the area in which he now lived. Fortunately, Paul had anticipated this problem and had installed satellite navigation software with speech output on his mobile phone. A particularly useful feature was that as he moved from one location to another, the street name would be announced.

Alex threw himself into the task as though it was a military exercise and, very soon, he had a mental image of quite a large area of London in his mind. Elsa was the perfect partner, negotiating all the obstacles which filled the pavements of the capital city, preventing him from falling down open manholes and colliding with hazardous road works.

Alex had also become accustomed to feeling the dog's movements through the handle on the harness and, gradually, gained more confidence in the dog's ability to guide him safely.

Within a few days with Kate following and observing them from a distance, she was confident enough to leave them to manage on their own.

Alex still felt nervous about trusting his safety to a dog, irrespective of how intelligent it may be. He did realize that he could leave his eyes switched on, but how soon would it be before a member of the public realized that he could see better than anybody else? It would be more convincing to onlookers if he had the occasional stumble or collision.

He had discovered that, within ten minutes walk from his apartment, there was a supermarket store where he could purchase his weekly shopping. Alex had asked the store manager if one of the assistants could help him find the items he required. "No problem, Sir. Sandra will help you to find just what you need. She has worked here for over eight years and will be happy to assist."

Sandra, a petite, talkative woman in her mid thirties, escorted him up and down the aisles pushing a small trolley, while describing what each aisle contained. She always seemed to have plenty to talk about and he found her ramblings, spoken in a high, Liverpool accent, quite interesting.

Very soon, Alex had a complete mental image of the store, making the experience quite straight-forward. At the check-out, Sandra would help to pack his shopping into a back-pack, allowing him to carry his shopping while leaving his hands free. Soon, this was a regular routine and one which Alex quite enjoyed as it made him feel "normal" again.

He was a man who did not like having to rely on others to carry out the simplest of tasks. His fridge and freezer were now packed with enough food to last for some considerable time.

High-energy foods were also now on his shopping list as he was determined to build up his body mass to what it had been before his injury. A lifting frame, weights and a running machine were delivered to his apartment and he soon had a daily routine of exercises. On top of these, he would have two daily sessions of fifty press-ups. He could feel the difference as his muscles became stronger, tighter and he knew that, if he had to use physical force, he could easily meet the challenge.

"Hmm, not bad", he thought as he looked at his naked body in the full-length mirror in his bedroom. "Not quite Arnold Schwarzenegger, but it will do for me."

The bond between Alex and Elsa soon became obvious and he found the dog good company. In the evening, Alex would relax, watching television, while Elsa lay on the floor at his side. It intrigued him how attentive the dog was, for, as soon as he made even the slightest move, Elsa would stand up immediately, always eager and ready to follow her master.

With his eyes "switched on", Alex could see the intelligence in the dog's face and the cobalt black eyes seemed to be both penetrating and understanding. Did she, somehow, understand why he had to pretend to be blind? Surely, this was impossible and yet, he was convinced that she knew far more than any dog could be expected to know.

Now that Alex's bank balance was quite healthy, he did not mind spending some and, one day, when he was going through his wardrobe, he realized that his choice of clothes was a bit limited. "I could do with a decent suit", he thought. He could have bought several suits "off the peg", but, instead, decided to use some of his newly-found wealth to boost his choice of clothes in real style.

Alex, together with Elsa, made the journey to Savile Row, by taxi. He had selected what he hoped was his best suit, as he did not wish to appear well-below the standard of dress expected by a top-ranking tailor.

"Which company do you want me to drop you off at?" asked the taxi driver.

Alex had searched extensively on the internet, when deciding which of the world-famous tailors to use. He was not surprised when he found that he had to make an appointment, even for an initial measuring. "Cad and The Dandy, please. It's at number thirteen."

"Good choice", said the driver. "I bring a fair number of clients to that tailor. I just wish I had the money to consider spending so much on a suit, myself." In truth, even if he had the money, he would rather have a good holiday for the same price as a suit. The cab driver pulled in at number thirteen, Savile Row and checked his meter.

Alex paid the fare, allowing for a decent tip, which, noticeably, pleased the driver. "It's okay to splash a little cash around", he thought, to himself.

The cab driver, temporarily, left his vehicle and directed Alex to the entrance doorway. Alex pushed the door open and walked upstairs to the first floor. He was surprised that, even in these times of austerity, there were still so many expensive tailors to warrant sharing an address on the famous Savile row.

Elsa's paws clattered noisily on the polished hardwood floor as they entered the premises. There was a dignified, yet not intimidating air to this world-class tailor's. "Can I be of assistance, Sir?"

"I have an appointment. My name is McCloud."

"Ah, yes. Please come this way, Sir. Would you like me to take your hand?"

Alex was pleased that this man knew how best to assist a blind person and relaxed his grip on Elsa's handle, letting it rest on the dog's back.

They walked into a measuring room, where the man referred to his notes. "I understand that you would like us to make a two-piece suit for you. Would you prefer machine-stitched, half-machine and hand, or completely hand-stitched?"

The young man knew that it was an extravagance, but had decided that if he was going to have a suit made especially for him, he might as well go for the best. "Hand-stitched, please. I am looking for a dark-grey suit and would be happy to follow your recommendations on the type of material and style."

The man breathed an inaudible sigh of relief. He preferred it when the client left the choice of material up to him, especially considering the problems in leaving the choice to someone who could not appreciate the many different types of material. "Very good, Sir. Would you please remove your jacket to allow us to take some measurements?"

"Of course. Lie down, Elsa!" Alex was enjoying this class of service. He observed, without it being apparent, as the man and his assistant made and recorded all the measurements. He remembered having a suit made to measure, several years earlier, but this was far more detailed than he had previously experienced.

About three quarters of an hour later, Alex was returning, by taxi, to his apartment. He had ordered a suit, three shirts and two ties, costing him around two thousand, five hundred pounds. It was a great deal of money, but he felt that it would be worth it and, providing he did not change his shape too much, the clothes should last him for many years.

He had paid a holding deposit, which did not seem unreasonable as, once the cloth had been cut for him, it would be useless for anybody else.

Over the next few weeks, he made several visits to number thirteen, Savile Row for fitting and completion of his purchase and, back in the privacy of his apartment, he admired the sheer quality of the product.

Life had now become more comfortable and "normal", but with this came a certain degree of boredom which Alex had never wanted.

However this was not to last for much longer. On one of his trips back from the supermarket, he was walking past Alexandra Park, when he heard a scream. It sounded as if it was quite close and he knew that he could not just ignore it and walk on as though nothing had happened. It sounded like the scream of a young female, but, what sort of person could strike such fear in anyone? He quickly "switched" on his sight and was just in time to see a man attempting to drag a teenage schoolgirl into the park.

Alex knew that he had to intervene and quickly, as there were no other people around. Whatever he did, he must avoid being discovered as a sighted person impersonating a blind man. The girl was still screaming, kicking and struggling, but she was no match for the greater strength of her attacker.

"What's going on?" Alex shouted as he approached the man who was already dragging the girl through the bushes.

Of course, nobody answered him, the man obviously feeling safe with only a blind person nearby. He had muffled the girl's screams with one hand, while the other was pulling her, roughly, into the park. She was putting up a good fight, but was no match for his greater strength and soon was overpowered by him.

Alex quickly unclipped the dog's handle. "Attack!" As soon as he gave this command, Elsa ran, with amazing speed, pouncing on the man, gripping him tightly by the leg with her powerful jaws.

The potential rapist let out a howl of pain and, as he relaxed his grip on the girl, she managed to scramble away to safety.

"Thanks, Mister. That dirty old git needs castrating!" she said in obvious relief.

"You're welcome. Get off home, quickly, before I release him." She took Alex at his word, picked up her schoolbag and rushed away

The dog's grip on the assailant was enough to incapacitate him, but not enough to do any real damage.

She was capable of biting much harder and could easily tear into the flesh of his calves, but Alex thought that this was not necessary and called to his faithful dog. "Elsa! Leave! Come!" Obediently, she loosened her grip and returned to Alex. "Good girl!" To maintain his guise of a blind person, he deliberately looked just to one side of the man who was cursing and rubbing his damaged leg. "Clear off before I call the Police, you fucking pervert!"

It was with some strange curiosity that Alex noticed the skin colour of the man. It looked somewhat unnatural. Of course, he could have just been unwashed, yet the greyish tone of the man's skin, with its slightly-blue tinge, seemed to be something more than just dirt. But, what? Alex had a distinct feeling that there was some significance in the strange skin colour.

As he pulled himself together, the man, similarly, stared at Alex in obvious surprise. Alex took advantage of the situation and, deftly, touched the contacts on his watch to find out if the facial recognition system would come up with anything. The top part of his vision remained frustratingly clear and Alex was about to cancel the function when details suddenly appeared. George Maxwell was only fifty-one, yet looked at least twenty years older. He had a police record mainly for indecent exposure and sexual assaults. "No change, there, then", he thought.

The man muttered some incoherent curse and it was a relief when he hobbled away, still holding his injured leg and, occasionally, looking back at the blind man with his now-passive guide dog.

Alex breathed a sigh of relief. He really did not want this incident to affect his role as a person within the Intelligence service, yet the offence could not be ignored. Maxwell was unlikely to tell anyone of his foiled rape attempt, but Alex felt obliged to inform Adrian, who would let the police know of this potentially serious incident.

As for the girl, she may boast to her friends that she had escaped a sexual attack with the assistance of a guide dog, but, hopefully, she would be more careful in the future, especially when walking home in the dark.

Alex bent down and clipped the handle on Elsa's harness. "Good girl", he repeated. He carried on back to his apartment and thought over the course of the past few weeks.

After Kate had satisfied herself that Alex and Elsa worked together to the standard she expected, Alex had, unknown to Kate, attended further instruction from a Military dog handler, organized by Adrian King.

This training had been much more difficult and intense than that at the Guide Dog training centre. Many different situations had been simulated where dog and handler would be tested under severe conditions. Tom was a disciplined military guy with twenty-three years experience of working with dogs in hostile situations. He taught Alex how to respond and how best to exploit the dog's capabilities.

Alex had never ceased to be amazed by Elsa's intelligence and devotion and thoroughly enjoyed working with her. Now their training had paid off and saved a teenage girl from the clutches of a rapist.

That evening, Alex tried to think about his future. When he had seen the old guy attack the girl, he was sorely tempted to use his own physical strength to teach the rapist a lesson just as he would have done a year earlier. The pretense that he had been asked to follow was difficult to maintain, yet he had not much choice. Eventually, he accepted that it was better to have superior vision while pretending to have none instead of actually being blind as he was before the prosthetic implants.

He decided to have an early night, reading in bed. Even this activity had become complicated. The woman from blind welfare had told Alex that he would be entitled to receive talking books from the Royal National Institute of Blind people, but Alex felt he could not use these resources when he could, in reality, still see. If he had paperbacks lying around his apartment, it would not take long for anyone to realize that he was concealing his true condition.

As a compromise, he had ordered audio books from Amazon. These came in the form of multiple CD's which could be played in any CD player. He had bought a neat player which he kept at the side of his bed. Using earphones, he could settle down into a comfortable position and read for an hour or two before sleep.

Alex had bought a selection of audio books by authors such as Stephen King, James Herbert, Dene Koontz, Lee Child, Tom Clancy, Nelson Demille and Robert Ludlum as these horror and action stories fascinated him.

After reading Lee Child's "The Killing Floor" he had found the character of Jack Reacher, a six-foot five, American ex-military policeman, someone who he could empathise with. Reacher was a loner who, without trying, managed to get himself involved in desperate situations where some mad, immensely powerful criminal killed without compunction.

In addition to eventually dramatically killing the arch-criminal, Reacher always found time to fall for some beautiful young woman who he would leave behind, ready for his next adventure and conquest.

Alex thought of his own situation when Jen had rejected his advances. None of Jack Reacher's women had ever said, "I'm sorry, Jack, but I don't think it's a good idea." Normally, they jumped into bed with him at the earliest possible opportunity.

Alex was now reading the next book in the Jack Reacher series, "Die Trying", which he found equally fascinating and one which was hard to stop reading. Eventually, at midnight, he switched off the player and settled down into an uneasy sleep.

The following morning, he phoned Adrian King. "Morning, Alex. What can I do for you?"

Alex found Adrian quite easy to talk to and explained what had happened the previous day. "It was so damn frustrating! I wanted to tear the man off the girl, yet I knew this would compromise my cover."

"Don't worry, Alex. You did the best thing. From what you have told me, you did what any concerned blind person would have done in the same circumstances and I will inform the Police of the incident. I'm certain that they will be paying a visit to Mr. Maxwell. Sounds like Elsa did a good job."

"She is truly amazing. I couldn't have wished for a better dog."

Adrian agreed. "I was going to phone you, today. There seems to be a lot of activity in London, at the moment, both in terrorism and in-fighting between criminal gangs. We have a job for you which takes advantage of your visual abilities."

This news came as a great relief to Alex. He had lazed about enough and, now, was hungry for action. "Good! I feel as though I need to get into doing something worthwhile."

For the next fifteen minutes, Adrian detailed everything relevant to this new mission. In addition, he sent an encrypted email to Alex's computer. This Notebook had been supplied by Adrian and had JAWS screen-reading software. This meant that Alex could still use the pc as a blind person, assisted by the speech synthesizer which would read any text appearing on the screen and even speak each character as it was typed.

Alex de-crypted Adrian's email and spent the rest of the day analyzing and understanding all the information about his task. It reminded him of his days in the British army, when he had to read and thoroughly digest the surveillance notes before embarking on a military mission. All the different forms of military intelligence were brought together in one, short, concise report, from which it would be his responsibility to determine which course of action should be taken.

CHAPTER THIRTEEN :

It was a cold, crisp yet dry, morning in late October, two thousand and eleven. Georgeo Petroski, a twenty-eight year old Albanian strode purposely along Oxford Street. Alex had been tailing him since the Albanian had left his apartment, ten minutes earlier. Although obviously noticeable with his guide dog, Alex hoped that Petroski was not aware of being tailed. He did wonder if anybody would ever suspect that they could be followed by an obviously blind person. Hopefully, this would not be the case.

Alex had his sight switched to surveillance mode, where the images he scanned were fed back to GCHQ headquarters to check images against a huge computerized bank of known criminals and terrorist images.

Petroski did not seem in any particular hurry. He was heading towards Piccadilly Circus, but, occasionally, would stop to look in the shop windows on this bustling street, obviously checking for anybody tailing him. Elsa normally walked quite fast, but, today, Alex kept coaxing her to move more slowly. Again, she seemed to know the importance of their task and padded along the crowded pavements quite casually.

Petroski stopped at one of the many stalls at street junctions dotted along Oxford Street. This was one of those dodgy stalls selling, quite blatantly, fake fashion products. Alex could not understand why the police still allowed these sellers to carry on plying their illegal trade.

Then, he spotted the two men moving towards the stall. They spoke to Petroski for a couple of minutes and, interestingly, he caught sight of petroski handing a small package over to one of the strangers.

Alex was now nearing the three men and, keeping his posture as though he was looking straight ahead, he glanced sideways at the strangers, aware that everything he saw would be relayed through GCHQ and, from there to MI6.

It was only a side-profile view of the unknown men and Alex knew that a frontal view would be far more valuable. Alex reached the edge of the pavement just near the stall and instructed Elsa to turn left. As they turned, he kept his eyes locked on the group of three men.

He walked slowly, down the narrow side-street, stopping at a narrow alley-way. There he allowed Elsa to urinate into an open grating. To the casual observer, this would be a natural occurrence for a man with a guide dog. After Elsa had finished, Alex again took hold of her handle and walked back along the street. Now, he was facing the three men, who seemed to be in deep conversation. He kept his eyes locked on their faces, zooming in for optimum viewing and, to his relief, text began to appear at the top of his field of vision.

It identified the two as Saaid and Mohammad Lalaki, two known, Pakistani men with long-established links to terrorist cells. Alex was taken aback when he realized that the skin-colour of these three individuals was, again, bluish-grey, just like George Maxwell, the potential rapist. "How strange", he thought.

He wondered which direction the men would move after finishing their discussion. Taking a gamble, Alex turned left, back onto Oxford Street. He was walking quite slowly, their progress being slightly hampered by the crowds of tourists. It came as a relief when the two Pakistani's overtook Alex and continued in the direction of Piccadilly Circus. Alex picked up speed, hoping to follow them close behind. He felt defeated when the two disappeared down the steps of Piccadilly Circus Underground station as he realized it would be impossible to follow them, without being noticed.

To his surprise, a message appeared at the top of his vision, reading "Do not follow any further – other operatives will take over".

Alex almost felt invaded by this anonymous message. It was now obvious that, in addition to the automatic facial recognition scanner, actual humans were also watching every little detail his eyes perceived. He was both in awe of the technology and, yet, at the same time, almost affronted by this invasion of his own, intimate, private world.

Was this the end of this shadowing task? It seemed so brief and, yet, hopefully, it had proved useful to MI6. Feeling somewhat downcast, he, slowly, worked his way back to his apartment. Was this to be his future? A brief assignment with others taking over and finishing the job? He knew that, as long as the mission was successful, there was nothing to worry about. But, why did he feel so empty and disheartened?

As if to add to his misery, the heavens opened and the rain bounced, noisily, off the pavements. By the time they reached their apartment, both Alex and Elsa were soaked and it came as a welcome relief to gain the shelter of their home. As soon as Alex removed Elsa's harness, she shook violently to rid herself of the rain, but, in the process, Alex and the walls were peppered with water. "Oh, thanks for that, Elsa! As if I wasn't wet enough!"

Elsa looked up at him with almost a soulful expression. "Perhaps she didn't like getting soaked, either", thought Alex.

He stripped off, had a warm shower and wrapped himself in a bath robe. Then he decided to dry Elsa, whose rain-sodden coat was beginning to feel a little matted. Ten minutes later, she looked and, presumably, felt much better.

After this, Alex phoned Adrian and talked through his mission, although his eyes had, silently yet effectively, already de-briefed him. Adrian was pleased with the information gleaned from the task and did his best to re-assure Alex of his usefulness.

Even after this, it felt quite an anti-climax for him and, once again, he felt lonely and desolate. He touched his watch and heard Jen's soft, pleasing voice. "The time is five twenty-three p.m." Another touch. "Today is Friday, the twenty-first of October, two thousand and eleven." Brief as it was, the sound of Jen's bright, pleasing voice temporarily lifted his spirit. He was missing the feeling he had experienced when Jen was working with him. He knew that he was attracted towards Jen and wished that she could have been there, with him.

That evening, he phoned home, speaking to his mother and Amelia. Lucy was not there, as she was now, in her first year, studying at Cambridge. Thankfully, this was not too far away, allowing her to spend weekends at home. As usual, his father was at a business meeting and not at home. How his mother had put up with seeing so little of her husband for so many years was beyond him. She had said, on many occasions, that he was not the easiest person to live with, so the absences may have helped to keep the marriage together.

To add to his frustration, Alex could not tell his family of his new-found career with Military Intelligence. Fortunately, they asked few questions about his work, accepting that he was assisting the Government purely as a military advisor and that he would be unable to reveal much of his daily tasks. The whole family was pleased that, even after his great misfortune, he was lucky enough to still have a career in the Army. If they had a greater knowledge of military matters, they would have realized that Alex was not experienced enough to be accepted as an advisor.

A few days later, there was another tailing through the now-familiar streets of London, but, sadly, it still did not satisfy his hunger for action.

After this, when he was reporting in to Adrian, Alex asked, "Adrian, is there any chance I could speak to Paul Marshall?"

There was a slight pause before he answered. "He's not in the country, at the moment, but should be back tomorrow. Is there anything I can help with?"

"It's not urgent. I would just like to find out if I can be utilized in a wider choice of assignments." He did not wish to speak to Adrian in any greater depth, preferring, instead, to raise his issues with probably the only person who could make a difference, the Brigadier General.

The tone of Adrian's voice had not changed and Alex felt that his contact did not mind being asked to refer to his superior. "No problem. I'll ask him to get in touch with you as soon as possible."

"One other thing, Adrian. I'm not certain the colour sensitivity within my eyes is working correctly. I still keep seeing strange colours on some, though not all, faces."

Adrian thought about this and said, "Sounds as though some checks need to be made. Leave it with me."

As Alex ended the call, he wondered just what he was going to say to the man pulling the strings at MI6. He had, at least, time to think how he should approach the subject.

For now, he needed to give Elsa some more attention as her coat was now dry. He had found great relaxation when grooming her and called the dog over. Eagerly, she came close to Alex when she saw him with the grooming brush. Although this brush seemed quite coarse, it did the job of removing loose hairs from her thick coat and, soon, the waste bin was quite full of discarded hair. Elsa really seemed to enjoy the experience and stayed relaxed while her master completed her grooming. Her coat felt smooth and silky to the touch by the time Alex had finished the job and, strangely, Elsa seemed to appreciate what had been done for her.

Alex mused to himself that, instead of giving all his attention to some delightful young female, he was, instead, sharing his life with a dog and this was certainly no metaphor for some tired, ugly woman. He supposed that he was lucky that this friendship only cost him dog food and was always appreciated. Still, he was only twenty-five and, hopefully, his love life could only improve. It would, certainly, be impossible to get worse as it was now completely non-existent.

It was two days later when he received a call from Paul Marshall. "Adrian tells me that you are looking for a different type of assignment?"

"I'm sorry to sound so ungrateful. Tailing someone for a short while and then handing over to somebody else leaves me feeling so empty and frustrated. I know that I am capable of much more."

The older man laughed, more in amusement rather than meaning that this was a ridiculous request. "Do you feel capable of carrying out a different type of work?"

"Yes! I know I can do more, if given the chance." Alex felt uneasy that his request may result in the ending of all work for the British Government and, in particular, MI6, but desperately hoped this would not be the case.

"Come in to the department, next Wednesday." Alex breathed a sigh of relief. "We need to assess your full capabilities before we can even think of other types of work."

"Thank you, Sir." Alex slept much better that night and just hoped that he would be up to the task.

Terry called promptly at nine, seven days later, as the Brigadier General had arranged. As they drove the twenty minute journey to MI6 at Vauxhall Cross, this now-familiar escort was still economic with conversation, which always gave Alex an uneasy feeling. He found it difficult to decide if it was terry's character or part of his job description not to converse. Perhaps he was just a sad, miserable, unsociable prick?

It was Adrian who met him and Elsa at reception and he guided them along the maze of corridors and, surprisingly, down several levels in the lift. This building on the South Embankment of the Thames was huge and, probably unfairly, nicknamed "LEGOLAND" because of its modular block construction with many different, stepped, roof levels.

As they left the lift, Adrian opened a door into a comfortable office. A smartly-dressed young woman introduced herself as Kelly.

Adrian said, "Kelly will look after Elsa while you are being assessed."

It was with some reluctance that Alex handed the lead over to this stranger. Could he trust this young woman to look after his canine friend? Would the dog think that Alex was abandoning her? Strangely, she seemed to understand and although a little quiet, she made no move to follow her master.

Adrian and Alex left the office and continued along yet another of the many winding corridors. "You can switch on your sight, now, Alex."

Wondering what to expect, he did as instructed. "Nothing special, here", he thought. "Just endless, boring corridors."

He understood fully when they entered the next room. Standing, smiling at him was Jen. "Hi, Alex! Good to see you again."

The smile on Alex's face said it all. "Great to see you." He very nearly gave her a hug, but realized that, in these surroundings and in the presence of Adrian, it would probably be construed as inappropriate. Instead, they shook hands warmly.

"What brings you back to England?"

Jen laughed. "You did! When you asked if you could be assessed for more complex duties, the Brigadier general asked if I could fly over to assist in your assessment." After a short pause, she added, "I also need to check the colour palette in the prosthetic eyes after you mentioned possible false colouring."

Now, Alex was feeling quite guilty, but still more than happy to see Jen again. Alex wished more than ever that he and Jen could have been an item. Dressed in a smart, blue trouser suit with crisp white shirt, she looked in great shape and that smile... Such a warm, inviting smile that any man who did not fancy her must really have been blind, which, in his case, was a little ironic.

She continued, "I was tasked to devise tests to fully assess your abilities in extreme situations and, hopefully, I have managed to think of suitable tests of your capabilities. My section leader was not too happy as I had only been back a short while, but he did understand why it should be me."

True to his lustful mind, Alex thought back to the fictitious Jack Reacher who, somehow, always managed to get laid in each story. How he hoped she was going to test his capabilities in bed with her, but knew this was just wishful thinking. "One day, perhaps", he thought.

"So, what have you devised for me?"

Jen handed Alex a pair of ear protectors. "The first is target practice, but you would do well to wear these. Your hearing could be damaged in these enclosed testing areas."

Gratefully, he took the protectors. "I'm going to stay in this control room, but will be in voice contact, throughout the tests. Now, start by entering the test area through the doorway in front of you."

Alex adjusted and positioned the ear protectors, which doubled as microphone and headphones, for maximum comfort. Warily, he pushed open the door to the testing room.

There was a choice of rifles at the end of a long room used as a firing range. Looking through what was available, he chose a SA80 as this was what he had used in Afghanistan. He set it to semi-automatic mode and told Jen that he was ready. She pressed a few buttons on a control console and, to Alex's surprise, a cloud of smoke entered the room through grilles positioned around the perimeter of the floor.

"Don't worry, Alex. It's quite harmless, yet very effective at obscuring the targets. Are you ready?"

Alex realized that this would be a good test of his ability to see clearly in low-visibility situations. "Okay, Jen. I'm ready."

By now, the room was full of this strange mist. Alex looked through his sights at the far wall. As he watched, a figure began moving across this wall, at first moving slowly, but gradually speeding up. He fired two shots and then noticed other targets moving into his visual field. One by one, he pumped the rifle until he felt certain that all had been hit.

Even with his ear protectors, the noise seemed extremely loud. In contrast, the sound of the electric pressure motors working hard was quite muted and, slowly, the mist began to clear and disappear.

"How did I do?"

There was a slight pause. "I'm just checking. You can come back in here, now."

He replaced the rifle, pulled off his ear protectors and walked back through the heavily-built door.

Jen was looking through data on a screen. All the hits were electronically calibrated and the results were displayed in tabular form.

"There were twelve targets and all received two hits in the head. Twelve kills! Congratulations, Alex!"

"What was the mist about?"

"We were testing your ability to see in low-light situations. The mist simulates a five per cent visibility level and you still managed to hit all targets accurately. Under the same circumstances, a normally-sighted person would have been lucky to hit one."

"Good! I still don't see why the lights could not have been switched off or, at least, dimmed, instead."

Patiently, Jen replied, "It would have been unfair to expect you to carry out the test in complete darkness and the mist is useful to replicate actual combat conditions. This test is used for other combatants, but not usually down to five per cent visibility. Okay?"

"Yes, fine. Is that it?"

"No, not yet. I want you to take a pistol and go into this other room. The obscuring mist is just being pumped into the next target room." She looked at her console to check the visibility level. "Okay, it's ready for you. Keep on your toes. In this room, the targets can pop up from anywhere. Just be quick and accurate as you can."

He was about to enter the room, when Jen added, "Oh, by the way, the red figures are enemies, while the black are friendly. Try to avoid shooting our friends!" She smiled coyly at Alex, after making his task even more complicated.

He grinned. "Thanks for that. Okay, I'm ready."

He pushed the door open and slipped through, closing it firmly after him. This room was full of low building facades and shells of vehicles. His eyes scanned the room for any signs of movement. Sweeping around, he spotted a figure, which seemed to be red, in a doorway and fired into it. The figure disappeared and then other figures began to appear from all over this large room. He walked fast through the maze of objects, picking up any enemy targets he spotted as he moved to the far end of the area.

After a few minutes, a siren sounded and the mist began to be sucked out of vents, leaving it clear once more. He walked back into the control room where Jen was, again, studying the results on a console.

She smiled. "One hundred per cent accuracy, again with a five per cent visibility factor." Then she added, "And not a single friend hit!"

"Have I passed, then?"

"With flying colours, Alex. There's no doubt that your bionic eyes have proved highly successful. In fact, far more successful than we had ever imagined."

Alex knew that his extensive training in the British Army and his experience in the battle field had proved invaluable in the accurate use of weapons.

"So, what now?" Alex wondered if she had any more tests for him. He was actually enjoying not only her company, but also the difficult exercises she had devised for him.

"I'm going to hand you over to our in-house psychologist, Susan Masters. She needs to determine if you are capable of handling greater stress. Oh, and after that we will do a colour calibration test on your eyes."

Alex had mentioned the bluish-grey tinge on the potential rapist and the terrorist suspects, which made her wonder if the colour palette had become mis-aligned.

A few minutes later, Alex was in the office of Susan masters. Jen had taken him to her room and then left the couple to their privacy. The psychologist was in her late forties, had shoulder-length black hair and looked remarkably fit. "Please lie down and make yourself comfortable, Alex."

He wondered just how she would assess his psychological profile. As he lay back on the sofa, she began to ask him to describe what he felt to be the major turning points in his life, even going back to being an infant.

She stopped him at many points, trying to elaborate on particular stages, where she felt it would help to assess him more in depth. After ninety minutes of asking deeply probing, sometimes personal, questions, she had a pretty good assessment of him, but still asked, "How do you feel about the Taliban bombing which injured you and killed your comrades?"

"Bloody angry! Is that so surprising?"

She replied, quite calmly, "No, it's not surprising at all. But, do you feel you are handling it adequately? Is the anger as strong now, as it was when you were admitted to hospital?"

He had to think about this. "How do you measure anger?"

"You can't! But, you probably can tell whether the anger is as strong now as it used to be."

"I suppose I feel just as angry, now, as I ever did and I honestly can't see that changing."

"What about your broken relationship with Helen? Tell me how you feel about it.

Alex took a sharp intake of breath at this most personal of questions. "Thoroughly pissed off! I can't ever forgive her." His forthright answer was made without any apology. "If her feelings for me were dependent on me staying fit and healthy, then it could never have been true love."

The psychologist did not make any comment, merely making notes on a pad. "Okay, Alex. I have finished my assessment. I'll call Major Sherlock to return here for you." Within a couple of minutes of speaking on the phone, Jen did return. From there, the couple walked to a laboratory for the next test

"This test is very simple", said Jen. She asked Alex to sit in front of a computer monitor. "All you need to do is look straight at the screen and try to avoid blinking as much as you can."

Alex did as requested. What he saw was what appeared to be a blank screen, but whose colour changed rapidly, running through the whole of the visible spectrum and then back again.

Jen explained. "The computer is comparing the colours on the monitor with the perceived colours transmitted from your eyes and through your wristwatch." She paused to study a report appearing on a separate monitor. "Good! What this proves is that the implants' perceived colours match precisely those presented on the monitor."

"So, where does that leave us?" Alex could not think why these results were so significant.

"Well, it does indicate that the implants are performing precisely as intended and, if you perceive any difference, as you did in the terrorist's facial colour, then it is your brain which is modifying the palette."

This made no sense to Alex. "But, how can that be? And, why?"

Jen took a deep breath, realizing that his question was not easy to answer. "Scientists do know a great deal about the human brain, but it still holds many mysteries. I do know of some research where people without sight can have a greater activity in part of the right-hand side of the brain which deals with intuition"

"So, you feel that my brain now has the capacity to change the perceived skin colour of an individual depending on whether he or she is good or not?"

Jen nodded. "That's about it. I know that it sounds a bit far-fetched and can not be scientifically proven, but, that's my personal interpretation. Of course, I could be completely wrong, but, frankly, I can't think of a better explanation."

Alex pondered on this remarkable observation. "There is a danger if this is what is happening. What if a person has a natural darker colour of skin? Or if they are unwashed? Could I mistake a good person for an evil one?"

Jen did not seem to be thrown by this obvious question. "Just think how many faces have you seen with your new eyes and, yet, only these few individuals had an observable difference?"

He could not argue with her logic and, yet, the concept of being able to identify potential criminals or terrorists filled him both with awe and dread.

Jen realized that this revelation was causing him some anxiety. "Don't worry, Alex! Just think how valuable you would be to British and American Governments."

He shrugged. "It's a hell of a responsibility and I may just be used as a filter without seeing any real action."

Jen now fully understood his anxiety. "Come on. Let's go and, first of all, report to Adrian and then get Elsa and go somewhere for a meal."

His face lightened. "Okay. That sounds good to me."

Adrian had a smile on his face when they entered his office. The section leader had been looking through the printed results of the shooting range tests. "Great work, Alex. Your ocular implants appear to be working superbly. As far as I am concerned, your eyesight is unparalleled in the human race."

"Does that mean that I can be used on more dangerous missions?"

"It means, Captain McCloud, that, if more difficult missions are presented, you will be one of several individuals to be considered for the task. I am also able to issue you with a Heckler and Koch MP5 carbine handgun with the complements of the British Government."

Adrian stepped over to a cupboard in his room, unlocked it and took out the weapon, together with shoulder holster and spare clips. "I just need your signature to acknowledge receipt of this weapon before you can take it."

"No problem." Alex signed the paper offered by Adrian. He took hold of the weapon, feeling the weight in his hand. "That feels good." He removed his jacket, fastened the holster in place and inserted the gun. "I feel fully dressed, again. Nice choice of weapon."

"Only the best for our soldiers. Just take good care of yourself and only use the weapon in extreme circumstances."

"Understood!" Alex and Jen walked back to where his dog was being looked after. He need not have worried about Elsa. She was fast asleep in Kelly's office. The German shepherd dog was obviously dreaming, her paws twitching as she, perhaps, was chasing some imaginary cat.

When Alex touched her back, the dog, like many humans in similar circumstances, recovered from her slumbers slowly and then shook her head, as if trying to clear it. By the time Alex had clipped on her handle, she was fully alert and ready to guide her master, yet again.

CHAPTER FOURTEEN :

The fresh, chilly air of the November day was welcoming after the air-conditioned offices of MI6. Jen knew the area better than Alex and, together, they took a taxi to a restaurant favoured by Jen.

Within twenty minutes, they were sitting opposite each other in a very busy Scott's Restaurant on Mount Street in Mayfair, with Elsa curled up under the table at Alex's feet. They were extremely lucky to find space, but, fortunately for them, there had been a cancellation.

Jen was recognized by both the bowler-hatted doorman and head waiter. She had used this renowned restaurant on several previous occasions, while working in London. Jen read the menu to Alex who chose roast Cornish lamb, while she opted for roast Gressingham duck with crispy bacon and Port wine sauce. Alex cheated by switching on his sight during their meal together, as he was still worried about making a fool of himself in this stylish restaurant by knocking his food off the plate, or worse still, spilling his glass of Gran Coronas Cabernet Sauvignon wine over the crisp, white tablecloth.

Alex, not wanting to be emotionally re-buffed again by Jen, kept the conversation light and polite, hopefully, without being boring.

Jen was just about to take a sip of wine, when she stopped, as if frozen.

"What's wrong?" Alex asked.

"That guy! He looks familiar."

Alex looked in the direction Jen had indicated, without making it too obvious. The man was quite tall, probably of similar height to Alex, had gingery, slightly-greying hair and wore a patterned shirt and velour jacket. There was a good-looking brunette on his arm and, from the way the head waiter was fussing around them, he probably was quite well-known. "He does look familiar", agreed Alex. He gently touched the display on his watch and, within seconds, a message appeared in the top of his vision. "Christopher James Evans, Nationality British, Marital status : married, Date of Birth : April 1st., nineteen sixty-six, occupation : Radio and television presenter"

Alex was constantly impressed by the facial recognition software available through the watch. "That's Chris Evans and his wife, Natasha", Alex whispered. "It must be some kind of celebration. Perhaps a birthday or anniversary."

"Oh, I remember where I have seen him, now. Sometimes, when I was in the hotel, before your operation, I would watch 'The One Show'. I'm fairly certain he was on every Friday."

"Yes", agreed Alex. "I watch that programme myself. Chris has quite an extravert, almost challenging manner, which, sometimes, gets him into trouble. I wonder who's looking after Noah?"

"They seem like a nice couple", commented Jen.

Chris and Natasha were escorted to their table, where the head waiter continued to take good care of them.

"This is what I like about London", said Jen. "It is one of the few places where you can rub shoulders with the rich and famous."

CHAPTER FIFTEEN :
NOVEMBER, 2011

Even for London, it was a bitterly cold evening, with a biting, icy wind, as they left the restaurant, together. Jen looked for a cab. "I'll find a taxi for you. My hotel is within walking distance, but it's quite a way to your place from here." They walked along Mount Street, looking for a taxi, unaware that they were being observed.

The man had followed them from M.I.6 to the restaurant and had patiently waited, without making it too obvious, until they had left Scott's. His eyes followed the couple. "Who was this tall guy with the guide dog?" There was no time to request new instructions and he was now entirely on his own.

At last, after a few minutes walk, Jen spotted a taxi driving on the other side of the road and waved her arm towards the driver. Luckily, he spotted her and, through a brief gap in the traffic, did a smart U-turn and pulled up in front of them.

Jen leaned in through the open front window. "My friend needs a cab to his flat about twenty minutes drive from here." She gestured towards Alex.

"No problem. Does he need any help?" The cab driver had noticed Elsa and understood his handicap. In London, it was not unusual for him to ferry blind passengers through the crowded city, but blind passengers with guide dogs were not quite as common.

"No, that's okay. I'll give him a hand, myself." Jen opened the taxi door and guided Alex into the cab. As he took a seat, Jen leaned in to speak to Alex, meaning to arrange when they would meet again.

"Jen! Quick, get down!" There was great urgency in his voice. To her surprise and shock, he grabbed the upper part of her body and pulled her roughly, downwards towards him. She was horrified and, angered, about to ask him what the hell he was playing at, when she heard the shot. Elsa gave a single bark as, with her thorough training, she knew how the sound of gunfire represented a dangerous situation for her master.

The top of the door frame of the cab splintered as the bullet hit it. A second or two earlier, the back of Jen's head would have been in line with the door trim.

"What the hell?" The driver was, obviously, not used to having his cab shot at.

Alex spoke wit great urgency. "Jen! Get in, quick!" She was half in and half out of the cab, sprawled without dignity, partly on Alex and the seat, but her legs were still outside. He used his strong arms to assist her. With his help, she managed to regain her balance and slammed the door shut. Alex swiftly touched his watch and stared out of the window, scanning the dark pavements where the shot could have originated from.

"Drive! Quickly!"

The driver was visibly shocked. "Where to?" His question was automatic, the same as he would have asked any of his thousands of usual fares, but there was nothing vaguely routine about this pickup. The driver wished he had taken a leak before this job as he now felt an urgent need to urinate.

"Hell, anywhere! Just get us away from this area. Quick!" The tension in Alex's voice was very apparent. The driver wasted no time, engaging the gears and pressing his foot hard on the accelerator. In his desperation, he nearly collided with the back of a bus, which was just pulling up at a stop.

Taking hold of the situation, Alex spoke again to the driver, giving him his home address and directions. "As quick as you can, please." He held Jen close. She was trembling with emotion, having come so close to a very grizzly death.

Nothing was said during the journey, both sitting in shocked silence. It was a relief when they arrived at the apartment. Alex paid his fare, including a generous tip, and, although his cab had been damaged, the driver did not ask for any compensation. Thankfully, the damage to the door frame was quite minor and could have been far worse, especially if Jen had been hit by the sniper's bullet.

Alex, Jen and Elsa wasted no time in entering his apartment. As soon as they were in the privacy of his living room, Jen asked, almost in anger, "How the hell did you know that a sniper was aiming for my head?"

During the journey, Alex had been pondering on this very question, knowing that it would be the first to be asked by Jen. "I really don't know. I had a sudden feeling, like a heavy pressure within my head, but I can't explain how I knew to pull you out of the sniper's sights."

Jen looked at him, not certain if she believed him. Then the emotion overcame her and she put her arms around Alex, pulling herself close to him, resting her head on his chest. The normally calm and controlled Major Jennifer Sherlock had disappeared and a warm, feminine vulnerable woman had replaced her. She said nothing, satisfied with just holding Alex close.

He could sense the change in Jen's demeanor. This was a strong woman, who had risen to the rank of Major and, yet, in front of him was a young, vulnerable, very feminine and frightened woman, gently sobbing on his chest. "Even though I can't explain how I knew, I'm just thankful that you escaped injury or possible death." Elsa sat quietly, looking up with some curiosity at the embracing couple. It was as though she sensed the change in her master's situation.

Jen lifted her head. "Thank you so much for saving my life, Alex. I'm so grateful." Then she kissed him full on the lips, lingering for what seemed like an eternity. Eventually, she pulled her mouth away, but still held onto him. Her normally pale golden skin was now suffused with a pinkish hue as she became more aroused.

Struggling to regain her composure, she said in a quiet voice, "I must phone Adrian and report this incident." Her voice, initially shaky, was now more controlled and calm.

"Yes, of course." Jen still held him close, as though finding it difficult to separate herself from the man she had not really wished to have a relationship with and, yet, he had just saved her life. Eventually, she loosened her hold on Alex and took the mobile out of her pocket.

As soon as Adrian answered, she quickly, yet precisely, described all the details of her near-assassination.

"Whatever you do, don't go back to your hotel, tonight. Who ever it was may know where you were staying. Tomorrow, go back to your hotel and check-out. Find another place, not too close and keep a low profile." Adrian sounded concerned for the American agent.

Alex intervened. "I'd like to have a word with Adrian." Jen handed the phone to him. "Hi, Adrian. Listen, I scanned the area where the sniper must have been. If you review the recordings around eight forty-five, tonight, it may give you some useful information." Now always aware that his vision was being recorded, Alex knew that it could now prove to be a very useful tool.

"Thanks, Alex. We'll check it out. Take care, you two." Alex handed the phone back to Jen.

"Do you mind if I stay here, tonight? Adrian thinks it may be dangerous to go back to my hotel."

"Of course not, you are welcome to stay as long as you want." Without a second thought, he added, "You can have my bed and I'll sleep on the sofa."

How gallant this Englishman was, but aware that she did not really want to be on her own, Jen replied, with a coy smile, "I'm certain your bed will be fine for both of us. That is, if you don't mind sharing it with me?" As if reading his thoughts about when she told him she did not want a long-distance relationship, she continued, "Tonight's experience was a stark reminder that, if I keep putting things off, I might never realize my dreams. I've always been too driven by my career, but I think it may be time to look a bit beyond my role within the C.I.A."

Was ne really a part of her dreams? The smile on Alex's face said it all. It was not anything triumphant, but one of tenderness and understanding. "That's fine by me, as long as this is really what you want."

"I think that may depend upon you." The excited look on her face made Alex feel better than he had for a long time. "But, for now, I'd like to freshen up. Can I use your bathroom?"

"Of course. There's no bath, but I do have a fantastic shower. The high-pressure side jets can be quite invigorating." He smiled at Jen, who he now saw in a completely different light. Then a sudden thought struck him. "Jen? Is there a way of stopping Adrian monitoring everything I see?"

At first she looked puzzled and then, with a sudden realization, laughed. "I can see why you asked the question. It could be quite embarrassing for both of us."

"I could imagine Adrian and his colleagues crowding around the monitor as unseen voyeurs, watching our every intimate moment. So, what can we do to foil them?"

Jen held out her hand. "Give me your watch, Alex." He slid the stylish watch off his wrist and dropped it into her open hand. Jen opened the battery compartment on the rear of the watch and took out the tiny lithium cell. "There! That will stop a peeping Adrian!" After a moment's thought, she added, "Though he will know that you are up to something, when he realizes that you have disabled the Internet connection." She handed the watch and battery back to a smiling Alex. Just don't forget to replace it when you are on surveillance work. There is a smaller battery for the time setting and other functions, so you won't need to reset it every time you remove the main battery."

Alex laughed. "I should have realized that the solution would be a simple one." He took the watch and battery, placing them carefully in a drawer. Jen had already gone through to the bathroom and, within a few minutes, Alex could hear the jets of water splashing noisily in the shower unit.

Alex took the opportunity to feed Elsa her nightly bowl of dog food and, not wanting to be disturbed by a desperate dog during what may happen in the immediate future, he took her outside to releave herself on the concrete run.

This duty done, he settled down in one of the chairs in the living room, with Elsa curled at his feet. Alex was deep in thought as he stroked the dog's head. What would the next few hours bring? Was his life about to change?

When Jen appeared in the doorway, Alex was stunned into silence. "I hope you don't mind me borrowing this?"

She was wearing one of Alex's t-shirts and, although it was far too big for her, it certainly looked far better on her than it had ever done on him. The bottom edge of the shirt was only a few centimetres below "C-level", displaying her long, firm, shapely legs. Jen was smiling, invitingly. Her eyes sparkled with the anticipation of what was to come.

"Was this the point where Lee Child's Jack Reacher gets the girl?" Alex mused to himself. He stood, walked over to where Jen was patiently waiting. Putting his arms around her, he drew her close towards him, kissing her lips with a passion and tenderness which noticeably aroused Jen as it did for himself.

They parted briefly and hurried towards the bedroom. Elsa stared after them, puzzled by this strange, human behavior, never to understand the pleasure derived from the act of coupling as the unfortunate dog had been neutered while still a puppy.

In the bedroom, Jen looked at the steadily increasing bulge in his trousers and tugged at Alex's belt, loosening it and unzipping the fly. Desperate for him, she unfastened the buttons on his shirt and pulled it up, assisted by Alex. He stepped out of his pants, kicking them sideways and then, with one swift movement, he pulled his tee-shirt off this beautiful, raunchy woman.

Jen had already pulled the covers back and nimbly jumped on the bed where she lay on her back, inviting Alex who wasted no time in joining her. She spread her legs apart allowing Alex's huge, erect member to enter her already-moist vagina. She gave a little gasp as he thrust himself deep into her. Her hands were on his buttocks, pulling him even harder and deeper inside her. Their tongues were searching each other's mouths, deriving every possible pleasure from this so intimate of kisses.

At first, his body moved in long, slow, tantalising movements, but, gradually, the pace quickened as their senses sought sexual climax. When it came, both their bodies moved convulsively and in unison, extracting every possible second of mutual pleasure in their orgasmic ecstasy.

Sleep came very quickly to the exhausted couple. It was one of sweet, satisfied love-making and they held each other close in their exhausted state.

He did not know how much later it was when Alex woke with a start. Something cold and wet touched his bare buttocks. He did not need to switch on the light to find out just what it was. Elsa's nose had burrowed through the covers and prodded him again and, as he put his hand out, Elsa allowed him to stroke her head.

He pressed the button on his bedside light and looked at the clock. It was six-thirty. Alex could not remember having such a deep, restful, untroubled sleep and was thankful to Jen for such superb sleep therapy.

She was still fast asleep as Alex climbed out of bed and, still naked, followed the dog to the kitchen. Alex smiled to himself, thinking that he had the typical, slightly-twisted, Jack Reacher smile after getting off with the girl.

The dog padded in front, eager to lead him towards the kitchen. "Poor Elsa! Are you desperate for a pee?" He unfastened the door and let her outside. She soon returned, happier that she had now expelled the contents of her bladder.

Alex checked the bedroom to find Jen still fast asleep. He grabbed some clothes and closed the door quietly so as not to disturb her. He shaved, showered and dressed and then moved into the kitchen and began preparation of breakfast.

His spirit was certainly better than normal. Within a twenty four hour period, his life had taken a new turn with the attack on Jen and it now seemed to have a purpose, but, would it last? Was he in the right place at the right time for Jen or did she have genuine feelings for him?

As if to answer this question, Jen appeared in the doorway. "Good morning, love. Mmmm... That smells great. I feel quite hungry."

"Good! Will scrambled eggs and coffee help?"

"Yes, that's fine. Can I help?"

Alex looked at her. "The eggs are almost done and the coffee maker is on. All we need is cutlery." He pointed to the drawer where she could find knives and forks. Unlike Jack Reacher, Alex preferred milk in his coffee.

During breakfast, conversation was easy and they both felt comfortable with their new, intimate situation. What was perplexing to both of them was the question about the reason for Alex's heightened perception. Even this was not a great description as a perception is usually observed after the incident, not before. Whichever way they looked at it, no explanations were possible.

Jen needed to return to her hotel to get her case and check-out. She felt it would be safe for her to make this journey on her own, but Alex felt that he should stay with her in case there was a further threat. She did not put up much resistance and, around ten thirty, they were in a black cab, driving towards Jen's hotel. Alex had decided they would be less obtrusive if Elsa remained at the flat. Poor Elsa was noticeably sad at the separation and, lying in the living room, kept a watchful eye on the door, waiting for her master to return.

Thoughtful of the situation the night before, Jen and Alex asked the taxi driver to drop them off a couple of streets away from the hotel. Now Jen had to act as his eyes, as Alex was determined to keep the "blind person" persona at all times outside his apartment.

She took his arm and walked swiftly towards the hotel. They avoided using the main entrance, choosing, instead, a little-used doorway which led into the reception hall, where they took a lift to the fifth floor.

Jen inserted her card in the slot at room five hundred and twenty-seven and gently pushed the door open, half-expecting to find some sinister figure inside the room. Everything looked normal to her and, thankfully, the room was empty. She swiftly moved to the bathroom and pushed the door open wide. Nobody there.

Jen then looked around the room, picturing it, in her mind, as it had been the day before. Again, nothing seemed disturbed or out of place. The bed was made, presumably, by the chambermaids, the day before.

Swiftly, Jen gathered up her few possessions and threw them into her suitcase. She travelled quite light and did not take long.

Alex had switched on his eyes and watched, interested but without comment, as Jen finished her packing. He had a feeling, though he knew that it may be nothing. Just a strange, incomprehensible, feeling that something was wrong. If Jen had this same apprehension, she did not show it, now looking quite relaxed.

It was then that Alex spotted it. A light was flashing on the bedside phone, indicating that there were messages. Jen spotted Alex looking at it. "A message for me?"

She was about to press the button to replay the message, when Alex shouted, "No, Jen! Don't touch it!"

She looked puzzled. "Why? It's only a phone."

Instead of answering, he asked her a question. "How does Adrian contact you?"

"On my mobile. Why?"

Again, another question. "Does anybody else know you were staying here? Your parents or other relatives, for example?"

"Why, no. But what should it matter?"

Patiently, Alex explained, "The fact is that the chance of somebody calling you on the hotel's phone line is quite remote. You said, yourself, that Adrian contacts you by mobile, so why would anybody contact you on the room phone? I had a feeling that something was wrong as soon as we entered this room, but I couldn't put my finger on it, until now."

She now understood. "You think there are explosives in the phone?"

He nodded. "Come on, let's get out of here." He opened the door, let Jen pass through and then grabbed the "Do not disturb" sign from the back of the door and placed it on the handle on the corridor side.

The wide, carpeted corridor was empty. Alex stopped. "Jen, can you phone Adrian from here and ask him to get the bomb squad to check your room? We don't want the next guest to find the surprise in your phone."

Jen paused and looked at Alex. "How certain are you about the phone?"

He did not hesitate. "Absolutely! At first, I couldn't place the smell. Then I realized that it was similar to the bombs in Afghanistan. That's why they use dogs to sniff out areas of danger. I think that, like my other senses, my sense of smell is also heightened."

Jen, now convinced, phoned Adrian and explained the situation to him. "Leave it to me. You two get out of there before the squad comes. I don't want any awkward questions."

Jen and Alex decided to walk down the stairs to the ground floor, leaving by the same doors as they had used when entering the hotel. Jen explained that she did not have to check out, as the details from her credit card were taken on registration, a few days earlier.

They did not leave unnoticed. The man saw them leave the hotel and raised his eyebrows in surprise. He followed them from a distance, Alex's build and stature assisting his task of following the couple. When they hailed a taxi, he did the same, determined to find their new destination. He was surprised when the taxi dropped the couple off, outside Harrods store in Knightsbridge. He did the same, but knew this location made his task that much more difficult.

CHAPTER SIXTEEN :

Jen leaned against Alex, cuddling up to him, as they relaxed on the sofa in his living room. "That's the first time I've been to Harrod's", said Jen. "Interesting place, but I was puzzled when you told the taxi driver to take us there."

Alex smiled. "It's a good place to lose a tail. I had a feeling that we were being followed, so decided to lose them."

"Your sensory perception is truly amazing." I never even realized we were being tailed until you told me and, how on earth did you smell the explosives in the phone?"

He shrugged. "It amazes me, as well", Alex agreed. "I really don't know why my senses are so acute, but, I'm grateful, if only to save you from what could have been a horrible, grizzly death."

Alex then remembered the words of the Neurologist, Peter Jacques. "Individuals with higher activity than normal in this area tend to be more aware, more perceptive and, in some cases, have an unusual talent, such as increased memory retention or the ability to mentally calculate complex mathematical calculations." He felt certain that his heightened senses were as a direct result of the impact on his skull in Afghanistan. "Behind every cloud, there may well be a silver lining", he thought.

As these thoughts were churning through his mind, Alex had not noticed the curious smile on Jen's face.

"Hello? Can you come down from outer space, please?"

"Sorry, Jen, I didn't mean to ignore you. I was just reflecting on something somebody once said to me."

"That's alright. I was just suggesting that we could do with a drink. Nothing strong, just coffee!"

"Yes, that's a good idea." Alex felt that this "new" Jen seemed so different from the formal, militaristic Major Jennifer Sherlock he had been introduced to only four months earlier. So much more feminine, seductive and extremely attractive.

While Jen began to make coffee in the kitchen, Alex was brought back to the real world by the sound of his mobile. It was Adrian. "I've had a look at the recordings from your vision, as you suggested. There is definitely a hazy figure that could have fired at Jen, but I'm afraid that it's not clear enough to make a positive identification." As if it was an afterthought, he added, "Not even with software enhancement."

"That's a pity. Especially since they seem determined to try and kill her. Somebody followed us from Jen's hotel, but we managed to lose them."

Adrian sounded concerned. "Best if Jen can stay at your place, for the time being."

"No problem, at all." There was nothing he would like better than to have Jen move in with him, but felt certain that this would only be for a short time before she felt that she had to return to the States.

"I have asked the hotel for a copy of their recordings of their security cameras and should get these later today. As soon as we have them, we'll do everything to identify the person who tampered with the phone in room five hundred and twenty-seven."

"Good! Let me know as soon as you get an I.D. on this guy, assuming that he's on the database." Alex ended the call. As Jen brought mugs of coffee into the living room, he explained to her what Adrian had told him. "Can you think of anybody who would want you dead?"

"None that immediately come to mind, but it's quite possible I've made some enemies over the years. After nearly seven years in the military, it's quite possible."

CHAPTER SEVENTEEN :
NOVEMBER, 2011

Danny Jackson and Paddy Conroy shuffled uneasily as they reported their failure to kill the American woman. They knew they had messed up and big time. Even more worrying was the fact that they had been instructed to meet their employer in person, rather than using a coded phone message, as usual. To actually meet the 'big man' gave them a distinctly uncomfortable feeling. Danny noticed how dry his mouth felt, but was certain that they were unlikely to be offered a drink by their demanding and, currently furious employer. This man reminded Danny of the business tycoon, Alan Sugar, but with a distinct Italian flavour.

The two criminals had worked together for the past thirteen years and, so far, had managed to look after themselves without being caught. They met as troublesome teenagers and, with similar backgrounds, found it profitable to work together. Most of their work came from contract killings and, to date, they had been quite successful. They had already completed several killings for Gianni, making this failure even more compromising.

They knew not to ask questions and carry out the jobs cleanly and efficiently. The money was good, allowing them to indulge in their passion for travel. Another few weeks and the two were due for a holiday in Thailand, something they were both looking forward to. Good hot climate, great food, cheap drinks and a few days of fun with sexy, young Thai girls, all added to the attraction. Danny had been thinking about this when he was, suddenly, brought back to the real world.

"This job should have been so easy, so how come you two idiots screwed up and managed to leave the fucking bitch alive?"

"Sorry, Boss." Beads of perspiration ran down Danny's face. He glanced briefly at Paddy, who was, in his mind, equally responsible for leaving the woman alive. Both men knew what could happen to those who fail Gianni. "The woman got lucky. She was in my sights and must have moved a fraction of a second before my shot would have hit her." He still found it incredible that she had moved just in time to avoid certain death. "Just my bad luck", he thought.

Gianni Lamancusa did not believe in luck, neither good nor bad, and could never have been described as a patient man. He looked stone-faced at the two men who had been given the role of ending Jennifer Sherlock's life. "Once was bad enough, but you two goons, somehow, managed to screw-up twice. Don't I pay you guys enough?"

It was Paddy who answered. Looking as uncomfortable as Danny, he replied, "Sure you do, Boss. We'll get her next time."

Gianni's normally placid face creased into a smile, which was unusual for this powerful, dangerous man. "Next time? You want another chance to fuck up? You don't even know where the bitch is!"

"Don't worry, we'll find her. She won't survive our next hit." Both men felt uneasy and probably wished they had gone for a leak before meeting Gianni.

"Relax, guys. Don't look so worried. I'm not going to hurt you. Just get out of my sight before I do something you may regret."

The look of relief on their faces was instantly noticeable. They headed for the door, Danny opening it, eager to escape. His eyes grew wide as he was confronted by the muscular, black torso of a huge man, whose body seemed to completely fill the door opening. Gigantic hands reached towards their necks. They were lifted completely off the floor and this giant of a man began to squeeze all life out of the unfortunate pair, even before they had chance to say another word.

The unconcerned Gianni, still smiling, spoke quietly. "I kept my promise, boys. I said that I was not going to hurt you, and I always keep my word, but our friend, Sam is going to do the job for me. Goodbye, boys!"

Sam, a giant of a man at six foot eleven, had picked up the two men by their necks and was steadily squeezing all life out of the now, ex-employees of Gianni. Black-skinned Sam, his polished, shaven head glistening with the close proximity of the ceiling lights, held up the unfortunate men. Their eyes were bulging, bones cracking and blood pouring out of their mouths. They never stood a chance. Sam dropped the two men on the floor, where they landed, unceremoniously, like a child's discarded, broken dolls.

There would be two empty seats on the Etihad flight to Thailand and those young Thai girls would never benefit financially for sex with the two British men.

Gianni's serious look returned. In an irritated tone, he said, "Get rid of them, Sam."

Sam's deep, baritone voice seemed to resonate around the room. "Sure, Boss. Do you have anywhere in mind?"

"I feel that the Thames is probably a fitting resting place for anybody stupid enough to disappoint Gianni Lamancusa." Obediently, Sam dragged the corpses away, as easily as if they were a couple of small suitcases.

Gianni leaned back in his chair, a resigned, depressed look on his face. He watched as Sam dragged the corpses away. He had to admire the strength of this huge man as nothing seemed to phase him.

Sam had been Gianni's 'muscle' for over eight years, after his life had been saved by the Italian mobster. Sam had upset another criminal gang when he prevented them from robbing a bank where he was one of the customers. The big man was surprisingly quick for his size and prevented the gang from completing their raid. They still managed to escape before the police had arrived, but a price was put on Sam's head. When Gianni heard of what had happened, he offered him a job and, very quietly, members of the opposing gang gradually disappeared. Their bodies were never found.

Gianni picked up a strange-looking phone, pressed a few buttons and spoke. Danny and Paddy have gone for a long swim. No sign of our friend, but we're still looking." The person on the other end of the phone clearly understood the message. "We will find her, eventually." He ended the call, looking annoyed, yet determined. He had clearly emphasized the word "will" and meant it in honour of his family.

He had the absolute belief that, if it was not for the interference by American Intelligence Services, Jennifer

Sherlock in particular, over three hundred of his family and compatriots would not, now, be languishing in high-security Italian prisons. He and about forty of his direct family members had managed to evade capture, but it had meant that they had to go underground in another country. The United Kingdom had not been their first choice, but the fact that it was physically apart from the main European countries gave it a distinct advantage.

The 'stealth' submarine had been expensive and far more sophisticated than the one found in Colombia by the authorities. The submarine had proved to be a valuable investment, as most of his immediate family had evaded capture by using this method of transportation. That was when he and his extended family had moved from Calabria in Southern Italy to London. It was a bold move but, hopefully, one which the authorities would never have expected.

Valuable contacts in the U.K. had provided information about possible locations for the family. Locations in which they could continue their luxurious life-style and yet remain hidden and undisturbed by the authorities. After all the necessary modifications had been completed, the "workers" had mysteriously disappeared.

In Italy, the phrase "Silence of the Lamancusa" had been used to describe the collection of numerous family members. One tended not to hear much from the family, but anyone found to have crossed them or leaked information would have their life terminated in a particularly gruesome way.

Gianni returned the phone to its cradle on his desk. There was no need to worry about his conversation being overheard. His phone was not connected to any conventional telephone network. Instead, it was a dedicated radio phone with all transmissions deeply encrypted. After the arrests of many of his 'Ndrangheta members in two thousand and ten, he had realized that even encrypted emails and mobile phone conversations were vulnerable to the sophisticated analytical methods employed by the CIA and, in the U.K., G.C.H.Q.

Gianni looked thoughtful as he relaxed, apparently unconcerned that the lives of two men had just been cut brutally short. He felt certain that these two contract killers, who had proved useful in the past, would not be missed.

CHAPTER EIGHTEEN :

Both Jen and Alex awoke, at the same moment, to the insistent sound of the musical tones from the mobile phone. Sleepily, Alex reached for the source of the noise. Through heavy eyes, he glanced at the screen and realized that it was Adrian calling him.

"Morning, Adrian. Any news?"

"We certainly have." Adrian sounded excited. "The video from the hotel has revealed the two guys who planted the explosives in Jen's phone."

"Great! Any idea who they are?" Alex was wide awake, now and Jen was cuddling close to him, trying to hear Adrian's words.

"Thankfully, they're on our database. The first is Daniel Jackson, a thirty-three year old dangerous criminal from London and the other is Patrick Conroy, thirty-two years old. He's Irish American."

Alex smiled and gave Jen a wink. "Have you managed to pick them up, yet?"

"Not yet. We have alerts out for them, but, so far, there's no sign of them."

"But, why would they want to kill Jen?"

"That's a very good question and one, for which we, as yet, do not have an answer. For now, you two had better keep out of sight, until we've caught these guys."

Alex agreed. "Adrian, can you send us their mug-shots?"

"Sure. I'll send them in the next few minutes. In the meantime, just take care."

Alex returned the phone to his bedside cabinet and lay back on the pillow. "What I don't understand is why these goons wanted you dead. Once could be a mistake, but twice is hardly likely. Too much of a coincidence?"

"Excuse me, Alex. I need the bathroom." As she climbed over him and walked, naked, to the door, he did not see the troubled expression on her face. Instead, Alex was admiring her long, powerful legs topped by a perfectly-formed, pert butt. Now that he knew her more intimately, he also realized that her blonde hair was absolutely genuine and not from a bottle.

He checked the time as she left the room and was amazed to find that it was ten-forty-five. Their love-making on the previous evening had lasted at least two hours, after which they had collapsed into a heavy, undisturbed sleep.

He lay there, quite relaxed, thinking of his new-found relationship with Jen and compared this with that of his three-year romance with Helen. It was difficult to compare the two women. Helen had been loving, tender and, until that day in the hospital, dependable. He could imagine that, once they were married, she would be a superb, reliable wife, well organized around the home and, probably, make a very good mother to their children.

Jen, on the other hand, had vitality, an energy, which really blew him away, especially while making love. As for what sort of wife she would make, he was uncertain, since he had not known her long enough to predict just what she would become. He knew that he must be patient and not expect too much of her, as they had only been really intimate for a couple of days. But, what was his future with her? He hoped that it would prove more long-term than Helen. It was difficult for Alex to admit, but he still had genuine, warm feelings for Helen, even after her change of heart.

Alex suddenly sat up. "Elsa!" He had forgotten about the dog, which, by now, must be crossing all four legs. The German shepherd had stayed in the living room overnight, as her presence in the bedroom disturbed Jen during their sexual antics.

Alex jumped out of bed and walked quickly to the living room. The dog had been sitting patiently near the doorway, waiting for her master to appear. He checked to see if there was an obvious wetting of the carpet, but, thankfully, found none. "Poor Elsa. Sorry for leaving you this late. Come on." She padded behind him as he entered the kitchen. As soon as the external door was opened, she ran, with some urgency, towards the concrete run. Knowing that he could not be seen, Alex stood, quite naked, in the doorway, undisturbed by the chill, November day. The dog returned and he made a fuss of her, still feeling guilty for leaving Elsa so long.

Within thirty minutes, Jen and Alex were sitting at the table, enjoying their breakfast, or should that, perhaps, have been an early lunch? They looked at the pictures of the two criminals, sent by Adrian. Alex had printed them, making the images much easier to see than on the phone's small screen.

"I'm certain that I've seen this guy, before." She was pointing at Conroy. "But, where?" Alex was, silently urging her to remember.

Jen did have a near-perfect photographic memory for faces. "I know! He was near the restaurant, the night when they tried to shoot me."

"Are you sure? I don't remember him."

Jen looked again at the picture. "I think so. I thought he looked a bit out of place in Mayfair, standing near Scott's when the two of us left the restaurant."

"Really? But I can't understand why?" Then he noticed her troubled expression. "Do you know something you are not telling me?"

Jen blushed slightly but still maintained that she had no idea why she had been targeted. Alex felt uneasy as he realized she was not telling him the whole truth, but decided to let it go, for now.

Jen, then, phoned Adrian to let him know that she had spotted Conroy outside the restaurant, the previous day, but even after ending the call, she still looked uncomfortable, avoiding Alex's gaze.

Changing the subject, Jen said, "I could do with phoning my parents." She checked the time. "My father gets up early, so now is probably a good time to call." Jen scrolled through the list of contacts on her mobile and touched the highlighted number. "Hi, Pop! I'm just calling to say that I am going to be in England for a while longer. No, I don't know just when I'll be back as I've got quite a bit more to do, here." She chatted for a few minutes, asking her father to let his wife know that Jen was missing them both. "Love you, Dad. Bye."

For the rest of the day, the couple just enjoyed each other's company, mainly in the bedroom. Even so, Alex had an uneasy feeling that Jen was concealing some important facts.

It was two days later before they heard from Adrian again. "We found these two", said Adrian with a cautious tone in his voice.

"Great! Where were they hiding?"

"Not really hiding. Their weighted corpses were recovered from the Thames, this morning."

Alex was stunned by Adrian's response. "You're certain it's these same guys?"

"No doubt about it. We have a positive I.D. on both of them and the two had been killed within the last seventy-two hours. I feel that it was probably retribution for failing to kill Jen, even after two attempts."

Alex thought for a moment and, even though he knew the likely answer, asked, "I don't suppose they drowned while having a casual swim?"

Adrian laughed. "No." His voice adopted a more serious tone. "They were dead before they entered the water. Their necks were broken. Initially, it looks as though someone with very powerful hands strangled both of them. And they were, themselves, quite big guys."

Alex shuddered. Even after seeing what the Taliban was capable of in Afghanistan, this obvious retaliatory killing in the heart of London sickened him.

Adrian again emphasized that both Alex and Jen should stay in his apartment, until they felt the threat may have eased.

Alex admitted to Jen, "I don't think the threat is over just because those two killers are dead. Whoever told them to kill you is obviously pissed off that you are still alive."

Jen agreed. "They do seem pretty determined."

Alex held his gaze steady on Jen's face, as he asked, "Do you know why these people are out to kill you?"

Her look was one of frustration. "I...I don't know."

Alex ran his hand through his hair in an unsettled gesture. For the first time since they had met, Alex angrily replied, "Come off it, Jen. You're not a very good liar! I know that you are hiding something and I want to know just what it is."

Her face reddened as she bowed her head in obvious distress. "I'm sorry, for getting you into this awful mess, Alex. Are you certain that you really want to know?"

"Of course I am. We're both in deep shit and, if I am going to die, I need to know why!" The silence emphasized the tension in the room. "How the hell can I help you Jen, if you don't tell me all the fucking facts?" He did feel sorry for her, but decided that he had to be firm. "Come on, love. No more bullshit!" He put his arm around her shoulder as she trembled with emotion.

Could she really tell Alex what she suspected? She knew it would not be fair to keep the truth from him much longer, especially now that they were beginning a much closer relationship. Taking a deep breath, Jen began. "Have you ever heard of the 'Ndrangheta?"

"No, I can honestly say I've never heard of it. What is it, some kind of STD?"

She gave a weak smile. "No, much worse. Like the Sicilian Mafia, it's a family-run crime syndicate based in Calabria, southern Italy. The word comes from the Greek, meaning courage or loyalty and even goes as far back as fourteen twelve to a gambling organization, The Garduna, based in Toledo, Spain. It's been in Italy since the eighteen-fifties, but, in the nineteen-nineties, it became the most powerful criminal organization in Italy, even beating the Sicilian Cosa Nostra, Neapolitan Camorra and Apulian Sacra Corona Unita."

Apart from the Mafia, Alex had never even heard of any of these criminal organisations and, yet, noticed how easily they tripped off Jen's tongue just as if she was a native Italian. He guessed that he was about to learn of the secret part of Jen's life before Moorfields.

"Income from drugs, prostitution, intimidation and money laundering for the 'Ndrangheta amounted to over three per cent of the Italian GDP, making them both immensely wealthy and dangerously powerful. Around two thousand and eight, the Italian Government decided they had to do something to curb the powers of the 'Ndrangheta, which would prove to be very difficult as they had many judges and politicians on their payroll. America was asked to assist in this task, called 'Operation Crrimine', and, since I had majored both in I.T. and Italian at High school followed by Internet studies at Stamford Research Institute, I was part of the team assigned to the job."

This was certainly a new side to Jen. Intrigued, Alex asked, "So, exactly how did you assist?"

Jen looked extremely anxious and played nervously with her hair. "Working for the CIA, I was on a team monitoring phone calls and emails between members of the families within the 'Ndrangheta."

Alex's face indicated great surprise at Jen's admission. "I thought it was illegal to monitor phones and emails."

Jen laughed, although a little nervously. "Most Governments monitor electronic traffic. They just don't talk much about it." Seeing the disbelief on Alex's face, she added, "The British Government intercepts far more electronic communications than any other Government. GCHQ is running an eavesdropping operation called 'Tempora' and it is proving very successful in combating terrorism." As an afterthought, she added, "The N.S.A. even monitors the mobiles of most European leaders, but keep that under your hat!"

Alex supposed that he should have known these facts, but was still surprised by her revelation about his own country and America's security agencies. "So, did your intercepts prove useful?"

She smiled, triumphantly. Oh, yes, the operation was very successful and, by July, last year, over three hundred 'Ndrangheta members were arrested."

"Good! So why is somebody within this Italian organization still trying to kill you?"

To his surprise, Jen continued to play, nervously, with her hair, which, for her, seemed to be completely out of character. "Unfortunately, they had a mole in the CIA who discovered the people involved. They were out for revenge."

Alex now understood and asked, with some trepidation, "Have any CIA staff been injured or killed because of the mole?"

An expression of great sadness filled Jen's face. Quietly, she replied, "Jason Barriman was my partner in the CIA, but, more than that, we were also in a close relationship." She had been uncertain about revealing her past lovers, but wanted to be absolutely honest with Alex. She owed him that much.

Surprised and uncertain that he really wanted to hear the answer, Alex asked, "What happened to him?"

Large tears began to flow slowly down Jen's cheeks. "He received a call, saying that his mother was ill, so he took leave to visit his parents in Fairfield, just over fifty miles away. It was a trap." She paused, finding it difficult to continue.

Alex put a comforting arm around her shoulder. "I'm sorry, Jen. You don't need to tell me any more."

"I must. You need to know just how ruthless members of the 'Ndrangheta are. When he did not contact me within a day, I informed my Section Head and a team was sent to Fairfield. I insisted on going with them, even though my leader did not want me there." She paused to take a deep breath. "We found Jason and his parents had been brutally executed. Their bodies were tied to dining chairs around the table." Jen's voice was very shaky and almost a whisper. "Their heads had been hacked off and placed on dinner plates in front of each body. The table had been set with knives and forks, as though they were about to eat their own heads. But, all the blood and the look of absolute horror in their eyes, was enough to break me and I had to be dragged out, screaming. It was the worst thing I have ever seen and it still, to this day, gives me nightmares."

She burst into tears and clung on to Alex. He now realized just what she had been through and sympathised. "I'm so sorry, Jen."

Still sobbing, she wiped her eyes with a tissue. "I had a break-down, after that. The Government gave me and my family protection and, after just over three months, I moved to the Augmented Reality Unit within the CIA, hopefully in a less-conspicuous position. I hoped that the 'Ndrangheta would forget about me, but it seems that there is a cell, even here in England and they are determined to kill me. Although most of the Italian family was arrested, their rackets continue in over thirty countries and their income amounts to billions of dollars."

Alex had a sudden thought. "Does Adrian know about your background?"

She shook her head. "He doesn't know about my involvement with the 'Ndrangheta. That information was highly classified and all he knows is my involvement in Augmented Reality at the CIA. I think Brigadier General Marshall probably knows."

Alex saw Jen in a completely new light and was, now, not surprised by her initial rejection. She was probably trying to protect him from a terrible fate similar to Jason's. The dreadful scene Jen had described was, now, firmly imprinted into Alex's own brain and it was unlikely that he would ever forget it.

Whether she liked it or not, he was now deeply involved and in equal danger of losing his own life. "I think we need to tell Adrian, so that he knows exactly what we are dealing with. My feeling is that we are both in deep shit!"

CHAPTER NINETEEN :

When Adrian heard of Jen's past, he then understood just why she was being targeted. "These criminals are probably looking for Jen at the airports, so I think she had better stay here in the U.K., for now. I don't want either of you to come here, since everybody knows exactly where MI6 is and these guys probably have look-outs for her."

Alex could understand the serious situation they were in, but countered, "Yes, but we can't stay hidden for ever. I'd much sooner do something to find them and neutralize the threat."

Adrian had a hint of impatience in his voice. "Alex, this is not Afghanistan. The 'Ndrangheta are even more difficult to locate than the Taliban. You don't even know where to start looking."

"We've fucking well got to do something!" Alex felt so impotent and just wanted somewhere to start.

"Okay." Adrian was thinking fast, anxious to help these two whose lives were, now, in extreme danger. "First, you two need different identities. I'll give you an address where this can be done, without the need to come here."

"Okay. We will need as much information about the 'Ndrangheta as possible. More than we could find just on the internet." Alex was now thinking like a soldier once again.

"That's no problem. With Christin's assistance, I can get all the data we need and send you files on them which will tell you everything there is to know, except their location."

"Great!" Alex had a sudden thought. "What about Elsa? She identifies me better than any I.D."

"That's true. It's up to you, really. If you wish, I can ask Kate to take her back for a few weeks. How would you feel about that?"

What Adrian had said made good sense, but he would feel guilty about sending her back. "Let me think about that." He looked down at Elsa. As usual, she seemed attentive and, since he had mentioned her name, apparently, listening to every word of his conversation. He knew that it would be unfair on the dog and decided that, somehow, they were going to have to work with her even through this present danger. Alex did know that, when necessary, he could leave Elsa in the apartment, without any problem.

The following day, Alex and Jen travelled, by taxi, to the address Adrian had given them. Alex had decided that it may make life easier if he went to this place as a sighted person.

Strangely, the place in Adrian's directions appeared to be a small, greeting card shop, but, when they asked for Pauline, as instructed, the person behind the counter escorted them into a back room.

Pauline was a small, dark-haired, middle-aged woman who welcomed them enthusiastically. "So pleased to meet you both." As she spoke, she was already studying them, assessing how she could give them plausible, new identities.

Her colleague, Rich, was given the task of assisting Alex with his new profile, while she would, herself, be looking after Jen.

"We'll leave the girls in here and use the spare room. Rich seemed friendly, but very effeminate. Alex could not stand men who shortened "Richard" to "Rich". It was almost a statement of pretentiousness. Shrugging off this uncomfortable feeling, Alex followed this strange tall guy with spiky blonde, hair into a separate room.

"Right! Let's have a look at you." It was an uncomfortable feeling, being studied by Rich. "You have some variations in your skin colour on your face and neck. Are they from burns?"

Alex longed for the day when the damage received from the explosion would not be noticed, but had to accept that there were still tonal differences. "Yes, burns."

"It's not a problem. I can provide you with a natural-looking skin tone which would cover the marks. A black hair colour would also make a big difference. I could colour your eye-brows as well and with a small moustache, your appearance would be completely different."

Alex was not particularly thrilled at the thought of changing his hair colour, but accepted that the 'Ndrangheta already knew what he looked like. In truth, he was a sitting target for any assassin.

His mid-brown hair had grown quite a bit since his operation and probably could do with thinning and re-shaping, hopefully disguising his appearance to some extent.

He allowed Rich to add colour to his hair, which took about twenty minutes to permeate throughout his thick hair. This was followed by a shampoo and rinse and, finally, a haircut. Rich stood back and looked at Alex, in a way that one may look at a famous work of art in some national museum. "I think you need to move away from the military-style cut. Let your hair grow longer and thicker. You would be surprised at what a change it would make."

By the time Rich had finished, Alex was amazed at the difference his new hair style and skin make-up had changed his appearance. As a finishing touch, Rich opened several small drawers inside a cabinet, searching until, triumphantly, he produced a small, neat false moustache. It was, apparently, the same, new colour as his hair. He held it in place on Alex's face. "What do you think?"

"To be quite honest, Rich, I don't like moustaches or beards. I think I'll take the risk of not using it."

Rich looked a little hurt. "Suit yourself. My brief is to change your appearance as much as possible, but it's your call."

Alex stood his ground. "How else can I change my appearance?" As he looked at Rich, he realised that he had, initially, thought this strange man was in his thirties, but now felt that he was more likely to be in his fifties. He felt certain that his face had undergone quite extensive plastic surgery in an attempt to make him look younger. Unfortunately, it had not worked.

"Your clothes. You give an impression of a neat, tidy guy. You need to look a little more relaxed. Perhaps, by wearing more casual, less close-fitting clothes." Rich disappeared behind a curtain and, after a few minutes of mild cursing, he reappeared holding a couple of hangers of jackets and trousers. Rich had a triumphant look on his face. "Yes! This is what I was looking for." He pulled back another curtain and switched on the light in the changing cubicle. "Try these on and see what you think."

Alex was relieved that he did not need to strip off in front of this strange guy and took the clothes into the cubicle. When he looked at himself in the mirror, he had to admit that his change of hair style and colour, together with the more casual clothes had managed to make him look completely different. He tried on both sets of jackets and trousers and, after a few minutes, chose one and stepped out of the cubicle. "What do you think?"

Rich had been relaxing in one of the chairs reading a P. D. James paperback and quickly stood up to inspect Alex's new persona. Oh, fantastic, darling! Even your own mother wouldn't recognize you."

Alex cringed at the guy's effeminate choice of expression, scowled a little, but tried to ignore it. "Yes, I think this will do fine."

"Right! Now we need to take your photo for your new I.D.'s. I suggest that you either wear a pair of ordinary spectacles instead of the dark glasses or, preferably, no glasses at all."

Alex had a sudden thought. "My eyes! I need to change the colour." "I could do with having a quick word with Jen. Is she ready?"

"We'll soon find out." Rich went to the adjoining door, knocked and opened it slightly. "Alex would like a word with you, Jen, if you are ready."

She was. Alex couldn't help but be amazed by the change in Jen's appearance. She was now a convincing brunette, with long, stylish hair. Like Alex, she had lost the formal, efficient look and was now far more casual. For a few seconds, they stared at each other, almost in disbelief, and, then, burst out laughing.

"Do you mind if Jen and I talk in private, Rich?"

"Not, at all. You two stay in here and I'll go and annoy Pauline."

"This may not have been far from the truth", thought Alex.

He quickly explained how he needed to change the colour of his eyes. "Can I wear contact lenses with my eyes?"

A smile lit her face. "No need. Pass me your watch, Alex."

He did as instructed and Jen touched the display several times. Satisfied that she had entered the correct option on the watch, she asked "What colour would you like your eyes to be?"

"You can change my colour as easy as that?" He was surprised and impressed at yet another function within his prosthetic eyes which he had never even considered. "Perhaps a dark shade of brown or black?"

"No problem. Look in the mirror while I go through the palette."

AS he watched, she stepped through the many shades of brown. It was fascinating as she stepped slowly, waiting for Alex's response.

"Can you go back a couple of steps, Jen?" She did as requested. "Stop! No, I think a darker shade may be better. Take it slowly and move darker again, please. Yes! That's the one."

"Right, that's set, now. It's very easy to switch between the original blue iris and your new choice of dark brown."

Alex was impressed by this use of technology. "You are truly amazing, Jen! To be able to program the eye colour so easily is a touch of genius."

"It's mainly down to Professor Goldman. My input is purely the interface electronics and software."

Alex replaced his watch, checked his image for one last time in the mirror and the two walked into the other room, where Pauline and Rich were relaxing, deep in conversation.

Rich looked up as they entered and, immediately, noticed Alex's change of eye colour. "Ten minutes ago, you had blue eyes and, now, they're very dark brown. How on earth did you do that?"

Alex cursed to himself and wished he had not been so observant. Jen came to the rescue. "I had some coloured contact lenses which suited Alex's new hair colour."

Neither of them knew if Rich believed this explanation, but they had to maintain secrecy about his artificial eyes.

Pauline interrupted. "Right! Let's get your new I.D.'s sorted." It took about forty minutes after having their photographs taken, before their new I.D. cards and passports were ready.

"Alex looked at Jen's new passport. Stephen Bancroft and Charlotte Ferguson. Where do you get these names from?"

Pauline hesitated a little and then decided that it would not hurt to let them know. "They were legitimate names, but both were from individuals who died in childhood."

This came as no surprise as both had heard of this method being used by the Secret Service.

"I think we should go back separately, as we are less likely to be recognized, even with our new appearances."

Jen agreed and left Pauline and Rich about ten minutes after Alex.

CHAPTER TWENTY :
DECEMBER, 2011

It was a sumptuously decorated room. Several tan-coloured leather chairs and sofas were arranged, carefully around the room. The lighting was subdued, yet the many elaborate, obviously expensive paintings which adorned the walls were easily visible, each with their own dedicated illumination. The floor was a rich, mahogany timber and a large hand-woven rug filled the space between the furniture.

Gianni looked quite relaxed, sitting in one of the large chairs. He had helped himself to a measure of single malt whisky from the well-stocked cocktail bar and sipped at his drink.

"No sign of the American woman, but we are still looking. It was sheer luck when she was spotted by Agostino in Woolpit at the Cannabis farm we had to abandon. We lost track of her two years ago when she and Jason Barriman meddled in our operation."

The man he was talking to, made no comment, but listened, intently, to what he had to say.

Gianni took another sip of Whisky and continued, "Although we would really like to eliminate Miss Sherlock,

I have to balance this against possible leaks about our organization, here in the U.K. I must admit that I don't want to bring in any more outside agents which may lead back to us."

The other man simply nodded in agreement.

Gianni continued, used to this strange, one-way method of communicating with his father, the Capo Crimin. It was not always a one-sided conversation, but the older man could be very moody, probably as a result of his confinement, and, on many occasions, just resorted to a slight nod of the head. Gianni knew better than to expect more of this very experienced and battle-worn leader of his family. The old man had a gold ring with a large, inset diamond on one of his fingers, signifying that he was an "Illumanati", which denoted that he was a leader rather than one of the henchmen. "For now, I feel that it is best to leave her alone and concentrate on our core businesses. We have done quite well, considering that the U.K. operation has only been going for a couple of years, but there is always room for improvement."

Again, a brief nod of the head assured Gianni that his judgment was accepted. This was enough for him and, after downing the last of his whisky, he returned to his own quarters.

CHAPTER TWENTY-ONE :

DECEMBER, 2011

Elsa had no difficulty in recognizing the changed Alex. As usual, she nearly knocked him off his feet, greeting him with many licks, her tail wagging excitedly. "I can't send her back to the training centre", Alex thought. He knew that it would not be fair on his canine friend to abandon her, even for just a short time.

Jen arrived a few minutes later and was similarly greeted by Elsa, who was now getting used to her master's new friend. All were, by now, hungry. Fortunately, Alex was well prepared and had plenty of food stored in freezer, fridge and cupboards. The couple decided on pork steaks with potato wedges and vegetables to satisfy their appetites. Elsa was equally hungry, but had to settle for her usual dog biscuits and water. The way she devoured the contents of her dish was enough to indicate, to anyone, that she enjoyed her regular diet.

During their meal, Alex was thinking of all the difficulties they were faced with now they had new identities and appearances. "I can't go to the supermarket, now that I've changed my appearance. It looks as if we will have to use home deliveries for our shopping, from now on."

Jen and Alex looked at each other with some amusement, their appearances now completely different, particularly Jen with her long, brunette wig. "You do look very different, Jen."

She smiled, coyly. "I was amazed what a difference a change of hair style and colour could make. How about you?"

"I just hope that none of my family and friends turns up, unexpected. I'm not sure how I could explain the change, especially the eye colour."

Jen had a sudden thought. "I didn't bring many clothes with me as I thought I would only be here for a few days. I could do with buying some spare clothes."

"That shouldn't be a problem, unless you want me to go out and buy them for you."

"Would you like to choose some new underwear for me, sweetheart?" Jen had a mischievous look in her eyes as she said this.

"Only if you want me to get the wrong size for you. I'd probably get them far too small."

She laughed. "I can imagine that you would enjoy yourself in the bra and panties section at Victoria secret in New Bond Street, but there is a simpler way. We just order online for a home delivery."

Alex felt relieved and a little excited by the thought of choosing Jen's underwear. "Good idea. Do you want to go on the website, now?"

"Might as well." For the next hour, the two of them looked through the numerous choices of lingerie on the web site, both of them feeling quite aroused by the experience. At last, they had chosen what to buy and clicked on the shopping basket ready to finalise their order.

It was then that they realized that their credit cards were still in their real names, yet the couple now had new identities. After all the time they had spent on the web site, they had to exit without placing the order.

"Never mind", said Jen, disappointed. "I'll have to manage with what I have, for now."

Alex realized that he would also need a replacement credit card in the name of his new identity, Stephen Bancroft. He would have to think it out carefully, withdrawing cash from his old account and depositing it in the newly-opened account, to prevent a paper trail leading back to him.

When Alex checked his emails, he found a message from Adrian. There was a huge attachment, which, hopefully, would give the couple all they needed to know about the 'Ndrangheta. Alex read through the document, re-reading it several times to absorb the vast amount of information. Jen had been sent the same files to her mobile phone and, like Alex, was studying the contents thoroughly.

By the time they went to bed in the early hours of the next morning, their heads were buzzing from the wealth of information about the Italian mob. What remained of the 'Ndrangheta after the police raid in two thousand and ten, had, seemingly, disappeared. However, the racketeering, money laundering and drug smuggling continued unabated. They were, obviously, still operating, but from where?

Too tired to read any more, both Alex and Jen agreed that they should try and get some rest. Alex was even too sleepy to shower and, within minutes, was in bed, next to, yet not cuddling up to Jen and then, nothing. It was like a mutual 'crash-out", where lights turned out immediately, only to be completely immersed in a deep, bottomless slumber.

Then there was light! Alex thought he had woken up, but, when he looked around him, he was certainly not in his bed, not even in his apartment. The space seemed very confined, the light dim and the floor, walls, even the ceiling appeared to be made of metal. He could almost feel the coldness of the metal on his bare feet as he stood, naked, in one corner of this cramped room. Stacks of strong, plastic bags were arranged along one wall leaving the narrowest of passages.

Alex jumped with surprise as a man entered the room. He felt certain that he had been seen, but when the man walked over his foot without any sense of pain, he realised that, like a ghost, he could not be seen.

The man was checking the packages, looking at labels and counting. He shouted something incomprehensible to someone else. Although he could not tell what had been said, it sounded unmistakably Italian.

A reply came back. There was some urgency in his voice, perhaps even a hint of excitement.

Picking up courage, Alex walked straight through the man and into the other room. This was a control room of some sort and, after seeing all the instruments, dials and controls, he realised that he was inside some kind of submarine.

The man in this control room was studying several screens and instruments, making small movements of the control levers.

Alex noticed that most of the monitors displayed images around the submarine, but the view through the curved observation window was spectacular, Alex finding it difficult to look elsewhere.

The water appeared to be fairly dark and murky, suggesting that the craft was at considerable depth.

Many colourful types of marine life seemed to glide, effortlessly, past the craft

The guy looked very relaxed as he used the fingertip controls to guide this mini-submarine. There were just two, leather, multi-position seats and both looked as though they could double as very comfortable beds. The guy who had been checking the bags returned and took his seat. Again, some incomprehensible conversation. They both laughed, Alex wondering what the joke was. Hopefully, not his naked torso. If only Jen was in this "dream" with him, she could have translated. A few minutes passed and the helmsman, seemed to be making even more delicate movements of his controls. Another glance at the window showed Alex that, where initially they seemed to be in open water, they now appeared to be in a narrow passage where precise control of the craft was essential.

Again, a few minutes passed and, to Alex's surprise, the view outside indicated that the submarine had broken through the surface of the water. Within a few minutes, the craft had docked and a hatch automatically opened, allowing the escape of the pressurised air within the submarine.

Shouts were exchanged with at least one other person at the dockside. Eager to see what lay beyond, Alex ventured through the hatch, although he felt certain that he could just have easily passed through the hull of the submarine. It was very weird trying to move. Not like walking. More like gliding and he could pass easily from one area to another and, best of all, he was completely unseen.

Alex was now on the dockside, watching the men unload the many bags of what must have been millions of pounds worth of cocaine.

Looking around the dockside, he realised that it was underground. This was certainly a highly organised method of smuggling drugs and, after what Alex had been reading before bed, must have been organised by the immensely wealthy 'Ndrangheta. The submarine itself must have cost millions, the whole operation perhaps even tens of millions. This was certainly a wealthy organisation.

There were four men in total. All were, now, on the dockside and the submarine had been tethered to bollards. Nearby, there was a floating hull of what looked like a canal narrow boat. The superstructure was suspended at least ten feet above the hull.

All four men were now busy, transferring the many bags of drugs from the submarine to the floating hull. They had obviously done this many times as they precisely arranged the bags within contoured pockets around the base of the hull. At last, every bag was in place. One of the men seemed to be in charge and closely inspected the final placement.

Satisfied that everything was correct, he controlled an electric winch to lower the superstructure back into position. Once done, all four men moved around the craft, firmly securing the superstructure to the hull.

"Incredibly ingenious", thought Alex. To outward appearances, it was just another canal boat, the superstructure even appearing to be old and weather-worn.

The four Italians seemed cheerful, exchanging what, to Alex, appeared to be pleasantries. The original two returned to the submarine, while the others loosened the moorings. Alex could not decide whether to return to the submarine or stay with the narrow boat. Which would provide more useful information? In the event, he did not have the choice as he seemed to be suddenly flying through a maelstrom of incredibly powerful wind. He shut his eyes and, when he finally opened them again, he was in his bed. Jen was sound asleep, her gentle breathing being the only noise. Had this been a vivid dream or had he really witnessed the criminal activities of the 'Ndrangheta?

He checked the time. It was three-thirty and Alex realised how incredibly tired he felt. It seemed only seconds before he was asleep, yet again and, this time, there were no dreams.

CHAPTER TWENTY-TWO :

When Alex told Jen, over breakfast that morning, of his strange dream-like experience, her first thought was that it must have been his vivid imagination. Alex remembered every detail and went over it many times in his mind.

"After reading all that information, last night, it's not surprising that you would dream about it. Even the submarine! Don't you remember how the authorities found a 'narcosa' submarine in Colombia? That could have triggered your imagination."

Alex had to admit that he had read that part of the report, but he still insisted that it was definitely no dream. "Perhaps it was a 'remote viewing' like Uri Geller? Even both the Americans and the Russians accept such possibilities."

Jen seemed to accept this as a possible explanation, but countered, "Those 'viewings' were never as detailed as you described. If it is really true, then you are unique."

"Ever since losing my eyesight, I have, somehow, been far more perceptive. I don't know why, but it could prove extremely useful to the Intelligence Services."

"It could also make you a perfect sitting target for terrorist assassination!" was her blunt reply. She looked nervous and genuinely worried for this man who, now, meant everything to her. She did not wish to find his headless corpse, one day, as she had with her previous partner.

"You said that they spoke Italian. Can you remember any words? Anything at all?"

Alex tried his best to recall anything useful, but shook his head. I could only pick out a few, occasional words, but without the context of the whole conversation, they were meaningless. They spoke very fast."

After breakfast, Alex phoned Adrian. He was even more pessimistic than Jen and had never been convinced about remote viewing. "Was there anything in this dream to locate this underground harbour?"

Alex had been thinking about this ever since his strange experience and wished there had been something to locate it. The narrow boat appeared typical of many he had seen in the United Kingdom, but, further than that, he had to admit that he had no idea where it could have been.

"What colour was the main superstructure?"

Alex pondered on this question. "The lighting was not very strong, but I would guess that it was a greyish blue."

"That should narrow it down a bit", said Adrian, sarcastically.

"Listen, Adrian, I'm sorry I don't have a fucking recording to play back to you, but I still believe it is an actual viewing of their activities."

Adrian backed down a little. "Sorry, Alex. I'm just used to dealing with facts, not visions seen during sleep. We don't even know if what you saw was in real time or a past event." Alex had not considered this possibility. "Apart from the two corpses in the Thames, we have precisely nothing. Our intelligence concluded that there was insufficient evidence to indicate the existence of a cell in the U.K."

"Well, at least we know that the assumption was incorrect", countered Alex.

"Okay. But next time you have a vision, leave the fucking battery in your watch and then we might even manage to monitor your 'vision' and do something useful about it."

Alex cursed himself for not thinking about this. Would it have worked? Could his visual cortex actually have transmitted the images from his 'viewing'? He blushed slightly as he thought of the reason why they had removed the battery. "Okay, I'll leave it in, tonight."

Adrian sounded cool. "Okay, keep in touch and don't do anything stupid."

Jen, only hearing one side of the conversation, still knew that it had not been a particularly good communication. She put her arms around Alex and pulled him close, kissing him softly on the lips. "Don't look so worried, Darling. Adrian can, on occasions, be short-tempered and a bit of an arse-hole, but he will get over it."

"He probably will, but I still feel as though I let him down. I've got to be more observant, but I'm still not letting Adrian snoop on our sexual activities."

"Perhaps he feels jealous of you." Again, she smiled coyly, an idea obviously forming in her mind. "Don't put the battery back in your watch, yet. We can make love in the shower together."

"Mmmm, that sounds like a very good idea."

"I must modify the software to add a 'switch-off snoopers' function." The two started, hurriedly, undressing each other, dropping their clothes in small bundles all the way to the shower.

They had just stepped inside the cubicle, when Alex's mobile rang. "Go play with yourself, Adrian! This is for my eyes only."

"That's almost a good title for a film", joked Jen. Alex turned on the powerful side jets. The water temperature was warm, yet not too hot. They held each other while moving around to allow the fine water jets to play on their buttocks, backs, breasts and genitals. Jen gently pushed Alex so that he was sitting on the cubicle seat, his strong erection being assisted by Jen's caressing hands. She straddled him, using the shower handrail to give her some leverage. She rode him vigorously, water jets still spraying the couple's torsos and splashing water in all directions.

It did not take long to reach a climax and their bodies writhed in pleasurable union. Jen dismounted and then began to soap both their bodies with shower gel. A final rinse with each using the hand-jet on the other made it a superb, exhilarating experience. The water was turned off and they stepped out of the cubicle.

As they dried, Alex noticed how happy Jen looked, even though her life was in extreme danger.

After drying-off and pulling on bath robes, they, once again, read through the 'Ndrangheta reports. A new one had been sent early that morning to add to the already extensive folders. "No wonder Adrian was grumpy. He sent this new folder at seven thirty-two, this morning."

"Have you not noticed that he answers our calls whether they are early morning or late evening? All work and no play make Adrian a dull boy."

Alex laughed at Jen's observation. "I take it that he isn't married?"

"Adrian? You're joking! I can't imagine any woman who would put up with him." When Alex looked surprised, she continued, "Don't get me wrong. Technically, he's brilliant and one of the sharpest minds in British Intelligence, but, socially, he's totally inept and still feels that women are a completely different race."

Jokingly, Alex raised his eyebrows and replied, "You mean they're not?" He saw the sudden flash of revenge in her eyes and quickly jumped up to, playfully, get out of her way.

She chased him around the apartment, Elsa looking, with some puzzlement, at this crazy couples' antics. "I'll get you, Alex McCloud!"

They were both just wearing bath robes and, as Jen reached him, she grabbed him by the testicles, squeezing gently.

"Okay, okay! I take it back!" Alex laughed.

Triumphantly, she exclaimed, "You see? It's not the man with his finger on the button who rules the world. It's the woman holding the balls of the man with his finger on the button!"

"Accepted!" The couple collapsed into laughter and then began, again, to kiss with increasing passion. Dropping their bathrobes on the floor, they returned to the bedroom, where, once again, they made wild, exciting love.

Sleep came very quickly after reaching their climax. The young lovers were holding each other close, as Alex's sleep turned, once again, into, what seemed to be, another dimension. He was on the narrow boat. Two of the men from his previous vision were sitting towards the rear of the craft. One of them was steering and the steady, 'chug chug' of the engine made it seem like a relaxing, comforting pastime. The man who was not in control of the boat was relaxing, looking very comfortable and reading a book. Nobody would imagine that millions of pounds of drugs were secreted in the bowels of this seemingly-innocent method of transport.

Alex moved as near to the men as he could and studied them closely. The one who was reading was, perhaps, in his early thirties, had thick, black hair. He was of medium build and his casual tee-shirt revealed strong, muscular arms. Interestingly, the book he was reading was Dan brown's 'Deception Point'. "A good book and a very apt title", thought Alex. "It's not one of Dan Brown's most recent books, so that does not help with a timeline."

The other man seemed to be slightly older, perhaps in his late thirties. There was a physical resemblance, indicating that they were, probably, brothers.

Although the two were silent, Alex could hear a man's disembodied voice. It sounded familiar. Then he had it! The voice was from a portable radio and it was Ken Bruce on Radio Two. 'Pop-master Quiz' was almost finished and a woman had just beaten her male challenger with a score of thirty-three points to his fifteen.

"And now, for a beautiful, BBC Radio Two DAB radio, I want you to give me, within ten seconds, Three hit singles by," There was an obligatory pause as the countdown timer started. "Glen Campbell!"

As the countdown advanced , the woman contestant said, "Wichita Linesman, Rhinestone Cowboy and..." She paused, struggling to think of a third. Just before the pips sounded, she, quickly, added, "By the time I get to Phoenix!"

"Yes! You just managed it!" Ken Bruce sounded genuinely excited and pleased for the lucky contestant and the recorded applause ended the item. As the woman started to name her friends and relatives, Alex pondered on what he had just heard. "So it is about a quarter to eleven, but on which date? I'm certain I can find that out."

Next, Alex began to look at the countryside they were passing through. It yielded no obvious clues, other than that the land was fairly flat. Few craft sailed on this stretch of water. He peered into the distance and could see another boat, but it may have been travelling in the same direction. "Direction!" Alex had nearly forgotten the basic principle in observation. "Locate the course of the canal by observing shadows." He looked at the two men, trying to observe which way their shadows were falling. Before he could determine anything useful, a large, grey cloud over-shadowed the craft. "Damn! Come on, sunshine!" He was willing the sun to re-appear and, then, it did.

From the shadows cast by the men and the time of the day, the boat was heading in a slightly west of north direction. The guy who was reading had a swig from a bottle of Coke and offered it to the other man. He took the bottle, had a large gulp, belched, noisily, and handed it back, saying something in Italian.

Alex jumped in surprise when a loud "Honk" sounded. It was from another canal boat coming in the opposite direction. A colourful craft which looked as though it could have been one used by a family on holiday.

This was reinforced by the appearance of two small children waving at them. A man and, presumably, his wife were in the rear, controlling the craft. This man shouted in the direction of the Italians. "Be careful at your next lock.

The turnscrews are extremely tight and the gates are a bit worn!"

To Alex's amazement, the older Italian shouted back, in what seemed to be, a perfect East End accent, "Thanks a lot, mate. We'll look out for that." He waved back at the children, who were, now, disappearing from view.

Before the entire craft was out of sight, Alex realised that a clue may lie in this boat. As well as being highly decorated, there was, on the side of the superstructure, a large picture of the head of a white cat with a red bow. Underneath the picture were the words, "Hello Kitty".

Even as he looked at the quickly-disappearing craft, the image began to break up into tiny fragments and, then, there was nothing but blackness.

As soon as Alex awoke, he climbed out of bed, careful not to disturb Jen, who looked serenely peaceful. Pulling on his clothes, he went into the living room and switched on the computer. "Damn! Why is it that it seems to take longer to start up, when you are in a hurry?" Eventually, the familiar Windows 7 desktop appeared. He clicked on "Internet" and opened the BBC Radio Two website. Jeremy Vine's programme was now playing. He looked at his watch. It was one-fifteen and he cursed himself for not waking sooner.

Anxiously, he selected the "Listen Again" option for the Ken Bruce show.

He had to admit that he was anxious about the results and moved the timer to ten-forty. As he listened, he began to smile as the same contestants were playing, as in his 'vision'. By the time the winner had finished the "three in ten" item, there was no doubt in his mind. What he had seen in his vision was definitely in real time.

Next, he had to identify the location. He searched for British canals and, not surprisingly, found far more than he had dared to imagine. Even when he looked at photographs of many canal routes, there was a great deal of similarity in them. Of course, the land had to be fairly flat for canal waterways to work.

Alex realised that he had wasted enough time and phoned Adrian.

His contact, always to the point, reminded Alex that his watch was still not transmitting.

"Damn! Sorry, Adrian, but I've had another vision.

"Another? During the daytime? What is it you don't want me to see, Alex?" As on the previous occasion, he sounded annoyed. Before Alex had time to think of an excuse, Adrian remarked, "I take it you are screwing the delightful Major Sherlock and you don't wish to share the experience?"

"Something like that", mumbled an embarrassed Alex. "God! Why did it have to be so fucking obvious?" he thought to himself. "Let me tell you about this vision. It's definitely in real time and I have an identification of another canal boat." He described the whole scene in great detail to the attentive Adrian.

"If we are quick enough, we may find this boat with the kitten on the side, but all it will give is a general direction. Do you know how many canals there are in the U.K.?"

"I know that it's a long shot, but it's all we have."

"Okay! Leave it with me."

As Alex ended his call, he noticed that Jen had wandered in from the bedroom. Still quite naked and looking superb, she sat next to Alex. He recounted the vision to her and saw the glimmer of hope in her eyes. Or could it have been, maybe, lust for his body, yet again?

When he explained that his visions were definitely in real time, Jen, with a smile, said, "It's a pity these visions are not ahead of time. Just imagine how you could make a fortune by knowing the lottery numbers in advance!"

Alex laughed, more out of resignation than amusement. "I never thought of that, but I've never been lucky, financially. I gave up doing the lottery ages ago as I never won a thing! Not even a measly ten pounds."

CHAPTER TWENTY-THREE :

Franco was not complacent about the dangers of moving such a huge quantity of drugs as was stowed in the hull of his narrow craft. His younger brother, Georgio, was a little too relaxed and assumed that they were smarter than the intelligence services seeking out contraband drugs. "That's how mistakes are made", he thought. They were making good progress and had been cruising along the waterways for about thirteen hours. It would take about another couple of days to reach their eventual unloading point, after which he could, finally, relax.

His phone began to play the start of "Popeye the sailor man", a ring-tone that he had felt, with a certain amount of amusement, was fitting to his role. "Yes?"

He listened, carefully, to the coded message and frowned in obvious annoyance. No response was necessary. He ended the call and, thoughtfully, replaced the phone in his pocket.

Georgio was asleep. This stretch of canal had no locks and, after taking the helm for three hours, he had decided to rest. "Wake up, Georgio!" He shook his brother in an attempt to disturb him.

The younger man woke with a start. The tone in Franco's voice told him that something was wrong. "What is it?"

"There's a change of plan. We are unloading our cargo earlier than originally intended."

Rubbing the sleep from his eyes, Georgio asked, "Why?"

"A message from headquarters said that there's a change in the plan. They want to get this load distributed quicker than originally planned, so we have to do the change at the earlier transfer point."

"Shit! You know that we won't get as good a price, if we unload early."

"It won't make any difference. We will just have to drive the cargo a bit further than usual, but all the stuff will still get to the centre of the city a day earlier."

"Good! That's okay, then.", Georgio conceded.

"And it's a damn site more comfortable in the van than in this tub", Franco added, feeling quite un-enthusiastic about these long, boring journeys. "See how much further it is to our new transfer point."

Obediently, Georgio pulled out a map from a waterproof pocket at the rear of the boat. He used a scale to calculate the distance and pronounced "About fifteen miles, perhaps another three hours or so. At least it will save us from going through over sixty locks."

Both men found the routine of changing level through the use of locks quite tiresome and wondered why canal cruising for leisure was so popular in the U.K. "Good." Thoughtfully, he said, "Let's see if we can do it less than that. It may make all the difference." He pushed the throttle lever fully forward, the "chug, chug" becoming a little more urgent and intense in its tone.

The noise of the engine drowned out the music from the portable radio, but neither Georgio nor Franco was concerned as they concentrated on their mission.

CHAPTER TWENTY-FOUR :

When Alex had described his vision, Adrian, for now, decided to believe there may be some possible truth in what Alex had said. He contacted the BBC and asked for an alert to be announced. Now, he was about to hear the result of his call.

Harvey Cook, the newsreader on Radio Two, which had the U.K.'s largest listening audience, began his report. "Police are asking the owners of a canal narrow boat, with a picture of a kitten on the side and the words, 'hello Kitty' to contact them. It is believed that they may have important information of interest to the police. It is understood that there is a man, woman and two children on this boat and they are asked to contact the police, urgently, on the following number."

It was five-twenty and the announcement had interrupted Simon Mayo's evening programme. Simon made some comedic comment about having a picture of a kitten on the side of a boat, but Adrian had already stopped listening.

He was now waiting for a response and just hoped there would not be too many hoax calls.

As expected, there were some cranks. Usually lonely people who sought any excuse to speak to a police officer. He smiled to himself when a woman told him that she had a beautiful 'pussy' on her boat and couldn't wait to show it to an officer. "Sad, lonely cow! She probably doesn't even have a boat or a cat", he mused.

After a few, fruitless calls, one came through which attracted his attention. "My narrow boat has a picture of a kitten on the side and the words, 'hello Kitty' underneath it."

"Okay?" So far, what the guy had said was what had been announced on the radio item, but, somehow, he felt this may be more promising. "Can I have your name, sir?"

"Sure, it's Paul Rogerson." The man sounded a little nervous and uncertain why his boat was of such interest.

"Were you on a canal waterway at about ten-forty five, this morning?"

"Yes, definitely. We were cruising most of the morning until we stopped at a hotel for lunch."

"Isn't it a bit cold for canal cruising in December?" The idea of freezing on Britain's canals certainly did not appeal to Adrian.

"It can be a bit cold, but there's not as much traffic at this time of the year. We don't sail as much, but enjoy the occasional cruise on the canals."

"Do you recall speaking to a couple of men on another boat, about that time?"

The man had to think about this and then exclaimed, "Oh, yes. We were going in the opposite direction and warned them about a particularly difficult lock which they would come across about ten minutes later."

"This is definitely the one", thought Adrian. "Perhaps Alex really does possess some inexplicable viewing power, after all"

He had paused too long and the man thought he had been cut off. "Hello?"

"Oh, sorry, Mr. Rogerson. I was just checking some of our facts", he lied. "Now this is very important. Can you recall just where this encounter was? And, where do you think the other boat might have been heading?"

"Let me think. It would probably have been somewhere well north of Brentford, closer to Braunston. The Grand Union Canal is a bit wider around that area, but, further north it is only wide enough for one canal boat. As for where it could have been heading, well, it could have been anywhere north of Braunston Junction. As its name implies, there are many different waterways branching out in that area."

"Not a lot of help", Adrian thought. "But it still may get us a bit closer to what's going on."

"What about the boat, Mr. Rogerson? And the men in it?"

Paul had to admit that there was nothing really distinctive about the boat and the men. "A grey hull and a greyish-blue superstructure. It had a rear well for steering and was one of the more recent designs, similar to a river cruiser, just like ours. As for the men, all I noticed was that both had black hair."

"Did either of them speak? Did they have an accent?"

"Oh, yes. One man shouted thanks for the warning. It was only a few words, but I think it sounded like an east End accent."

This fitted in exactly with Alex's report. "Thank you so much, Mr. Rogerson. Can I take your number, in case I need to get back to you?" He noted the number. "If there is anything else you think of, please get back to me as soon as possible."

Clearly puzzled, the man asked, "What is this about? Were those two men criminals?"

"We are, as yet, uncertain. Just following up some information. Thanks, again, for your help."

Adrian relaxed. He called the switchboard and asked them not to put any more calls through unless it was Paul Rogerson. "I've had my fill of crank calls, today."

He requested detailed maps of the canal network in the area Rogerson had mentioned. The subject of narrow boats was a new area to him and he used his Internet search engine to provide as much information as possible. "How fast could they travel and just where could the boat be, now? It was six-thirty and, if they were quick enough and had a certain amount of luck, they may find the boat. If it could not be found soon, the chances of finding it at all were minimal.

CHAPTER
TWENTY-FIVE :

At six thirty-five, that evening, the boat glided slowly into the docking area of a large, un-imposing metal-framed building. Doors had closed automatically after the boat had passed through into the building and away from the normal canal routes.

Georgio wasted no time and jumped, deftly, onto the quayside and was mooring the boat to the bollards. It was obvious that this was a well-practiced routine.

Once secured, Georgio returned to the boat and, together with Franco, they moved around the vessel in an organised, well-practiced fashion, loosening the many retaining bolts. Two other men had appeared and now began to position the mobile crane to raise the superstructure. As soon as it was locked in position and a good ten feet above the hull, all four men jumped into the boat and began the, now, obviously routine, task of removing the many plastic bags of drugs. The men spoke little, the transfer process requiring their full attention.

Once the hull was empty, the superstructure was, slowly, lowered into position and the bolts tightened. Again, as if it was a well practiced routine, they, next, began to peel off, what could best be described as a 'skin' off the superstructure. What had before been a drab, greyish-blue exterior was slowly being transformed into that of a smart, bright, yellow and green appearance. It truly was a floating chameleon.

The 'peeled' skin was then, separated into smaller areas before being carefully, laid in shallow baths of acid, reducing the plastic to an unrecognisable piece of waste. The pulp would be dumped many miles away from the warehouse, all possible links being carefully thought out. No evidence could be left to incriminate the group of drug dealers. This was certainly a well-planned exercise, but it was not yet complete.

The forty, five kilo bags of drugs had been placed on trolleys. These were moved to another area within the warehouse, where ten, gleaming white Hotpoint washing machines were lined up. The ballast weights, normally used to provide some stability as the machines were working, had already been taken out. The back of each machine had been removed, allowing the men to insert the drugs, four bags per machine, into specially-prepared mouldings attached to the chassis.

Franco reminded the others to take extreme care not to catch the plastic bags on anything sharp within the machines. They were all aware of the vast wealth in pure Asian Cocaine they were handling so routinely. These four men, again, exchanged few words as they carried out the task of concealing the drugs within their new hosts. When all the backs were replaced, the men, again, used the trolleys to put them into a white van. The whole military-like operation of transferring the drugs from the canal boat into the washing machine delivery van had taken just forty-five minutes to complete.

Franco and Georgio now exchanged places with their cousins, Alfonso and Pedro, who entered the cabin of the canal boat to rest for the night. The other brothers would have to wait a while for their rest. They had ten addresses in the Birmingham area where they had to deliver the washing machines. They might manage to deliver, perhaps, one or two this night and the remainder on the following day. After all, who would want to take delivery of a washing machine after about nine o'clock in the evening? Everything they did had to be above suspicion and their task was to blend in with everyday life. It only needed one little mistake for their whole operation to be compromised.

Franco started the engine of the van, the electric, sliding doors raised just long enough to allow the van to pass through. Georgio was already entering the first delivery address into the sat nav and, once again, they were ready to deliver another shipment.

Within forty-five minutes, they had arrived at their first address.

Jimmy Warburton was not surprised to see the delivery van arrive at his apartment in East Birmingham. It had been due two days later, but he had received a call, telling him that the delivery would be re-scheduled earlier than expected. He smiled as the two delivery men wheeled the smart, new washing machine from the van into his ground-floor apartment. The men returned to their van and came back, carrying a couple of boxes, supposedly containing all the accessories for the new machine. "So, there's nothing unusual in having a washing machine delivered, even at this time of the evening", he thought.

Once everything was inside his kitchen, the two men, saying little, unscrewed the rear panel off the machine and, carefully, slid the four plastic bags, temporarily used as ballast. These were replaced with the real, manufacturer's ballast from the cardboard boxes and the panel replaced.

Jimmy's thoughts were on the vast amount he could charge for the twenty kilos of high-quality cocaine in these four, inconspicuous bags. No negotiations were necessary as he had already agreed the price for the drugs, well in advance of shipment.

Jimmy Warburton, a forty-one year old, stocky, muscular man, had been a drug dealer in this part of Birmingham for over fifteen years and had made a comfortable living out of the business, never once being foolish enough to take the drugs himself.

His supplies had been uncertain until about two years earlier, when this new gang offered him a steady supply. He knew little about them apart from the fact that he knew not to cross them.

Jimmy had numerous business contacts and had put most of his money in off-shore accounts and, when the time was ready, he would retire, either to Portugal or Spain, where he could spend the rest of his life with his wife, Jacquie and their children, in reasonable comfort in a climate far superior to that of Britain.

"Can I offer you two a drink of tea, coffee or something a little stronger?" , Jimmy's Birmingham accent was unmistakable, having grown up in this part of England.

"Thanks, but, no. We have many deliveries to make, but it's good of you to offer." Franco preferred to say as little as possible to their customers. "Bank transfer, as soon as possible, Jimmy."

"Of course. I'll do it tomorrow, first thing." Jimmy knew not to play games with these people. Before they came along, he had dealt with other drug importers who had not been quite as well organized or efficient. When he learned of the grizzly demise of his usual supplier at the hands of this new organisation, he realized that they really meant business. He shuddered as he remembered how the bodies of the drug importers had turned up in a huge, industrial mincing machine within a slaughterhouse. Police had never been able to discover the truth behind the killings, but it was a poignant reminder that he needed to toe the line. He did not even know who was behind the organization, preferring not to ask too many questions. He was aware that there was an Italian connection, but that was as much as he wanted or dared to know. Jimmy was a family man and the thought of his wife or children being slaughtered was all ne needed to keep his mouth firmly shut.

CHAPTER TWENTY-SIX :

Alex and Jen had heard the message broadcast on the radio and wondered if anything would come of it. It came as a great relief when Adrian phoned and told of his conversation with Paul Rogerson. To have his 'vision' validated so precisely, gave Alex a feeling of, at least, being of some use again. It was also satisfying that Adrian now actually believed him.

Jen, meantime, had been taking the time to read the vast volumes of information about the 'Ndrangheta. Sadly, it re-opened many old wounds to think, once again, of Jason's terrible death. She remembered all the times they had spent together, both of them analyzing the 'Ndrangheta's electronic traffic, but also some of their more intimate moments. She was already comparing Jason and Alex and had to admit that she was falling deeply in love with him. True, the sex was superb and she could never get enough, but there was also a much deeper emotional bond with him that she knew was absolutely genuine.

She, like Alex, wanted to do anything which would bring down the hated, Italian family of crime.

Of one thing, Alex was absolutely certain. He was going to have to learn Italian and without delay. He downloaded a translation course and, with Jen's assistance, began to pick up the language quickly. Jen was amazed as to how fast a learner he was. Again, Alex felt that the blow to his head and the increased cortex activity within his brain had improved his ability to absorb new information, just like a sponge. Within this first day, he was even able to speak and understand simple sentences in a dialogue between him and Jen. She was amazed at his speed of learning and knew that, in normal circumstances, it could take several weeks to reach this same level of competence.

That night, Alex followed Adrian's request and left his eyesight switched on to test if his 'visions' could be transmitted to Adrian's computer. It proved far more difficult than he had thought, to avoid looking at Jen as they prepared for bed, but Alex felt that he had not revealed anything which may have caused her any embarrassmen.

They refrained from making love that night, but, much to Alex's annoyance and frustration, he awoke the following morning, well rested, but without either dreams or 'any visions'. What determined if a vision should appear while he slept? Was the fact that they had made love on both occasions essential? Perhaps coitus lifted his awareness to a level which allowed him to see activity from a distance?

Since it was now obvious that the visions occurred in real time, Alex realized that it would be far more useful to experience them during the day, rather than at night-time when the Italians were, themselves, probably sleeping. For this reason, he did his best to tire himself by strenuous exercise during the morning and, after lunch, went to bed for a short, hopefully fruitful sleep.

He asked Jen to try and stay awake to observe him during sleep, as this may also prove useful. She noticed that, at first, he seemed quite restless, turning several times. There followed a restful stage, during which he was probably experiencing normal dreams. Watching Alex sleeping and recording times of the different stages was making Jen tired herself, but she persisted, occasionally sipping a drink of water to keep awake. Alex was lying on his back, his breathing deep and regular. "Sleeping like a baby", Jen thought.

What happened next nearly caused Jen to spill her drink. His eyes had, suddenly, snapped wide open and seemed to be staring at the ceiling. She moved her hand over his eyes. He showed no indication of having seen her. It was as though he was in a deep, hypnotic trance, she thought. Quickly, Jen made a note of the time. He stayed absolutely motionless and was in this trance-like state for just thirteen minutes. His eyelids slowly closed and his body seemed noticeably relaxed. It was a relief when he awoke an hour and a half later.

"Did you have another vision?" Jen asked, eagerly.

Still a little groggy, he replied, "Yes. A very strange one." Jen explained how his eyes had opened, presumably during his vision.

"Tell me what you saw." She was curious and impatient to learn of his new experience.

Alex put a hand to his head and groaned a little. "I don't know if it is because I am seeing these visions, but I have noticed that, when I wake up, I have a splitting headache."

Jen looked concerned. "Would you like something to take to relieve the pain?"

"No, thanks, love. Once you start taking pain relief tablets, it is very easy to get into the habit and I don't want to get hooked."

Jen nodded in agreement. She remembered the cocktail of drugs she had been prescribed when she suffered depression after Jason's death. Thankfully, that was, now, all behind her. "Take your time, sweetheart."

Alex's memory of his vision was, as yet, completely intact and he knew that, once he had recounted it to Jen, it would be even easier to retain. He closed his eyes and tried to completely immerse himself back in the vision.

The two guys from the canal boat were in what looked like a Ford Transit van. The one who had been steering the boat was driving, while the other was trying to give him directions by using a portable sat nav. It seemed obvious that the driver was unfamiliar with the area. Alex looked through the windscreen at the roads ahead. There was a great deal of traffic and, somehow, the busy roads seemed vaguely familiar. There were many junctions off this complex network of roads. At last, the driver found his way out of the confusion and headed down, what still seemed a busy road, but, at least, it seemed to be heading in some positive direction which satisfied the man at the wheel. The repetitive rhythm of the windscreen wipers was almost hypnotic as they worked hard to improve vision. Driving conditions were, indeed, difficult on this stormy December day.

The driver glanced at his watch, cursed and put his foot harder on the accelerator.

Suddenly, the guy in the passenger seat shouted to the driver to turn left at the next road junction, but he had left it a bit too late. The driver seemed to panic and turned sharp left without noticing that a cyclist was on the nearside of the van. The female cyclist hit the side of the vehicle with great force and was thrown, heavily, to the ground, her tangled bike falling on top of the unfortunate young woman.

With a look of panic, the driver realized what had happened, but, instead of stopping to assist her, he accelerated down the road. The two men started arguing and, this time, there was not a hint of an East End accent. They were, obviously, speaking in fluent Italian and seemed to be frantically looking for a way of escaping. This time, Alex could understand some, although not all of their heated conversation. One of them spotted a narrower road off to the left and pointed to it. The driver turned sharply into the road, looking for somewhere to abandon the vehicle. A passageway between two buildings seemed to offer a solution to their problem. The driver turned smartly into this passage, drove about fifty metres into it and braked, sharply. The two remaining washing machines rocked, unsteadily, with the shock, but, somehow, managed to remain upright.

Both men quickly gathered all personal belongings from the vehicle to prevent any identification. They moved swiftly and, strangely, coordinated in their actions, as though the possibility of an accident had, at some time, been considered and subsequent actions decided in advance. Next, they took off their jackets, turned them inside out and put them on again. This simple action had, significantly, altered their appearance.

Satisfied that they had left nothing of use to the police, they locked the front doors and, with some caution, climbed out of the back. Before locking the doors after them, one took something out of his bag and attached it to the inside of the rear door.

They walked away, trying to put on a casual air.

Alex had watched this in shock. He wanted to rush back to where the woman had been knocked off her bicycle, but decided to follow these two men, if only to provide Adrian with as much helpful information as possible. To his surprise, Alex watched as each man took a different route, a clever ruse should the police be on the lookout for two men.

"Now, who do I follow?" Alex decided to tail the older man on the chance that he may reveal more information. It was strange, trying to control his movement. It was neither walking nor flying, but more like ice-skating, but with far less control of his movements. He found it extremely difficult to keep up with the man, but concentrated all his effort in staying as close as possible. The man took a cap out of his pocket and placed it on his head, making identification even more difficult.

Alex nearly collided with the Italian, but, instinctively, knew that he would probably just have passed straight through the man's body, like a ghost. Alex was close enough to hear a mobile phone conversation.

"Had to abandon delivery. Two machines left, but alternative plans are in place." Alex realized that the device on the rear door must have been a bomb, timed to detonate when the criminals were well clear. "Will organize transport to return to base." With that, he ended his brief, seemingly innocent call.

Alex thought how professional and organized these men were. He was hoping that he could follow this man and discover just where his base was located, but, just then, the sound of a huge explosion reached his ears and, with that, his vision abruptly ended.

He was disappointed when Jen told him how long he had been asleep and, more importantly, how long it was since his vision had ended. "They could be miles away, by now. Must phone Adrian."

The Intelligence Officer answered his call quickly on seeing Alex's name appear on the display of his phone. "Do you have any more information?"

"Yes!" Alex was excited and told Adrian of the events in his vision, earlier that afternoon. Adrian listened with interest as Alex recounted how the two guys had been driving in a van, had an accident, hidden the van which exploded, allowing them to escape. "Do you have any idea where all this happened?"

Alex thought carefully. "I'm certain that I recognized the road network, but, where?" He turned the images over and over in his mind and, then, exclaimed, "It's Birmingham! No wonder they were lost. That complicated road network could only have been Birmingham's Spaghetti junction!"

"Great! Hold on while I check news reports for Birmingham." The forty seconds or so that it took Adrian to find the news item on the internet seemed much longer to Alex. "Yes! I found it." He read it to the fascinated Alex. "At two forty, this afternoon, thirty-two year old, mother of two, Jessica Turner was knocked off her bicycle as a van turned sharply off the A456, near to Birmingham's city centre. Mrs. Turner is in Intensive Care in Birmingham Hospital, suffering from severe abdominal and chest injuries. It is understood that she is four months pregnant and, at this stage, the condition of the fetus is, as yet, unknown until further tests can be carried out. The two men driving the van have disappeared and the van, believed to be a white Ford Transit, was destroyed in an explosion. As yet, the police have not established the cause of the explosion, but it is thought that it may have been deliberate."

"That fits exactly with what I saw in my vision. Poor woman." Alex now wished that he had returned to the scene of the accident, thinking that he could have done something to help the woman and her unborn child, even though he knew it would have been physically impossible.

Alex had another thought. "Adrian, did the monitor show my vision?"

"Not a thing", he had to admit. "I've already re-played the monitor recordings for this afternoon and, for the whole time you were asleep, there was absolutely nothing!"

Alex felt both relieved and, yet, strangely, disappointed by this news. A video of his visions would have been extremely useful in determining the absolute facts and, yet, somehow, it would have felt like an even greater intrusion into his personal privacy.

Alex was, still, replaying the vision in his own mind, trying to think of anything which could be of assistance. "We do know that these two guys were in all three visions and, although they spoke in an East End accent for most of the time, they were obviously Italians."

"Adrian agreed. Yes. Which brings us back to the 'Ndrangheta. My guess is that the drugs from the submarine were transferred into the canal boat and, later, into the washing machines for delivery in the van. Since there were only two machines left, the question is how many other machines had already been delivered and where to?"

"What strikes me is that these two guys were obviously unfamiliar with that part of Birmingham, which may mean that this is not where the drugs were originally intended to be delivered. Either that, or this was their first time in Birmingham."

Alex remembered the conversation between the two men while in the van. "One of them had mentioned a change of instructions, complaining about this on their route towards the Midlands. That could be why they ended up in unfamiliar territory.

"This is all fitting together like a jigsaw, but we are still missing many of the pieces. I've been looking at the canal system in the U.K. and it's quite fascinating. By the way, we have carried out a search for the canal boat, but it seems to have completely disappeared." Alex listened with interest. "The Grand Union canal starts at Brentford, north of London. At Braunston Junction, the canal system heads towards Birmingham and, surprisingly, it even runs under Birmingham's Spaghetti junction. From there, there are many branches, which could have taken them anywhere within a seventy mile radius."

"So Birmingham could still have been their ultimate destination, even with the change of plan."

Adrian agreed with this supposition. "Keep on having these dreams, Alex and we may, yet, manage to put all the pieces together."

Jen had been listening to this conversation with interest and, as Alex ended the call, she said, "I think you may be better to sleep during the day, if only to get more useful visions, like this one, today."

Alex looked thoughtful. With a feigned look of innocence, he asked, "But, what can we possibly do during the night?"

Jen's eyes sparkled with excitement, a smile lighting her beautiful face. "I know exactly what you have in mind, Alex McCloud, and I think it may be a very good idea."

"At least, we now know that Adrian can't monitor my visions, so we can just remove the battery when we don't want him to see us together."

CHAPTER TWENTY-SEVEN :

DECEMBER, 2011

At fifty-eight, Gianni Lamancusa had never been a patient man and the news of the partially aborted drugs run to Birmingham had angered him far more than the usual petty irritations he encountered in his line of business. "Six fucking million lost through this stupid mistake. It's bad enough when fixers outside the family fuck up, but when it's your own family, it's even worse!" He coughed, a deep, throaty, retching cough, made worse by smoking heavily.

"Don't worry so much, Tesoro. Your blood pressure is already too high! Please, try and calm yourself." Gianni's long-suffering wife, Carina, knew the pressure her husband was feeling, but since their flight from Italy, she knew that it had increased, significantly, thanks to their unusual way of life. "What was the point of all this luxury, if one's health is compromised?" This was a question she often asked herself.

His stomach ulcers could be treated with medication, but his blood pressure was, on occasions, dangerously high, despite taking daily tablets to, supposedly, help keep his pressure to an acceptable level.

Even getting hold of proper medication had proved difficult. As fugitives, they did not have the luxury of a

G.P. to monitor their health and prescribe medication. Of course, with money, anything could be bought, but it was becoming ever more difficult to live in this underworld, despite all their luxuries.

She was tired of permanently hiding away from the authorities. The worst aspect of their life was the boredom of living unseen, hiding away like rats in a sewer, even though it was a somewhat comfortable one, at that.

This life was not what she had expected when, thirty-eight years earlier, she had married her cousin, twice removed, as was the custom within the 'Ndrangheta. Gianni was, then, tall, ruggedly handsome, physically strong, and Carina had welcomed their union. She had known, even at the tender age of eleven, that they were destined to marry, their parents carefully planning the long term future of the family. Life had been much different then, as they could carry out their illegal activities, unhindered by authorities, thanks to the bribes paid to a few, select senior officials.

"Where are Franco and Georgio?" Carina was concerned that two of her four children were in danger of being caught by the authorities.

Gianni looked downcast, sharing his wife's concern. "They are on their way back. Franco is on the Inter-city train from Birmingham to London and Georgio is coming back by coach."

Carina knew that neither of them would feel at ease until their sons had returned safely and tried to engross herself in her book, a biographical work describing the turbulent relationship between film stars, Richard Burton and Elizabeth Taylor.

What Carina did not realize was that her husband was not only suffering from these current problems, but was also missing the relative freedom they had enjoyed back in Italy. Although not risk-free, they were happier times when everybody showed them some respect, even if it was fear-inspired.

The door opened and an energetic, attractive woman in her early thirties briskly entered the room. "What's the matter? Why are you two looking so glum?" It was Francesca, the fourth of their children and their only daughter.

Carina explained the problem in the Birmingham drug run and how they were worried about the safety of their sons.

"Don't worry! They'll be okay. They can handle themselves and, at least, they are brave enough to do the run." It was plainly obvious that she admired her brothers.

Gianni found his daughter's irreverence annoying and asked, "What do you want, Francesca?"

She looked taken aback by her father's brusqueness. "Nothing! I just came to let you know that the Casino had a record evening, last night. Since you let me take control, eighteen months ago, profits have trebled." She had been tired of having nothing to do and had begged her father to let her do something worthwhile. It had been with some reluctance that Gianni conceded that she could look after the Casino operations, feeling, like many Italian men, that women were much better having babies and carrying out domestic duties, leaving the men to do the 'hard' work. Gianni, clearly, had not yet joined the ranks of enlightened males who felt that their female counterparts deserved equal opportunities. It was also doubtful that this would ever change within Gianni's lifetime.

Carina gave her husband a disapproving look, which, without words, said, "Don't be too hard on our daughter."

Seeing this, he softened a little. A smile crossed his lips, yet his eyes gave no impression of softening. "Good. How did you manage to improve profits?"

Francesca knew that her father was not, normally, interested in detail, as long as the money came in, yet she humoured him. "In two ways. In all seven casinos, we have reduced the size of the lounge area, making room for more tables. Secondly, we are keeping a greater check on crooked staff. We've sacked seven croupiers over the last six months for taking bribes to help players win." It was quite ironic that, probably what was the most crooked gambling organization in the U.K., considered these greedy croupiers to be "crooked". Still, Francesca felt proud of her achievements and contributed as much to the family as any of the men around her.

"Keep a watch on those who have been sacked. We don't want any come back because of staff with a grievance." Back in Italy, if Gianni had caught anybody cheating on him, they would not be sacked. Instead, they would literally "disappear", without trace. Building sites with deep, concrete foundations had always proved to be very useful. It annoyed him that, here in England, he did not yet have the resources nor the numerous crooked officials he could depend on as in Italy. He did hope that this situation would improve in time, as he spent a great deal of effort identifying corruptible officials in all political parties, Police and civil servants.

What Francesca did not tell her father was that she had her own method of ensuring silence of those who had been sacked. The threat of violence against someone close, parents, husband, wife or even children, was more than enough to keep their mouths firmly shut. She was, indeed, her father's daughter.

CHAPTER
TWENTY-EIGHT :

A lex felt elated that his visions were far from that. It was as though he was a camera-man able to capture a scene where the criminals were in the act of carrying out their crime. The worst aspect was that he had absolutely no control of what he could observe. He had to take whatever was given, but he now had a hunger for more detailed information. If, somehow, he could "fine tune" this new-found ability, it could prove to be essential to the Intelligence services, making his existence seem more worthwhile.

He and Jen had lengthy discussions, where they both tried to work out just how best to utilize his visions to improve his usefulness. The worst aspect was that it meant sleeping during daytime and evenings to gain any useful information.

What they agreed on was that they could try and adjust their sleep patterns to start about two in the afternoon until roughly midnight, followed by vision analysis, if any. This would be followed by taking Elsa for exercise about three in the morning, when the streets were empty.

There was no point in Jen staying awake while Alex slept, as she could only record the times he was having visions and, now they knew they were in real time, there was little point. It was already after five o'clock, so for today, they would have dinner and then an early night. When Alex awoke at two thirty in the morning, he felt that he had had enough sleep, but, this time, there were no visions. Jen had slept badly and was already awake. Alex looked outside. It was a fine, cool, clear, December morning and Alex felt that he could do with some exercise. "Do you feel like a walk, this fine morning?"

Jen felt tired from her uneasy sleep and was not certain that a walk would improve how she felt. Still, she did realize that both of them needed exercise after being confined to the apartment over the past few days. "As long as you promise not to walk too fast."

Alex laughed. Although Jen was quite tall, she had, on the few occasions they had all been together, found difficulty walking at Alex's pace. "Do you hear that, Elsa? Can you slow down for our new friend?"

The dog, on hearing her name, looked up, with curiosity, at the two of them, turned over and put her head down, ready for another sleep.

As soon as Jen and Alex had showered and dressed, they, together with Elsa, ventured out of the apartment, where they had spent most of their time over the past few days. It was three in the morning and the roads in the area were quiet, apart from an occasional taxi. Alex managed to keep Elsa to a manageable speed for Jen's benefit and the three walked for about an hour, taking a route that would follow a circular path, bringing them back to the apartment. They talked little, finding it intriguing to just listen to the sounds of London at a time when most people were sleeping.

All three felt better for the exercise and fresh air, but, once Alex had relaxed in his chair, his eyes became heavier as he fell into a light slumber.

Jen returned from the bathroom to find Alex asleep and gently snoring. "This won't help with our new sleep regime, if he is dozing already", she thought. She looked at her watch. It was four ten and dawn was still a few hours away.

Elsa was lying down, her eyes following Jen and Alex. "Elsa! Come on and wake up your master!" Jen encouraged the dog to come closer to her master. Alex was sitting with his legs slightly parted, the steady breathing noises indicating that he was quite settled.

"Get him, Elsa! Come on, get him!" Jen's words did the trick as the powerful dog pushed her long snout firmly into Alex's crotch, causing him to wake up with a start.

"What the..."

Jen laughed. "Good girl, Elsa! Sorry, Alex, but you need to keep awake until this afternoon. It's no use sleeping now, when you need to stay awake."

"I suppose you're right." He stroked Elsa's head. The excited dog was now licking Alex vigourously.

"I'll make us coffee and toast. That will help to keep you awake.

"Okay. Good idea. It's going to take some time for me to get used to my new sleeping pattern."

The morning seemed to drag along but the couple kept busy, mixing domestic chores with necessary paperwork. Alex did phone Adrian, but neither of them had anything new to report. Alex told Adrian of his new sleep pattern, in the hope that it may provide many more visions. It was also a reminder that Adrian needed to phone them in the morning, rather than the afternoon.

By one thirty, both Jen and Alex felt ready for sleep, but, this time, remembered to let Elsa out for relief without interrupting them.

As the couple relaxed in bed, they were both hoping that, this afternoon would prove fruitful in having another glimpse into the murky world of the 'ndrangheta. So far, these visions had proved to be completely unpredictable, without any obvious pattern.

Alex had been asleep for several hours, when his mind latched onto a new vision. He was standing in a shop of some sort. It seemed to be a general store. Looking at the shelves, Alex spotted packets of cereals, chocolate bars, sweets and other confectionary. Another group of shelves had numerous types of vegetables and fruits. Muted displays of packets of cigarettes were along most of the wall behind the counter.

There was just one customer who had just bought a bottle of Vodka, which, Alex noticed, the person serving had pulled out from under the counter. "Probably not a legitimate manufacturer", Alex thought.

The customer seemed unconcerned that he may be purchasing a dangerous Vodka substitute and, with shaky hands, passed over the money.

Clutching his purchase, the man pulled the door open. Before he could escape, two men pushed their way in, almost knocking the customer over as though he did not even exist. Seeing the grim look on their faces, he escaped as quickly as his legs would carry him, while still clutching his precious Vodka. One of the two men closed the shop door and turned the sign to indicate that the store was now closed. The shopkeeper, a small, Asian man in his fifties appeared to know the men. He almost seemed to shrink on seeing them and wore a very nervous expression as they approached the counter.

One of the men, a tall, bear-like, stocky guy held out his paw, inviting the shopkeeper to hand over cash. Alex, at first, thought they were attempting to steal the man's takings, but it was the fact that he recognized them that led Alex to the only possible conclusion. They were demanding protection money.

With shaky hands, the shopkeeper opened his till and extracted a small bundle of notes.

The guy who had held out his hand greedily grabbed the notes and swiftly counted them. A broad smile lit the face of this hugely-obese man. "That's a good boy, Masseud. Same time next week."

What surprised Alex was the fact that this guy spoke with a strong, Scottish accent. "Probably, Glaswegian", he thought. This puzzled him as he felt that these tough guys were not connected to the 'Ndrangheta, so why was he having a vision about them? Some accents were easier to copy than others, but, in addition to the accent, these men did actually look as though they could be from Glasgow.

Pocketing the money, the guy turned around and headed for the door, closely followed by the other. Masseud looked relieved to see the back of them.

What happened next, took them all by surprise, including Alex. The door burst open and two men suddenly appeared in the doorway. "Police?" wondered Alex. He could not have been further from the truth. These two were holding small weapons, yet they were not revolvers. Each fired at the two Scottish criminals. There was no explosive sound from the weapons, more like the whoosh of compressed air. A small dart appeared in the neck of the two targets and, with a look of surprise, they collapsed to the floor, in obvious pain and struggling to breathe.

The two men, seemingly unconcerned, retrieved the darts from their victims' necks, placing them into small containers, which they pocketed. Next, they rifled through the pockets of the men on the floor, removing any money, credit cards and even driving licences. It was obvious to Alex that any identifying documents were being deliberately removed. "But, why?"

Masseud, meanwhile, was frozen to the spot, finding it difficult to comprehend what was happening in front of his eyes.

One of the men approached the terrified shopkeeper. "You have seen nothing, understood?"

Masseud nodded his head vigorously. "I see nothing, at all." A forced smile appeared on the terrified shop-keeper's face.

"You won't be troubled by these guys any more."

Masseud had a feeling that this was no cause for celebration and, nervously, asked, "Who are you? Why did …?" He looked down at the prone figures on the floor.

"We will take good care of you from now on. How much did you pay these guys?"

"A hundred and fifty every week."

The man, almost dismissively, said, "Is that all? From now on, you will pay two hundred and fifty every week. Cost of living increase, okay?"

Meekly, Masseud replied, "I don't earn much from this place. Are you trying to put me out of business?"

"No, not at all, my friend. We are here to look after you and we know you can afford it, especially from the dodgy spirits you sell." Although these men were smaller than the two Glaswegians, they appeared to be far more sinister and worrying to the Asian man. It had not been difficult for Alex to detect an Italian accent in the man's words and he now understood. "This must be the connection", Alex realized.

"It seems that I have no choice." Masseud worried about the future for him and his family. He was married, with three children and, on many occasions, his wife had begged him to find another, less-precarious occupation. Faced with attacks by petty criminals and extortion by the crime syndicates, he had, also, thought of closing his business, perhaps becoming a postman or delivery-van driver.

He may have to re-consider his options again if the demands made it impossible for him to earn a decent living from his store.

"I'll let you off this week, thanks to the money I found on him." He pointed to the prone figure of the bigger of the two unconscious men.

"What about those two? Are you going to leave their bodies here?"

The man smiled. "Oh, they're not dead, yet. Go to the other room and give us ten minutes. When you come out, again, we will all have gone." As if with an afterthought, he added, "Just do not tell anyone of what you have seen today or you will live to regret it. We will return next week, okay?"

Masseud gave a little nod, a sad, defeated expression overpowering his normally impassive features. As instructed, he opened the door to the room behind the shop and, quickly, disappeared, pulling the door shut behind him.

As soon as he had left the room, the two intruders acted without hesitation. Each pulled a hypodermic syringe out of their pockets and, skillfully, injected the contents into the vein in the arms of the two men. One of the figures on the floor began to moan and attempted to lift his head. Gradually, the sedation began to ease and both figures sat up, looking glassy-eyed, unaware of what was happening to them. The two intruders helped them to their feet. Alex watched in horrified fascination. Was this an elaborate setup? Yet, if this was the case, why take the money and documents from their pockets. Slowly, he realised that the Glaswegians had a vacant, glassy look on their faces. It was a strange sight, seeing the intruders assisting the more heavily-built Scottish men, walking like zombies, out of the shop. Not wanting to lose them, Alex moved to follow the four men, but, to his annoyance and frustration, the vision melted away into nothing and he returned to normal sleep, back in his own bed.

CHAPTER
TWENTY-NINE :

Even though Alex was unable to continue with his vision, the incident at the shop continued. Tom and Barry McTaggart had a tough reputation in this part of London, especially for their strong-arm tactics in their protection racket, but in their present subdued state, they were unrecognizable as the same two men. Their captors led them towards a car parked nearby. Obediently, they took a seat in the back of the Vauxhall, the two Italians taking the front seats.

The driver wasted no time and, after turning on the ignition, he put his foot hard on the accelerator, obviously in a hurry to escape the area. The car sped off in the direction of the North Circular Road at South Woodford, heading towards the M11, which continued northwards towards Cambridge.

The front passenger kept turning to look at the two guys in the back, but was satisfied that the drugs they had used were powerful enough to stop them becoming a problem. Had they become difficult, he had a spray, which, if directed towards their faces would have been inhaled, deepening their drugged state.

They drove about eight miles on the motorway and, making certain they were not in an area covered by cameras, the car pulled onto the hard shoulder.

The driver put on his hazard lights and stayed there while his partner climbed out and opened the rear-nearside door. "Come on, you two. It's time to go for a little walk."

Again, obediently and without argument, they left the car, standing looking quite confused as the traffic sped past, many headlights illuminating the area.

Once he was satisfied that he had done his job correctly, the Italian slammed the door shut and, hurriedly, took his seat in the front, Even before he had chance to fasten his seat-belt fully, the driver put his foot down hard on the accelerator and they sped off towards the next junction, from where they could return to London and dump the stolen Vauxhall. No forensic evidence would be left, as the car would be torched, allowing the two Italians to escape.

Meanwhile, the two abandoned men, obviously drugged and confused, cowered on the hard shoulder, watching, almost spell-bound, as cars and heavy vehicles thundered past with monotonous regularity. Gradually, they began to wander, somewhat aimlessly, onto the traffic lanes, seemingly oblivious to the potential danger.

The brakes on the forty-four-ton, articulated truck were well maintained and efficient, but still did not manage to stop the huge vehicle in time to avoid a disastrous collision with the men. The impact crushed many bones and sent their bodies flying high, like spinning toys, into the other lanes, where they were hit many times by several other faster-moving vehicles. By the time the police and emergency services had arrived to discover a multiple pile-up, the bodies of the two Scottish men were broken, battered and completely unrecognizable.

CHAPTER THIRTY :

When Alex did wake up, it was ten past midnight. Jen was sleeping, her gentle, rhythmic breathing sounding comforting to the still-sleepy Alex. He remembered his vision and went through it several times in his mind, in the hope of remembering all the details. While doing this, he fell asleep again, cuddling up close to Jen and it was after two o'clock before he awoke fully.

Excitedly, he recounted his latest vision to Jen, who listened, fascinated.

"Your previous visions covered drug distribution by the 'Ndrangheta, but this seems to be about their protection rackets. I wonder what the Scottish guys were injected with?"

Alex had been thinking about this. "It was the way he said that they were 'not dead, yet'. So either the drug would eventually kill them or they would be killed in some other way when the drugs wore off."

Jen agreed. "I wonder if it is the injection which eventually kills them. If it was a stimulant just to bring them around, they would have been pretty angry, but, you said that they went 'like zombies' with the Italians. Perhaps something which attacks the nervous system."

What she had said made good sense and Alex agreed with her, but the big question was "Where was the shop and, more important, the Scottish guys?"

As soon as he thought Adrian would be in his office, Alex phoned and detailed his latest vision. It was frustrating that his vision had not given enough information to locate the shop, but Adrian would keep a check for any information which may seem to link the incidents.

It took three hours and a great deal of searching before Adrian phoned back. "Alex! I think I have found a news item which could relate to your latest vision." Alex listened with interest. "I've checked the news items for anything that happened in the London area, early in the evening, yesterday. There was quite a big incident on the M11 at seven twenty-five. There was a multiple pile-up and, fortunately, there were only minor injuries amongst the people within the cars."

"So, what's the connection?"

"I'm coming to that! There were the bodies of two men who appeared to be wandering on the motorway. The driver of a heavy artic saw them, but it was too late. He is in shock and is finding it difficult to get the images of the men out of his mind. He distinctly remembers that the men almost looked lost and puzzled as they stared at him."

"That must be what the two Italians planned for these guys! Was there any identification?"

"Not a thing! Which fits what you saw. The two guys were quite big, probably about six feet and well-built. Can you remember what they were wearing?"

Alex thought back and said, "I'm pretty certain they were wearing long, dark-grey coats. I remember how alike they looked and dressed."

There was an excitement in Adrian's voice. "That matches what the police report stated. I think these are the Scottish guys."

"It would be interesting to know what the post mortem finds in their bodies. The chemicals must have been quite powerful."

Adrian agreed. "I'll keep a check on the p.m. results. These Italians seem quite resourceful."

"Dangerously so", Alex said, part in admiration and yet so revolted by their actions. "How about mug-shots of these guys to show around likely areas of London?"

Adrian gave a noticeable sigh. "I wish that could be possible. There's not much left to recognize after a forty-four ton truck and several fast-moving vehicles had collided with and ran over them. I don't think the artic driver would be able to describe them, either. The only chance would be from an artist's impression from your own description."

"I'll try, but it's not going to be easy when you consider how little I saw of them and the fact that it all happened in a vision."

Adrian knew this but hoped that Alex's military training would assist in the process of accurately describing their features. "Presumably, these two guys also had family, so, sooner or later, somebody is going to miss them."

Alex felt that this would probably be more fruitful than his descriptions, however, Adrian said he would organize an artist to visit Alex, that same day.

"I didn't get much of a look at the second man. I was mainly concentrating on what the main guy was doing, but my guess is that they were probably related."

"That's alright. We'll just concentrate on him. Just keep me updated on anything new." Their discussion ended, the call was disconnected and, for a while, he and Jen carried out domestic chores, just as if they were a married couple, which, to Alex's mind was quite comforting.

"I don't know what I would do without you, Jen. Everything between us feels great."

She smiled, again with that flirty yet coy look. "Same here. I never thought I could fall in love with anybody again after what happened to Jason, but I feel so happy with you. And, on top of everything else, you've twice saved me from certain death."

As they held each other close, Jen noticed a look of pain on his face. "What's wrong, sweetheart?"

He gave her a tender kiss, saying, "Nothing to worry about. Just one of these damn headaches."

Alex did not know if it was the strain of these increasingly disturbing visions, but he was suffering daily headaches and Jen was concerned about him. She insisted that he take pain relief. Reluctantly, he agreed and had just taken a couple of Paracetemols, when the artist arrived.

Samantha Parkinson was an attractive, twenty-six year old with long, black hair which almost reached her nicely-shaped backside, who, to Alex's mind, actually did look the "arty" type. Taking the seat offered to her, she removed a sketch pad from her bag and arranged several pencils, ready for use. "Now, Mr. McCloud, can you briefly describe the man you saw?" Adrian had decided it would be better to avoid telling the artist how Alex had seen the man in his vision, as the fewer who knew the real situation, the better.

"I am guessing that he was in his late forties, about six feet tall, perhaps even as much as six feet two. Weight I guess would be about seventeen or eighteen stones. I would definitely describe him as being obese. Hair colour is black, quite thick, yet shortly trimmed. His ears are quite large and his face is a bit fleshy. Heavy-jowled, quite large mouth and nose."

"Good description." She reflected on his words for a moment and asked, "Could you say what colour his eyes are? Any distinguishing marks?"

Alex thought, before answering. "I couldn't really tell what colour his eyes were, but my impression was dark. Probably black, but that's a guess. As for marks, I think he had a small scar above his right eye. Oh, and I think his nose may have been broken at some time."

Samantha smiled. "That's quite a good description. She wasted no time and began sketching. Within minutes, she had a rough outline. "How does this look?" She turned the pad to face Alex, who studied it carefully.

"Close. Perhaps a little less depth in the forehead and the jowls need to be a bit heavier." Alex laughed. "He gave me the impression of a bit like a slobbering bulldog."

Samantha quickly modified the sketch and, within minutes, again showed it to Alex.

He studied it closely. "I think that is pretty damn close. Yes, I think you have perfectly captured the image in my mind." He admired Samantha's talent as an artist, something he had never been particularly good at, when at school.

"Excellent! I'll take this to Mr. King."

Jen offered Samantha coffee, which she gratefully accepted and, for about thirty minutes, they chatted, again bringing an air of normality to Alex's strange life.

Shortly after Samantha had left, Alex's mobile rang. Jen had to admit that she did not like his ring-tone as it sounded too sinister. The start of Gustav Holtz's "Mars" from the Planet Suite was certainly striking and, for Alex, a suitable tone, noticeably different from all the rest. He did not get many calls, but was pleased to see the caller display indicate his sister, Lucy.

"Hi, Sis! How's University?"

"Great! The first week or two were difficult, but, now, I'm getting quite used to University life and I've made lots of new friends. Anyway, I phoned to see how you are. I was going to phone tonight, but had an early finish in lectures, so thought I'd give you a call. How are you coping?"

Alex smiled to himself as he could hear the concern in his sister's voice. How he wished that he could tell her the truth. "Absolutely fine. Elsa, my guide dog is terrific and helps me to be quite mobile. On top of that, the Army is keeping me really busy."

Jen, realizing that Alex would not want her presence to be known, was keeping very quiet, but, at that instant found it impossible to restrain a loud sneeze.

Lucy heard it and, somehow, knew that it was not from her brother. "Sorry, Alex. I didn't realize that you had company."

"It's alright. A business colleague has called to discuss some work with me", he lied, hoping that his words would be accepted.

Lucy, however, was a perceptive young woman and realized that the sneeze had sounded distinctly feminine, if that was possible. She smiled, convinced that her older brother had a girl-friend living with him. In truth, she felt relieved knowing how depressed he had been, following the breaking off of their engagement by Helen.

She thought about congratulating him, but, instead, told him about the medical course she was studying at

Cambridge University. "I'm managing not to vomit when being shown gory bits of the body specimens. I'm looking forward to finishing for the Christmas break, when I can stay at home for a couple of weeks and, hopefully, see you there. Anyway, I'd better go and let you get on with your 'work'."

As she ended the call, Lucy was wondering whether she should tell Amelia and her mother of Alex's so-called business colleague. There had been a time when she could extort money from her older brother just to keep quiet about his indiscretions. In the event, she decided to keep this information to herself and, perhaps, share it with her University friends.

As Alex disconnected the call, Jen said, "Sorry about the sneeze, sweetheart. I just couldn't stop myself. Do you think she realized that I was here?"

"I don't know, but don't worry about it, love. If I know my sister, she probably won't say anything, anyway. To be quite honest, I wish that I could come clean about everything, but I Won't."

CHAPTER
THIRTY-ONE :
DECEMBER, 2011

It was about four in the afternoon before Alex and Jen could settle down for bed, after their somewhat unusual day, especially the call from Lucy. When they awoke, around two in the morning, Alex realized that he had not only slept a comfortable, dreamless sleep, but that he had also not experienced another vision. On top of this, his headache was gone. He felt good, but wondered if the visions had ended and, if so, why?

Later on that morning, he received a call from Adrian. The Identity sketch had been shown on the television news the previous evening and, to Adrian's relief, there had been a response. "Sixty-eight year old Margaret McTaggart, a Scottish woman living in London, had seen the news and realized that the two dead men were her only sons, forty-four year old tom and forty-one year old Barry. This morning, she had identified the bodies, mainly from their clothing, having been spared from seeing their battered and crushed faces. The mother was in shock from their deaths, but probably expected them to be caught either by the police or competition, at some time in their lives. Adrian sounded pleased that, thanks to Alex's vision, the identities of the two Scottish men had been revealed without undue delay.

"What do the police know about the McTaggart brothers?"

Adrian was enthusiastic about the identification. "They have a long track record for violence and extortion in London and have been in prison three times over the past fifteen years. They were, without doubt, the guys from your vision and the world is probably better off without them."

Alex was surprised by Adrian's insensitive comment. "I don't know about you, but I would not want to die in that way and I wouldn't wish that on anybody." He paused, thinking of what it must be like to be killed in the horrific road accident described so vividly by Adrian. "And that still doesn't get us near the Italian family."

"No, perhaps not", admitted Adrian. "But, as long as you are still having visions, the chances of identifying where they are hiding are improving. Anything in your sleep, yesterday?"

How he wished that he had more revelations, but Alex had to admit that he had no new visions. He would let Adrian know as soon as he had any valuable information.

This day, following another intensive Italian language lesson, Alex and Jen did not get to bed until about six fifty-five and within just a few minutes, Alex was fast asleep. Jen was still awake and, after about another fifteen minutes, she felt Alex's body go quite rigid. Unfortunately for her, there was just one part of his body she liked to feel stiffen and that part still felt quite relaxed. She realised he was having another vision, but knew that, with it, there would be a painful headache for the man who, now, meant so much to her.

For Alex, the scene before him appeared to be different from what he had seen in his other visions. He could not decide if the female he was now watching was a girl or a woman. She was sitting on the edge of a bed and seemed quite good-looking, with long, black hair framing delicate, typically Eastern European features. She seemed almost anorexic, with her unusually thin limbs. The black dress did not leave much to the imagination, but the main impression was one of abject terror. She had been crying and kept dabbing her eyes with a tissue, an anguished expression spoiling her naturally-beautiful features.

She stood and, shakily, walked towards a window and, gently, pulled the curtains back. It looked like any other bedroom window, except that, the lower part had been boarded up, leaving a narrow strip of glazing only visible at high level. Standing on her toes, she could just about see out through what was left of the window and gazed, longingly, through it. Alex stood beside her, following her gaze. It was dark outside, but lights from various shops illuminated the scene. Alex was much taller than the girl, which he had now decided she must be. Probably only about fifteen or sixteen years old. With the advantage of his height, he could clearly see the group of shops on the opposite side of the road. Then it suddenly hit him! He recognized the location. Checking the order of the five or six shops visible, he was convinced that he knew exactly where he was. On the days he had been shopping from the supermarket, he had passed along this very road and had, on occasions, left his eyes working to see just what lay along this route.

Tearing her gaze from the window, the girl, with sudden resolve, walked with shaky legs cautiously, to the door. Opening it slightly, she listened for any sounds and then crept, slowly and purposely, onto a landing and began to descend the stairs. Trying to keep her in his sight, Alex moved to follow her, which, as he had discovered from previous visions, was not easy.

The girl had almost reached the bottom of the stairs when, even with her slight build, the step creaked. A door flew open and a man emerged, looking, with stern features, up at the terrified girl. She turned and tried to clamber her way back to the bedroom. The man was quick and grabbed her roughly as she tried to escape. He pushed her back up the last few steps and, once inside the room, he slapped her hard across the face, the force of his blow sending her reeling backwards onto the bed.

"What the fuck are you trying to do? Why do you want to escape? Do we not look after you?"

Alex's impotent frustration boiled over. "Leave her alone, you bastard!" His shouts, of course, went unheard. His fists, directed towards this brute, simply met no resistance as they punched the air.

Tears ran down the girls face. She held her hand against the area where she had been hit so violently. "Please let me go back to Romania to my family. You promised me work when I came here."

Roughly, he dragged her to a standing position and shouted, "Go and clean yourself. If you are a good girl, you can eat well after tonight's clients.

Alex heard the emphasis on the word "clients" and wondered just how many perverts were going to screw the unfortunate girl, this evening.

With a resigned look, she walked, defeated, into the tiny bathroom. She rinsed her face with cool water and then dried it, gently. The expression in the mirror was that of a broken person. The man had returned downstairs, secure in the knowledge that his sex slave would not attempt to escape, again.

The girl used the toilet, ran a comb through her long, black, silky hair and then returned to the sparsely-furnished bedroom. The bed, bedside cabinet and a couple of flimsy chairs were the only furnishings. Then Alex noticed a clock-radio on the bedside cabinet. He peered at the display and saw that it was seven twenty-five. At least, he had a positive time for this particular vision.

Within a few minutes, the man came back up the stairs, followed by another person. This man was about five feet nine and noticeably overweight. He was sweating in spite of the cold night and Alex knew that it was the excitement and anticipation of sexual relief with this under-age girl. It made Alex so angry, he felt as though he was going to explode from the sheer frustration at not being able to intervene.

The girl's pimp spoke excitedly, "This is Jacqueline. She will look after you." He then left the room, closing the door after him.

Alex was trying to determine if the pimp was Italian and, thinking of how he had spoken to the girl, rather than the client, he felt certain of the connection. This was yet another branch of the 'Ndrangheta. Drugs, protection and, now, forced prostitution, there just had to be some way of stopping them.

Staring at Jacqueline with obvious lust in his eyes, the client took off his jacket, put it on the back of a chair and then unfastened his trousers. He almost seemed embarrassed as he removed the rest of his clothes. The girl watched the man with a look of dread in her eyes. She looked at his erection and knew that she was soon going to have that awful "thing" inside her.

Nervously, the man said, "Come on, er, Jacqueline. Take your clothes off." With a half-smile, he looked the kind of guy who could soon turn nasty and, perhaps, even violent.

She stared at him, with a pleading look in her tear-filled eyes. With sudden resignation, she unzipped her dress and let it drop to the floor. She wore no bra, just a brief pair of panties, which she dropped on the top of her dress. Her breasts were quite small, adding to the skeletal appearance of this young girl.

She climbed onto the bed and lay, ready, with her legs apart.

The client looked wide-eyed at her youthful body and climbed on top of her, not even bothering to use a condom. The pain could be seen etched on her face as he pushed himself inside her. As he began to move, Alex felt sick and wondered why he had to watch this depraved act. As if in response to his revulsion, the scene faded and he returned, once again, to a restful sleep.

CHAPTER THIRTY-TWO :

It was several hours before Alex awoke and, as before, Jen was still fast asleep. Snuggling up to her warm body, he tried to avoid disturbing her.

When she did, eventually, wake up, he quickly related his latest vision to her. She was equally revolted. "Are you certain that you know where this place is?"

"I think so. As soon as I can phone Adrian, I'll see what we can do for that poor girl."

Later that morning, Adrian listened with interest as Alex recounted his latest vision. "Can you pick me up so we can check the address of this place?"

"Are you certain you can recognize the road?" asked a skeptical Adrian.

"I think so. It really reminds me of the shops on my journey to the supermarket."

Within an hour, a smart vehicle with blacked-out windows pulled up outside Alex's apartment. Jen had wanted to join them, but Alex was worried that Jen may be seen by members of the 'Ndrangheta and insisted that she remain at the apartment, for her own safety. Reluctantly, she agreed to stay with Elsa, giving Alex a hug of encouragement before he left.

As Adrian drove along the route he had described, Alex peered through the windows at the shops. "Yes! I'm pretty certain these five shops are the ones I could see through the bedroom window. It does look different than it did at night with all the lights on, but I feel certain these are the ones. There's a coffee bar, fast-food place and a betting shop all next to each other."

They pulled up to the kerb in front of the shops, allowing Alex to look across the road. He scanned the first floor windows until he spotted the partially-boarded up windows. "There! That must be the window I was looking through!" He pointed it out to Adrian, who had a register of the various properties along this road listed on his notebook computer.

"That belongs to number two hundred and seventeen." He laughed. "It's supposed to be the premises and showroom for a taxidermist.

Alex laughed. "I'm certain there's a great deal of stuffing going on in there, but not of dead animals! From what I saw, this poor girl is a sex slave."

"You would be surprised how many sex slaves there are in the U.K.", Adrian seemed quite knowledgeable on the subject. "Gangs have been bringing in young girls, for many years, usually from eastern Europe. They con the girls, sometimes pretending to be their boy friends, and, once they are here, their passports are taken away and they are locked in seedy rooms and forced to do what their masters tell them. In many cases, the girls are doped full of heroin, to make them more submissive."

Alex shuddered at the thought that Jacqueline was only one of many and wished that he could do something to help these unfortunate victims. "Well, it would be a start if we could help some of them."

"We can't even help here until we have a search warrant." Adrian made a call on his mobile, requesting a warrant to be issued immediately. "We are a bit conspicuous sitting here. I think we'll drive around for a while." He gave instructions to the driver, who pulled into the traffic and drove away from the area.

Within thirty minutes, a motor cyclist drew alongside their car. Both vehicles parked up as soon as they could, considering the heavy traffic. The cyclist dismounted and took an envelope out of his carrier. Adrian pressed the control to lower the passenger window and was handed the envelope by the cyclist. No pleasantries were exchanged, the cyclist returning to his machine and, within seconds, he had disappeared back into the heavy traffic.

Adrian opened the envelope and, carefully, read the official-looking document. "Good! This is what we need to get in that Brothel, without breaking any laws." He gave instructions to the driver, who skillfully drove the large vehicle, returning to the address where, hopefully, Jacqueline was still imprisoned. Adrian turned to face Alex. "I know this may seem hard, but I want you to stay in this car while we go in."

Alex opened his mouth to protest, but, seeing the serious expression on Adrian's face, changed his mind and said, quietly, "If I must. But how will you identify Jacqueline?"

"I just don't want to take the chance that any of these criminals may see you, as this will put you in even more danger." Adrian touched a screen in the car and, immediately, an image of Alex appeared on the display. "Don't worry. What you are seeing is the feed from a camera in my jacket. I'll keep in voice contact with you, so you can tell me if you spot this Jacqueline on the screen."

"I'm impressed", Alex admitted. "Very high tech."

"It would have been even more helpful if we could have monitored your visions in a similar way, but that's probably asking a bit too much." Adrian turned around and looked through the rear window. Alex followed his gaze and could see that another, similarly blacked-out car had pulled up behind them. Adrian pulled open the door and stepped out. He approached the other car and, within seconds, four men piled out, following Adrian.

He led the way to the door, tried it, but, as expected, it was locked. One of the men produced a silenced gun and shot at the lock. The men rushed through the opening with Adrian following. Alex turned to look at the screen in the car and could see the mass of men quickly forcing their way through the building, weapons at the ready. There was a great deal of shouting and confusion with doors crashing open, revealing surprised men. One scene reminded Alex of his vision as he saw a naked man being given a blow-job by a young woman. As the two realized what was happening, the half-naked girl, obviously frightened by the intrusion, bit hard on the man's penis. He howled in pain, blood spurting from his organ and was about to slap the girl, when Adrian pointed a gun at him. "I wouldn't do that if I were you! Get your clothes on!" The man scowled and did as directed, hastily stuffing tissues into his underwear to soak up the blood. Alex looked at the girl. It wasn't Jacqueline, although she did look to be of similar age and ethnicity.

"That's not Jacqueline, Adrian. It looks as though she is not on her own."

Adrian left one of the men to keep control in this room, while he moved to another. It looked, at first, as though there was nobody at all in this room, but when Adrian pushed the bathroom door wide open, he could see a terrified Jacqueline trying to get as far away from the door as possible, almost as though she could, somehow, squeeze her emaciated frame through the solid wall. "That's Jacqueline!" called Alex. He felt relieved that they had not caught her in the middle of providing sexual favours for a customer.

Picking up the prompt, Adrian asked, "Are you Jacqueline?"

Still looking terrified, she looked at the gun in his hand and nodded, tears already streaming down her face. She must have felt that this was to be the end of her short life, killed by an unknown assassin.

Now certain that there were no men in this room, Adrian put the gun away. "Don't worry, Jacqueline. Please stop your crying. You are safe, now. Have you a coat? It's quite cold outside."

The girl's face lightened. "You are here to help me? No more sex?"

"No more sex." Adrian looked down at what looked to be nothing more than a child. "How old are you, Jacqueline?"

"Fourteen, just two weeks ago." The fact that she knew her birthday was so recent, did not, understandably, give her cause for any happiness. Her large, sad eyes said it all.

"What about the other girl? How old is your friend?"

"The same as me. Fourteen."

Adrian shook his head in disbelief that anybody could take advantage of girls so young. "The men who controlled you are under arrest. You are now free." Alex was quite impressed by Adrian's calmness. "Come on. Bring your possessions."

Jacqueline moved towards Adrian and hugged him. "Thank you. I dreamed of this day for so long."

"It's over, now, but I'm not the person you should thank. You will meet him in a few minutes. Come on, now."

With a renewed energy, she retrieved a small bag from under the bed, opened the zipper and pulled out a coat. It was only thin and more like a cheap, plastic raincoat, but it was all that she had. She put this on, picked up the bag and followed Adrian. At last, there was a hint of a smile on her young, proud face.

As they went downstairs, the guy with the damaged manhood was angry, demanding his money back and even some compensation for his injury. "What am I going to tell my wife when she sees teeth marks?" He looked a very worried guy.

One of the Secret service men lost his patience. "Listen, I don't give a fuck what you say to your wife, but the people here are under arrest and, if I were you, I would not make a fuss, otherwise we may just take you along as well."

Adrian interrupted. "The girl you were with is only fourteen. Having sex with a under-age girl is committing a criminal offence, so we have enough against you to make an arrest. Quite honestly, I think you should have your dick cut off for what you have done. Would you like to explain that to your wife?"

This was enough for the middle-aged man, who was hastily fastening his blood-spattered clothes as he left through the still-open doorway.

Through Adrian's camera, Alex could see another young girl and two handcuffed men. He recognized one of the men. "Adrian! The man with the short, black hair is the one who slapped Jacqueline. I think he may be Italian." Adrian turned to this man. "What is your name?" He glowered at Adrian, but refused to say anything. "Suit yourself. We will identify both of you no matter how long it takes, so it makes no difference. You are both under arrest." Adrian read them their rights and three intelligence officers took both men out to their car. One officer remained, still checking for any other evidence he could find. He took his time, making certain that there were no concealed areas within the old building. Cupboards were searched thoroughly and, if there were any signs of loose floor boards, these were also investigated. Eventually, satisfied that nothing had been overlooked, he carried a bag with the few items he had found and secured the outside door to prevent drunks and vagrants from taking over the building.

The two girls followed Adrian out of the place in which they had been imprisoned and into the cold December day. Some people, aware that there had been a raid on this building, were watching with a mixed curiosity. Thankfully, there were no press people yet and all Adrian wanted to do was get these girls away from this place. He opened the door of the car where Alex was waiting. "Please have a seat, Jacqueline and ...?"

The other girl spoke. "My name is Rosita. Are you certain we are really safe?"

"Absolutely. This is the man who helped. I would prefer not to reveal his name, but I can assure you that, without his help, we would not be here, now."

Alex felt quite embarrassed by Adrian's praise and spoke quietly. "I am so pleased that we could help you both. How long have you been trapped in that place?"

The car was quite spacious and the two girls, simultaneously, hugged Alex. "It is hard to keep track of time, but I think it will be about eight months." It was Jacqueline who answered. "How did you know about us?"

It was an obvious question and Alex did not know how to respond. They would never have believed him if he had told them of his visions. Even he still found it incredible that he had developed this ability since the disaster in Afghanistan.

Again, Adrian came to the rescue. "I'm sorry, girls. That information is classified, but I can guarantee that, without this man's help, you could have been trapped in that hell-hole for years."

Jacqueline wondered if there had been hidden cameras in their rooms and if so, if this man had been watching them perform all sorts of sex acts for their clients? Even if this was the case, she would not have been ashamed as she felt that she could trust him and he would have been far more preferable to some of the weird creeps she had to endure. Jacqueline felt strangely comforted by this tall, good-looking man.

She blushed at these intimate possibilities. In this thought, she was not far from the truth, but she would never discover just how Alex had learned of their activities.

Trying to take the pressure off him, Alex asked, "Were those men violent towards you both?"

This time it was Rosita who answered. "Oh, yes. If we did not do what Barry and Phil said, they would hit us. We have both been raped many times by both of them." These thoughts brought fresh tears to her eyes. "I still find it hard to believe that we are really free."

"Listen, girls. We are going to take you somewhere you can rest, clean yourselves up and have a good sleep. Then, after that, help will be given to start the process of getting you back with your families. Please take a seat and fasten your belts." Adrian certainly sounded re-assuring and Alex hoped the nightmare was over for these two young Romanians. They followed his instructions and, very soon, the car was moving through the heavy traffic.

Jacqueline and Rosita leaned back, one on either side of Alex. No words were necessary. The fact that their ordeal was over was enough.

Jacqueline's thoughts returned to the poor area of Bucharest in Romania, where she and her cousin, Rosita, the only girls in a male-dominated family, had been born in nineteen ninety-seven. The two girls had been very close for most of their lives and were equally determined to break out of their background of poverty and hunger. Both had learned to speak English, convinced that, one day, it would prove useful.

When the advert for junior secretarial staff based in London appeared in the local paper, it seemed like a dream come true to the girls. Together, they replied to the advert and were amazed to be invited for an interview. Even more surprising, they both passed the interviews and were told that transport to London and accommodation would be provided as part of the contract. Their parents were delighted and looked forward to the money their daughters would be able to send for family support. They were even given financial help to acquire their passports by the agency which, supposedly, was to provide their future employment.

They and six other teenage girls were transported by mini-bus over the mainland from Romania to France and, from there, by ferry to the United Kingdom. The level of excitement was high amongst all the girls who had quite willingly handed over their passports to the two men, Barry and Phil, who had organised the journey.

It was only when they reached their final destination that the truth had dawned on them. Their passports were withheld, they were locked in and forced to work as prostitutes. The secretarial work had been a ruse to get the girls into England and the pimps found plenty of clients to earn them a profitable income.

Of course, the girls saw nothing of the financial benefits. These two men, who, initially, seemed friendly and caring, turned out to be sadistic beasts, looking on the girls as their property, just like domestic pets. Any sign of dissent was dealt with harshly, violence against the girls being carried out in a way that would not leave bruises to frighten off potential clients.

The other six girls had been 'sold' to other pimps, while Jacqueline and Rosita were retained, because of their exceptional looks, by the two Italians.

After eight months of absolute hell, all the two girls wanted was to return home to their families.

Adrian had made a call, requesting medical and social carers to be on hand to look after these two damaged, teenage girls and had given directions to the driver.

Meanwhile, Alex was talking to Jacqueline and Rosita, being careful not to ask too many probing questions as they would soon be asked the same questions by the professionals. "What are you both looking forward to?"

Without hesitation, they both replied, "A good meal!" Apparently, they had been given the minimum amount of food during their captivity. "I would really like a Big Mac with lots of fries."

"And lots of sticky-toffee pudding with thick fresh cream", added Rosita. Both girls looked as if they were in heaven, just at the mere thought of good, nutritious food. Alex laughed. "I'm sure you will get plenty to eat, when we get you to a safe place. I am not surprised by your choice of food. You are making me feel hungry for a Big Mac, myself!"

He could almost see the girls salivating at the thought of food and noted that both were now laughing at his admission.

Rosita looked thoughtful and said, "I suppose I really don't mind what I eat as long as I can get some food inside me. We are so hungry." Alex was in no doubt that these two girls, who resembled prisoners in Hitler's death camps would soon improve with adequate supplies of good, nutritious food.

Eventually, they arrived at the centre Adrian had chosen as the closest source of assistance. "Okay, girls. I'm afraid our friend, here, will not be able to accompany you." He was pointing to Alex. "I'll take you inside to introduce you to these people who are going to look after you and then I will leave you in their care."

Once again, they both hugged Alex, Jacqueline even giving Alex a kiss on his cheek. "Thank you so much, mystery man." The smile on the faces of these two damaged girls made Alex feel very proud of what had been achieved, today.

Alex laughed. "I will ask for a progress report on getting you both back to your families. Take care, girls."

Adrian escorted the two into the care centre and, ten minutes later, he returned to the car. "Right, Alex. I'll take you back to your apartment. It's been a good day's work."

Within thirty minutes, they had arrived back. "You will keep me informed, won't you?"

"Of course. Don't worry. We will do everything possible for those two young girls."

Jen and Elsa were equally pleased to see Alex. Alex was feeling quite hungry and, together, he and Jen prepared a meal, all the time he was explaining what had happened as a result of his vision. At last, they had succeeded in foiling the 'Ndrangheta's crime syndicate, at least in a small way.

CHAPTER
THIRTY-THREE :
DECEMBER, 2011

Gianni was furious and in a foul mood when he heard of the arrest of two of the younger members of the family clan. "How the fuck did Brando and Carlino let themselves get caught? I thought they could handle themselves! I'll have to speak to the Capo Crimine about this. Our phone line may have been compromised. Let everybody know that the security code on our phones needs re-scrambling." He threw the phone on the desk in obvious disgust.

Events did not seem to be going their way, recently. The failure to kill the CIA woman, the loss of forty kilos of cocaine and now, this. Gianni did not really believe in luck, whether good or bad, but he was not used to losing and fumed, inwardly. He sat at his desk for a few minutes, as if in deep contemplation. Finally, he rose and walked out of his room and along the corridor to a door at the far end.

He knocked and a voice said, simply, "Enter." It was the voice of an elderly man and someone of obvious authority. Gianni pushed the door open and walked in to the luxuriously-furnished room. "Take a seat, Gianni. You look troubled." This man was in his late seventies and still had a good head of hair, although the black had now turned a silvery-grey. His black eyes looked as sharp as those of a much younger man, but the lines on his weathered face belied this.

"We have a problem, Papa. Carlino and Brando have been arrested. They were running one of our brothels in the East End."

"So, what went wrong?"

Gianni shrugged his shoulders. "It seems that they were raided late morning, but, from what I understand, it wasn't a police raid. Brando seemed to think that they were secret service officers."

Gian Battista raised his eyebrows in surprise. "Do you think we have a leak?"

Gianni pondered on this question and then shook his head. "I don't think so. If the secret service knew of this place, I'm certain that we would have been raided, by now."

"I hope you are correct. There is a great deal at stake here and I have no intention of giving up without a fight. The location of this place must remain a secret." Even at seventy-eight, Gian Battisto had a sharp mind and a determination not to be caught by the authorities and imprisoned as had happened to many members of his family, two years earlier.

Gianni was certain that his father, even at his age, would fight with his life, should there be any threat on his empire. "Is it worth putting a bit of pressure on our friends in high places?"

The old man frowned. "I need to think about that. It would be a last resort, but, if I feel it necessary, then it will be done. Just make certain that Brando and Carlino are comfortable while in custody and, when it comes to the court case, the barristers on our payroll should manage to get them a lighter sentence. In the meantime, let everybody know that they must be alert and not to compromise the family in any way."

Gianni took heed of his father's words. He had seen how, over many years, his father had, ruthlessly, crushed any opposition. Even in his seventies, he was a formidable opponent and deserved the title of "Capo Crimine".

After a thoughtful silence, Gian Battista added, "Of course, if something was to stop them ever getting to a court case, that could solve many problems."

A thoughtful smile appeared on Gianni's face as he took in his father's comment. "I'll see what can be done."

CHAPTER THIRTY-FOUR :
DECEMBER, 2011

By now, Alex had a good working knowledge of Italian and, determined to master it, he asked Jen to converse with him in this beautifully expressive language. She was amazed at how proficient he had become in such a short time and now accepted that his brain had switched into super-absorbency mode. Alex was determined that, should he have any more visions involving the 'ndrangheta, he would be capable of fully understanding what they were saying.

He was also concentrating on getting his body in shape and had a running machine delivered, a few weeks earlier. His bedroom was quite large and the machine was permanently positioned and ready to use in one corner of the spacious room. Jen was also feeling the effects of insufficient exercise and was as committed as Alex in keeping fit. As part of their morning routine, both Alex and Jen spent at least twenty minutes each on the machine, by which time, the sweat was pouring off them. Both Alex and Jen ran in shorts and tee-shirts and were equally fascinated watching the other running. Alex particularly enjoyed watching the athletic Jen, admiring her superb physique.

He particularly liked to watch her long legs, topped by a perfectly-shaped butt as she ran to keep up a fast pace.

The shower which followed the exercise was refreshing and stimulating, both succumbing to intense sexual activity within the confines of the shower cubicle.

Jen felt very comfortable living with Alex and was always singing. Her current favourite was Kelly Clarkson's "Stronger", which she sang at every opportunity, particularly when preparing food in the kitchen. Alex always enjoyed listening to her, yet did not join in, as he admitted that his voice did not lend itself to singing.

By late morning, Alex was wondering about the two Romanian girls and phoned Adrian for a progress report. Apparently, both had been in contact with their parents, who had given up all hope of ever seeing their daughters alive again, after such a long time without hearing any word from them. Obviously, they were, now, delighted to hear from the girls and were looking forward to having them home again, hopefully, in time for Christmas. This would not happen for a few days until they had rested properly, eaten well and given statements about their time in captivity. Apparently, their request for a Big Mac and fries was granted, much to the girl's delight.

In addition, Adrian said, "As for Barry Jones and Phil Turner, the two who had been arrested, the I.D.'s they were carrying had proved to be fakes and they were saying nothing." This did not surprise Alex. "One of the guys phoned a solicitor for representation. He came to advise them, but mainly told them to say nothing. Since we are pretty certain that they are Italian, we've sent their photos and fingerprints to the Rome authorities in the hope that they can identify them."

"I'm sure the Italians will soon come up with their true identities and, hopefully, a link to the other members of their families."

Adrian agreed and added, "By the way, one of the men was carrying a mobile, but it was not your average phone." There was surprise and curiosity in Alex's face. "Oh? How was it different?"

"It was not connected to any of the usual network providers. Our analysts are taking it apart to find out more. It seems that members of the 'Ndrangheta have their own private phone network with deep encryption, presumably to avoid detection."

"They do seem very well organized and resourceful." Alex thanked Adrian for the information and told Jen of his news.

She smiled broadly. "I feel very proud of you. If it wasn't for your visions, those poor girls would still be sex slaves." Jen checked her watch and found it was nearly two-thirty. "I think it's about time for sleep, and, hopefully, another vision."

"Now that you said it, I probably won't have one, today", laughed Alex. He was always hopeful and within another twenty minutes, was fast asleep.

This time, he was lucky and a new vision started. A man, who Alex recognized as one of the two men on the canal boat and the delivery van, walked out of a room and into a wide corridor. He was wearing slacks and vest and had a towel around his neck. The corridor was long and had many doors, but there was no clue as to what was behind them. At last, the man arrived at another anonymous door and pushed it open. Alex followed as close as he could and was astonished to see a room about five by eight metres, full of exercise equipment. With running machines, exercise bikes, rowing machines and many weight-training machines, it made his exercise equipment seem quite tame, by comparison.

There were two men in the room already, one, who looked vaguely familiar, on an exercise bike and the other on a rowing machine. Alex recognized the second guy. It was the other one from the canal boat. Both men seemed pleased to see the new arrival, who took a second rowing machine. Now that Alex understood Italian, he realized that the new guy was challenging the other to a race on the rowing machines. The electronic data displays on both machines were initialized and, after a short countdown, they both started rowing vigorously. Both men were quite fit and of similar strength and Alex watched with interest to see who had superior strength. The guy on the exercise bike had stopped pedaling and was also watching this challenge of strength, a slight smile on his lips. Alex was trying to think where he could have seen this man and, then, it came to him. Thinking back to the day in Woolpit, where they had discovered the cannabis farm. He felt certain that this was the man he spotted entering the house. "So the cannabis farm was run by this family of Italian criminals", he thought.

As an electronic noise was heard, the two stopped rowing, instantly. The third man dismounted from the bike and inspected the displays. The guy who Alex had followed had rowed twenty-seven more metres in the set time and was declared the winner. Both men were breathing heavily, their competitiveness ensuring maximum effort.

Their next challenge was on wall-mounted machines. The idea was to pull down on a horizontal bar, with variable weight settings.

The man raised his voice, calling, "Sam! Have you a minute?" Alex was surprised that this was spoken in perfect English and Alex looked around, wondering where this "Sam" could be. Alex, who had been standing near a door, with his back to it as he had been watching the challenge, heard a door open. Suddenly, he felt enveloped in a huge, dark mass, almost as though someone had turned off the lights and, then, he realized that Sam had walked straight through him. Alex stared in astonishment at the huge, ebony-coloured man. He was the tallest person he had ever seen and must have been about seven foot tall, making Alex feel quite small by comparison. The man strode, confidently, over to the lateral bar machines and began to adjust the tension to calibrate them to provide equal resistance.

"Thanks, Sam."

"No problem, Franco." The voice was as big as the man, with a deep, resonant, baritone quality.

The two men pulled down on their bars, both managing, without too much effort, to pull it down to the same level. They released their grip and Sam, again, adjusted the weights. The two men tried once again, but this time, it was obviously much harder. The competitiveness between the two was apparent and muscles rippled and sweat poured down their backs as they pulled down as hard as they could. Sam was watching closely and, seeing Franco's bar had moved slightly more than his opponent, declared him the winner.

"You are still the champion, Franco, but your brother is improving and may soon overtake you." Sam's voice boomed around the room, the hard walls adding to the resonance.

Alex suddenly realized that, while this friendly competition had been going on, he could have been looking around this place, finding out as much as he could while his vision lasted.

Cursing himself for his stupidity, he moved back into the corridor, chose a door on the opposite wall and walked straight through the wall adjacent to it. He was shocked to find himself in a large shower cubicle, sharing it with a young woman. If he had been solid, their bodies would have been touching and Alex smiled to himself at this erotic thought.

There was background music playing in the cubicle, the woman, sometimes, joining in as she showered. She could well have been Italian with her long black hair and Mediterranean complexion. This was confirmed when she started singing "Moves like Jagger" by Maroon five and Christina Aguilera. Although her words were plainly English, her accent could only have originated from Italy.

He tried to assess her age and, after studying her body, perhaps a little too closely, he thought that she was probably around thirty. Her breasts were small and firm and, with a slim waist and nicely-rounded buttocks, felt this to be a reasonable assumption. Alex, of course, was, equally, naked, but he had the advantage that this woman could neither see nor feel anything of his body, not even his erection, stimulated by her vision.

It seemed completely strange being in a shower with a good-looking woman and not feeling the water cascading down over his body. If only he knew her name, it could be another clue to the identity of this large group of Italians, but with nobody else in the room, he was unlikely to find out. Alex was about to drag himself away from this location and, perhaps, discover other useful information, but, to his annoyance, the vision quickly faded. What determined where, when and for how long these visions lasted?

CHAPTER THIRTY-FIVE :

Jen found Alex's latest vision quite intriguing and incredible and, after hearing that he had shared a shower with a beautiful unknown woman, wondered if he was teasing her. Eventually, she believed him and, together, they tried to analyse the vision. Alex had not seen any windows in the few areas he had encountered and felt that all the family members were living underground. But, where? He felt that it was probably in London, but that did not help in any way. In a city of over eight million people, it literally was like looking for a needle in a haystack.

Jen agreed. "The question is, how do they get to this underground base? There has to be some way that members of the public and the security services are not aware of, but, where?"

"Just what do we know?" asked Alex. "We know the names of two of them. Franco and that huge guy, Sam. I don't fancy my chances against him. Anyway, I'd better update Adrian."

The Intelligence officer was now getting used to Alex's weird visions and was hopeful that, soon, they would give them some useful information, such as the one which led to the freeing of the two Romanian girls and the capture of two of the British-based 'Ndrangheta. When he heard of the shower incident, he laughed and said, "You lucky bastard, Alex. I wouldn't mind a vision like that!"

Alex felt like saying "Get a life, Adrian! Find yourself a good woman and stop being so frustrated!" but he thought better of it. "These Italians obviously like to keep fit, judging by all the equipment in that fitness room. If we are lucky enough to find their location, we'll have to be careful with that huge guy! He's obviously, their muscle to stop people like us from invading their territory."

Adrian agreed. "Keep on having your visions, Alex."

Alex was about to disconnect, when he had a sudden thought. "Adrian! Those two criminals who were found in the Thames! Didn't you say that they had been strangled by somebody who had great strength?"

Sudden realization dawned on the older man. "Yes, of course! I feel quite certain that Sam could be responsible. Well thought, Alex!"

CHAPTER THIRTY-SIX :
DECEMBER, 2011

*"*I think it may be a good idea for you two to take a break from the drugs runs." Gianni was looking quite relaxed as he spoke to Franco and Georgio, in his comfortable lounge area. His sons, however, were not quite as relaxed. When their father had called them in for "a little chat", they knew that significant changes were about to be made. Changes which would have a dramatic effect on their immediate future, perhaps even in the long-term as well. Neither of them liked changes, preferring to stay with what they knew and had done over the past few years.

Georgio looked annoyed. "I suppose that's because we lost forty kilos of high-grade cocaine on that Birmingham run!" He was still hurting from his father's harsh words he had to endure for this unfortunate incident.

Gianni remained quite calm and impassive. "It's not just that. Experience of other areas would benefit both of you in the long term."

Franco appeared to be more restrained than his younger brother and accepted that they had made a serious mistake in losing so much of their valuable cargo. "So, what do you have in mind?"

Gianni smiled, grateful that Franco would be more cooperative and "flexible" than his younger, more volatile brother. "The supply of weapons is proving to be very profitable and we have recently sourced a new supplier in Russia. They are very keen to increase volumes and their prices are unbeatable."

"What about demand? I would have thought that most gangs had sufficient weapons."

"You would think that, wouldn't you, Franco? The truth is that, right now, the requirement for more weapons is at an all-time high. There have been many recent police raids in London, Birmingham, Manchester and Glasgow, where large caches of weapons have been seized and, right now, they are ready to re-arm and they are willing to pay good prices for reliable weapons with no questions asked."

Georgio still looked doubtful, but Franco had no such reservations. "Okay, Papa, we are ready to move on the weapons circuit."

Gianni breathed a sigh of relief. He had anticipated some resistance to his suggestions, particularly from his younger son, but, thankfully, Georgio made no further comments. "Good! There is only one thing you must remember. If a customer in London is keen to buy, supply him, but tell me and I will inform our friends."

Georgio looked startled and was puzzled by this request. "Why?"

Gianni looked directly at his son. "It's quite simple. The probability is that, if someone is after a gun in London, that it may be used against us. There are many who are envious of our wealth and power. By revealing their names to the Police, we are letting the authorities do our dirty work for us by removing the problem. Think about it. After all, we still make the profit on the arms we supply."

Georgeo smiled at his father's plan. "Very useful having friends in high places to help in removing competition", he thought.

Gianni had decided to use this tactic with great caution, since he did not wish to be the person responsible for the riots again, as had happened in August. There had been no way that he could have predicted such an unfortunate outcome, but would be much more careful in the future. "I want both of you to talk to and learn from Francesco. He has many years experience in the supply of weapons, so please be open to taking his advice." Gianni knew that he was asking a great deal, as Georgio and Francesco had always been confrontational. Francesco was the older of the two cousins and had far greater experience but had an unfortunate way of expressing his assumed superiority.

Alex had been watching this, his latest vision with interest, but was disappointed that it only lasted for a couple of minutes. He recognized Franco and Georgio from the canal drugs run and the delivery van in Birmingham, as well as in the gymnasium, but this was the first time he had seen their father. How he wished that he had known the older man's name, but the only names he had mentioned were those of Franco and Francesco.

When Jen awoke, Alex eagerly told her of his latest vision. "Drugs, protection, prostitution and providing illegal weapons. No wonder the 'Ndrangheta is so rich and powerful. If only they were honest, they would probably do a better job than the present British Government."

Jen laughed. "I thought you were a fan of David Cameron and the governing Conservative party?"

"Oh, don't get me wrong. Of all the political parties, the coalition between the Conservative and Liberal Democrats is probably making as good a job as possible. I just meant that, if the 'Ndrangheta were legal, their experience would be of great benefit to the British economy. Just think of all the taxes they would have to pay into the Government coffers!"

She gave a dismissive laugh. "Well, there's not much chance of that. At least, your visions are helping to build up a better picture of the 'Ndrangheta, but I'm certain that there is a great deal more. It's like an iceberg where most of the bulk is still hidden. If only your visions could locate their headquarters."

"That is exactly what I am hoping for. As soon as I see a vision which locates their underground bunker, I will be doing everything possible to end their reign of terror."

Jen knew that the discovery of the Romanian girls forced to work as prostitutes, had touched a raw nerve and deeply affected Alex. "I'm certain that they will be found. It's just a matter of time."

Adrian was excited when he phoned, later that morning. "The Italian Police have provided us with names and mug-shots of the members of the 'Ndrangheta who managed to escape arrest. The 'Capo Crimin', their head man, is a guy called Gian Battisto Lamancusa, aged seventy-eight. We can only assume that all of his extended family members are holed up, here in England."

Alex was thrilled at this news. "Great! Can you send us the full details of this family of criminals?"

"Of course. I'll send it in a few minutes. Just keep on having your visions and we may, yet, find out where they are."

CHAPTER THIRTY-SEVEN :
DECEMBER, 2011

According to the Italian Authorities, there were thirty-eight members of the Lamancusa family probably living in the United Kingdom. Three generations of this dangerous family had escaped capture when a large contingent of Italian Police swooped down on all Calabria-based known members of the 'Ndrangheta. There was a suggestion that news of the raid had been leaked by an insider, but not in time to save almost three hundred members of the organisation.

As Alex scanned through all the information, he recognized eight faces. Gianni was the older man in Alex's visions, while the two men on the drugs run were Franco and Georgio. The two men charged with holding the Romanian girls as sex slaves were Brando and Carlino. Scanning through all the photos, Alex also recognized the two men who killed the Scottish protection racketeers to take over their territory. He could not be absolutely certain, as many of the family, understandably, had similar features, but Alex recalled his vision and felt certain that the two men were Lorenzo and Paolo.

The last one he recognized was Agostino Lamancusa. It had been such a brief glimpse of the man entering the house in Woolpit, four months earlier, but he felt certain that this was also the same person who he had seen on the exercise bike in the gym.

As they were looking at the details of this family of criminals, Jen realized that some of them could have been responsible for Jason's brutal murder.

As she looked at the pictures, some of them bearing a satisfied smile, she wished that she could line up every one of them against a wall and mow them all down with a high-powered automatic rifle.

Alex noticed the grim determination on Jen's face and was about to ask what she was thinking, but, instead, refrained, guessing just what was going through her mind. Seeing all the members of this group of criminals must have brought back bitter memories of Jason's murder.

In an attempt to distract Jen from her terrible experience, he said, "There doesn't seem to be many females in the group." The faces of nine women stared out from the screen

Jen agreed. "The question is, are they active members of the 'Ndrangheta or just wives and sisters of the members?"

Alex thought for a moment. "It doesn't really make any difference, does it? Even if they did nothing illegal themselves, they knew exactly what all these men were doing."

"Very true", Jen agreed. "Either way, I would like to see all of them behind prison bars." She did not mention to him what she would really have liked to do to these criminals.

Alex had decided that he had seen enough of this large, Italian family and was about to close the file on his computer, when he suddenly realized something. He pointed to one of the younger women and exclaimed, "That's the one I shared a shower with!"

Jen's eyebrows raised in a quizzical smile. "You do sound as though you enjoyed the experience?"

Ignoring her taunt, he said, "I nearly didn't recognize her with her clothes on, but, I feel pretty certain that she was the one."

"I suppose that you weren't really looking at her face while you were showering together?" Jen wasn't really envious, but enjoyed teasing her lover with the strangest of his many visions.

A broad smile appeared on Alex's face. "Okay, so I was a bit distracted by her nakedness, but, I can tell you this, her body can not compare to yours, honey!" She accepted his compliment with satisfaction, feeling very happy with their relationship.

In two thousand and ten, Christmas had been spent on active duty in Afghanistan and, now, this year it seemed that, for Alex, Christmas would pass without any celebrations. In truth, he did not mind, as long as he was with Jen. However, Lucy phoned to remind him of her wish for him to spend the festive period at home with his family.

Alex felt as though he could not relax until their mission to find the 'Ndrangheta was complete. "Sorry, Sis, but I'm in the middle of a project and have to wait a bit longer before I can take a break."

"Really? Over Christmas? Is it that important?" Lucy felt that this was just an excuse to spend more time with the mystery female. She did not believe that his work as a military advisor would take so much of his time.

"I am sorry, Sis, but I promise that, very soon, I will see all of you and enjoy a meal together."

Disappointed, Lucy relayed the message to her sister and parents. His mother worried that he was working far too hard and blamed the Army for taking so much of his time. At the same time, she did feel very proud of her son's contribution to the safety of British army personnel.

Alex, together with Jen, ordered items to be delivered to both his and Jen's family in time for Christmas, hopeful that this may help to stop both families from worrying.

As for themselves, they ordered plenty of festive-type food to be delivered and both helped to prepare a memorable Christmas dinner of turkey with all the traditional trimmings and even Christmas pudding with cream, to follow.

Alex was hopeful that new dreams would help in locating the 'Ndrangheta's hideout, but, annoyingly, over the next few days, he slept peacefully, without a single vision. Frustrated, he and Jen experimented with different sleeping patterns, indulging in heavy sex before sleep and, sometimes, refraining from sex, altogether. It made no difference, at all and he began to worry that he had lost the power of the revealing visions.

As an alternative, he and Jen spent hours reading through the mass of information on the 'Ndrangheta during their reign of power in Italy. Ever hopeful of discovering something useful, they read and reread all the text. Drugs, prostitution and protection rackets were similar to what they had discovered in the U.K., but then, Alex realized there was one area in Italy which, to their knowledge, had not been apparent in England. Alex, smiling, asked, "Gambling has been a major earner in Calabria, so, why would they not be doing the same here?"

Jen shrugged. "They probably are, but, how can you find out?"

Alex, in reply, carried out an internet search on high-end Casinos in London. As expected, it brought up quite a list.

Avoiding the on-line Casinos found in his Internet search, he selected each Casino, in turn, to discover more information and, eventually, had a list of the most probable venues run by the 'Ndrangheta.

"It's only a guess, but I think there are eight possible locations."

"So you have a list of possible Casinos, but, what do we do about them? Tell Adrian?"

Alex pondered on this point for a moment. "The trouble is that Adrian can only deal in hard facts. If I hadn't been able to identify the location of that brothel, those girls would still be working as sex slaves. No, I think we have to do a little investigation, ourselves."

"How? What can we do?" Jen looked worried at the prospect of doing something themselves, worrying, not unreasonably, about the dangers if they were discovered by the Italian family.

Alex looked at Jen. "I think I need to do this on my own, since they may still be looking for you, but I feel that I should pay a visit to some of these Casinos."

Jen looked concerned. "I'm not certain that's a good idea. You could be putting yourself in extreme danger."

"I don't think I have much choice. My visions seem to have dried up, for some reason. I've just feel that I must do something!"

Jen could tell that Alex had made up his mind, but this gave her great concern about the new man in her life. The last thing she wanted was to find Alex's body hacked to pieces by the dreaded Italian mob. "What about Adrian? Are you going to tell him just what you are planning?"

Alex again considered Jen's question. "I think not. It's such a long shot that there would be little that he could do to assist."

This did not ease Jen's mind and she knew that Adrian would try to talk Alex out of the idea. She watched him as he selected the clothes for his evening out in London. He really did look good in the suit he had bought from the "Cad and the Dandy", giving him quite an air of sophistication.

Alex was equally pleased with his tailor-made suit. The material and colour were perfect and the fit was better than anything he had previously experienced. "The expense had definitely been worth it", he thought.

Alex had, again, died his hair black, making him look very different from the man Jen had first met five months earlier. "You look like James Bond."

Alex arched his eye-brows in true, Roger Moor style. "Really? Which one?"

Jen laughed. "You could have passed as Daniel Craig, until you had your hair dyed. Now, perhaps more like piers Brosnam or Roger Moore." Her face took on a more serious expression. "Listen, Alex. I feel that it would be more natural if we both went, together. I can use my wig and, with one of my better dresses, would be completely unrecognizable."

Alex thought on what she had said. It did make good sense, while a man on his own could appear to be a little strange and out of place. "Okay. I'm sure Elsa will be fine for a few hours." He looked at his watch. "I would like to get to this place by nine-thirty and, perhaps, stay for a couple of hours."

Happy with his change of mind, Jen began to prepare for her night out in London.

Elsa seemed to know that she was going to be left on her own and looked, with some sadness in her eyes, as the couple prepared to leave. "Sorry, Elsa, not tonight. Be a good girl." Obediently, she remained still, watching as the door closed behind her master.

CHAPTER
THIRTY-EIGHT :
JANUARY, 2012

The couple walked for about ten minutes before hailing a taxi. Within twenty more minutes, they had arrived at the Rendezvous Casino on Old Park Lane, Mayfair.

Alex had chosen this casino as the first to visit, as he felt certain that this was not one controlled by the 'Ndrangheta, since it had been well established for many years. His thought, by coming here, was to establish a standard by which he could compare any other Casino.

Dress code was, obviously, important, confirming Alex's idea of purchasing a suit of high quality. He had to admire Jen as she looked very classy and absolutely stunning in her evening dress and brunette wig. As he glanced around, he noticed that everybody was dressed smartly, with not a single pair of jeans in sight.

The place was busy, with many people collected around the numerous gaming tables. Alex walked over to the Cashier desk and purchased a couple of hundred pounds worth of chips. He had decided to watch some of the other players before taking part.

Next, he bought drinks for Jen and himself, casually sipping as they watched several players losing their money. These players always seemed to think that they could always win on the next spin of the wheel. Of course, they became more and more despondent as their losses mounted.

Jen and Alex were careful not to use their real names in conversation and tried to give the impression that they could not decide whether to play Blackjack or Roulette. There were quieter areas where three-card poker or stud poker were being played, but Alex thought it best to avoid these games, partly because he was uncertain of all the rules and did not want to lose money because of his lack of knowledge.

Eventually, he decided to take a chance on the Roulette wheel, placing a few chips on one of the squares on the table. He had no idea why he chose red eighteen, but was both surprised and delighted when the ball landed in his chosen slot. The croupier slid an increased pile of chips towards Alex.

Jen smiled at him. "Beginner's luck, Darling?"

"I don't know. We'll have to see." He placed some, though not all of the chips on black eleven and was even more surprised when the ball locked into this very slot on the wheel's next spin.

Jen clapped, enthusiastically. "Well, done! You could be on to a winning streak!"

Alex, not wanting to draw too much attention to himself, gathered his chips, but did not place them on the table, preferring, instead, to sip his drink while watching the other players.

After a gap of about fifteen minutes, Alex, again, placed some chips on red fifteen, fully expecting to lose this gamble. He was more surprised than anyone when he, yet again, had picked the winning number. He, now, had four times as many chips as when he started and decided not to place bets on any more numbers.

Of course, the Casino owners wanted players to put all their winnings on one last number, which would, almost certainly, result in loss of all their chips. Alex had the good sense to stop while ahead and, after watching players on the blackjack tables, cashed in his chips. He was thrilled to discover that his two hundred pounds which he had, initially, converted to chips, had now grown to eight hundred and forty pounds.

"Not a bad return for a few hours", he said with a broad smile. He could understand the almost, hypnotic attraction to gambling by millions of people, but had more sense than the average player.

"Are you hungry?" asked Alex, thinking of the restaurant owned by the Rendezvous Casino. He knew, from the Google search of Casinos, that it had a good reputation.

Jen checked the time. It was eleven-thirty. "Okay, as long as it's just a light meal."

"Okay. A light meal it is." They entered the restaurant and did not have to wait long for their meal. It was superb and both left quite satisfied and ready for home.

The couple collected their coats and walked, arm in arm, out into the chilly January night. Again, they walked for a while, before looking for a taxi.

It was a great feeling as they entered the apartment, after a night out, a meal and over five hundred pounds in profit, even allowing for the meal and drinks. "I didn't expect to come home with more money than I started with", said Alex.

Jen agreed. "I've never been in a Casino in my life, but I quite enjoyed it. But, how did you manage to keep winning?"

He shrugged. "I don't know. I've never been lucky enough to win anything in my life before, but I wonder if it is related to my improved intuition, since my injury. Just the same as when I sensed that bullet aimed at your head."

Jen gave a little shiver as she remembered how close to death she had come on that night. "Same as with the bomb in the hotel room."

The couple agreed that, each night, over the next two weeks, they would visit a different Casino, in the hope that, eventually, they could discover which were run by the Italians.

What Alex had overlooked was the connection between his eyes and Adrian's monitoring system. The following morning, Adrian phoned. "What the fuck do you think you were doing, last night?

Realisation dawned and Alex cursed himself for not thinking about his "transparent" eyes. He explained how his visions seem to have dried up and they just wanted to find out some information for themselves. "We did adopt our different identities", countered Alex.

"I still think it was a fucking stupid idea, disguised or not!"

Alex felt angered by Adrian's hostile remarks. "Listen, Adrian, We've got to do something. We just can't wait in this apartment for ever, waiting for all the 'Ndrangheta family members to die. I'm sorry if you don't like it, but we have to do something!"

Adrian had to admit that, if it led to the Italian family, then it would have proved worthwhile. "Just take extreme care and don't attract too much attention by winning, against the odds."

"He's just envious of my winning streak", thought Alex. "Don't worry, Adrian. We'll take great care."

Jen heard both sides of the conversation, Adrian's voice being noticeably louder than usual. She also noticed how Alex's face coloured at the criticism aimed at him. "Poor Alex", she thought. "He does seem sensitive to Adrian's harsh comments."

After this, Alex's mood deepened a little, but, with Jen's encouragement, particularly in the bedroom, he soon recovered to his more usual, relaxed style.

CHAPTER THIRTY-NINE :

Brando and Carlino Lamancusa were relaxing on their bunk beds in their remand cell when they heard their door being unlocked. Two stony-faced, armed officers entered. Both were over six foot in height and quite muscular, but one was about ten years senior and probably in his mid-forties. The older officer, a dark-haired man with a sallow complexion, spoke. "Right, you two. Time for your courtroom appearance." Neither of the men made any attempt to move. The policeman's tone was a little sharper, now. "Stand up! Both of you!" Without any sign of urgency, the Italians got to their feet, saying nothing. The officers attached handcuffs to the two, after which, they led the men out of the cell and the remand centre. The rear door of a police van was opened and the two bundled, roughly, inside. Their cuffs were removed from the officers' wrists and fastened to bars within the van. Bench seats ran along both sides of the van and the officer indicated that their prisoners should sit down and not to make any trouble. The two prisoners said nothing and looked, impassively, at their confined surroundings.

The rear doors slammed shut and were securely locked, after which, the policemen took their places in the front of the vehicle.

It was eight-thirty on a Wednesday morning as the van pulled out into the slow-moving, yet busy, London traffic. The journey from the remand centre to the courts was only about three miles and, considering the location, nothing should have gone wrong with the transfer. With only about half a mile before their destination, the van turned into a narrow road and, to the surprise of the two officers, their path was blocked by a council refuse truck. Unable to pass, they had no option but to wait and no reason to doubt that it was a genuine traffic problem.

Suddenly, their van was rocked by a huge explosion. The rear doors had been blown completely off and two masked and helmeted figures quickly jumped inside. They fired stun darts through the metal grill at the two officers in the front, taking them completely by surprise. The policemen were unharmed, yet unable to prevent their prisoners escape as they collapsed, unconscious from the effects of the quick-acting drug.

The assailants acted swiftly and without hesitation. Using a bolt cutter, they sliced through both sets of handcuffs, releasing the criminals. It was as though they had been expecting this attack and both jumped out of the van, following the men who had released them.

Passers-by gawped at the scene in disbelief, but made no move against the obviously-escaping criminals. Could this really be happening in the centre of London? By the time people had realized what had happened, the four men had escaped on motor-bikes, which had been concealed in nearby side-roads.

When Adrian heard of the escape, he was, understandably, furious. An alert had been put out in an attempt to re-capture the criminals without delay. He phoned Alex and told him of the bad news. His first thoughts were for the girls who had been used and abused by these criminals. With anxiety in his voice, Alex asked, "Where are Jacqueline and Rosita?"

"Don't worry. They are already home with their families in Romania. They are quite safe, now. The girls asked me to thank you again, for helping them."

"Good! I'm just happy that we managed to save them, but it's a pity those bastards escaped. I imagine they will be back in their underground bunker, by now."

"Don't be so pessimistic, Alex. They will be caught", Adrian said, with conviction in his voice.

CHAPTER FORTY :

The next evening, the couple repeated their visit to a Casino, but this one was not as quite up-market as the Rendezvous. Alex had drawn up a list of Casinos in Central London, from the internet and had chosen one at random. The place was still busy with punters who, although always hoping to win, were destined to be losers. The only winners, of course, were the owners of the Casino. Some did win, but, as Alex had already noticed, all their winnings were lost in subsequent games. "Why do they never know when to stop?" thought Alex.

As with the previous night, he played the Roulette wheel. Again, his luck was in and, Adrian's words still ringing in his ears, he stopped before his good luck was noticed

Even so, Jen spotted some envious glances, usually from those players who had won and then, inevitably, lost all their chips after feeling "lucky".

In the background was the constant noise of slot machines, with greedy punters always hoping for that elusive jackpot. Both Alex and Jen glanced, hopefully unnoticed, at the staff, looking for any signs of the faces they had now in their minds. Of course, the actual

'Ndrangheta members were not likely to be seen walking around the casino. They would, more likely, be in other rooms, watching closed-circuit television cameras trained on the gaming floor, in the hope of spotting troublesome punters.

Jen was amazed to find a young woman trying to chat up Alex. This woman had played and lost, but had noticed Alex winning several times.

"What's the secret of your success?" the woman asked, admiringly.

Alex looked at the woman. She had long, genuinely-blonde hair framing delicate, possibly Scandinavian features and bright blue eyes. She was wearing a very close-fitting black evening dress which left very little to the imagination. "This gets more like a Bond movie", thought Alex, smiling. "Luck, I suppose." As an afterthought, he added, "and knowing when to stop."

She gave him a coy, inviting smile. "I could do with a guy with your luck. What's your name?"

Alex was surprised that this woman had not noticed Jen, who was not far away. He gave her an apologetic smile. "I'm sorry, miss, but I am with my partner." He indicated Jen, who lifted her glass in a mock toast to Alex.

The woman looked disappointed for a moment. Regaining her composure, she said, "That's a pity. If you ever fancy a bit of fun, you'll find me here on most nights. Just ask for Lindi."

She gave Alex a lingering last look and then disappeared into the crowds.

Jen returned to Alex's side. "Interesting conversation?"

"I can't help it if I find women attracted to me", he said, with a mischievous smile on his face.

Jen could understand how any woman would be attracted to the man who was, now, such an important part of her life. His height, build, handsome features, calm manner and, now, so well-dressed that Jen had to accept the situation.

She imagined that lindi would have been even more attracted to Alex if he had spoken a few, romantic words in Italian. This beautiful language can be very seductive.

After another drink, Alex cashed in his chips, ready to leave the Casino. Making their way through the crowds, Alex caught a momentary glimpse of Lindi. She was watching another punter playing Blackjack. She spotted Alex and gave him a wide, inviting smile, as if to say, "Please come again. I so want to see more of you."

Alex smiled to himself. "She certainly doesn't give up easily", he thought.

Back at their apartment, both Jen and Alex realized how these late evening visits to the Casinos were tiring. They had both slept late, as it had been between one and two in the morning before they managed to get to bed.

After five nights at different Casinos, both were beginning to realize just how difficult their task would be. For all they knew, they could already have been in one run by the 'Ndrangheta, yet, somehow, Alex felt that, eventually, their search would prove fruitful. On the sixth day, Alex looked at his list of Casinos, looking through the remainder which they had not yet visited. Talking to himself, he said, "Come on, which one should we pick, for tonight?"

Jen heard his frustration. "Don't blame yourself, Alex. I'm certain that we will get lucky, if not tonight, perhaps tomorrow?"

"I just wish we had some clue."

Jen was thoughtful. "Listen, Alex. If I cover the ones we have been to and you close your eyes? At least your choice will be completely random and not influenced by the name."

"Okay! We can only try." He placed the printout so that Jen could use her hands to cover the ones they had already visited. Then he closed his eyes and brought his finger down on the paper, in a somewhat exaggerated, dramatic style. "That's the one!"

Jen laughed. She lifted his hand and both looked at the name he had selected. The King Louis Casino was not far from the one they had visited two nights earlier, but the decision had now been made.

"Okay, the King Louis it is, tonight." In truth, he had little confidence that anything would come of their visit and felt that Adrian would be gloating at their failure.

The entrance to the casino was hardly impressive, but the interior was quite a surprise. The place was richly decorated in the decadent style of the last ruler of France and the staff continued this theme with their extravagant costumes and wigs. As usual, Alex exchanged two hundred pounds into chips, ready to see how his luck went in this place. As usual, he watched others playing roulette before trying his luck. When he thought the time was right, he placed several chips on black five. He never ceased to be amazed by his good luck and gratefully accepted his winnings when the ball fell into this particular slot.

Resisting the impulse to immediately put more chips down, he waited a while before making his choice. Again, he was correct, but, as he took his chips and placed them in his pocket, he was distracted by another punter.

This was a bald, rather-rotund man in his late fifties, who had, obviously, been drinking a bit too much, as confirmed by the redness of his fleshy face. He reminded Alex of the comedian, Harry Hill, without the usual giant collar. He was loud and did not seem to care who heard him. The man was a little unsteady on his feet and, as he rushed to put down more chips, he caught the hand of a smartly-dressed, younger man standing just to his right. The man's drink was spilled and chips were knocked onto the floor. "Get the fuck out of the way!"

The drunken man's face reddened even more and, in a slurred voice, he retorted, "There's no need to talk to me like that! It was an accident!"

This inflamed the man even more. "No, you're the fucking accident! Get out of my way, you idiot!" He bent down to pick up the chips off the floor and, as he descended, so did the drunken man. Heads collided and the scene was reminiscent of a "Laurel and hardy" slapstick sketch.

Unfortunately, those involved did not seem to think it humourous at all and the offended man grabbed the other by the lapels on his jacket, drew his hand back, clenched it and was about to hit him in the face, when security men, who seemed to appear out of nowhere, grabbed him from behind. Reluctantly, he loosened his grip and dropped the older man, who fell heavily to the floor.

"There's no need for that, sir. Please calm down."

"Get your fucking hands off me!" He struggled against the stronger force of two burly, security men, while a third assisted the drunken man who, by now, was lying flat on his back, with blood pouring down his face. He was moaning quite loudly, while holding his injured head. Apparently, his nose had collided with the head of the other guy

Suddenly, a space opened around these individuals and a woman seemed to take charge. "I'm sorry, ladies and Gentlemen. The game is suspended on this table, for now. Please use other tables to place your bets." She then addressed the offended man with a calm, relaxing voice. "I'm sorry, sir. Please calm down and the casino will make certain that you are not out of pocket." This woman was, obviously, in charge and appeared to resolve the situation quite amicably. The drunken man was helped into a chair, where his damaged nose was attended to and, soon, gaming resumed, as though nothing had ever happened.

Jen excitedly tugged on Alex's sleeve and spoke quietly. "Isn't that the woman you showered with?"

Alex had been watching the almost humourous sequence of events of these two men while sipping his drink and nearly choked on hearing Jen's unexpected question. Recovering himself a little, he now looked at the woman. Of course, she looked different with her clothes on, but Alex had to admit that Jen could be correct. She had long, black, curly hair, had typically southern-European features and could have been in her early thirties. As if to confirm this, a message appeared in the top of his vision. "Name : Francesca Lamancusa Date of birth : 21st. November, 1979 in Calabria, Italy. Member of the outlawed 'Ndrangheta." The face-recognition software was working well.

"Bingo!" whispered Alex to Jen. "Well spotted!" The couple, though excited by their discovery, did their best to carry on as normal, casually sipping their drinks and watching punters lose their money. Once the two men were seen to be placated by the efforts of the woman, she disappeared into one of the "back" rooms. Alex assumed that she only came out when situations such as this one, demanded her special attention.

What Francesca said about these two men once she was in her own space was far less comforting and certainly not lady-like. These incidents were an irritation, resulting in punters being temporarily distracted from gambling, which was not the idea of this high-earning establishment. The people working for her kept their distance from Francesca as she cursed. Her words could have made the swearing heard on a building site seem quite tame, by comparison.

In normal circumstances, she remained in the background, keeping a watchful eye on both staff and punters, but had, on this occasion, decided to assist in bringing everything back to a peaceful conclusion. Francesca had grown up in a family of tough individuals in the Italian Calabria gangland and was quite capable of looking after herself, as her employees knew by experience.

The man with the injured nose had sobered up quite quickly after the confrontation and staff had arranged for a taxi to take him either home or to an accident and emergency unit. The other man had, similarly, calmed down and accepted a voucher for two hundred pounds of chips, as compensation. It was not really a hardship, as this would soon be recouped on subsequent visits to the gaming tables.

As soon as they could, without drawing undue attention to themselves, Alex and Jen cashed in their chips, collected their coats and, quietly, slipped out of the casino. Both were excited as they walked away from the place. "So, what do we do now?" asked Jen.

"I think we need to speak to Adrian. There's no point in waiting until she comes out of there. She could be hours and we don't have transport to follow her. Come on, let's get home."

The following morning, Alex phoned Adrian, as soon as he thought his section leader would be in his office. "Adrian! We found a Casino run by the 'Ndrangheta, last night."

"How do you know? Are you certain?" Adrian sounded skeptical, but, at the same time, he hoped that Alex and Jen's visits to the Casinos would turn up something useful.

Alex described the altercation between the two men and how Francesca Lamancusa had emerged from the back room to calm the situation. "Check the video from my eyes for last night. It would have been around eleven-thirty. It was at the King Louis Casino near Leicester Square."

Adrian had known that there was little chance of finding the correct casinos just by visiting them at random, but, if Alex had really seen one of the 'Ndrangheta, then, he had to admit, that the young Captain's intuition had proved to be correct. "Okay, I'll check the videos as soon as we finish this call. The next step would be to place an observer outside the casino in the hope of spotting her leaving."

At last, Alex felt as though he had achieved something. Adrian, like Alex, found it amusing to watch the confrontation between the two men in the casino, but was intrigued to see the young, Italian woman doing her best to resolve the problem. "Pity there's no audio to add to the video recording", thought Adrian. This would have been far too intrusive and Alex would never have agreed to this level of monitoring.

CHAPTER FORTY-ONE :

Adrian had arranged for two of his men to keep a watch on the King Louis Casino, but was disappointed when they reported back, the following day. They had been issued with pictures of Francesca, taken and enlarged from the videos captured through Alex's eyes, in addition to the photo released by Italian security forces.

Even though they had watched from six in the evening for a twelve hour period, the two had no sightings of the woman.

The intelligence man decided to keep his observers in place for the following nights, in the hope that they may still be lucky. The two men found this to be an extremely boring and tiring task and took it in turns to be on the lookout from their car, while the other rested.

What none of them realized was that, Francesca ran seven casinos and spent one night in each and, if Adrian had not decided to keep his men for a full week, they would have completely missed the Italian woman.

Michael, one of the two assigned to keep watch, was using night-vision optics and noticed a woman, who certainly looked like the Italian, leave the club around three-fifteen in the morning. She took a seat in the back of a large, black Volvo. Michael shook his sleeping colleague, who was gently snoring. "Wake up, Jim! The target has appeared."

With a sudden rush of adrenalin, his partner quickly jumped out of his slumbers and switched on the engine. It was difficult to follow without being noticed, but they did their best to follow the route taken by the Volvo.

They were frustrated to realize, after a tortuous, thirty-minute route to find themselves back at the casino. "Fuck! It must have been a trick!" To add to their frustration, the male driver left the Volvo, locked it and entered the casino on his own, seemingly oblivious that he had been followed.

"The woman's not there!" Michael could not believe their bad luck and knew that he was going to be asked some awkward questions. He could imagine Adrian asking, "Why is it so difficult for two of my officers to follow a lone woman around central London at three in the morning? After all, she can't suddenly disappear."

Jim scratched his head. "She must have been dropped off somewhere, but why didn't we spot her?"

That was the first question Adrian asked when they reported to him, later that morning. "We couldn't follow too closely, or else she would have spotted us. The Volvo took many turns and we were very lucky to keep track of the car at all", Michael explained.

Adrian knew this was true and what they were trying to achieve was a very difficult, if not impossible task. Even though these two men were experienced in surveillance techniques, the Volvo driver may have spotted them. "I need to know the exact route that the Volvo took. Perhaps we may spot likely drop-off points."

Fortunately, their route had been electronically recorded and Michael replayed the data, all three watching the display on the monitor. A road map of London, starting at the Casino, indicated the route taken by the undercover officers. Times were displayed at each point on the journey, but this still did not yield any helpful clues. "I'll send this data to Alex and see if he can spot anything significant about the route she took."

Alex was, equally, frustrated and disappointed to discover that Francesca had evaded their surveillance. He studied the details of the route taken in great detail, but, after over an hour, had come to the realization that they were no further forward. Since it would do no harm to have another pair of eyes to study the problem, Jen also followed the data outlining the now, so familiar, route around London.

"There just doesn't seem to be any part of the journey where she could have left the car without being noticed", Jen admitted. After a moment's thought, she said to Alex, "Why don't we ask Adrian if the surveillance guys could take us round the route during the daytime? We may just spot something useful."

Alex thought this was a good idea and phoned Adrian with the request. The older man, at first, felt it would be a waste of time and resources, but, eventually agreed. "On one condition."

"What's that?" Alex wondered just what his boss was going to demand.

"That you wait until tomorrow. Michael and Jim are resting now after their overnight surveillance and I don't feel like disturbing them out of their slumbers."

"I don't have a problem with that", Alex conceded. This was not an unreasonable demand and one more day would, surely, not make any significant difference?

Alex had seen no more visions for a couple of weeks and, as he lay in bed, that night, wondered why they had dried up. Jen was already fast asleep, her gentle, rhythmic breathing sounding, somehow, quite reassuring. His thoughts, however, were with another woman, Francesca Lamancusa, who, he reasoned, was, probably, only on the fringes of crime as a result of being born into the Lamancusa family. His thoughts were still with her as he fell into a deep sleep.

The two women looking at the bank of screens were scanning through all the images of punters playing roulette, poker, blackjack and even the slot machines. Sometimes, they would adjust controls to zoom in or pan around the punters. There was an air of calmness and strict organization in this viewing room. To his amusement, it struck Alex that, in this instance, he was actually snooping on the snoopers.

"Look, there! The tall guy in the dark pin-stripes on camera seven, Angela!" Francesca was obviously in charge as she directed the other woman to take a closer look.

"Yes, you're right. It is the same guy. What do you want to do about him, Fran?"

"Let's just watch him again to make absolutely certain."

Alex was puzzled by their interest in this one man. What were they looking for? The tall man in pin-stripes looked a bit like Alan Rickman in his younger days, slim build and neat, black hair. Alex remembered him as Severus Snape in the Harry Potter films. He thought that it was also the air of confidence and composure displayed by the man which added to the impression.

"See, there!" said Francesca, who seemed to be, now, known as Fran, excitedly. "He's moving around until he is behind one of the players." Alex could not see closely enough to make out what the man was doing, but was intrigued by the interest shown by the two women.

"Watch what he is doing with his left hand!"

Angela followed her boss's directions, zoomed in and said, "His left hand is in his jacket pocket, but are you certain that he is up to something?"

"Well, there's no smile on his face, so I don't think he's playing with himself. He is definitely using something in his pocket to relay the player's cards to the opponent. I've been in this game long enough to recognize an illegal operation."

Alex had to smile to himself at the double-standards of this strong-minded Italian criminal.

"Just keep an eye on the game and, if the guy being assisted wins, then we will take care of both of them."

It did not take very long for their suspicions to be justified. The man who, presumably, was receiving the signals, made a substantial win.

Francesca spoke into a microphone, connecting her to the earpieces worn by her employees. "Okay, Greg and Dan, I've seen enough. Moved towards the group of people surrounding the gaming table. You know the guys we're interested in. Take them into the interview room, please."

The two women and Alex watched closely as two heavily-built men, presumably Greg and Dan moved towards the gaming table. One of them put a hand on the shoulder of the tall man, while the other moved to the opposite side of the table. It was obvious that the couple were surprised and, seemingly, offended by the confrontation, but they complied, knowing better than to try any violent moves. They were escorted, looking somewhat sheepish and uncomfortable, to a door at the back of the room.

As soon as Francesca saw this, she jumped up and made her way across the studio. She pushed a door open and walked, confidently, into the interview room. The heavies pulled chairs out from a desk and offered them to the two punters who seemed surprised to be facing the good-looking, young Italian woman.

"Please take a seat. Good evening, Gentlemen. I take it you had a good night, playing in my Casino?" Her voice was strong, calm and confident, with only a slight trace of her native Italian accent. She took a seat in a large, comfortable-looking, leather chair. "I'm certain that we can clear this matter up, quickly."

It was the Alan Rickman lookalike who spoke. It was obvious that he had been rattled by the confrontation, but tried to remain calm as he spoke. "I must admit that I find it surprising that you feel we have anything to say. I was just enjoying an evening in your superb casino, so what am I doing in here with this man?" He looked at the other man with obvious disdain, trying to emphasise that they had absolutely nothing in common and did not know each other in any way.

"Ah, well, I'm sure we can soon settle this matter. Please empty your outer jacket pockets, sir."

He looked surprised and began to object. The big guy behind him bent over and, ignoring his protestations, reached into the man's left pocket and pulled out a small device, about the size of a mobile phone. He handed it over to Francesca, who studied it with interest.

It was thicker than a standard mobile and, instead of the usual display and keypad, had twelve buttons and a two-line Braille cell matrix on its upper surface. "What is this?" She sounded more curious than angry. That would come later.

The man cleared his throat. "Ah, that is my Grandmother's Braille-phone. She's both blind and deaf and is lost without her communicator. I have had it repaired and will be taking it to her, tomorrow."

"Really?" She sounded surprised and nodded very slightly to the heavy behind the other man. On this simplest of commands, he reached into the pocket of the other man, who had not yet spoken. He retrieved an identical device and handed this to his employer.

Francesca smiled. "What an amazing coincidence! Do you also have a Grandmother who is both blind and deaf?"

The man seemed lost for words. "No, I..."

"Come on, gentlemen. Don't piss me off. We have been watching the pair of you on the CCTV and it is obvious that you were communicating with each other by using these clever, little devices to win unfairly." She looked at the now, noticeably nervous men. Scooping up both devices she offered them to one of her heavies. "It was an ingenious plan and the first time we have encountered these devices. We will pull them apart for our own amusement and analysis. Unfortunately, there won't be much left by the time we have finished with them."

One of the men began to protest, but stopped when he, once again, felt the heavy hand on his shoulder.

Francesca smiled broadly, yet her voice was strong and menacing. "Let me give you some good advice, gentlemen. I don't want to see either of you in the Prince of Clubs Casino ever again. Nor any other of my Casinos, either. Ignore this advice and both of you will end up just like these clever little gadgets, broken and incapable of anything! Do I make myself clear?"

Both men seemed to have noticeably shrunk over the past few minutes and nodded meekly.

"She really does know how to make them feel small", thought Alex.

The 'Ndrangheta family member spoke calmly. "Please escort these gentlemen off the premises. Nice meeting you both." Francesca stood and returned to the observation studio. Alex began to follow, but, at this point, the vision faded and he returned to his sleep, once more disappointed that the vision had not lasted long enough to discover where she was living, along with her other family members. Why was it that these visions always stopped before any useful information could be gathered?

Jen was intrigued as Alex described his vision, over their breakfast. "Now, that is a really clever way of cheating at cards. I had no idea that Braille mobiles existed."

"Same here", admitted Alex. "I don't think Francesca had come across them, either, judging from what she said.

CHAPTER FORTY-TWO :

Alex was eager to relay the information about Francesca to Adrian, who listened, with interest. "So, she has other clubs, as well?"

"Seems like it", agreed Alex. "But, we don't know how many. Are we still okay for the journey around London, this afternoon?"

"Yes. Michael and Jim will be at your place around one o'clock." With a firmness in his voice, Adrian added, "Just observe and try to avoid being seen, Alex."

"No problem." Alex knew how important this exercise was, but had a feeling that they were getting closer to the 'Ndrangheta's hiding place. Was it misplaced confidence? He felt certain that there would be a break-through, before very long.

The Intelligence service was always very precise and it was exactly at one when the two men arrived. Alex bent down to talk to Elsa, who watched with keen interest. "Sorry, Elsa, but you can't come with us. Be a good girl and keep a watch on this place for us, while we are out." Her reaction was much the same as a child's and the German shepherd's shoulders seemed to drop at the realization that, once again, she was going to be left on her own. A mournful look in her eyes made Alex feel guilty. "I'm sorry, Elsa. We'll be back soon."

Elsa lay down, resigned to her waiting role and watched as Alex and Jen closed the door gently behind them.

Michael was driving, with Jim in the passenger seat while Alex and Jen sat in the rear of the dark-grey Toyota Prius. Even the Government's intelligence service realized the advantages of driving a hybrid car in Mayor Boris Johnson's busy London roads. From Alex's apartment, they drove to Leicester Square, where, just over a week earlier, Alex and Jen had spent the evening at the King Louis Casino, run by Francesca Lamancusa. From there, they drove west, along Panton Street, turning left onto Whitcomb Street, following the route taken by these two men.

All four were scanning the roads along their route, looking for anything that could give them a clue. They took a few turns until they drove along the famous or, in the light of recent revelations, notorious Fleet Street, along Ludgate Hill and then left past the Old Bailey.

The traffic was heavier than it had been during early morning, but, in less than thirty minutes, they were back at Leicester Square.

"Can we do it one more time, please?" asked Alex, who was already feeling frustrated by their lack of progress.

"No problem", replied Michael. "But, any more and somebody may notice our journey."

"Agreed." Alex had to concentrate all his efforts on finding the point where Francesca had left the Volvo and this was to be his last chance. The car moved at a leisurely pace and, again, followed the route precisely. Shortly before Newgate Street, they had to wait for traffic lights to change and it was this that gave Alex an idea. "Michael! When you were following the Volvo, did you have to stop at these lights?"

The surveillance man had to think, recollecting the early morning journey. "Yes, I'm pretty certain that we did! I remember cursing that the Volvo had just got through the lights and turned right, while we had to wait for them to change."

Jim added, "Yes! We were worried about losing the Volvo, but, when the lights changed and we turned onto Newgate Street, we managed to pick it up, again."

This encouraged Alex to study the surroundings as the lights turned to green, allowing them to turn. Jen was using her I-phone to make a video recording of the journey and she recorded all the buildings as they passed.

Alex could feel the pressure on him as they studied everything closely. His head was spinning as he forced himself to look ever more closely, before the traffic took them out of the area. Then, from the corner of his vision, he spotted the railings on the island at the west side of Newgate Street where there was a junction with King Edward Street. "What are those railings for?"

The others turned to look where he was pointing. It was Jim who provided the answer. "I'm pretty certain that it is a ventilation shaft for the Tube."

"Of course!" These ventilation shafts were dotted all around London, providing fresh air to the deep, underground tunnels used by London's famous Tube system. "Any idea which line it is for?"

Jim shook his head. "Sorry, I've no idea. I don't use the Underground, if I can help it."

Taking his gaze off the surroundings, Alex switched on his I-pad and quickly entered a search item in Google. "That's strange. The nearest station is St. Paul's on the Circle line." After a few more searches, he exclaimed, "That must be it! It says that there used to be a station on Newgate Street, but this was closed many years ago with the station moving to what is now St. Paul's." He read on a bit more and exclaimed, "And get this! During the Second World War, the Electricity Board had a Control room for the whole of London and the South-east built within the service hall beneath that ventilation and lift shaft!"

All inside the car fell silent as they realized the significance of this discovery. If Alex had found the information so easily, the 'Ndrangheta could, equally, have found it and seen its potential as a hiding place.

Jen did see a flaw in this supposition. "But, how would they get into it? I can't imagine Francesca getting her leg over the railings to climb down to the service hall."

Alex smiled to himself at the image of this cultured, Italian woman doing what Jen had just described. "I accept that", he agreed. "But there must be another way into it. When we get back to the apartment, we'll study the videos, particularly of Newgate Street and, hopefully, find our entrance."

Within twenty minutes, they had returned to the usual, boisterous welcome from Elsa, as if they had been away for weeks. Her tail was wagging vigorously, as she greeted her master and mistress.

When she had calmed down, Alex and Jen sat together on the sofa, to study the video footage. Jen re-started the recording and then fast-forwarded to the junction before Newgate Street. The buildings were quite tall, fairly anonymous and quite old-fashioned in appearance. After re-playing the recording several times, they agreed that, from what they had seen, they still had no idea where Francesca had gone after leaving the car.

Alex, now feeling a little less confident, decided to phone Adrian to let him know just what they had discovered.

Adrian was in good humour. "Leave it with me, Alex. I have access to many historical files about London. What we need to know is where the original underground station was sited on Newgate Street. In addition, I'll get Michael and Jim to keep a watch for this woman close to where we think she is going. Good work, Alex!"

The praise was gratefully received, but just how close were they to the truth?

CHAPTER FORTY-THREE :

Once again, Michael and Jim were on night duty, parked where they had a good view over a large part of Newgate Street. They had arrived around two thirty in the morning and, using night-vision equipment, began their vigil. Francesca arrived early, shortly after three. As before, she was in the Volvo. Her car stopped, briefly, and then moved quickly away. The Italian walked, quite casually, towards what looked like an apartment block. She pressed some buttons near the doorway, entered the building and disappeared inside. The place looked quite old, but, presumably, had been re-furbished internally to provide modern apartments. Satisfied that they had the information, Michael pressed the ignition and, using battery power only, the Prius glided away, silently.

It was Adrian who phoned Alex, the following morning. "Good news! We have the address where Francesca entered the building and, thanks to the archived data, we know that it is adjacent to the site of the old Underground station."

"Fantastic!" Alex felt elated at the news. "I feel that we are really getting somewhere, at last.

Adrian agreed. "What we must not do is to rush in to this. We need to find as much information as possible, before we make any move."

"Of course. It reminds me of Afghanistan, in a way. Just because we knew where the Taliban were hiding, we wouldn't rush in with an attack. It still took time to work out the best line of approach."

What Adrian said next, took Alex's breath away. "I would prefer it if you could leave this operation to us, now, Alex.

"No way! You know fucking well that, over the past two months since they attacked Jen, I've thought of nothing else except finding where these bastards are hiding and, if you think I am going to hand it over to you on a plate, you can get stuffed!"

Adrian had expected some resistance, but was surprised at the strength of Alex's feelings. "I'll need clearance from the Brigadier General."

"I don't care, even if you need the queen to approve it, just accept that I am going in with you guys." Alex turned to see Jen who had been listening, with some interest, to this heated conversation. "Do you want to go in with us, Jen?"

"I wouldn't want it any other way. I need to see these killers caught. I owe that, at least, to Jason."

Alex again spoke to Adrian. "The deal is that Jen, Elsa and I must be included in the raid or else I will kick up such a stink that you won't ever be allowed to forget. Don't forget, my eyes could be our best asset."

Adrian was tired, not only of this battle with one of his operatives, but also internal difficulties within the department. Ever-increasing demands were getting him down. Wearily, he said, "Okay, I'll see what I can do. Just don't do anything until wee are absolutely ready. It's going to take a few days to prepare for an assault."

"Understood", Alex agreed. After a moment's contemplation and a slight change of heart, he said, "Sorry, Adrian. I didn't mean to..."

Adrian sighed. "It's okay. I did have a feeling that you would want to go in with us."

The call ended and Alex turned to face Jen. "It looks as though we're getting close to the 'Ndrangheta and their underground bunker."

She smiled, a smile which Alex always enjoyed seeing on her beautiful face. The trouble was that he was, now, even more concerned about her safety, knowing that she also wanted to join in the attack. After what he had said to Adrian, it would be hypocritical of him to try and prevent Jen from joining in with the attack.

Adrian now had plans of the apartments on Newgate Street and was studying them in great detail. Apparently, after the Underground station was closed, the buildings remained derelict for many years. As London was becoming an attractive place to live and work, it became ever more viable to develop new offices and apartments. Newgate Street, with its proximity to important areas in East Central London, was no exception and, even though many buildings were of listed status, developers spent millions on providing comfortable accommodation and office space behind the preserved facades.

What puzzled Adrian was how the 'Ndrangheta had managed to use the apartment block, which would house many innocent people, to suit their own ends. Then he spotted it. Looking through all the ownership records, it was obvious that, after development, the apartments had been owned by several different property companies, sometimes through financial difficulties and others by pure future speculation. The present owner was a private, venture capital company based in Calabria, Italy. This was far too much to be a coincidence and, of course, what better way to launder the millions gained from their illegal rackets in what appeared to be a perfectly legitimate investment? What did surprise him was that the purchase of this particular block of apartments was made in two thousand and seven, long before the swoop and arrest of most of the 'Ndrangheta in two thousand and ten. Was this an insurance policy that had been planned well in advance, or was it just a lucky coincidence?

Armed with this new information, Adrian called Alex and explained his findings.

The excitement could be heard in the young soldier's voice as he heard this news. "Any chance you could email the building plans to me? Preferably, both before and after the property was changed into apartments?"

"No problem." With a note of caution in his voice, he added, "Just promise me one thing. I don't want you going to look at this place for yourself. Any tip-off, at this stage, could compromise the whole operation."

Alex smiled to himself. "Adrian! Would I do such a thing?"

"I've been in this business long enough to know that it only takes one mistake by one person to fuck up the whole operation."

Alex could hear the stress in Adrian's voice. "Don't worry. I would just like to see the plans and I promise not to do anything stupid."

When Alex received the email with the plans of the apartments on newgate Street, he forwarded a copy to

Jen's notebook, giving both of them opportunity to study the drawings.

Alex found the original Underground station drawings fascinating, the style of drawing contrasting sharply to that of the modern plans for apartments. By the end of that day, both Alex and Jen had heavy eyes after hours of studying many drawings on what were, relatively, small screens. Within minutes of putting their heads on the pillows, both were sound asleep.

Alex felt very confused, when he found himself standing on a pavement, stark naked. Francesca had just stepped out of the Volvo, thanking the driver. As the car drove away, she walked over to the entrance door to the apartment block. After pressing a few keys, the door opened, automatically. The Italian stepped inside and Alex rushed to follow her, although there was no need for haste. He did realise that he could probably have moved straight through the solid door or, even through the wall. Alex followed her along a corridor, almost slipping through her body, when she stopped at a doorway. Francesca removed a key from her handbag and inserted it into the lock. To his surprise, there was already a light in the room, although it did seem more like emergency lighting since it was of low illumination.

She locked the door behind her and began moving around the room. As he followed her, he thought it was just a storage room, judging from the amount of items stacked all over the tiled floor. Then he saw it. In the far corner, there was a low, concrete wall which separated the room from a staircase leading downwards.

Francesca wasted no time and began to descend the steps. Again, Alex followed, although moving about in his visions had never been easy. It was a bit like swimming, but in air, rather than water. It meant that his progress was hampered, as there was nothing to provide much purchase to aid his progress. "Oh, come on, you idiot! I mustn't lose her, now."

Francesca was not rushing, but seemed to move with great purpose and confidence. "If she only knew that I can see everything she does, she wouldn't appear so bloody confident", thought Alex.

After four flights of stairs, the Italian and her unseen stalker were now moving along quite a wide, tiled corridor. Occasionally, there would be an arch, which, originally, would have taken the passengers towards the Underground platform. These arches were now built up, providing no choice but to continue along this obviously-still maintained hallway. After a few minutes, the end of the dimly-lit corridor lay in front of the couple. "Where to, now?" thought Alex. All that he could see was an old-fashioned gate to a lift, but, to his surprise, Francesca opened the gates, walked in and pulled them close behind her. Quickly, Alex followed and very nearly, walked straight through the back of the lift cage. Francesca pushed a button and the lift began to descend. There was nothing derelict about the lift. The movement was smooth, indicating that someone was maintaining the electrics and hydraulics. The lift halted and Francesca opened the doors to let herself out. Alex was praying that this vision would not end until he had more useful information for Adrian. The area in front of the lift was not large and had just one door in the opposite wall. Again, she retrieved a key from her bag and inserted it into the lock. Opening it, she walked through and locked the door again, behind her. They were in yet another corridor, but, strangely, this one looked vaguely familiar. Alex thought of the vision where he had passed from the exercise room into a corridor and then into Francesca's shower. This was that same, almost hotel-like, corridor. There were many doors on both sides of the corridor, but she walked another twenty metres or so, and pushed the door open. It led into a small hallway with five doors leading off it.

Francesca opened one of these, as though she was trying not to disturb the occupants. Alex was more curious than ever to discover the secrets of this huge underground labyrinth.

"Mama?" The head of a small child lifted off the pillow and looked towards Francesca, now framed in the doorway.

"Gemma! Why are you still awake?"

"I couldn't sleep, Mama. I keep having bad dreams. A really big monster keeps following me everywhere."

From what Alex could see of the girl, he guessed that she was probably about five years old. To his surprise, another voice could then be heard.

"Gemma's a real nuisance, Mama. She keeps waking me up."

Again, another girl, but this one was about eight or nine.

"Right! I'm back, now, and I want you both to settle down." She walked over to the younger girl and gave her a hug of reassurance. "Come on, now, Gemma. There's nothing to be afraid of and I'm here for you, now. They are just silly dreams. Okay?"

"Okay, Mama." There was a slightly happier tone in the young girl's voice, now that her mother had returned.

"And try not to disturb Serena. She needs her sleep as much as you."

The girl yawned and relaxed back on her pillow. "I'm okay, now, Mama."

"Good! Just remember, I'm only in the next room." Francesca kissed both her daughters and, quietly, closed the door. She pushed another door open, switched on the light, and walked into what looked like her own bedroom. "I wonder where the husband is?" thought Alex. There was something about the room which made him think that this was more like a single woman's room rather than that of a married couple. He moved around the room looking for any helpful clues. On a bedside table there was a photograph of a young, handsome man, who was probably in his late twenties. Another photo showed the same man, holding a beaming Francesca close in a warm embrace. Alex recognised the older girl in the photograph, looking a little bored, but she would only have been around four years old. A baby, probably less than a year old was sitting in front of her mother, trying to attract her attention. This must have been Gemma.

Alex had guessed correctly. Francesca and her husband, Grecco, had been blissfully happy, together with their two young daughters until two thousand and eight, when Grecco had been killed in a gun-battle with Italian police forces. An informer had revealed the mobster's location, but, thanks to the loyalty between 'Ndrangheta family members, the informer did not live long enough to enjoy the substantial bribe offered by the authorities.

As he turned around to study the rest of the room, he realised that Francesca had started to remove her clothes. Standing quite naked, she was hanging her dress in a wardrobe. What was it that made this woman want to remove her clothes whenever Alex was around? "Ah, well, mustn't complain. These fringe benefits are all part of the job!"

She walked into a bathroom, where she used the toilet and then brushed her teeth. Alex had, gallantly, stayed in the bedroom, not wishing to see every intimate detail of this attractive Italian's private life.

Francesca returned to the bedroom and removed something from a drawer, placing it on the bedside cabinet. Suddenly, Alex realised what it was. A vibrator! "That does suggest that the man in the photo is not around, any more." Francesca slipped into her bed and, pulled up the covers after taking hold of the vibrator.

Alex was thinking of what he could do for this lonely woman, when the vision suddenly faded and he was back in his own bed.

CHAPTER FORTY-FOUR :

When Alex told Jen of his latest vision, over breakfast, she said, with a resigned sigh, "Why is it that when your body is in bed with me, your spirit is somewhere else with another woman?"

Alex smiled at her comment. "Sorry, sweetheart. You know that it's beyond my control."

"I bet that you would have liked to replace her vibrator with something of your own?"

A somewhat disguised look of innocence crossed his face. "Me? The thought never crossed my mind!" he lied, crossing his fingers as though it would make any difference.

"Liar!" She laughed, always enjoying teasing Alex. "Only a gay could resist such a temptation." Neither was dressed yet, Alex in his boxers and tee-shirt, while Jen was wearing a somewhat brief nightdress. She jumped up and ran round the table and pulled at Alex's boxers, exposing his manhood. "See! You've got a hard-on just telling me about your vision."

"You know that's beyond my control. What do you want?" All thoughts of breakfast had suddenly disappeared and he was laughing, as she ran her fingers along his erect member.

"I want you inside me, not in that Italian woman!" She was giggling as she pulled him towards her. Placing a towel on the cold, granite worktop, she slipped off her underwear and sat on the edge facing towards Alex. "Come on, now, Romeo! Do what you can, just for me and nobody else!"

Elsa watched with curiosity at the humans doing strange things in the kitchen, of all places. Both Jen and Alex were laughing, but Elsa could not understand why.

Alex felt quite elated by Jen's crazy, energetic sexual antics, being completely sexually driven, unlike the more reserved Helen. Alex realised how unfair it was to compare these two very different women, as Helen had many good qualities and would probably have made a very good mother for their children. On the other hand, Alex had difficulty imagining Jen changing a baby's nappy, taking children to school and all the other things that went with parenthood. "I don't want to think too far ahead", thought Alex.

After this somewhat vigorous exercise, both were extremely sweaty and needed to shower. Once Alex had dressed, Adrian had to be informed of this latest vision. When Alex phoned, the older man listened with interest, the only omission being Francesca's vibrator. "Don't want to get Adrian over-excited", he thought. Of one thing, Alex was certain. His knowledge of the underground bunker and its access made his role in the assault even more essential.

"There's just one thing that bothers me", said Alex.

"What's that?"

"Those two young girls. We can't just go in with all guns blazing. We can't have the deaths of two innocent girls on our conscience." With an afterthought, he added, "And, for all we know, there may be other children in other rooms."

Adrian agreed. "It does complicate the assault, but, we'll do everything to avoid any collateral damage."

Alex did not like this term. Calling the deaths of innocent children "collateral damage" is the military way of avoiding a difficult issue. Alex remembered his time in Afghanistan, when the Taliban used innocent people to shield them from assault, like the cowards they were.

Adrian continued. "The other difficulty is that lift. It's going to be pretty difficult getting to the target without alerting them. For all we know, they may have cameras close to the lift. Leave it with me to work out a plan of action and I'll call you, when we are ready."

It was two days later when Adrian phoned back. "Right, I'd like you all to come here for a briefing, ready for the assault. I'll send a car for you, this afternoon."

As before, it was Terry who arrived at their apartment. Alex had thought it may be him and had warned Jen about this strange, un-communicative, man. Still, he was always efficient and, very soon, Alex, Jen and Elsa were at MI6, where Adrian was waiting for them. He took them to a briefing room, which already seemed to be full of young, though experienced intelligence officers.

Many pin boards adorned the walls and, on some of these, the photographs of all the 'Ndrangheta family who had, so far, evaded capture, were pinned. Pictures and maps of Newgate Street and, in particular, the address where Francesca had been seen entering the building, were also on these boards.

Adrian addressed all within the room. "This exercise, Ladies and Gentlemen, is aimed at capturing, preferably alive, all the remaining members of the 'Ndrangheta, currently living underground in the Newgate area of

London. You have seen the records of all these individuals and, believe me, they are extremely professional, dangerous and well organised."

"We will start our operation at 02:15, tomorrow morning. We will wait for Francesca and, hopefully, with her help, enter the complex. Two officers will remain in the apartment block, just in case anybody else turns up." Adrian looked at the attentive faces in the audience and added, "Now, the Italian Police have sent us photos of thirty-eight members of the family who escaped to the U.K., but we do know that there are at least two small children, maybe even more. For this reason, extreme care must be exercised to avoid injuring any children."

"Don't forget about Sam!" interrupted Alex.

"Of course. From what officer McCloud has observed, Sam is a man of African origin. Estimated height and weight is two point one metres and about one hundred and twenty kilos." The thought of a man of this size showed in the officers' faces, yet each person would like to be the one to "bring him down to size".

Adrian continued. "The biggest problem we have is the lift access. My thoughts on this is that, myself, officers Mcloud and Sherlock, Elsa the dog and two other officers use the lift first to reach the lower level and the others follow by flexible ladder through the lift's emergency access. In this way, we are not wasting time in waiting for an ancient lift to go up and down, several times."

Alex felt both excitement and fear as the plan of action was outlined. It reminded him of the times in Afghanistan when attacks on the Taliban had been planned and discussed. There was always an unknown factor. A "what if" factor. What if there are booby-traps? What would they do if Francesca refuses to co-operate? What if the lift will not move? "So much to think about", thought Alex.

Adrian continued, his tone sounding more like that of a maths lecturer to a class of young students. "The priority, once we have reached the level where the targets are living is to terminate the power source. We all have night vision and, with that advantage, it should assist us to complete the operation without too many casualties." He paused for effect. "Any questions?"

One of the officers asked, "Why are we going in at two fifteen?"

"This is only a short while before Francesca normally arrives back and the hope is that we can surprise her as she enters the apartment block.

Hopefully, she will co-operate with us and, when the noise of the lift is heard, the Italians will just assume that it is her returning.

That's why the timing is critical. I suggest that you all get some rest, now and be ready to leave here at one-thirty, precisely."

CHAPTER FORTY-FIVE :

Alex found it difficult to sleep, but, at least, he was rested, when all officers were called to prepare for the assault. Jen was not the only female officer. She and three others were issued with the same dark tunic as the men. Black and light in weight, the suits were reinforced with Kevlar. This super-strong material was also used in the headgear, giving the wearer maximum protection.

Even Elsa wore a Kevlar-reinforced suit and headgear, giving her an unusual, almost supernatural appearance. Alex was uncertain about Elsa's feelings in wearing this strange suit, but, at least, her tail was still wagging, which was always a good sign.

Once everybody was ready, they filed into the underground car-park of the MI6 building. Three black, mini-buses were waiting for them, Adrian, again, organising who went into which vehicle. The engines were already started and, as soon as everybody had taken their places, the vehicles moved out into the darkened London streets. They moved at a leisurely pace. Alex was sitting next to Jen and Elsa relaxed on the floor between them. Alex looked sideways at her and smiled to himself on seeing her camouflaged face. She certainly looked different and had the confidence of a very determined individual. Jen sensed that Alex was looking at her and smiled at him. Everybody was tense and ready for action. They arrived near to Newgate Street exactly on time and, swiftly, all the officers left their vehicles. Aware that the underground criminals may have cameras close to the apartment block. The team split up into small groups, in an attempt to blend in with the surroundings.

They did not have long to wait. Within minutes, the black Volvo turned into Newgate Street, allowing the young woman to exit the vehicle. She looked around as the Volvo drove away and began to head towards the apartment entrance. As soon as she opened the main door, Alex and Adrian, who had been hiding nearby, ran, silently, up to the woman. Alex put his hand over her mouth to silence her and quickly dragged her inside.

"Don't scream if you want to see Serena and Gemma, again!"

The mention of her daughters' names did the trick. The woman's tensed body relaxed into submission. This had been Adrian's suggestion, knowing that any mother would do anything to protect her own children.

"What do you want?"

Alex could see the fear in her eyes and knew that he had guessed correctly in using the names of this woman's two young children. He knew that exploiting weaknesses was the best way to survive. As he restrained her, he could feel her pounding heart as he held her tight. "You will help us to reach the underground base where your family members are hiding."

"I... don't know what you mean", she stammered.

"Yes, you do! I know that you go down stairs in this building into the old underground station and then into a lift to reach your base."

Francesca stared at him with incredulous eyes. "How do you know?"

"Never mind that. Just co-operate with us and you and your children will be safe. Okay?"

She nodded, submissively. As she looked at Alex, she realised that many others, all dressed like him, had entered the building, including one large, weird-looking dog. Thankfully, she did not recognise him from the time he and Jen had visited her Casino, probably because of their military-style camouflage.

Alex held out his hand. "Now, give me the keys you are carrying in your bag."

She opened her Louis Vuitton bag and took out a key ring with several keys, dropping them, reluctantly, into Alex's outstretched hand. "Which key opens the door in this area?" He spread out the five keys towards her.

"That one." She pointed to one of the keys. Alex used this in the lock of the door which he had seen in his vision. Again, Francesca looked surprised that he knew, exactly, just which door to open

The room was just as he had seen in his vision, containing many large boxes and crates. He did wonder what was inside them, but would leave that until later.

Still holding on to Francesca, he walked across the untidy room and found the staircase leading downwards. "Are there any cameras between here and your rooms?"

Francesca shook her head. Now, she wished they had taken that precaution. "What is going to happen to my family?"

It was Adrian who answered. "The 'Ndrangheta members will be arrested and eventually, deported back to Italy, assuming they put up no resistance. But, if you help us to capture them without any problems, we will keep you out of prison to let you and your children stay together. That's a promise", he emphasised.

Alex wondered just how far this woman would go against her extended family to save the lives of her children and herself. From what he had red about the 'Ndrangheta, there were severe punishments for any traitor within the family. The fact that she was giving the information under duress may help to keep her safe.

He led the group slowly down the stairs, aware that it would be foolish to assume that she would not lead them into a trap. As they reached the underground platform, there was a low level of illumination from occasional wall lights, which, presumably, were left on permanently. Floors and walls were tiled and, considering how old this station was, they seemed to be in remarkably good condition.

Alex noticed the lift gates on a wall at the end of this long concourse and wondered how many years it had been since commuters on the London Underground had used this ancient station. He could imagine crowds of commuters filling this space with noisy, excited chatter as people made their way to their places of work. Now, there was just the muted sound of this group of officer's footsteps as they followed the Italian woman.

As they reached the gate, Francesca seemed to hesitate, realising just how close they were to her family's hideaway. Impatient to move on, Alex pulled open the two sets of metal gates and strode into the lift, pulling the woman along. Adrian, Jen and Elsa followed. When they realised how large the lift was, four of the officers also entered. Pulling the gates back into position, Alex motioned to the Italian to press the button, but, then, had second thoughts. If one of these buttons was to alert the 'Ndrangheta members, their task would be that much more difficult. He remembered from his vision just which button she had pressed. Without delay, he pressed it and the lift began to descend to the lower level. For a brief moment, his eyes met Francesca's and, to his surprise, her facial skin colour appeared quite normal. Did this mean that she was not as criminally-minded as the others? He reminded himself to check the facial tones of the main members of the 'Ndrangheta, assuming he had the luxury of time to study them.

As soon as the lift stopped, Adrian opened the gates, allowing all but two of the officers to leave. These men, together, managed to lift the access panel in the roof of the lift cage. As soon as they had done this, a lightweight, coiled ladder dropped through the opening and, within seconds, the remainder of the officers began to climb down to the lower level.

After only a couple of minutes of activity, all the officers were now assembled within this, now somewhat cramped, ante-room.

Alex held out the small group of keys in front of his captive. "Which key, now?" The Italian woman, again, hesitated a little. "Remember, Francesca, we are very close to your children and I know exactly which room they are in."

She stared at him, incredulous that he could know such detail. "This is the one", she replied, in a somewhat nervous tone. Alex realised just how close they were to a highly-organised and dangerous group of criminals and turned the key in the lock.

CHAPTER FORTY-SIX :

After Alex had, gingerly, unlocked the door, it was Adrian who led the way. The officers spread out along the dimly-lit corridor, with at least two outside each door. Alex indicated the room in which the young children were, presumably, sleeping. There would be no need for their room to be invaded, but Alex hoped his memory was correct.

At a signal from Adrian, each door was kicked in and flares, together with smoke bombs detonated. The officers rushed into each room, shouting and trying to intimidate the occupants into rapid submission. Not surprisingly, it was not going to be that simple.

Several of the men had weapons at their bedside and fired at the intruders, probably as an instinctive reaction.

Jen escorted Francesca into her room to look after her two girls, who, not surprisingly, were terrified by the explosions of gunfire in a confined space, together with all the shouting and confusion. Tearful Gemma and Serena Were sitting on the bed, holding on to their mother, obviously wondering what was to become of them.

Jen had a sudden thought. "Are there any other children down here?"

Francesca shook her head. "No other young children like my two", she said with a strong sense of fear in her voice. In some ways, it would be a relief to end this underground existence. It had been a welcome reprieve to work in her casinos, if only to escape this ever-lasting confinement. Yet, her own daughters had not had this same luxury.

Without her husband, she had spent her days educating the girls, probably more extensively than if they had attended a state or even a private school. Every evening, she had left the children in her mother's care, while she worked at the casinos. Francesca also realised that her management of the Casinos would probably have to cease, but, as long as she could stay with her children, either in the U.K. or Italy, this was a sacrifice she could live with.

Alex had been looking for any signs of the huge form of Sam, but, as yet, had not seen anything of the man. "He had to be somewhere down here, but, where?"

Purely by chance, Alex, together with Elsa, burst into the bedroom of Gianni, who was in bed with his wife. Strangely, it was Carina who seemed to resent this intrusion. She, with a typically fiery, Italian temperament, began to throw anything she could lay her hands on towards Alex. Books, shoes and even a bedside lamp crashed into Alex, who, with apparent ease, brushed them to one side. In addition, she was cursing him, in Italian, using words which Alex had not even heard of while he had been learning the language.

"Attack!" he shouted as he was bombarded by even more books and part of a trouser press. Both Gianni and his wife were out of bed, now and Elsa, thinking that Carina was the greater threat, sank her teeth into the woman's arm, effectively disabling her. The woman screamed and Gianni pulled out a drawer, grabbing a weapon to defend himself and his wife. That was when Alex noticed that Gianni's weapon was aimed directly at Elsa's head. Even with her Kevlar protection, Alex still worried about the dog's vulnerability. With only a fraction of a second to spare, Alex shot at the Italian's gun hand. Gianni's weapon fired, missing Elsa by mere inches and then fell harmlessly to the floor. Alex fired another shot, hitting Gianni in the leg, effectively disabling him. "Must keep the bastard alive", thought Alex.

The noise was sheer hell as gunfire, screams and shouts reverberated throughout the warren of rooms.

"Where is Gian Battista? Where is the Capo Crimin?" Alex demanded.

Gianni had collapsed to the floor, where his wife was trying to support him.

"You seem to know so much, so you find him, if you're not too late."

"Too late for what?"

Gianni smiled through his pain. "That would be telling.

At that instant, all the lights went out, plunging the maze of rooms into complete darkness. Presumably, one of the officers had found and disabled the power source, as instructed. For Alex, this made no difference at all, his implanted eyes still able to discern all objects, even people, in complete darkness. Similarly, the other officers had their night-vision goggles on, so should be able to cope equally well.

Alex wasted no time. He picked up the weapon Gianni had nearly used on Elsa, tucked it into his waistband and ran back into the corridor, followed by Elsa.

Adrian had burst into the room where the two brothers, Lorenzo and Paolo, were sleeping. "Out of bed, you two!" They did as instructed, both standing in their boxer shorts. Suddenly, Paulo made a dive towards the bed and, smoothly, threw a knife, which had been concealed under his pillow. It had been directed towards, Adrian's face with remarkable accuracy. Adrian, instinctively, dropped down. The blade skimmed over his head, missing him by a few millimetres and embedded itself in the door frame. Adrian had intended just to disable these two, but soon realized that they were not going to give up without a fight. Adrian's weapon fired at Paolo's arm, but, with the Italian's movement, the bullet entered his chest. Blood spurted everywhere as the man sank to his knees.

"Paolo!" Lorenzo grabbed his brother, holding him close. Blood was gushing over both of them, the life draining away from the young man. As he held his dying brother, Lorenzo stared at Adrian with horror and absolute hatred in his eyes.

Adrian had no need to apologise, yet did manage to say, "Listen, I'm sorry about your brother, but if he had not thrown that knife at me, he would still be alive. There may still be a chance as we have medical support coming soon." Adrian called for another officer to make certain that Lorenzo did not try anything else to cause them a problem. By the time medical support had arrived, Paolo was dead, the loss of blood being too great to allow any chance of survival.

During all the noise and confusion, a large figure slipped silently along towards the end of the corridor, assisted by the darkness. The man quietly opened the door and entered one of the rooms. With cat-like precision, he made his way towards another door.

In this bedroom, Gian Battista had been enjoying a rare, alcohol-assisted deep sleep, when he awoke to find Sam, shaking him. "Wake up, master. The place is being attacked."

"What? Are you certain?" As he listened, he could hear the shouts of the officers in the corridor and was now in no doubt about the truth of Sam's warning.

For his age, he was quite quick in pulling on a pair of trousers, shirt and jacket, assisted by the huge man. It was made that much more difficult with the absence of lighting, yet he prepared himself with great urgency.

Sam had locked the door to delay any attack and quickly helped Gian into his shoes. "You'll need a weapon, sir." He handed a gun to the elderly man who tucked it into his belt. Last of all, Gian Battista grabbed an envelope, containing a large amount of cash, out of a bedside drawer. Hastily, he stuffed this into his jacket pocket, ready to, hopefully, make his escape.

While he was doing this, Sam had already opened a hidden door in one wall. He ushered the old man through the opening, saying, "I will do my best to delay them to give you time to escape."

"My stick! I need my stick!" Sam soon found the walking stick and placed it into the old man's grasping hands." "Thank you, Sam. You have been a great help."

The big man knew that this comfortable way of life was about to end, especially considering his employer's parting words. This faithful servant closed the secret door and, effortlessly, moved a large chest of drawers in front to conceal the opening. Sam was sweating and, unusually for this huge man, a worried look crossed his face. He knew it would only be a matter of time, now, but, at least, he had done his best to save the Capo Crimin.

Some of the officers were dragging many of the Italians out into the corridor.

As Alex turned to look the other way, he spotted the huge bulk of Sam, purposely striding towards him, a look of grim determination on his face. This man seemed even bigger than when Alex had seen him in his vision. He must have weighed well over a hundred and twenty kilos, but it was all well-toned muscle and the man's fitness could not be doubted. Alex had been standing with Elsa watching the other officers controlling the 'Ndrangheta's members and, unfortunately, was the closest to the approaching mountain of a man.

Elsa did not need to be given the instruction to attack, as the threat to her master was obvious and imminent. She ran, swiftly, towards the fast approaching giant, who barely flinched as the dog sank its teeth into his calf. If this had been any other man, he would have collapsed, submissively, but not Sam.

He simply swatted the dog away, as if it was merely a troublesome fly and Elsa crashed into the wall with a howl of pain. Alex then made a potentially-fatal mistake. He aimed his weapon at Sam's leg, in an attempt to cripple rather than kill, and pulled the trigger. To his amazement, Sam hardly flinched as the bullet sank into the firm flesh, allowing blood to trickle down his leg. The giant ran, somewhat clumsily, towards Alex, ripping the gun out of his hand and tossing the weapon to one side. Before Alex could reach to get the other gun out of his waistband, the huge figure put his hands around the young officer's neck and began to squeeze. Alex felt the strength draining out of his body as the grip of this huge man became ever tighter. He cursed to himself, realising that all the Kevlar protection on his body and head was useless against somebody determined to crush the vulnerable neck area.

Lights were flashing through his brain and the realisation that he was close to death pervaded his mind, blocking out all his other senses.

Unable to escape from the iron grip of this giant, Alex felt as though he was about to lose consciousness, death coming ever closer, when a huge explosion ripped through the air. The pressure on his neck slowly diminished and he sank to his knees, his body feeling completely drained.

"Alex!" He wondered if he was dead and, yet, he could still hear Jen's voice, sounding, somehow, very distant. "Alex! Come back, please!"

He shook himself and staggered to his feet, with the assistance of Jen, who was looking very concerned for her partner and lover.

Alex looked very puzzled. "What happened to Sam? I thought he was breaking my neck." Then he looked down at the floor, where Sam's huge body seemed to fill the entire width of the corridor. As Alex's senses returned, he realised that the whole of the back of Sam's head had been shattered, both blood and brain matter spilling out onto the expensive carpet.

Alex felt very relieved to see that there would never be any life left in the big man to strangle anybody else. "Who shot him?" Alex asked in obvious relief, although he had a very strong idea who it may have been.

Jen smiled. "Just returning the favour of when you saved my life. I managed to get several rounds into his big head, while he was concentrating on strangling you."

"Thanks, Jen. I owe my life to you."

"No, you don't. We're quits, okay?"

He gave her a huge kiss of gratitude. "Okay!" As he gathered his thoughts together, he remembered seeing Elsa flung aside by Sam. "Elsa! Is she alright?"

"I guess so. See for yourself."

A warm nose, muzzled Alex's hand. "Elsa!" He stroked the dog's head and felt a wet patch where a small trickle of blood was already congealing. There would be a scar, but, thankfully, she seemed to be in no immediate danger. "Thanks, Elsa. You were great!" Suddenly, Alex realised who he had been looking for when Sam had intervened. "The Capo Crimin! I think Sam was meant to delay me to give his master time to escape!"

"But, where? I'm certain that we have checked all the rooms."

Alex looked at the end of the corridor from where Sam had appeared. "There! There is another door. I think there is, perhaps, another way out of here."

Elsa had just about recovered from Sam's attack and was standing, loyally, by Alex's side, looking up at her master, seemingly aware how close he had come to death.

Alex, followed by Elsa, raced to the end of the corridor and pushed open the last door, which was set back slightly from the main wall surface. The doorway opened into a large, luxuriously furnished room. It was obvious that there was nobody in here, but there was another door, presumably leading to a bedroom. He wasted no time and crashed the door open, but, again, was disappointed to find the room completely empty. Even his superior vision had not detected the concealed door opening in the bedroom and, together with Elsa, he ran back into the corridor, where Jen had been waiting for him.

At this end of the corridor, there was just a blank wall. He was about to give up when he had a sudden thought. Alex ran his fingers over the surface, tapping the wall with his knuckles every so often. "I think there's a hidden opening in this wall."

"What makes you think that?"

"At this stage, it is part guesswork and part intuition. If you try to think like these people, wouldn't you have an emergency exit?"

"I suppose so", admitted Jen.

Alex looked back down the long corridor and spotted Adrian. "Adrian! Can you come here, a minute?"

The older man jogged towards them, his way now clear after some of his men had moved Sam's huge body to one side. "What is it?"

"I think this may be an emergency way out for the Capo Crimin. Can you use some explosive charge to blow a hole in it?"

Adrian smiled. "No problem." He called one of his men, Pete, who brought a small container of plastic explosive. Adrian explained what they wanted and he began to spread a thick, waxy substance between floor and wall. Then he pushed a small detonator into the substance. "You would be as well to stand well back. We don't know just what the explosion will bring down." Once everybody was at a safe distance, he pressed a small button. The noise in the confined space was deafening, a cloud of dust spreading along the corridor.

Alex breathed a sigh of relief that the roof had not fallen in. "I wonder what is above us?" he thought. His intuition had been correct. There had been no solid, concrete or brick wall behind the plasterboard. Instead, another corridor opened up in front of them and a smaller one led sideways towards the concealed door to the bedroom. Knocking off some loose, hanging debris, Alex, with Elsa, stepped through, followed by Adrian and Jen, both holding flash-lights. This corridor was about two and a half metres high by two wide, quite rough and basic in comparison to the luxurious living quarters. There was a cement finish to the floor, walls and ceiling, but no attempt had been made to give it a smooth finish. It was what it was. An emergency exit, but, just where did it lead?

Alex quickened his pace, not running, yet walking at a speed which allowed him to scan around for hidden dangers. There was still no sight of the old man, but Alex was convinced that he had come this way from the little disturbances in the dust on the concrete floor.

Alex had not bargained for what happened next. The corridor split off into two different directions. Fuck! "Now, why would they do that?" Alex thought, aloud.

"Probably a delaying tactic", answered Adrian.

Alex looked closely at the floor, scanning the surface in minute detail. "Well, it didn't work. He pointed the direction they should take, while explaining. "This Capo Crimin is nearly eighty and, I'm certain that he is using a walking stick." Adrian and Jen both looked at the floor, but their eyes were unable to discern the regular disturbance in the floor dust where the old man's walking stick had been used to support his weight.

Once again, Alex silently thanked Professor Goldman for making his artificial eyes powerful enough to spot these minute tell-tale signs.

All three quickened their pace an, after about another hundred metres, they came to a door. To their annoyance, it had been locked from the other side.

"No problem", said Adrian. "Just stand back, a minute." They did as instructed, allowing Adrian to shoot at the lock mechanism. There was an ear-splitting explosion and it shattered, allowing the door to swing open.

They stepped through the opening and, to their surprise, they found themselves on a London Underground platform. The three turned around in amazement to see that they were at St. Paul's station on the Central line.

At three-fifteen in the morning, the platform, one of only two, was, understandably, deserted. In comparison to the dark corridors they had come through to reach this place, Lighting was good and it was Jen, who spotted a figure slowly climbing some stairs. "There he is!"

All three humans and one dog ran towards the staircase, their footsteps echoing around the empty area. The elderly man realised that he was not fast enough to escape and turned to face his pursuers. That was when they noticed the gun in his hand.

Jen quickly dodged behind a ticket machine, although it probably would have offered very little cover. Alex and Adrian pressed themselves against the wall, but none of them was ever in any real danger. Gian Battista Lamancusa, realising that he could not evade his pursuers any longer, leaned heavily on his walking stick and put the gun against his own head, pulling the trigger. Again, the noise of the gun firing seemed even louder, the noise reverberating around the hard surfaces of the subway. The weapon, walking stick and, finally, the old man, himself, tumbled down the nine or ten steps onto the platform. The King of the 'Ndrangheta had, finally, fallen from his throne. This was the end of his sixty-year reign, since being baptised into the "Honoured Society" at the age of eighteen.

CHAPTER FORTY-SEVEN :

Adrian used his radio to call for medical assistance, but it was quite obvious to anyone that the old man was well and truly dead, blood and brain matter spilling from his shattered skull.

The senior intelligence officer decided that he had better stay at the crime-scene until somebody could take charge of the old man's body. "You might as well return to the underground rooms to see if they need any further assistance."

Alex took one last look at the upturned face of the old man and realised that even with the damage to his head, the darkened colour was not just that of the face. It was more like an aura, extending slightly beyond the head. Yet, as he watched, this aura was diminishing in intensity as the life ebbed away from the physical being. Alex turned to Jen and asked, "Did you see something like an aura around his head?"

She looked closer at the upturned face of the old man. "No, nothing." She was clearly puzzled. "An aura?"

"Yes. It's just about gone now. It faded as he died."

Jen looked again at the old man, but saw nothing, realising that Alex's powers of observation were far beyond her own capabilities. To her, it almost seemed supernatural and a little scary.

There was not much conversation as Alex, Jen and Elsa walked back, re-tracing their steps through the narrow corridor until they reached the junction in the passage. "I think we should see where this leads."

Jen could understand Alex's curiosity, but said, "I think we should check if everything is alright, first. We can always come back here."

"Okay", Alex conceded. They walked further until they reached the carpeted area, where they found many of the criminals in handcuffs all looking somewhat sad and defeated.

Again, Alex studied their faces and, as with the Capo Crimin, they all had this same dark, brownish aura surrounding their faces.

Alex recognised a few of these men. Agostino, the first of the Italian family seen by him at Woolpit, was, like everybody else, shocked by this intrusion into their "home".

Brando and Carlino looked equally dejected, their escape from the prison van had only given them a few, short weeks of freedom. For what they had put Jacqueline and Rosita through, they deserved a very long prison sentence.

Adrian's second in command, Mike Edwards, saw Alex and walked towards them. As the man reached him, Alex asked, "Is everything okay, now?"

"Yes, fine. We are certain there is nobody else here, now. There are thirty-nine of them, including the two children."

Alex felt relieved, saying, "Look after those children and, don't forget, I promised Francesca that she would escape punishment if she assisted us. Take care of her."

"Don't worry. She will probably just get a suspended sentence to allow her to stay with her children." It was obvious that Mike was excited to show Alex something. "Come and look what we have found in one of the rooms." The three followed Mike into quite a large, well-stocked room which had needed explosives to break through the heavily reinforced door. "What the ….?" What stopped Alex in his tracks was a veritable treasure trove. It was like an Aladdin's cave, stacked with piles of gold bars, packages of many different currencies of banknotes, other bags full of drugs and, within large wooden boxes, many different types of guns and rifles, together with a great deal of ammunition.

Jen drew in a sharp breath. "There must be millions of pounds in here. What a fantastic catch!"

Mike smiled. "It's been a very good day, so far. Quite a haul!"

"We have one other passage to check on, Mike. Can we borrow your man with the plastic explosives, just in case there is another barrier?"

"Of course." Mike went to the door opening. "Pete! Go with Alex and Jen just in case they need some assistance."

A tall, quite slim officer, in his late forties, came over to the small group. "Fine! Lead the way and I'll follow."

The trio and dog returned to the end of the corridor and stepped, once again, into the roughly-hewn passage. They walked until they found the fork in the passage. Taking the other route, they set off, wondering what they would find next. It was a long and meandering journey, the passage, in places sloping down to a deeper level and quite low , making it necessary for these tall individuals to bend forward.

Alex estimated that the passage was at least a mile in length before it opened out into what seemed to be a huge cavern.

It was in darkness, yet Alex, with his ultra-sensitive eyes, instantly recognised the view in front of them. They were in an underground cave with water lapping gently against a low, harbour wall. A submarine was securely fastened to low bollards on the quayside. The craft was of a very sleek, low profile and with the strange, black plastic-like finish. This, presumably, would make detection by under-water sounding equipment very difficult.

"This is what I saw in my first vision, where they were transferring the bags of cocaine from the sub to the narrow boat."

Pete and Jen did not have Alex's super vision and had to use their powerful torches to make out any detail within this area, yet the sound of the water lapping against the concrete quayside was unmistakable. Alex pointed his torch towards the roof of the cavern and picked up the outlines of the mechanical hoist which had lifted the superstructure of the canal boat. "Look! That's the hoist used by the Italians on their drugs run."

As he shone his torch around, Alex spotted a row of switches on the rear wall. He walked over and soon found those which controlled the lighting. He pressed a few switches and soon, the underground cavern was fully illuminated. The three gazed around the huge area. "This is truly impressive", Jen said, in wonderment. "It must have cost a fortune to set up all of this."

Pete was more interested in the stealth submarine and had walked down the short gangway onto the deck. "This is quite impressive. A cable ran across the ground and into a hatch on the top of the submarine. "Looks as though the batteries are being charged, ready for a journey."

Although he had no sense of imminent danger, Alex called out, "Careful, Pete! It may be a booby-trap!"

The older man paused and looked, cautiously, through the part-open hatch. He shone his torch around the interior of the submarine and decided that there were no signs of possible traps. "I think it's okay. You two stay there while I check." The explosives expert opened the hatch fully and climbed down into the interior of the craft.

Meanwhile, Jen, Alex and Elsa explored the jetty area, curious to discover more about this underground marina. At one end of the quay, the water lapped, lazily against a vertical wall. "No obvious way of escape here", said Jen.

"Unless it's under the surface. I remember, from my vision, the submarine moving carefully through a tunnel and then surfacing over there." He pointed towards where the craft was now moored. "Let's check the other end." The trio walked about a hundred and fifty metres to the far end of the quayside. In some places, the quay had been about ten metres in depth, but, at this end, it was less than two metres wide. Alex was surprised to feel cool, fresh air on his face and shone his torch around the wall near to them, searching for an opening. "There!"

"What is it?" Jen could see nothing of special interest.

"I think this is where the canal boat enters and leaves this area. There is a tunnel in that wall surface which must lead to the canal system. I can feel fresh air coming from that tunnel"

"This is fantastic! How on earth did they manage to create all this, undetected?"

Alex had a sudden thought. "I don't think they did! My feeling is that it was constructed during the Second World War, to provide safety and shelter during the Nazi bombings."

Jen was surprised by this possibility. "Really?"

"During the War, many subway stations were used as emergency evacuation areas and that tunnel leads directly to St. Paul's Tube station. This may even have been an emergency exit for senior Government officials or even the Royal family."

They were discussing this as they walked back towards the gently-floating craft. Pete emerged from the submarine with a wide grin on his face. "What a fantastic toy! Come and have a look."

Jen, Alex and Elsa walked along the gangway and followed Pete into the craft. It brought back memories of Alex's first vision and, now that there were no bags of cocaine, it seemed less cramped than he remembered.

Pete showed them the controls in front of the helmsman's comfortable seat. "This craft must have cost a fortune! It's very sophisticated and crammed with very high-tech navigation and stealth technology."

For the next few minutes, the three of them looked closely at every area within the craft. It even had a compact, yet well-designed toilet and wash room, which would have been necessary for longer journeys. Eventually, they left the submarine and headed back along the winding passage to the underground 'Ndrangheta rooms.

Some of the prisoners had been removed, while others looked downcast and defeated.

The underground habitat's lighting had been restored, now that the criminal gang were, safely, under their control.

Alex spotted Mike and quickly told him of their discovery. "This is quite a catch in many different ways. Come and see what else I have found."

They followed him into what would have been the lounge area for the Capo Crimin. It was luxurious in every detail from comfortable seating and obviously-expensive ornaments to richly-decorated walls and concealed high-tech LED lighting. "Do you recognise anything?" asked Mike.

The others looked around the room, wondering just what they were supposed to see. Then, all of a sudden, Alex spotted them. "Those paintings! They look vaguely familiar."

"Well spotted, Alex. Over the years, many famous art masterpieces have been stolen and we are now looking at two of them." Mike Edwards had several interests to occupy him when off duty and, as a lover of fine art, he had quickly recognised the treasures hidden away in this underground habitat.

Alex looked at the first of the two paintings. There were three musicians, a young woman playing a harpsichord, a man playing a lute and another woman singing.

"This one on the left is 'The Concert' by Johannes Vermeer and is reckoned to be worth over one hundred and thirty million pounds. It was stolen from the Isabella Stewart Gardner museum in nineteen ninety."

Alex looked again at this painting. True, it was impressive but who would pay a hundred and thirty million for just one painting? Alex could never understand how paintings could command such high prices, but, as long as there were billionaires with money to spend, the prices would continue to be over-inflated.

Mike continued as though he was the guide at a national art gallery. "'Poppy Flowers' was painted by Vincent Van Gogh in the late eighteen hundreds. It was stolen from the Cairo's Mohammed Mahmoud Khalil Museum in two thousand and ten and is worth about thirty-five million pounds. The reward, alone, for these two paintings would be several hundred thousand pounds!"

"This gets even better. What a superb catch! The 'Ndrangheta and a veritable treasure trove all in one day."

CHAPTER FORTY-EIGHT :

All the news channels were covering this huge story, but Alex preferred to watch Fiona Bruce on BBC television news, as she always seemed to have a sexy way of presenting news items. He felt that it could have been the seductive twinkle in her eyes or the slightly-teasing tone in her voice, but, whatever it was, she fascinated him, even though she was probably double his age. "The Intelligence Service, yesterday, apprehended over thirty members of an Italian family. Similar to the Mafia in ideals, they were called the 'Ndrangheta, originally based in Calabria, Southern Italy. The family was ruled by Gian Battista Lamancusa, a seventy-eight year old ruthless gangster, who committed suicide when he realized that capture was inevitable. Several members of the family have suffered gunshot wounds and are being closely guarded in hospital. The large family evaded arrest over two years ago when Italian Police forces managed to capture and arrest nearly three hundred members of the same syndicate. At this stage, little is being disclosed by the Security service, but it appears that this large number of criminals, together with family members, including two small children, have managed to travel illegally to the U.K. and have been living underground in a luxurious dwelling actually based underneath the Old Bailey."

At this point, the image changed from Fiona to that of the superbly-comfortable living room where Gian Battista had spent most of his time.

"Apparently, there was a secret passage underneath the famous legal courts to move prisoners towards Newgate Prison, sometimes for public executions, in the nineteenth century, but, this passage had been abandoned for more than a hundred years."

The picture switched from the newsreader to show images of the world-famous law courts and Alex wondered if the members of the 'Ndrangheta would face trial in the very same building under which they had been hiding and living. "That would be true justice", he thought.

"Adrian was not surprised by this disclosure", Jen commented. "He said that the Ministry of Defence has a building over Brompton Road Underground station in West London. The station is also owned by the M.O.D. and hasn't been used for over eighty years. Perhaps there is also an illegal operation running there, right under the noses of the M.O.D."

Alex agreed. "I now believe that anything is possible, so who knows?"

Fiona continued with her report. "How these Italians managed to discover this place and actually take up residence is still a mystery. From this secret location, the family have been running a three hundred and fifty million pound business, based on illegal immigration, prostitution, protection rackets, providing weapons and importing drugs for distribution throughout the United Kingdom. Security forces also found a room containing many gold bars, currency, drugs and weapons, presumably collected by the 'Ndrangheta members over many years. Two valuable paintings which had been stolen several years ago were also recovered. The final discovery was a five million pound mini-submarine, which the family had used to smuggle both the family and drugs into the United Kingdom. The submarine was found in an underground cave with a connecting channel to the open sea. It was packed with high-tech 'stealth' electronics to avoid detection by the authorities."

As an image of the submarine appeared, Alex switched the television off. He had, already seen the report several times and felt quite satisfied by the coverage.

He and Jen were cuddled together on his sofa, while Elsa lay at their feet.

Alex felt quite infuriated at the bold approach of the large, Italian family. "What a bloody cheek! Actually living underneath the Old Bailey and nobody was any the wiser. That took real balls!"

Jen smiled. It was a cheeky smile, especially for the man she had lived with for the past three months. "You mean that yours are not real?"

"Of course they are real! Do you want to find out?"

"Perhaps I should investigate and get down to the truth?" She jumped up and chased him, again, into the bedroom, Elsa relaxing in the living room. She was, by now, quite accustomed to her master's strange antics with this woman. She could never understand the crazy behaviour of these humans and closed her eyes. She knew that she would be undisturbed for quite a while.

EPILOGUE

It was the first time that Alex's family had visited him at his apartment in London and all were impressed after looking round the tidy rooms. Alex hoped that he had not left any of Jen's personal items lying around for them to spot or else he would always be teased and reminded of this by his ultra-observant sisters.

Lucy was sitting on one side of him on the sofa, with Amelia on the other and his parents relaxing in the armchairs. All four had taken a liking to Elsa and made a great fuss of her. Of course, Elsa enjoyed all the attention and, for some reason, favoured Amelia, relaxing on the floor near to the young girl's feet, which pleased his younger sister.

There was an uncomfortable moment when Amelia, running her hand over Elsa's head, noticed the scar, where she had been injured when Sam had thrown her off him in their recent battle. They seemed to accept Alex's story that a huge Rottweiler had attacked her while out walking. Attacks by other dogs on guide dogs were not particularly uncommon and the family accepted this story as the truth.

They had all commented how well Alex was looking. "It's a good job that the marks on my neck, from Sam's attempt to strangle me, have become less visible", he thought. Still, to be certain that it was not noticed, he had decided to wear a smart, black polo-necked sweater.

The occasion was Amelia's fourteenth birthday and, when she had been asked what she would like as a gift, all she wanted was to visit her big brother and see the sights of London. Her parents and Lucy also, thought it was a great idea and had made arrangements with Alex to visit him on the following Saturday.

Of course, he would have to revert to his original brown hair colour and blue eyes to avoid awkward questions, but that would not be too difficult. He needed to check with Jen on how to change his eye colour by himself, in case he needed this for the future.

When he had told Jen of this arrangement, she felt it better if she was not there at the same time as his family. "They would jump to the wrong conclusion."

"Is that conclusion so wrong?" asked Alex, somewhat naively. "Do you not want to stay with me?"

She looked at him and, with a great deal of sadness in her voice, said, "You know that it's not that simple. Christin has, on my behalf, been keeping the States up-to-date, but I am already well over my allotted stay here in the U.K. My job is based in the U.S. and my family live there. I have to go back soon, so I think it better that I go before your own family arrives."

Alex's heart sank, visibly. He looked, sadly, into Jen's beautiful, blue eyes. "Will I ever see you, again?"

Her answer was so matter of fact, as if the question was not even necessary. "Of course you will. I'm not that far away and I'll visit whenever it's possible." It was definitely not an afterthought when she added, coyly, "And you could always come and stay with me for a holiday, whenever you wish."

Jen had really caught him by surprise. He knew that he wanted to be a major part of her life, but had an uncomfortable feeling that they may never meet again. He had no idea why this thought should have been so strong, yet he was certain that, for some reason, it was the truth.

Alex thought of Jack Reacher in Lee Child's novels. In each adventure, he would find a beautiful woman to bed, but, by the end of the story, He would be moving on, leaving the woman behind. "It's not quite the same situation, but the effect is the same. A fantastic short-lived relationship and then one has to move on to a new chapter in my life!"

SEE ALL EVIL :
PRESS RELEASE

"See All Evil" is the latest novel by John Raynor due for general release in paperback and E-book formats in December, 2015.

A brief synopsis follows :

When British soldier, Alex McCloud is injured and blinded in Afghanistan during 2010, he is offered the chance of sight using bionic implants, developed by Professor Goldman of Moorfields Eye Hospital in London, in conjunction with Augmented Reality specialist, Major Jennifer Sherlock of the C.I.A.

These implants not only provide him with sight, but much, much more, proving to be of great interest both to the M.O.D. and the C.I.A.

His new life as an intelligence officer based in London brings him many challenges utilising his unique abilities.

The author is currently writing a sequel with more adventures of his main character, Alex McCloud.

John Raynor has already published two novels, two autobiographies and three children's short stories. Aged seventy-one, John is registered blind and has used his personal experience, together with a great deal of research and a vivid imagination to make "See All Evil" an unforgettable story.

John enjoys reading many of the books available through the Royal National Institute of Blind people's talking book library.
He intends to continue sponsoring new talking books to assist the many blind people unable to read printed books.

John can be contacted for interviews and book signings by

phone on 0(44) 161 969 2663

or by email at computential@btconnect.com.

His web site is www.jsraynor.co.uk.

Address :
70 Norris Road, Sale, Cheshire, M33 3QR, United Kingdom.

Please find the enclosed complimentary paperback copy and hope that you find it possible to read this story and give your welcome comments in a review.

Lightning Source UK Ltd.
Milton Keynes UK
UKOW01f0416031015

259748UK00001B/2/P